by ULRICH BECHER

THE WOOD- CHUCK HUNT

TRANSLATED BY HENRY A SMITH

crown publishers, inc.
new york

Rowohlt Verlag GmbH, Reinbek bei Hamburg, 1969

English translation © 1977 by Crown Publishers, Inc.

Inquiries should be addressed to Crown Publishers, Inc., One Park Avenue, New York, N.Y. 10016.

Printed in the United States of America

Published simultaneously in Canada by General Publishing Company Limited

Designed by Shari de Miskey

Library of Congress Cataloging in Publication Data

Becher, Ulrich, 1910-
The woodchuck hunt.

Translation of Murmeljagd.
I. Title.
PZ3.B387416Wo (PT2603.E16)   835'.9'14
ISBN 0-517-51624-1   77-3063

Cast of Characters in order of appearance:

Albert (Trebla) von———
Thirty-nine-year-old Socialist Austrian journalist; son of a nobleman Field Marshal in the Imperial Army, and himself a Baron; took part in the uprising of 1934, and has fled to Pontresina, Switzerland.

Roxana (Xana) Giaxa von———
Trebla's wife, a twenty-seven-year-old philologist and translator.

Adelhart von Stepanschitz
Former WWI colleague of Trebla's.

Joop ten Breukaa
Wealthy Dutch businessman; owner of the "Spahi"; he and his wife live on an estate near Pontresina.

Pola Polari ten Breukaa
Joop's wife; Jewish; a former music hall soubrette; as nurse in WWI, nursed Trebla after he had received a serious head wound.

Madam Fausch
Postmistress, Pontresina; Trebla and Xana are renting a room in her home.

Dr. Tardueser
Pontresina physician.

G. Mostny & J. Krainer
Two Viennese who Trebla suspects have been sent by Laimgruber to kill him.

Zarli Zuan
Local printer.

Police Corporal Defila

Police Commissioner Dumeng Mavegn

Mr. Fitzallan
Retired Irish jockey.

Dr. Gaudenz de Colana
Alcoholic attorney.

Dr. Maxim Grabscheidt
Half-Jewish, Socialist physician in Vienna; aided Revolutionary Uprising of 1934; friend and underground colleague of Trebla.

Elsabé Giaxa
Konstantin's wife.

Konstantin Giaxa
A world-famous circus equestrian of anti-Establishment sympathies.

Lenz Zbraggen (Soldier Buddy)
Soldier in Mountain Machine Gun Company.

Fräulein Tummermut
Fiancée of Lenz Zbraggen.

Teresina Clavadetscher
Men's wife; former fiancée of Men's brother Peidar.

Men Clavadetscher
Proprietor of Chesetta Grischuna, who killed his brother, Peidar, in an ambiguous hunting accident.

Bonjour
Servant-chauffeur of the ten Breukaas.

Pina
Waitress with whom Trebla has brief affair.

Benedetg Caduff-Bonnard
Proprietor of Cafe d'Albana; hunting companion of Men and Peidar Clavadetscher.

Henriqe Kujath
Anti-Nazi Swiss mill owner referred to as Grandpa. Close friend of the Giaxa family and of Trebla. Active in spiriting anti-Nazi resistance fighters out of Austria.

Señor and Señora Ithurra y Azkue
Anti-Franco Basque brother and sister whom Kujath is helping to escape.

Valentin Tiefenbrucker
Former anti-Nazi Social Democrat representative in the Bundestag; escaped from Dachau.

Standartenfuehrer Giselher Liebhenschl
Detention Camp Director.

*Balthasar (Balz) Zbraggen and
Andri Zbraggen*
Lenz's brothers.

Captain Heinzwerner Laimgruber
Former WWI colleague of Trebla's; now with Viennese Gestapo.

Count Aurel Tességuier
Aristocrat neighbor of the Giaxas; helped Elsabé escape to Switzerland.

"Spahi"—a painting by Gauguin.

book one

The
Off Season

1

"You see, madam, there is really no point in being sentimental."

The phrase wasn't mine. Just a line from the puppet play *Punch and the Doughnut Baker's Widow*. A witless line, really, as it was croaked out by Punch. But it always got a laugh at Professor Salambutschi's Punch and Judy show in Vienna's Prater, at the little theater set up halfway between Kolarik's Swiss Chalet and the New Ghost Train.

"You see, madam, there is really no point in being sentimental," I croaked on that damnable evening at the end of May—what May? why did I say May? With my keen eyes I spied the boulder by the path along the water's edge, a rock that jutted out like a diving board over the almost invisible water—and saw something whitish that might be her saffron yellow tricot dress; she had brought along a bright blue one, but this evening she had worn the yellow one when she stole away from Acla Silva. On all fours I sprang onto the rock, slipped on the cold, slimy stone, slightly scraping my right palm and bruising my left knee, and clawed my way up over the cold, spongy moss, then slid forward on my knees to the "diving board," a dull pain in my bruised knee that did not hurt, and touched something round, white, and cold, something like a half-frozen peach (the woman's cheek), and embraced her and hugged her close to me as she crouched there apathetically. And the cold, wet shiver that came from the dark water and the machine-gun throbbing of my racing pulse that beat in the hollow scar on my forehead, and the sweat trickling down under my shirt, and the rasping voice that sounded foreign to me, disguised, like the voice of the puppeteer Professor Salambutschi: "Really, madam, being sentimental is pointless. Because they—because *they* killed Maxim Grabscheidt in Dachau, *you* want to jump into the ice-cold water just like a pregnant servant girl in an old-fashioned dime novel? Be more contemporary, madam!" (None of that was ever heard at Professor Salambutschi's.) "You of all people, one of the best thousand-meter swim-

3

mers at Millstatt Lake? Down there on the island, at Hvar on the Adriatic, those thousand meters were risky on account of the sharks, but you tried it anyway; of course your Papa-Rose drove along beside you in Duschan's motorboat, armed with a giant rifle and a harpoon, to protect you from 'Oh the shark has/pearly teeth, dear,' "; yes I sang Brecht-Weill on this Mayless May night. "And do you really think, Madam Xana, tht you would be doing anyone but Maxim Grabscheidt's murderers a favor with your spur-of-the-moment cold-water suicide?"

From Xana's whimpering I gathered something like, "I only wanted to sit here awhile," and I said in the direction of her barely visible face, "No, you were sort of halfway planning to, ah, to take a little jump off this big rock diving board," and she whimpered in a low, sniffling voice something like, "How can you keep on living in a world where they treat people like *that?*" And I croaked, "That's nonsense, madam." (Which was not part of Salambutschi's text either.) "It makes absolutely no sense whatever to become sentimental about these murderers. Because they'll all be dead before long. After they've got twenty to forty million lives on their, um, nonexistent consciences, they'll be dead themselves, and there'll be no shovel. There won't even be a shovel to dig their graves."

My dear Trebla,

No doubt you are surprised that an old comrade from the Boroëvić regiment is dispatching such a lengthy epistle to pursue you into your newfound exile. Ascertaining your Zurich address was a simple matter, because the friends of the newly risen German Reich are increasing everywhere and have their eyes and ears open. And thus I come at once to the salient point of my letter. As you are no doubt aware, I was never one to mince words—a quality that in our old army (may she rest in peace!) earned me the nickname "the Prussian," a nickname about which today I need no longer feel ashamed. For, thanks to the brilliant resolve of our Chancellor and Fuehrer, our old internal conflicts—despite all the foreign plots to perpetuate them—have finally been laid to rest; the Anschluss has become an irrevocable fact; and we, whether Prussians or Austrians, may call ourselves—according to the right of the strong—and may it never again be taken from us—Germans!

You may ask yourself how a nobleman who for years wore the red and white ribbon of the Fatherland Front on his lapel could stand so completely behind the Fuehrer today. To this I can answer that I always wore that ribbon with mixed emotions! What moved me primarily to wear it was the loyalty of Chancellors Dollfuss and Schuschnigg to the idea of the Monarchy, a loyalty that I, as a former officer of the Imperial Army, felt duty-bound to support; and there were also—and not least important—the decisive measures taken by both these statesmen against—forgive my frankness—your political associates.

How you, who had been one of us, were able to align yourself with this godless company remains a mystery to me. But I shall return to that. In any case I can reveal to you in passing that, after the Red revolt of February '34 was beat-

en down and you were in a bad, I must say, very bad way, an anonymous mentor intervened for you at the highest level, in consequence of which your life was spared. This mentor was I, Adelhart von Stepanschitz—but I do not desire your thanks at this late date. What I want from you is merely—if you please!—an unbiased attitude toward the proposal that I am officially charged with making to you.

Yesterday while I was strolling down the Graben and gazing up at our dear old St. Stephen's Cathedral, I said to myself suddenly, no, Stepanschitz, you have not been disloyal to the idea of the Monarchy! You are the faithful subject of a yet uncrowned ruler, who, with his iron hand, is building the new Reich as a bulwark of Aryan Christianity against the international league of Untermenschen. And I vowed that I would thank the Almighty on my knees the day this ruler would accept the Imperial Crown in the sanctuary of St. Stephen's.

As I have already indicated above, it was, dear old comrade—and I trust you will allow me, despite all that has divided us in the past decades, to address you thus, in affectionate remembrance of our wartime adventures together—it was always a riddle to me that you, on returning from the front, threw yourself into the arms of that rebellious mob, which, led by seditious Jewish elements, dared to vent its Asiatic lust for destruction on the very foundations of morality and property, in short, of our entire Christian civilization. You, the son of a general, you, on whose chest a Boroëvić pinned the Silver Cross and a Tuelff von Tschepe und Weidenbach pinned the Iron Cross First Class! You, who were allowed to sit at the same table with Field Marshal von Mackensen!

At first I attributed your sympathy for the November Criminals to the ignorance of your tender twenty years. But when you, whose ancestors had repeatedly taken up arms for the honor and glory of the Empire, began to founder completely in the disgraceful Marxist ideology, I came to suspect that the head wound you received from that British bullet had . . . impaired your sanity—again, comrade, forgive my openness.

With shock and disgust I turned away from all the literary sins you committed in those years: booklets, tracts, inflammatory satirical poems—with the single exception of that truly poetic work "Cormorants of Lobau," which occupies a place of honor in my library, a fact that should speak for my impartiality.

Then came the February revolt of the Vienna Commune!

With horror I learned from the newspapers that you—along with a certain Koloman Wallisch (who was to meet his just reward on the gallows)—had organized the armed rebellion in Styria. I shudder to think what your father would have done had he known this! My suspicion that you were not in full possession of your senses now seems confirmed. After your arrest, this, and my affection for you dating back to the Isonzo campaign, inspired me to intercede on your behalf. Thus I succeeded in maneuvering you out of the danger zone of martial law. My efforts, in view of your previous service as an officer, to arrange for a mere confinement to quarters, were unsuccessful. Nevertheless you were spared the worst.

Incidentally, in view of the overwhelming, epoch-making changes that

have just occurred in our Fatherland, I now see your participation in the Febru-
ary revolt in a somewhat different light.

*It is now clear that the policies of Dollfuss and Schuschnigg were harmful
to the extent that they ignored the demands of the hour and turned a deaf ear to
the call by eighty million voices for the unification of all Germans; thus I now
suspect that your defiance of such antinationalist policies was not provoked by
outside forces alone, but that in this defiance reposed the germ of the same
"healthy folk-instinct"—unconscious to be sure—which today is taking the history of the world in hand.*

*Several days ago I met with Captain Laimgruber, and by chance we began
talking about you.*

*Laimgruber, your commander in Brăila, is by no means unknown to you.
The Captain related a great many things about you from the old days, and there
was no laughter missing. He confided to me, among other things, the story of
your encounter in Countess Popescu's salon, when, unable to locate the privy,
you p—d on the potted palm behind the grand piano! Thereupon I recounted
your adventures on the aerial tramway at Novaledo. We stopped for champagne
at the Sacher, and laughed ourselves to tears over your escapades, my dear
Trebla. In the end, the Captain, expecting imminent promotion, declared it was
indeed a shame that such a devil of a fellow—forget his juvenile mistakes—was
doomed to spend his time out there with that mob of amateur revolutionaries instead of taking an active part in the rebirth of the Fatherland.*

*Captain Laimgruber today ranks high among those headquartered at the
Hotel Metropol, i.e., he serves in a position of trust with the Viennese Gestapo.
(I am authorized to reveal this to you.)*

*Apropos this, you should not believe the fairy tales about the Gestapo that
the Jews are spreading around outside Germany. At one time even I was taken
in by such blather, and can only laugh at myself today. For this institution in-
conveniences no one who has a good conscience about his People and Fuehrer,
and it serves, with laudable selflessness, a single cause, that of preventing another "stab in the back" such as the one that brought on the catastrophe of 1918.*

*The Captain has, despite his inconclusive encounter with you this past win-
ter, recently decided to review your case. Among other things he has contacted
several old National Socialist campaigners who now hold well-deserved positions of authority but who once served time with you in Woellersdorf, and despite their complete disagreement with your ideological position, could report
nothing unfavorable about you. In addition, he learned that you are living in
Switzerland under wretched circumstances and that your residence permit is
due to expire in a short time. And what then, my dear Trebla?*

*Do you propose to let yourself be chased or cajoled from country to country
like a destitute Wandering Jew? Or perhaps in your desperation you might even
get the suicidal notion to go to Spain and join that nationless brigade of bandits,
and to fight—perhaps to die—alongside church-wreckers and nun-rapists for a
cause that is—thank God!—already lost.*

*Out of this desperate situation there is only one honorable escape, one that
your former comrades wish to make available to you—a return to your homeland!*

6

Laimgruber has authorized me to make the following proposal in good faith: You are granted a maximum period of fourteen days to consider the proposal, after which time you must travel to Vienna. The Captain, on his word of honor, guarantees you safe conduct. You will be required to complete a two-month political reorientation course, during which you will be guaranteed—again on the Captain's word as an officer—complete freedom of movement. Of course your previous writings, which—alas—deserved the public burning they received, will remain forbidden, with the exception of the "Cormorants," whose republication is now being considered at my suggestion. May you consider it your sacred obligation to add to this volume still other verses inspired by a real bond with the German soil and filled with the new spirit of racial and national community. The poisoned fruits of your youthful delusions, including the grotesque attacks against the National Socialist State and its Fuehrer, will then be forgiven.

Let this unique and magnanimous gesture bear witness to the fact that the Fuehrer State is always generous to those of its opponents who rediscover their true German hearts and who are prepared to help build the New Reich—forged in blood and iron, the proudest bulwark of civilized humanity.Loyalty for loyalty!

Heil Hitler! And let me add as well a reverent kiss for the hand of your dear wife. Since the weaker sex is blessed with the advantage of following the heart's command, I am sure your dear wife will concur in my wish that this long epistle might fall upon fertile soil.

Yours,

Adelhart Stepanschitz

Vienna, the 21st of May, 1938

P.S. Herr Dr. Livesius from the Consulate General of Greater Germany, 12 Zurich I, has been instructed to provide you and your wife with passports as well as two paid first-class Zurich-Vienna train tickets.

Two days before Uncle Adolf in the company of Quartermaster-General Franz Halder raced toward Vienna in the armor-plated Mercedes ... "Wien/Wien, nur du allein/Sollst die Stadt meiner Traeume sein"; but no, that's by a Jewish composer!...two days before the Birthday of Greater Germany I appear in the courthouse in Graz and ask Councillor Zoetlotener to release the documents that had been confiscated by the Security Services of the Christian Corporate State: my passport, doctoral diploma, and driver's license. Strangely, or perhaps typically enough, the Councillor, a monarchist, pale with excitement, feels like making a joke. "You want your driver's license *now*, when the Fuehrer is coming to take over the wheel for us? Technically you're still under police surveillance, you know."

"Technically, I suppose so. But I imagine there will be a great change in the police force after a day or two—"

"I expect that too. That is why I'm ready to close both eyes and assume that you intend to depart the country."

"I can only endorse that assumption, Herr Councillor."

"I *also* plan to go," Zoetlotener announces rather formally. "To Belgium. Stenokerzeel. To Emperor Otto's. And if you will have me extend your most humble greetings to His Majesty, I'll turn over those impounded documents within a half an hour."

"All right, fine. Please give my best regards to Herr Dr. Otto von Habsburg-Lóthringen."

"It's a deal." Zoetlotener smiles. And in a half an hour I really do have my documents again. Things could not have gone more smoothly. Two days before the annexation of Austria there occurs OPERATION OTTO, under the surprising classification State Secret. But getting out was, as I discovered, not quite so easy.

Exactly a week after Adolf proclaimed on Vienna's Heldenplatz, "with history as his witness, the return of his homeland to the Rrreich," my Xana is traveling with Joop and his wife Pola ten Breukaa toward the Swiss border in a first-class compartment of the Arlberg Express. I am riding in a third-class section of the same train, my skis laid between the baggage nets, disguised as a skier, wearing a black stocking cap to conceal my "identifying mark."

As was agreed in Vienna's Western Station, Joop and "his ladies" are ignoring me until we reach Bludenz, Vorarlberg.

Pola, who had her debut as Pola Polari at the theater Beim Leicht in the Prater around 1912, almost became famous as a soubrette, but only almost; she was mentioned in the same breath as Mlles Massary and Zwerenz; the Apollo and the Theater an der Wien were the later "stages" of her rise to almost-fame. In the third year of the World War she interrupted her career and enlisted as a nurse. At a mineral spring in the Carpathian forests where serious casualties were sent to convalesce—I already had behind me two operations on my head wound by Chief Medical Officer von Rohleder and a third by Admiral's Staff Surgeon von Eiselsberg—she cared for me, and I had the honor, the dubious honor, of losing my virginity to Pola. (Dubious only because I never in my life was really sure if I—barely eighteen—had not lost my virginity at an earlier date.) In postwar Vienna "Miss Populari's" fame dwindled, and so she married the elderly Count Orszczelski-Abendsperg, who forthwith—during the honeymoon at the Hotel Royal Danieli in Venice—expired. Pride, however, did not allow her to return to the operetta stage. And so in 1927 the widowed Countess Orszczelska-Abendsperg (which she called herself despite the fact that the First Austrian Republic had abolished the use of titles) married Joop ten Breukaa, a more or less inactive partner in an Amsterdam shipping company. Part of his youth had been spent in the Dutch East Indies on his father's kapong, a colonial mansion between the harbor of Surabaya and the Vorstenlanden of Java. Later the office of his father's shipping concern was unable to hold him. Off and on he handled overseas business for the firm, studied art history in various parts of Europe, collected paintings by Dutch and French masters, some Far Eastern and Etruscan sculpture, and made himself a name of sorts among artists and art dealers in Europe as a lover of well-known paintings and of little-known actresses whom he "promoted." Because he was not exactly stingy as a patron, the lively artists' community decided to tolerate his proverbially boring company. He could offer Pola a large house in the residential area of Vienna as well as a country estate called Acla Silva in the Upper Engadine and a tiny city apartment (nine rooms) in Amsterdam. In 1936 he had already evacuated a Jacob van Ruisdael, a Solomon van Ruisdael, a G. B. Weenix, an S. de Vlieger, a J. de Momper, and a Dirck Hals from Vienna, partly to Amsterdam and partly to Acla Silva, but most important, The Spahi which he called his "bodyguard."

When the ten Breukaas decided on the eighteenth of March, 1938, to leave the newly begotten Greater German Reich (and to take Xana with them), it was not because Pola had "a few drops of the forbidden blood in her veins," as Joop might wearily remark, but because he feared reprisals in the foreign currency market.

The reprisals *I* had to fear were definitely not in the foreign currency market.

In Bludenz I climb off the Arlberg Express and shoulder my skis. Glancing back across the skis to the first-class car, I receive not the slightest wave of good-bye from the window. That too is according to plan. Even so I feel a slight twinge in my heart, and in the same second a slight pain in my forehead.

Everything familiar and yet new. *This* situation *is* new.

And so it develops, this new situation. I take the bus to Schruns (where Ernest Hemingway is said to have spent some happy days), stay overnight with a comrade (a doctor), and next day go through Montafon up to Sankt Gallenkirch. There I spend the night with Toni E., the head of the local smuggling ring. Haven't met many smugglers who were active in the movement, and who remained so; Toni was one of the few. In a low-ceilinged room lit only by a kerosene lamp he gives me instructions over a glass of mulled wine. The brand-new SS ski patrols in the Montafon-Silvretta area are from Bavaria. They are not yet totally familiar with the "arctic" Silvretta region. The local gendarmerie that serves with them has not become nazified yet, and the snow conditions, above 2,000 meters, are at the moment excellent for skiing. The border between the—now German—Montafon and the Praetigau in Switzerland is marked across the Silvretta snowfields by long stakes projecting from containers in which the exact path of the boundary line (to the meter) is delineated on papers sealed in waterproof envelopes.

Toni will take me to this border at 4:00 A.M. As he gives me my instructions, Toni tests the strength of each of the four narrow sealskin strips we will attach to our skis for the ascent, then expertly begins to wax both pairs of skis with the help of a flat iron. Either the whole thing runs smoothly—an essential aspect of good skiing, haha, says Toni. Or if there is imminent danger up on the Silvretta (it's a risky stretch), Toni will stay behind me and move the border stakes that are spaced a hundred meters apart. Will pull them back toward Montafon, Vorarlberg, toward Austria, excuse me, Germany, just the way slalom stakes are shifted at certain championship events, hahaha ... And our friends from Bavaria will be fooled and won't follow me onto what they believe to be Swiss territory. On the other side the ski patrols of the Helvetian Border Police were reinforced a week ago. "Everything clear, Trebla?"

"All clear, Toni." I am a crack skier, almost first class. Born in Olmuetz, I was surrounded by rugged terrain: High Tatra, Ore Mountains, Giant Mountains; my father sat on his horse and laughed at skiers; my mother loved the new sport; at twelve I attempted a schuss into a grove of trees to impress some on-looking lady—and "made kindling"; i.e., I broke my skis to pieces. After the war I learned from Hannes Schneider, founder of the Ski School at St. Anton, how to ski downhill in the Arlberg crouch. (Toni E. informs me that Hannes has just emigrated to America.) It was all over with flying after my war injury, but I could still do something on skis, even on a long descent. Pressure changes in skiing are not *quite* so rapid as those in flying.

They almost took me prisoner. Took me prisoner? Am I already in the Second World War? A risky stretch, risky, ski, ski, ski! Just as Toni expected, out of the snowy distance (the name of a Tyrolean peak facing Bavaria) emerges the SS ski patrol—the Bavarians; Toni moves the "slalom stakes" minutes before they whisk by in the powdery snow, and I whisk away from them, flanked by the cracks of a few carbine shots. *That* is certainly nothing new to me, and I don't even feel a throb in my forehead.

I hope Toni gets away. Ah, don't worry. He skis like a young god.

"It's war again, and I desire/To bear no blame for it" (Matthias Claudius). Above all, in this war I desire not to be killed. Not on the Silvretta. To see Xana again in Zurich (the ten Breukaas continued on to the Engadine). To live two months in Zurich's Seefeld quarter, in the hotel At the Sign of the Rear Falcon, a third-rate house, known as The Rear for short. That is in keeping with the new situation. One shouldn't be complacent, certainly not after seven years of marriage, but I have a suspicion: Xana loves me, and not only that, she seems absolutely infatuated with the Man Who Came Over the Silvretta. Until a bad hay-fever attack with asthma banishes me a second time—into the Upper Engadine, where in Pontresina we rent (from Madam Fausch, the postmistress) two relatively cheap rooms with a shower over the post office. No sooner have Xana and I set up house there, I mean here, than we receive word from Franz S., editor of the *Ostschweizerische Arbeiterzeitung* in St. Gallen that Dr. Maxim Grabscheidt, one of our best friends, a doctor from the Lastenstrasse in the working-class section of Graz, a Socialist (and according to the latest Nazi terminology, a half-breed of the first order), three or four weeks ago was deported to the concentration camp Dachau near Munich and murdered.

Xana, it seems, takes the belated news with complete composure. That afternoon Madam Fausch hands me another, less belated message. The yard-long handwritten epistle of Adelhart Edler von Stepanschitz. A really typical piece of shit, something for the connoisseur. I decide not to show it to Xana.

The ten Breukaas have invited us for the same evening to Acla Silva. In situations like this I am in favor of distraction, therefore against turning them down.

Shortly after dinner Xana disappears.

Pola tells about the last "divine première at the Burgtheater before the Anschluss," which makes me sick, and Joop praises his Spahi to the skies, which makes me sick. In French, Pola orders Jean Bonjour, her Vaudois gardener-servant-chauffeur (a somewhat overcrowded profession), to serve the coffee and not to forget le sucre, which makes me sick, and I leave the overheated living room with its enormous English fireplace devouring half a forest of Swiss pine, leave without a word like someone heading for the toilet, and hope *that* was the reason for Xana's departure. But she is nowhere to be found in the house, and her three-quarter-length camel's-hair coat is hanging in the vestibule closet, and there is no sense in making a visit to the kitchen where Jean Bonjour is clattering with the coffee, because the house door, the thick front door of the imitation Scottish country house, is standing half open. Illuminated by the two lamps outside, the cold night mist seeps into the doorway, as palpable as it is visible, night-mist, night-fog, yes, fog, damp and cold.

My eyes search across the steps to the terraced garden. The wrought-iron gate is also ajar—by the little covered bridge with the green glass lantern hanging over its entrance—the garden gate that, if not locked (in the special interest of the Spahi), can be opened from the vestibule by means of a button. Obviously Xana used the button and went out the garden gate in her saffron yellow tricot dress—or was it the blue one? No, the saffron yellow dress—with no coat, no coat, headed for . . . where? *WHERE?* I leap down the long steps like a steeplechase horse, gallop over the wooden bridge (with a brief burst of hoofbeats), and halt outside the wall surrounding Acla Silva beneath the single light bulb that marks the ten Breukaas' garage. I halt like a reined-in horse, scan up the road that loses itself in the darkness of the Staz forest; don't think she went that way, so down the road leading to the northeast corner of Lake Moritz I run. It's the end of May and what a nonspring! Leaving the ten Breukaas' garage behind me I glance upward as I run through the cold, moonless night and glimpse the stars, flickering ghostly through the frosty night mist, emergency lighting for my racecourse.

It's not my instinct alone that sends me in this direction, but logic as well. Before dinner Pola, Xana, and I went for a walk along the shoreline promenade leading down to the Stahlbad (while Joop chose to stay with his Spahi). I race down the shoreline path where we had gone before, so that my pulse hammers in my head wound—nothing unusual.

More ominous, no, more alarming, no, more ominous is the realization that there is no point in calling her.

No point in calling her name.

No point. (One of her childhood sayings: "The more you call me, the less I'll come.") Xana!—shouting would be senseless. It all depends on the instinct, and the intuition, and the intelligence, and the fitness of the runner. (The way it is in every sport. Luckily my hay fever is gone.)

And then at about 10 o'clock on that completely unspringlike May night the runner reaches a sort of goal. On top of a rock at the water's edge, on a block of boulder chipped from the Rosatch that he noticed earlier that evening, there sits a—a shimmer of saffron yellow in listless motion.

Now the pulsebeat of the runner with the thrice-operated brow, the pulsebeat in his hazelnut-size, hollow scar goes wham-wham-wham-wham. He was not even eighteen when he was shot in the head, and so they called him—his fellow soldiers and later on his comrades during the peacetime that was no peacetime—called him "Trebla, whose heart beats on his forehead."

On the morning after the night I had groped my way to the boulder she was running a 102° fever and coughing. The ten Breukaas sent over their family physician, Dr. Tardueser. Slight bronchitis, injection, a few days' bed rest. During our long acquaintance Xana had seldom had a cough and was an inept cougher. Her coughing distinctly reminded me of the hoarse, voiceless barks of stray dogs in Turkish cities.

"Do you know how you cough, my dear?"

"No."

"Like the half-starved stray dogs in Constantinople used to bark. Exactly. You know, I always asked myself why they couldn't bark properly. It's funny, but they just couldn't."

Xana's laugh became a coughing fit. She brought it under control and said hoarsely: "A stray Turkish dog yourself."

"Who?"

"You," she rasped.

"Aha," I said. "They were also very pathetic and lovable. Even though they had lots of fleas and ugly hairless spots covered with mange."

"So do you."

"What?"

"With all your fleas and mangy spots," she rasped, "you're very —echechech—pathetic and lovable, little mother."

She smiled up at me wanly from her pillow. Today she had less temperature and more face than yesterday, I noted with some satisfaction. (When she was sick Xana always lost her face, and I seriously wondered if anyone would have recognized her in a brief, chance encounter with this faceless visage.) Into this illness she had fled from the truth that Maxim Grabscheidt was murdered.

When she gets up tomorrow she will have gotten over both of these things. And while I was thinking of the truth, Stepanschitz's letter crackled in my shirt pocket, and I went from our small bedroom into the adjoining one that I had set up as a workroom, closed the door and typed my answer on my small Remington portable.

Pontresina, May 24, 1938

Previously esteemed Adelhart!

Tell your Captain, tell him he can kiss my ass.

No longer yours, Trebla

I closed the envelope and typed the address: Schwarzspanierstrasse, Vienna IX.

After three gloomy days (the postmistress had supplied us with an electric heater) spring finally crept into the mountains. In the pasture beneath our windows grazed several well-groomed pepper-colored cows, herded by a red-woolen-outfitted child who was so small we couldn't tell whether boy or girl. Around 11:00 A.M. an energetic knock at the door. Dr. Tardueser stepped in with his black bag, dressed very much for the city—today I noticed something shiny sticking out of his vest pocket that seemed to be not a medical instrument but a tuning fork. He listened to Xana's breathing, then said tersely, "At noon today we get up."

"Can my husband also get up, Doctor?"

"Your husband? Is he sick too?"

Xana inspected her virtually restored face in her tarnished Biedermeier hand mirror (an heirloom): "No, but he isn't getting up."

Tardueser examined me through his pince-nez. I stood there in Bosnian slippers, wrapped in the burnoose (woven through with broken gold threads, faded from many trips to the cleaner's) that I had picked up in Smyrna in 1916 and that had served me as a bathrobe ever since.

"That is, ech-ech," she coughed, "he is recuperating. He had a bad attack of hay fever in Zurich. With asthma."

"Asthma!" snorted Tardueser in unexpected delight. "Asthma. Hay-fever asthma! A fellow suf-f-ferer! I myself am aler-r-rgic to pollen! Do you know what would happen if I went down to the lowlands this time of year. I'd suf-f-focate! Literally suf-f-focate!"

"I feel much better up here."

"I should say! I should say it's better for you here, young man. Ppon-trressina! The pparadise of asthmatics! And don't lie around in the sack till noon, young man! Get up! Go out and walk around in God's own sub-blime Alpine landscape!" He snapped his bag shut, and before I could open the door for him, planted his natty, gray felt hat over his silvered hair.

"Young man—and me thirty-nine! How can you make such a fool of me in front of a complete stranger—and a real dunce at that? Xana, I don't understand you any more; as far as I can remember you have *never* made fun of me before, then all of a sudden you ask this . . . medic, this tourist-healer in the sub-blime Alpine landscape if your husband can *also* get up. Is that supposed to be a lead-off number à la Giaxa and Giaxa?"

"Please don't," she whispered into the antique mirror. "Please don't say anything about Giaxa and Giaxa. Please, not now."

She had a strange way of looking at me sideways while keeping her head in profile (her widespaced eyes allowed for that), of looking at me with *one* eye, silently, softly withdrawn, and at the same time alien and suspicious like a mustang foal.

The doctor had insisted she pull her nightgown over her head. He was "not about to confuse a stethoscopic examination with a lot of rustling clothes—especially when we're dealing with a bronchitis." Warmed by the electric heater, Xana sat half naked in bed with her knees drawn up under the blanket, one temple resting on her concealed knee, as with long, slow movements of her bare arms, she tried to pull the nightgown back over her head. A saffron-yellow one, of all things, the same color as the dress she wore as she crouched on the boulder. The lanky roundness of this twenty-seven-year-old woman-child always surprised me, since there was not the slightest conflict between length and curve, but a harmony instead that was marvelously attractive, and even bizarre. A long back; sometimes I get the feeling she has no backbone, she can curl herself up so tightly—a "snake woman" in the jargon of acrobats. But her breasts—in the second before she slips on her nightgown—are spectacular in another way, almost heavy, almost buxom, something you can, no, something *I* can get hold of—just made to nurse a baby (though we had none). Around her slender neck a bright rose-colored scarf. High-set cheeks inspired the nickname "Reine Patapouf" (in memory of the French fairy tale of King Fat-Cheeks, which my nanny in Olmuetz had mercilessly retold to me over and over again), cheeks that showed the tint of ripe peaches now that her illness was over, the right one resting on her knee as she looked up at me with *both* her smallish eyes—eyes that beamed a color somewhere between violet and gentian blue beneath rounded, almost crescent brows. Xana's hair, which could dry, even during milder illnesses, into a kind of dull, greenish spider web, fluffed out once more in a cloud of hazelnutbrownblond—and so once again I capitulated to this impressionistic beauty-of-the-bed. (She once replied to a Viennese admirer, "I'm not really pretty, I just look that way.") I shuffled over to my Remington.

"Trebla."

"Yes?"

"How old was he, actually?"

"Who?"

"Maxim Grabscheidt."

"Two years older than me. Forty-one."

For three days Xana, wrapped in a woolen blanket and a coat, relaxed on our little wooden balcony in the sun. Following Dr. Tardueser's advice she had decided to delay working on the translation job she had accepted. Even without the doctor's advice she would have been prepared to do absolutely nothing—and then at other times, a great deal. She was a wild poppy who could change without warning into a mule. She was working on a "Metamorphosis" very much in the spirit of Lucius Apuleius, born A.D. 125, whose *Golden Ass* she had contracted to translate from its Latin (tinged with North African Greek) into up-to-date German. (One reason for undertaking the translation was the frequent use of the word "Forsooth!" in the translation by August Rode.) La Mistinguett, mistress of the music hall Moulin Rouge in Montmartre around 1930 (soon thereafter it became, by way of all flesh, a movie house), diagonally across from the Circus Médrano where Giaxa, up to his farewell appearance in '36, always performed—La Mistinguett had nicknamed his daughter, a student at the Sorbonne, Xana Coquelicot, "wild poppy on a long stem." At the Pontresina post office, while typing, I asked occasional questions of the wooden balcony, How is Miss Poppy, or Fraulein Doktor Elephantophile? Xana, who loves wild elephants, replied, just fine, Aviatishek, or Kometishek, both nicknames hearkening back to my days as a wartime flyer. This name cult was started by Xana's Russian-German mother Elsabé. And so, for example, we called each other *kukulaps* (Estonian for "cuckoo-child"), or "little mother," an ironic comment, perhaps, on our own childlessness. For three days Xana rested in the noonday sun, and I knew that the sweet sorrow that enveloped her like her woolen blankets was no longer related to the death of Maxim Grabscheidt, but to the living: Konstantin and Elsabé Giaxa, who were always on her mind. And once as I gazed at her profile my heart stood still on my forehead. Hadn't it been reckless of me to keep Stepanschitz's letter from her? And to answer him behind her back with my laconic quotation from the young Goethe? No doubt she would have advised me to ignore the letter from Vienna, but now the rude answer was on its way. Suddenly the dreadful word *Hostages* came into my head. No, I calmed myself, they wouldn't dare. His name conjures up volleys of laughter out of the past; they wouldn't dare lay a hand on him. Not only that, but he had been so quiet lately—an old man in his mid-sixties living in solitude in his country home at Radkersburg, devoted to chess and jigsaw puzzles, and Giaxa the Last munching his retirement oats in Giaxa's stall . . .

"One coffee grappa please, and one plain."

"Coffee grappa for me too, please."

I am mildly surprised. "You too?"

Xana calmly: "Me too."

We ate in the common room of the Morteratsch Hotel in the company of servants and truck drivers. (We chose the common room so as to escape the Hay Fever Society.) The waitress served us two glasses of black coffee laced with grappa.

"Cuckoo-child, shouldn't you give Pola a call? She did send you her family doctor and a thousand rhododendrons. Just out of politeness, shouldn't we go over to Acla Silva and say hello?"

Xana: "Not yet . . . Not yet . . . I—"

"Whatever you say, little mother."

Pensively she blew into the glass. Then she emptied it in long swallows like a thirsty person drinking water. "All right."

"It's agreed?"

"No, I mean this coffee grappa of yours. It's all right."

"Really? Since when are you sympathetic to alcohol?"

"Since today."

Less than a week after I had dispatched my answer to Stepanschitz/Laimgruber, two gentlemen from Vienna checked into the Morteratsch Hotel. Blond fellows in their mid-twenties. They added their names to the C.H.P.P. (Club for Hay Fever Patients at Pontresina) "membership list" that hung in the hall outside the dining room:

> J. KRAINER
> G. MOSTNY

2

Thursday, June 2, Radio Beromuenster (overheard in the common room) announced that Dr. Hans Froehlicher had been named Swiss ambassador to Berlin; around four that afternoon the First Encounter took place in Roseg Valley.

On the Russellas Promenade cirro-cumulus clouds gave the sky a quilted appearance; lower down, in the Valtellina, the first hot day of the year may have arrived; here in the Roseg the brooding sun pressed its warmth through the gaps in the clouds and milked the smell of resin out of Swiss pines, Scotch pines, and larches. "Breathe," I said. We encountered no one. Out of the south, down from the glacier foamed the Roseg Brook, swollen rather high in its banks, and when the trail passed near it we felt its fresh, icy breath. The road that followed the opposite bank was also empty, except for a lone rack wagon drawn by two mules trotting slowly in the direction of Pontresina. Large zinc milk cans, obviously empty, rattled against each other, but the rushing torrent drowned out their clanging. Past and gone.

16

The pine forest grew sparse and stunted; we were nearing the tree line. But there *was* a sign of life up there.

In the midst of a boulder-strewn slope, matching its surroundings so well as to be almost indistinguishable, crouched a grayish orange, furry woodchuck. No, it wasn't crouching, it was standing there erect on its hind legs, arrow straight, with its forelegs, or rather its short arms, hanging at its sides. Much like a cautious, curious little man dressed in a full-length fur coat, standing expectantly, on the lookout, as if waiting to say "Who goes there?" As we approached—a soft, piercing whistle, and he was gone.

Xana, in her low-heeled shoes, wandered five, then ten, then fifteen paces ahead of me. She was wearing her blue sweater-dress with a matching scarf as a turban, and the dress seemed designed to go with the blue that showed between the clouds. She sauntered, with a barely perceptible rolling of her slender hips, toward the glacier. On our right we had the Alp prima, and high above us on our left, just as the postmistress had described it, rose the Alp seguonda, checkered with pink from the first blush of rhododendrons, and I inserted my horn-rimmed monocle, one of two monocles, the other my reading glass (intended, not to symbolize my connections to the Old Empire, but to remedy a real problem: the occasional weakness in my right eye—a consequence of my head wound—which particularly impairs my distance vision, while my left eye remains as sharp as a hawk's). I estimate another half hour's walk to the Hôtel du Glacier. A house at the foot of the blackish glacial moraine with ghostly fumes rising from its roof. Unconsciously I glanced behind me and saw . . .

What I saw left me rooted to the spot, as the saying goes, no longer than a second. Then I reacted.

About sixty meters away, from behind a boulder standing on end and capped by three dwarfed stone pines, projected an arm clothed in bright-colored wool.

It seemed to be an Egyptian pattern, Tutankhamon to be exact. A hand held a long object and slid slowly away from it. Something gleamed dully in the diffused sunlight, something like a slender burnished steel rod whose end was slowly shifted in my direction.

With three bounds I took cover behind a man-sized boulder, at the same time warning Xana with a restrained shout. But very close to the curving Russellas Promenade roared the Roseg Brook, swollen with snow—and she couldn't hear. Now some thirty meters upstream, she tramped toward the foot of the Alp seguonda.

When she didn't hear I felt afraid for the first time. A possible headline flashed through my mind: **DOUBLE MURDER IN ROSEG VALLEY—CULPRIT UNKNOWN**.

I picked up a flat stone and gave it a good heave in her direction. It flew over her head and landed on the path just in front of her, so that she turned around (she seldom turns around) somewhat bewildered, it seemed, and I waved at her vigorously with the alpenstock I had borrowed from the postmistress. Then I pantomimed a demand for her to get off the promenade and take immediate cover.

For a moment she seemed puzzled. Then with an unexpected reflex she glanced quickly up at the Alp seguonda: was my pantomime a warning of a rockslide? I shook my head and saw her open and close her mouth. Now she seemed to want to come back down the path to me, and again I urgently waved her "offstage."

Finally Xana decided to follow my sign language and, balancing over the rock-strewn ground, disappeared in a dip between the path and the stream.

All this had happened within two minutes. Peering up over the jagged edge of my cover I looked downstream. The arm with the barrel of burnished steel, probably a Flobert rifle (what else could it be?) had disappeared behind the up-ended granite block.

The only weapon at *my* disposal was Madam Fausch's gnarled alpenstock with its iron tip.

I put away my monocle and stole down to the wild gushing brook that foamed a milky, iridescent blue green, as if it were carrying down pieces of sky and rock crystal, and its rushing, roaring, hissing overwhelmed the sound of my cautious footsteps.

A two-pound, sharp-edged rock—a puny, miserable substitute for a hand grenade—I picked it up, shoved it into my left pants pocket, and still bent low, crept along the bank through clumps of grass mixed with soldanella and over water-smoothed stones, trying to pass unseen the point where the arm with the Tutankhamon pattern lay in wait. Then I could approach the culprit from behind.

I stayed close to the bank of the stream, jumping from one torrent-flattened rock to another. Then I caught sight of it between two Swiss pines, the canted boulder alongside the Russellas Promenade.

From this point the three stone pines looked like one.

For several seconds I squeezed my monocle in my weak eye. One of the two blond fellows who had recently checked in at the Morteratsch Hotel lay on his belly, his hobnailed boots in my direction, a knapsack within reach. The other one was turned away from me, kneeling sentrylike with his right shoulder against the rock.

He seemed to have a handgun at the ready.

Both wore sweaters with the same Egyptian pattern, knickers, and white woolen knee socks. Next to the kneeling man was a camera. Mounted on a tripod of burnished steel. So it could have been a leg of the tripod I had seen projecting from behind the rock.

It *could* have been.

Stalking through the low grass. They didn't notice me until I stopped five paces behind them, with the middle of the stick in my right hand, ready to slash or jab, and my left hand gripping the stone in my pocket.

"Well, gentlemen, how's the hunting?"

The one on his knees jerked his face toward me. A face not particularly handsome, but anonymous to agreeable. An attractive average-boy's face, his carefully parted ash blond hair slicked down with brilliantine, his medium sideburns typical of the petty bourgeois Austrian dandy. In the hotel I had already noticed this en passant, as well as the fact that the other fellow was straw blond.

The latter, here and now, was lying prone on a plaid blanket. Pushing himself up with his arm he turned his head much more slowly than his companion, and I saw his doughy face close up for the first time, and the many moles dotted across his skin. It was not as if he were turning around of his own volition. But as though he were merely imitating his friend. And now, now he seemed to want to prove his own initiative. Rising to his knees, he stretched out his left hand toward the open knapsack (mustard colored, seemingly brand new). A brief gesture by the ash blond—clearly the act of a superior—and the straw blond retracted his hand.

The weasel-quick eyes of the ash blond were fixed on my left pants pocket. I moved the hidden stone into position like a "trigger happy" gunman in an American gangster film who enjoys shooting holes in his pocket.

One-two-three, the ash blond was on his feet. The straw blond followed him, a bit less smartly. I took a step back. Both were about six feet tall; the ash blond made an athletic impression, the other seemed more lax. They both wore the same insipid sweaters, the same herringbone-tweed knickers, the same white knee socks. Who would go around in such a uniform? Twins perhaps. Or homosexual lovers. Or "special units in civilian clothes."

The one with the agreeable face: "Hunting? Whad'ya mean, hunting?"

"You seemed to be looking for game."

"Game? That's funny. Sometime I *would* like to shoot somethin'."

"Aha. You want to shoot some-thing."

"Sometime. A woodchuck."

"Aha. A woodchuck."

"Sometime. With the Leica there. A snapshot."

"A snapshot. I see. Wouldn't it be better then to put the tripod *on* the rock. Instead of behind it?"

"That's *awr* business, a'think," said the ash blond, and I really couldn't disagree. He alone kept up the conversation with me and his Viennese accent was unmistakable. Having spent so many years in that city, I thought I could even guess the part of town he came from: zone VII, the very Neubau district where at noon on July 25, 1935, the Eighty-ninth SS regiment had assembled and disguised themselves in federal army uniforms, so that they could be transported to the Ballhausplatz, could enter the chancellery courtyard unhindered and murder "Millimetternich," the dwarfish chancellor Dollfuss. "Awr business, isn't it, Shorsh?"

Shursh, Shorsh: a variant of George. So it was the straw blond whose name was Mostny. Until now he had not uttered a word, just stared at me—not at my eyes, but at a point in the middle of my forehead. On his doughy face an expression that I took to be dull-witted hate. Even after the rhetorical question of his apparent superior, of J. Krainer (so he had entered his name on the hay-fever list), he said nothing, and I didn't like his expression, his silence, and in this context I didn't like the nearby roaring of the Roseg Brook at all.

All of a sudden the game I had started to play seemed to be full of REAL potential danger, but I said, "Naturally it's your business. It just seems a bit odd that, mm, when you've got your camera mounted five feet off the ground you'd get down on your knees to take a picture. So I asked myself if maybe—sometime!—you might be wanting to 'shoot' yourself a woodchuck—not with a Leica, but with, mm . . ."

The spokesman, raising his voice somewhat: "With?"

"With . . ." I made a slight but demonstrative movement with the stone in my left pants pocket, "with, let's say, a Luger pistol . . . or a small-bore rifle."

"What if!" the man who had registered as Krainer replied still louder. (Though his tone couldn't be called aggressive yet.) "What if we went n' shot us a woodchuck with a Luger—whadda you have to say about it? You a game warden or somethin'?"

"No, I'm a hay-fever patient like you."

"Whaddaya say about that, Shorsh? Three hay-fever patients inna group."

For the first time the ash blond and his companion traded glances that were full of secret understanding, whereupon the quiet one twisted the corners of his mouth into a foolish grin.

"If you went and shot yourself a woodchuck, as you put it, I would be obliged to intervene, even though I'm not a game warden. Because I'm a woodchuck hunter-hunter."

"What' sat?"

"A woodchuck-hunter-hunter."

"D'you hear that, Shorsh?"

The roar of the mountain stream. Crazy. If I had made a mistake about these two, they would have to think I'm crazy. Even if I hadn't made a mistake, they'd think me no less crazy, perhaps even a potential suicide.

Without warning the ash blond turned his back to me and began removing the camera from its tripod, at the same time signaling to the still grinning "Shorsh" with a jerk of his chin.

The latter immediately lost his grin and stepped off the plaid. I had not time to lose. Thrusting the point of my stick in the grass, I bent over quickly and whipped the blanket off the ground.

No weapon to be seen. There remained the half-open, mustard brown canvas knapsack.

Grasping Madam Fausch's stick, I took a brisk jump to the knapsack, the plaid in my left hand, the stick in my right, caricature of a torero. Both the blond fellows stared at me.

Holy Laudon! What would the next few seconds bring?

The next second came with a crack.

The crack of a whip. Returning up the road across the stream came the rack wagon pulled by its two mules. Proceeding uphill, the driver, his cornflower blue shepherd's blouse hanging down over his pants, walked next to his slow-moving team and cracked his whip, cracked it louder than the roaring water, in an apparent effort to greet "us three." With my alpenstock I sent him a fencer's salute, which he answered by means of a second whipcrack; then I folded the plaid and said, like a ham actor miming politeness: "Since I have disturbed you gentlemen, allow me to be of assistance." I handed the plaid to the straw blond.

Two others, two.

Unmistakably English, both around fifty, long and lean. The man was lugging a greenish, weather-beaten, almost moss-covered knapsack hung with a coiled rope and a canteen, wearing snow goggles around his soft felt hat, weathered breeches and, like his female companion, dusty mountain climber's boots fixed with heavy crampons; a pointed nose, wire-rimmed glasses—here too he resembled his lady. Both trotted down from the glacier world, their heavy-booted toes turned slightly inward, and although they were anything but handsome, they seemed radiantly likable, at least as far as my impressions were concerned. The pickax the man carried, point forward, next to his bicep, gave his figure not only an unobtrusive but a definite militance. He was cleanly shaven, whereas his lady possessed a little stubble of whitish whiskers around her chin and cheeks. So they trotted down the Russellas Promenade toward the village, and came out from behind our slanted boulder as if emerging from a grotto. And between them strolled . . . Xana.

"That's my husband," she said in English, ignoring our two blond friends.

"Webster," said the man with friendly, dry reserve. "My wife. How do you do."

"How do you do," I said with a slight bow in the direction of Mrs. Webster. Very nice that they didn't consider shaking hands.

Meanwhile the young men from Vienna had left without a word and hiked up the path toward the Alp seguonda and the glacier. The straw-blond carried the knapsack with the plaid strapped to it; his "superior" had two leather cases slung over his shoulder, camera and tripod.

Pizzagalli's Sporthotel lay on the road to Campfèr. It was not one of the pretentious giants, but one of the cheapest hotels in the rather metropolitan village of St. Moritz, and one of the few that stayed open during the off-season. Painted pinkish beige, it had a table-flat roof on which laundry often fluttered, and an *American Bar & Buendnerstube*. The bar, a longish, wine red room with a zinc-plated counter, Russian billiards, and a series of bright colored photographs of Italy (cypresses, cypresses). Adjoining it was the Buendnerstube, a dark-paneled back room with its showpiece, a wreathlike chandelier of intertwined ibex horns. Along the back wall of the hotel ran a covered boccia lane. The Pizzagallis, Italians from Lake Como who had long been citizens of Switzerland. The proprietor was a stocky, jowled man with stubbly gray hair, slightly apoplectic, with rolls of red flesh on his neck marked with the fat, wormlike scars of once-punctured boils. The hotelkeeper's wife was a head taller than her husband, a massive matron with a pug-nosed face. Whenever she pondered something her eyes rolled up under her lids leaving only the whites of her large eyeballs still showing. Faustino, their son, was at the moment attending the "refresher course," i.e., the maneuvers being held around Bernina Pass. Annette was a neat, slender woman from Geneva who served the customers of the American Bar and the Buendnerstube with masterful agility. The wife of a watch-factory worker and mother of five children, she had taken a temporary job in the Engadine in hopes of curing her anemia. She had a quince yellow complexion and a very French pointed nose; she was dressed all in black with no jewelry; the sweater she wore as a sign of her chronic chills fell flat from her shoulders, revealing a complete absence of bosom.

The tourist-healer Dr. Tardueser called from the Buendnerstube: *"Du rouge, Annette, du rouge! Et deux Brissagos!"*

Annette served us cups of light brown caffè espresso and gave Xana a light pat on the shoulder. Then jumped behind the bar and filled a two-liter carafe with foaming, violet wine. In the side room sat a table full of notables having their premature evening drink along with a never-ending card game. Mr. Dumeng Mavegn, police commissioner, a giant with a tendency toward goiter and silver-graying hairdo complete with bangs, towered over them all. The owner of the printing press, Mr. Zuan, with his well-groomed full black beard, was reminiscent of a turn-of-the-century advertisement for hair-grower. Police Corporal Defila (Annette had whispered the names and professions to us in passing), a somewhat oversturdy man with a baby face. Orange colored insignia on the collar of his blue uniform. The fourth cardplayer in the group beneath the ibex horns was Dr. Tardueser, who hardly managed a nod for his patient Xana (and her late-rising husband), just a side-glance from his pince-nez: strangely animated, almost obsessed with his involvement in the foursome. *"Un 'Jass' à quatre, vous savez,"* Annette informed us as she balanced the two-liter carafe alongside a box of Brissago cigars. "Nonparticipants are required to shut their traps," Tardueser snarled occasionally at the silent kibitzers in exaggerated High German (while the others spoke a brand of Graubuenden German I found only half comprehensible). Whenever he, together with his—by contrast rather apathetic—partner Zarli Zuan (with the splendid beard), succeeded in winning a hand, he would pull the tuning fork out of his pocket and, while Zuan chalked the score on a small blackboard, would intone in tremolo: "De-e-e-p in-n the cel-l-ler, he-e-ere I sit . . ."

One of the kibitzers was Fitz, who didn't really seem to belong there. A quiet, fidgety little man who usually—even at the table with his cronies—wore a canvas cap with a projecting bill. As Annette had let us know during an earlier visit to Pizzagalli's, years ago he (Mr. Fitzallan, of Irish descent) had been one of the private jockeys of King George V. He had won X number of winter races on the ice of Lake Moritz. Then, entangled, so to speak, in his wilting laurels, he decided to stay here, opened up a sporting goods shop, and began giving lessons every winter in skijoring and curling. He never played cards, just kibitzed a little, rocking back and forth astride his chair.

Now Fitz rose from his "saddle" to his full height of five feet and strode bowlegged out the swinging doors of the bar, paying no heed to us. And today, now, during a pause in the service, Annette told Xana, who was leafing through about ten pounds of international magazines and newspapers, and me that it was Fitz's mania to approach standing horses and talk to them for fifteen minutes at a time. English-speaking guests had verified that such lectures consisted entirely of a long series of obscene insults. Whether saddle horses, draft horses, or mules, when Fitz encountered them he scolded and cursed them gently, and with incredible endurance. An eccentric well known all the way from Zuoz to Maloja. And he wasn't the only one in the area. Had we met Decolana?

"Decolana?"

Xana glanced up briefly from her page-flipping. "The name sounds like a circus act."

Annette must have carried the comment to the Buendnerstube, for the men there suddenly burst into laughter; Dr. Tardueser came over to our table.

"Cirrrc-hus!! There, my beautiful young lady, you have, if I may say so, blindly hit the nail on the head. How's our galloping consumption? All cured now?"

Xana smiled up at him.

"And our candidate for hay fever? Do we find ourselves free of asthma? Have we stopped lying around in the sack till noon? Do we get up bright and early now?"

"Instead of dull and late, you mean?" I replied. His pince-nez gaped at me as if he hadn't understood the joke (where there was no joke to understand). Suddenly reserved: "Stop by my office soon, madam, and let me check your respiration." With that, the resort physician returned to his table, where the term "Decolana's circus" seemed to have brought the card game to a halt.

"D'bear-red," remarked policeman Defila with an undertone of rude pity, stood up, took his white gloves from the chair, and stamped out of the room.

"The pear-head," said Tardueser. "Yes, the man does inde-e-ed have a ra-ther degenerated skull. A ra-ther degenerate patrician. After all, his family has been sit-ting in Bergell and Domleschg since Anno-o-o 1100. That's a matter of histo-o-orical record."

The giant (commissioner) Mavegn puffed on his long, thin Brissago. "Hey, noo, was a time when Decolana wasn't a bad lawyer. But noo he's gone t'th'dogs. *Gone to the dogs."*

Bursting, wheezing laughter, in which the grandly bearded printing-press owner Zuan did not participate.

"An animal trainer!" Tardueser added. Bursts of laughter.

Then the two hoteliers chimed in as well.

I: "One question, Signor Pizzagalli. What's with this Mr. Decolana?"

"Il avvocato Bow-Wow? Yes, what's with this Dottore Decolana?" Pizzagalli asked his wife. She began to cogitate, rolled her pupils up beneath her eyelids, let the whites shine for a moment, then dropped her pupils into view again.

"D'you want to buy a doggie?"

Xana, as if entranced by reading, scarcely looked up.

I: "What do you mean? Does this Dottore Decolana own a kennel?"

"Is not necessary you buy a doggie," Pizzagalli decided. "Say you maybe *want* to buy a doggie. That you *solamente*—that you alone are *un interessato*. An interested. Basta! You know where is the schoolhouse yard? There lives Dottore Decolana. *Ecco, ecco.* Maybe"—now he puffed up his shiny jowls—"you get a nice reception."

Through a very short street, past the police station, its windows trimmed with hanging carnations, I reached the schoolyard. Here there were no towering hotels. A formless group of soldiers in ill-fitting olive green uniforms and heavy boots disappeared into a small bar, the Café d'Albana, located on the corner of the little street. Then it was as sunny and quiet as the piazza of a little Italian town in the afternoon, except tidier and cooler, and into this cool, tidy stillness the deliberate bell of the nearby Protestant church struck five o'clock.

Dr. Jur. Guadenz de Colana
Attorney

To the right of the steps leading to the aerial tramway station I found, on a stately but neglected Graubuenden-style house, the weather-beaten enamel sign with its cracked letters. No hanging flowers pushed through the bars covering the narrow, fortresslike windows. Almost all the green paint had peeled off the huge door with its rustically carved baroque rosettes. Moldy black, it stared at me with its old wrought-iron knocker—the handle strangely fan shaped—and seemed permanently shut. Above it on the stained white plaster wall I was greeted by an epigram, now meaningless after the brush of time had scrubbed half of it away: IL SEGNER BENEDESCHA

I had occasion for some serious doubts about myself. What was I doing here? Buying a dog I didn't want? But I had already grasped the iron fan—it felt ice cold. The hard hammer-strokes made hollow reverberations inside the house. Then silence, I waited, and used the cold knocker a second time. Now, far inside, a dog began to bark, its voice weak, sleepy, and hoarse.

The following second shattered the pall of silence that had seemed to envelop the place. A hellish barking broke loose in the house, and, provoked by its own sound, swelled to ever wilder intensity, seemingly amplified in its hollow echoing by some sort of stone-walled chamber. Metallic yelps, roaring woofs, yaps that sounded like asthmatic chirps, all against the counterpoint of the angry-deep-gravelly bark of some giant beast I took to be a St. Bernard or a Great Dane. All this noise rushed up like surf against the door, and I pressed down the cold, heavy door handle and . . . "An animal trainer," Dr. Tardueser had announced. "Maybe you will get a nice reception." The sly, vibrating undertone in Pizzagalli's words echoed in my ears.

Why had I pressed down the door handle? The door was unlocked and creaked open. Wasn't I, a perfect stranger, an unwelcome intruder, just asking—oh why, why—to be torn apart by a Great Dane trained to attack?

My head shrank down between my shoulders. "Ai!" In a compromising reflex my hand jerked toward the stone in my pocket. The vicious Great Dane: a fat little spaniel with shaggy, tattered fur, at one time probably black, now almost green with age, and matted, hanging ears like the side-flaps of an old judge's wig, obviously the ancestor of a teeming brood of six, seven, eight children, grandchildren, and great-grandchildren. While the youngest ones, quick to make friends, jumped at me through the door's opening, bounding, whining, sniffing, whirling their stumpy tails, the elders preferred to bid me a disdainful welcome without leaving the hallway. "Yayayayaya. Okokokokok," I warded off the leaping, scrambling little rascals and, taking care not to step on any of them, slipped quickly into the house, to the growling displeasure of the Spaniel patriarch.

The intruder looked about him. He stood in a spacious, hall-like entranceway, a stony chamber floored with dirty tiles, topped by a low, Romanesque vault, and pervaded by the cold, sour smell of mold. Dusk filled the place. Only through the cubical window-holes flanking the entrance and through the half-open door at the end of the hallway was a slight vestige of sunny afternoon able to penetrate the gloom. The light fell on a hanging, crisscrossed arsenal of maces and halberds that might have been swung at the battle of Marignano, and on which the dust lay thick as grayish snow. Fell on the oscillating pendulum of a decrepit rustic baroque grandfather clock that ticked in dull, dragging beats like an ancient heart. Fell on a sarcophagus that, upon closer examination, proved to be a monumental chest crammed to its unclosable lid with stacks of yellowing file folders. A few of these had overflowed onto the tiles. And all about the floor lay, as if scattered by vandals, a yellowed, crumpled, shredded litter of old ledger sheets, no doubt the playthings of the spaniel pups.

The storm of barking had subsided.

I cleared my throat.

"Hello-o?"

The stony chamber carried off the echo of my call.

"Excuse me, is anyone home? Is Dr. de Colana there? Oh Doc-tor . . ."
No answer.
"Hello there. Could I disturb you for a moment? I say, hello-o-o?"
"Ho-o-o," rang the echo. Then a cool, dusky silence. Wasn't it obvious that I had to turn around and leave the house? It was obvious, but I couldn't bring myself to do it.

Half followed, half led by the uncombed congregation, their big paws padding about me like oversize slippers, I shuffled ahead, accompanied by a few perfunctory growls, across the paper-strewn tiles. Only the patriarch felt dutybound not to be taken in by my soothing words and continued his deep-voiced baying, which, soon exhausted, degenerated into a kind of gutteral howl.

The yawning doorway drew me on.

To make myself look more respectable in case I was caught by surprise, I inserted my monocle. Albert the Absurd.

The first thing I noticed upon peeking through the doorway was two mudencrusted, black button-boots projecting motionless beyond the foot of a wooden bed.

Quickly I stepped closer.

Into a room whose disorder was almost insane. A disorder so fantastic that it seemed almost intentional, almost rigged. Dominated by an enormous wardrobe—like the bed, apparently a genuine Renaissance piece of considerable value—a wardrobe that stared gaping, as if recently plundered by feverish, searching hands, at two dilapidated high-backed chairs by the opposite wall, both richly ornamented in late Gothic style, at a worn-out Biedermeier wing chair, a blocky, rustic table, and a rococo secretary—all wildly strewn with pieces of clothing, stained ties, crumpled shirts, scattered newspapers, overflowing ashtrays, open books, sugar-crusted teacups, as well as several containers of empty and half-empty bottles labeled Zuger Kirsch, Grappa, Marc de Bourgogne. Dangling over a reproduction of Michelangelo's *Last Judgment* was a pair of long-legged, poison-green underpants. On the floor lay trampled eggshells and two or three large, gnawed-up beef bones. This chaotic still life of valuables, rags, and garbage—the likes of which I'd never seen before—lay exposed at the mercy of the afternoon sun. The window, larger than the ones in the hall and fronted with wrought-iron bars, looked onto a disheveled terrace garden in which lay two garden elves once brightly painted, but now washed gray by the rain.

In the rumpled bed lay a fully clothed man.

Skin bluish red. With a head that tapered scalpward like a pear. He didn't move. His mouth, a dark hole beneath an untrimmed, yellowish moustache, gaped unnaturally wide, as if his jaw were out of joint. He was not snoring. Hardly seemed to breathe. Lay completely motionless.

". . . Oh—ah, hm . . . Oh Doctor?"

He moved not a muscle.

3

I stood there feeling rather uneasy. If this man were breathing he was doing it more imperceptibly than anyone I had ever seen. For a few seconds I even felt justified in wondering whether a murder hadn't taken place here. In broad daylight? two steps away from the police station? in the safest country in Europe? It was a theatrical notion, virtually impossible in reality. I saw myself as an actor in a melodrama, playing the role of a thoroughly unlikely detective, the hero of a whole series of stage mysteries, who, in the most abstruse play of the lot—entitled perhaps *Murder in the Spaniel Sanatorium*—had just discovered the first corpse.

Then I saw how effortlessly the spaniel pack assumed their customary places amidst the chaos, and all my thoughts of being an actor in a murder mystery vanished. One dog jumped into the wing chair, two snuggled down on a coat pulled from the wardrobe, others started busily licking one another. One began a self-important scratching of his floppy ear and soon found imitators. Meanwhile the patriarch, after several vain attempts, succeeded in hurling his corpulent body onto the place of honor, the bed. With a very gentle, very soft, drawn-out "hoo-oo-oo," a loving sigh from his puffing jowls, he slithered inside the sleeper's arms, bedded his graygreen muzzle on the man's stone-motionless chest and closed his lids after giving me a last, suspicious glance from his half-blind, white and bleary eyes.

The dog's touch released the sleeper from his total paralysis. He moved his arm, and a rattling wheeze escaped his open mouth. No sooner had he given these feeble signs of life than the whole pack sprang from their places. The grownups jumped onto the bed amidst subdued yelps of joy and snuggled up to their master, while the smallest ones, unable to make the leap, began a mournful whining.

The rattling wheeze grew louder, then stopped abruptly, and the man's jaw snapped shut. His eyes opened squinting—inflamed, bluish white eyes not unlike those of the spaniel patriarch. A totally benumbed gaze stared up at the stained ceiling. The dogs on the bed had all taken up a sitting posture, and with their round eyes gleaming expectantly, observed the awakening with almost scientific interest.

"Pardon me . . . Dr. de Colana?"

"Grrunngg-gungg-heh?" A mucoid gargling. His gaping stare wandered from the ceiling and came to rest stupidly on me.

"Please excuse me for disturbing you, Doctor, but I've come to—hm—ah—inquire . . ."

"Aaa . . . aww . . . waah . . ." A groaning yawn. His inflamed eyelids fell shut. Now his chest rose and fell steadily, and I thought he was asleep again. Then he stared at me once more, dumbly gaping.

"I've come to inquire about buying a dog. I might be interested in a spaniel."

Now the expression of complete bafflement gave way to gradual comprehension. Yes, something like hostile arrogance began to peer at me from out of his bleary eyes. Amidst colossal groaning and applauded by nine joyfully wagging tail-stumps he raised his muddy boots from the foot of the bed, reeled into a sitting position, and stopping on the edge of the bed where, with numbly inept hands, he adjusted his loosened black tie and buttoned his long-tailed black jacket. The light shone on a gleaming violet pimple that disfigured the left nostril of his otherwise rather nobly shaped nose.

"*Vacca Madonna*," he grunted, squinting at me even more unkindly than the patriarch. "How did you . . . who sent you here?" He spoke almost pure High German.

"Mr. Pizzagalli."

"Pizzagalli, heh?" Groan. Suddenly he was on his feet, pursing his straw-covered lips to make a kissing sound. "Pf-pf, Sirio! *Venga qui!*"

A roughly one-year-old spaniel with a pitch-black, shining coat scrambled obediently over the bed. De Colana grabbed him by the scruff of the neck, moved totteringly closer and shoved him brusquely in front of my nose, almost striking me in the face.

"Twelve hundred francs!" he growled. The sour smell of liquor fanned out from beneath his fringed moustache.

I didn't have any intention of buying a dog. How could we, as homeless refugees, tie ourselves down with a house pet? Still, the price amazed me. I examined Sirio. He hung in front of my nose without struggling, all patient, suffering innocence, and stared at me with his round, young onyx eyes.

"Twelve hundred? Isn't that a bit expensive?"

With a caution that was touching due to his unsteady condition, de Colana set Sirio back onto the bed. Then he began to rub the matted, splendid ears of the patriarch who was nestled up against his thigh.

"Expensive, *mein Herr*, but genuine. A Scottish cocker spaniel, ancient pedigree, King Charles . . . Sirio of Bannockburn . . . Try going to Milan or Zurich, and if you can find a dog like this—ech!" a grunt of arrogance, "I'll put twelve hundred on the table and no questions asked . . . I won't sell him cheaper. If he's too expensive for you, all right. You don't have to buy him."

With a wave of his hand, a scornful shaking of his arm, he turned his back toward me, to which a few bed feathers were sticking, and squinted, still scratching the patriarch, out at the faded garden dwarfs. I was dismissed.

"Then once again excuse the interruption and thank you very much for the information. Your dogs are really superb, I must say, but twelve hundred—that's out of the question. You see, we're from Austria . . . ex-Austria . . . The special conditions these days, you know. I think you understand . . ." Why was I, the unwanted guest, making such a long speech instead of just leaving?

Then he turned toward me and, teetering slightly on his feet, peered at me—my monocle, then my forehead.

"My respects, Doctor." I nodded ceremoniously, turned and walked out of the chaotic room, this place—half museum, half rubbish heap, across the echoing, rustling tiles of the hallway. Then his shuffling steps were behind me and the clicking of a cane.

"Hey! Mr. Austrian," he groaned, echoing. He wore a broad-brimmed, black felt hat that lent him a rustic dignity as well as a certain priestlike quality. About him swarmed the spaniel pack. "Where are you going?"

"Me? Oh, back to Pizzagalli's. My wife is waiting for me."

He shuffled up to me. His hostile arrogance seemed to have evaporated. From under his unkempt, hanging moustache peeked a nimble grin. He was nibbling on a peppermint tablet that had purged his schnapps-laden breath. "So . . . Isn't tomorrow Pentecost, heh?"

"Right."

"How would it be if we allowed ourselves—echech—a glass of Chianti Antinori to celebrate the day?" Despite the drinker's boil that gleamed on his nose he did a convincing imitation of the puritan philistine who allows himself a glass of wine once a year before Pentecost. "Might I have your company for an evening drink?"

"I'd be delighted."

Leaving the spaniel pack turned out to be a small ceremony. Not in Romansh, but in beautiful Florentine Italian, he gave a rather unctuous speech, which he ended with a gesture like a benediction. Only the patriarch Arcibaldo had the privilege of accompanying us. Sadly submissive looks from eight pairs of cocker spaniel eyes, then de Colana closed the door and locked it using a key as long as a toothbrush. Propped up by an amber-handled cane with worn-out rubber tip, he set himself in motion. I calculated that at such a trot it would take us twenty minutes to walk to Pizzagalli's. Then he asked me to wait and tapped, followed by the waddling patriarch, around the corner of the house.

The hum of a starter and an engine coughed into life. Around the corner jerked a mud-spattered Fiat limousine. Hesistantly I squeezed in next to the patriarch who sat enthroned in rigid dignity beside the driver. To my mild surprise de Colana drove safely across the schoolhouse square and took the curve from the short alley into the unvillagelike main street Via Maistra with a certain elegant verve. At the same time he announced that he knew Austria well, having studied law at the universities of Graz and Innsbruck around 1905, later in Heidelberg as well. When I told him that fifteen years later I too had studied law at

Vienna and Graz, he snorted a short laugh through his nose and crowed "Fellow student!"

I found Xana as before engrossed in her newspapers. The Buendnerstube had become rather empty, most guests having gone home for dinner. Those who remained could not suppress a burst of laughter as I introduced Xana to Dr. de Colana. Signor Pizzagalli scratched his boil scars and giggled. Then he tramped up to us and asked with strained seriousness if we wished to have our evening meal in the dining room. But we preferred to stay with Annette and ordered the cheapest dish on the menu, eggs *à la russe*, and de Colana ordered the same (out of politeness I suspected) and invited us to share a half liter of Chianti, Marchesi Antinori Firenze.

Arcibaldo the patriarch had obtained a wicker chair for himself. Xana admired his ancient green muzzle and spoke to him gently. Flattered, the country lawyer laughed through his nose, and when he heard that Xana had studied classical philology at Graz a quarter of a century after he'd been through, he again remarked happily, "Fellow student!" The wine made him recover fully from his afternoon binge, and he showed us a small dueling scar on his temple he had gotten as a member of the Saxoborussia fraternity in Heidelberg. His casual waves to Annette brought more and more basket-covered Antinori bottles to the table.

The "celebration" ended with me carrying Xana more or less piggyback to the lawyer's limousine. Once again I sat next to the driver, ready at any moment to help him steer if necessary. But the drive to Pontresina, accompanied by close and distant cowbells, passed without incident. At times de Colana stretched up to look in the rear view mirror at Xana who was sleeping curled up in the back seat; then, if anything, he drove even more cautiously. In the reflected glow of the Fiat's headlights I caught a glimpse of his gleeful grin. That a young woman had let herself be overcome by wine (how could he know it was the first time in her life?) may have seemed to justify his own weakness for alcohol.

Yes, he drove with caution.

The ten Breukaas had invited us to go for a little excursion with them on Pentecost Sunday. Because of Xana's "alcoholic excesses," I had to phone them and call it off; the excursion was postponed. I spent the holidays and the following Tuesday and Wednesday behind the typewriter. My cigar consumption began to menace our budget. Maxim Grabscheidt's present was buried, as always, in my manuscript trunk. Yes, by now it seemed foolish to go running around with a gun in my pocket. The absurdity of my previous suspicions seemed every day more blatantly obvious. If someone had planned to assassinate me, then certainly they would have been ordered to do it quickly and would not spend idle days waiting around at the scene of the crime.

On the Thursday after Pentecost between 2:00 and 3:00 P.M. came: The Second Encounter.

The Swiss Alien Police had granted us a temporary residence permit and had, at the same time, strictly forbidden me to work. At the Zurich city hall, following my dramatic entry into Swiss exile, I was informed that so long as we remained in Switzerland I was to refrain from all work as a writer. I put it to them directly. Was this for political reasons? The Threat to Neutrality Posed by Foreign Elements was a favorite theme of the Swiss Alien Police. I was brusquely rebuffed. As an alien on a temporary permit I had no choice but to follow the order of the authorities. This order was clear and to the point: no writing. Aha, but could I at least, with your kind permission, make notes? Notes, notes, growled the official, for all he cared.

So I made notes.

They were published under the pseudonym Austriacus Babeuf simultaneously in the *Ostschweizer Arbeiterzeitung,* the Bern *Tagwacht,* and the Lugano *Libera Stampa.* I recounted the history of Austria between February 1934 and March 1938 from my own point of view. The addressee and fee recipient: Henrique Kujath of Luzienburg in the Domleschg.

When I finished them, the commentaries of Austriacus Babeuf appeared in serial form under the title "After February Comes March."

"Xana."

"Mm."

"Do you want to come up to the Corviglia with me?"

"Cor——what?" A woebegone peep.

"Corviglia. You take the cable car from the St. Mo schoolhouse square. From the top you can see the Dolomites. In the other direction, they say, all the way to the Matterhorn when the weather's clear. The weather is great today and I can't get anywhere with typing. You know me. After I've typed for four days——"

"Oh Trebla."

"What is it now? Ah! I know. Last Saturday, in front of de Colana . . . That's really no reason to feel conscience-stricken for days on end. As we—as we were loading you in the car, Annette told me that it happens to the finest ladies of high society here in the Engadine. Apparently because of the thin air. Come on now, forget about that little high of yours, little mother."

"Little mother."

"Yes?"

"That wasn't just a high. I was —unconscious." Xana was hunched over on the edge of the bed in her new, cheap flannel robe, her hands in her lap, head down; a shock of hair hid her face from me. Now she tossed back her hair.

"What—did you say—that Annette said? That it comes from the thin air?"

"That's what she said."

Her gaze wandered off; it was as if she had stopped to listen. Suddenly she looked at me again, intently. "You *hate* my robe, Albert."

"Me?" I stood there as if caught red-handed. She had read my thoughts exactly. "These stylized flowers don't exactly suit my taste. They might be sores instead of flowers, but—"

"It's dreadful, I know!" she interrupted me, yes, almost sharply. "But cheap and warm. Down there you told me to buy a warm robe for the mountains. This was the cheapest one I could find. In the Catholic Department Store Mondial."

Since when do you go shopping in Catholic department stores? I almost said. Now I know what kind of a pattern it is. Reminiscent of the martyr St. Teresa of Konnersreuth. (I didn't say it.) Oh Xana, with her pangs of conscience, in this devotional dressing gown, dear Xana.

Along the fronts of the Engadine houses in the lower village the hanging carnations pushed through the bulging, freshly painted window bars. The sun spent its completely unoppressive heat, but was unable to warm the shade. Stepping into the shadows of rooftops I was bathed in cold.

In front of the Morteratsch Hotel the fountain (where the cows paused for their evening drink) splashed, and on its edge sat the marble-white waitress from the common room with her black-stockinged legs dangling playfully, and chatting with the Two Blonds—and while the pimpleless one murmured something in her ear the pimple-faced one contented himself with a continuous grin, which vanished as soon as he saw me.

"Greetings, Miss Pina!" I made a sort of fencer's salute with Madam Fausch's stick. Pina nodded slightly and smiled at me sadly.

The Two Blonds didn't look my way. Nevertheless I succumbed to a faint twinge of anguish. The melancholy smile and those two large, deep-dark eyes pierced me like a small pain.

I had never really looked at her when she served us in the common room although we had carried on brief conversations. From these we learned that she was from a wine-growing village in the Valtellina. I had briefly noted the contrast between her black hair and pale complexion. Now I saw her for the first time outside, with her apron off, in the powerful midday sun. She sat on the edge of the fountain, leaning back against the pillar which was topped by a container overflowing with geraniums. After nodding to me, she dropped her head back into half profile and stared into the splashing water while the pimpleless blond continued talking to her. Rarely had I seen hair of such pure obsidian blackness. Apronless in her black taffeta dress, and so pale, so marble pale, like a statue of sadness. But she was smiling. This pallor framed by the darkness of her dress; the furtive swinging of her slender legs, her—now look at that—Roman profile; and the way she smiled, looking sad and yet touchingly flirtatious. It got to me.

The train from Tirano was not due for another ten minutes; the station lay abandoned at the bottom of the valley. Only an adolescent wagon driver in his shirt sleeves rolling great zinc milk cans onto the platform. I waited in front of the ticket counter. In the ticket office a tiny bell rang and a man's voice, loud and alone, spoke Romansh—apparently into the telephone. Then the agent appeared in an unbuttoned uniform jacket at the ticket window. I bought a ticket to St. Moritz. Through the window of the little waiting room I saw the agent step out and turn the crank on a little box; again there was a tiny ring.

I strolled out onto the square in front of the station. The serpentine road that wound toward the village lay empty of traffic. Here and there gleamed the Flaz Brook that flowed down from Bernina Pass. Then, far above on the bridge over the Flaz that I had crossed a few minutes before, I saw two men walking. Their white stockings shone brilliantly in the sun. What did I care? Half consciously I breathed a little sigh of relief that these two brothers (they actually could have been brothers, but what did I care) were hiking out of town—perhaps to the Roseg Valley again—out of the town where Xana was at home alone. It was like a physical disgust. Or was it jealousy because they had just been so involved with Pina?

I shifted my gaze to the post office, identified first the pepper-colored cows on the meadow beyond it, and then our hotel window. There . . . just then Xana stepped out onto the wooden balcony. Her devotional dressing gown sent brilliant greetings into the valley; the distance had swallowed up the stylized flowers; her face was a spot of light. She stood there perfectly erect, gazing motionless. I waved my stick. She didn't move. I began jumping up and down and swinging my arms in wild signals. Now, slowly, she lifted her arm and moved it once to the left, once to the right. Oh Xana.

I sat down on a bench in the waiting room and waited without looking back at the village until the electric train came sliding up, sled-quiet. The midday glare had made my right eye ache. I inserted my long-range monocle, which didn't help at all. Whenever I looked into the light the right side hurt. It was a familiar pain.

In the winter of '29/'30 my parents were snatched away, as they say, by the great flu epidemic. My father, a retired Lieutenant Field Marshal, and mama had lived in an attractive apartment (with an attic) in Graz near the Paulus Gate. By ironic chance the Gestapo later established its headquarters just two doors away . . . In 1925 I had, merely to please my father, completed my *Doctor juris*, with no intention of using it professionally. Shuttled back and forth between Graz and Vienna as a correspondent for the Vienna *Arbeiter-Zeitung* and made it my business, as a disabled war veteran of twenty-five, to help train the Republican Defense Corps. Mama to me: "Albert, Papa and I have nothing against you making the attic into your own private castle . . . We have absolutely no objections, but does it have to be *five?* Can't you be satisfied with *one?* Or even two?"

"But Mama, they're always the *same* five. If they were always different, always new ones I could understand your being against it. But when it's been the same five for the last two years? You know, in this respect at least, I'm conservative."

"Ah, what's the use," my mother said, applying a brief kiss to my "head injury." Then my parents (she 55, he 66) had both fallen victim to that infernal flu epidemic—almost on the same day. It had hit me rather hard; no longer restricted to the attic, I roamed about the large apartment and never allowed any of the "five" to come in again. Just then *she* appeared on my gloomy horizon.

Xana. Liberal arts student Xana Giaxa.

I had known the girl (born 1910) since she was seven. In the early summer of 1917 she had literally "crossed my path" while I, the eighteen-year-old "casualty," was convalescing in the Slovakian resort of Trentschin-Teplitz. In the course of a dozen years (during which I never saw her) the child "Xaninka" had developed like a blooming hyacinth. At seventeen Xana had effortlessly passed her school examinations and studied the first semesters of classical philology at the Sorbonne while the Giaxa family headquarters were set up in Paris, where the famous act long stood on the program of the Montmartre Circus Médrano. Then Xana studied a summer semester in Graz, lodging with her Aunt "Za," Giaxa's elder sister (in her own way as strong a character, will, and talent as he himself): Dr. Miliza Zborowska, by no means a beauty, with her wide brimmed black hat, her starched white collar and black habit, she looked at first glance like an undersized country priest. And Za was a personality the whole city knew. In the 1890s, equipped with a scholarship, she had studied medicine in Zurich, later married the (now long deceased) Imperial Staff Surgeon Wladimir Zborowski; as the first Social Democratic woman doctor in the Austro-Hungarian Empire she, together with her husband (no Socialist), had directed the health services in the "protectorate" of Bosnia-Herzegovina. The woman doctor of Banja Luka had spent years riding around on donkeys to provide injections and obstetric services to Moslem women . . . One day in June 1930, shortly before the beginning of semester vacation, Xana and I were walking through the city park in Graz and hit on the subject of Aunt Za's strong personality and her donkey-riding midwifery—when Xana announced rather suddenly but casually as we stood across from Café Glacis: "By the way, did you know I'm in my second month?"

The ticktick in my brow. The only thing I could think of: Maxim Grabscheidt, M.D., to the rescue.

At first Xana resisted: she liked Maxim as a friend; it was "awkward." Then she gave in. Doctor Za was told that her niece was taking an excursion to the High Tauern with her fellow students. Instead of this, Maxim Grabscheidt, after performing the operation, concealed liberal arts student Xana Giaxa for two days in his ground-floor apartment-cum-medical office on the Lastenstrasse near the working-class district of Graz.

Then we went down to Radkersburg, to the Murauhof, Giaxa's rather modest country home on the left bank of the border river Mur.

Hardly had she left when I was overcome by the decision to marry her. It seemed completely absurd: neither of us had ever considered it. If I *had* considered it, Maxim's help might—who knows—even have been unnecessary. But of all times now, after everything had been set right according to the hypocritical conventions of bourgeois society. Absurd. Absurd, but imperative. The way Xana had said good-bye to me at the station, tall and slender, yet not quite so erect as usual, a little bent over by the aftereffects of a pain that was more than physical, pale, smiling, rather faceless, without a hint of accusation: this image followed me day and night and even in my dreams. I had never felt so enchanted by her as I was now by this memory of her, the parting sufferer. Marry Xana! All at once I was obsessed with the decision. It was a command, a law, a categorical imperative.

But exactly how I was to obey it was a complete mystery to me. Cursing myself a licentious coward, I telegraphed Pola Polari. HELP! In a few days Pola came bustling in, and we took off together for Radkersburg.

Elsabé and Konstantin Giaxa received us with unaffected cordiality. Xana had recovered astonishingly quickly, blossomed as before like a Renoir portrait, and showed not the slightest surprise at our sudden arrival. The master of the house did me the honor of allowing me to ride Giaxa VII. In the company of both namesakes—the man and the horse—I trotted along the banks of the Mur past Slovenian farmers who saluted us smiling. Although I (as a former cavalryman's son) was not bad on horseback, I was ashamed to ride on the famous, almost magically beautiful Lippizan gelding, and all the more since Xana's nearly sixty-year-old father, who was making do with the black horse he used to pull his dogcart, sat poised in the saddle like a god. When I returned from the ride I suffered a hay-fever attack. Attacks of sneezing and gasping hindered me in the most insidious way from carrying out my plan. Pola, whom I had chartered as a mediator, hissed at me that I was impossible in this condition, simply impossible. I avoided Xana, avoided the sunny summer days with their billions of swarming pollen grains, huddled away in a shadowy corner of the den, and with my host, an excellent player, waged countless games of chess, most of which I lost.

Giaxa played in complete silence and with incomparable concentration (one of the secrets of his success). His play mirrored the character of the player: it showed strategic training and abounded with startling, absolutely whimsical tricks, and with mathematical hocus-pocus the likes of which no chess partner had ever shown me. Sometimes I could not avoid laughing aloud, between sneezes and gasps of "Excuse me!" at a move that broke my king's neck. At the same time I had an unprecedented opportunity to study closely his un-made-up, undisguished face—a martial face with ice gray, bushy brows, like Bismarck's and Garibaldi's rolled together, fenced over with hundreds of creases and wrinkles, warning signs of the basic element in his nature: creative mockery. It was as if all the laugh wrinkles from all the faces he had ever made to laugh were preserved, chiseled into his own countenance. Despite this it was almost a beautiful face and reminded me distantly of Xana. I ascribed the little, secret-playful, wrinkling smile he always maintained to his satisfaction over his unremitting victories at chess. Incorrectly, as I later learned.

Thus ten days of sneezing, snorting, wheezing, chess playing, taking bitter ephedrine tablets and soaking countless handkerchiefs passed by without my ever announcing the reason for my visit. Elsabé, the Livonian, regaled me with Russian hospitality. Finally Pola had to return to Vienna. On the evening before her departure, during dinner, she finally came out with it. To *my* considerable surprise, no one else showed the *least* surprise, neither Giaxa nor Elsabé. Nor Xana. Over roast chicken Pola performed her duties to perfection, and over crepes the details were already being discussed.

I had left the Catholic Church after the war, about the same time that I joined the workers' movement. Giaxa, as a devout liberal, was a miserable Catholic, and Xana was Protestant like her mother, whose ancestor, a supporter of Melanchthon, had carried the Reformation to the Baltic provinces and had translated the Bible into Estonian. The first Austrian Republic had not succeeded in introducing civil marriage. Thus the Socialists, in order to avoid church weddings, had thought up an expediency called "life companionship." Even before he answered me I knew Giaxa would not dream of letting Xana become my "life's companion."

"All the names they called me before and during the war—the good people! Anarchist, nihilist, Bolshevik! I took it in my stride, was even a bit proud of it. But at home, you understand, Trebla, at home I'm as conservative as they come. I could care less whether you marry Catholic, Protestant, Greek Orthodox, or Moslem. But you'll marry in a church, that much I insist on. I've given it some thought, and, well, in short ..." Jovial sarcasm beamed from all the wrinkles in his face: "I had your banns published in Vienna ten days ago. At the Reformed Church in District One. Wanted to be ready for any eventuality, you know. Of course I didn't have any of your papers, but I managed anyway. What's our old Austrian slackness good for anyway, if not for things like that? And then it'll also be good later on when you—ah—I mean, in case of a divorce. Tell me now, how long do you give this thing?"

"When I look at impossible Trebla," Pola spoke up, "all I can say is, a year at most."

"And you?" I asked Xana. "How long do *you* give the thing?"

Xana replied with a foal-like gaze: "One year."

That was eight years ago.

Although Dr. Grabscheidt could not be accused of a professional error—the gynecological verdict was "completely normal"—since that first unborn child I took from her, Xana has remained childless.

From the station platform at Bernina an underpass led under the tracks to the open square. I groped my way down the steps. In the darkness of the passageway it was easier for me to open my obstinate right eye. And I saw—two pairs of white stockings jogging up the exit stairs ahead of me. White stockings. Aha!

Why: aha? If you hadn't kept your eyes shut you'd have known *eo ipso* that they were riding with you on the same train. In any case, you should have taken the Walther along. Oh, what's the difference. Let it lie in the manuscript trunk. Just then Madam Fausch's walking stick slipped out of my hand. The sudden clack echoed in the tiled passageway and was immediately drowned out by a heavy thundering overhead that caused the underpass to shudder. I bent over and received a push that knocked me off balance.

My hand jerked toward the tiled wall and I glanced up to see a stocky young girl standing in front of me, bareheaded, with a platinum blond "Titus" hairdo. She was saying something I couldn't understand over the roaring of the train. I picked up the stick and she looked me over curiously, her hands in the pockets of her bright green, unbuttoned fleece coat from which a generous bosom protruded, and I laughed and thought it ridiculous that my laughing was completely inaudible above the noise of the train, and laughed louder, and in a sudden silence my strained laughter reverberated through the concrete underpass.

"Eeee-eee!" she squeaked, almost like a piglet. Conspicuous coral earrings, cute, sassy turned-up nose; the exact opposite of Pina's enchanting somberness. Then she sauntered casually past me, and her ample bottom, which she accentuated by stretching—hands in her pockets—the frog-green fleece around it, shone in the early afternoon sun.

In a pharmacy on the main street in St. Moritz I bought an ink-blue celluloid sunshade to fit my monocle.

The funicular railway had just been reopened; I bought a ticket to Corviglia and took my seat in the uppermost compartment of the step-shaped, blue-lacquered gondola with very few other passengers. Five minutes until departure. I pulled a crumpled newspaper from the pocket of my Manchester jacket and began to read. When occasional steps echoed over the cement platform of the clean, bare, miniature station I automatically glanced out of the gondola window. If a passenger entered one of the compartments below my own I couldn't see him from where I sat.

HUNDREDS DIE IN GRANOLLERS NEAR BARCELONA

Heavy footsteps echoed emptily across the concrete steps. An Alpine herdsman, a Senn, stamped into my compartment carrying a heavy bundle tied to a wooden frame on his back. Around his neck like a fantastic ruff hung two large, brand-new wooden hoops the Senns use as cheese molds. He wore a shepherd's blouse of cornflower-blue linen covered in front with red and white embroidery. His small, contented, impish eyes flashed in his leathery, brownish red face. Bareheaded, dark-haired, with thick, tightly curled locks. A glint of sunshine reflected on the station window and gleamed on a gold button in his left earlobe.

With a graceful swing he heaved the pack frame onto the bench, sat down opposite me, dug out a short pipe, clamped it between his teeth without lighting it,
planted his blocky boots wide apart, crossed his sinewy arms across his embroidered chest, smiled at me contentedly and growled: "So so." (It sounded like
"sow sow.") Which apparently had no connection to anything in particular. The
brief ringing of a signal bell chimed through the station.

"Sow sow," repeated the contented Senn.

A second signal bell.

Hurried steps clatter across the concrete steps. I lean out the gondola window and see a white-stockinged calf disappearing into the last compartment.

A set of gears begins an unsteady grinding. The cable pulls taut; the gondola creeps up the mountain, cogwheels engaging the toothed rail with a click.

"Sow sow."

After a short ascent the gondola stops for a few minutes at the intermediate
station Chantarella. The Senn swings his pack onto his back, and, mechanically,
I get out behind him, pace after him across the steps of the little station. The
gears are silent. Against the Senn's heavy trudging I hear lighter footsteps behind me. Signal bell; the gears begin to grind; the gondola rolls forward and
crawls up the mountain toward Corviglia.

In front of the station the Senn shifted the cheese hoops dangling around
his tanned neck, finally lit his little pipe, and examined the three men who had
gotten out behind him: The Two Blonds and me. Growled "Ciao!" and
trudged, bent forward, with bouncing agility up the path leading along the railway embankment.

Minutes crawled by in slow motion. Deserted lay the terrace crowned by
Chantarella Sanatorium, a long building, its rows of windows and doors closed
tight, barricaded against the off season. Deserted, the station building with its
monotonous hum of gears. Up across layers of green wound the black, narrow
line of track on which the gondola crept steadily skyward, blue as the shirt of the
Senn. On its vigorous climb it grew noticeably smaller. Overhead rose the massive head of the Piz Nair (Black Mountain), a sparsely covered giant granite
hump, sparkling brownish black in the overbright sun.

The two didn't move from the spot. With a leisureliness that was
provokingly obtrusive they stood next to me, their arms crossed over the tops of
their ski poles, supposedly engrossed in the view of Black Mountain.

Then came a cry.

A long, drawn-out, exultant yodel. The Senn was still within shouting distance. I began swinging Madam Fausch's walking stick with exaggerated carelessness: "Out shooting woodchucks again?"

The ash blond with the agreeable, ordinary face stood up straight.

"What?"

"Are you out shooting again," I asked nicely, "with your camera? I don't
see the tripod."

The almost good-looking ash blond turned to his companion (perhaps his "comrade-in-arms," if one only knew), the straw blond with the mole-speckled dough-face: "Hey Shursh, ya remember the woodchuck-woodchuck-hunter from Roseg Valley?"

The pimply-faced one didn't answer.

Shursh didn't answer. Brushed a strand of hair off his forehead and put on (what seemed to me) an exaggeratedly foolish-malicious smile. He gave a barely perceptible nod.

"Gentlemen," I said, swinging my stick emphatically up toward the Senn (their eyes followed it), "there's been a slight error. I'm not a woodchuck-wood-chuck hunter—which would, of course, be nonsense . . . but rather a wood-chuck-*hunter* hunter. And that is by no means nonsense. At least in my eyes. I hunt hunters. You understand?"

"The man," said the ash blond to the straw blond, "hunts hunters, and says it isn't nonsense. And he wonders—Shursh!"—his half-suppressed shout seemed intended to rouse the other from the numb fascination with which he stood staring up at the blue-shirted Senn—"if—we—understand."

The straw blond with pimples made another slight nod and showed again his put-on, arrogant, foolish-malicious, indeed rather horrible, no cruel, no horrible smile.

"We understand," announced the ash blond. "What could we wish the gentleman now? Maybe we should just say . . . good hunting."

His dough-faced companion laughed with a closed mouth, apparently so slightly amused that his laugh was a mere sniff through the nose.

"The hunter thanks you."

Since I didn't move they stepped past me on my left and right: marching steps (so it seemed) that had been tamed into hiking steps. As they withdrew I turned around.

Now I was behind them.

Peace, thy name is war.

There was no peace in 1918. In Poland, Silesia, in Russia, in the Near East the fighting went on into the twenties; then a few brief minutes of world history echoing with League-of-Nations prattle; at the end of the twenties Japanese imperialism struck at China. 1938: for two years now Adolf's Germany and Benito's Italy had been using the young Spanish Republic as their proving ground. *When* did the *defenders of democracy* start shooting in Europe? In Austria, February '34, and Trebla was there.

The memory of that night (from the twelfth to the thirteenth) flashed through me on that overbright day like a lightning bolt in the dark. While Dr. Engelbert Dollfuss, by the grace of Musso (breeder of *Il Fascismo*) and with Papal blessing, Chancellor of Austria—while Dollfuss (himself soon to be a victim in history's bloody comedy) was having cannons positioned on the Hohe

Warte to spray shells on the huge districts called Karl Marx and Goethe—model communities of the Viennese workers—I was racing on my motorcycle over the dark, icy highway from Leoben along the Mur, bypassing roadblocks at Frohnleiten and Peggau, toward Graz. At my back, groaning, bobbed the limp body of Franz Scherhack.

"JesusMaryandJoseph," groaned Franz Scherhack, though he was a sworn atheist.

"How's it going, Franz?" I yelled over my shoulder above the howling, icy wind that blew against me as thick as an unyielding blackwetcold tent wall. "Can you hang on a little longer?"

"JesusMaryJoseph," he groaned behind me, shoving his hot, blood-sticky mouth next to my cold ear. "Much farther, Trebla?"

"Come on, Franz boy, hang on just a little while," I shouted over my shoulder. "It's not much farther." It was far enough.

On the night before, Koloman Wallisch, Union secretary in Leoben, had decided to take up armed resistance even though he realized that our military potential was weak. As third in command of the Republican Defense Corps in Styria, I had rushed over from Graz to Leoben. I see Koloman's broad-boned face, his pale brow and bushy black hair in the muffled lamplight of that mine inspector's shack, hear his deliberate, encumbered voice with its slight accent (he was from west Hungary), hear his "Wait and see, I tell you." I was excited; we argued with each other. When he learned that they were shooting at us with cannons in Vienna he changed his mind. He stood up behind the lamp like a bull from the stable floor . . .

During a clash at night between the Leoben Defense Corps and the Federal Army—supported by the gendarmes and the Austrian "Storm Troopers" (so-called "Tabernacle Bugs")—Franz Scherhack was shot in the lung.

Scherhack was a railroad watchman on the line from Graz to Bruck, father of six children, and although not an old man, suffered from a respiratory disease. "I got nothing to lose but my TB," was the excuse he gave for his fearlessness, "why should I be careful? Let'm try and get me, the damn reactionaries, what do I care?" Now he had a bullet lodged in his bad lung and was coughing up blood.

I pulled him out of the fray, dragged him—he could barely walk—to my motorcycle, a one-cylinder four-stroke BMW with 13 hp, that I had hidden behind the giant warehouse at the coal mine. I must bring him to Dr. Grabscheidt (have to go back to Graz anyway)! I tried to hoist him onto the rear seat but he was unable to hold on. Then I hunted down a clothesline, hoisted Franz onto my back, then, gasping and sweating, wrapped the line around both of us again and again and tied it in front. I sputtered away over the bumpy, icy road. He hung there on the back seat, shaken up and down, bound to my back, and from time to time he vomited warm blood on the back of my neck.

I drove with my headlight on low beam. Sometimes the front wheel began to slide. I caught it in time.

"Jesus Mary," gurgled Franz in a small voice.

The east wind blew hard against me, then it began spraying fine hailstones that bit into my skin. My cap had long since blown off my head, and I heard an indefinite, hollow, horrible sound. Yes, it was as if the wind were playing my punctured brow like a flute.

"D'you hear it?" mumbled Franz Scherhack thickly, warmly in my ear. "Sounds like a siren. Hey Trebla, I think they're chasing us, the miserable bastards, they're going to catch us."

I was startled to find out that Franz had also heard the sound. Then I smiled. It could be the telephone wires that paralleled the road.

"It's just the telephone wires, Franz boy," I yelled. "You know, the wind."

No answer. Then, "Jesus Mary, is it far?"

"No, Franzl, just hang on; we're almost there!"

"JesusMaryandJoseph," groaned Franz Scherhack.

Night traffic on the highway seemed to be at a complete standstill. We met only a few farmers' carts, lanterns swinging beneath their shafts, as they rattled sluggishly to market. Finally the few lights of the Ruckerlberg flickered into view. On the outskirts of town I saw far ahead another roadblock with guards in long coats and carbines over their shoulders. I knew the area well and bypassed the roadblocks on the side streets that lay strangely darkened, over rutted cobblestones that made the cycle bounce.

"Jeez-us! . . ."

Near the railroad terminal in Graz I heard, or thought I heard, the asthmatic barking of a machine gun from the rolling mill. Covered with blood, tied to a seriously wounded man with a clothesline, I didn't dare drive down the Annenstrasse, so I raced down side streets to the Lastenstrasse. And all the time an incurable pantheist inside me who always turns up in times of need had been praying—praying impatiently to the stubborn east wind, to the shadows of the cart horses plodding to market, to the bare trees that haunted the roadside: let Maxim Grabscheidt be at home; don't let him be arrested; don't let him be fighting, wounded, flown; let him be at home so that he can patch up Franz Scherhack.

Maxim was home.

Franz had stopped moving. He seemed to be fast asleep. Carefully I rolled myself off the saddle and lugged Franz on my back into the mezzanine-apartment (which also served as an operating room) of the poor-man's doctor. Maxim received us calmly, as was his way. Franz was not the first man brought to him that night. In his one-room office divided by curtains into several "tents" he ran, in those days, a regular field hospital. The quiet coming and going behind the curtains, the soft groaning and cursing caused me no small amount of worry, for I expected a police raid at any moment.

Fanny, Maxim's wife, a very attractive Viennese woman who played the role of a mundane country girl, was shocked at this "Granada bivouac" and hissed that her husband's nocturnal deeds were "madness that will cost us all our heads." In her heart she detested all the impoverished patients sent to her husband by the relief agency or the workers' health insurance. My family's title and military tradition, on the other hand, impressed her petty-bourgeois sensibilities. (Her father had been a Christian Social pastry shop owner in the Alsergrund district of Vienna.) My frozen blue face and my blood-encrusted jacket seemed to frighten her far more than the unconscious man who hung on my back like an Eskimo child. After Maxim had untied him from me, she insisted on giving me a glass of Slivovitz and one of her husband's bathrobes. Then she washed my face—first with cold, then with warm water, along with complaints about our "madness," and not without some flirting with me.

"Don't you realize it's war?" I asked abruptly.

"What do you mean, war?" she pouted. "It's just foolishness, it's madness. Now, in peacetime . . ."

"It's war, you'll find out soon enough, Fanny," I snapped breathlessly, turned, and hurried to the operating table where Maxim had laid out the seriously wounded Franz. He had examined and bandaged the undressed, emaciated man, standing phlegmatically (though he was anything but phlegmatic; it was part of his nature to exhibit placidness as a kind of professional camouflage).

"Our friend Scherhack," he said gazing at me from his beautiful, somberdark eyes and thoughtfully stroking the bluish stubble beard that masked his narrow, El Greco face (I suspected him of not shaving so as to avoid looking handsome amidst the very unhandsome poverty that surrounded him in his practice). "Did you know, Trebla, that he has tuberculosis?"

"Of course I know."

"And a bullet lodged in his lung, hm. I'm afraid there won't be much we can do."

"Try anyway," I blurted impatiently. "After I hauled him all this way."

Grabscheidt seemed to daydream for a few seconds. Then he threw off his calmness like a piece of clothing and, assisted by his wife and by two only slightly wounded Defense Corps men, half children, that he conjured up from behind the curtains, began the operation, while outside I threw myself onto my motorcycle . . .

Maxim Grabscheidt brought Franz Scherhack back to life.

After two days the Defense Corps offensive against the clerical dictatorship collapsed. The leadership of the Social Democratic Party had failed, the general strike was neither unanimously called for nor unanimously carried out; the dictatorship had the military machine on its side, the cannons, the regional militia (drilled in the Mussolini-Italian fashion), and not least, the disunity of the Socialists. I went into hiding for a short while at St. Lambrecht on a farm run by the brother of the cook who had worked in my parents' home for years. Maxim was arrested and released on the same day. Thousands were thrown into prison. In the Graues Haus in Vienna the pulleys were oiled on the gallows. Warrants were issued for the arrest of Wallisch, Stanek, Scherhack, myself, and the other leaders of the Defense Corps. A search of Dr. Grabscheidt's apartment and operating room was made—without result—while Franz Scherhack lay gasping in the coal cellar of the house in the Lastenstrasse. (The caretaker was one of us.) Maxim had succeeded in removing the bullet and preventing any complications. The secretary of the metalworkers, Stanek, was taken prisoner in Graz, tried by military court and hanged. Wallisch was recognized and turned in to the authorities near the Hungarian border by a railway worker, a traitor from our own ranks—returned to Vienna, tried by military court and hanged. (The railwayman did not live to enjoy his reward; he was found stabbed the next day.) On the very same morning Franz Scherhack would have been well enough to be moved, and the time was right to take him out of the cellar hole where he had proved his will to live, and smuggle him into Yugoslavia . . .

While I was sneaking down from St. Lambrecht I found out. Nine hours before the suspension of martial law, while Fanny was in Vienna with their eight-year-old son, Grabscheidt was arrested again (perhaps on the word of an informer) and a second, more thorough, house search was undertaken.

That night on our secret printing press in the Auenbruggergasse I set up the text of the handbill I had written, which—when it was published—was the cause of my landing in military confinement. It bore the title HEALED FOR THE GALLOWS!

Four hours after they hanged Franz Scherhack, martial law was ended; the shabby carnival went on.

The Two Blonds shouldered their ski poles; I did the same with the walking stick—and marched behind them at a distance of about forty yards. On the curves leading down to St. Moritz a train of mule carts hauling long planks up the mountain appeared; the pleasant smell of the long-eared beasts moved past me, the drivers trotting alongside as if they had deserted their wagons. At each curve a new load of planks. Then I lost sight of the two Tutankhamon sweaters.

At the door of the country lawyer's house stood de Colana's unwashed Fiat limousine. Should I use the knocker on the door? The fan-shaped grip like a miniature peacock's tail? I looked the Fiat over. The front bumper was bent in on the left, the fender dented; the left running board dangled out of its mountings. In the back window hung a good-luck charm I'd failed to notice before. A strange feather-duster-like object that looked like the packed skeletons of large trout or almost completely hairless peacock feathers. Across the schoolhouse square shuffled the country lawyer—without a hint of unsteadiness.

"My respects, Dr. de Colana!"

"My respects," he mimicked me in his creaking voice, "Mr. Black-White-White-Black." He carried a stick and a briefcase and was obviously sober. The pimple on his nostril seemed paler, his moustache seemed to have been combed and his rustic priest's hat brushed.

"Did you have an accident?" I nodded toward the dented fender and the bent bumper. "Did you run into something?"

"Pppp-fff!" He puffed through his moustache. "*I* run into something! Something ran into me, a *camion*, my dear Black-White-White-Black. Ech!" He waved his stick over the Fiat: "Have to get it washed sometime . . . Now I must drive down to Poschiavo. On business," he concluded brusquely, opened the door and began straddling his way across the damaged running board.

"Poschiavo? Puschlav? Don't you go by Pontresina?"

"Climb in, Black-White-White-Black."

With some vehemence he threw his stick and briefcase onto the back seat—which was covered with a veritable pelt of dog hair. As the starter whined, several octaves of riotious barking and howling broke loose behind the house door. As if automatically, the lawyer's hand reached for the door handle, but he pulled himself together and guided the rattling Fiat over the schoolhouse square.

He drove with almost annoying caution.

"Allow me to ask—why have you decided to call me Black-White-White-Black?"

"I have my reasons—eh . . . once in a newspaper I read, ech, one of your short stories . . . The final point had, eh, something to do with Black-White-White-Black."

"Impossible. Black-yellow or red-white-red or just red—that might be possible. Besides, my short stories are famous for their pointlessness."

"Nonono," he insisted stubbornly, "that was the point. You published it under the pen name Albert Trebla, didn't you?"

"It's not a pen name, it's an anagram. Albert is my first name and Trebla the reverse. Spelled, quite simply, from back to front."

"Wait a minute . . . *that* could have been the point as well."

"What?"

"Quite simply from back to front."

Celerina and the short bridge were behind us. On the left a solitary hill with a little church on it. Two towers—the taller one protruding jaggedly was a ruin. Its pointed roof might have burned out a few years ago. Or a few centuries. The smaller one, attached farther back along the nave, resembled a shrunken Italian bell tower.

Campanile. (I thought of the tall, beautiful campanili in Italy—a place now taboo for me.) The whole church surrounded by tall larch trees with slender, naked trunks, their tops like the coarse hair of reddish blond women.

We had passed the Punt Muragl and were clattering along the banks of Flaz Brook when the driver growled something about a "coma," and I asked him if that, too, was a point to one of my stories. He nodded peevishly toward a rolling landscape in front of a forest (Staz Forest?) on the right.

"Plaun da Choma."

Just before we entered the lower village of Pontresina I noticed, also on the right, several long ridges nearly as high as a man: heaps of layered compost, peat or something. To me they seemed rather like trenches.

4

I didn't find Xana in our two-room apartment. Locked both doors to my "private chamber," opened my wardrobe trunk filled with books, manuscripts, and notebooks, dug the Walther pistol out of the bottom drawer, checked its magazine, and put it in the back pocket of my Peyatchevich trousers. From my stock of twenty-five pairs of Peyatchevich trousers Giaxa gave me as a wedding present—he had once been given them by an admirer—I was only able to give away a dozen pairs to unemployed friends . . . not even unemployed friends want to wear thirty-year-old (though indestructible) cavalry pants of light beige twill, narrow at the bottom, as was the fashion around the turn of the century, with gaiters that buttoned around the shoe soles. On a tip from Madam Fausch I found Xana in an alcove of the antique-laden Confiserie Jann. As in X number of prior reunions, I could never quite imagine her face before I saw her again. It was a surprise every time (whereas imagining a classical woman's face, it was sometimes a slight disappointment for me).

She had shed her melancholy along with her dressing gown. She leafed through and read the Brief Classical Dictionary (Bern, Sammlung Dalp) and made notes in a small notebook. Beautifully turned hazelnut-brown-blond locks fringed her forehead; she wore a slightly faded scarab-green velvet dress. Following our joyful reunion I was able to contemplate the curve of her cheek in profile while she made a few last notes. I told her about the panorama I had enjoyed in Corviglia. After she had listened for a few minutes, she said, keeping her head turned in profile, that I never went to Corviglia, never went, never went.

Omschena in the Eastern Carpathians, May 1917. Pola Polari (real name Paula Popper) had made her debut as a soubrette in the outdoor theater Beim Leicht in Vienna's Prater. In 1912, at the age of nineteen, she was already an operetta star in the Theater an der Wien, acclaimed by enthusiastic admirers (primarily from the officer corps) as "Miss Populari." Five years later she was a Red Cross nurse serving at the Carpathian resort of Trentschin-Teplitz where I, with my official Imperial head wound, had been ordered to rest and recuperate. Within walking distance, for a time at Dukla Pass and then again at Sillein, the

MPHQ had set up its tents, the Military Press Headquarters, where Konstantin Giaxa worked as a war correspondent.

At that time I hadn't yet made his acquaintance.

One afternoon in May Miss Populari and I, the eighteen-year-old wreck, take a carriage ride out to Omschena: a Slovakian village with thatch-roofed cottages, bucket wells in front of the doors, and a village pond full of romping ducks and geese. Old peasants in flat felt hats decorated with tufts of what they called "orphan girl's hair," and young women in broad, short peasant skirts, all wearing white felt boots. Next to the talkative Red Cross nurse—Pola was at the height of her form in those days—I lounge in my blue gray flyer's blouse; instead of a cap I wear a black silk cloth around my head that emphasizes the hollow-cheeked pallor of my face; my lips are frozen in a thin smile. (I still have a snapshot from those days.) All at once shouting disturbs the idyllic scene at the pond.

Rolling slowly past we are witness to a shrill scuffle involving about two dozen children. One mob is made up of village boys, the other of street urchins from Teplitz. They flail at each other with sticks and branches; soon the game is no longer a joke and the first stones begin to fly back and forth. Always eager for a sensation, Pola orders the driver to halt.

Suddenly the combatants seem to decide that a duel between their two leaders would be better than a general free-for-all. The boys, all about ten years old, form a circle around the two gladiators. The leader of the village gang is a tall country bumpkin with a shock of red hair, while the gang from the town—my indifference turns to mild surprise—is headed by a sturdy little girl no more than seven years old in a sleeveless red dress, wiry braids protruding from her round head. Nimble as a flash she rushes at her opponent, jumps at him, wraps her arms around his neck, and despite the boy's desperate efforts to shake her off, holds fast. In a shrill voice she cries: "Viselovich, I'm going to kill you!"

"For goodness' sake!" Miss Populari cheers in horror, "do you know who that little girl is?"

The boys' shouting swells to a wild howl. The bumpkin with the red sack tied to his neck spins around again and again until he stumbles and falls on his back. The victory cheers of the Teplitz gang are met by threats from the Omscheners who begin to receive reinforcements. They grab sticks to revenge their leader's fall and then charge the Teplitzers. Seeing the village boys' growing superiority the girl gives the shrill command to retreat. Chases her troops straight in the direction of our carriage. The pursuers fan out to either side to cut off their escape.

Zip! In two bounds she is with us in the wagon, hoping to use it as a springboard for her escape—while her band is involved in a new scuffle, which the driver (in his Franz Josef beard) vainly seeks to break up with curses and whipcracks.

Nurse Pola grabs the girl by the wrist before she can get away and orders the driver to proceed: "Xaninka! Those bad boys will do you in! Come on now, ride along with us."

Wordless, panting and straining with dogged determination the girl tries to free herself. In contrast to her reedlike slimness her plump round cheeks glow as red as her disheveled dress. One beribboned braid has come undone during the fight and hazelnut-brown-blond hair blows over hot, shiny violet—yes, violet— eyes. Which suddenly change to an expression of mild surprise when she looks at my black headband and then at my face.

"Come now, say a nice hello to the Lieutenant," warbled Miss Polari (illustration from a book: *How not to talk to children*).

The little girl, still out of breath from running and fighting, says nothing at first. Before I can, so to speak, bow to Pola's cliché-demand and extend my right hand, a featherlight and, despite the scuffling, strangely cool little hand is laid, just for a moment, on the back of mine; a child's hand . . . no, just a hand; yes; yes . . . telling me it's all right.

The immediate result was so queer I could hardly believe it.

Pola Cannot Conceal Her Jealousy. "Xana! Didn't I tell you," sternly rings the trained soprano voice of the nurse soubrette, "to say a proper hello to the Lieutenant and make a nice curtsy?"

"One nice curtsy," says the girl thoughtfully, without a hint of impertinence, "and I'd fall out of the wagon."

The driver, his torso turned our way, laughs aloud and gives vent to his merriment in Slovakian, shaking the "orphan girl's hair" on his hat. I too feel a laugh coming on (the first for some time). But the little girl says, "You're wounded, Mr. Lieutenant."

"It's no trick," hisses Pola to me, "for her to figure that out. You with your headband."

"How did you know that, Xana—that I'm wounded?"

"You're wearing the green ribbon for it," says the girl; "besides you've got the golden one too."

Pola whispers: "She knows all that from her father. From Giaxa."

My whisper back: "Of Giaxa and Giaxa?"

The little girl, ignoring Pola's nodding: "Of course your golden one could be a combination of two silvers."

Pola's hiss: "She has it all from *him*."

"That's exactly what it is," I say. To change the subject: "And did you really want to kill this enemy of yours, this . . . Viselovich?"

"That was just a game," the little girl said seriously, moving ever farther away from the backrest of the carriage seat, gently swaying as if ready to jump.

"Xaninka, jump on down now and go back to your boys . . . It's all just a game. They won't do anything to you."

"Your wish is my command, Nurse Pola."

As amazing as the Xana of seven years had been to me (when she, literally, crossed my path), she was just as amazing when I found her again, so changed, after her adolescence. At large gatherings she could simply lean back in her chair without contributing a word to the conversation . . . like something just bloomed, yes, something belonging more to flora than to fauna. In her eighth year of marriage she was certainly more talkative in company, but still her being involved was less important than her being *there*.

This eleventh of June 1938 was gray cold and rainy. A leaden sky that smelled like snow had swallowed up the mountaintops and hung across the valley. We were not far from being smothered by heavy fog. But in the Buendnerstube hung another kind of fog, a warm fog—the mildly biting smoke of long, thin Brissago cigars. Players' fists slammed down on the green tops of the card tables, sometimes so vehemently that the chandelier of ibex horns began to dance. From the side room, the boccia lane, echoed the dull thuds of the balls and a loud Italian palaver that would burst out at times in a raucous din of shouting. From the common room rumbled a wine-soaked *Ladin*, and the American Bar was garrisoned with weekend vacationers from the Sixty-first Border Regiment (not one officer among them). As I soon discovered, the atmosphere was charged with a kind of electricity that caught up everyone in the motley assemblage. As if they had all come (or fled) here to jabber, drink, and play games in order to escape something threatening, the unsummerish, season-scorning, almost prewinterish melancholy of the bad weather outside in this titanic landscape.

"Sit!"

Joop spat out the order, a brand-new, splendid dog leash wrapped around his hand and held under the table to something that occasionally broke out in miserable moans and high-pitched whining. On the telephone, while arranging our meeting at Pizzagalli's I had told ten Breukaa incidentally about my visit to de Colana, about his spaniel breeding, the charming young Sirio, the shameless price demanded by the country lawyer. Whereupon the Dutchman went and plunked down fourteen hundred francs on de Colana's table. For two days now Sirio had been constantly whining at Acla Silva for his beloved and now suddenly lost companions. "Incorrigible Trebla, you really lured us into a smokehouse this time!" Pola rapped the back of my hand in mock chastisement. She wore a cap and jacket of ocelot fur, the latter wrapped in calculated jauntiness around her shoulders, on her bosom a diamond-studded cross with a crown atop it—whether it was worn to commemorate the late count or to demonstrate her Habsburg loyalty, it was all the same to me. She coughed in simulated agony, as if stifled by Brissago smoke. Whenever a player's fist slammed down or a new burst of laughter rattled from the nickel-plated bar she flinched on cue as if being physically struck. Then she rolled her antelope eyes toward the ceiling and batted her black-lined eyelashes in distress. And then she put on an animated smile again. Her expression changed constantly. Her face had to be called "prepared" rather than made up; so carefully was an entire palette of colors applied to a base of ocher powder it seemed as if she was putting on, like an ancient actor, a whole series of masks—but in unbelievably quick succession with the help of some hidden mechanical trick—masks of agony, of shock, of chaste innocence, of ecstatic happiness.

"Why didn't we go to Café Hanselmann?"

Next to her, Xana in an ice-blue sweater with a high turtleneck collar, which, when seen from a distance, looked like the hairshirt of a squire. Next to her, Joop in a worn-out homespun jacket. (When you earn over 300,000 gulden a year you can afford to wear worn-out jackets.) His longish bald forehead surrounded by a yellow gray fluff like chick down reminded one, in its rosy high gloss, of the "skin" of a Punch and Judy doll. No wonder Pola liked to address her husband with the nickname "puppet." Decked out in a gray flannel suit, I completed the foursome; and every time I changed my position in the wicker chair I felt the gentle pressure of the Walther pistol against my thigh.

". . . why not Hanselmann?"

"But Pola," said ten Breukaa, lengthening the lower half of his face in a closed-mouthed yawn, "it's quite tolerable here . . ." (Since he was born rich, it was much easier for him than for Pola naturally to avoid snobbery.) "Even Commissioner Mavegn seems to be a regular customer here. And our Dr. Tardueser."

It struck me how heavy his Dutch accent was—with its guttural sounds so similar to Alemanic Swiss—despite all the years he had spent outside the Netherlands.

"Sit!" he added sharply.

"Sit? Do you mean me?" teased Pola, winking at me eagerly.

"I mean Sirio," Joop corrected her joylessly and allowed himself a piqued pseudosmile.

"Aha," Pola kept on teasing. "Trebla, look at the good Commissioner Mavegn! What an old rogue! Look—look how he's making eyes at Xana."

"Looks like the old man of the mountains in Schiller's *Alpenjaeger*," I confirmed. "In a modern edition."

Mavegn caught our glances. Lifted a giant arm and waved slowly with his snarled cigar. Joop, in greeting, rocked forward in his wicker chair. Pola nodded about twelve times in a row so fast I could hardly believe it.

"Sayhellosayhello," she cackled under her breath.

"Me? What for. I don't even know him."

"This Mavegn is a big cheese in the cantonal police. You've got to stay on the right side of him. A close friend of Rothmund's, Xana; smile, *smile!*"

"What?" asked Xana, and attempted, her head held slightly to one side, to look at Pola with polite attention. It was obvious she hadn't been aware of Mavegn's admiring glances and hadn't heard our conversation. Judging from her absentminded aloofness you could conclude she was thinking of the Giaxas. And yet today it was a different aloofness, a new variety, as if she had set up a transparent partition between herself and me. Could it be really that she had seen through my white lie about being in Corviglia and was mad at me for that? She who was so unlikely to hold something against me, especially a trifle—but then again you could never tell exactly where and when she had set her limits—beyond which she did indeed begin to hold things against me. Damn it all, I couldn't explain *why* I had gotten out at Chantarella even though I had bought a ticket to Corviglia.

"Who is Rothmund?" I said to change the subject.

"What, you don't know who Rothmund is? Did you hear that Joopypuppet? He doesn't know who Rothmund is!"

"Well so what?" I mumbled, lighting a cigar. "So what if I don't know. Would it irritate you if I smoke?"

"Did you hear that, puppet? Would it irritate me if Trebla smoked. As if it makes any difference in this d-read-ful pea soup fog if one more person smokes. And as for Rothmund, Trebla," Pola patted the back of my hand, "he's your last resort."

"My last resort? I thought that was the Fuehrer, now that I'm a citizen of the Reich."

"Rothmund, dear Trebla, is-your-master-over-life-and-death." With these last words she patted my hand seven times.

"What?" I asked amused.

Joop had lowered his polished dome. He lifted up the corner of the tablecloth and squinted under the table with an insulted mien. "Dr. Heinrich Rothmund is the chief of the Swiss Alien Police," he lectured. "For my part I've had very pleasant experiences with him."

When you earn over 300,000 gulden a year you're inclined to have pleasant experiences, I thought. "And the mountain spirit is a friend of his, I see. Do you know him well?"

"His brother-in-law arranged the sale of Acla Silva for Joop."

Joop's fallow eyes turned toward the Buendnerstube where Commissioner Mavegn was just joking about a lost hand of cards. "Och ja, och ja. Mr. Mavegn would make a good model for the King of Bernina."

"And who was that," asked Xana suddenly (apparently trying to come out of her shell).

Ten Breukaa did not hurry to answer, but glared once more under the table. Now the fact that Sirio had given up howling and had curled up for a nap seemed to insult him. "A great chamois hunter. A giant of a man. Legendary figure around here. In his normal profession," a feeble joke, "he was an excellent poacher and a large-scale smuggler of contraband. Gian Marchet Colani."

"Colani?" I asked. "Could that be an ancestor of our Avvocato Bow-Wow?"

"Salut, Mijnheer ten Breukaa, beautiful ladies!" Dr. Tardueser's pince-nez flashed joviality; no doubt he was so merry because he had just won a hand at Jass. "Could old pear-skull be a descendant of Marchet Colani, the Bernina King? N-n-not a chance. The de Colanaaas have nothing to do with giant Gian. It was a de Colana who murdered the brilliant Swiss statesman Ppomppeius Pplanta. In Riedberg Castle, anno sixteen hundred and twenty-three. Ah yes, our inebriated pear-pate is a di-rect descendant of this aristo-cratic as-sas-sin!" Amazing, the tourist-doctor's animosity for the country lawyer . . .

According to what Madam Fausch had told me, her husband was presently serving as an officer in the Sixty-first Border Regiment. But she never revealed the difference between the "introductory" and the "refresher" course. I figured it out this way: the introductory course was a refresher course in unfamiliar terrain, in this case the glacier-world surrounding Bernina Pass.

Behind the nickel-plated bar stood Sergeant Faustino Pizzagalli, the perfect pug-nosed image of his mother (though he was thinner and wore glasses) and ordered free beer to be passed around to the members of his battalion who were enjoying their weekend leave in the bar. They all belonged to a battalion of Mountain Fusiliers, which consisted (ignoring the headquarters—and what battalion can ignore its headquarters?) of a headquarters company, four companies of Mountain Fusiliers, and a Mountain Machine Gun Company. The units were not only identified by the numbers on their embroidered epaulets, but on the right sleeve of their swampy olive green uniforms the Mountain Fusiliers wore a dark green patch like the cross section of a bluntly pointed pencil. The sleeve of Sergeant Pizzagalli, Jr., was also decorated with two silver chevrons beneath an embroidered Swiss cross. He spoke Italian, Graubuenden German, Romansh—all equally well. He obviously enjoyed playing the generous barkeeper and showing off his skills in beer-pouring and foam-wiping. The soldiers had made friends with two country policemen from Samedan, their rolled capes slung over their shoulders; all were involved in various kinds of strength-testing like arm-wrestling and finger-wrestling (called *Fingerhakeln* in Bavaria and Austria), to the giggling amusement of Faustino Pizzagalli: "Another glass, Soldier Buddy?"

"Yessir, Sergeant sir. Hahahaaa!" The man he had asked laughed raucously as though his answer had been amazingly clever.

This soldier was strikingly handsome. Unlike the others, he wasn't wearing a "pencil" sewn to his sleeve but a patch that looked like a three-pointed meat cleaver without a handle, with a tiny triangle in the middle, the symbol of a mountain. A mountain machine gunner. Tall, broad-shouldered, narrow-hipped; a powerful young Achilles, his cap pushed back on his head; a bush of pitch-black hair atop his face, tanned bronze by the mountain sun; an almost brutally stubborn-looking, protruding jaw with a cleft chin and very white teeth. If someone came over to challenge him he would lock middle fingers with

the opponent and drag him across the table with the greatest of ease. "Haaaa."
If he reached out his hand to someone who refused the challenge: "Hahaaa."
Carousing, he laughed almost constantly, and his face dimpled when he smiled,
took on a strangely wild, humorless, indeed almost lecherous expression.

A frog-green fleece coat swung through the barroom doors. The buxom
young girl who ran into me in the underpass. She was greeted with a boisterous
chorus of hellos. The handsome soldier promptly grabbed her under the arms
and lifted her playfully into the air, and started her pummeling with her short,
plump legs, brandishing a short umbrella in the air, screeching and squealing
like a piglet. All the soldiers laughed, and in the boccia lane the balls thudded,
and in the Buendnerstube the fists banged on the gaming tables and shouts rang
out like pistol shots, "A three!" "A four!" or "Hundred!" or "Four jacks on a
jack-ace!" "Two hundred."

While the handsome one was holding the girl in the air his cap fell off his
head. A fellow soldier picked it up and waited until the squealing girl was slowly, with a great show of arm muscles, lowered to the ground. Soldier Buddy then
slipped his hand under her open fleece coat, embraced her swelling hip, and
drew her close to him with the obvious pride of ownership.

"Fräulein Tummermut, a beer?" asked Faustino grinning.

"Okay with me," the frog-green girl said saucily.

Then she looked my way.

She winked over at me, wrinkled her turned-up nose and, puffing air out of
her puckered lips, pulled her head down between her shoulders. She bedded her
cheek against that of Faustino's Soldier Buddy and chattered up at him, still
puffing. He thrust out his jaw and looked around at me; the girl, stupidly peeping with joy, began telling the soldier a story while the other men turned around
laughing to look my way.

"Hoho, Xana, look." Pola tattled in delight. "Look at that soldier's honey
by the bar—the way she's winking at Trebla. Cats won't give up mice. I know
him. I'll bet you a hundred to one he's made himself a little friend on the sly."

"First of all you know I'm not very sly," I parried, "and second—that little
platinum blond there? I don't know who she is. Maybe she's the same one who
knocked me over in the railroad underpass when I—uh—was on my way to Corviglia."

Miss Polari: "You rascal, now we've got you!"

Now Xana looked at me in mock sympathy. "Knocked you over, did she?"

"Nothing worth mentioning."

"Oh *really?*" intoned Pola skeptically.

"On your way to Corviglia?" Xana scrutinized me sympathetically through
our invisible partition.

"Yes." I jerked out my pack of cigars.

"On your way to Corviglia," Xana repeated piously, "you were bowled
over by happiness. Poor boy."

I stared at her. She met my gaze calmly. Two things occurred to me. For one I verified an old impression: Xana's violet eyes were variable, as changeable as the color of the sea in changing weather. Today in the mouse-gray light that fell through the windows of the American Bar they seemed almost mouse gray. Second, the irksome little smile that exposed her very pearly, shimmering front teeth revealed a slight defect in her beauty that I had long ago learned to ignore; one incisor slanted a tiny fraction of a millimeter in front of the other. In this unhappy moment I couldn't avoid feeling glad about any flaw.

Krainer & Mostny hung their peaked loden caps on the clothes hanger and took off their windbreakers; the Tutankhamon pattern once again. They ordered coffee from Annette and went directly over to the neat little set of Russian billiards.

Without paying the slightest attention to the other guests they took cue sticks from the wall rack, rubbed the points with blue chalk, threw a coin into the slot, and pulled a lever, whereupon a chain of ivory white balls (and one red one) rolled into the retainer. The pimply, dough-faced one (Mostny), called "Shursh" by his friend (Krainer), set up the balls—on directions of the latter—across the green-felt-covered surface and placed a red wooden mushroom in the middle. Krainer bent forward, made a few trial strokes, and began shooting.

The green surface had several holes in it. The object of the game was to shoot the red ball and knock all the white ones into the holes without touching the wooden mushroom. When one player failed to sink a white ball the other player took over. A player who knocked the mushroom over lost all the points he had won so far. A few soldiers sauntered over and began to kibitz.

"Watchout, watchout, hahaha," yelled the handsome soldier in crude High German and laughed lecherously. Some of his comrades called him Lenz, others Soldier Buddy, others by a name that sounded to me like "Brocka." He stood there with his thumbs hooked on his Sam Browne belt. Fräulein Tummermut had hooked her arm into his. "Watchout that y'don't knock over Hitler! . . . Owww, kee-rist, that one just missed Hitler by a hair, hahaah . . ." He had nicknamed the red mushroom "Hitler."

The players ignored his warning completely. The two policemen from Samedan, bulging holsters at their hips, joined the onlookers.

In the Buendnerstube the card game was drawing to a close amidst the protestations of Dr. Tardueser. "You should have trumped with the jack," he scolded the somber printing press owner Zuan who waved his prize beard in dissent. "And nonplayers should kindly refrain from exercising their tongues," continued the tourist-healer, his pince-nez gleaming chastisement at the Irishman. Fitz hadn't opened his mouth for a half an hour. He straightened his canvas cap. Got up, hardly adding to his height, and pursed his lips.

"Ff . . . Ff . . ."

Yes, in resigned fury he repeatedly mumbled something that began with a sharp "F." He stopped next to the Russian billiards to kibitz again. Almost seemed to be kibitzing through Soldier Buddy's widespread legs. That's how short Fitz was.

The leaden light of the afternoon fell on the billiard table by the windows. Between the surrounding kibitzers I caught sight of the two players in profile. First one and then the other, they bent down to the table, made a few piston-rod motions with the cue and took their shots. As soon as one missed a hole he stood up and chalked his score on a little blackboard while the other one bent over the table. They played, insensitive to the advice and laughter of the onlookers, in ostentatious, sullen silence. There was some sort of secret agreement between them. When not playing they both would stand leaning on their cues in the same present-arms pose. The one with bad skin had a strand of bleached blond hair dangling over his forehead. It was as if they had practiced the game in advance. Two robots playing. Bending forward, shooting, watching the results of the shot, dour, deaf, dumb to the world around them. Bending forward—shooting—

I lit my cigar. Got up quickly. Went to the billiard table. I ended up standing next to Fräulein Tummermut, but didn't look at her.

"Heil Hay Fever!" I said, the cigar between my teeth, which made me mumble a bit. "Heil Hay Fever in Pontresina."

Shursh, now playing, brushed me with the most fleeting, empty glance, made a few piston strokes, aimed and shot. Wouldn't it have been proper for Messrs. Krainer and Mostny to make some sign of recognition, at least a sarcastic comment like "Careful Woodchuckwoodchuckhunter!" Nothing of the kind.

I stepped closer, between the soldiers, and commented, chin on hand: "Hitler will fall."

Shursh bent over, touched me again with his glanceless glance. They didn't smile, the two of them, didn't even exchange glances. Shursh kept playing; the ash blond, sly-looking athlete looked on, resting on his cue.

"No matter how you play," I mumbled, puffing occasionally on my cigar, a talkative kibitzer, "Hitler will fall. As a matter of fact—just wait and see—the red ball will get him."

"I don't know about that," Lenz objected firmly. "You shoot with the red one. It takes orders, that's all. More likely one of the white ones will knock off Hitler. I'm good at this game, you know; got thirty-seven points in a row one time, hahaha," boasted Soldier Buddy and laughed lecherously down at the Tummermut girl.

Fitz moved over to the Kurierstube and I returned to our table. In a curiously lame gesture Joop's right hand began polishing his rosy-shiny, bald forehead to a high gloss. No doubt he missed his Spahi.

"Watch Hitler, watch Hitler!" excited shouts came from the group of kibitzing fusiliers and machine gunners. Suddenly howls of laughter burst from the crowd. "Boom, hahahahahaaah! I'll be damned, Hitler got knocked off!"

Pimply-faced George stood up. Wiped a few hanging strands out of his face with the back of his hand. Stared unbelieving at the table.

"So, how 'bout it, haha," the handsome soldier brayed and winked in my direction, "the man over there called it right, didn't he?"

The pimply dough-face, unmoved, wordless, turned toward the blackboard, took the chalk and wrote down a number.

"*Ohhhh* no!" objected Soldier Buddy violently. "Erase it *all*. Erase ev-ery-thing! You can write down a zero, my friend, and that's all."

Now the sporty good-looking fellow deigned, for the first time, to speak to the onlookers. He stared at Lenz with grim hostility. "We use different rules," he glowered. "We only subtract half when the mushroom goes down."

"You mean Hitler?" Lenz waved his powerful hand aggressively. "Not a chance. I know the rules. When Hitler gets knocked off, *you* lover there, you lose the whole game. Understand?"

"Bravo Brocka," a comrade cheered him on.

The loser's ears began to turn red. The other gave him a sign. It was obvious that a scene should be avoided. He (Krainer) shrugged his shoulders, and with cheek muscles grinding marched to the blackboard and erased both scores.

"So, that's better," said Lenz in condescending triumph. He detached himself from Fräulein Tummermut, strode with smoothly rolling steps to the nickel-plated bar where Faustino had prepared another round of beer, grasped a mug and, bending backwards, drained it in a single draft, then laughing, grabbed another, and swinging it aloft, sent a toast from one billiard expert to the other: "This one to your health!"

I raised my glass with its lapping contents of kirsch-laced coffee and toasted back.

A car drove up; a polyphony of barking swelled and ebbed away with the slamming of the car door. Then the country lawyer burst into the room. Close at his master's heels waddled the patriarch Arcibaldo.

Something, something that looked like a black, hairy ball shot out from under our table toward the newcomer—chirping, whining, yowling for joy—and jumped at him like a rubber ball, then threw himself on the patriarch, pulling him up on his hind legs where both embraced each other with wildly wagging tail stumps in a paroxysm of reunion rapture. In mad revelry they scrambled through the legs of the loudly laughing soldiers; Sirio became caught up in the trailing leash, flipped over on his back, shook himself free. And the country lawyer looked on; standing a little off-balance he rotated around his cane and, puffing up his shaggy moustache, put on a stolid bourgeois demeanor befitting the director of a successful traveling circus.

Joop had shaken off his apathy, jumped up, jabbed his index finger toward the floor in front of him repeatedly, and roared in a breaking voice: "Sirio! *Sirio*. . . . *Sit*, Sirio! *Heel!* . . ." Which had not the slightest effect on Sirio.

The alert Sergeant Pizzagalli, Jr., sprang from behind the bar, stepped quickly to the dragging leash, caught Sirio up and carried him over to us grinning. I snatched the wriggling bundle from under Joop's blanched nose—I couldn't understand what it was about a young dog's exuberance that made ten Breukaa so indignant—settled the overheated, silken-smooth pup on my knee, stroked him and whispered: "You're a naughty boy, Sirio. If you don't learn to behave I'm afraid your master is going to beat you."

"*Ecco, ecco, il Avvocato Bow-Wow! Salut,* Mr. de Colana, Doctor of Laws ... Greetings, greetings, oh noble patrician!" These and other malicious compliments, all led by Dr. Tardueser, echoed from the Buendnerstube as the country lawyer shuffled toward our table. Behind him, totally exhausted, dragged the patriarch, his twitching, dripping tongue dangling from his mottled-green mouth. De Colana's bloodshot eyes, the purple swollen boil on his nostril, his citified, outmoded black topcoat with its gnawed velvet collar, unbrushed, incorrectly buttoned, tassled with threads where a button was missing: it took no great powers of observation to see that he had been through another drinking bout.

With a careless wave of his stick he signaled his contempt to the name-callers in the next room. Beginning to sway, then pulling himself up straight, he bent forward and with his amber cane-handle tapped (gently, almost tenderly) on my chest and whispered in a sly voice—a foul gas of booze and peppermint fuming out at me: "Ah, Black-White-White-Black, that I should meet you here ... *benissimo.* I have an invitation to deliver."

He straightened up ceremoniously; strained clumsily to assume the rigid pose of a Heidelberg student. Attempted to click the heels of his dirty button boots. Doffed his clergyman's hat. Snickers from the Buendnerstube. De Colana, in complete disregard of his mockers, kissed the hands of Xana and Pola (the latter suffering this—no doubt because of the man's rather unsavory moustache—with an expression of mild revulsion) while I rose quickly and said with loud, exaggerated cordiality: "My dear Dr. de Colana, may we have the pleasure of your company at our table?"

"*Merci* very much, Black-White."

He extended his hand to Joop, who took it with an air of sullen peevishness, obviously looking for a polite opportunity to get Sirio away from me and give him a taste of discipline. Annette took the lawyer's coat, hat and stick, and pushed up a wicker chair for him. Groaning slightly, he sat down with barely perceptible unsteadiness, and Miss Polari fixed her rapt attention on the man's lapel, which was spattered with a whitish liquid, apparently condensed milk.

De Colana seemed to be in excellent spirits, his dignity enhanced by the lucrative Sirio transaction. Strangely enough, he showed his gratitude not to the buyer, but to me, the go-between: he half turned his back on Joop, and while he made a few pronouncements on the weather in his croaking, drinker's voice, reached over to me again and again to stroke, at first timidly, then with confidence, the spaniel's pitch black silken coat from neck to stubby tail. "Yes, yes, Joseph, sold by your brothers—hng!" He snorted a contrite little laugh through his nose.

As if touched by magic Sirio grew completely relaxed. With luxuriating moans he reveled in the caresses. Meanwhile the patriarch had recovered and crouched at our feet, hind legs clamped between his front paws. His half-blind eyes were riveted on Sirio.

"What can we offer you?" I smiled. "A coffee kirsch?"

"Kirsch—no, no, no, no. In the afternoon—ech—em—eh, I make it a habit, hum-rrum, never to touch alcohol." To make this bombastic lie seem more plausible he added, "Virtually never, hng, hng."

"A caffè espresso then? . . . Madame Annette, an espresso for Dr. de Colana!"

"May I be so bold, dear ladies and gentlemen . . ." De Colana got up halfway to attempt a Heidelberg-student-bow, then plopped back in his chair. "As a small tribute to the weather's inclemency," he forced out a stilted speech amidst suppressed groans and coughs, "in the form of a convivial gathering, ech, hem, it would be most appropriate . . . So may I be so bold as to request, ech, that you all do me the honor, hum, rrum, of being my guests for dinner at the Chesetta Grischuna? . . . Use, dear Black-White," he turned to me, "use your influence on your friends . . ."

"Where is this Chesetta Grischuna anyway, my dear Pink-Purple?" I asked brightly.

"Black-White? Pink-Purple? What kind of a secret code is that, Trebla?" bubbled Pola, with a gesture to her husband. Under no circumstances was he to accept the invitation of this leper. "You and Dr. de Colana seem to be the best of friends."

"A-aah," said de Colana with a sly grin. "You ask where the Chesetta Grischuna is. Well, it's in Sils. In Sils Maria on the hill. Nowhere in all Graubuenden will you find a more bull-foddied," he became tongue-tied, grimaced in embarrassment, "full bobbied, ech, full-bod-ied Valtellina wine."

"How about it?" I asked the group. "Shall we all go?"

"To Sils, how wonderful!" rejoiced Pola and clapped her hands. Confident that her signal had functioned properly, she begged, "Oh Joopypuppet, please, please, can't we all go?"

"No." Joop had indeed functioned, rubbed his bald forehead. "I have to work on my catalogue this evening."

"Oh, you and your old catalogue," sulked Pola, still playing dumb. "Please-please-please can't we go?"

"Sorry, but I have my commitments."

"Well that's that," I commanded. "The two of us will go alone, doctor. We can leave immediately."

"And Xana can have supper with us," Pola suggested impulsively.

"All right? And Trebla will drive to Sils with the doctor, okay? And then he can pick up Xana, and Joop will give you the Chrysler to drive home in."

I had stood up, placed Sirio on the tiled floor of the bar, pressed the leash into Joop's hand, carefully buttoned my flannel jacket over the black pullover Elsabé Giaxa had knitted for me, and avoided looking at the table. Why watch the heartbreaking farewell between de Colana and Arcibaldo on the one hand and Sirio on the other? Why watch Pola, who had just called Signor Pizzagalli over and asked him: "My good man, could you tell me who that handsome, *wonderfully* handsome soldier is over there?"

"Him? Over there? Mountain Machine Gunner Zbraggen," I heard Pizza-galli reply obligingly. "Lenz Zbraggen. He's got a lumberyard here in town with his brother. Was just called up for the refresher course. My boy Faustino is a sergeant in his battalion."

"Zbraggen! He delivers wood to us! I only know his brother Balthasar."

Printing press owner Zuan was obviously not one of de Colana's mockers; while the latter fumbled with his coat buttons Zuan came up to him, spoke Romansh to him in hushed tones. The country lawyer listened patiently, pulling on his moustache, made some reply, and rapped his amber cane-top reas-suringly on the man's shoulder. Then Zuan turned, thoughtfully milking his beard, and went back to his cronies.

"*Avanti a gletsch,*" rasped de Colana eagerly. And broad-brimmed hat in hand, performed an expansive farewell gesture in the direction of the table. We strolled through the American Bar in single file: the country lawyer, the patri-arch Arcibaldo, myself. Behind us buzzed Tardueser's wisecracks and Mavegn's guffaws and Pola's clucking and Sirio's yowling and Joop's "Sit! Sit!" Past the Russian billiards. The kibitzers had drifted off. The balls had disappeared into the table. Only the wooden mushroom—Hitler—was set up again in the middle of the green tabletop. Turned toward the blackboard the Two Blonds were pull-ing on their windbreakers.

Fräulein Tummermut was still hanging on the arm of the soldier Lenz Zbraggen. By the crowded bar I was accidentally pushed against her, and for a second my arm could feel her bulging bosom; she snapped one eye shut and looked me over with the other (green iris) and peeped, "Bye-bye."

Lenz: "Say, y'know those pretty ladies over there y'just walked out on —the older one's a customer of ours—would'ya mind if I gave 'em a little bou-quet? Some heart's-beard? A little bouquet of heart's-beard from Soldier Bud-dy."

"Heart's-beard?"

The mountain machine gunner unbuttoned his blouse, reached inside his undershirt and—rip, zip!—held out a tuft of blue black chest hair in his fist.

"Try your luck with it," I said.

"Only a joke." With a lecherous laugh—contagious as usual to his fellow soldiers—he opened his fist. "*Ciao!*" he shouted exuberantly after us. "Soldier Buddy hopes the gentlemen have a pleasant Sunday."

5

Not that the man was *of* leather. But he was certainly *in* it to an extravagant degree. A kind of beret, but of black leather; maroon brown leather jacket, black shirt—or, to be more exact, blackshirt; high, golden brown jackboots. A moustache shaved so small it made you think of a liver spot on his upper lip. Which, on closer examination, looked more like a *leather* spot. He swung from the saddle of his heavy, sidecar-equipped motorcycle. When it comes to motorcycles I know a thing or two: German make —Zuendapp. A twin-cylinder four-stroke with over 20 hp. He shook hands with Krainer and Mostny, first with the "spokesman," then with the silent one.

Ten Breukaa had two cars—a cinnamon-colored Chrysler cabriolet and a seven-seat Austro-Daimler limousine, a long, black-lacquered snobmobile with cream-colored upholstery and a separate driver's seat. In which sat gardener-servant-chauffeur Bonjour over a crossword puzzle. Between the parked cars a team of mules waited. Standing in front of them, Mr. Fitzallan, the dwarfish Royal Jockey, Ret., coat collar up, mouth corners down—and completely oblivious of the other three: Krainer, Mostny, Leather Man, and us three, de Colana, Arcibaldo and myself—was giving the mules a dressing down.

"Fffuck you," he cursed them, squeezing out every word. "You blasted goddamned donkey bastards . . . Go to hell! You sons-of-bitches, listen to me. To hell with you, you goddamned ffucking . . ."

The two mules absorbed his maledictions with a deep and alien impassiveness; only their fuzzy ears twitched gracefully.

There, parked askew to the curb, stood de Colana's unwashed limousine. Behind the mud-spattered back window seven spaniel snouts crowded over, under and beside each other in a kind of posed family portrait. Upon seeing us the picture came to life and began a breathless, joyous yapping. With an inscrutable mien that failed, however, to conceal his fatherly pride, the country lawyer opened the door. At once the pack tumbled out and fanned out into seven tiny, shaggy flying carpets. For two minutes he let them romp; then he put the housekey to his lips and called them back with an unconvincing whistle. Only three obeyed and jumped into the back seat.

"Arcibaldo, *avanti!*" shouted de Colana, but even this stern command was undermined by a certain kindness in his voice. Immediately the patriarch trotted off to act the experienced sheepdog. With menacing growls and snorts he rounded up the four renegades and drove them back to the car. The amber-

handled cane, it turned out, could also double as a shepherd's rod; a few featherlight raps and all were settled down in the back seat.

De Colana straddled across the damaged running board and squeezed behind the wheel; I helped the patriarch get in (to the seeming annoyance of his
master) and the three of us were soon settled in a row on the front seat; the starter whined several times without success before the motor finally sputtered into
life.

A leaden gray afternoon, but with a glimmer of hope! There above the en-
shrouded Fuorcla Surlej gaped a tattered hole in the heavy cloud; within it
shone, infinitely far away, the cornflower-blue sky of the south, in the midst of
which, seemingly framed by a capricious hand, shimmered the promising,
ivorylike disk of the nearly full moon.

Then the swollen ring of clouds squeezed in and smothered out this un-
earthly omen of hope.

We drove along a hillside covered with larches and stone pines; higher up
the slope the outlines of trees dissolved in fog. When clouds come down from
the sky they're called fog, I thought simplemindedly; I stretched my neck and
peered into the rear-view mirror, without, it seemed, distracting the driver's
fixed attention from the road ahead. The peacock feather swayed gently in the
back window, and the road reeled out behind us—empty. We drove rather fast,
the loose running-board rattling. On the left we had a last view of the resort and
its row of hotel boxes; everything appeared quite dead. Then we drove deeper
into the Suvretta Forest.

"Black-White-White-Black? Are you asleep?" de Colana's voice rasped
from afar.

I pulled myself up straight. "No . . . I'm just a little, ah, dazed you might
say. All this gray—the weather I mean. Maybe the coffee kirsch too. When I
drink during the day I sometimes get a little drowsy."

"Aha. What did I tell you? I make it a rule, hm-rrum, a rule—" His forward gaze turned my way and the sour stink of booze and peppermint billowed
out at me: "During the day, not a drop of alcohol."

"Don't preach at me, Doctor. I'll bet you a million pounds sterling that
you've got at least half a liter of schnapps in you. As a matter of fact—just a minute," I sniffed, "um, Marc de Bourgogne. Am I right?"

"Me? *In* me? A half a liter of Marc de Bourgogne? Where did you ever get
such an absurd idea?

Meanwhile the patriarch had done me the honor of spreading out his floppy ears—those fantastically mangy hanging ears—on my knee. Though he had
assumed a sleeplike pose he wasn't sleeping; his half-blind eyes squinted up
slyly into the grayness beyond the car window. Again I stretched over to look in
the mirror. We had left behind the last houses of the village of Campfèr. Now
we were driving along the shore of Lake Campfèr. In front of us, still small, the

houses of Silvaplana. The cloud masses hung low, almost within reach, over the lake, and just under this impenetrable, grit-gray cotton blanket sailed a large, black bird of prey (a golden eagle, I presumed) flying with weary, dragging wingbeats over the motionless, utterly colorless water, like a symbol of this Cimmerian landscape, like a messenger from the Underworld.

The rear-view mirror was set for the driver's eyes and limited my view of the road behind. I twisted around as if to check on the well-being of the spaniel pack. Two of the youngest were sleeping. The rest of them—some using the backs of others as chin rests—stared into space in sullen resignation. All their enthusiasm had evaporated.

Through the dirty rear window, past the denuded, barely recognizable peacock feathers, I peered out at the shoreline road trailing out behind us with its wrought-iron posts topped by an improvised railing of barkless stone-pine trunks. No vehicle was following us.

De Colana gave me a brief side-glance. "Now tell me," he asked in drawn-out, rasping tones, "fellow-student Black-White, what are you always looking for behind us, eh? Did you, hech-hech, lose your heart in Heidelberg?"

"I think that applies more to you."

"Have you been taken with the idea that your friends, ech, may have changed their minds? eh? and are roaring after us in their, ech, official state limousine?"

"I doubt that very much. I wanted to ask you, though . . . Just now, while I was dozing, did someone pass us? A motorcycle with sidecar, a Zuendapp for example?"

Once again his red-rimmed, bluish white eyes, their tint and expression so similar to the patriarch's, gazed at me for a moment. "While you were dozing?" An indulgent grin crept out from under his gray brown moustache fringes. "A motorcycle—not that I'm aware. No one passed us. Not a Zuendapp in sight. You were dreaming, Black-White."

I looked at de Colana furtively out of the corner of my eye. The flat-brimmed black hat was jauntily set a little off-center. Perhaps he was once a smart-looking student whose family name had opened the door to one of the first-rate Wilhelmine fraternities. If you took away the swollen, violet quality of his face and the chronic drinker's boil—if you rimmed away his messy sea-lion-moustache, he had, amazingly enough, an almost handsome male profile. Suddenly I wondered if I shouldn't take him into my confidence about the Two Blonds. But feeling too dull-witted to make a decision, I leaned back in the seat. The patriarch gave out a deep groan. The loose running-board rattled.

"Don't you remember, Doctor?" I persisted sleepily. "Back there . . . in front of Pizzagalli's hotel . . . there was someone waiting with a motorcycle. A man in a brown leather jacket."

"Ah so. Ah that one."

"You know him?"

"And how! That's Paretta-Piccoli. 'The Fascist,' as the St. Moritzers call him . . . Hng, and *how* I know him."

The running board rattled. "Fascist?" I asked sleepily, incapable of any coherent thought.

"Oh yes . . . The fellow once ran the Crestalta sawmill . . . Embezzled some money . . ." His monotonous rasping sounded far away. "At the time I represented the co-plaintiff . . . He spent three years in Chur Penitentiary, Paretta did. And ever since he's gotten out, hng-hng, he's been a big follower of Mussolini's. Now he's taken up local hauling."

"Mussolini?" I queried very sleepily.

I didn't realize that I'd been really fast asleep this time until we were entering the village of Sils Maria, situated on a neck of land between two lakes; the patriarch was sitting up beside me and de Colana's voice was croaking, "Black-White, shall we go see Nietzsche?"

I raised myself off the back of the seat, stretched, and yawned into my elbow, blinking uncomprehendingly at the country lawyer.

"Good morning," he grinned patronizingly. "Hope you rested well . . . I wondered if you might want to see the house where Nietzsche went insane."

"Hm?"

"Anno eighty-eight. Shall I take you there?"

"No."

"No?"

"I'm not much of a Nietzsche man."

"Not . . . ?" His brows disappeared beneath the hat brim. Something like surprise, or rather disappointment, flickered in his grinning face. No doubt the Heidelberg student Gaudenz de Colana had been a Nietzsche follower. Later on Nietzsche probably became less helpful to him and had to be replaced by schnapps.

We jerked past a weathered sign with the inscription VAL FEX & MARMORE, then up a little hill, and the neuralgic pain that stabs at my forehead every time I wake up began slowly to dissipate.

We stopped in front of a stately whitewashed inn painted with Rhaeto-Romansh benedictions. Under the projecting gabled roof a large fishnet was hung out to dry.

Not a soul in the gloomy entrance hall. Frosty cold tasting like milk. This corridor was long, tunnel-like, on its walls a shadowy parade of neat little chamois antlers and boldly curved ibex horns. Its other end led outside again, and the exit framed a view of drying laundry and the pepper-colored posterior, the full, swollen, rosy udder of a tail-flicking cow. Then a sturdy, red-haired farmer appeared, girdled with a milking stool whose single leg projected from his buttocks; appeared and disappeared as if absorbed in work, without giving a sign of recognition.

The country lawyer opened a door on the left; burned into the wood: STUE-VETTA. A neat dining room, empty. Wood paneled walls, a few tables scrubbed to a shine, wall benches running around the entire room, everything made of unfinished, reddish stone-pine that breathed out an unforgettably sweet-acrid scent of resin. A giant tiled stove took up nearly a quarter of the room. In anticipation of a cold evening it had been stoked with split logs that crackled quietly.

As in all true Engadine houses, built as they were as rustic strongholds against the long upland winters, the windows resembled the cubic embrasures of a fort. The depth of the windowsills showed the walls to be at least four feet thick. Whereas double windows kept out the cold in the winter, outside windows were enough in the summer—though one must have had to lie on his stomach to close them.

Between the windows, a glass case displaying several silver trophies surrounded by colored pennants and wreaths of artificial oak leaves. A red and silver brocade ribbon was embroidered with the inscription *Swiss Fed. Shooting Match Luzern;* a yellow, blue, and white one bore a rampant ibex, the heraldic symbol of Graubuenden. Enthroned atop the chest was a paper-mâché construction that was supposed to represent a rocky cliff; upon it, sitting on its hind legs, stood a stuffed woodchuck whose pepper-colored, vaguely orange-tinted fur almost blended into the paneled wall behind it.

De Colana, grunting, pulled off his coat, rapped his amber cane-handle against a sliding door in the wall, plopped onto the bench by the stove, slid groaning behind the table, and with a spiraling hand motion invited me to sit down. As I took my place at the corner of the bench, Maxim Grabscheidt's present was pushed out of place in my back pocket. I reached in to straighten it out. The mother-of-pearl grips felt cool to the touch.

Part of the spaniel-cortege jumped onto the bench to devote themselves to the (soon imitated) business of flea-scratching and belly licking. Others went on cautious reconnaissance patrols among the chairs and tables. Wherever you looked, there a dangling, uncombed ear, here an oscillating tail-stump, there a bizarrely long paw on a short, befringed leg.

A wooden, clattering shuffle in the hall. A wooden kick pushed wide the door. In plodded a massive St. Bernard as big as a calf, large headed, with red-underlined eyes and slobbering jowls. As soon as he saw the pack he began to whip the air with his great switch of a tail. The shaggy crew jumped off the bench and out from under the tables, crowded together and began cursing the enemy with an incredible storm of barking—first, like Homeric heroes, from a safe distance, then venturing closer, then swirling back on stiffened front paws. All the while this excitement had an air of unseriousness, and I realized that this little battle had often been waged before—only to end in universal goodwill.

Only the patriarch Arcibaldo refused to take part. It had taken some effort to get up on the bench and it was befitting his age and dignity that he maintain his place. Poised like a field marshal he surveyed the contest.

As soon as the advanced guard came near him the St. Bernard plumped himself down on the floor and began rolling on his back in boorish delight. At once the hostile yapping turned friendly, and the pack began dancing around him, planting swift kisses on his stubby muzzle, bounding over his rather loathsome, big, blondish belly. Adding to this scene from a canine *Gulliver's Travels* came the surging-rising-falling screams of an infant around six months old cradled in the arms of a young woman who, clacking along in wooden clogs, had followed the St. Bernard into the room. De Colana leaned back against the stove and laughed—shoulders jumping—his almost inaudible laugh. Snatched up his walking stick, banged it on the table and crowed, *"Fermati adesso!"*

On this command the pack withdrew from the St. Bernard. The latter raised his giant body onto his feet and trotted over to sniff the newcomers.

"Yayayayaya," I said. "Good dog, big dog, v-e-r-y good, big dog."

The St. Bernard bedded his heavy stump-nose on my leg and slobbered all over my pants.

"Barrrrri," the woman scolded with a heavily rolled "r."

Barri kept on slobbering. No doubt he liked me.

Holding the bawl-baby in her bare arm she stood on one leg, pulled a wooden *zoccolo* from her bare foot, threw it, and struck the hindquarters of my newfound friend with a well-aimed shot. Barri freed me at once from his soggy intimacies and, tail between his legs, bounded like a clumsy rocking horse out the door. The woman slammed it shut behind him, and limping on her shoeless foot, padded and clacked over to us, slipped into the cast-off *zoccolo*, showed us a gap in her teeth and shouted above the baby's crying (but in pleasant, well-modulated Italian), *"Ecco, ecco, il Dottore de Colana! Buena sera. Come sta, Dottore?"*

Without waiting for an answer she flicked off one of the blankets the child was wrapped in—a piece of murky pink wool—bent over the heavy table and began zealously rubbing Barri's slime-deposit from my Sunday trousers, whereby I got the chance to breathe in the not unpleasant smell of infant urine and soured milk. At the same time it was somewhat embarrassing to have a young mother, and a complete stranger at that, start dabbing around on my upper thigh without a word of warning. The country lawyer could read my expression, but sank back against the stove and snorted his nasal laugh. Then in a comical bow he bent down across the grainy, knot-covered tabletop: *"Grazie, Donna Teresina, molto bene, mmm. E come sta la signore e suo marito?"*

"Abastanza bene, grazie, Dottore," she said, finishing me up.

"Grazie, grazie," I tried to smile. De Colana was relishing my slight embarrassment and puffed air through his moustache fringes in undisguised glee, while the woman rewrapped her offspring in the cleaning rag.

A sloppy, black-haired woman, greasy-shiny braids coiled like seashells about her ears, a scarf around her neck that seemed to have been made from an old stocking. A sleeveless, wine-red woolen bodice with a few unraveled threads, so stretched out at the top that her bare shoulder was revealed, not un-pretty, rounded, olive-gleaming, baring several shoulder straps, and the upper-most shadowy space between her breasts as well, emphasized by a brassiere too tight for her heavy bosom. Several ribbons crept out from beneath the bodice, and a stained and faded cotton skirt reaching barely to the knees stretched over a rounded belly. Her stocky, bare legs were spattered with manure. Despite all this the slovenly young black-eyed woman had something thoroughly feminine and attractive about her. If you overlooked the bad teeth revealed by her surly smile, her careless attire, her unflattering hairdo: she might have been one of those southern village beauties who, as soon as they have children, rapidly dete-riorate, as if from intentional neglect.

Hissing and hushing she rocked the child so vigorously that it suddenly broke off its crying. It bore little outward resemblance to its mother. Much lighter-skinned, with pepper-colored, almost orange-tinted fuzz on its head—very like the stuffed woodchuck on the case, I thought—it gaped at us with eyes of unusual color and expression, reddish, almost albino eyes that held an oddly unchildlike, seemingly inborn suspiciousness.

"*Un' bambino?*" I asked.

"*Si, signore. Un' bambino.*"

"*Ech-hemm-m, cominciamo con due Strega.*"

"*Sta ben,*" the woman said to de Colana and clattered out of the room.

"Pph-hng!" his grin burst out, as the pear-shaped skull approached me. "Now show me—show me the exact place where, ech, this mammoth creature dribbled on you. Show me the precise location where Donna Teresina dried you off, where—where—"

"Heehee."

"Hng-hng."

"Heeheeheehee."

"Hng-hng-hng."

"Don't worry, Doctor. No taboos were violated there."

"Taboos! Pp-hng! That's an original way of putting it. You and your taboos, Black-White . . . Humm, yesyes, Teresina Clavadetscher . . ." In antici-pation of an evening snack the spaniels were posed in a polite circle on the bench and the floor; the patriarch had hung his paw in the crook of his owner's arm, and as patient as they were eager, all stared up at their master with gleam-ing, rounded eyes. "Yesyes, Teresina . . ." De Colana held his leaning pose against the giant stove in which the crackling had grown still. He tugged on his moustache and stared silently, motionlessly through the fortlike window into the leaden twilight. He seemed to have grown suddenly very pensive, and it made me glad to realize I was one of those rare people in whose presence one feels free to keep silent.

Very distant, as if smothered by the pressing cotton blanket of the sky, came the dull clang of a mournful evening bell. Then the nearby bell of Sils

Baseglia took up its dark, prolonged pealing. After a few last listless humming strokes it fell silent, and only the far, far half-smothered ring of the other bell kept up its lone lament, on and on. Finally it too was quiet. Now it was very still in the little guest room.

The owner of the farm stepped in. The milking stool unbuckled, two schnapps glasses and a slender bottle in his blocky hands, he stamped across the creaking floor.

De Colana creaked too, "*Salute.*" He picked up his cane, but not by the handle, which he carelessly swung in front of my chest: "*Un' amico di Vienna,*" he introduced me. "*Poeta-giornalista exiliato.*" Now the amber handle swung toward the farmer: "*Segner Clavadetscher, padron' della Chesetta Grischuna.*"

The farmer didn't say a word. Placed the bottle and the glasses—clink!—on the table. Extended his hand to the country lawyer, jerked it away after a single shake, and grasped mine. His hairy block of a hand felt rough and calloused. An imposing man, he wore clay-encrusted boots, patched pants, but a snow-white shirt he had obviously just put on, and over it a clean, black, unbuttoned vest. He was remarkably fair-skinned with pepper-colored, bristly hair that tended toward orange (woodchuck fur like his son's) wetted down and freshly combed: he must have just taken time to clean up. His eyes, almost albino eyes, had a reddish glow about them, strange and animal-like, suspicious, overly watchful, like the eyes of his son.

Without giving us another look he poured quick as a flash and with dead aim, virtually flinging the pale golden schnapps into our glasses; his watchfulness seemed directed at nothing in particular. Such oily liquor was probably meant more for dessert, but I decided not to say anything about it. De Colana shoved his glass carefully under his fringed upper lip, closed his eyes and tipped it up, groaned aloud as if completing a hard but pleasant task, slapped his hand to his face and vehemently wiped his moustache, and then, with a careless wave, ordered the *padrone* to pour him another.

"Strega! Black-white, why aren't you drinking? It's evening already," he added slyly. Slop! The *padrone* had refilled his glass. "Cheers, fellow student." With an expansive gesture the country lawyer clinked his glass against mine, then emptied it again in a single gulp. Toasting to my blissfully groaning companion I too drank out my glass. The Strega tasted sugary, vaguely like hair tonic and reminded me of Kaiserbirn, burning not unpleasantly in my chest and then in my stomach. Clavadetscher refilled my glass. His watchfulness wasn't meant for me.

De Colana drew him into a brief conversation, which (for me) shifted from somewhat familiar Italian into almost incomprehensible Romansh. Old memories crept up on me as I listened to this dialect—according to Xana a true remnant of Vulgar Latin. Yes, the farmers in the Brenta Valley had talked like this—back when we took up quarters with them after the Thirty-sixth Reconnaissance Company had been transferred from the Eastern Front.

While they were talking I thought I noticed that the country lawyer, unlike myself, very often found himself in the wandering searchlight beam of Clavadetscher's suspicion—this suspicion, which pretended to be so inborn, organic and natural, but which possessed deep down and carefully concealed—or was I wrong?—something restless and unstable. Now this ray of mistrust strayed off to search the room, seeming to find itself verified in the form of a disheveled ball of yarn that lay, skewered with knitting needles, on one of the mighty windowsills. Even though the *padrona* had seemed careless, the farmer appeared to insist on rigid orderliness. He marched briskly to the windowsill, snatched up the ball in a snap and stuffed it in his pants pocket. Jerked open the door of the stove, peered in, found his suspicions confirmed again. Marched out the door, elbows wide, forearms swinging their red-haired, blocky hands.

"This Clavadetscher has hair like a woodchuck's," I said, and felt a warm, golden sweetness inside that was beginning to lift my spirits.

"All ... the Clavadetschers here have red hair ... Even his, echhh," groaned de Colana slowly, "brother Peidar—even Peidar Clavadetscher had red hair." He stared out through the window embrasure. In his bloodshot eyes was the pale reflection of the long-lasting summer light of this unsummerlike evening. "Four or four and a half years ago—echhh—this Peidar was shot to death."

"The farmer's brother? Shot?"

"A hunting accident."

He read the question in my face and rumbled, "*Vacca Madonna*," then wagged his pear-shaped head to shake off his pensiveness and nodded mischievously at the Strega bottle that the *padrone* had left on the table, and when I failed to take the hint, nodded more sharply, this time without a trace of mischievousness, whereupon I granted his wish and refilled his glass. "*Salute,* Black-White." He placed it under the fringes and tipped it up, grunted contentedly, and shooed away a nonexistent fly from his face.

Behind the sliding door there arose a clatter of wooden shoes and pans and plates. The muffled voices of the two proprietors could be heard exchanging one-word sentences. The spaniel pack crouched obediently, a monument of expectation. I sipped my Strega.

"Well now, what was it you wanted to ask? If I have many clients?"

"No, that's not what I wanted to ask," I smiled. "But do you?"

"Do you know the Alpetta Brewery in Celerina? Well now, I was legal representative there until—six months ago." A shaking motion with his hand. "Now they employ a younger man. Colleague Tardueser."

"A relative of our tourist-healer?"

"A cousin of Pompeius's, yes indeed."

"Is Dr. Tardueser's name Pompeius? Rather archaic-sounding appellation."

"That's the gentleman's name, yes." Again his jellyfish eyes mirrored the sluggish, pale twilight, which was so little different from the light of the dull afternoon. And again, a question forced its way to my lips. But it remained unspoken, and instead I asked:

"And this what's-his-name . . . this fabulous full beard that talked to you before, this walking advertisement for hair grower—?"

He let his fingers fall fluttering from his chin. "Zarli Zuan."

"Zuan, yes. Also a client?"

"M-hm. A very ori——, original stroke of bad luck—hng-hng, he came up with, old Zarli. You could write a story about it, Black-White. With the title, hum-rrum, the title, 'Hairy Christmas.'"

"Pardon me. *Hairy* Christmas?"

His inflamed, mucoid eyelids winked cleverly. Puffing out his shaggy moustache he said: "Mhm! Exactly. Now listen here, old man . . ." Laboriously he dug all kinds of objects out of his coat pockets: a box of Laurens cigarettes, a pencil stub, a medicine bottle, a glass tube with a rubber squeezer wrapped in a wrinkled handkerchief. "Listen here, old boy . . ." He dipped the glass tube into the bottle, let it suck in fluid, jerked down his eyelids one after the other with practiced agility and gave himself an eyewash. "So listen here . . ." With compressed eyelids he groped for the handkerchief, touched it fleetingly to his eyes, then squinted cautiously and put away the bottle and the eyedropper. "I, uh, violate no lawyer-client confidence when I tell you of the misfortune that befell poor . . ." He stopped, let his nose hang over the table as if something had failed him. ". . . Poor," he snapped his fingers feebly, "ah, poor Zarli Zuan. A well-known misfortune, so listen carefully."

The country lawyer turned over the cigarette box and, bending over, began to scribble on it with the pencil stub, while at the same time beginning to tell in more or less coherent fashion—albeit often interrupted by pensive nose-hanging, soundless laugh-snorting and gargled throat-clearing—of how Saluvers, the "greatest hoteliers far and wide," had contracted printer Zuan to produce a total of twenty thousand New Year's cards. It was a yearly business practice for the Saluvers to take out their guest registers and send off thousands of New Year's greetings to the "international set"—on the finest paper, no less, a variety that the storyteller could identify only after considerable nose-hanging. "Japan!" he announced at last, raising his pencil in triumph. "Japan paper."

De Colana pushed the cigarette box in my direction. With some difficulty I succeeded in deciphering the shaky scrawl:

"Happy New Year nineteen hundred thirty-eight," I read aloud. "Indeed. Do you realize, my friend, that we are in the midst of World War II?"

"Mrm," he growled, continuing his story undaunted. In November Zuan's youngest daughter had caught pneumonia. For days her father had torn his beard in worry and had neglected his duties in the printing shop. But when the order stood stacked and ready for delivery he made an unfortunate discovery. A typographical gremlin had been at work and had made an M into an H. On 20,000 sheets of expensive Japan paper stood the proud inscription: HERRY CHRISTMAS.

"Sad story, that," I murmured. "And so . . .?"

And so naturally the Saluver Hotels refused to accept the order from Zuan. On top of that, one maître-d'hôtel had dropped a remark that reached the printer while it was still warm: Zuan must be of the erroneous belief that the Saluvers were manufacturers of hair-growing tonic. Zuan flew into a rage, sued his typesetter and accused him of taking revenge. The latter was supposed to have committed the error intentionally in order to pay back his employer for a reprimand he had received a few days before. But the complaint was rejected on the grounds of insufficient evidence. Furthermore the plaintiff was declared to have been remiss in his duties as a supervisor. The whole matter got Zuan into considerable difficulties.

"He'll get himself untangled from his hairy Christmas, hng-hng . . . Doesn't need to turn gray over the affair. It would be too bad for his beautiful black Capuchin beard," the country lawyer concluded.

The sliding door rattled upwards. Onto the sideboard slid a giant frying pan that steamed with the splendid odor of melted butter—next to it a two-liter decanter of sparkling deep purple wine. Soon Clavadetscher marched in swinging his arms, his shirt sleeves now rolled up, fetched heavy plates, two thick glassed and wooden handled utensils, scattered all this onto the table as if to say, "There, take it!" Then he swung the giant pan onto the table and grunted "*Maluns!*" It was a steaming mountain of finely chopped fried potatoes dripping in butter. Now came a massive chopping board piled with gnarled Salziz sausages, delicate Salamettis and paper-thin slices of transparent, rosy Graubuenden ham. Then two angular loaves of white bread like feet in plaster casts. Finally he let the purple-sparkling Valtellina wine gurgle into our glasses, banged down the decanter, placed his hairy hands on his hips and raised his chin with a jerk that commanded, "Eat!"

For the first time he took a closer look at me and fixed his reddish gleaming eyes on my forehead. Suddenly his imperturbable, impassive face revealed a hint of curiosity (I was used to that); but then astonishment, then—yes—a touch of horror. He gasped. As if he wanted to ask something. De Colana noticed it too. With a turn of his head he followed the other man's gaze and glanced at my brow. A barely noticeable but absolutely demonic, clever smile hid behind his moustache as he piled fried potatoes onto my plate. The farmer whipped the Strega bottle off the table, turned on his heel, slammed down the sliding door and marched out of the room.

"Why was your friend Clavadetscher looking at me so funny?"

A disdainful flutter of his hand. But his devilish, sly little grin still lurked behind the matted bristles of his moustache. Then my host raised his much-too-full glass. In the incredibly slow-fading, grayish glow of the day the wine sparkled in the glass like an enormous ruby. Slowly, devoutly and carefully, de Colana lifted it, trying hard not to tremble. The attempt failed and the wine slopped over, staining his shirt and tie with two ugly, violet spots—an accident that he completely ignored. Raising the glass in front of his nose he intoned ceremoniously: "*Salute*, Black-White-White-Black."

"*Salute.*"

We drank; the pack followed our movements as if hypnotized. He raised his glass and stared at me expectantly. The dogs did too. The wine did not have the volatile taste of great age—like that of ten Breukaa's Valtellina. Glowingly full-bodied, yet tart and pure and as fresh as an iron-rich mountain stream, it shot raging into my limbs and gave me a slight cramp in the forehead.

"Excellent."

"Ah yes, the Valtellina grape. Conrad Ferdinand Meyer sang its praises . . ." He leaned his head to one side and flabbily snapped his fingers. "And now I will recite a poem for you, just a moment . . . 'Purple grapes of Valtellina/Ripening in the noonday sun/On this day . . .' mm, wait a minute . . . well now, and so forth and so on . . . Hum, and then, 'Now the restless soul inside me/Brimming o'er with nature's pow'rs/With the grace of heav'n to guide me . . . guide me . . .' no. I can't do it any more. . . . But yes!—'Bursting forth from leafy bowers/Fire-filled . . . F-i-r-e-f-i-l-l-e-d . . .' No. No, I can't do it any more. No. Only last year I recited the whole thing. On August first, last year . . . I guess I'm just getting—echhh—old . . ."

"I like him very much, old Conrad Ferdinand," I bantered casually, "but I can never remember poems. Even when they're my own."

This was no consolation to him.

All at once the farmer was in the doorway, a bundle of firewood in his arms. He stood there peering over at us suspiciously. Now I was included in the searchlight beam of his mistrust. Since we continued eating and drinking without a word, he dropped his load of wood rattling in front of the stove. Jerked

70

open the door, dropped pliantly into a squat, threw in a few logs, blew at the coals. Stood up and trudged out the door. It began to crackle quietly inside the stove, inside this heat-radiating house of a stove; the fried potatoes steamed their crispy smell, the country bread and the massive half-round golden cheese gave off their fragrances, the scent of stone-pine paneling filled the room, and the wine "fire-filled" the drinker, it really *fire-filled* you. (Thanks be to Conrad Ferdinand Meyer for this verb.) I should have been able to lose myself in pure enjoyment. What prevented me from doing this was hard to define. It was not any concern about the Two Blonds, Maxim's death, Xana's behavior, no secret worry about Giaxa or about tomorrow's uncertainties: the more I indulged in the Valtellina, the more these things disappeared in the fire of the moment. It was the moment itself—this moment that seemed to promise a brief span of forgetfulness and pleasure—that was the source of my uneasiness. It could be that the twilight was to blame, indistinguishable as it was from the gray afternoon, without a beginning and, so it seemed, without an end. It simply remained light; interminably this pale sheen peered in the fortress windows, by God, as if the earth had stopped to rest on its journey around the sun. Of course only ten days separated us from the longest day of the year. But the fact that this fading June day in the mountain valleys appeared as pre-winterish, as buried as a day in late November, seemed unreal. Again my gaze fell on the dull iridescence of the display case with its marksmanship trophies and on the stuffed woodchuck

"By the way, the hunting accident you mentioned before," I chatted amidst our rustic feast, "I think I know—"

But de Colana—who had washed down all his troubles, his moustache tips gleaming with melted butter—twinkled at me roguishly and interrupted me by rapping his cane against the sliding door. Clavadetscher soon appeared in the room. "*Pronto!*" he banged another two-liter decanter onto the table, although the first was not yet empty. Whack! the door slammed behind him.

"Archie! . . . ," crowed the country lawyer. "Principe! . . . Borgia! . . . Felice! . . . Saxo! . . . Borussia! . . . Lucretia! . . . Concetta! . . ."

He had cut three sausages in pieces and now he called the spaniels up one by one, as sharply as a sergeant at a company roll-call (even though this sharpness did sound a bit rusty). As each dog's name was called he jumped up immediately and began dancing eagerly on his hind legs. A piece of smoked sausage flew through the air—he snapped it up and disappeared. Those not yet called remained crouched at the ready, unwilling to risk the attempt to steal his piece, unmoving, frozen with envy.

"Bravo. I must say, Doctor, you could be in the circus. Like my father-in-law."

"Your, hum, father-in-law? Who's that?"

"Giaxa!" I almost shouted. The "fire-filled Valtellina grape" was really potent. I took another drink. It girded me.

"You don't mean, ech-ech—'Giaxa and Giaxa'?"

"You guessed it!" I cried.

"You don't say! Well, well, that's really an honor, hum-rrum . . . With the honest-to-goodness son-in-law of—hng-hng-hng. A genius in his field, if I may say so."

"You may."

"Wait a minute, when—when did I see him . . ." He wiped his napkin carelessly across his whole face. "Back in O-seven! Nineteen hundred seven in—ech—the Circus Schumann in Berlin. Could that be?"

"That could be."

"High astride a horse—and what—and what a horse—*per bacco!* Not just a horse, a glacier-white steed, I should say, an Arabian thoroughbred, a noble steed. Obristi Obraski! Peals of laughter, Black-White, that I can swear. *Peals* of laughter . . . Yesyesyes, Giaxa and Giaxa . . . that says it all! A name, ech-ehum, from another age . . . with a great sound today too, but . . . Perhaps you can no longer understand, Black-White . . . Today people don't laugh any more . . . I maintain," he crowed, suddenly almost indignant, "that today people don't laugh any more!" He hesitated. "Where does your father-in-law live?"

"Radkersburg, South Styria, right on the Yugoslavian border, not far from Hungary."

"Ah so," he smirked in satisfaction. "But—but he doesn't perform any more?"

"No. Not for two years now."

"Um. Will you do me a favor, Black-White?" His butter-dripping moustache tips flashed. "If you write to him . . . would you pass on a special greeting from, mmm—Advocate-Doctor-Gaudenz-de-Colana—an old admirer?"

"Will do!"

"Aaah . . ." He grabbed both two-liter decanters by the neck and refilled our glasses, thereby slopping some wine on the table; he took his glass and struggled to his feet by leaning against the stove. "To the great Giaxa—long may he live," he croaked solemnly, his glass held aloft before his nose.

I got up too.

"Long live Giaxa," I said with a curiously feeble voice; my forehead was beginning to act up again.

Then I clinked my glass against his, we drank, and he fell back onto the bench and snatched up the decanter again.

"This Peidar Clavadetscher . . ." I said to change the subject. "Once a lively young man, if I understood correctly before. Then one day, bang-bang, dead as a doornail?"

He stared at me stonily, no twinkle in his eyes. Slowly his mind regained the present. The effort it required for him to overcome, in this case, a total loss of memory distorted his face to a grimace. Hoarsely: "Peidar Clavadetscher?" He resolved to nod slowly.

"Yes. May I do a bit of guessing, my discreet friend?" I asked tipsily. "Let's say I knew *who* . . . was responsible for . . . bang-bang . . ."

Then it slipped onto his face, this concealed, arch-clever grin. With start-ling quickness de Colana flicked his index finger in front of his lips: "Psh-sh!"

The farmer marched up to the table, threw open the sliding door; through the opening seeped the feeble shimmer of a light bulb. One-two-three, he cleared the table—except for the country lawyer's wineglass, which remained locked in the latter's grip—wiped up the wine puddles with the napkins, shoved everything onto the sideboard, was handed a sky-blue coffeepot from the kitch-en, two bowl-shaped cups, a whole trough of sugar cubes, and a glass containing sticklike pastries.

"Ah, Totenbeinlein," croaked de Colana at the fresh-baked sticks.

The two schnapps glasses from before returned freshly washed, then a li-quor bottle in which a vinelike plant was floating as if in an aquarium.

"A very special grappa," said the country lawyer, introducing me to the bottle-aquarium, "Alla Ruta."

The farmer asked something in Ladino and received a negative reply. Re-calling my high school Latin, I figured out that Clavadetscher's offer to turn on the lights had been rejected. The farmer swung his arms indifferently and start-ed to leave, but de Colana croaked at him again. The farmer nodded, and for the first time a dark, sullen smile passed across his face. He turned toward the wall opening, but once again de Colana croaked something and the other stopped. My host shakily grasped the bottle and filled his empty wineglass al-most to the brim with grappa. Then, without delay, the farmer took the bottle, filled both schnapps glasses, lifted one—while again his glowing stare paused for a few seconds at my brow—and said, "*Evviva la Austria.*"

"*Austria erit in orbe ultima,*" the country lawyer replied ceremoniously.

We emptied our glasses, the farmer and I; de Colana took a long drink from his wineglass, as if he were drinking wine and not schnapps. Then he puffed up his moustache with a groan of wonderful satisfaction that ended in a couple of joyous gasps, expressions of the same elemental pleasure a baby might experi-ence at its mother's breast. Clavadetscher refilled our glasses.

"*Evviva la Svizzera,*" I said and lifted mine.

"*Evviva la Grischa,*" the farmer replied. "Long live Graubuenden." Again the dark smile flickered on and then went out. For a moment he stood there be-fore us, scratched his red-haired arms, then went to tend the fire, poked around in the embers, slammed the stove door, then the door to the room.

As soon as we were alone the arch-clever grin came to life again. "Well then?" de Colana whispered brusquely.

"Pardon me?"

"Well then?"

"Well what?"

His inflamed, viscous, watery eyes—yes, they dripped with roguishness.

"Who, in your opinion, mmm—went bang-bang . . . with Peidar Clavadet-scher . . .?"

"Oh, I see," I whispered. "Well maybe . . ." I nodded in the direction of the door the *padrone* had just closed.

"*Vacca Madonna*, but you're a sly fox. Hng-hng-hng!"

"As a matter of fact, in the head," I whispered eagerly. "Smack in the middle of the forehead; am I right?"

His amazed gaping stare hung almost stupidly on a place above my eyes; wandered off, grew sly again and literally sparkled with craftiness. "Hng! An absolute fox you are, Black-White. A great detective in the eyes of the Lord. Hng-hng-hng. Have a Totenbein. They're delicious."

The farmer's hairy hands appeared through the opening in the wall and cleared the sideboard. The sliding door clattered down. De Colana craned his neck, looked toward the left past the side of the stove, and then to the right. After reassuring himself that both doors (the one to the room and the sliding one) were closed, he indicated with a nod that I should come over and sit next to him on the stove bench. As I stretched my way over the slumbering patriarch I realized that I was rather nicely drunk. I stepped on something soft that yowled sleepily.

"Beg your pardon, terribly sorry," I mumbled.

"Don't mention it," croaked the country lawyer. "Now listen here . . ."

I suspected he was about to give himself another eyewash. Instead, he offered me a cigarette, helped himself to one, then held out a ghostly flickering match. At long, long last the twilight had come to an end and a sluggish darkness crept through the fortresslike windows and began to erase the contours of the room. But the boil on his nose still glowed at me, close at hand, as we sat there on the bench, our backs bathed in the heat of the stove, our heads not far apart. A vapor of wine, schnapps, coffee and tobacco wafted toward me. Overhead—in the Clavadetscher bedroom, I calculated—dull, heavy steps echoed far away, then closer, then farther off again: it had to be a large room. I had shoved my glass to the far edge of the table so as to avoid—in deference to my head wound—any further temptation. At the same time de Colana served himself again and again from the grappa aquarium. His hand no longer trembled, his harsh half-whisper grew more and more fluent: the surest indication of a notorious drinker. At times, with a disdainful wave, he tossed his cigarette ash carelessly into the air.

. . . Four and a half years ago it was, in the fall. Not long after the previous owner of the Chesetta Grischuna had died: Toena Clavadetscher, a widower, father of Peidar and Men. Peidar was the firstborn.

At that time Men was acknowledged to be one of the best sharpshooters in the canton—de Colana pointed to the glass case where the gleam of the marksmanship trophies was visible. Since that unlucky day he never visited another shooting match, never went hunting again, even though he had been a famous marksman and was envied for his hunter's luck. Stubbornly he applied himself fully to fishing and dairy farming.

On the ill-fated day, a twelfth of October—the country lawyer knew the date from the documents—the Clavadetscher brothers, in the company of a certain Benedetg Caduff-Bonnard, owner of a small inn opposite the police station in St. Moritz, had embarked on a hunting expedition in the region of Fuorcla Surlej.

"In case you—mmm—have a taste for preserved snails, I recommend Caduff-Bonnard's Café d'Albana."

In the course of this hunting trip Peidar split off from his companions (mark you! without a prior word between the brothers; according to Caduff's later testimony, all three were in the best of spirits before the hunt) and had disappeared from view along a boulder-strewn slope overrun with woodchucks. A clear, transparent day. All around the reddish mountains. Red? Yes, indeed: the lustrous blue of the southern sky, the white of the fresh snow on the peaks and under it the moss-covered slopes in the flame red of autumn. A tricolor, as it were. Not bad—"hng-hng"—blue-white-red, the tricolor of October in the Upper Engadine. Tricolor, not bad.

And everywhere the whistling of the woodchucks. Here the country lawyer made an effort to imitate a woodchuck-whistle, but was thwarted by his fringy moustache and could only bring forth a half squeak, more like a hiss than a whistle, so that not even the dogs took note of it. Yes, everywhere the warning whistles of the invisible creatures. One listening post reported the approaching hunters to the next: one shrill peep and they disappeared in the gaps in the rocks. It's no easy matter trying to bag a woodchuck.

(Woodchuck Hunting Season Sept. 1-Oct. 15.)

"Hum-rrum—have you ever hunted woodchucks, Black-White?"

"No. I'm no hunter."

You're no hunter, Albert Woodchuck-hunter-hunter? The pressure of the Walther pushed gently at my thigh. The stuffed figure on the glass case between the windows had lost its shape. But still—still visible: the reddish glow of the dusty fur lump. And it began to happen again as it had several times before during these past few days: a feeling of unreality crept over me. Like one of those momentary lapses that kept recurring ever since I was wounded like a post-traumatic disturbance. I was no longer capable of *grasping* the moment; it slipped away from me like a book I had just put down, as if I were unable to bridge some enormous gap between the last page and what I had read before.

Something like a spasmodic urge for self-preservation threatened to overwhelm me. The fortress windows through which the night sank formlessly into the room were like portholes. Portholes were for shooting. I got an itch to draw Maxim's pistol, to stalk through the room, to bolt the door and take up a firing position on one of the windowsills. Evil seconds that were broken by a

trifle—something like a feather-quiet, momentary click and creak from an unknown source—feather-quiet, but so obvious that it seemed to be a noise in *this*
room.

The dogs in their keen-eared slumber must have heard it too; a sleepy
growling arose, then fell away. Without a word I squeezed out from behind the
table and strode past the stove to the door; touched the door handle.

The door was closed.

So I was wrong about the source of the noise. It couldn't have come from
this room, but rather from upstairs, or perhaps from the kitchen. I went back to
the table, reassuring myself on the way that the sliding door was still shut, and
slid back onto the bench beside de Colana. "Hee," I snickered dourly. "That
weed there in your grapp-a-quarium is real poison."

"Mmm, don't you feel well, Black-White?"

"If you mean my stomach—it's fine." I allowed myself a generous gulp of
lukewarm *café au lait*. "Now then, this man, the one with the snails—what's his
name—?"

"Caduff-Bonnard."

"Right, yes. So he went with Peidar Clavadetscher. Excuse me, Doctor—which one went off by himself? At the moment I'm a bit muddle-
headed . . ."

No. Caduff had remained with Men. Peidar stalked off alone. For a long
time the two lay quiet as mice, rifles at the ready. Suddenly Men nudged his
companion and whispered, "There's one!" Witness Caduff-Bonnard later test-
ified before the district court in Maloja: three hundred paces ahead "something
like reddish fur" had peeked up from behind a rock, something that had looked
"precisely like a woodchuck." In that same second he had heard Men's rifle
crack beside him.

Then up ahead, as the shot echoed against the rocks, to Caduff's dismay a
figure jerked up from behind a boulder; a rifle fell from an outstretched arm;
then the figure dropped like a sack between the rocks.

"Peidar, God the Father, my brother!" Those had been Men's words.

Here I profaned the climax of this dramatic report with an irrelevant question: "Does Men speak good German?"

The storyteller, somewhat indignant, grunted in the affirmative. Men, followed by Caduff, had scrambled across the boulders like a man possessed. They
had found him there, Peidar, at the foot of a small ravine, lying on his back with
a bullet hole in the middle of his forehead.

"Precisely the place," de Colana whispered eagerly, "where y-o-u, Black-
White—you yourself—"

"I knew all along," I reminded him with false modesty.

"You see? That's why the *padrone*—hmm—was looking at you so—so oddly."

Caduff and Men had carried the body down past La Motta into the valley.

Both were immediately questioned by the police in Sils. Men had declared in evidence that "by awful mischance" he had mistaken his brother for a woodchuck; the statements of the two hunting companions agreed in every detail. On the basis of this police report the famous shooting champion was first charged with negligent homicide. Soon all kinds of stories began to circulate among the lake villagers. Hey, hadn't father Toena Clavadetscher just recently died? Hey, hadn't he left his farm to Peidar, the eldest son, and given Men only a few thousand francs and the fishing concession? Hey, hadn't Men even thought of emigrating to America? If it hadn't been for Teresina . . . Teresina, the daughter of a shepherd from Bergamo, a well-to-do wandering herdsman who spent the summers with his large flock on a mountain pasture near Isola in the Fedoz Valley? Wasn't it true that both Men and Peidar had vied for the hand of this Teresina—then an unusually pretty girl, a natural beauty—hey, wasn't it so? Before long Men Clavadetscher was accused of murder, fratricide. Dr. Gaudenz de Colana had taken over his defense and, thanks to the testimony of the respected Caduff-Bonnard, had obtained an acquittal of the charge of murder. The accused was sentenced to a short prison term for negligent homicide, which was waived in view of the time he had spent in pretrial custody. That was all.

Oh yes, one thing more. A full two and a half years later Men took Teresina home as his bride.

"A real Graubuenden melodrama!"

Meanwhile it had grown almost dark in the room. The long drawn-out moaning of a cow. The clatter of wooden shoes across a bridge, the crying of a child that stopped when a door was slammed. The distant, brushing sound of a car. Once again the nearby melancholy mooing. I looked at the shadowy profile beside me. Our cigarettes were out. Only the boil on de Colana's gleaming nose was shining; it shone like a lamp in the last, fading, yellow trace of daylight.

"What are you staring at me like that for, fellow student? . . . Aaaah! Aha. You're wondering . . . you're wondering how such an old—has-been—mmm drunkard . . . hng-hng, how somebody like me could be defense counsel in a big trial like that . . . then even manage to get an acquittal, hey? Well . . . well . . . *carissimo amico* . . . four or five years ago, then—then I was still . . . then I was still . . . Five years are a long-long time . . . hum, for somebody like me . . ."

"But that's not what I was thinking at all, Doctor," I whispered. "Not at all, really. What I was thinking . . . was—were you . . . *you* . . . completely convinced of your client's innocence?"

I had to wait for the answer and during these seconds of waiting I thought I heard, just as before, a slight noise; this time like the briefest imaginable sniff through the nose; not from de Colana or the dogs, but *from the top* of this room.

I peered up at the massive shadow of the stove. Could it be that a cat was hiding on its roof? Could it have been a cat hissing? Not a chance. The spaniel pack would long ago have scented it and chased it away. But something else confirmed that my ears had not deceived me: from the floor a silhouetted muzzle rose toward the ceiling. The phenomenally faint sound, like the one that bothered me before, came perhaps from the chimney of the stove, was perhaps no more than a tiny draft in the stovepipe.

". . . Hng-hng-hng. Black-White, you are a sly old fox indeed—I already told you. *Naturally* . . . of *course* . . . Otherwise I'd never have . . . hum, never ever have taken on, hum, his defense. Just think a moment . . . think of Caduff's statement . . . The man is on the city council . . . Naturally I *was* convinced . . . then . . ."

"So, you were . . .? Really? *Then* you were convinced?" Once again there was a tiny puff in the stovepipe. "And today, Doctor? . . . Today you're no longer—so sure?"

The glowing nose came closer. His breath reminded me of an ether mask before it's placed upon your face. "What I am about to tell you—em—you—a stranger to this area . . . What I am about to tell you *cum grano salis*, is not to be repeated. In strictest confidence. A matter of honor, you understand? . . . Understand? . . . No . . . *No*. Today I—am of a different opinion."

"So you believe that Men *intentionally* . . .?"

"M-hmm."

"And despite that you make this Chesetta Grischuna your favorite haunt? You keep on patronizing a common—?"

"Hng! Hng-hng-hng." The shadow's shoulders danced. "I said—*cum grano salis*—I *believe*. Not—mmm— I *know*. Besides, he has the best—the very best Valtellina in the whole area. Doesn't he? . . . Hng. What do you want? . . . Don't talk to me about morality!" A shaking movement of the shadow's arm. "I don't believe in your 'progress,' ech . . . Even in the Bible there is fratricide—there is . . . and the Bible is certainly a—a—a . . ."

"You mean, a moral codex?"

"Mhmm. And what happened to this fellow there, hupp—"a fat hiccup—"this Cain—who killed his brother—what happened to *him*, hupp? He was *damned*, to be a wanderer by the sweat of his brow—no wait, that was Adam . . . Yes!—a fugitive and a wanderer, hupp, shalt thou be on earth. As long as men have lived they've wandered the earth as fugitives—murderers and non-murderers alike." A shaking of the shadow arm. "You . . . *you* are a fugitive and a wanderer, aren't you? Phng! You know what kind of punishment that is! . . ."

I said nothing.

"Hupp, morality, fellow student! Morality and reason! . . . It is something *completely different* that drives men on. Something inside. Deep inside . . . perhaps in the gut, hng! In the intestines, hng-hng. Some sort of crazy . . ."

"Yes?" I asked hesitantly.

". . . some sort of crazy force," croaked the shadow.

6

The cold, foggy-damp night air sharpened my awareness of how drunk I was. Fog, fog. The country lawyer, visibly relaxed and at the same time fortified by his immense consumption of schnapps, having reached a stage that many would consider normal, could not conceal some difficulties in walking. But he refused my offers of support. It was as if he had somehow managed to put on lead-weighted boots and was trying to do an imitation of a clown doing an imitation of a drunkard. Despite his objections I managed to help him down the front steps. Now he stopped, walled in by fog in the glow that seeped through the wide-open door from the dim hallway, his clergyman's hat pulled down to his eyes, and I couldn't remember ever seeing anyone who was able to sway so far—first forward, then back on his firmly rooted feet—without falling, In doing this he twirled his cane and crowed over and over again: "'Bursting forth from leafy bowers/*Fire*-filled. . .! *Fire*-filled'. . .No! *Vacca Madonna*, no, no, I can't do it any more . . . *Porca Miseria* . . . I can't any more . . . *Sono un' vecchio cretino . . . troppo affaticato . . . troppo ubriaco . . .*"

The spaniel cortege presented a touching picture of concern. No sooner had they all done their business than they crowded together, fearless of the twirling cane, about their wildly reeling master. Despite their fur coats the smaller ones were trembling from the damp-cold breath of the night fog. Tail stumps lowered, concerned eyes glancing up at him, they steered him steadily and with guide-dog discipline toward the limousine.

Despite the fact that I was warmed to the core with drink I pulled up my coat collar. I opened the driver's door, and de Colana stumbled belly first against the side of the car and stayed there; then he began rotating his lead-weighted boots and made a face as if he intended to head back for the entrance.

"*Un' bicchier' de vin'*," he mumbled.

While the pack, unanimously keen on going home, slipped into the back seat, I grasped him by the arm. "'*Bicchier'* nothing. We've had enough of that for one evening. So climb in. And please allow me to drive, Doctor, me. With your kind permission I'll take the wheel for a change and drive this noble company home. Agreed?"

With his amber-handled cane he pushed his hat up from his eyes: "Are you—mmm—qualified?"

"My friend, I was a military pilot. I can chauffeur you around with a motorcycle, a car, a plane, whatever you like. Just take your seat."

"Military pilot, eh? Hng! Hng-hng-hng. I . . . myself . . ." he rapped the cane against his chest. "I *too* am a military pilot, Black-White . . . a trained army pilot . . . a great army pilot—I am. I am!"

He sank down almost to his knees and, for better or worse, I helped him roll behind the wheel. "*Evviva Nero-Bianco-Bianco-Nero—evviva te.*" Soon the headlights flared up and bounced off the wall of fog in front of us. In the reflected glow I could see his cryptic smile. "As an army pilot I was decorated, hum, with the Pour-le-Mérite. By General Ulrich Wille—at the request, hupp, of Kaiser Wilhelm. Hupp, or vice versa."

"But—"

"Come-on-come-on-come-on. Colonel de Colana—a decorated war pilot. . . . Just listen here . . ."

Now I saw that all the persuasiveness in the world wouldn't help. It was pointless to say: "You're drunk; so am I, but not as much; so let me take the wheel," or: "I'm not in the mood to break my neck tonight," or something of the sort. He would counter every argument with this insane pilot-joke I had unwittingly planted in his mind.

I waded through the fog-enshrouded headlight beams, unlatched the passenger's door, climbed over the unusable running board, shoved a warm bundle—the patriarch—to one side and slammed the door shut. "So all right, drive on for God's sake!"

So he drove on for God's sake, across the crunching gravel, and I had to give him credit. He shifted gears so smoothly, took the exit curve so correctly that I began to suspect he'd been deceiving me all along with his crazy balancing act—that I'd been duped by a mischievous bit of playacting. *Advocatus diaboli*—today couldn't be the first time the devil had gotten into him. Perhaps, I thought, he had really drunk himself to the point of soberness, to that ice-cold, starlit sobriety known only to true alcoholics, who fall to pieces when they are really sober.

I cast a brief glance back at the Chesetta Grischuna. In the Romanesque arch of the wide-open door, silhouetted against the meager light of the hallway stood Men Clavadetscher, his biceps spread, his forearms hanging free; next to him stood the silhouette of the St. Bernard, and both cast long bizarre shadows that oozed out through the fog onto the front yard of the house. The farmer stood erect and motionless. He made no sign to us. No wave. No nod.

We rattled at a leisurely pace through Sils Baseglia, past the church. De Colana took the curve from the village street onto the main highway according to all the rules of law and safe driving. Fog hung thickly over Lake Silvaplana and the shoreline and walled in the headlight beams. Now and then, between the shadowy forms of the railing posts that went marching past us there appeared a towering larch tree, its branches distorted weirdly in the fog, its top fading out in an illusion of enormous height. Hat pushed back on his head, body bent forward, the driver stared ahead. I kept a constant eye on the road and the steering wheel, alert, always poised to grab the wheel if I had to. Gradually my tension abated. He continued to drive with caution. The loose running-board rattled.

Only once a pair of half-blind headlights crept toward us. De Colana sent out a couple of drawn-out horn signals—rusty, croaking, like his voice, I thought—and was answered in kind. He brought the car to a halt and waited until the other vehicle crept past us. We were on the lake side and the road ran close to the water's edge; it was by no means a senseless precaution. Meanwhile I calculated that it would take an hour at this snail's pace before I could see Xana . . . Xana! Impatience rumbled inside me.

"Nero-Bianco . . . I'm driving—mmm—too slow for you, yes?"

"No, no," I hastened to assure him. "You are driving extremely well."

"But you don't believe me . . ."

"What's that?"

"You don't believe that I was a great army pilot . . ."

We were driving up to Silvaplana when it happened.

Now the fog floated somewhat higher, canopied the road; here and there a stretch lay free of fog. We glided through formless mountains of fog that vanished unexpectedly. The suddenly unmasked headlights threw a stretch of the shoreline road into glaringly sharp focus; on gentle curves the lights flashed out across the water. De Colana drove just noticeably faster.

In the reflection of the lights his twinkling side-glance brushed me. "Am I a great army pilot or am I not?" he asked in rude, quarrelsome tones. "Well, out with it!"

I began to tire of the joke. "You're the greatest army pilot of all times," I said.

"A-*ha!*" His side-glance stared at me, sparkling belligerence, with a kind of sardonic cunning. "You're mocking me, aren't you, Mr. Poet? An incurable empiricist, eh? . . . You can only be convinced a-a-a-a," he gasped, "p-o-s-t-e-r-i-o-r-i, eh? *Ecco, signore . . .!*"

The car leaped forward. He had floored the accelerator.

We plunged into a cloud covering the road and the headlights grew near-sighted, almost went blind. He held his foot on the gas pedal, never letting up. The loose running-board began clattering wildly.

Along with the first shock the bewildering thought struck me: This diving through the clouds is indeed like—flying. Night flight. The pilot attempts to keep his aircraft clear of the clouds, to hold his course above them or between them. He doesn't always succeed; often he has no choice but, just as now, to shoot right into the formless, yawning monsters made of water vapor. Only the shudder of the wings as they strike the "airborne water" is missing . . . Once the cloud bank is punctured, the vista of the Black Sea opens up far, far below . . . the beacon lights of Constanta and Sulina are seen blinking, and then the ones at Brăila, on the Danube, Brăila, our home base . . . Brăila, autumn 1916 . . .

We shot out of the bank of fog. The greenish glare of the headlights licked unhindered over the first flat-roofed houses of the village of Silvaplana. We'll crash into these houses. This is no airplane. This is a drunken, careening automobile. No airplane.

A horizontal crash.

I began to think desperately. The running-board rattled wildly. I stared at the illuminated speedometer. It danced between 70 and 75 mph; beneath it was the ignition key.

A flash of hope.

Twist the ignition key, pull it out! He anticipated my grasp. Devil's advocate . . . *Advocatus diaboli* . . . lawyers are trained to weigh all possibilities and to head off the opposition . . . While holding the dancing wheel in his left hand he jerked out the key and stuck it in his pocket.

"Pphng-hng-hng!"

I began to realize my complete helplessness. A scuffle with him at this speed could hasten an accident rather than prevent it. Then the horn croaked. With a series of dissonant horn blasts we shot toward the village with its few lighted windows.

Just before the first houses he savagely slammed on the brakes. The car went into a slide. He caught it skillfully.

"Phng!"

Constantly blaring the horn we careened through the abandoned village street at barely reduced speed, brushing by a sleepily waiting mule team with only inches to spare.

"Phng!"

For an instant a phosphorescent *mene-tekel* flashed before us: JULIER. Then Silvaplana dropped into nothingness behind us, devoured by new banks of fog that we roared into with ever increasing speed.

We were lucky. We got through. After a short stretch of marshland it lay before us again—the shoreline road, this time skirting Lake Campfèr, an absinthe-green gully, a living tunnel drilled by the headlight beams, a tunnel that we, like Tantalus, could never get through, no matter what fantastic speed we reached. Yes, suddenly I was frozen with the ridiculous thought that this mad ride would never end.

I had felt like this before in moments of great danger. The sudden, obsessive thought: there is no end. Even death is no end. Everything goes on and on, beyond what we think is the end, and everything is continued in a mysterious, cruelly persistent way, everything lives on. Applied to the moment this fear became the fear of having to race down the shoreline road forever.

I leaned back in the seat. De Colana's profile still revealed his incessant, cruel-crafty smirk. He bent over the steering wheel, hunched, his pear-head jutting forward (the hat had fallen off). Out of the depths of his chest now swelled a half-gargling, half-roaring singsong like a horrid howl of triumph—drowning out the insane clattering of the running-board: "*I—am—a—famous—army—flyer——a—famous—pilot—am—I—*"

Marshland again to the right. The flat roofed houses of Campfèr, licked by the absinthe beam. De Colana flipped his foot off the gas pedal, kicked in the clutch; the car coasted along a high speed, slowing gradually. Shall I jump him now? Already we were sucked into the pipe of the empty village street.

A rear wheel scraped the curb, the car fishtailed slightly to one side and de Colana caught it—"Phng!"—and stamped his foot onto the brake. With squealing tires we skidded up to a brilliant road sign: a pole supporting two illuminated boxes of ink-blue glass with white lettering announced a fork in the road at the village exit. On the left the road branched off to St. Moritz; on the right toward the Stahlbad. If de Colana chose the fork curving up a rise to the left this insane ride could end safely; he would have to shift into second, and I would have a chance to overpower him.

He flung the wheel fiercely to the right. The Fiat leaned hard to one side on groaning springs. We had passed to the right of the sign and were rocketing toward the spa.

The road headed downhill; the fog was higher here; we were no longer sweeping through it. The threat of the lake was past too. We flew along close to the banks of the Inn Lake between meadows and larch forests whose trunks flared up in the absinthe beams while the treetops stayed in darkness. What difference does it make if you run into a lake at 75 mph or hit a tree . . . To race along a downhill road at this speed: suicide. He wouldn't be able to hold the car on the road . . . Curves were waiting ahead . . .

Then it jolted through me: my Walther pistol!

Pulling it out, waving it at his skull, screaming in his ear, "Stop this car now or I'll blow your head off!"—would it snap him out of it? I could imagine his answer to such desperate words, could hear his voice grating, "Go ahead, Black-White, shoot down a famous army pilot!" and his rattling laugh. On a foggy night. Roaring along a precipitous road. Pulling a pistol and holding it to the head of a maniac driver. Wild West thriller. Pulp novel. Unreal . . . unreal . . .

The Inn bridge, built into the turns. Just before entering the right-hand curve he gave the brakes a gentle tap, so gentle it seemed impossible that his feet had ever worn "lead-weighted boots." Then we were across the Inn bridge and I could not avoid—no, I couldn't avoid feeling boundless admiration for his driving skill. Any race driver would have envied the talent of this old souse. It was scandalous to admit it, scandalous but unavoidable: he was right.

He *did* have the stuff to be a military pilot, by God, he did. The determination, the cold-bloodedness, the "finely tuned nerves," and the contempt, yes, the fanatical contempt for his own life and the lives of others—everything that is commonly known as "bravery."

book two

The Light in the Lake

1

The speedometer sank, sank. The spa, a sparsely lit resort. Through the sparsely lit arcades of wrought-iron art-nouveau frippery strolled a lonely couple in raincoats. The race driver halted his machine next to a sign inscribed: TATTERSALL. In the reflected glow of the undimmed lights he stared at me expectantly. Since he obviously expected an indignant explosion I casually remarked, "I'm out of cigarettes. Can you give me one?"

"Hng-hng."

"I must say," I said to myself. "I must say . . . in the past few weeks I've passed up more than one chance to make my wife a widow. You're all I needed, Dr. de Colana." Other words hovered on the tip of my tongue: You don't belong behind the wheel, you belong in an institution for drunkards. Instead I repeated, "I must say, you're all I needed."

"Hng-hng-hng-hng."

His sniffling laugh was beginning to irritate me—when I made an alarming discovery: it was no laugh. It was a sob. He slumped down toward me, his gaping eyes blurred. He wept with eyes wide open. Shoulders shaking with sobs, he slumped down onto my shoulder.

"Hng-hng-hng, *perdonate mi*, Nero-Bianco, *perdonate mi* . . . forgive me, please, please, hng-hng . . . You're so good to me, Black-White . . . I know you hardly at all, hng-hng, but so well . . . the only—yes, on-ly f-f-friend I've had f-for years . . . for years . . . Up here, hng! hnnng-hng—up here I'm nothing but—an object . . . an object of ridicule . . . *un' vecchio ubriacone*, n-n-nothing more . . . Not a soul, not a l-living soul will have anything to . . . Only the dogs! Only the dogs, hng-hng . . . And sometimes, s-sometimes—it just comes over me—up h-h-here . . . You just don't know . . . hnng-hnng-hnng."

Nose and mouth pressed into the flannel of my shoulder, he gave vent to this painful, half-stifled mixture of stammered words and whining sobs: as if vomiting tears and words that lost their articulation and sank into a mumbled gurgling like the last utterance of someone drowning. A man's crying is taboo, but *his* seemed grotesquely touching to me. I held him against my arm like a loved one and soothingly patted his heaving back over and over again: "It'll be all right, Doctor. Just calm down now, allrightallrightallright . . ."

I had gotten out and settled the now helpless figure down in the passenger's seat. From the back seven round pairs of eyes glowed a magical dull, ruby red in the brilliant sheen of the headlights. The patriarch cowered beneath the steering wheel, his giant tassel-ears trembling. I dug the keys out of de Colana's coat pocket and got behind the wheel.

On one side of the de Colana house a single, dismal light bulb was burning, smoldering above the abandoned stairway leading to the tramway station. A bat fluttered through the damp shimmering light, darting up into the foggy gloom above the rooftops, then swooped down again.

"Doctor! . . . Doctor de Colana . . . we're here . . ." He didn't move. The bat darted and dove. "You're home, Doctor!" I shook his shoulders. He sank down still further. I got out:

"Hey, Doctor!"

The cocker spaniels crept and hopped out of the Fiat. A timid bark, brief and sharp, was soon multiplied. Clearly they wanted to help me wake their master.

Finally I succeeded in lifting him out the door and onto his feet. He had to brace himself with one hand on the car. This could never have been the fearless race driver with his "finely tuned nerves," the daring curve-taker who had just been racing hell-for-leather through the night. Never. This was just an old souse, a babbling old cretin hardly able to keep his feet. I planted his hat on his head, pushed his cane into his hand, and holding him up, dragged him to the front door. The spaniels pressed around his feet.

"Your housekeys, please!" The bat darted and dove. I gave him a quick frisking, found the bunch of keys, unlocked the door with the largest of them, threw the keys into his baggy coat pocket and shoved the man inside the door. "Good night, *Buona notte, Avvocato Bow-Wow.*"

The last I saw of him he was tottering into the darkened hallway surrounded by the worried, upturned noses of his padding spaniel pack.

From the corner house opposite the police station lights were shining through gingham curtains. The shadowy, florid script on the milk-glass panel in the door:

CAFE D'ALBANA

BENEDETG CADUFF-BONNARD

PROP.

That was the name of the defense witness in de Colana's "Cain and

Abel" story of the woodchuck hunt. "Good evening." A narrow, corridor-like small-town cafe filled with wooden tables stained dark orange, all empty except for the ones at the rear. Mr. Zuan engrossed in the newspaper *Foegl d'Engiadina*, which concealed his splendid beard. Next to him Fitz, the Irish dwarf, the ex-king's jockey, or rather the king's ex-jockey, sucking on a short meerschaum pipe. (Always the same faces. A real village.) A waitress, bent over her knitting, completed the speechless trio.

"Oh miss, may I use your telephone?"

Her pimply face reminded me of a ventriloquist's dummy in Vienna's Prater, and to my nebulous discomfort, of something else as well . . . The high, fat cheeks, the turned-up nose, Holy Laudon!, a fairly good caricature of Xana.

"Surely." With a clumsy flirtatious walk she led me to a wall telephone behind the bar. "Can I place the call for you?"

"No. Thanks a lot. Amazingly enough, I'm not injured."

Then the voice on the telephone, dark and beautiful, a bell with a velvet clapper: "Where in the world are you, Trebla?"

"Xana Coquelicot! Doctor Elephantophile!" I yelled so loud that a bit of black beard peeked out behind Mr. Zuan's newspaper. "How did you know it was me?"

"I've been waiting for you to call. Are you very drunk?"

"By no means very. Of course this crazy lawyer *did* try to . . . oh well, I'll tell you all about it later. Maybe tomorrow. How do we get to Pontresina? The last train is already gone."

"Where are you anyway?"

"In a little joint on the schoolhouse square."

"Bonjour has gone to bed. Pola wanted to lend us the Chrysler—I've got my international driver's license. Joop doesn't seem to mind. Wait a second. I'll let you talk to him."

"Ha-aw, yes?" came ten Breukaa's voice, obviously suppressing a yawn. "Though it's not a good idea to lend out women and cars, h-aw, I suggest you meet your wife at the train station in twenty minutes."

"Thanks a million, ha-aw," I slurred.

"What's that?"

"Thanks a million, Joop; I kiss Pola's hand and yours too."

The station was fast asleep; I sniffed the fog and shivered and waited. Beyond the tracks the discreet hum of an approaching motor. Two astonishingly large, yellow headlight eyes peered through the fog, pushed beneath the viaduct, and I jumped up in the glare like a wing-flapping penguin. An ideal target, I thought momentarily. Then the lights were dimmed, the car brought to a halt. From the driver's window of the cabriolet a hand reached out to me, a gentle hand whose gloved back I covered with a salvo of smacking kisses. She gave me a little shove.

Next to the driver, his chin buried in a cashmere scarf that reminded me of the Spahi's jellaba, sat ten Breukaa.

"Greetings! How nice of you to keep Xana company. Now we'll just quickly drop you off at Acla Silva."

"Won't be necessary." He climbed out somewhat stiffly. "I'll walk."

I sank into the Joop-warmed seat and thought, a real bore this Trying Dutchman, but sometimes very nice indeed. And Xana said, as the car cruised effortlessly up the steep village street: "A bit of a limp dishrag, Joop is, but sometimes very nice. Seems a little mummified by all his riches—money-fied you might say."

Thick fog blanketed the summit. "Shouldn't I drive for you?"

"No, little mother," said Xana, "you're plastered."

While she drove, her powerful yellow fog-lights—yes, now that she was driving they were "hers"—pushing back the fog, she suddenly let her cheek rest for a moment on my shoulder. The same shoulder de Colana had cried on not an hour before. Strange.

A quick little tongue-kiss flicked warm and damp in my ear. With the agility of a contortionist, a "snake-woman," she sprang back into driving position. Around midnight we drove into the long village of Cresta-Celerina, and she said: "Now we have to watch out, Pola said. Just before a sharp left turn in the middle of town—with an oval mirror like one from the fun house in the Prater. She said. Watch out that we don't turn left or we'll be heading for Samedan. We have to turn right onto the road to San John."

"To San what?"

"Gee, I, A, N. San Gian. Like Giaxa."

During the night I woke up.

It was pitch dark in the room and very cold and completely still; too still.

Suddenly wide awake, I sat up and leaned over toward the other bed. Now I could hear Xana's very gentle, regular breathing.

My hand groped for the chair next to the bed, ran across my flannel pants hung over the back, felt, in the buttoned hip pocket, my present from Maxim Grabscheidt. Whom they had just killed, yes. Dragged him off to Bavaria and rubbed him out, yes. Herr Maxim Grabscheidt, M.D., doctor in the workers' quarter of Graz. Yes . . . I continued to listen hard.

Why; for what?

One of the immutable night noises of the village was missing: the persistent splashing of the fountain in front of the Morteratsch Hotel. Listening carefully as a lynx, I was finally able to make it out: a barely audible, steady whisper, much quieter than usual. Outside, the all-devouring fog. I thought, it even smothers sound.

Now for the first time I became aware of the rapidly beating pain in my forehead—a pain that spread out from the center of my forehead and pounded through my skull with machinelike steadiness—and of a parching thirst. I'll

90

have one hell of a hangover tomorrow, I prophesied, and a bitter memory of de Colana flashed through my mind. Miserable drunkard, miserable . . .

I crept out of the covers, crouched on the end of the bed and reached for a very cold glass of water on the night table; drank it dry. I would have liked to turn on the night table lamp, but didn't. Barefoot I crept through the pitch darkness in the direction of the door, touched the ice-cold handle, pressed it gently, gently downward. The door was locked; good. (Xana never locked a room, a closet, or a suitcase—so I must have done it.) I was cold in my pajamas. Groped over to the clothes rack, slid into my Bosnian slippers. Felt the material of my twenty-year-old burnoose, put it on, crept over to my den, bumped into a chair that squeaked noisily, and I knew that in the next second Xana would call out to me, for she was a very light sleeper. Her sleep was as shallow as a rabbit's—which had earned her the nickname "Miss Slumberbunny" from Elsabé Giaxa, that habitual inventor of rather silly pet names. I waited. Miss Slumberbunny didn't make a sound.

The outside door to my workroom had been locked from the time we had moved in—not a precaution then, since the doorway was the only place I could find to put my manuscript trunk. My groping hands found the trunk in its place. I moved ahead with tiny steps, trying hard not to make another sound, toward the balcony door. Its wooden shutters were closed. I opened the door soundlessly, but as I gently pushed against a shutter, its hinges creaked abruptly. Now I would hear from Miss Slumberbunny. But I heard nothing.

Then I peered out into the foggy darkness. Beyond the wooden ledge of the balcony I could see vague lights, a gray-blurred suggestion of lights in the valley. But between me and the lights something was swirling. Moving wisps of fog? In the dull, cloudy ice-breath of night no wind was stirring. I stood in the balcony door, both hands stretching the old burnoose tight across my chest, and stared intently down at the blurry ghosts of light in the valley.

Yes, it was snowing. It was snowing in the foggy darkness, snowing over every sound and burying the whisper of the fountain.

I crept back into bed, slipped, still in my burnoose, beneath the covers. Once again I leaned toward the other bed and listened to the gentle breathing of the motionless sleeper. I lay quite still, and again the headache began its rhythmic pulsebeat. I was an opponent of sleeping pills and of remedies for bearable pain, so I sought to escape my misery by falling asleep. Without success. But encouraged by Xana's wonderfully deep repose I began rolling back and forth, making anguished faces in the dark. Then I lay still again and listened . . . yes, I listened again "like a lynx." What the devil had wakened me from the depths of my alcohol-numbed sleep?

Then suddenly I knew. Nothing but a dream has wakened me. And in the moment of certainty the memory of this dream leaped into my consciousness like the memory of a real experience.

Like a lynx . . . I was no lynx, no nocturnal beast of prey, nor was I a human being. I was small, furry, soft, easily wounded—but had one thing in my favor: I was fast.

I was a little animal, but at the same time, myself, Albert. A hybrid. Woodchuck-man. Someone was hunting me. I didn't know who. And, unlike other woodchucks, I was unable to escape with a warning whistle. Whom was I to warn? No one to warn, no one to warn me. I was a poor, lonely, defenseless, harassed little woodchuck-man, alone and afraid on an empty plain, alone with my formless pursuer.

One thing was certain: I had to take cover. Again and again—thanks to my protective quickness—I had managed to hide, again and again I had been flushed out. Panting desperately, completely out of breath, I darted toward the last available hiding place, a cave, whose entrance was blocked by a—yes—by a golden concert harp.

The harp lay pressed against the mouth of the cave as if it had been welded on. So I made myself very thin and slipped between two of the resilient strings. There beneath the low ceiling of the cave, whose only entrance was barred by the harp, I crouched with wildly pounding heart. Crouched and panted and listened. And then I heard music. A jangling swipe across the strings, something like an accidental, atonal arpeggio.

And then I saw it.

A gigantic orange-furred claw, larger than I was, thrust between the harpstrings and into the cave.

The hand of Men Clavadetscher.

2

A hung-over Sunday. Bonjour came and got the cabriolet. Snow.

On Monday morning a cold rain was pouring down. I listened to the rain and felt its chill and heard Xana click on the electric heater and slept a little longer and announced my awakening with a roguish, groaning moan of satisfaction. My giant hangover was *passé*. All the while Xana had moved about noiselessly; now she stood by the half-open window shutters in her new, cozy, dreadful devotional dressing gown with a long, pretty nightgown showing beneath it. With a kind of gentle, self-caressing motion she lethargically brushed her hair. On the breakfast tray was a letter. Sent to the hotel At the Sign of the Rear Falcon and forwarded here; return address: ALIEN POLICE OF THE CANTON ZURICH. OFFICIAL BUSINESS! I decided to read it later. Was there any more mail, I asked thoughtlessly. No, that's all; Xana continued brushing her hair. No letter from Radkersburg. No sign—no sign of life from Radkersburg (whereas at the

Rear Falcon in Zurich a letter or card in Elsabé Giaxa's hurried scrawl had reached us almost daily—half drowning Xana in maternal affection, and also, in deference to the postal censor, completely void of information). At that moment I decided to write Konstantin Giaxa this very day, perhaps under the cover name Gaudenz de Colana LL.D.

"If you look at her closely," said Xana. "That marble-white complexion. That Roman nose. Those slim legs. She's actually . . .beautiful, that girl Pina. Her name is pretty too. So girlish and Roman. By the way, I'm going over to St. Moritz at two o'clock."

"Wha-at? In this weather? Even the smugglers stay indoors on days like this. I can't let you do it."

"The bus from Poschiavo stops right in front of our door. I can be back by five."

"And get a *second* case of bronchitis? Along with another visit from our dear friend Tardueser?" I advised her strongly to put off her shopping trip until a better day, got out a thick, oilcloth-covered binder and began outlining the final article in the Austriacus-Babeuf series; looked out the window of the common room in the Morteratsch Hotel and saw my wife in her raincoat, beneath a topaz yellow umbrella, hiking toward the post office. I wrote undisturbed for forty-five minutes; got up, unhooked my loden cape from the wall. There stood Pina to help me into it. Mumbling thanks I refused her offer and threw the cape around my shoulders with a show-offish fling. Pina untied her very small, white apron. (No more than a figleaf if she'd been nude.)

"I've-a gotta do da roomss now," she said.

"Signorina Pina," I announced, coming to attention. "You are a true *bellezza*. At least, that's what my little sister says."

"Your-a sister?"

"*Ecco.*"

Without further ado I walked past the entrance to the corridor leading down a few steps to the glass-covered veranda. Through the opening I could see one-and-a-half uncovered dining tables, and at the one cut in half two sweaters with Tutankhamon patterns hunched over a collection of little black blocks.

The Two Blonds were playing dominoes.

Clamped in my old Remington was a typed note:

> *Kukulaps,*
> *Am in St.M. Back soon.*
> *X.*

Water gurgled through the rain gutters on the roof and I trotted about our two unheated rooms in my Bosnian slippers, choking on my rage; I felt wronged, irritated out of proportion to the (in itself) none too tragic fact that my Xana, despite vigorous dissuasion, had slipped off to St. Moritz for reasons she felt obliged to conceal. Suddenly my forehead began to register a heartbeat.

What if. What if she had gone to "St. M." to get on the train and travel, via Chur and Buchs, back home to Radkersburg? (She manages our finances.) As if drawn by two magnets: her parents. We hadn't heard a word from them for fourteen days; and now she could wait no longer. Hadn't she stared at me for a moment in the common room as if in a trance? "Back soon." Couldn't that mean two years as well as two hours? Yes, it was a baseless, nonsensical supposition. Nevertheless I felt abandoned, shivering all alone in the two tourist rooms of the postmistress Fausch.

SUMMONS

ZURICH, *10 June 1938*
You are hereby ordered to report to room 27a of the Kaspar-Escher Building at 9 AM, *14 June 1938. You will be required to present the following documents: a* <u>*valid*</u> *passport; any certificates of good conduct you may possess.*

ALIEN POLICE / CANTON ZURICH

Through my teeth I began whistling the Rákóczidetzky March, Giaxa's self-composed parody that always marked the beginning and end of his opening number. The underlined word "valid" was no less than an order for me to crawl into the German Consulate in Zurich, grovel before the swastika, and do everything I could to get a passport embellished with that nice little emblem. And what sort of "certificates of good conduct" did the gentlemen of the Alien Police wish to examine? Perhaps one issued by the Gestapo in Vienna, perhaps signed by the good Captain Laimgruber himself? Whisper-whistling a complicated rhythmical mélange of the Hungarian Rákóczi March, the one composed by Johann Strauss the Elder in honor of "Father Radetzky," I shoved the electric heater next to my improvised writing desk, sat down in front of my old faithful Remington, unbuttoned my shirt collar and sleeves and typed an answer to Room 27a of the Kaspar-Escher Building:

PONTRESINA, *13 June 1938*

At health resort. Will return on report.
    (Signature)

P.S. Typing error: Will report on return.

As I was about to start typing a new letter, I stopped whistling. Brainstorm! In my flannel jacket I found the folded slip of paper Pola had handed me the day before yesterday—with the sneering comment: "Here's what the bill of our

94

dear doggy lawyer looks like. It's priceless!" Beneath the country lawyer's letterhead stood the ruins of a once impeccable script, a hopelessly chaotic pencil-scrawl.

RECEIPT

I hereby thankfully acknowledge the receipt of 1450 sfr. (one thousand four hundred and fifty Swiss francs) from Mr. Joop ten Breukaa in payment for the male Cocker Spaniel Sirio of Bannockburn (pedigree guaranteed).

Dr. Gaud. de Colana

Underneath this, like a seal, was a splattered stain of red wine that bore an odd resemblance to a peacock's tail. A curiosity made even more obvious by the addition of several shaky pencil strokes and dots. I erased the text without difficulty, leaving only the signature and the improvised "seal," then slipped the paper into my typewriter.

GAUDENZ DE COLANA

*dr.jur., advocat e vicenotar
ex-cussglier guv. pres. dal
tribunel districtual Maloegia*

ST. MORITZ, *13.VI.1938*
Mr. Konstantin Giaxa
RADKERSBURG
Germany (Ostmark)

My dear Kosto!

With fond hopes that you now find yourself in the best of health I am pleased to inform you of my imminent departure for the island of Hvar. As you know, the tourist season commences for us in these altitudes at the beginning of July, by which time I must, in view of professional commitments, be back from my visit to the beautiful Dalmatian coast. I will expect you and your charming wife to reach the island no later than the 19th of this month and have, confident of your approval, already taken the liberty of reserving accommodations for the three of us at Duschan's place.

Forgive me, but there can be no question of a refusal on your part. I repeat: no question! So no excuses!

Good-bye until our joyous reunion. With respectful regards I remain your old admirer

The chaotic pencil scrawl: Dr. Gaud. de Colana

I locked myself in my room; got my ski boots ready, my swamp-green loden cape, my old Styrian hat, five sheets of typing paper, a bottle of typewriter oil, the Walther pistol. From a case packed full of ties and belts I drew a black leather belt that looked, at first glance, very much like the others. Only after opening several snaps could one see that it was filled with 6.75mm ammunition. I counted: forty-three *Fisolen* ("cartridges" in Viennese wartime slang; as third in command of the Republican Defense Corps in Styria I had had the camouflaged belt made up by a discreet Socialist leathercrafter). I exchanged the belt I was wearing for the camouflaged one—which also possessed a no less camouflaged holster on the right side—and slipped the magazine out of the Walther's pearl-handled grip. Maxim's present was manufactured in Germany by the famous Thuringian gunmaker Carl Walther, Zella-Mehlis.

I let a few drops of typewriter oil drip into the barrel, then oiled the sear spring and shell ejector. On each of the five sheets of typing paper I inked a massive black dot and surrounded it with three fat concentric circles in red. Improvised targets.

POSTA E TELEGRAF. Madam Fausch sat framed in the window of the postal counter and eyed my loden cape. "Ei, ya. Nine months winter and three months cold, that's what we say up here."

"When I'm near you, Madam Fausch, the cold cannot touch me," I parried, whereupon this mannish little woman, this mountain troll actually blushed a little. Her weathered skin looked for a moment like dyed leather.

"Fiddlesticks!" she grumbled.

I handed her the two letters to be weighed—the one to the Alien Police in Zurich and the disguised warning to Konstantin Giaxa.

Marching out of Larèt, the lower village, across the muddy main street of Upper Pontresina (called the "Spiert" in Romansh) I felt well insulated and maneuverable in my heavy ski boots, cape and Styrian hat, well-armed for my own private refresher course, and hummed the overture to Giaxa & Giaxa's opening number, the Rákóczidetzky March. The rain had settled down to a cold drizzle. Still, there was hardly a soul on the street, hardly a soul. The geraniums hung stiffly, as if frozen, through the bowed wrought-iron window bars of the well-kept, fortlike Engadine houses. The piles of firewood under the balconies breathed out a spicy, damp scent of pine forests that was mingled with the odor of burnt wood. The rain, drizzling down from nothingness, congealed to form a heavy blanket of fog that pressed the chimney smoke down over the gabled roofs. At the Engadiner Hof I turned into the puddle-covered path that snaked up through the stone pines to the Alp Languard, trudged up the slope above Giarsun farm and past the pentagonal ruin of Spaniola tower that stood like a remnant of Saracen times, as if the Moors had somehow managed to build an outpost way up here. Then through the pine forest with an occasional rainy view through the trees to the valley. Suddenly the view vanished in clouds; I had passed the fog line. Groping along as close as possible to this invisible boundary, I left the path, stamped across slippery moss, and bent forward, pushed my way through the underbrush. The hat brim pulled low over my eyes fended off the wet, whipping branches; several times I had to jerk my cape free of the tangled brush. The new snow, long washed away by the rain in the valley, still clung to the ground in sparse patches. I stopped and listened in front of a larch tree with high-set branches.

All around, the faint, irregular sound of dripping. It was not the drizzle—that remained inaudible; all I could hear were drops that fell from moisture-laden boughs with a constant, gentle tap-tap-tap.

In this no-man's-land between the rainy forest and the upland fog the visibility was no more than twenty paces, just enough for my purposes. I unbuttoned my cape and pulled out the five homemade typing-paper targets, unfolded one of them and pasted it on the trunk of the larch. It clung to the sticky resin of the tree like a poster on an advertising pillar.

Bending over, I stalked across the slippery ground through whipping pine branches and counted my steps. Just like a pistol duel, I thought, seven, eight, nine, ten, eleven, twelve. I turned around. The red circles and the black bulls-eye stood out well enough from the rain-soaked paper. Once again I stood motionless and listened. Only the dripping, the ever-present tapping sound. I drew the Walther, switched off the safety, squeezed my unreliable right eye shut and forced the pistol in front of my left eye, aimed and fired. Peng! Peng! Peng! and the three shots sounded oddly flat and unresonant, like three slaps of a wet dishrag on wood or three shots behind an insulated door.

I put on the safety, checked the magazine, verified the normal functioning of the shell ejector and pulled three *Fisolen* out of the pistol belt, filled the magazine, and trudged over to the tree to confirm that all three shots lay within the outer and middle circles of the target. I crumpled the paper and glued another one to the sticky tree trunk and pushed my way, lashed by sharp, cold branches, back to my firing line. This time I took more time to aim. Off they went, five shots like rag slaps. I flicked on the safety, wiped my face with the corner of my cape and balanced my way across the slippery ground to the larch. Two shots were in the black.

I had slapped a third target on the tree trunk and turned to load the Walther when I made a discovery. A little below the place I had left the Languard trail stood a double-something amidst the pines. Something I hadn't noticed before, something out of place in the mental picture I had made of my drizzly surroundings.

Almost shapeless. Hardly a shadow. But the shadow of two man-high stumps. Two. Man-high. And now, now in this foggy-misty forest where not a breath of wind was stirring the two shadows drew closer together and merged into one. Then the entire specter vanished.

And the dripping, dripping, like an ever-present tap-tap-tap.

Tap. Taptap. Madness. Like playing with fire. Literally playing with fire. Sending myself off on a one-man maneuver into the forest in miserable weather.

To calm my restlessness. Restlessness, why? Because of Xana. Because Xana had gone away.

Taptap. Tap.

For nearly five minutes I stood leaning gently against the larch tree until the cold began gnawing at my bones, and I sniffed the etherlike bitterness of the fog and the spicy pine odor of the forest, today strangely without the usual bad-weather smell of moldering earth and mushrooms. With undiminished intensity I listened to the tapping drops and came to a conclusion.

It was very well that I had checked my impulsiveness to act—and my curiosity to know. Even if they weren't policeman or foresters (who would have challenged me without a moment's hesitation) they might have been lumbermen or perhaps even hardy members of the hay-fever club from Pontresina. Whoever it was. If I'd let them have a clear look at me they might have recognized me later in the village and turned me in for poaching. So lie low.

Taptaptaptap. I stood, my back protected by the broad tree trunk, and peered, eyes right! left, right, left, waiting (I had pulled down the third target and crumpled it into my pocket) until my ears had grown accustomed to the cryptic rhythm of the dripping-tapping drops. Soon the wet gravel of the Languard trail was crunching beneath my boots. At the five-sided tower, I left the path leading to the upper village and headed down a side trail. On the way I discarded the wads of paper, joined the main street near the Protestant church, a few steps away from POSTA E TELEGRAF.

It was five o'clock and Xana was still not back.

Mr. Duschlett, Madam Fausch's assistant at the post office, had nothing to report. Over to Confiserie Jann. No Xana. Loitering on the wooden balcony of my workroom, still wearing my cape, spouting curses without ever repeating myself. Hearing the whistle of the train just arriving at the station; cursing the lack of a telescope; with hungry glances searching the milling crowd by the station as it breaks up into small groups of black mushrooms moving up the street. There! There, a topaz yellow mushroom standing out from the rest.

"Aviati——Aviati——Aviatishek!"

My first impression: she must be drunk. Her smooth complexion tinted violet from the cold, her bangs pasted willy-nilly over her forehead, the water-darkened, dripping hair on her neck hanging matted and shaggy. As if she had never used her umbrella, much less the hood of her raincoat. She tugs on the latter in a half-hearted attempt to take it off. With a kind of unconscious hesitation she steps toward me, and it seems on the verge of coming out: the reason, the real reason for the agitation, the excitement, yes, the rapture that makes her expression seem to vibrate. An experience. Something completely unexpected. Unique and fantastic. Something miraculous. That lingered as a trance of indestructible contentment or satisfaction. Then it catches me by the throat, the exasperating, stupefying sensation of jealousy.

My Xana has just gone off to St. Moritz for a splendid little tête-à-tête. *Revenge for Corviglia!* had no doubt been her motto. How do I know what happened in the feverish, bad-weather atmosphere of Pizzagalli's American Bar after I had rattled off to Sils with de Colana? Perhaps Pola had called the handsome soldier Lenz Zbraggen, Soldier Buddy, over to the table where he had squeezed in with his lecherous laugh next to Xana. Perhaps Pola had found it entertaining to play the matchmaker. This Lenz fellow had a splendid Dinaric skull; no injuries there, no . . . Now the young woman has taken off her raincoat and her hands want to grasp my shoulders and she wants to tell me something, but I reel back, my scolding voice filling the small apartment.

"My Ex, my Ex, my Ex, after I told you expressly not to do it you run off in this horrible weather to some marvelous little rendezvous or whatever it was—you who are supposed to be recuperating, you who were in bed fourteen days ago with pneumonia—!"

"Albert! Madam Fausch."

"I couldn't care less about Madam Fausch. Shall I show you? *There* . . .!" Launched from my right foot, a Bosnian slipper flew over the wooden balcony and out of sight. "I've been worrying about you! For hours! Been tearing my hair out over you! For hours! And finally here you come, dripping wet from head to toe with this silly—moon-eyed—lovesick look on your face!"

Xana goes over to our bedroom, sits down on a chair. Her lowered head rests on her hand, her eyes covered. Is she crying? Peering through the doorway I discover: she's smiling. Her whole wayward, chilled, rain-soaked being is smiling with this newfound, obscure, miraculous contentment. It gets to me.

"I was afraid my Ex was gone *for good* because she'd gotten tired of being banished here with an old war casualty! Why didn't you? Slam-bang—like *this* . . ." With a solid heave the second slipper goes flying out over the balcony. "Home to the Reich! Home to your retired circus rider——"

The young woman gets up with a gentle start, still smiling, and gently but decisively closes the door between us. There I stand, Othello in socks.

I got dressed, went out and searched the side terrace of the post office building and the long concrete stairway leading down to the basement laundry room. There where Madam Fausch used to hang her laundry on sunny days, I found one Bosnian slipper—one. Feeling not a little contrite, I gave up searching for the other slipper. Up in my workroom again, leaning far over the balcony railing I spied the second slipper. It had landed on Madam Fausch's balcony. From a string and a bent paper clip I manufactured a fishing line. After a long game of patience I finally hoisted the slipper on board, knocked on Xana's door and heard her immediate response, "Come in!" She was sitting on the edge of the bed in her horrible devotional dressing gown, got up without further ado, flung her arms around my neck and nestled her plump cheek against my cheekbone with a soft but definite pressure. Her hair—now combed, but still stiff with dampness and hanging in unintended pigtails—gave her a very girlish appearance, something like an Illyrian Cinderella's, and I went out to buy an inexpensive, cold evening meal, and while Xana set it out and I helped her (in reality I set it out and she pretended to help me) I said, "Hvar." (Pronounced "Kva.") "In old Illyria. How long do you suppose the island's been inhabited?"

"I imagine about six thousand years. Didn't you ever visit the caves at Pokrivenik and Grabak?"

"No."

"There they found fragments of old ceramics. I think the oldest pictorial representation of a ship—in Europe. In China there may be older ones."

"How 'bout that. Why do you think" (this was my leading question) "people moved to the island six thousand years ago?"

"I ima-a-agine," came her long, slow reply, "to escape their enemies on the mainland."

"To escape their enemies on the mainland. Well, of course, that was in the Stone Age. By the way I wrote to Papa-Rose today. On some special paper I got ahold of, the official letterhead of Gaudenz de Colana, Attorney at Law. Even de Colana's signature is there, right under the text I wrote."

"Why the big production?" In the same second Xana realized. "Because of the Nazi censor."

"Of course. In the disguise of de Colana I let the message come through loud and clear: that they should come down to Hvar, to Duschan Mlisz *now*. Now. Not in two weeks."

"Now, Trebla? In the middle of June, not at the end? That wouldn't fit the program at all."

"Programprogram. Circusprogram—"

"Now don't get excited again. Don't throw any more slippers off the balcony. In this rain it'd be no pleasure to go looking for them—"

"Rainrain, I'm not getting excited and I have no plans to go looking for anything. Quite to the contrary, I have some definite plans, as I said, in regards to Mr. Konstantin Giaxa."

Aside from the Slavo-Romano-Germanic influences that had inspired some amateur morphologists to define Giaxa as a kind of hybrid of Garibaldi and Bismarck, this medium-sized man had something primordial about him; he seemed to belong to a much older race than, say, the Jews. Despite his energetic cleft chin, the almost semicircular line of his nose and his bushy eyebrows lent his face a quality that was vaguely prehistoric, paleoanthropine (or in mythical terms, centaurian)—something of which he was well aware, as revealed by one of his caustic *aperçus:* "After I die I want you to mount a brass calling card on my skull: GIAXA: I don't want to be dug up thirty years later as Neanderthal number two."

The dozen of times I walked into his dressing room in a circus or theater somewhere in Europe, he was always there a full hour before the beginning of his opening number in order to gather his strength and to get a message from

"Rittmeister" Magrutsch, whose normal concern was the fitness of the other Giaxa, the Lippizan stallion. During this hour he enjoyed the company of his family, of the impresario, of fellow performers, or of a theater critic in search of an interview. The first time I visited him in his dressing room in the Circus Renz near Vienna's Karlstheater he was in his mid-fifties. Pola Polari, who had shown me the way there, confided to me that *after* his 35-40-minute performance he never wanted to see anyone except Magrutsch and the wardrobe attendant—not even Elsabé or Xana. This was the time he needed to overcome both his exhaustion and the back pains that recurred with increasing frequency as he grew older. For Giaxa, like myself, had his own special wound, his permanent injury left over from the army. Around 1900 he was kicked by a horse in the small of the back, an incident that led to his transfer to the reserves—kicked out, as it were, from the regular army. Entering his dressing room from behind him as he sat before the mirror, his nose already concealed behind the violet half-pomegranate with its oversized hanging moustache so reminiscent of two foxtails on the chair next to him the coat of Obristi Obraski or Colonel Dubouboule at the ready, his torso bare, a towel around his shoulders—I was not so much surprised by the sinewy leanness of the aging man as by the blondish gray growth of hair that covered him. Chest, underarms, shoulder blades were thickly forested, autumnal with a hint of gold, and out of the forest everywhere, and even on his back, peeked the bluish lettering in all sizes and designs: the multiple, indelible tattoo AIDA.

Giaxa never stopped returning to the island of his birth where his childhood friend Duschan Mlisz later opened a vermin-free hotel. From an early age when he happened to examine some ancient amphorae from a neighboring island Kosto (Konstantin) had been preoccupied by a nagging question: What ancient instinct was it that drove men to move in circles?

And when he, already famous, came to Hvar with his new bride in 1910—the mildest January nights anyone could remember, "the roses began to bloom again"—Elsabé discovered on his body the stigmata of an earlier passion, now long forgotten: AIDA. It didn't bother her. (Almost nothing ever bothers her.)

A short time later in Budapest, where Giaxa was appearing at Favörosy-Nagy, Elsabé noticed that she was with child (as people said in those days). After a gynecologist from the Lukatsch Spa in Buda had confirmed this fact in writing, she and her husband made the climb to the sacred tomb of the Moslem sheik Gül-Baba, i.e., Papa-Rose. It must have been an auspicious moment when Elsabé, the incurable dispenser of nicknames, chose to assign the name Papa-Rose to her husband—in a spontaneous act of gratitude (for *one* unborn child had already been taken from her).

Whenever the great Giaxa paid a visit to Hvar the islanders made no great fuss over him: he was just a local boy who had come back to enjoy some peace and quiet. In July of 1936, however, one of the greatest in the field came over from Venice, Paolo Fratellini, whom I had seen for the first time in street clothes during our wedding at the Reformed Church in Vienna's Dorotheergasse. He had a completely shaved head and finely modeled features (his brother Albert was even handsomer) and a neat little pair of Mephistopheles eyebrows. At that very time the Lilliputian Gypsy Band Husseindinovich from Zagreb had stopped off in Hvar on their way to Dubrovnik with the intention of giving a little nocturnal serenade in honor of Giaxa. Sitting next to Paolo in the loggia of the Hotel Split, Giaxa witnessed the evening ceremony, and a great crowd assembled at the Marina to see the Lilliputians unpack their instruments: quarter-size violins the size of the one Grock had used to fiddle himself to fame, a bass-viol as small as a viola, a toy xylophone. I was astonished by the fortissimo the dwarfs managed to squeeze from their instruments.

The next day at high noon Giaxa, Mlisz, the Lilliputians and I undertook a little sailing excursion. Paolo didn't come: a serious bibliophile, he was trying to locate a first edition of the Croatian humanist Hannibal Luchich. Elsabé and Xana, the two white thin-skinned ladies, stayed behind under the shade of a giant Baghdad pine. In a rare gesture of extravagance, perhaps a rudiment of his island childhood, Giaxa wore a cherry red Herzegovinian cap. The boat left Palmizan behind and sailed for Jerolim, on whose shores grazed a large herd of sheep. Giaxa took the protesting first violinist Husseindinovich on his arm and jumped ashore. Two baskets of delicacies were deposited beside a stream in an olive grove: pickled Kaivar peas, roast chicken, baked octopus, ewe's milk cheese, halvah, an assortment of bottles of Smederevka white wine placed in the stream to chill, and for spirits, Vlahovach and Maruska. Following a Croatian drinking-custom Duschan appointed Papa-Rose and me *stoloravnatelj* (marshals) and the Lilliputian concertmaster a *vunbatzitelj* (bouncer).

"Allow me, my dear Treblian" (as Giaxa sometimes called me), "to take you *bras-dessus-bras-dessous*." He rarely took anyone by the arm. "Let's forsake this jolly gathering for a few minutes."

I grew somewhat uncomfortable. I knew that Giaxa knew. Since February '34 my passport had been in the hands of the "Christian" regime in Austria. Now he would probably ask me how I had managed to outfox the Viennese police and whether I had traveled to Yugoslavia on forged papers. But instead he pointed through the wonderfully gnarled olive trees toward the city of Hvar across the channel, whose ancient wall seemed to rest on a bank of golden cloud in the late afternoon glare: "Behold, my dear Progressive. Three hundred and fifty years *before* Christ that was a *polis*. A free city-state. A brilliantly functioning island democracy. Archons and scribes. A legislative body. A popular assembly with the power to pass resolutions. Politically independent. Free. Delegates to the Olympic Games . . . 350 B.C. And today? So-called Olympic Games in the capital of the Third Reich. With over four thousand sports addicts from all over the world, the greatest number of participants since Baron Coubertin first warmed over the old idea. The whole world is making a kowtow to a petty-bourgeois nincompoop who not only misunderstood Nietzsche, but Karl May as well. Hitler-Hatler, Uncle Adolf, or whatever you call him."

Unsure of what he was driving at, I got set to reply. Then he asked suddenly, "You plan to go back to Vienna?"

"Of course."

"Wouldn't it be better if you two stayed here? You know how hard it is for Elsabé to be separated from Xana, but. . . without wanting to interfere in your affairs: this in and out of internment camp, in and out of jail, doesn't your . . . not to mention your marriage . . . doesn't your writing suffer from all that? You realize that I'm privileged to consider you a great writer."

"Thanks a lot, Gül-Baba, but I *must* go back."

"You must. And if our friend Adolf has himself crowned Emperor of Germany in St. Stephen's—these days anything is possible—what do you do then? You, who made a personal attack on him in your *Tale of the Robber Who Joined the Police?*, the ballad you signed with your own name and had smuggled into Germany as a pamphlet—"

"If he does come back to Vienna . . . whether or not he's crowned King of the Yahoos . . . I've got to go."

"*Good.* Just be careful you're not sitting in the Black Hole when the brownshirts arrive."

"I'll do my best, Gül-Baba."

"Gül-Baba advises you to visit Grandpa," said Giaxa. "Who has a particular fondness for you." Henrique Kujath, owner of the Luzienmuehle in the lowlands of Graubuenden, who had helped Giaxa himself out of more than one tight situation, would be more than happy to help us out. His connections were legion, beginning with those to certain key positions in the German Wehrmacht. If we wanted to go to Latin America, for example. By the way, it was not advisable to enter Switzerland on a forged passport. The Swiss authorities had little sense of humor when it came to things like that . . . "Now, my Treblian, forget your troubles for a minute and look over here."

Trudging through a sparse grove of olive trees and flowering ash, we cut across to the other side of the little island. On the marble gravel in front of a white ridge and barely standing out from it was a motionless white horse. So motionless that at a hundred paces it looked like an effigy on stone: *The world's most ancient depiction of a horse.*

We crunched across the gravel toward the ridge. Giaxa stopped for a moment, then called out in his unmistakable bassoonlike voice (full in the bass, nasal in the treble range), whose sharply clipped or octave-spanning commands had echoed throughout circus tents all over Europe, "Argon!"

The white horse, vaguely outlined against the marble ridge, still like a contour chiseled in stone by the hand of a prehistoric artist, remained immobile.

"Ar-gon!" called Giaxa, pressing something of the Obristi-Obraski sharpness into his voice. The contour's only reaction was to raise its head slightly.

Having approached him to within twenty paces, I took him for an unusually fine, young horse—judging from size and build a thoroughbred, an unbridled, perhaps barely tamed white stallion. Would he gallop away in the next seconds, striking sparks from the gravel?

"Argon?" I asked, benumbed by the *dolce far niente* of the hot afternoon. "Do you know him?"

Giaxa kept me waiting for an answer. After we had come cautiously nearer I finally realized: my weak right eye had fooled me. It was a well-preserved old hack whose great age could not detract from its noble bearing, an ancient nag of almost ghostly beauty.

"Shouldn't I know my old Argon? Giaxa the Fifth," Papa-Rose introduced me. "Retired Lippizan stallion. Pensioner number six, as you remember, broke his foot on Hvar three years ago and had to be . . . dispatched. This is number five, my inflation horse. He used to get a little nervous before we went on. Me too, for that matter, when I considered that my evening's fee would lose half its value by the next morning. He lives here on Jerolim now, along with the sheep; Duschan has someone looking after him every day . . . Argon," he murmured to the ancient stallion, which stood with head erect, hardly moving its ears, as he stroked its jawbone. "yes-yes-yes-yes-big-boy-don't-get-excited-easy-easy-easy."

Knotted veins ran from the Lippizan's eye to his nostril. The nostril gave the caressing hand a very faint and unfamiliar snort. The eye stared motionless, dead, glazed over with milky white: The iridescent Adriatic day was reflected there as on something inorganic, like a piece of milk glass. Blind.

Giaxa checked the other eye. "On the left he can still see." He felt the swollen foreknees, uttered a brief growl, then grasped the noble nag by the muzzle with both hands. Hand-shy, the horse lifted his head, but then, soothed by a steady flow of calming words, let the man force open his jaws. What Giaxa saw there made his bushy gray brows flinch upward for a moment. He bent over effortlessly, rinsed his hands in a pool of seawater and dried them on a freshly ironed handkerchief, spoke matter-of-factly, without a trace of disappointment or sentimentality, rather somewhat sternly, "My old partner Argon doesn't recognize me any more. *Andiamo.*"

We crunched across the marble gravel. "You've had some experience with horses, my Treblian. A dog recognizes his master after years have gone by—think of Odysseus. When the crafty one, the singer of many songs finally returned to Ithaca disguised as a beggar—who recognized him? His dog. His horse, never."

We had surmounted a low dune where some agaves thrust out their sword-like leaves, and saw up ahead a crowd of curious sheep flocking around Duschan's camp; turning around we saw the ancient Lippizan walk stiffly away across the crescent strip of beach.

"Ah, Argon really is a proud beauty. I'm not exaggerating, he was truly magnificent. He was the first one I got from Piber near Graz after 1918 spelled the end for Lippiza, the Imperial Stud Farm in Istria. A direct descendant of the famous stallion Conversano. An unregenerate aristocrat."

Winking, I said: "Why are you looking at *me* like that? If my grandfather hadn't married a Slovakian peasant girl—strapping giant of a woman—I might have turned out as small as our friend Husseindinovich."

"Haaa-haaa," said Giaxa. (It was no laugh.) "An aristocrat *and* an acrobat. *Sapristi*, when I think how he could pull off a half capriole *passo e salto* straight ahead! A ballotade on a volt to the left or a *courbette a la droite sur la ligne*. And then the full capriole! It was like flying on a Pegasus . . ."

Argon was standing. He lifted his head, turning it slowly and holding it as if sizing us up carefully with his one good eye, and from beneath his belly something that looked like a dead tree limb began to dangle. Constantly eyeing us he let forth a trembling whinny that was almost lost amidst the gentle beating of the surf.

"Well I'll be—" said Giaxa quietly. "Like a voice from another world."

"You see, Papa." Involuntarily I touched his shoulder. "Don't you think he really *did* recognize you . . .?"

The tree-branch disappeared.

"Hardly. Still, he looks as if he knew. That it's all over for the circus. Admit it, in the age of radio and film it seems old-fashioned. And after the animal act good old Shitler is putting on—"

"Please, you mean Uncle Adolf."

"—there's a chance that animal training might go completely out of style. During the next few centuries. The circus might disappear altogether. Just think, the horse has served mankind for over six thousand years. Six thousand years ago man invented the wheel, and when he had that he had the wagon and caught himself horses to hitch to it. Not to mention the much earlier centaurs—of which I, of course, am one." For the first time all day Giaxa uttered a chuckle sounding like a bassoon staccato. "The first book on horses was written by a Hittite long before the Trojan war. Speaking of the Trojans, Agamemnon and Co. didn't ride into those breastplate-battles at Ilion, they drove. The great cavalry charges didn't come into vogue until later, and, as you know, the great military monarchies of the pre-Christian era would have been unthinkable without the horse. No other creature has been so tangled up in human history. And what has human history been most of the time up to now—well?—*war*, that's what. If it wasn't such a dunce by nature the horse would never have allowed itself to become so attached to man. What possible good can come of being attached to *that* villain? You might be asking yourself how such a devout pessimist—misanthropist would perhaps be saying too much—could spend his whole life making the villain laugh. Well, one of the main reasons is wicked Mammon. Do you know, being hungry once gave me a nice little childhood trauma. Whenever a hailstorm ruined my father's vineyards we lost more than a few grapes. So his son decided to become . . . an expensive joke . . ."

Papa-Rose had seldom been so talkative with me as he was now. Argon shook himself out of his backward-looking stance and, head down, paced stiffly away toward the point of the crescent beach.

"After six thousand years comes a turning point for the horse. The end. One indication: the Fuehrer of the Master Race, this Herr Nit-ler . . ."

"Uncle Adolf."

". . . who, despite his fatal penchant for heroic poses and phony romanticism, never dares mount a horse. He can't afford the risk of being thrown off—his earth-shaking aura would be ruined. Just imagine Napoleon without a horse. After six thousand years its job is done. It's suffered enough. Look, there goes the old codger, trotting away in peace . . ."

Now far away, Argon cleared a row of agaves with a leap so lame it was more like a creeping stretch and continued on toward a cabana surrounded by mulberry bushes.

Duschan's call: "Come on!"

Giaxa's answer, a bassoon fortissimo, gruff and brief: "Coming!"

He glanced up at the sky and I followed his gaze and suddenly, yes, suddenly, we saw it hanging in the boughs of a Mediterranean pine, the thin-fine sickle of the young moon—the hazy afternoon had concealed it from us. "Ave Luna—greetings, fair moon-goddess!" In Bosnian-Moslem fashion Giaxa threw a kiss to the slender crescent, a thoroughly gallant gesture. "The sun feminine, the moon masculine—one of the great misunderstandings of Germanic mythology. Look, now if that isn't a delicate little luna-moon-maiden up there, and over there Mr. Helios the charioteer with his team of seven fiery steeds . . ."

Papa-Rose lit his rosewood pipe, then pointed over at the big island of Vis, and where sea and sky merged in the mist I *saw* something like the fading image of a chariot pulled by six or seven horses. Yes, it seemed as if the image were *driving slowly away* in a cloud of rose-colored dust. And I saw Argon in the distance standing among the mulberry bushes, *a rose-red yearling foal ready to sprint away with sparks flying from its hoofs.* Eager to know if my companion was suffering from the same optical illusion I looked over at him and discovered that his red cap had lost its color in the redness of the sunset.

"Now Argon looks like a mustang foal," said Giaxa. "Don't you think?" A chirping of cicadas and then something else: from the east marina of Jerolim the incredibly high piccolo-fluting of a fiddle. "Husseindinovich. Or Pythagorean music of the spheres, hm? A little philosophy and mathematics, that doctrine of Pythagoras, a little music and astronomy and poetry and peaceful rivalry and theater, yes playacting and death."

"Beg your pardon?"

"Uncle Adolf's Olympics—ha! 'Seeking the Grecian homeland with his petty-bourgeois soul,' as Goethe might have put it. Orpheus the Thracian (in short, a Balkanese) serenaded the wild beasts with his lyre and in the end was even allowed to play in Hades—out of sheer love. In all seriousness, that means a great deal! No doubt you're aware that the first Olympiads were nothing less than an Orphic cult of the *dead.* The most cultivated form of variété. They played music, philosophized, extemporized, recited, debated, calculated, juggled, threw the discus, or ran races—in honor of the beloved shade—"

Without a further word he left me standing alone on the agave-covered dune. The easy fluency (like that of an experienced lecturer) of this normally taciturn man, his adept and unique use of German, unique not just for its Austrianisms, not just for its strongly rolled South Slavic "r," but which contained something of the timber of *all* the languages in the old Austro-Hungarian Empire—yes, something like the *entire Danube* echoed in my ears and faded away into the unreal, high-pitched fluting of the tiny violin. Through the crowded trunks of pines and twisted olive trees I was unable to make out the soloist, but could see the large, milling flock nearby in which the Lilliputians were wandering about, their Panama hats barely projecting above the fleecy backs of the black and white sheep. But whatever color they were, all was changed to rosy red in these few minutes of sunset.

About to follow Papa-Rose along the path descending into the mossy turf, I watched him trudging toward the herd of sheep. His light gray linen suit, like everything else, transformed in the redness of the slowly fading day, resembled—I noticed it now for the first time—the hide of a Lippizan stallion. He wasn't swinging his hands, but kept them, in his usual promenading manner, clasped behind his back. Perhaps it was because of the yielding moss underfoot, but with each step he raised his foot with bended knee exactly the way an "ambler" lifts his forehoof, like a Lippizan stallion with a flawless *pas d'amble.*

"That's nice of you, Trebla, to be worried."

"Worried?"

"About him."

"I'm not worried about him. I just don't want him to—"

"I understand just what you mean. But I'm sorry, you don't know him very well."

"Don't know him very well? I've known Papa-Rose since—"

"Still, you don't know him very well if you think—disguised as a Swiss lawyer—or a Swiss emperor for that matter—you can persuade him to run away."

"Who said anything about running away? I just want to get him to take a trip. To Hvar. *Now.*"

"He's got reservations with Duschan for the twenty-ninth."

"Very simple. Instead of on the twenty-ninth he arrives on the sixteenth. My Colana letter went special delivery."

"Look . . ." Xana's silence.

"I'm looking."

"Look . . ." (As if she hadn't heard me at all.)

"I'm still looking."

"Look. One of the hack writers who works for Goebbels wrote in the *Angriff* . . . I think the character's name was Widukind Weisskohl. Well this writer character in Goebbeles' *Angriff*—"

My involuntary (always too shrill) laugh: "Hee! Where did you get 'Goebbel-e-s'?"

"Didn't you notice that Maxim Grabscheidt never called him anything else? 'Goebbeles the Germanic dwarf, student of Jewish Professor Gundolf, onetime Stefan-Georgian, Goebbeles who once tried unsuccessfully to get an editor's job from James Joyce's Jewish publisher Daniel Brody in Zurich—'"

"Maxim told you that? I've never heard of the Brody thing. How did Maxim know about it?"

"He knew Daniel Brody personally. Didn't you know that?"

"He never told me," I mumbled.

"He did me. Back when I was . . . how shall I say . . . undergoing treatment with him."

My silence; her silence; our silence; only the patter of the rain outside. Then Xana: "Well this Weisskohl, or whatever his name was, raised a storm in the *Angriff* against Giaxa & Giaxa because the Obristi-Obraski number in the Scala supposedly 'undermined the German folk-concept of militance' or something—"

"The concept of folk militancy."

Xana: "Or the concept of military folk-dancing for all I know. 'Giaxa and Giaxa are undermining the concept of military folk-dancing, and we must put an end to this outrage,' was approximately what this character Weisskohl wrote. Whereupon Papa Rose broke his contract with Duisburg and, as you know, left Germany in the same cattle car as his horse . . . a rather show-offish way of demonstrating his solidarity with Giaxa VII."

"I never knew the details."

"You had your hands full with the Defense Corps then. Anyway he said to the German customs officials at the Czech border, 'Gentlemen, take a good look at that Lippizan stallion. That's your ancestral foe, the inferior race.'"

"Grotesque. I never heard about that episode—"

"Now you've heard about it. But he'll never leave Austria in a cattle car. First of all because, if I know him at all, nobody can talk him into or out of doing something. If he's decided to travel to Hvar on the twenty-ninth he will *not* go on the sixteenth . . . And second, there's the taboo."

"Taboo?"

"His taboo, no . . . his . . . Papa Rose's feeling that *he* is taboo."

"Hmmmmmmmmm?," my inarticulate question.

"His conviction that he's an Austrian institution. Almost, almost a legend. And that no one who rules in Austria, even his archenemy, would dare to touch him."

I kept silent, but not without reminding myself that it was a petty silence. On Tuesday it was pouring cold rain and I sat at my old Remington and began to put the finishing touches on my Austriacus-Babeuf series, while in the next room Xana sat on the bed with her knees up, dressed in her devotional dressing gown, writing on a piece of paper backed by a magazine, whose full-page crossword puzzle she had just solved in what seemed to be three minutes. She was working on the translation of Lucius Apuleius's "Metamorphoses," which the Amsterdam publisher Allert de Lange had commissioned her to do. While typing, I sent over the following remark: "I'm not sure Mr. Rothmund of the Alien Police is going to grant you permission to translate a single line of that enchanting but sometimes rather lewd work."

The answer did not arrive until some five minutes later: "Rothmund can go jump. How do you translate 'phallos'?"

"With 'phallus.'"

"That's not . . . allegorical enough for me."

"Then try 'tail.'"

"That could lead to misunderstandings, especially since it has to do with a donkey."

"Then translate it as 'campanile.'"

"Why *that*, of all things?"

"I'm thinking of the leaning tower of Pisa. And the leaning tower of St. Moritz-Kulm."

"His campanile? Do you think they had campaniles in the second century?"

"Call up Joop and ask him. Maybe he has a better idea."

My cigar supply was getting low; I threw on my cape, splashed over to the common room of the Morteratsch, bought a pack of Fivaz from the concierge. Pina was nowhere to be seen. Presumably she was "doing da roomss." As I walked out the door a detatchment of mountain machine gunners from the Sixty-first Border Regiment was just passing by, not quite company strength. Eight mules bearing olive green tarpaulins, which no doubt concealed machine guns. Behind the mules a troop of about forty men wearing hoodlike molded helmets and olive green ponchos.

One of the men had left the formation.

His poncho hanging askew, his steel helmet dangling from his arm like a shopping bag, his carbine bouncing from its sling across his chest like a trinket, he ducked beneath a large umbrella held by an old peasant woman who was on her way to the upper village. Now he hooked his arm inside hers, and with a stupidly flattered look she let him do it, and I recognized the man as soldier buddy Lenz Zbraggen. At the same time he recognized me and gave me a thoroughly familiar wave, his young Achilles face gleaming with moisture and merriment.

"*Brocka!!*"

The rain poured and poured so dense and heavy that the well and the watering trough had overflowed. Did the harsh voice that had just shouted the name Zbraggen belong to the sergeant marching next to the mules? Or was it the snarl of the officer in the shiny leather coat who was bringing up the rear on his gray stallion?

For a single moment the face of Mountain Machine Gunner Lenz Zbraggen was transformed—so it seemed to me, although the rain may have distorted my vision—into an expression of intense hate. Quickly he ducked out from under the old woman's umbrella and trudged back into the formation. The column moved off in the direction of Bernina Pass and soon disappeared as if washed away by a current of water.

3

A Wednesday in mid-June. Across the Rosatsch blew the southwest wind that overnight had swept the rain and fog from the upland valleys, and all about the mountain peaks stood frosted with fresh snow, sharply outlined against the cerulean blue of the sky with its wispy clouds that sailed overhead like flotillas of snow-white rafts. The steady wind brushed the ridge lines and sent the powdery new snow swirling into the valley like dissolving silver smoke.

"Where did you leave Sirio?" I asked Xana.

"With Uorschletta."

I: "We've hardly gotten a look at her."

Miss Polari, the widowed Countess Orszczelska-Abendsperg, leaning back in the Isabela-brown back seat of the Austro-Daimler: "The kitchen help belongs in the kitchen."

"And the chambermaid in the chamber and the chimneysweep in the chimney. But Spahis belong in the living room," my clumsy joke. "Tell me, Joop, don't you ever worry a little about the fellow?"

Ten Breukaa's jaundiced stare. "What fellow? Sirio? Why?"

"Not the *spaniel*. The *Spahi*. I mean like today for example, when you're out for a ride. Aren't you afraid that he might, ah, get lost?"

"He's insured," Joop grumbled.

"But remember the Mona Lisa affair," I stuck to the subject. "That happened in the Louvre before the eyes of a dozen guards. Let's suppose there is someone—not necessarily a professional criminal, just a passionate Gauguin enthusiast—who is just as enchanted by your famous Spahi as you yourself. He waits and waits for the opportunity—"

"You've got a persecution complex."

110

"All right, I've got a persecution complex. The man waits for the opportunity, breaks into Acla Silva while you're away, cuts the Spahi out of his frame with a razor blade, rolls up the canvas, and carries it out of the house under his coat. Then he keeps your Gauguin. Keeps it hidden in his house without ever thinking of selling it. For years. And sometimes at night when he's alone he takes it out and admires it and is blissfully happy. Just like Balzac's *Unknown Masterpiece*. It's conceivable, isn't it?"

"You're living in a detective story."

"All right." Joop could not suspect that his grumbled objection had touched a weak spot in me. "Maybe, hm, maybe we're all living in a detective story these days. Let's stay with the hypothesis: the amateur thief does not get caught. The insurance money is paid but it doesn't make you any happier, Joop. Your Spahi is gone for good."

The vein that snaked out of the fuzzy down on ten Breukaa's brow suddenly became more prominent, and I felt Xana's hand lightly touch my neck.

Up in front next to Bonjour sat another man, bareheaded and dark-haired. His starched white collar protruded from his high-buttoned, shiny black jacket: a priest's habit. When we had gotten in the car at Pontresina he had been sitting there in the driver's compartment and had given us only a reserved nod. Maybe it was Pola's father confessor (two prelates, one abbot and a papal nuncio, had been among her regular guests in Vienna). But since no one introduced him to us I decided that the young priest was a casual acquaintance of the ten Breukaas who had simply asked to ride along to the Hospice of Bernina.

MORTERATSCH was the inscription on a small gray building of rough-hewn stone blocks. Next to it, a freshly painted sign bearing two skulls over crossed bones with a warning in four languages not to enter the maneuver area. Two guards in steel helmets with carbines slung over their shoulders.

Ten Breukaa put on an oversized pair of dark violet sunglasses and led us up to the iron railing. The priest made no move to join us. Bonjour raised one of his mirror-shiny knee-length boots onto the running board and struck up a conversation with him.

"Bernina—Crastaguezza—Bellavista—Palue," Joop introduced us to the row of icy pyramids with the lethargic gestures of a museum guide. The Morteratsch Glacier lay spread out toward us in its colossal granite bed like a gigantic skeleton with countless riblike fissures: emerald-green crevasses. The nearer the eternal ice approached us with its frozen waves and eddies the dirtier it looked until it melted away into the blackish rubble heap of the moraine, eternal filth, in which shone the bright reflections of a few scattered symbols of our transient world, broken beer bottles.

"Do you know the Morteratsch legend? You don't? Tell it, tell it to them, Joopypuppet!"

Ten Breukaa told and told and told the old mountain legend in a manner as dull as it was protracted. Long ago a young man disappeared on a trip across the glacier. His lover set out to search for him. But she too did not return. If one stands near the glacier when the ice begins to melt in early summer one can hear the girl calling her lover, "Morteratsch, Morteratsch!"

"And now listen closely everybody." Pola feigned a childish expectancy. "Maybe we can hear her calling. Shhhh! . . ."

An ice-fresh glacier breeze ruffled Pola's voluminous shaving brush hat decoration. God, how I hated the damn things, and she had to go and wear the biggest one I'd ever seen. Nevertheless I did her the favor of listening politely. And the breeze died down and there was not a sound on the road behind us. A great, strange silence—and then I heard it. Very far off, and yet borne through the ether with minute clarity: tacktacktacktacktack. And then something else. My forehead reacted like a seismograph:

"Did you hear *that?*"

"Ooo-eee," exulted Pola, "I heard it!"

"A machine gun," Joop enlightened us. "They're holding alpine maneuvers up there. A machine gun on the Diavolezza."

I held my breath and listened. The tack-tack had fallen silent and remained so. "A machine gun, no doubt about it; but that's not what I mean. The other sound a second later . . ."

"Ooo-eee, old Trebla heard it, the voice of the glacier bride!"

"Just a minute, Pola. Xana, did *you* hear it?"

"Hear what?"

Then I realized that she hadn't even pretended to participate in our little listening game.

Ten Breukaa's sunglasses flashed at me. "What do you think you heard?"

"Pardon me. Not what I *think* I heard. What I actually *did* hear. A cry."

"A cry?" His lips, in contrast to the owlish seriousness of his sunglasses, twisted into a thin smile: "Was it maybe—ah—Morteratsch?"

"Don't be ridiculous! It was a hideous scream. Like—like a stuck pig. But it lasted only a second . . ."

"Och zo." Ten Breukaa turned back toward the car and removed his sunglasses. "Interesting. Interesting case. First you want to convince me that my Gauguin will be stolen. Then you hear a stuck pig squealing on the Diavolezza." He emitted a half chuckle like a dry cough. "Console yourself with the knowledge that you're a poet, Trebla."

The pass highway moved up through the rocky wasteland alongside the narrow railroad track. The last larches, hardly trees any more: like charred smokestacks hung with spiderwebs.

Right in front of my nose stood the open sliding window of the chauffeur's compartment and through it I could hear Bonjour's subdued *français fédéral* and the hesitant one-syllable answers of the priest in more melodic French. Bonjour, who addressed him as "*monsieur le Curé,*" didn't realize he was being overheard.

112

"Do you know the joke about the window without a curtain, *monsieur le Curé?*"

The priest shook his head feebly.

Bonjour leaned slightly toward the priest and whispered something, then sprang back behind the wheel, "*Pas mal, hain?*" Not bad, eh?

The priest smiled.

> "*Le chef de la gare*
> *Est en rétard,*
> *cocu . . .*"

hummed Bonjour, then stopped with a suppressed snicker.

The priest smiled again.

On the right a lifeless-looking pond came into view, a small lake that flowed northward into the Bernina Brook, a grayish black pool like liquid lead, separated by a dam from a larger lake extending toward the south that, strangely, had a completely different, creamy yellow color. We had crossed the watershed.

"Lago Nero—Lago Bianco," ten Breukaa, the morose travel guide, introduced us to the lakes.

I said, "Nero-Bianco, that's me."

"That's *you?* . . . Those two lakes? *You?*" He seemed intent on exposing me as a lunatic.

"Nero-Bianco, Black-White—that's what de Colana nicknamed me."

"Whatever for?" asked Xana.

" 'Cause he was soused," decided Pola. "Anyway you two are really a good match; you're both nuts."

"Yes, we two nuts are really a good match," I concurred obligingly and felt a slight longing for the company of the country lawyer. I felt more at home in his rattling Fiat than I did in this official state limousine. Inconspicuously I turned my attention to my listening post at the sliding window.

"Do you know the corner of the Rue Blondel and the Boulevard Sébastopol, *monsieur le Curé?*"

The priest shook his head weakly.

"*Numéro sept, rue Blondel, Paris!*" said Bonjour in amazement. Didn't everyone know this address?

"No," murmured the priest.

"You walk through a swinging door," Bonjour whispered enthusiastically. "*Une chaleur*—heat like in a Turkish bath. About twenty-five girls, all *toute nue. Complètement nue.* Stark naked as they live and breathe, just wearing high-heeled shoes and a kind of pink figleaf. And a cheap thrill too, *monsieur le Curé, une trouvaille!* For a hundred francs, French francs . . ." Bonjour leaned over toward him, whispering.

113

"Inexpensive indeed," the priest mumbled shyly.

"You really don't know *numéro sept, rue Blondel?*"

"I really don't, I'm sorry Monsieur Bonjour," whispered the priest. The conversation seemed to annoy him. Disconcerted, he stuck his finger inside the starched white collar that projected from the black soutane.

"But the Sphinx," Bonjour insisted. "You must know that place. Anyone who's ever been to Paris knows it."

"Sphinx?" asked the priest hesitantly.

"*Oui.* On the left behind the Gare du Montparnasse. You know where I mean, right?"

"I'm very sorry," sighed the priest, "but I don't know the Sphinx either."

"*Zût alors.* You've missed something. I figure there must be about fifty of them there, not stark naked of course, only half naked, that's the one disadvantage compared to the rue Blondel, *je l'admets.* But real young ones with bare boobs. Boobs, I tell you—*des seins formidables!*"

The priest said nothing.

"On the other hand it costs more than *numéro sept.* Around twice as much. But much more elegant; *beaucoup plus chic.* You dance on a glass floor with lighting underneath. *Sans faute,* it's worth the price."

The priest said nothing. About the eastern shore of Lago Bianco by a snow-lined pond rose the Ospizio. On the road below the pass a couple of mountain fusiliers trotted about chopping away patches of ice and strewing ashes. The priest took courage and whispered, "Sphinx? Where is that, Monsieur Bonjour? Behind the Gare du Montparnasse?"

"*Exactement, à la gauche.* You can't miss it. Go and try it, *monsieur le Curé.* You won't be sorry." Bonjour parked the giant limousine next to a swamp-green army truck and the priest shook his hand and smiled discreetly through the sliding glass.

"*Merci bien, Messieursdames,*" he called. "*Au revoir.*"

Miss Polari gave him a condescending wave and the priest shook hands again with Bonjour, who winked at him. Then he climbed out and put on a black billed cap, and I discovered to my amazement that what I had taken to be a soutane was really a livery jacket of shiny black material with covered buttons. He wore breeches and glossy polished knee boots in which he trudged over to a wine-red Citroën.

"Holy Laudon!" I exclaimed. "*Ecoutez,* what did you call that man?" I barked at Bonjour, who was opening the door for us. "Didn't you call him *monsieur le Curé?*"

The servant-chauffeur, a bit flabbergasted: "*Lecaure, c'est ça.*"

"Lec-a-u-ré?"

"*Mais oui, monsieur.*" He spelled out the name. "*Un copain de Genève.*"

"He's chauffeur for Tronchin, the Geneva banker," Pola commented as she got out.

"Hee!" my too shrill laugh.

"What are you laughing about?" asked Xana.

"I thought he was a priest."

"W-h-o?" squeaked Pola, her shaving brush blowing in the wind. "That chauffeur over there?"

"Hee, yes. The black coat, the high collar—it fooled me. But the funniest thing. . ." I broke off, unwilling to inform on Bonjour, who was about to help ten Breukaa over the running board.

"Hho-hho," he went; it sounded like a thin echo of a laugh. "A highly interesting case. First, you see a criminal Gauguin enthusiast breaking into my house. Second, you hear a pig squealing on the Diavolezza. Third, you confuse a chauffeur with a bishop, hho-hho-hho." He gave my shoulder a prim little slap. "You've been caught in the act, my dear friend." His jaundiced, scoffing glance rested fleetingly on my forehead. "Admit it now; you've been seeing ghosts."

"I'm seeing ghosts. I'm caught in the act. I'm seeing ghosts."

After a "collation"—Pola insisted on this technical term for lunch at the hospice—ten Breukaa revised the plan of our excursion (which was to have taken us down to Poschiavo) with the shabby excuse that the road over the pass was dangerously icy and that he had forgotten his cap and couldn't stand a draft on his bare head. He directed Bonjour to drive back to Acla Silva, and from there down to Soglio in the Bergell region.

Bonjour drove up to Acla Silva. The property was surrounded by a ditch and a six-foot-high wall built, like the house on the hill above it, of sienna brown brick. Ten Breukaa had us wait in the state limousine. Shortly after he disappeared into the house I watched the three open living-room windows that looked out on the gray alder trees and saw them being closed one by one. (Aha, the flea I had put in Joop's ear with my talk of the Mona Lisa affair *did* have its effect, despite all his sneering about my "seeing ghosts.") As he left the house dressed in his cream-colored travel cap the little spaniel shot out the door and plunged down the garden steps like a black flying carpet. At first annoyed, Joop called him back, then he changed his mind. After he had stopped on the little wooden bridge and carefully checked the lock on the wrought-iron gate (my flea!) he tried to convince us that he had returned to Acla Silva so that Sirio could take part in our little excursion.

After Maloja and the Maloja wind were behind us and we had spiraled down the four descending valleys of Bergell the growing compactness of the air caused such a liberating release of tension that I began to be annoyed by the gentle pressure of the Walther against my thigh. Our rapid descent into the Italian summer put color in the faces of my fellow passengers, a gleam in their eyes, even in Joop's as he pointed out the rune-like vestiges of the old Roman road. Just before Promontogno he pointed out a wildly romantic hilltop castle he called Castelmur.

"Castelmur? The castle we passed a while back near Stampa—didn't that have the same name?"

"That was the ancestral seat of the counts of Castelmur. This one originally belonged to the Colana family. Och zo, and there is supposed to be another castle of theirs in the Domleschg."

"That? the ancestral home of Avvocato Bow-Wow? A ruin is the ancestral home of a ruin!" I sensed an undertone of respect in Pola's joking. (No doubt she would invite the country lawyer for tea tomorrow.) Behind Promontogno the first walnut groves, fields of mulberry trees, cornfields and, sensation! the first vineyards and grape arbors. On either side, divided into neat squares by moss-covered stone walls, the freshly mown fields covered with haystacks. A sure sign for me: no hay-fever attack. No attack . . .

Then Joop suddenly suggested forgetting about Soglio and instead making a short excursion across the border to nearby Lake Como. He countered my first objection (that Xana and I would never get across with our invalid Austrian passports) by asserting it was just a quick hop across the border and his Dutch passport would do for everyone in the car. With peculiar stubbornness he insisted on his whim of "driving a little way into Italy." Although relieved of my irritating "*Qui-vive* complex" I flatly refused to set foot in the realm of *il Fascismo.* After some discussion we agreed that Xana and I would stroll up from the border town of Castasegna through the chestnut groves to Soglio where we would meet the ten Breukaas in the marketplace at eight o'clock.

Through the forest of Spanish chestnuts, Sirio always some distance ahead of us. A spacious forest of deciduous trees: *leaves,* leaves, not the blue green needles of the close-ranked stone pines, not the rust red spiderwebs of isolated larches, but sun-drenched leaves. In the dead leaves and underbrush Sirio rolls on his back and grunts deeply, blissfully, then jumps up, and round eyes sparkling beneath his thick black lashes, trots over to us, ceremoniously wreathed in brown. Then dashes off quite unceremoniously, out of sight. Somewhere in the distance his boyish, throaty, aggressive bark, his first bark since being sold by his brothers to Potiphar. We round a curve in the path. Sirio, not without a certain *grandezza,* is barking at a herd of coal-black goats grazing in a small clearing, a herd watched over by a wrinkled old hag dressed entirely in black. She laughs silently at Sirio but hardly looks at us; the old fairy-tale witch—she is knitting something—maybe a magic stocking to cure gout.

A very small cemetery on the edge of the great chestnut forest, somewhat off to the side of the path snaking up toward Soglio, surrounded by a rectangle of moss-covered, crumbling wall just higher than a man. The gate, a bent and rusted set of bars, is standing wide open. No more than twenty paces across, that's how small it is. And out of use—not a single grave, not a single trace of a grave. Only weeds, moss, and two wild elder-bushes. All the plaster has long since crumbled from the inner wall except for a shapeless white spot with the barely visible vestiges of an old fresco. A portion of a child's leg in weathered pink hovering over the fragment of a mauve-colored cloud; above this a hint of ocher angel's wing. The centuries-old, happy little ghost of a fresco.

116

"This would make a good resting place."

"Thinking about dying, Trebla?" (Somewhat mockingly.)

"Why do you say that?!"

"Because you'd like to be buried here. I never think where I'll be buried. Never. I couldn't care less."

"Who said anything about being buried?"

"You. 'This would make a good resting place.'"

"I was trying to say, this would make a good *camping* place."

"Ah, I see."

"Come on, let's take a break here." I throw my cape on the moss (Xana has left her coat in the car). "Let's drink our Nebiolo here." At a grotto in the border town I had bought a bottle of red Piedmontese Spumante.

"Do you want to get drunk on somebody's grave?"

"There hasn't been a grave here for over a hundred years, look. Anyway, if somebody wanted to get drunk on *my* grave it would be just fine with me."

"Cut out all this grave talk."

"Yessir-ma'am." The neck of the bottle is draped with shiny red paper like a champagne bottle. As I tear it off and unwind the wire securing the two tin cork-retainers I can't help thinking: this is something like pulling the pin on a hand grenade.

The shaking the Nebiolo bottle received on the walk up from Castasegna through the warm cisalpine summer afternoon (so unlike the Engadine) has built up an amazing amount of pressure. Unexpectedly. The cork shoots out like a bullet and seven-tenths of a liter of highly carbonated red Piedmontese wine (alas, almost all of it!) gushes out onto Xana's snow-white blouse.

"Thank you. Very nice of you."

Her reaction irritates me all the more because it contains not a trace of irritation.

"Nice of you to serve me the Nebiolo in such a charming way."

"Sorrysorry, I feel terrible, but, but the compression from the heat, we should have cooled it off, maybe back at the waterfall, Caroggia or whatever it's called." I raise the bottle; at the bottom of it a small pool of Nebiolo sparkles in the sun.

"That quantity can't hurt me."

"Of course not."

"Although Tardueser got rather angry when I told him I had drunk so much Antinori at Pizzagalli's that I had to be carried piggyback—"

"You went to see Tardueser again?"

"Ye-es."

"Day before yesterday you went to see h-i-m in the pouring rain?"

"Ye-es."

"And this, this tourist healer thought it was all right for you to go out in the cold rain?"

"Ye-es."

"But he got mad about you having a few glasses of wine?"

"Ye-es."

She takes the bottle out of my hand, places it on her lips and, like a trooper, bends back and empties it, then flings it over the wall with unexpected verve.

"Anyway your Piedmontese compression was a complete success. Just look at me."

"Holy Laudon, that's a pity," I say, my voice full of pity (or pretending to be). "Your shiny white blouse looks like a raspberry batik. Take it off and we'll hang it on the elder-bush to dry."

She glances around: "Am I supposed to . . . *here?*"

"If you slipped off your tunic on *my* grave—"

"Just please cut out all this grave business, Kukulaps. I'm getting sick and tired of it."

"Me too."

Through the gaping iron gate—which really is beyond being merely bent and rusted and looks more like a tattered spider web—comes Sirio, ears flying. He stops, looks, sees us, waddles straight over to us and sniffs at Xana's white sandals.

"Look! Even my shoes"—she's not wearing stockings—"have got that raspberry stuff on them."

The cocker spaniel sniffs as if slightly surprised; sneezes in delight; looks up and smiles at us. Unlike horses, dogs can smile. (But unlike dogs, horses can laugh.) I say, "That's right boy, how nice it is to sniff a little spilled wine again, right? Never get a chance to do that at ten Breukaa's, do you?"

Sirio smiles. He waddles out of the onetime cemetery, gives us a meaningful backward glance from the spiderweb gate that says, Don't worry, I'm guarding the door. Cautiously Xana unbuttons her long tunic-blouse; I take it off like a trained coat-checker and stretch it over the elder-bush to dry. To dry the dye beneath the sky. In the wink of an eye. Perhaps the sun in the Italian sky (still hot after five o'clock) will dry the dye in the wink of an eye.

"No! No!! *No!!* You really . . . liquored me up from head to foot. Externally I mean. That one swallow was nothing. Even my bra is soaking wet."

"Take it off. The dye will be dry in the wink of an eye."

"And my skirt t-o-o! That Nebiolo soaked right through my tunic."

"Take it off. The sky will dry the dye in the wink of an eye."

"What are you mumbling? N-o!" She has opened the zipper of her skirt. "Even my panties got it! *Quidquid agis, prudenter agas ac respice finem.*"

"The end, yes I'd say so. Let's have it all. Don't be shy. The sky will dry the dye in the wink of an eye."

"Have you got sunstroke, Trebla?" Slowly she steps out of her skirt, bends her lily white arms behind her back, unhooks her white brassiere (with a delicate lacy pattern), slips off her white panties (of the same material) along with her sandals, her last "articles of clothing." Steps into my loden cape, stands with her

118

back to me, her arms crossed in front of her bosom while I play coat-checker and decorate the elder-bush like a Christmas tree.

She loosens the knot of her violet blue silk headband and lets it flutter onto the moss.

"To stand here dressed *only* in a scarf would be obscene." Vigorously she shakes her cloud of hazel-nut-brown hair. A few minutes later, up from the valley of Chiavenna comes the distant cling-clang—hardly to be called bell-ringing—of a campanile, swinging through a whole octave in its beguiling, sleepy, secret melody full of so many halting ritardandi. Like atonal, almost twelve-tone music, sometimes sounding like the cling-clang-clong of a xylophone player improvising in his sleep.

"Ah, a campanile."

". . . are you laughing at me?"

"Not at you. I'm just thinking of the translation tip you gave me yesterday. Oh. Oh campanile-oh-campanile. Aren't you afraid that . . . that we might get arrested for desecrating a cemetery—?"

"I already told you. This little place has been out of service for a long time. Retired. Obsolete. Besides, I've got a lot of experience at getting arrested. Nobody will catch us here. Want to bet?"

"I'll never make the mistake of betting with you again. But really, what if somebody comes by?"

"Sirio will start barking right away."

"All right, come on. But be gentle with me today."

"Gentle? All of a sudden you seem to think I'm a real ogre. How come?"

"Because I asked you to."

"What kind of an answer is that?"

"No answer. Just be a little careful, okay?"

"Xana, since when are you made of glass?"

"What a godforsaken hole! A real robber's den," whispered Miss Polari as she looked about with an air of naïve horror at the pine-paneled dining room of the Chesetta Grischuna, its fortress windows hung with faded, mended, gingham curtains. Her wide-staring, thrill-thirsty eyes shone darkly in the light of the single weak bulb inside the rustic wrought-iron lamp hanging from the low ceiling.

A gust of wind blew with a sound like distant thunder through the chimney of the massive tiled stove in which, today, no fire was crackling.

"A real murderer's den . . ."

I gazed over at Men Clavadetscher's marksmanship trophies. They gleamed dimly behind the glass of the wall case, on top of which the stuffed woodchuck still sat erect.

"A murderer's den," I added obligingly. "You may just have hit the nail right on the head."

"Don't kid around, I'm really scared!" swore Miss Polari. "Why Trebla had to drag us off here for dinner, of all places, here by the Fex Valley in the middle of nowhere..."

"Was it bad, the dinner?"

Ten Breukaa aimed his nose at the heavy plate that Bonjour, in the absence of the proprietor, was about to remove from the table. "Graubuenden home cooking," he grumbled.

"And the Valtellina?"

"Too fiery. I prefer my own brand, Grumello."

The sliding door rattled upward. Teresina Clavadetscher, daughter of a shepherd from Bergamo—bone of contention between two brothers, one of whom lay in the Sils graveyard with a hole in his head, victim of an ill-starred woodchuck hunt—Teresina Clavadetscher placed five thick-walled cups filled with foamy-warm, Marsala-laced Zabaione on the sideboard. Bonjour, who, by dessert time, had finished his dinner in the kitchen, set four cups on the table and held the fifth awkwardly in his hand.

"One serving too many," Pola remarked. "*C'est à vous, Jean?*"

"*Bien sur, madame,*" mumbled the man from Vaud, turning to replace his cup on the tray.

With a polite "*Mais prenez place*" I had him sit down at the next table. It was set very close to ours; so it happened that the servant-chauffeur began spooning his Zabaione not far from Pola Polari. She gave me a horrified glance, then stared expectantly at her husband. But Joop, with an almost ceremonious fussiness, had begun stuffing his pipe. Once again a wind gust evoked muffled thunder in the stovepipe.

"Jeezus, Jeezus," hissed Pola, distracted. For her the slovenly Teresina, loitering with hands on hips behind the sliding window, did not exist.

"*Buono—il Zabaion'?*"

"*Molto gustoso,*" I praised the hostess. "*Come va il bambino?*"

Her gap-toothed smile: "*Grazie, signore. Bene, bene.*"

And how was her *marito*, I asked incidentally.

"*Bene, bene.*" He'd just gone out with the *camion;* delivering a load of wood to Samedan.

With a side-glance at Sirio I asked a third casual question. Ever since we had entered the room the young Spaniel could hardly cease sniffing the floors and benches, oblivious to Joop's reprimands and uninterested in the sausage rind I tried to tempt him with. Had, I asked Signora Clavadetscher, Doctor de Colana turned up in the Chesetta Grischuna since our last visit together?

"*Questa sera.*" This evening he had come with his whole *circo di cani* and had left only *una piccola mezz'ora* before we arrived.

He had probably *bevuto bastante,* drunk a fair amount, hm?

"*Si, si, bastante.*" With a strange sensuous-melodic giggle Teresina drew back into the kitchen.

Bonjour stood up, removed the cups and left the room, giving me an obvious wink.

"I'm afraid we'll have to invite him to tea tomorrow," announced Pola.

Ten Breukaa drew on his pipe. "Who? Bonjour?"

"Ha, Trebla hasn't made me a Socialist yet, even though he just made the chauffeur my table partner. No, I mean Dr. de Colana."

Old snob, I thought.

After we had met the Italian returnees as planned in Soglio: the palazzo of the patrician family de Colana, a nobly weathered Renaissance palace, obviously uninhabited, seemed to have impressed Pola even more than the ruins of the family castle. Result: In her eyes the country lawyer had automatically qualified for high society. The Salis Palazzo had been remodeled into a restaurant, and Joop had expressed his intention to eat dinner there. Following Pola's objection that Xana in her sullied condition was in no shape to visit a better establishment, I had suggested the Chesetta as an alternative. Now the wind thundered once more in the stovepipe as Pola pressed Joop, "Come on and pay so we can get out of this haunted house," and I remembered suddenly that other hushed, deceptive sound that I, and the dogs as well, had heard as it rustled down from the top of the massive tiled stove . . . Today it was not de Colana who sat leaning against it, but Xana. De Colana was absent. Until an hour ago he had been reveling here with his pack of dogs and then, no doubt, had driven home. Xana was absent too, really. On the drive back up the mountain road she had slipped further and further out of the present—something I had seen her do several times in recent days. The Chesetta Grischuna, which had inspired Pola to her performance of girlish jitters, left Xana apathetic to the point of drowsiness. But despite her trancelike state she had shown an unusual appetite for the Graubuenden home cooking, without, however, touching a single drop of Valtellina and without smoking her usual after-dinner cigarette.

"W-e-l-l-l . . . let's go-o-o kids," she said in long, lazy tones. "I'm a bit drow-w-wsy . . ."

Bonjour had parked the Austro-Daimler on the meadow in front of the house. With great white headlights probing powerfully ahead, lighting up sections of the dark pine forest, he drove up to the door.

"Cool," said Xana slowly and sleepily. "C-o-o-o-l . . . ti-i-i-red . . ." and let me button up her coat collar.

Teresina hadn't seen us to the door; from the depths of the barren-dismal hallway echoed the whining cries of a baby. Then from somewhere the melodic voice of the farmer's wife called through the wind, "*Buona notsch!*"

As Bonjour drove the limousine away from the house we met a truck growling up from the village below. Before Jean could dim them, the powerful headlights struck the front of the oncoming vehicle. Behind the windshield of the driver's cab two red eyes flared up like cigars burning side by side in the dark. As we drew closer I could see they were the eyes of a St. Bernard sitting beside the driver.

Bonjour let the horn's pompous chord blast pizzicato. Whining along in first gear, the oncoming *camion* steered to the side. A fleeting glimpse as we passed by in semidarkness was not enough to allow me to recognize the driver. But I was sure it was Clavadetscher, the owner of Chesetta Grischuna.

Behind me Miss Polari gave out a suppressed cry: "Terr-rible! Did you see his *eyes?* Flame red!"

"Sorry, but those were his dog's eyes, not his. He had his St. Bernard sitting next to him, a gigantic beast. By the way—hee!—this Mr. Clava——actually does have, ah, reddish albino eyes."

"What'd I tell you? They were *his!* Jeezus, Trebla, I think you took us to the *devil's* place for dinner! Joop, hold on to me, I'm going to have a heart attack!"

The big, heavy car rode before the wind. Yes, the mountain wind assailed us once again, this time not in front of us, but from behind. As if it were beneath his dignity to be rushed by it, Bonjour maintained a steady speed of 35 mph. The wrought-iron railing posts along the shoreline moved toward us, sharply outlined in the powerful headlights. Through Silvaplana. A few blurred lights behind drawn curtains. A well-lit though abandoned hotel vestibule announced that the off-season would soon be at an end. Past. Marshland, then the shoreline road of Lake Campfèr.

Above the Rosatsch sailed a very pallid, green-tinged moon, rather egg-shaped as it began to wane. Beneath it endless rafts of cloud drifted to the northeast. Their swift procession made the shapeless moon seem to be sailing rapidly southwestward, appearing and disappearing as it plunged through banks of clouds. Once obscured in darkness and before it reappeared the moon sent a magic emerald glow flickering over the tattered edges of the clouds, and the lake-mountain landscape brightened and dimmed in the restless fluctuation of the light.

It was quiet in the car. With hardly a curve, the shoreline road ran on toward Campfèr. The closed windows began to steam up from the body heat of the passengers, and I, seated beside Joop on the front folding seat nearest the lake, rubbed the window with my sleeve and stared out fascinated at the ghostly glint of moonlight playing across the choppy water.

A larch tree along the shoreline road interrupted the procession of iron posts. It flitted past and then I saw it, the light in the lake.

Convinced by a sudden ticking signal in my forehead I asked Bonjour to stop. Joop objected immediately. He wanted to go home. I had obviously been fooled by a reflection of the moonlight. I countered immediately that the moonlight now, just look, was a greenish color, while the light I had noticed was a strange reddish glow that flickered out across the lake from somewhere near the shore, ghostlike, you might say. Miss Polari, in the back seat, sitting in a triumphantly maternal pose with the half-slumbering Xana in her arms, took it for a fisherman's lamp from Campfèr. Which I very much doubted in view of the high wind. Joop clung to his theory, moon reflection, and finally even Xana went against my wish to stop by mumbling at me in her deep, sleep-heavy voice, "Al'ert . . . Kuku'aps . . . Let's g'ome."

After passing thrugh Campfèr Bonjour did not turn down de Colana's racecourse to the spa, but instead steered up through the Suvretta Forest, past Pizzagalli's Sporthotel to Acla Silva, where the green Biedermeier lantern on the roof of the bridge gate greeted us as if being waved by a railroad stationmaster. With a restrained sigh of satisfaction Joop noted the brightly lit, closed-curtained front of his manor house (no doubt he'd instructed cook Uorschletta to display such extravagant illumination). He pulled his cashmere scarf out of the pocket of the car door.

"Bonjour has had a hard day's driving. Therefore, Trebla, you may have the Chrysler to drive home to Pontresina. Bonjour will pick it up tomorrow morning. *Gelt?*"

In the back seat an intense, female whispering that ended in a decisive "No!" by Miss Polari. "Xana dear doesn't feel so good. I insist they stay overnight with us."

Ten Breukaa seemed agreeable. As he said good-bye to Bonjour in his clumsy Dutch-French I helped Xana out of the car. "You don't feel good?"

She hung limply on my arm. The cold night wind blew rushing through the alder trees of Acla Silva and made her scarf flutter. Her upturned face, unusually pale in the "flashing" moonlight, was shaped by the thought of something, by a little smile that squeezed her eyes to shadowy slits. Then she whispered darkly, scarcely moving her lips, "No, Kometishek, I don't feel so good. But it's hardly anything, really. Maybe it's a very good thing that I don't feel so good. A very good thing."

"That's still the effect of her bronchitis," Pola interrupted. "Uphill and downhill and all that change in altitude; it's been too much for the poor child. Now let's trundle her off to bed and tomorrow our little *beauté* will be as fit as a fiddle."

Bonjour said, "*Bonne nuit, messieursdames,*" and Joop said, "*Bonne nuit, Bonjour*" and took Sirio on a shortened leash up to the covered bridge, opened the special lock on the iron gate and waited until the three of us had passed through, then locked it again with great care. I hoisted Xana up the stone steps, afraid she might fall asleep in my arms, unable to let her know what was on my mind, and Pola unlocked the front door and took Xana away from me.

I waited for ten Breukaa between the burning candelabra by the door, still wearing my cape, annoyed by a constant, gentle ticking in my forehead.

He came up the stone steps and let Sirio loose. "March!" The young cocker spaniel waddled sleepily into the house.

"Joop," I said, "I have to take you at your word. Let me borrow the cabriolet."

4

Ten Breukaa seemed rather surprised. "You want to drive to Pontresina alone? I thought you were going to stay overnight with us."

"With pleasure, thanks very much. All I want to do is take a quick jaunt out to Campfèr and back."

"To Campfèr? A quick jaunt? Now? Haven't you had enough driving around for one day?"

"Lend me the Chrysler for half an hour?" I parried with another question, disguising my rising impatience in forced friendliness.

He stood between the milk-glass candelabra. Under the brim of his cap his now pointless sunglasses glittered at me like something from a masquerade. "Och zo. You want to take another look at that light in the lake. That natural phenomenon. Or rather, I should say, that product of your overstimulated imagination." His choice of phrase seemed to please him. In a pose of self-satisfied indulgence he strode through the vestibule, opened the glass double-door to the gaily lit living room where the Spahi's red trousers gleamed from the wall, and pointed to the painting. "*Voilà*. I suggest we indulge in a whiskey soda before going to bed. That will settle your nerves."

"Please call me a taxi then."

"Omm. Let's recapitulate. First you want to convince me that my *Spahi* might have been stolen. Then you hear a horrible scream from the glacier, a scream nobody else can hear. Then—"

"—I confuse a chauffeur with a priest, then I refuse to risk a trip to Mussolini-land because I imagine somebody might arrest me, then I get obsessed with a will-o'-the-wisp in Lake Campfèr, IknowIknow. Joop, will you lend me the cabriolet or not?"

Ten Breukaa pulled the front door shut. Began walking down through the rock garden, wordlessly jingling his key chain. Once more we passed the bridge under the swaying lantern and he locked the garden gate behind us, tugged his cashmere scarf over his chin and walked down the road with me against the wind, my cape flapping, his hand gripping the brim of his cap; our steps were barely audible in the stormy rustling of the alder trees, steps something like the rolling gait that sailors have. For not just the treetops, everything was swaying or seemed to sway on this restless, bleached-green, pallid moonlit night, even the ominously close, black-sparkling Rosatsch Massif, above which the egg-shaped moon flitted in and out of the racing banks of cloud, and even the naked light bulb on ten Breukaa's garage, though firmly mounted, was swaying, and so was the lighted window over the garage door. My companion unlocked the double door that was caught by the wind, throwing both sides of it open with a loud groan.

Bonjour's torso, clothed in a white shirt, leaned swaying over the window-sill.

"Tout va bien, Bonjour," Joop shouted up to him, and his voice, overwhelmed by the wind, had something of the quality of a baby's wailing. "*Allez vous coucher!*" He switched on the light in the two-car enclosure and, without a word, handed me the ignition key. I squeezed past the massive Austro-Daimler and into the cabriolet, backed it out of the garage to Joop's croaking admonitions, "Careful. More to the left! Stay to the *left* . . .!"

"I always stay to the left, as a matter of principle," I tried joking casually to conceal my agitation. "My humble thanks for loaning me the car." But ten Breukaa, after locking the garage door, unexpectedly got in beside me and pulled a pair of fur-lined gloves out of the door pocket.

"You're coming along, Joop?"

"I'm coming along to see that you drive safely and to see that you admit it."

"That I'm admitted? To an asylum?"

"To see that you adm-i-t i-t. That you've been seeing ghosts."

Soon I was driving down along the lake to the village.

"Even our lake has lights in it tonight. Optical illusions everywhere." Joop exhibited his dry sarcasm.

I glanced briefly to the side and saw Lake Moritz "swaying." This still, deep body of water that otherwise lay like a placid eye beneath the brow of the Mauntschas. Even though the waves were not capped with white the water still drove oceanlike toward our shore, and on the crests of the waves glinted the moon's pale green flashing and fading, a ghostlike sparkle and glitter.

The wind blew through the railroad viaduct with a muffled boom like a tuba, and through the Posthotel's "Bridge of Sighs" like the distant howls of a moon-struck gang of tomcats.

"Say, Trebla, didn't somebody call out?"

"Nope, that was just the Maloja wind, as they call it. Anyway the Suvretta Forest is protecting the town. When we get beyond it, closer to Campfèr, it's going to be even less pleasant."

"Yes, but—you're not driving to Campfèr at all. Where are you headed, anyway?"

"Be patient for five minutes, Joop."

The main street of the village was swept clean of any signs of life and swayed in the light of three hanging lamps. No bats were darting around them. Through the short street past the blacked-out police station, past the prematurely darkened corner café of Benedetg Caduff-Bonnard. The schoolhouse square, set as it was against the mountainside, was fairly well shielded from the gale; thus the play of light and shadow across its surface seemed all the more ghostly. The bells of the Protestant church, whose sound contained something of a distant howling noise, struck eleven as I drove up to the country lawyer's house.

The blemished white facade glowed as if phosphorescent in the flashes of cold moonlight. Not a shimmer of light behind its barred fortress windows. I jumped from the driver's seat, ran to the massive front door, and without hesitating, pushed on the cold metal handle. Locked. I grasped the icy knocker, the worn, wrought-iron form in the shape of a peacock's tail. My knocking echoed hollowly inside. I listened hard for some sound from the interior. Nothing.

Several times I struck iron against iron. Listened. Nothing. Then another knocker began to function: the one on my forehead.

Joop had remained in the car. "... Didn't you just hear whining?"

"Dogs whining?" I asked electrified.

"Presumably dogs whining," he nagged. "Cows rarely whine."

I listened. Banged off another salvo with the knocker ... "Wait a minute!" Now I *did* hear something. An irregular, dull, very brief whining coming from the back of the house. With fluttering cape around the corner, over cobblestones, then over gravel—I was inside de Colana's neglected terrace garden. The whining had stopped.

There stood the two rain-bleached garden dwarfs; they too seemed to sway in the wild spasms of light and dark. I tried to orient myself with them. Here, this deep-set, shadowy window fronted with bowed-out bars had to be the country lawyer's bedroom window. Above it a coat of arms in sgraffito, its colored plaster long since washed away. Still, one could just make out the heraldic animal, a spread-tailed peacock. In this light the scratched-out emblem seemed more like the *skeleton* of a peacock.

"De Colana! ... *Dottore!* ... Gaudenz! ..." Then I called the names of the spaniel pack as well as I could remember them. Collected pebbles and began throwing them with no great caution into the deep window-cavity. In the pauses between throws and shouts I waited for the slightest whine, growl, or bark—I *longed* to hear something. But there was only the roaring of the wind as it strayed, somewhat subdued, through the yard of the house. In the house everything remained silent.

I turned and saw the two phosphorescent garden dwarfs, and it looked as if they were grinning slightly in their dun-colored beards, not about me, but about a private joke, a perfectly confidential little secret. Then a brief whine close at hand made me turn around. In an adjoining building, in the shadow of a deep, tunnel-like archway, a double door. One of the ponderous doors was open wide, and swung slowly on its hinges from time to time: the whining sound. I groped my way inside, struck a match that went out immediately. But I smelled the

126

cold odor of gasoline. De Colana's garage. It was empty.

Through the Suvretta Forest, which was one great, furious roaring, through Campfèr. As we passed a massive barn on the way out of the village a door slammed shut. Like a shot fired after us. Along the marshland whose bluish surface was swept by a wind that charged toward us with a hundred galloping phantom carriages, the shadows of the clouds. Then Lake Campfèr.

Here the waves that rolled past us along the road had emerald crests of foam, as if a piece of the South Sea night had been magically transported to the mountain valley. The moon's reflections, constantly erased and revived by the chasing clouds, created an unnatural brightness like that produced by magnesium flares. How could anyone, on such a blinding-flashing night, search for *one* light in the lake? Of course, a fool in the advanced stages of a post-traumatic disturbance whipped up by the brutality of current events to the point of hallucination. But the country lawyer's dead-quiet house, his empty garage? What if he had returned to Sils Baseglia and was carousing in the company of his spaniel family?

There was the lonely larch tree standing by the shore, bent like a gigantic bow beneath the blowing storm. I braked, steered the cabriolet onto the mountain side of the highway where I discovered emerging from the forest a narrow road that I had overlooked before.

"That leads up to the Orchas," ten Breukaa was able to tell me.

"You want to wait in the car?" I yelled.

"I came along to rid you of your delusions, Trebla! Your *delusions!*"

Joop was obviously pleased to be able to use this word. He climbed out of the car like a ghostly scarecrow, his cap pulled low over his eyes—which he had shielded behind his black-sparkling sunglasses—his cashmere scarf bundled around his mouth; his scrawny pointed nose was all that remained of his face. Leaning against the wind we groped straining across the highway that stretched lifeless in both directions, as barren and bonelike as the Cimmerian shore Odysseus had seen. My cape fluttered wildly about me; Joop's traveling cap swelled up like the bulbous caps that caricaturists once used to symbolize the Social Democrats. On ten Breukaa, of all people, I thought; then I forgot he was there.

The unbroken procession of railing posts was interrupted by the larch tree. From its trunk to the next post a sizable length of the highway lay unprotected. Here and there cascades of silvery spray struck the barren road. A new flash of light revealed that the bark of the tree was carved up as if by careless ax blows.

Holding onto the wet tree trunk I clambered down onto the narrow shoreline ledge as ice-cold splashes of spray soaked my face, then I let go of the tree and crouched on all fours on the slippery ledge so as not to fall into the sea (what am I saying, just an Alpine lake), and my vision was impeded by tears of spray that drowned my air supply, and the spray was hurled at me again and again until finally my ears were better able to detect it than my eyes—the sniffing, whining and yowling of a hundred voices, like the cries from a canine hell.

The clouds were torn open. The moon threw down a broad, wavering bridge of light upon me, but no more than ten yards from where I crouched something like a blunted peak rose up out of the water, glinting like metal, washed over again and again by spray. Then the clouds concealed the moon completely and threw my vantage point into sudden darkness.

Then I saw it again, the light in the lake.

Two reddish underwater beams of light having nothing to do with the reflections of the stormy moon stabbed slantwise toward the shoreline where I stood and were reflected back across themselves to reveal an image obscured every few seconds by the boiling surf and constantly distorted like an accordion in action.

A crashed limousine underwater . . . one corner of the top projecting aslant from the waves . . . closed windows, through which a lifeless, twisted, shadowy thing was visible against the steering wheel . . . the pear-shaped skull, unmistakable . . . around which numerous woolly giant flounders swam lazily . . . hardly recognizable as drowned cocker spaniels . . .

. . . a grisly, monstrous aquarium.

The Morse code of my heartbeat ticked away on my forehead, drowning out the Maloja wind. This unreality was horribly real. It had happened.

At my furious waving ten Breukaa had ventured down onto the ledge with me. His sunglasses shattered on the wet rocks. With an iron grip his fingers sought a desperate handhold on my cape.

"*Chodverdomme* . . .!" he croaked. "*Chodverdomme!*"

5

Not yet eighteen years old, Konstantin Giaxa reported for duty as a one-year voluntary cannoneer in the Thirteenth Imperial Artillery Regiment Prince von Lobkowitz at Agram. Captain of his battery: Wenzel Hrubasky.

Anyone so unfortunate as to come near Wenzel Hrubasky was sure to get acquainted with the Provost Marshal. Eighty days of arrest were the order of the day, randomly distributed among eighty one-year volunteers—almost always the maximum allowed. You served your sentence sitting on a plank bed in a flea-ridden cubbyhole; "solitary" was rotated to a new prisoner every day: six hours in shackles with your right arm chained to your left ankle.

(From Giaxa's memoirs *Clown on Horseback*)

No matter how hard he pestered Kosto, the Captain could not, a year later, prevent him from being sent to Graz for the reserve officers' examination, from which he emerged in the top rank as a "One Year Voluntary Platoon Leader, Titular Artificer, pre-selected to be evaluated for transfer to duty as a regular officer." Nevertheless, Hrubasky sabotaged his promotion to second lieutenant by rating him "qualified" instead of "very qualified." So Kosto took leave and went to see Janko Peyatchevich, his father's former commander. Who put in a good word for him with two cousins of his in Vienna, Field Marshal Count Uexkuell-Gyllenband and a suffragan bishop ("ex-killer Guilty-hand and a suffering bishop"). Under such patronage the corporal's son advanced to the rank of artillery lieutenant at the same time Captain Hrubasky was promoted to major.

Major Hrubasky, slave-driver, bullet-eater and ball-buster, senile at forty-seven, with a short, reddish gray full beard designed to cover his goiter, a bulbous drunkard's nose (by no means a result of intemperance), a booming voice that soared to a high falsetto shriek, in short, an insufferable jackass.

After the imperial maneuvers at Belovar, Lieutenant Giaxa left the artillery for the cavalry and soon won his first two races on the Sisak Heath; his chestnut gelding Gad was victorious in the steeplechase at Chakovek. After numerous "affaires d'amour et d'honneur" he fell in love with a heroine of the Burgtheater, who was doing a guest performance in Agram. After driving her around the fortress all night in a four-horse carriage he resolved, firmly and unshakably, to marry her. Officers of the Imperial Forces who desired to marry actresses had to obtain permission from the highest authority. When he was finally ordered to Vienna for an audience, the famous lady had forgotten all about the little lieutenant from the Balkan garrison. Yet he had no choice but to put on his full-dress uniform, march into the Hofburg and present some abstruse petition to the old—even then old—Emperor. (The petition dealt with the exploration of the sea bottom around the island of Hvar.)

The aides-de-camp had informed me that I could address the emperor in military fashion with the words "your obedient servant" or in the courtly manner with "your most humble servant"; at the conclusion of the audience I could either do a soldierly about-face or walk backwards (civilians being required to perform three bows) toward the door, which would then be opened by the royal attendants.

Lieutenant Giaxa addressed the Emperor—who had posed stiffly, head inclined to the right, through several hours of morning audiences—as his "obedient servant," but withdrew in the courtly manner (as a soldier, without having to bow), whereby both his eight-pointed spurs became imbedded in the sliding door: the royal attendants had opened it too late.

Now, under the stony gaze of the monarch, he had to be lifted up and extricated from the door.

Suddenly the motionless Emperor could be heard to utter something like a brief cough.

"His Majesty seems to have a slight cold," one of the attendants whispered to the unfortunate petitioner after the door finally separated him from the august presence.

But Giaxa knew. The old fellow had laughed.

His frustration in love embittered him to further service in the Agram garrison, so he had himself transferred to the Imperial School for Instructors of Riding, Driving, and Fencing in Wiener Neustadt as the youngest instructor. "May God go with you," growled Major Hrubasky in farewell. Since it was a habit of his to repeat his orders word for word, Giaxa blared, "Yes sir! May God go with me!" Hrubasky's gaze was muddy ice.

During the next summer it came to pass that a uniformed rider jumped his mount across the ivy hedge of the Eisvogel café in Vienna's Prater and crowned his leap with a rearing *levade* amidst the frightened screams—soon followed by wild applause—of the guests, among whom was a certain Mr. Ratay, brother of the Budapest circus director. "Lieutenant, if you should ever happen to leave the service, come and see us," said the illustrious circus man. "Ratay will make you one of his star attractions!" Giaxa trotted, pensively grinning, out of the Praterau.

Later he returned to his regiment as a first lieutenant. Wenzel Hrubasky was still a major. The gap between the two had narrowed, a circumstance Hrubasky found unforgivable. Meanwhile a consumptive schoolmaster had taken up lodgings in an upstairs room of his old quarters, and Giaxa occasionally discussed Lucian with the old gentleman. One night when a drunken mob of officers with their hired band of gypsy violinists reeled singing and fiddling up to the house, the rudely awakened professor voiced from the window his fervent wish that the whole mercenary pack might proceed directly to the underworld.

Any officer, when insulted by word or deed in the presence of a third party, must promptly avenge this wrong with his sidearm.

Equipped with such an honor code, the senior captain among the drunkards drew his saber. But Giaxa rushed to restrain him and advised the terrified schoolmaster to make an immediate apology. Which the latter, stuttering, was only too happy to deliver. The affair appeared settled, but had given Major Hrubasky the longed-for opportunity to convene a regimental board of honor. A "preliminary inquiry" was initiated against First Lieutenant Konstantin Giaxa for hindering his comrade in the "defense of his honor." Giaxa "behaved like a clown before the Board of Honor," was removed from active service and placed in the reserves. Wenzel Hrubasky appeared to have won.

Twenty months later a cavalry captain who had just spent several days' leave in Budapest returned to Agram, and laughingly told his comrades in the casino about a brand-new, widely acclaimed attraction appearing nightly at the Circus Ratay, a clown on horseback who called himself "Obristi Obraski." The performer wore an illuminated pomegranate nose the size of a fist, a great, bright red moustache that hung down over an enormous goiter, an oversized saber and a fantastic uniform, which with its shako crowned by a yard-long plume of black horsehair, its coffee-brown tunic and sky-blue knickers, bore a striking resemblance to the uniform of the Thirteenth Artillery Regiment Lobkowitz. Swaggering gravely toward his horse, he stumbled over his saber with such vehemence that he bounced with a somersault into the saddle and bellowed with a voice like a bassoon until his goiter (a rubber balloon) burst. His props were hidden in the saddlebags of his Lippizan stallion: a trumpet, various kinds of headgear, and uniform pieces for various ranks. He was not only the "Obristi," but also his staff trumpeter who sounded the attack so blunderingly that the Obristi flew into a rage. He was a mounted gunner who, instead of a cannon blast, produced nothing but the ringing of an alarm clock. He was cannoneer, corporal, lieutenant, captain, major and colonel all wrapped into one, and he not only accomplished the miracle of "chewing himself out" in a voice ranging from a bassoon staccato to a tuba-like boom, he even managed the illusionist's trick of standing at attention in front of himself.

In all his slapstick stunts and acrobatic tricks he showed himself a consummate equestrian, absolutely first rank, worthy of Vienna's Spanish Riding Academy. The captain from Agram had no doubt. It must have been Kosto Giaxa. But after the performance when he had tried to find out the clown's real name and had asked to speak to him, he had despite loud protestations, been refused on both counts.

Major Hrubasky nearly had heart failure when he heard about it. He screamed bloody murder all the way up to the Ministry of War. But it was hardly possible to throw a reservist out of the army just because he had become a circus performer. Even the name, that absurd bowdlerization of "Obrist" (the outmoded German word for "colonel"): "Obristi Obraski" (which was later immortalized as a kind of trademark like Grock's "No-can-do" or the Rivel Brothers' "Bee-yootiful Acrobat")—this name was hardly illegal. For Wenzel Hrubasky, whose person was so fantastically satirized in the Giaxa number, was no colonel, but had remained a major (notwithstanding the promotion he received at the hands of Ratay's clown). Nevertheless the board of honor decreed the following reprimand: demotion.

Kosto, who had moved to Munich—in those days a bastion of artistic freedom—and was now doing the lead number "Giaxa & Giaxa" in the Circus Krone, got wind of the matter from one of his old Lobkowitz comrades. When the reprimand notice reached him via registered letter he cleverly refused to accept it. The Ministry of War bombarded him with twenty registered letters.

Twenty times he refused delivery. Finally, with the help of time-honored Austrian negligence, the document sank beneath the bureaucratic dust. But no matter how loudly Giaxa ridiculed the run-down black and yellow barracks, they had been his home, reeking of horse urine, soldiers' sweat, and Tokay wine, and resounding with Gypsy violins and the carping of nasal voices—a home that he had spun inside a web of hate-love, much professional mockery, and a bit of sentimental affection.

The Baroness Elsabé von Hahnspor-Fermin was born in the Czar's Baltic province of Livonia on her family's estate Tiflisana. Her grandfather on her mother's side, General Vladimir Fedorovich Fermin, had served the Czar as governor of Transcaucasia-Georgia in Tiflis, where he had married a local girl. Georgian women are famous for their beauty; even in her old age Elsabé's grandmother was as pretty as a picture, and rather eccentric too. When the retired general died at an advanced age she concealed the death and burial with elaborate care and moved into the Fermin's town house in Dorpat without telling a soul that she was a widow, and had her husband stuffed. That is, his general's coat with its board-stiff epaulets. She set his service cap atop a rolled feather-comforter protruding from the collar and placed the dummy in a wing chair facing away from a front window.

Standing in front of the house, she would tell acquaintances who asked about the general, "See, there he sits, the good Vladimir Fedorovich, with his chronic gout, not fit to go out or receive visitors."

In this manner Elsabé's grandmother was for years able to collect the full pension, which, had her widowhood become apparent, would have been cut by half.

Elsabé's father was Chief Forester of the Realm. A quiet gentleman who seldom shot an animal himself. Elsabé's childhood: sleigh rides with her father across the immense Lake Peipus, behind them a pack of hungry wolves, before them cracking ice, but they got away unscathed. Grand balls at the family home, to which a hundred relatives arrived in coaches from surrounding estates. There, in a little room next to the main hall, a shoemaker worked all through the night to mend the dancing shoes worn through from ceaseless gallopades and waltzes and mazurkas. Elsabé was gripped by a girlish moon-madness—cold, green, Shakespearian moon of the North! Every evening she roamed through the forests of Tiflisana riding sidesaddle, her face turned toward the greenish glow, a habit that earned her the name "Moon Girl" among the Estonian peasants. Around this time Elsabé entered into seven secret engagements and earned herself a reputation as a heartbreaker and bluestocking who devoured the German and Russian classics, handed out unserious promises to Baltic country squires, and dreamt all the while of being married to a knight in moon-green-shining armor, an actor, a poet, or a musician from the Great Outside World.

But before she knew it she had fallen prey to a young knight-errant—the

132

young Courlandish Baron Henricus Carlovich von Cock—called "the frivolous Cock" at the University of Dorpat; barely eighteen, she became the Baroness von Cock. Her husband, equipped with a diploma in agronomy, made a nuisance of himself at Tiflisana, and after soon tiring of this he induced Elsabé to embark on several successive honeymoons. During a summer masquerade at the casino in Zoppat the foolish, impetuous couple danced Elsabé's unborn child to death, a miscarriage. Next winter came the second blow, and then the third.

The Chief Forester broke through the ice on Lake Peipus and drowned along with horse and sleigh. Elsabé's mother, hard hit by the misfortune, succumbed to a case of influenza. Now Baron von Cock was the sole master of Tiflisana, and after a few "business trips" to St. Petersburg, Warsaw, and Berlin he had soon gambled and caroused away the inheritance that had accrued to Elsabé, who, inexperienced as she was, never guessed what he was up to.

Suddenly the process servers descended on the house like a plague of locusts and seized the young couple's property literally down to their last nightshirt. Even the wick of their last remaining kerosene lamp went dry.

"I'll go get some kerosene, Moon-Girl, kerosene," said the Baron. Strolled with an oil can out into the grayish light of the midnight sun and never was seen again . . .

The family counsel was urging the abandoned girl to sue for divorce when the news arrived that Henricus von Cock had settled the divorce in his own way.

He was found shot through the heart in the boudoir of a demimondaine in Riga.

The twenty-year-old had lost everything: her unborn child, her parents, her husband, her money, her property. The sum total of her young life amounted to zero plus scandal. But she was a type who always suppressed unhappiness and her optimism, a vegetative optimism that thrived far from reason or experience, remained intact. Completely penniless, she moved to Berlin and began working as a typist for the International Theatrical Agency Marinelli. In the impresario's office she met Giaxa, who had recently left the Circus Schumann to join its main competitor, Busch (for reasons she learned of only later). After fourteen days the now famous "equestrian eccentric" proposed to her. And she accepted immediately. Now she had the man she had always dreamed of, even if he wasn't exactly a knight in moon-green-shining armor.

The story about Xana being born on a roller-coaster during the 1910 Munich Oktoberfest is apocryphal. It is true that Elsabé visited the Oktoberwiese with a fellow Livonian, a dwarfish Schwabing painter and passionate collector of Toulouse-Lautrec posters, while Giaxa was making a return appearance in the Circus Krone, this time on the Lippizan Giaxa III. Xana was not born until a week *after* the October festivities. Two decades later, after I myself had entered the Giaxa family album, Elsabé told me very candidly about her first marriage "because you write stories, after all," and concluded, "You see, the way this fellow Cock told me 'I'll go get some kerosene, Moon-Girl, kerosene' . . . and walked away with his oil can into the twilight—you know the North? the summer up there? the midnight sun—the way he walked away and left me all alone in our cleared-out house, never to return again—that, you see, is a very Baltic story."

It was no accident that Giaxa had fallen out with Albert Schumann (whose Berlin Circus was then the largest in Europe) and had gone over to his prime competitor, Busch. To "initiate horses in the secrets of equestrian art" required six months to a year and a half. Whenever an equine beauty (the successful ones he coddled like mistresses) turned out to be a slow learner, Herr Schumann would demand capital punishment and have the unfortunate animal carted off to the slaughterhouse. Giaxa wouldn't stand for that. His horse partners (all white Lippizans) Giaxas I-III he obtained from the Imperial Stud Farm near Trieste, and after the fall of the monarchy, Giaxas IV-VII from the Piber Stables in Styria. Except for Giaxa VII, called "the Last," he had them all pensioned off to the island of Hvar to spend their declining years.

With the outbreak of World War I the Hrubaskys thought their hour had come. It was rumored that the centaur clown would be called to active duty as a mounted artilleryman without rank and be sent to the eastern front with a combat battalion. Then something typically Austrian happened. As the declaration of war on Serbia was being fired off from the Ballhausplatz, Viennese gazettes were discussing the following issue: Can an artist of Giaxa's caliber be left to the mercy of a few stuffy military bureaucrats? An admirer of his entreé number, General Hoehn, chief of the newly established Imperial Military Press Headquarters, requested the services of the "clown and erstwhile officer" (who also wielded a proficient pen), exasperating all the Hrubaskys. The liberal *Neue Freie Presse* was quick to obtain his services. For two years Giaxa rode back and forth (sporting a huge fur hat in winter) along the front lines of the eastern theater. Once he telegraphed the full text of Schiller's *Lied von der Glocke* to his office in order to tie up the lines and thus allow his paper to report the fall of Lemberg an hour before their competition. But other things began to raise the eyebrows of the "higher-ups." He never neglected to report the virtues of the enemy, to write for example that Russian peasant soldiers would rather be exposed to fire than trample down a wheat field in search of cover; or to report the Austrians' indiscriminate, paranoid executions of Serbian civilian "spies." Also he made no secret of his pessimism concerning the war's outcome. And then, in the third year of war, came the great scandal.

A Giaxa article bore the title: "How Much Longer Can the War Go On?—The People Have No More Suspenders!" Even though the headline was printed in quotation marks and the following article revealed the words to be nothing more than the heartfelt sigh of a loyal artilleryman Giaxa had interviewed, this did not prevent the Hrubaskys (now sensing their imminent demise) from crying out in indignation, screaming bloody murder amidst the din of cheers and battle cries that echoed above the carnage. The left wing of the Viennese Social Democrats, led by Austerlitz, inspired by Karl Liebknecht's recent stand in the Reichstag against war credits, took up the suspenders slogan. Benedikt, the editor-in-chief of the *Neue Freie Presse*, feared for his job. And once again Giaxa was punished—with the revocation of his war correspondent's license. Then Grandpa Kujath arranged for him and his family to go into Swiss exile.

I see Giaxa waiting with Giaxa on the sandy sawdust of the arena entrance behind the giant curtain of the circuses Favörosy-Nagy, Renz, Hagenbeck, Busch, Krone, or Knie—all the places he appeared as Obristi Obraski. (In Romance countries he did guest appearances as the Foreign Legionaire Colonel Dubouboule, in Anglo-Saxon ones as Colonel Mac Mac, dressed in a Scottish kilt that reached almost to the toes of his riding boots. From the heights of the (here invisible) balustrade the circus band blared the entrance march—that parodistic mixture of Rákóczi- and Radetzkymarch. In his huge, black riding pants, patent leather boots with oversized comic spurs, on his left a gigantic saber dangling almost to the ground, in a black shako with a four-headed brass eagle and horsehair plume, coffee-brown tunic with gold buttons, scarlet collar and cuffs, wearing the pomegranate nose with its twin-foxtail-moustachios, his own eyebrows painted flame red—stands the equestrian clown and pats the Lippizan's neck and jawbone, strokes its mane down to the withers before swinging up into the saddle. The blaring brasses, the applause of thousands when Giaxa enters the ring at a perfect trot—into a circus tent totally lacking in the anachronistic dignity of the Spanish Riding Academy. Thoroughbred Lippizans are nothing like cold-blooded Belgians, which explains the equestrian eccentric's care in pacifying his snow-white steed before the act. With a gentle swing he mounts the saddle while a circus hand, traditionally a Czech, holds his saber. Behind him wait two black Arabians, each hitched to a featherlight imitation gun-carriage bearing a not quite man-sized dummy cannoneer. The rider gives the Czech the signal to give the signal. The curtain, a house-high affair of purple velvet and gold lamé, furls upward to either side. The little cavalcade appears in a *trot du manège à la muraille tout droit:* Giaxa & Giaxa's entreé.

"The whole thing is just dreadful, don't you think? How anyone could think up such a thing! To get soaking wet like *that.*"

"What do you mean, soaking wet? Don't you think I would have stripped to the skin and waded out into the cold water if this damned light in the lake hadn't shown me, shown me beyond any doubt, that it was too late to do anything? So Joop and I just called the police in Campfèr and they notified this Commissioner Mavegn. I told you the whole thing already, how they drove out to the *Orchas* in the middle of the night with a tow truck and hauled the Fiat onto land. The statement Mavegn drafted was signed by Joop alone, because—"

"The terrible thing," said Xana. "The terrible thing about it is to see how suddenly a person can die. A man gets drunk in a tavern and then, mm, he thinks he falls asleep and has a terrible dream—that someone is tearing his heart from his body—and then afterward he feels perfectly all right again and continues on his way, and then suddenly he's near the water—"

"*In* the water, you mean to say."

It was as if she hadn't heard me at all.

"—near the water. Near. And then he drinks the water, drinks it because he suddenly has such an afterthirst . . . just before that he'd eaten a big piece of cheese . . . and then he drinks the water . . . and spits out a bloody sponge. Spits out a bloody sponge in place of his heart . . . which they'd taken out of him before. And then he's dead. The bloody sponge floats away on the water. It's so old . . . and so terrible."

We were standing on the little wooden balcony of our lodgings in the Pontresina post office where Bonjour had dropped us off a few hours earlier. Thursday toward evening, and Xana was gazing over at the tip of the Palue Glacier, and the way she was talking bewildered me so much that I kept silent.

"And the bad part of it is," she added, "that it happens again and again."

Then I: "What do you mean, again and again? It is, it was a completely unusual accident, and if the Fiat's doors hadn't jammed shut he might have succeeded in saving himself *and* his dogs."

"There weren't any dogs around," said Xana and looked at it, at the piece of Palue Glacier as it began to redden in the fabled Alpine twilight, looked at it as if it were something quite nearby. "Just two men traveling together. Two men who were happy to have left this—this cursed tavern behind them. But one of them—yes, as they came to the water, one of them threw up something, as I just explained to you. And the thing drifted away. Not his heart, but a bloody sponge, as I said . . . and the other one had no need for the police or a tow truck. His new friend was dead."

"His new friend? What in the world are you talking about? It almost sounds as if *I* was with de Colana in the crashed Fiat—"

"The man's name was not de Colana, but Socrates. And his friend wasn't Trebla, but Aristomenes. The *latter* was the one who got soaked in this awful tavern, and do you know how? The two witches had stood spread-legged over the sleeping what'shisname, Aristomenes, and pissed all over him. Imagine that. And the next morning what'shisname, Socrates . . . without the slightest idea what had happened—that his friend's heart had been torn out and replaced with a sponge . . . Socrates said jokingly to Aristomenes, 'Don't come any closer; you smell like a chamber pot.'"

Solution to the riddle: "This charming editor-in-chief, Mr. Landauer, wrote me a month ago when we were living at the 'Rear' that he had to have the Apuleius translation by mid-July."

"Holy Laudon, I've never been so far off the track listening to you! You're talking about your Golden-Apuleius-Ass! This time the ass is me."

"What did you think, Trebla? I saved the first chapter until the *end*. Do you know, if I were a novelist, I'd always write the first chapter last. So I'm only getting to the first chapter *now*. And right at that point, even before the author

136

changes himself into an ass—now don't look at me like that; you know how *much* we like the ass, you and I—comes this dreadful story. Can you lend me your typewriter?"

"With pleasure, *madame*. I'll go down to the common room in the Morteratsch—"

"To fair-skinned Pina from Valtellina."

"To Pina from Valtellina, and I'll try to draft the conclusion of my Austriacus Babeuf. Since I'm writing a historical *reportage* and not a novel I think I'll write the last chapter last. I could call it, mmm, *You Never Saw So Many Bloody Sponges* or *The Linz-Potsdam Axis*." Downstairs in the hall between the stairwell and the post office I met the postmistress. She handed me a letter. It had arrived earlier in the afternoon but she had held it for us. "Because you people spent the night out of the house and I didn't know when you'd come back. Ahh, and now our friend Dr. de Colana will never come back! What do you think of it . . . It never rains but what it pours! Of course it's no surprise to anybody around here that old Avvocato Bow-Wow went and drove into the lake. He was just too fond of the bottle. But that German artist-fellow Kircher, that he took a pistol and shot himself yesterday over in Frauenkirch by Davos—"

"Madam Fausch, do you mean Ernst Ludwig Kirch-ner by any chance?"

"That's him. And not only that but there was the incident up on the Diavolezza where Captain Vaterlaus came within a hair of getting himself shot to death. I tell you, it was an unlucky Wednesday. Go over to Jann or to the Morteratsch and read the newspapers."

The envelope she had handed me was postmarked in St. Moritz the day before; there was no return address. Strolling over to the common room of the Morteratsch, I opened it in the miraculous Alpine twilight.

A letter from a dead man.

GAUDENZ DE COLANA

> *dr. jur., advocat e vicenotar*
> *ex-cussglier guv. pres. dal*
> *tribunel districtuel Maloegia*

ST. MORITZ, *Wednesday, 15th Junius MCMXXXVIII*

> *La schort digl poet*
> *Sez scretg e sez stampo e sez ligia*

o'l l'atagna tgera poesia.
El e parchegl gist scu la gaglinetta
tgi maglia sez sies ovs, povretta.

My dear Black-White!

'*Tis hoped you will take no offense at the above epigram by Lozza and its allusion to your noble art. In the unlikely event that your honored spouse, the classical philologist, should find difficulty in translating a Rhaeto-Romansh text, I hereby proffer my humble services as* traducteur:

The poet's fate:
He writes, he prints, he reads, he sings
Himself the poetry he pens.
In this he's very like the hens
That eat the eggs they lay, poor things!

In addition I should like to take the liberty of a repeat performance of our convivial soirée à deux *at the Chesetta Grischuna in Sils next Saturday (before which time I am, alas, o'erburdened with* obligations professionelles*). A refusal will on no account be tolerated, whereby the undersigned pledges a solemn oath to conduct his vehicle—whose arrival you may anticipate at vespers before the Posta-Pontresina—at a civil tempo.*

After the words "liberty of" in the foregoing passage the writer neglected to include the phrase "inviting you to"—which passage he hereby amends and corrects.

Upon completion of my labors this evening I foresee a brief call at the Chesetta in order to collaborate with Donna Teresina in concocting a menu for our souper.

So then, until Saturday night, my friend! (Believe me, Black-White, to know that you are this affords me greatest satisfaction.)

Should we both live so long, let us look forward to a pleasant meal, a pleasant drink, and a pleasant conversation until the hour of midnight.

Arcibaldo, Concetta, and the other canine creatures send their greeting via oscillations of their vestigial appendages.

Ciao!
Yours, Gaudenz de C.

P.S. Do you know the "Drunken Song" by Nietzsche? I presume you do, but nonetheless allow myself to refresh your obvious erudition with the following transcription:

Oh man, heed take
Of what the deepest midnight spake!
I sleep, I sleep—
From depths of troubled dreams I wake!
The world is deep,

With deeper sense than day can make.
Deep is its woe (!!!)—,
But lust is more than misery!
Woe bids us go!
Yet lust must have eternity,
The deepest, deep eternity!

P.P.S. Addio! Addio!

By the age of seventeen I had already seen too many violent deaths.
"Unnatural deaths make me feel lascivious"—this open confession of mine
had earned me much misunderstanding, mistrust, indeed even hostility. So be
it. But did I stay in the Morteratsch common room until long after eight o'clock
on that Thursday (June 16) just to be near waitress Pina, pretty Pina from Valtellina? In my mind, i.e., superego, I found another justification for my presence
in Pina's domain. If I was able to see the dreadful reality behind *the Light in the
Lake*, why then should I be wrong in my suspicions about the Two Blonds?
Thus it was important here and now to investigate the doings of my "coun-
trymen" Mostny and Krainer in their chosen abode, Hotel Morteratsch—to
keep a sharp, yet unobtrusive eye on them like a good private detective. As if I
were working for Captain (Ret.) Heinzwerner Laimgruber in his Vindobona Detective Agency—Laimgruber, who was no longer a private eye but had become
a most unprivate big wheel in Uncle Adolf's Gestapo HQ, Vienna.

INCIDENT DURING ALPINE MANEUVERS

*Headquarters, 61st Border Regiment. Around noon yesterday a near trage-
dy occurred during a firing exercise by Mt. MG Co. IV in the restricted maneuver area Diavolezza-Bernina. Mt. MGr. Lenz Zb., ostensibly blinded by a reflection from the glacier, turned his weapon and fired on the observation stand occupied by Capt. Urs-Dom. Vaterlaus. Reacting with great presence of mind, the
Capt. managed to save himself with a leap, taking cover behind a boulder and
calling on gunner Zb. to cease fire. The offender was immediately placed under
arrest to await the results of an official investigation.*

Only a single light above the bar remained burning in the empty common
room; the chairs stood legs upward on the tables, above them the pungent
smoke of burned-out Brissaghi and Nazionalihing. Pina was nowhere in sight.
Then she emerged from the half darkness of the corridor: in a cheap evening
dress, long and dark, that fell in heavy, togalike folds; around her shoulders a
short black jacket. "*Ecco, Alberto, finita la giornata,*" she said without the least
surprise about my reappearance. "I'm offa now. I'ma going up to Giarsun."
"What will you do there, Pina?"
"Da domestics are-a gonna dance over by da 'Mountain Buck.'"
"The domestics?"

"Da 'otel girlss."

"Are you sure it isn't the other way around?"

"Whada you mean?"

"That the mountain bucks are going to dance over by the domestics?"

Pina whispered: "*La luna montera sopra la Schela del Paradis.*"

I turned the common room into an improvised stand-up bar by inviting her—regardless of her evening plans—to pour out two glasses of Valtellina and drink a little toast with me. She poured me a glass, but having little use for wine outside of mealtimes, filled herself a liqueur glass with Strega, and I sniffed it and remarked that it smelled like hair tonic, and this feeble joke she understood immediately, giving out a laugh and allowing herself, at my encouragement, two additional Stregas. It was my bitter duty to question Pina about Krainer and Mostny, with whom I now had to come to terms regardless of how nasty a job it was. I paid and asked Pina if I might escort her part of the way to Giarsun. I might.

Glowing midday marble, marble heated by the pressing sun, hot enough to burn your hand—memories of Hvar. Glowing midnight marble, a new experience for me as I stood in a pine grove above Giarsun leaning against the ruined wall of Spaniola tower, the girl in my arms with her back against me, as she willingly let my hand steal beneath the gathered fabric of her gown and clasp her firm, young, girlish breast.

The late moon was rising. It was still hidden from our view by the Languard peaks, but across from us it was already spreading out its coppery, almost orange sheen across the Roseg Valley.

Pina whispered: "*La luna monterà sopra la Schela del Paradis.*"

"Pardon?"

"The moon will come up over the Schela del Paradis."

"What is that, the Schela del Paradis?"

Pina gazed up the steep fire-break to the Languard peaks, whose outlines appeared chiseled and nearly transparent in the growing, indirect, orange glow. And again her whisper: "If we walk up da hill, way up, den we come to da Schela del Paradis, Alberto."

Then the moon crept over the ridge—tonight, as it waned, even more shapeless than the night before—and put a sparkle into Pina's large black eyes, and I asked her if she was cold, and she whispered, "*Fredda?* No," and as my right hand rested on her breast my left easily undid the snaps beneath her arm that fastened the bodice of her evening gown, and she not only let me do it, but helped me a little by shaking off her jacket. Working gently from behind I soon had her undressed down to the hips, and Pina's head sank far back across my left shoulder, and what I embraced and caressed was a perfect female torso made of marble, burning at midnight, as if glowing from the heat of a summer noon at Hvar.

Then Pina's left arm curled up around my neck as the hot marble of her face pressed against my cheek, and her sparkling eyes grew blurred from close-

140

ness, and I lifted her other arm over my shoulder where it clasped me tight, and her mouth opened and I kissed her as gently as I could in my frenzy and she uttered a guttural cry that vibrated on my tongue like a rough, ecstatic laugh and I felt no sense of remorse in that timeless moment, of that I am sure. There was no forgiveness to be sought for what I did—from the living or the dead. By an unforeseen lucky chance I had landed here with Pina tonight, equipped with a written warrant from the World Beyond:

> ... *Woe bids us: Go!*
> *Yet lust must have eternity* ...

Then all too suddenly a screech owl hooted right above us in the roofless tower of Spaniola; a first, mournful cry, surprisingly close at hand, like the starting signal for a thousandfold fluttering of wings. Not the hushed beat of owl's wings, but a rapid, hectic chaos of floppy ears, a swarm of featherless little bodies pouring as if moonstruck over our heads toward the orange disk. Pina pulled her lips away.

"*Pipistrelli*," she whispered. "Batsa."

"Are you afraid of bats, Pina?"

"No afraid. Inna my town-a-home, *nella Valtellina ci sono anche molti pipistrelli durante le notte di luna*. No afraid, Alberto, so long dey not come inna my hair. *Santa Madonna*, so much—so very much batsa ..." Adeptly she covered her hair with her hands. Then, no longer whispering, she said calmly: "I'm a litta bit cold."

"*Poverina!*" I held her and felt the hot, smooth marble become cool and rough with gooseflesh, and I myself registered the growing cold that came with the rising moon and pulled up her hanging gown and redressed her (once again she made subtle, helpful movements) as quickly as I could. Picked up her jacket. With it wrapped around her head and shoulders she looked, in the coppery moonbeams, like a young Tuscan peasant girl on her way to church. Holy Laudon, why of all places had I taken her to this infernal Spaniola tower where every bat in the area had its roost. The answer lurked in my subconscious. Because its wall afforded better rearward cover than a tree trunk ... the hell with cover, take Pina away from this bat sanctuary, take her off into the pines, lay her down ... Yet I knew the magic minutes, barely utilized, were past. Cold.

As we walked above the lights that blinked through the trees from Giarsun, retracing our steps back down the path I said: "Now *la bella Pina* can go to the 'Mountain Buck' and catch up on some of the dancing that nasty old Albert's kept you away from."

She leaned against me as we walked, whispering again: "I dancing tonight no more. You're-a not nassy, Alberto. It's good wis you."

"Pina ... couldn't we go to your place?"

"My-a place?"

"The two of us—go to your room."

"Now?"

"Yes."

"We canno do it."

"Why not?"

"We canno. Angelina from-a kitchen sleeps in nexta room."

"Aha, from the kitchen."

"Listen, Alberto . . ."

"Yes?"

"Can . . ."

"Yes?!"

"Can we go to your-a place?"

"Not a chance."

"'Cause of your-a sister?"

"No, 'cause of Madam Fausch."

"Ya, I see," said Pina. "Ya, I see." After a pause: "Saturdi Angelina goes to Bianzone, to her-a town. Saturdi at-a twelva clock you can come to me, Alberto."

"Saturday. So . . . the day after tomorrow—no, tomorrow; today is already Friday. Saturday at twelve, on the stroke of midnight." I kissed Pina's jacket-nestled face.

"Wait-a for me by da fontan."

"By the fountain in front of the Morteratsch."

"*Ecco.*"

"Where Signorina Pina sat a few days ago and listened to some sweet-talk from two gentlemen named Krainer and Mostny."

"*Geloso?* Are you a jealous Otello, Alberto? Shouldn't be. Dose boring guys-a from Vienna. Dey gone yesterday."

"Gone? Where did they go?"

"No far. Dey gone over to St. Moritz-Bad."

"Hm . . . You don't know their address by any chance?"

"I sink . . . I sink Villa . . . Villa Muongia."

In front of the Stefani I met printer Zarli Zuan.

"Hello. Excuse me—how do I get to the Villa Muongia?"

He stopped, but at first did nothing but stare into space. Pine needles were sticking to his violet-colored business suit as if he had just finished an off-trail plunge through the forest. He grasped his black beard and began stroking it absentmindedly, then his shadowy eyes touched mine, eyes that showed what seemed to me a kind of helpless-insane confusion, momentarily suppressed by a squint of astonishment.

"Villa Muongia—what would *you* want to go *there* for?"

"Oh . . . to visit some friends."

"Friends, I see. Well now, you take the bus to the spa. Bus to the spa, bus to the spa. Go on past Tattersall. Then you follow along the lakeshore toward Sur Punt."

"Sur Punt."

"Acla Silva, you know that place; you're a friend of Mr. ten Breukaa's, right?"

"Yes."

"Sur Punt is directly across from Acla Silva. On the southeastern corner of the lake," Zuan continued his gloom-shrouded lecture. "Keep going along the water until you cross a little bridge. Then you'll be right in front of the Villa Muongia." Then an unexpected dry laugh sprouted from his mournful beard. "But just watch out. *Watch out*. That you don't fall off the little bridge! Our lake is deep. Unlike Lake Campfèr . . ." Zuan surveyed me in a kind of bitter, even malicious, yes even rather insane amusement, and added suddenly, "You know that I'm having business problems now, don't you?"

"No," I lied. "How should I?"

"He must have told you."

"Who?"

"Your drinking partner. Il Dottore Bow-Wow, God rest his soul." Exaggerated beard-stroking. "After a few drinks he would even tell business secrets. Yes, he would do that. I once told him straight to his face, eh—: 'Your blabbing is going to get you into *serious* trouble, Doctor.' . . . And today they're carting him off to the grave. *If*, that is, *if* the argument is settled in time."

"What argument?"

"The argument that started up over his will. Haven't you heard about it?"

"No."

"Come over to the schoolhouse square at five o'clock if you're interested. You'll be treated to a spectacle the likes of which you've never seen. That's right, a spectacle." The printing-press owner trotted two steps farther, then turned around; with a vague gesture: "He's a beastly fellow, this . . ." The name was lost in his beard. "Isn't he? He presses and presses."

"Pardon?"

"He presses down on you from up there, the brute."

"What brute?"

His long index fingers pointed up at the mountain sloping jaggedly down into Lake Moritz. "Aye, the Rosatsch."

There was the covered bridge. It resembled the one by Acla Silva except that it was longer, for it spanned more than a mere ditch: a tiny lagoon that gazed up as slatey black as the Rosatsch it reflected, black despite the cloudless afternoon, but with an undertone of mermaid green. (Unlike ten Breukaa's estate, the property stood right next to the deep water.) Crossing the bridge I glanced momentarily down across the railing of slender pine logs.

Gliding lakeward the shadow of a fish—a giant pike. Or the compacted shadow of a swarm of trout?

As it dove downward with a sudden thrust and disappeared in the mermaid green it seemed to me (was my weak eye fooling me? I hadn't time to insert my monocle) as large as a shark, but with the bullish head of a giant catfish.

VILLA MUONGIA stood on one of the gray stucco posts of the open gate. Under the sign several penciled marks of various sizes. Although someone had tried to scratch them off with a knife they were still recognizable: swastikas. Close by the gate posts a pier jutted into the water.

Then I heard a quiet, irregular tick-tack that I diagnosed as a bouncing ping-pong ball. I walked cautiously across the gravel. A short row of mountain ashes concealed the house from view. On the lawn in front of the veranda stood a ping-pong table where a game of doubles was in progress. One team—I recognized them at first glance through the squat, berry-laden trees—was made up of Messrs. Krainer and Mostny. They opposed two younger men, one with a fox-red, the other with a curly black beard, both with braidlike locks hanging at their temples and billowing caftans; possibly rabbinical students.

RIT . FAMILIENPENSION

MORDECHAI KATZBEIN-BRIALOSZYNSKI

PROP .

Coffee, Tea, Homemade Pastries. Kosher Cuisine.

Specialty: Gefillte Fish

"Good grief, this empty, yawning wall over the mantelpiece! Where in the world's the Spahi?"

"Yesterday Joop put him in his bank vault in the village."

"Pardon me, dear lady, but it must be even *more* boring for him there."

"For whom? Where?"

"The Spahi. In the bank vault."

"All right, enough of your little jokes, and don't call me 'dear lady,' either, when Joop isn't around," said Pola rather irritably. "All the masons and locksmiths and electricians I have running around the yard and the house on Saturday afternoon earning expensive overtime, it's enough to drive a person crazy. And whose fault is it? Yours!"

"Why me, dear lady."

"Now just stop that dear lady business, do you hear? It's all because *you* convinced him that his Spahi might get stolen by burglars. First he thought, and he told you, too, that you were completely out of your mind. But after you dragged him out the other night to your spooky light in the lake, and after he read in the paper that this what'sisname, the handsome soldier we met at Pizzagalli's who gave Xana a bunch of hair from his chest—"

"Lenz Zbraggen. And his heart's-beard bouquet, as he so curiously called

144

it, he offered to *both* ladies, that means you too."

"What's it matter. But that this fellow almost shot his captain with a machine gun at the very same moment ... so that the scream, the scream you heard up on the Diavolezza was *not* something you imagined ... that the scream at midday and the light at night were *not* figments of your imagination—well, it was too much for him; he's got no peace."

"My peace is gone," I declaimed, "my heart is sore."

"Oh get out of here with your Gretchen from *Faust;* you, Trebla, you are to blame for the whole thing. That he's suddenly having the wall raised and broken glass put on top of it and an alarm system installed and new locks put on the gate and the front door and I don't know what all—can't you hear all the hammering? It's that way all day long. Yesterday afternoon he went off to Zurich on the train to a police-dog show, all because of you, because of you, and just now he called me from Baur au Lac saying that I have to come right away and look at two Great Danes trained to attack."

"To attack whom. Me?"

"Oh be quiet. In an hour Bonjour will drive me down to Zurich in the Daimler. In *this* weather!"

"Only a little rain this time. The barometer's high."

"Great Danes! When we already *have* a dog. I guess Joop thinks the Spahi's too small to guard the spaniel."

"How's that?"

"See, I'm just all mixed up. Of course I mean the spaniel is too small to—"

"Pola, do you realize," I said in a different tone, "that he's the last one? The sole survivor of an entire family?"

For the first time today she looked at me with her "questioning antelope eyes."

"Sirio."

"Uorschletta has him out for a walk in Staz Forest."

"Mmm, apropos Sirio. Could I perhaps borrow the Chrysler? I've got an appointment. In Sils for dinner."

"With whom, if I may ask?"

"With the Honorable Dr. de Colana," I replied formally.

"Are you crazy?"

"Beg your pardon, maybe I'm just a little confused—like you. The procession is at five o'clock in the village."

"The funeral? I never even read an obituary."

"Neither did I. Zarli Zuan just told me about it. Now it's a quarter to."

"Have you got your international driver's license? Yes? All right. I'll give you the Chrysler. The garage key I can't give you. Just go ahead and take the car home and bring it back day after tomorrow." With that she planted a little kiss on the right corner of my mouth. "Kissproof."

"Who?"

"My lipstick, you silly Trebla. Go on to your procession."

On the short drive to St. Moritz I reconsidered what had gone through my head as I walked along the shoreline path from the spa to Acla Silva: Why in the world was the two-man death's-head team in "mountain climbing civvies" playing ping-pong with a couple of rabbinical students in the front yard of the Villa Muongia? One of Maxim Grabscheidt's maxims gave me a plausible answer. The hateful Nazi interest in the Jews is a kind of demented hate-love, something perverted, something lewd. Lewd interest. Adolf would like to transfer the Jews' status as "chosen people" to the Germans. In his subconscious he sees Moses as the first absolute Fuehrer in history, one who led and controlled his people every waking and sleeping moment, whose laws extended all the way down to washing instructions for women during their periods. Hitler didn't want to be Napoleon or Caesar, Alexander or Xerxes; Hitler wanted to be Moses.

I came too late for the procession. Met Miss Tummermut in her green fleece coat with matching frog-green umbrella in front of the Café d'Albana as the crowd was breaking up on the schoolhouse square. She coerced me into buying her a sherry brandy. Touching on the Diavolezza accident involving her fiancé: "Ooh, yeah, for three days he's been under arrest. In the hole. 'Cause he was so careless. Young men just seem to do that, even the ones that aren't careless. First they're in the hole, then they're out." She, a great winker, said this without the trace of a wink. "What do you think about those piano movers?"

"Piano movers?"

"Yeah. It seemed to me like a crate they put a grand piano in. I watched the show out the window here. Fantastic!"

After I told her I'd come too late for the ceremony she related a grotesque story which she claimed to have heard directly from Commissioner Mavegn. Yes, old Advocate Bow-Wow really *had* once been a clever lawyer, and a little of this legal savvy was still spooking around in his booze-soaked brain (according to Mavegn) when he wrote his will. Yes, that paragraph, that one hair-raising paragraph. (A): In the event of the testator's death all of his dogs were to be "sacrificed by means of a painless injection." (B) In the event the testator and his dogs all perish together, e.g., as the result of an accident—"*voilà*, the high point of the hairy paragraph!"—the mortal remains of the testator and his cocker spaniels are to be interred *together* in a "receptacle fashioned of stone pine." Should the rightful heirs refuse to carry out these directives they shall be declared disinherited and the entire legacy shall pass to a certain Mr. MacIntosh (or something like that), the owner of a cocker spaniel kennel in Aberdeen, Scotland.

So that is why they just took this giant crate out of the house over there and put it into a big, black-draped moving van. "They're driving down to Bergell with it." Down there in Soglio on the family property there's a queer little cemetery where the family has been burying its hunting dogs for centuries. "Avvo-

cato Bow-Wow is going to be laid to rest in a dog cemetery. Isn't that the limit?
Naturally no clergyman went with him."

"The last words of *Young Werther*," I said.

"Young Werther?" asked Miss Tummermut. "Don't think I know him."

I dropped her off at Pizzagalli's as Dr. Tardueser ws just going in. With a
strange, triumphant smirk he called over to me: "Sad, but amu-sing! At last the
P-protestant p-peacock has met his match."

As I rolled down the highway between Campfèr and Silvaplana (once
again) and saw the towering larch tree between the guard posts (rising like a
monument on the site of the accident) across from the path that came down out
of the Orchas d'Albanella, I steered the Chrysler off to the side of the pine-
flanked road and stopped. What did I want here?

The rain clouds had disappeared as if by magic and the valley was dipped
in gray shadow; soon the obligatory alpine twilight would set in. Motorized traffic had almost ceased at the vesper hour. From the direction of Maloja a column
of motorcycles with Genoese license plates raced past, the drivers mostly hel-
metless with African hairdos and garbed in colorful, piratelike outfits. Their
rumbling faded off into the distance and left the quiet sound of waves lapping
against the stones—stones I had crouched on with ten Breukaa to peer out at the
eerie scene revealed to us by the Light in the Lake.

Around the gashed trunk of the larch, traces of blue chalk; similar traces,
faded but still recognizable, remained on the asphalt. No doubt leftovers of the
measurements taken by the police. Yes, the police had done their duty.

I trudged back across the pavement and stopped on the path coming down
from the Orchas. It came out diagonally across from the larch tree, a few paces
down the highway toward Campfèr. It was no road for vehicles, nor a hiking
trail, just a path for the Senns, the woodmen, and their pack animals. I bent
down. On the pine-needle-strewn, rain-softened humus were fresh tracks: a
large farmer's boot and some neat little hoofprints. I took a few steps uptrail.
Here fresh mule droppings, neater little "apples" than those of horses. Following the afternoon shower a Senn must have led his pack-mule up into the Orchas. But there was another, older track.

Truck tires.

Three or four days old, but barely washed away by today's rain: they were
too deep for that. Not automobile tires. Parallel double tracks like the rear tires
of a heavy truck. Someone had backed a heavy truck into the forest here. But
not to turn around, for that there was no need to back in so far. Someone had
backed a truck in here—to hide it in the woods?

I drove on. Before Silvaplana a signpost pointed up into the stone pines:
ova del vallun. Backed into the entrance of the trail was a gigantic truck, so
well hidden by the forest that I noticed only the massive radiator (with the
brand name saurer) as I passed by. Piled high with long tree trunks on which
the woodmen—all dressed in gentian-blue peasant shirts that fell below their

waists—balanced as they hoisted up additional logs on chains. I considered turning back to Pontresina. And drove on to Sils.

The sky was a cool mass of flames descending behind the blackened mountain peaks. Paleozoic landscape, but the forests were already formed; the Devonian period had certainly begun: age of ferns. And the age of trucks? A disturbing thought. What was the word on the nose of the monster that waited patiently among the ferns: *Saurer?* Or *Saurian?* And the monster I had seen in the forest near Silvaplana merged with another I hadn't seen, but whose massive footprint I had discovered at the scene of the accident. A saurian; three days ago a saurian had lain in wait for its unsuspecting prey.

7

THE RED EYES OF MR. CLAVADETSCHER

I had parked the cabriolet in the village of Sils Maria and walked the short distance up to the Chesetta Grischuna. Across the front courtyard paved with cobblestones. Into the hallway where there was a chill of stone-surrounded air, a scent of milk, just like the week before at exactly the hour de Colana had first brought me here. In the pine-paneled Stuevetta not a soul. In front of the stove, curled up to a massive bundle of dirty-white-orange fur, the sleeping St. Bernard. His blowing, whistling snores persisted as I walked up to him. Then he uncurled and stretched, glaring up at me sleepily with his bloodshot, running eyes and giving out a rumbling bass growl. Whick! the sliding door by the sideboard snapped open, whack! then shut. I had been noticed. Snuffling asthmatically the massive roundhead approached me, then began wagging his fringed switch of a tail. He had recognized me. Hardly had I removed my coat and seated myself (mechanically) on the bench by the stove, when he bedded his heavy muzzle on my knee and slobbered on my pants. Just as I had the week before I tried to ward him off: "Good-dog-good-dog-good-dog," and in my mind I heard the country lawyer's wheezing laugh.

zoccoli, she clip-clopped into the room. (She didn't appear to have attended the funeral.) Without a trace of familiarity, almost rudely—was she trying to conceal embarrassment or even fear of my presence, or was it just the impatience of a busy housewife—she asked me: "*Che desidera mangiare?*" I ordered trout.

"*Che bibita desidera?*"

To drink? "*Il vino preferito del Dottore de Colana,*" I said in a most matter-of-fact way.

"*Va bene,*" the woman muttered, eyes lowered.

148

"*Oggi* . . ." I collected my Italian to explain to her that the country lawyer had invited me to dinner here this very evening. All the farmer's wife had to say in reply was, "*Il poverino* . . ." Poor man.

Followed by the St. Bernard she clattered out of the room. I was alone in the Stuevetta, alone with the stuffed woodchuck that stood guard atop the display case housing Men Clavadetscher's shooting trophies. A different twilight than a week ago. Outside the cubic window-shafts swam an iridescent blue that intensified as the day began to fade: *l'heure bleue*. I sat still at the roughhewn table and the emptiness of the place beside me where de Colana had sat yawned at me in the twilight blue, and twilight blue collected in the corners of the pine-paneled room, and I thought of the spaniels' romping mock-skirmish with the St. Bernard and imagined I could hear the sonorous battle cries of the Homeric warriors. Then the rumbling roar of an approaching truck.

I stepped to the window, the short tunnel of a window that I would have had to climb into to open. The roaring swelled lazily up the hill. I waited with a strange eagerness, and as I waited my gaze wandered away from the jumbled, hundred-year-old cobblestones of the courtyard, from the large well, from the pile of stripped, thirty-foot pine logs like those I had seen on the truck below the Ova del Vallun. Beside me, almost within reach, stood the "begging" woodchuck on its papier-mâché stand. It too was coated in blue fur: the dusty orange of his pelt could not resist the magic glow of the *heure bleue*, but the glass-beady eyes held their own. Red gleaming little eyes, glowing like the rear reflector on a bicycle, their dead, lookout's gaze staring out over my head.

At last the truck appeared. With a vague sense of relief I saw that it was not coming from the woods. Stacked on its flatbed stood huge fishnets that hung down dripping over its flanks *(flanks?)*. Among the nets six men stood spread-legged, looking like woodmen in their now *very* blue, long peasant shirts equipped with hoods which they had all pulled over their heads. In the driver's cab sat Men Clavadetscher; like the others, he wore a peasant shirt. Although its hood concealed his face, I recognized him at once from the way he let his paw-like hand hang down beside the driver's door after using both hands to haul the heavy steering wheel around for the turn into the courtyard. The roaring ceased; a light hammering sound persisted.

The St. Bernard bounded out of the house, now blue himself, though not wearing a peasant shirt. His tail switch waved to greet his master, but the latter hardly noticed him as he gave the dismounting men a sign, whereupon they began dragging the nets off the truck amidst guttural heave-ho cries.

The roaring began again as I made a half-conscious discovery.

The fender over the right front tire of the truck—wasn't it damaged? Now Clavadetscher drove the unloaded truck off the courtyard, at a bouncing snail's pace to be sure, but my vision was blocked by the St. Bernard trotting along next to the front wheel. Dog and truck disappeared outside the cubic window's narrow field of view. The motor raised its voice briefly, then once again, and then the roaring stopped for good.

Soon the Chesetta's proprietor trudged back into my field of vision and lent a hand with unfolding the water-heavy nets. The fishermen ducked their heads beneath the gathered mesh—that's why they had put on their hoods—and dragged each net single file over to a row of wooden pegs. Each net sixty feet long and more, sagging down across the heads and backs of the carriers so that only their steadily pacing legs were visible, the end of each net unrolling like something organic, with mesh resembling scales, like a monstrous lizard's tail that dragged out snaking behind them; and everything dipped in swimming blue. A dinosaur . . . Then the fishermen hung the nets on the pegs to dry.

"*Pronto, Signore!*"

Behind me a rattling of the sliding door, a clattering of wooden slippers and the rough melodic voice of Teresina. Before I could turn around she had clattered out of the room.

There stood the steaming blue trout surrounded by fist-sized buttered potatoes, there the Valtellina sparkling in its carafe, and its dark radiance was transformed in the ever-intensifying *heure bleue* to a peculiar violet shade. The six fishermen marched in in single file, their heavy shoes making the floorboards creak. The Chesetta's proprietor was not among them. They said not a word of greeting, nor did they speak to one another. Pulled off their hoods, which together with their silence, rather gave them the appearance of a secret society, hung their jackets over chair backs, sat down at a table by the window and began silently waiting, stroking their animal-like faces. (Three of them had long moustaches, three, short scraggly full beards.) None of them took any notice of me.

Teresina clacked into the room with a half-dozen neat little earthenware mugs from which she carelessly allowed red wine to spill as she served each of the fishermen, murmuring, "*Salute* Gion—Andrea—Giacomin—Simon—Zampieri—Toena."

The men nodded wordlessly, and after the woman had left the room, raised the mugs and drank and wiped their beards and said nothing. No one thought of turning on a light; it wasn't necessary. Three days until the longest day of the year: now it took even longer for darkness to fall than a week before.

"*Salute*," Clavadetscher greeted me. His shirt had merged with the blue hour-blue that had even changed the color of his hair. But not his eyes. Like the red bead-eyes of the woodchuck, they maintained their color.

He stepped up to the fishermen's table, in his fist a leather purse, which he opened as he sat down. Silver five-franc pieces jingled onto the table; he distributed them among the fishermen, who stashed them away with silent nods.

He sprang supply to his feet and led the foot-stamping file of men—for whom I was still no more than part of the bluish haze—out the door. In the stony entrance hall their monotonous farewells echoed and reechoed. Clavadetscher's voice, full of domineering energy, suggestive sharpness, evoked the same brief reply from each man—uniform, meekly imitating the man before, with an undertone of forced submissiveness.

Domineeringly: *"Ciao, Gion!"*
Submissively: *"Ciao,* Men."
"Ciao, Giacomin!"
"Ciao, Men."
"Andrea, *Ciao!"*
"Ciao, Men."
"Ciao, Zamper!"
"Ciao, Men."
"Ciao, Toena!"
"Ciao, Men."
"Simon, *ciao!"*
"Ciao, Men, *ciao!"*

Tapping footsteps of the group as they withdrew across the cobblestones. And suddenly, like a signal of their freedom from an evil curse came a Romansh chorus of almost frenzied gaiety that broke into yodeling superdominants. The song grew quieter until it ebbed beneath the ringing evening bell from the nearby church. It had rung like this the week before. Exactly like this.

Who could possibly object to a guest wanting to smoke a cigar in the courtyard after dinner? The opening and closing of the door, my cautious footsteps in the hallway—all that was certainly drowned out by the nearby pealing of the bell. The bell stopped. I began to step even more carefully across the bumpy cobblestones in the direction Clavadetscher had disappeared in with the truck. There was a giant, wide-open barn door; the "driveway" approached at a slant—a broad, grass-covered ramp over blocks of stone. The cigar wouldn't draw. I threw it away.

Inside, the faded, sweet-pungent odor of last year's hay mixed with gasoline fumes. A dangerous mixture. The barn owner, it seemed, did not go out of his way to avoid risks. There stood the truck parked on two long boards as if on rails, its rear end toward me. I groped my way forward along its right-hand side into the half darkness vaguely lit by the dull reflection of the "blue hour" that shone in through the barn door, and it seemed to me that I was stalking alongside the longest truck in the world.

At last the radiator. The reflected twilight was enough to allow my good eye to see: the right front fender was damaged. I ran my hand across it in disbelief. The paint was stripped off the entire front curve of the fender as if scraped away by a heavy glancing blow. It was possible that the collision had bent the sheet metal back far enough to jam the front wheel and that an amateur had hammered it back into shape, for the surface felt wavy, as if dented by many hammer blows from the inside.

Suspicion ticked in my forehead. Get out your matches! I told myself, heedless of the dangerous fumes. Before I could react I heard feather-quiet, grass-muffled steps approaching. In a reflex my hand jerked toward the pistol in my hip pocket. In the high, hazy-blue doorway stood the blocky silhouette of a man with long, dangling arms.

"Segner, waas wenderi mym Gaada?" asked the shadow in domineering tones.

I didn't understand him; my hand rested on my hip. "I'm looking for," I began lamely, "the whachamacallit—the—"

"Pissoir?" the shadow asked suggestively.

Following the farmer across the entrance ramp I commented: "I seem to have lost my way."

Without a word in reply Clavadetscher led me across the cobblestones to a side building attached to the house, a shed constructed of very thick pine boards with a door bearing the letters "p.p." He pushed it open, turned on the light and marched away without giving me even a side glance. I waited eagerly to see if he would disappear around the corner of the house or turn into the courtyard. Instead he went to the edge of the meadow and stayed there, his back toward me, in the blurring blueness that was gradually turning to ink. The only explanation for his sentrylike stance was that he was determined to keep a close watch on me, to see that I didn't "lose my way" on his property again. Then from down by the lake I heard, quiet as a chirp of a sonorous chord, the liberated singing of the fishermen, farmhands, or smugglers (whatever their main profession might have been). It seemed to fix the attention of the Chesetta's owner, for he bent forward and stiffened in the pose of a man on listening post.

The bleak light inside the outhouse fell on its inwardly opened door. After the "p.p." someone had inked a "c." and scribbled three words. What was p.p.c. supposed to mean? Perhaps the old diplomatic abbreviation of *"pour prendre congé"?* The three following words: *"de ce monde."*

"Pour prendre congé de ce monde"?

"To take leave of this world . . ."

The scrawled inscription was fresh, but unobtrusively placed.

Unmistakably de Colana's handwriting.

The little cell enclosed a chestlike seating arrangement above the latrine and a urinal improvised from a section of tin rain gutter; the reddish pine plank above it was covered with a motley assortment of messages—some scrawled in pencil or pen, others carved with a pocket knife—immortalized sentiments of the most diverse kinds: infantile, sentimental, obscene, and political manifestations such as:

EVVIVA IL NOSTRO DUCE BENITO MUSSOLINI! MARIO ZOPPI, MILANO
LOOKING FOR A NICE STRONG PRICK NOT MORE THAN 25 YEARS OLD, BRITISH
OR AMERICAN PREFERRED. ASK FOR RONNEY KIRKPATRICK MALOJA-KULM
IN THE CHESETTA GRISCHUNA I DRANK THREE LITERS OF BEER

HEIL HITLER!
JULIUS

P.S. I WANT TO PHUQUE PHRAEULEIN HOCKENJOS (YOU SWABIAN SWINE!)

Engraved in a clumsily carved heart:

BARBLA, LA BRAMA M'ARDAIVA
ZOPPAD AINT IL COUR,
BARBLA, ED EU CHI T'AMAIVA
NU POSS PLUE DIR OUR! GAICHEM
JUDA VERRECKE! HEIL HITLER!(the "I" changed to an "A", so as to read:)
HEAL HITLER!—FROM HIS INSANITY, DEAR GOD!

Finally I found what I had been looking for, almost feverishly looking for as a complement to the words on the door: de Colana's inked scrawl, hastily tossed off in block letters (probably an attempt at camouflage—making his inscription resemble the others, careless, hurried, but except for a few missing punctuation marks, free of errors:

CARO NERO-BIANCO! IN CASE WE MISS EACH OTHER HERE ARE FOUR
MAXIMS BY ABBE GALLIANI A FORERUNNER OF F.N.:
MAN SHOULD NOT SEEK AN ALLIANCE WITH NATURE. IT IS TOO UNEQUAL.
WE ARE NOT CREATED FOR THE TRUTH. IT SHOULD NOT CONCERN US. WHAT
CONCERNS US IS OPTICAL ILLUSION.
ONE MUST LEARN TO TOLERATE INJUSTICE AND ENDURE BOREDOM.
DEATH IS CERTAIN. SO WHY SHOULD WE NOT BE MERRY?

15. VI.

(no signature)

I stepped outside and struck two or three matches in an attempt to light another cigar; I did not succeed. My dexterity seemed hampered by a kind of jitteriness. At last I got the cigar to begin smoking. The blue hour was fading now; in its absence the planet Venus sparkled unnaturally large and bright like a glitter-star on a Christmas card. *Pina, my rendezvous with Pina at midnight . . .* I strolled puffing in the direction of the meadow's edge. Men Clavadetscher had left his listening post; there was no one around. I breathed a sweet-spicy smell of freshly cut, damp pine wood, but my senses did not respond to it. And the increasing cold corresponded well to the mood I was in—my dull, cold suspicion.

Someone had pulled the red gingham curtains in front of the windows of the Stuevetta, and through the fortresslike openings shone a muffled, glimmering light that reflected dully on the courtyard's cobblestones. There, a round gleam of metal; as I went to step over it something held me back. What was it? I bent down and picked it up: a fuenfliber, no doubt about it, a silver five-franc piece.

I weighed the sizable coin in my hand. It was not hard to explain the find.

153

One of Clavadetscher's latently reluctant helpers—each one had gotten several such coins—had dropped the fuenfliber. I could give the coin to Clavadetscher and ask him to return it to its rightful owner; I could; yet I could hardly imagine him as the honest manager of a lost-and-found bureau. It was better to look at my discovery from a different, more irrational aspect—not as a welcome addition to my meager finances, but in the light of my dinner invitation this evening—the invitation of a dead man; yes. *Advocatus de Colana, advocatus diaboli mortuus*, this was just the kind of gesture he would make.

The empty dining room. The blueness of the slow-fading twilight had made it appear bigger; the electric light of the single, dimly burning bulb hanging unshaded from the low ceiling so emphasized the bulk of the massive tiled stove (in which no fire was crackling today) that the entire, shrunken room seemed nothing more than a pine box in which it was packed. The slovenly Teresina had not taken the trouble to remove the plate with its trout skeleton. I knocked on the sliding door and ordered a coffee grappa from her, and soon amidst a clatter of *zoccoli* she brought in the steaming glass along with the "grappaquarium," from which she poured (holding it in both hands) a careless splash of liquor into the coffee—increasing my suspicion that it was less a question of carelessness than of some sinister anxiety. (What was she afraid of?) I asked for the check, *l'addizione*, and she muttered like someone laboring under the aftereffects of serious argument: "*Quatro franchi settante, servizio compreso.*"

I let my "find" clink onto the table.

Teresina took the fuenfliber, murmured "*Grazie*" and hurried out of the room.

With careful, slow-motion steps, trying to be as noiseless as possible, I walked around the stove, and it seemed as if I was going around the largest stove ever made by man since that memorable day (it was probably night) when Prometheus stole the first fire from Mount Olympus. At the very back of it, deep in shadow, stood a hidden ladder. Without hesitation, as if irresistibly drawn, I climbed up the few worn rungs until I saw it—or rather felt it—the trapdoor in the ceiling. The massive stove blocked off any light from the room's single lamp. Climbing cautiously higher I pressed open the trapdoor; my head and shoulders pushed hesitantly into stuffy darkness, and all was quiet except for the gentle creaking of the hinges. Not a glimmer of light, just the compressed stench of a farmer's unaired sleeping quarters: moldy straw, leather, sweat. Struggling to keep the door propped open I leaned the edge against my shoulder, got out my matches, struck one, then another. Close by the opening a low alcove, apparently not used as a place to sleep. There were no sheets, just a stripped feather comforter of grayish ham color, but so disheveled that it appeared to be serving someone as a resting place. No bedroom; instead a comfortable resting place for an eavesdropper to wile away his time. A cleverly hidden little listening post.

"*Segner, waas wender dett dooba?*" said the farmer.

"Excuse me." I blew out the match. "But I thought I heard a cat purring on top of the stove. I like to play with cats."

He stood there with dangling arms and looked up at me, his eyes shooting out a steady, coppery, flickering like that of the "eternal light" in a church—even though he was completely hidden in the shadow of the stove.

Things were at full swing in the Café d'Albana (Benedetg Caduff-Bonnard, Prop.), for the alpine maneuvers of the Sixty-first Border Regiment were over this Saturday. In the corridor-like room a few Mountain Fusiliers were dancing to loud radio music with Italian hotel maids who had just arrived for the tourist season—most of them short, plump, black-haired girls who, grinning tipsily, revealed their filling-laden teeth. Little beauty to be seen here, and nothing of Pina's marble melancholy. *Pina.* The waitress with the pimply face and turned-up nose (a malicious caricature of Xana) waved at me while dancing with a beerily grinning corporal, broke away from him, and pushed her way, smoothing the little apron that hung over her belly like a piece of bouffant curtain, over to the last free table where I had just sat down: "What'll the gentleman have? Wine? Beer?"

"Coffee grappa. Tell me, my pretty"—her ventriloquist's dummy face beamed—"is Mr. Caduff-Bonnard around?"

"*Le patron* is in Kulm at the *bal des gastronomes.* In an hour he'll be *retour.* Tonight before midnight he's going fishing—because of the waning moon."

"What's he doing before midnight?"

"Fish-ing! Why do you want to talk to the *patron?*" she asked curiously; the blaring radio forced us to speak as if both of us were hard of hearing. On the opposite wall, two posters. One, yellowed, bore the silhouette of a snail and the words: EAT SNAILS! ESCARGOTS PRÉPARÉS À L'ALSACIENNE!

"I'd like to buy a shell from Mr. Caduff-Bonnard."

"A *shell?*"

"You see, on nights like this I come so far out of mine that I need a new one. A snail shell. If Mr. Caduff-Bonnard happens to have one vacant."

Just as before she gaped at the hole in my forehead, then skipped over to the bar. I waited for my coffee grappa, and the ventriloquist's dummy served it to me. The beer-soaked Fusilier tapped her on the shoulder and patted her flat behind, and she took this as an invitation to dance, and I sipped on the coffee with its steaming, winy fragrance and waited for Benedetg Caduff-Bonnard to return from the ball and above the blaring radio I heard the heavy droning of a truck driving in first gear.

The other wall poster was an old-fashioned polychrome print, yellowed but colorful, divided into two halves. On the left a man, starved down to a skeleton, wearing only his baggy underwear and a Toulouse-Lautrec-beard, cowering hopelessly in front of an empty safe and watched over by two hungry-looking rats. Caption: I GRANTED CREDIT TO MY FRIENDS—AND NOW I FACE THE BITTER END! The other: a fat man in a fancy dressing gown, bedded down in an uphol-stered rocking chair after a gargantuan meal (whose remains are visible on a table), smoking a floor-length pipe in supreme satisfaction. Caption: "NO CRED-IT" WAS MY POLICY. NOW EVERYONE LOOKS UP TO ME. The noise of the truck's en-gine roared up briefly, then ceased.

Eat Snails I Granted to My Friends Préparés à l'Alsacienne Eat Credit Was My Policy and Now Escargots Look Up to Me à la Snails My Friends Granted Eat Policy Now Everyone Faces the Bitter End.

The curtains of the Café d'Albana were closed, only one window at the end of the room remained uncovered—the one displaying a stuffed chamois. The schoolhouse square was dimly lit. From my seat I could look out over the back of the chamois and see the shadow of the darkened de Colana house. Again and again it attracted my gaze, but the chamois made me think of another stuffed creature.

Suddenly the telegraph key on my forehead began sending an alarm signal.

The darkened windowpane above the chamois back was now enlivened by a flickering glow. A reflection of room lights constantly erased by the shifting shadows of the dancing couples? Or was it two cigar-smokers standing outside, momentary onlookers at the improvised dance hall. Or was the window creating an optical illusion? But the moment before it disappeared it seemed to be alive, to see, to rest—not on the dancers—but on me. . . like albino eyes.

"Is the gentleman leaving so soon?" squeaked the dancing ventriloquist's dummy. "The boss will soon be *retour!* Where are you going in such a hurry?"

"Just to get a breath of fresh air. Be back in a minute."

Just outside the door I almost stumbled over Zuan. Hatless, coatless, his violet suit-jacket collar turned up, he bent down next to a ladies' bicycle leaning against the doorpost and busied himself with a bulging knapsack he had depos-ited on the threshold.

"Good evening. Pardon me—do you smoke cigars?"

He stood up, reeling slightly. "No need for cigars." The words were a thick-tongued mumbling emerging from his unusually disheveled patriarch's beard.

"I mean, did you happen to be smoking a cigar just now—over there by the window with the stuffed chamois."

"No need for a chamois."

"Or did you see anyone there? Just now? Excuse my curiosity. I'm ex-pecting a friend."

"No need for friends."

"You see, I thought I saw, just this minute—"

"No need for minutes."

His obsessed, one-track answers, the wet sparkle of his eyes (not albino

156

eyes) allowed one to guess that he was on a bicycle tour of the local bars.

"Or did you happen to see a truck drive by here?"

"No need for trucks. They'll never carry m-e off in one of those things—not m-e!"

Without warning he burst out with a hollow laugh, a chilling cackle that shook his messy noble beard. Robbed of his gloomy decorum he was almost exuberant as he slammed the café door shut behind him; the ladies' bicycle crashed to the pavement. I lifted it up and leaned it against the doorpost, then looked around in all directions and made my way past the police station toward the main street of the urban village. I never reached it. Out of a darkened doorway the eye stared at me, the red eye. It scarcely flickered. Its coppery beam rested on me. From its blurred iris the coppery sheen overflowed the entire fist-sized eyeball. It stared at me calmly, waiting, out of the depths of the shadowy doorway, an albino cyclops eye, and scarcely moved.

My weak right eye must have been playing tricks on me again. A brief, closer look had revealed the "albino cyclops eye" phenomenon as something utterly trivial. The neat little brass sign of ENGLISH HAIRDRESSER, hanging free on a red-white-and-blue striped rod, dully reflecting a streetlamp on the Via Maistra, the main street of St. Moritz. *What concerns us is optical illusion.* This saying of Abbé Galiani's that de Colana had bequeathed to me on an outhouse wall—I was not about to accept it and certainly not to exemplify it into practice; yes, even began to suspect my suspicion of Men Clavadetscher. Nevertheless I did not give up my intention to sound out Mr. Caduff-Bonnard, Men's companion on the woodchuck hunt during which Men's brother Peidar was ostensibly mistaken for a woodchuck and shot dead. And Xana? She was *not* waiting for me. (Instead of me she had the *Golden Ass* of Apuleius.) But Pina from Valtellina? with whom I had a midnight rendezvous? with this girl of marble, this marble Roman statuette just waiting to be turned glowing midnight hot? If I could catch Caduff before too long and if he were talkative I might still be on time for this nocturnal demarbleization.

"*Ciao,* ladies and gentlemen! —And a H-A-I-R-Y Christmas to you all, H--A--I--R--Y C-H-R-I-S-T-M-A-S!" Printer Zuan slammed the door of the Café d'Albana so hard that I was afraid the glass would break. He grabbed the handlebars of his ladies' bike: "Hey there, you!" he flew at me. "No need for stuffed chamois cigars! Mahahaha!" Suddenly he turned off his reeling and cackling; forced himself back to his air of gloomy dignity. "Please help me tighten the straps on this pack, my good man."

I did him the favor, a little surprised at the weight of the knapsack. Holy Laudon, that's well over fifty pounds, I thought, and packed so full and hard. What was he lugging around in there anyway?

"Waste paper," Zuan answered my unspoken question. "You need any waste paper? You don't, but I do, mahaha." He swung, no, rolled himself onto the saddle. "*Il Avvocato Bow-Wow* was done away with."

"How do you mean that, Mr. Zuan?"

"Well now, I mean simply—the way of all flesh. *Ciao*."

I could ask him about this comment of his later—when he was sober. Now he would pedal away, but not run away from me. No, Zarli Zuan won't run away from me.

Steering a slightly zigzag course he rolled down the side street toward the Via Maistra, pedaling with fanatical zeal, presumably to the next bar. A bit of beard fluttered over his left shoulder.

The ventriloquist's dummy, the waitress, said, yeah, yeah, Mr. Zuan was drunk, completely stoned, which was something unusual for him. Wasn't he a hazard to himself and others, cycling around in his condition? Hardly, she said optimistically. He was an excellent *vélo* rider who went on all the *vélo* tours—usually on a ladies' model, so that he didn't need to wear bicycle clips. But was he in the habit of making such tours loaded down with a heavy backpack? No, she never saw him cycle with a back-pack. And by the way, *le patron* had just come back. He was just now changing his clothes to go night fishing.

Mr. Caduff bore little resemblance to the "no credit" fat man on the yellowed color print. An obviously friendly man of dark, almost North African complexion, wearing boots and a coat of reddish brown rubber.

"I'm told you would like to try my snails. *Excusez*, but I'm afraid it's too late for that. I cook them myself. Right now I have to go out on the lake. Before midnight with a waning moon, you know, that's when the pike bite the best."

"How interesting." I passed myself off as a sportswriter. "I've already eaten this evening—in Sils. In the Chesetta Grischuna run by Mr.—what's his name? Clava?—yes, Clavadetscher. You probably know him."

Caduff-Bonnard's very by-the-way reply: "I know every *restaurateur* in the Upper Engadine."

I paid my check, walked out the door with him. "Fishing and hunting, those seem to be the hobbies of a lot of restaurant owners around here. I've heard that this Mr. Clavadetscher is a great hunter."

Caduff-Bonnard: "Was, was. As far as I know, Men hasn't been hunting for some years now." Period. (Too direct, too direct, my approach to the subject.) "Besides it's closed season now. Otherwise I could recommend a good chamois stew for tomorrow. If St. Peter is willing I'll hook a big pike tonight, and tomorrow there'll be *quenelles de brochet*."

Pike dumplings. I feigned a sportswriter's interest in the enterprise. Would he object to including me in the fishing party. He did not.

Toward midnight, as the rays of the waning June moon at six thousand feet above sea level created a magical brilliance, my new companion's boat with outboard motor steered toward the southeast corner of the lake. To our horror, Mr. Caduff and I suddenly observed printer Zuan, his beard clearly recognizable, as he raced his bicycle down the pier of the Villa Muongia, the bulging knapsack on his back. With a single splash the tin horse and rider sank into the lake.

1

The next morning, Sunday the nineteenth of June, at 9:15, I was arrested.

Two gendarmes from Samedan hauled me out of bed. As a passive specialist in arrest-making I was no more surprised than Xana was. We were agreed that the tenth hour of the morning was a fitting time to arrest hay-fever patients at a mountain resort.

On the office door of the Samedan police station a multilingual sign announced SPECIAL SERVICE. The room was divided in half by a wooden barrier. On this side a few stools without backs, on the other side three desks with leather-upholstered swivel chairs. Three locked windows, all like giant embrasures; to the right of them a door that opened to admit police big shot Dumeng Mavegn. Yes, a bigger shot than I had imagined. He had to bend down a bit to get through the door. Perhaps no older than his mid-fifties, prototype of the Big Old Strongman. Black vest hanging open, snow-white shirt sleeves; his enormous, broad starched collar held together by a comparatively small, chic bow tie (houndstooth check). He made himself as comfortable as possible in the chair and burst out with his booming bass voice, which, like a damaged organ pipe, betrayed a trace of a wheeze. "Takhe a seat."

He opened up a heavy dossier. Papers of various sizes and colors. Carbon copies, pages of typed memoranda (the length of legal briefs) intermingled with memo sheets, handwritten notes, stamped papers, bound papers, all being flipped through by his tree-root-knotted fingers. Then he slowly turned his large face toward me, and the light falling through the massive fortress windows made it appear like a brownish, chiseled rock. And then there were the ice blue, shaggy bangs that fell across his forehead and, somewhat to the left beneath his chin, an inconspicuous but recognizable goiter sprinkled with moss-colored flecks. Yes, a glacial moraine was staring at me.

"Your passport."

He flipped cursorily through the booklet.

"Yeahno, this pass is invalid."

I did not reply.

"You're aware, off course, that cirkha three months ago the Republikh of Aushtria, *Républiqhue d'Autriche*, ceasedh to exisht, both *de jure* and *de facto*.

"I'm aware. Rather more *de facto* than *de jure*."

"That is no-o khoncern off mine. For the p-hurpose off obtaining a validh passport you w'r supposedh to rep-hort to the Cherman Khonsulate in Zurickh and app-hly as a citizen off the Reich."

"I refuse . . ." I broke off. "I flatly refuse."

"You fhlatly refhuse." He noted something with a heavy fountain pen. "'R you a Joe?"

"A what?"

"Joe-ish."

"No, are you?"

The moraine stared at me. Suddenly Mavegn swung way back in his chair and emitted a whistling, thundering laugh of real amusement. Then pulled himself back to his upright position.

"It's no-o business off yours. Yeahno, it really isn't. But if you really want to know, I'm a ffree citizen off Rhaetia. My ffamily goes backh to the old-est in-ha-bi-tants off ourr beautifful Engadine. Ihhappen to be a di-rekht descendant off the Etruskhans."

"Oi vay."

"What's that mean?"

"Excuse me, but I happen to know a little about ethnology and history. It's a proven fact that the Etruscans were a people who migrated from Asia Minor to the Apennine Peninsula. From Rome to Florence, I mean in the whole area we now call Romagna, Umbria, and Tuscany they built up a fabulous culture."

"*Ekkho*," said the Commissioner.

"Then the Etruscans were defeated by the Latins."

"De-*ffeatedh?*"

"The ones who didn't surrender. They were forced out of Rome. Forced into emigration."

"Emi-*gration?*" he rumbled like an approaching glacial thunderstorm. (Once I was overtaken by a thunderstorm while crossing the Moine Glacier above Chamonix—unpleasant memory.)

"Yes. The Etruscans moved north. Up here into the southern Alps—Friuli, Trento, the Engadine—was where they emigrated."

"*Emi*-gratedh?"

"*Ecco*," I said politely. "From the beginning the Etruscans were a *non-Ar-yan* people, Commissioner Mavegn. No more Aryan than the Jews. Sort of Jew-ish emigrants."

"Yeah-*no-o*, now I've hhadh enufff!" The heavy fountain pen stabbed out at me. "'R you a Khommunist?"

"No, are you?"

Then the thunderstorm broke loose with lightning flashing from his eyes and thundering fist-blows on the desk top. "A-n-s-w-e-r m-y k-h-w-e-s-t-i-o-n-s or I'll have you hhauled away!!"

"All right. I was a member of the Austrian Social Democratic Party until it was declared illegal by the Dollfuss regime."

"Illegal akh-tivities seem to be your shpeciality. At the endh off March you illegally overshtepped the Swiss border."

"Overslid."

"What?"

"Came across the Silvretta on skis. And reported immediately to the police in Klosters-Platz. Despite my fatigue."

"Your fatighue doesn't khoncern me. What do you mean, overslid?"

"Starting from the highest village in Montafon, from Sankt Gallenkirch. Even though I'm a passable skier, it was no fun. Hot on my trail was an SS ski patrol with carbines. Death was hot on my trail, if you want to make a note of that."

"Why? That doesn't khoncern me." Dictating to himself he scribbled, his "root," his mandrake hand still trembling slightly with slowly dissipating rage. "'The suspekht's mentality in-khlines him to makhe things ekhs-sessively dra-ma-tikh.' Fooh, so then, you count on being rekhognized as a politikhal refu-gee."

"My status."

"A fugitive." Now Mavegn turned a page. "Embezzlers khan be fugitives too." His mandrake hand carefully smoothed out a sheet of typewritten paper. "Did you, immediately before your, eh, es-khape from Vienna khommit an akht of emb-hezzlement?"

"I beg your pardon?"

"I see no reason to kheep the fakhts in this khase a sekhret," said massive Mavegn. "The shtate's attorney's office in Vienna is reqhuesting your extra-dition, fooh, based on ffindings off the khriminal police to the effekht, fooh, that you imbezzled ffunds off the Social Demokhratikh Party off Aushtria."

I peered across the barrier. In the bright light from the windows my good eye quickly recognized the signature on Mavegn's document. The intitial "L," whose cross-stroke jerked pompously upward behind the last letter of the name. "This libelous denunciation is signed by an intimate *enemy* of mine. Heinzwer-ner Laimgruber, Secret Police Headquarters, Vienna I."

Mavegn began turning pages—all too quickly. "These dokhuments w'r sent to us by the Vienna khriminal police. Not by the Geshtapo."

"Just part of their little trick."

"That remains to be seen. What means off ffinancial sup-hort do you hhave hhere?"

"I write. I mean I've been writing for various Swiss papers for years. Partly as Vienna correspondent, partly as a short story man. I haven't been paid directly but have had my fees deposited by Mr. Henrique Kujath of Luzienburg in the Domleschg. For a rainy day. Which has arrived."

My disclosure seemed to disappoint and even startle the Commissioner. "This matter will be checkhed out." Scribbling. "Since y'r entry into Swiss territory you've been forbidden to write." Leafing. "A-n-d to shoot."

"Pardon me."

"Do you poss-hess a fire-harm?"

"No."

" 'R you trained in the use off fire-harms?"

"I would say so. But it seems that others were better trained than I. Don't your files show that I have a war wound? Since you've forbidden me to ask questions you can take that as an answer."

"Wounded in the war." Mavegn's mandrake fingers flip pages. "In what place?"

"Between Brâila and Konstanza."

"That doesn't khoncern me. Answer my khwestion precisely."

"I can't be very precise—because I was flying more than six thousand feet over the Black Sea at the time—there was a thick layer of cloud below me—"

"What part of y'r b-o-d-h-e-e was wounded!"

At the same moment his gaze touched my forehead. Obviously a completely new discovery for this criminologist. Suddenly he slammed the dossier shut. "It remains a k-hurious fakht that you always seem to be around when a ffatal akh-cident or the likhe okkhurs. Lawyer de Kholana, in a drunken shtate, drives into Lake Khampfér—

Excuse me, but I question whether he was drunk that evening and question whether it was an accident. Listen to what I have to say. Why didn't I come out with it, here and now?

"—and off all people you're the one," he continued, "who khomes along and diskhovers this light in the lake."

"I was in the company of Mr. ten Breukaa."

"We know that. Three days later, yeshterday before midnight, the printing press owner Zuan khommits suicide, and you off all people 'r a witness to the occ-hurrence."

"I was in the company of Mr. Caduff-Bonnard."

"We know that. We have information to the effekht that you w'r the last person to talkh to Zarli Zuan."

"I exchanged a few words with him as he came out of the Café d'Albana—"

"About what?"

"He asked me to help him put on his knapsack."

"Why did he re-khwire y'r assistance?"

"In the first place he wasn't very steady on his feet. In the second place the knapsack was rather heavy."

"Rather heavy. That interests us."

"That concerns you?" I asked.

Mavegn sharply: "On this occ-hasion did you have occ-hasion to identify the khontents off the knapsackh?"

"No. But whatever it was felt hard and angular. I thought of blocks of paper. Or books. A natural assumption since I knew Mr. Zuan's profession. And he actually did ask me if I had any need for waste paper. But a little later when he, Mr. Zuan, sank out of sight before my very eyes—like a sack on wheels—"

"Ffooh, ruckh-sackh on wheels!"

"—I thought back. Thought, no, *too* hard, *too* angular. More like big stones."

My speculation appeared to satisfy Mavegn; he uttered something like a gurgle of contentment. "On the hhighway to Chantarella next to Zuan's printshop two guard shtones 'r missing from the khurb. These same shtones w'r dug out by an unknown party sometime after dark lasht night. The khase is khlear. Khlear. Zarli digs out the shtones. Fills his ruckh-sackh, puts it on, and rides his *vélo* into a, ffooh, into a watery grave. *Ekkho.* The weight drags him to the bottom. So that we khan't find his body, yeahno, we khan't find it."

"You can't find it."

The moraine stare struck me. "Did I askh you anything?" The desk telephone jingled. The Commissioner picked up the receiver. "Mavegn! . . . Baur au Lac, Zurickh? . . . Aaah." In a moment he was out of the chair and leaning his buttocks against the edge of the desk, one leg extended as a prop. "*Salut, Madame, salu-u-ut.* What khan I do for you? Yeahno, as you see, I'm on duty Sundays too." (How gallant a glacier can be.) As unexpectedly as it had brightened, the face of the telephoning interrogator went dark again: "Yes, that's exactly what happened. We had very good reasons . . . About that, madam, I khan give you no infformation." After Mavegn had listened quietly for some time: "R-e-a-l-l-y? . . . Ah . . . That is indeedh something new to us. . . . I see . . . Yeahso. . . . Yeahnono, in that khase I am preparedh," he hesitated, snorting with a whistle, "fffhoo, to place the matter backh in the hands off the Zurickh authorities . . . Nothing to thankh me for; eh, what won't a gentleman do for such a pretty pair off eyes. Wish you and y'r husband a pleasant Sunday. *Aadieu.*"

Mavegn hung up the receiver, took five giant steps to the window, glanced, bending over somewhat, out the "embrasure" with his back to his prisoner as if he had forgotten about him. Startled, a fat fly began to buzz around him, a beetle of a fly, as oversized as the man himself. He took a halfhearted swat at it, turned toward me, sat back down at the desk, scribbled for some time, his head pushed back farsightedly, ripped the finished pages from his note pad and deposited them in the dossier, which he then slammed shut.

"Bekhause you have ignored the second summons of the Khantonal Alien

Plice in Zurickh you will be charged with this offense in the lokhal police khourt there. By the way, I didn't know you w'r related to . . . you may go."

"Hallihallo," Xana greeted me as I got out of the bus. "How did I organize your release this time?"

"It was ingenious. You sicked Pola onto that glacier Mavegn."

"Right." After my arrest she had called up Pola in Zurich and asked her to intervene; the latter had remarked: "Arrested again? That seems to be normal for him," and, "Mavegn! I'll have him eating out of my hand in five minutes." In the meantime a telegram had arrived for me. Madam Fausch was gone. Mr. Duschlett had brought it up to her. Naturally she had opened it. I could imagine why.

"From! —your! —pa! —rents!" My exclamation like four shots from the Walther pistol.

"Nnno-o. Just from Grandpa Kujath."

DEAR TREBLA URGENT BUSINESS REQUIRES THAT YOU VISIT ME TODAY SUNDAY EVE-
NING AFTER 8 PM ALONE IF POSSIBLE   GRANDPA

I: "Maybe Grandpa is about to sell my Austriacus Babeuf series to a Swiss book publisher and doesn't want to discuss it on the phone." Since Pola had lent me the Chrysler for the weekend, it was my plan to drive the 100 kilometers down into the Domleschg early in the evening and return the same night. "Unfortunately the 'Special Service' cops forgot to serve me breakfast. Come on, let's go eat something. No, not in the Morteratsch."

"Embarrassed to go in there, aren't you?"

"Why embarrassed? By whom?"

"Pina. As an ex-con . . . with your sister . . ."

"Mmm. Come, let's go to Jann. They have eggs *à la russe* there *too*."

From two-thirty until five-thirty I "stored up some sleep" by means of an extended nap. When I awoke Xana was standing next to my bed. To my, at first groggy, then wide-awake surprise she was dressed in her dark green evening gown, gently, tenderly, narcissistically stroking the fans of dark green rooster feathers fastened to the straps.

"Holy Laudon."

"Why do you always say Holy Laudon, Trebla?"

"You ask me that after having known me so many hundred years? Gideon Laudon. A Scotsman born in Livonia."

"In Livo-onia?"

"That's right. Maybe a distant relative of Elsabé's. First he served with the Russians, then he became a Field Marshal for Madame Marie Thérèse. Do you know that she never signed her name as, you know, 'Maria Theresa,' but always the *other* way. Not the German way, but in the French version, pro-

166

nounced in court Thérèse."

"I think Papa-Rose once told me that Laudon lived in the Hofburg . . . and that people said there was some sort of secret passageway between his bedroom and the chambers of the widowed Madame Empress—"

"Viennese gossip. But maybe there was something to it."

"Do you really think there was *ever* anything to Viennese gossip?"

"If I had shoulder feathers like yours, I'd probably shrug them. Anyway Gideon in his early fifties seems to have been a dashing fellow—Holy Laudon, they were *both* born in seventeenseventeen—and Marie, despite her seventeen, I mean sixteen children, had a fabulous bosom. And now unfortunately I have to start getting dressed to drive down to the Domleschg. Say, why have you got that evening gown on? I never dreamed you'd packed that in with everything else."

"I even packed your old tuxedo."

"Really? When I see you in *that* dress I always think of Feather-Elsie. The gun moll in the George Raft picture."

"That's a compliment, of course."

"Of course. And I think of something else, too. Your shoulder feathers look just like the helmet plumes on captured Bersaglieri officers as they trotted through Novaledo in 1918. Novaledo in the Brenta Valley. I had ended up with the old Thirty-sixth Reconnaissance again—which had been transferred from Brâila to Trento—and I was no good for anything but ground duty."

"Will you give me a lift to St. Mo?"

"What are you going to do in St. Mo with your Bersaglieri feathers?"

"I have a sort of halfway date with Pola. She told me on the phone that she wanted to be back here by 8:30; and if she isn't too tired—there's a sort of a thing Badrutt's giving at the Embassy Room of the Palace, a sort of gala soirée to open the season."

"And Pola invited you?"

"Sort of halfway. She said you could bring me over in the Chrysler, though we won't take Joop and Trebla, she said. But if you have to go see Grandpa earlier I can always take the train."

"Why in the name of all the atheistic gods do you want to go tonight to some idiotic-snobbish-goshawful-crash-boring-gala-soirée-embassy-open-season-season-opening-galagala?"

The Bersaglieri feathers began to vibrate imperceptibly.

"'Cause I've had 'nuf." (She swallowed the "e.") "'Cause I want to make 'zelf feel bedder 'nzide. 'Zides the awvul zdory of Magsim Grabscheidt . . . zun'ly you gum home with a dreadful zdory 'bout Mr. Lana and his Zbaniels all drowning in a zord of a 'quarium. Then zun'ly there's the zdory of how Mr. Zuan drove his bizyggle into the wadder . . ." (When Xana swallows the first syllable of a word or voices unvoiced consonants—*s* changing to *z*, *k* to *g*, *t* to *d*, etc.—it can be a sign either of contentment or irritation.)

"And you want to make yourself feel better inside at Bedrutt's soirée?" Hello jealousy! After a short discussion we agreed to forget Pola's half-invitation and to drive to the Domleschg *together*, despite Kujath's dissuasion; and on our return "to do a few turns on Badrutt's parquet if possible"—as Grandpa would say. So in the name of Laudon I put on my tuxedo and left the building alone to check the tires and the gas gauge of the Chrysler. Mr. Duschlett, the postal official, came up to me in his Sunday best. With a disgruntled "Here's *another* one for you!" he handed me a telegram.

It had been sent from Murska Sobota, Yugoslavia, just a stone's throw across the border from Radkersburg, South Styria.

OUR DEAR OLD CIRCUS HORSE WAS REQUISITIONED A WEEK AGO STOP
NEGOTIATING HIS RELEASE STOP SPECIAL DELIVERY LETTER FOLLOWS
AUTES

It wasn't a ticking on my brow that struck me this time, but something *tearing* in my forehead, like a torn ligament above my eyes.

Tearing. I tore up the yellow paper into tiny scraps—like a bill forger afraid to be caught with his wares.

We drove into Thusis at around 8:30 that evening after passing over a suspension bridge; Thusis was not much of a town. The signal bell chimed from the railroad station, the arpeggiated chord of seconds that rings from all Helvetian stations, and in a decrepit old pharmacy with night service I located some Merck's ephedrine and swallowed three tablets with some water served to me by the woman at the drug counter. She resembled Madam Fausch. She inspected my face closely, unabashedly, then she gaped at my tuxedo, then through the glass door at the long hood of the cabriolet. Suddenly she said straight to my face she knew who I was. Really? Who? I asked; and she said, a king, and I asked, a king of spades or diamonds, and she said, no, a real one, and I asked, one with or without a throne, and she took on Madam Fausch's teasing masculine tone and said, *excusez*, but Your Highness knows that better than anyone else. (That's the way she said it, without irony, so it seemed.) I got behind the wheel and announced that I'd been taken for a hay-fever-suffering king, and Xana said, "That on top of everything else, you poor soul. How do you feel now?" I replied that the stuff didn't take effect that quickly.

We drove out of Thusis and into the Domleschg Valley, and the dry south wind not only made the sparse lights strewn across the foot of the Heinzenberg appear deceptively close but it magnified sound as well, the rushing sound of the Hinterrhein coming out of the monster gorge of the Via Mala.

'Bad road."

"Hm?"

"Can't you hear the roaring of the Via Mala behind us, Xana? Via Mala, right, Miss Ancient Philologist? means Bad Road. I hear its roaring/but I know not/where it leads us."

"New poem?"

"Hay-fever poetry."

"How are your little voices doing?"

"...Weaker." Although I sniffed the stinging smell of freshly mown hay the crackling constriction of my breathing began to abate. I knew that the effects of the ephedrine would begin to wear off in two hours and the attack would return, unless of course I took still more ephedrine and so brought myself to the threshold of that state the Americans call "drugged." A hapless euphoria for me that, especially tonight, I wanted to avoid.

TARTAR said a lantern of blue lead-glass disguised as a signpost.

"Tartarus, subbasement of the underworld, right, Miss Primeval Philologist? Would you buy a castle next to a village with a name like that?"

"I don't think Grandpa is bothered by having such a little Tartarus for a neighbor."

Below the village of Tartar on a foothill of the Heinzenberg a loose bundle of hectically blinking lights: the Luzienburg. I turned away from the bed of the Hinterrhein up a gravel road rolled flat by truck tires, up two rather steep spirals to the top of the hill. Almost vertically overhead, unlighted and shadowy, towered the castle's outside walls. Then the road leveled out and snaked into a half ravine. Built into this ravine with the skill of a fortress architect or a camouflage artist and invisible from below, something white rose quite unexpectedly out of the stacked shadows of the pines to a height of a hundred feet. Something like a narrow skyscraper squeezed in between the cliffs, its front windowless. A lonely light bulb illuminated a sign with discreet, small lettering:

HENRIQUE KUJATH
LUZIEN-MILL & SILO

Beneath it, a very closed off, seemingly unreachable door that led out onto a raisable loading ramp that was hoisted into its uppermost position. On the plateau in front a pair of two-wheeled truck trailers draped in large tarpaulins.

I stopped, listened. "... Usually the mill works until midnight during the summer. How quiet."

"Today is Sunday."

"'All the turning wheels will stop/When your mighty arm decrees.' —Holy Laudon, that slogan of ours has turned out to be a horrible mistake in Central Europe."

"Not in Russia," said Xana.

"Perhaps because wheels were comparatively rare in Russia back then."

I drove around the last curve and the double headlights glared against a mighty door covered by a barnlike roof: the gate to the Luzienburg. There, the veritable drawbridge, Kujath's pride. Like his predecessors he had refused to tear it down, but had its load capacity strengthened instead, and "kept the winches oiled in case the process servers, in Swiss, the *Betreibungsbeamte*, try to storm the castle." I said, "The gate seems to be shut. Don't be startled when I give the signal."

Twice I let the pompous minor-third fanfare sound, and wondered whether Xana suspected something about the telegram Duschlett had given me two hours ago, which had been sent from Murska Sobota and signed "Autes" and which I had promptly torn to pieces? My forehead acted up again.

"Aha, da Red Baron. G'd evenin' ladies 'n gentlemen 'n comrades."

After Pfiff had carefully, very carefully closed and bolted the heavy, iron-plated doors behind us he swung himself sidesaddle onto the hood with a jockey's agility. Although bigger than the English king's ex-jockey, he reminded me of Fitz. I let the car roll slowly across the cobblestones of the Pfauenhof, the Peacock Courtyard (as the inner yard of the castle had been called for centuries). Illuminating it were several baroque candelabra that seemed to have been removed from the Place Stanislas in Nancy. Past the well, the wrought-iron gate Kujath had put across the sixty-foot-deep shaft (for the protection of his grandchildren) gleamed dully. Two cars, a coupé and a limousine, were parked beneath the bricked-up alcove window, through which no white-veiled woman glided. (Today I resisted making any jokes about the legendary castle ghosts.) The rest of the windows in the Peacock Wing, as the main building was called, had heavy shutters with wavy red and yellow stripes; in the pale glow of the candelabra they looked like tired watch fires.

The windows on the ground floor were alight, on the second story, only one next to the bricked-up alcove (which had been left with its wooden shutters) was alight. From it a child's bawling monotone could be heard.

"Lots of grandchildren here, Pfiff?" I asked over the top of the windshield.

"All nine of 'em. 'Cause of d' boss's birthday t'morra."

"Didn't know that."

"T'morra all d' poppas come rollin' in here too, Herr von Querfurt, Herr von Preznicek and Herr Dokta' Heppenheim wid his wife." ("Wife" meant Sedina, Kujath's only daughter, who had already seen two of her marriages go on the rocks.) "Just between us, d' boss is a little sour 'bout d' big celebration. An' dat's not d' only thing he's . . ."

Pfiff broke off abruptly and sprang down off the hood as I halted in front of the narrow outside staircase. Grandma Kujath came rustling down in mouse-gray taffeta, her "little" bit of an evening dress that seemed unpretentious despite her mink stole with its rather stunted-looking collection of tails. With her usual whining, cracking, almost whimperingly squeaky voice she called out, "There they are at last, the seldom-seen little couple! Oh, how splendidly they're dressed! Our studious little Xana-kins with her cute little model's waistline, and Trebla, the gallant little knight of the proletariat!"

"Of the *little* proletariat," I was tempted to correct her. Grandma Kujath—nee Diethelmine von Plessenow, daughter of a Brandenburg country gentleman and dubbed "Helma, the Kummersdorf-Cuirassier's-Child," or "*die Burgfrau*" by Grandpa—belonged to the type of Prussian woman who loses her face when she grows old. Her once pretty features were more than sunken; they had all but disappeared. Her once graceful figure, next to which the young self-made man Henrique Kujath had seemed all the more massive, had not become obese, just shapeless. Grandma's personality manifested itself primarily in her voice, in which since girlhood she had cultivated a tearful undertone. "Even as a teenager she used to whimper a lot, and now that she goes tottering from one sanatorium to another her chronic blubbering is getting worse by the day," confirmed Kujath with exaggerated heartlessness. "Whereas in the tropics I only got a case of malaria plus an enlarged heart, the Kummersdorf Child has collected so many maladies that she'll certainly live to be a hundred." Once Grandpa had told me in detail how he, the just-returned "Rubber King" of the Amazon, had met little Diethelmine at the Berlin Alpenball around the turn of the century, and how the financially insolvent country gentleman had granted the Germano-Brazilian pioneer his daughter's hand in marriage; and what a scandal (a well-kept secret up to that point) had blown up when Kujath's father was revealed to be a retired teamster from the Badstrasse in North Berlin who carried on a small business selling porcelain imitation bread rolls with money slits, "piggy-banks made for smashing."

"Madam Kummersdorf can't stand you, Trebla, because you're an Austrian," Grandpa had snickered, amused by his indiscretion. "She only whimpers your father-in-law to the skies because it's just good form to rave about a world-famous clown; in reality she's written him off as an Italian. And then about your wife she once whined: 'This little Roxana-kins has developed into a real *beauté*, but for all her philology she's still something of a little dummy.'" (Which Xana, oddly enough, took as a great compliment. She took malicious pride in being considered dumb and beautiful.)

Grandma Kujath reveled in diminutives, but these were nothing like the endless pet names Elsabé Giaxa had transferred from Russian into her charming eccentric Balto-German. Grandma's diminutives, cultivated among her brood of grandchildren, could have hooks and barbs.

"Good evening, Grandma," we said with one voice. I climbed out quickly, kissed Grandma's hand, which felt like paper, and murmured, "My respects, dear Lady," knowing full well that she despised such "Viennese frillsy-willsies," and out of the corner of my eye caught a glimpse of Pfiff helping Xana out of the cabriolet (a gesture Grandma usually refused).

"Have the 'parentless children' dined this evening? No? Well, come right in! There's a little cold snacky waiting for you."

With an air of embarrassed secrecy I'd never seen him show, Pfiff announced: "'Scuse me, Miz Kujath, but d'boss ga' me strict orders t' take d' gentleman straight up to d' silo-studio—and be sure he's alone, d' boss said."

"Then let's leave these little know-it-all mennikins to themselves," whimpered Grandma. "Trebla will be able to get a little sandwichy in the tower. Would it bore you terribly to spend a little whilesy with a sick old ladykins, Xana-deary?"

"I'm never bored, Grandma-deary," said Xana.

"Well then! First I have to put the Heppenheim kiddies to beddie-bye and then we can have a little chat, but not in ancient Greek, pretty please," a whimper-giggle, "but I must lie down."

"Me too," said Xana.

"Wha-a-at?"

"Mmm," I said, "Xana's just gotten over a case of bronchitis."

"Oh Goddy, oh Goddy," whined Grandma cheerily, "nobody ever tells me anything."

I parked the Chrysler by the well from which no severed woman's hand appeared and from the building I heard the monotonous staccato of a ping-pong ball and, glancing quickly around, I just managed to catch sight of a reddish shimmer from Xana's crimson evening jacket. It seemed like the farewell wave of someone departing on a long journey . . .

Without hesitation Pfiff adopted a familiar tone with me. "Dat slick lookin' Yankee rig belong t' you, Comrade?"

"Good grief no."

"Rented?"

"No."

"Borra'd?"

"No."

"Heisted?"

"Heisted," I said. "Should I put the top up?"

"It's not gonna rain."

"I mean, so I can lock up the car."

"Got somethin' value'ble in dere? You're safer here dan Schicklgruber in his 'Eagle's Nest.' "

"No valuables. Just an unregistered Walther pistol."

"Nuttin'll happen to it. What's d' rod for, Comrade?"

"It's wartime, Comrade, and not only in Spain."

"Class war y' mean. Dat neva stops."

"I mean the Second World War."

"Seccon?" Pfiff turned away and pulled a flashlight out of his pocket, grumbling over his shoulder: "Y'could be right. D-i-s kinda peacetime ain't wortha nickel, as I always used to tell my buddies in Berlin."

Pfiff made a brief motion with the switched-off flashlight. In the light of the candelabra I discovered the shy seriousness in the face of the ever-faithful boy from Berlin. Hans Pfiffke was a factory worker's son from Reinickendorf; on May Day, 1929, after the traditional May Day parade had been ordered cancelled by Berlin's Social Democratic Police Chief Zoerrgiebel, the wiry little

172

man marched to the Lustgarten with the Red War Veterans' Union, which had defied the order. A street riot; a cracking of nightsticks; shots; dead men. Hans Pfiffke dragged himself into the bushes of the Tiergarten with a bullet wound in his upper thigh. Driving out of the Grosser Stern came a gentleman driving a roadster with Swiss license plates, a Herculean man in his sixties wearing a bright-colored spring suit, obviously a spectator, perhaps a reporter. With astonishing quickness he carried the wounded featherweight from the bushes to the car before Zoerrgiebel's cops could close in, turned around despite the police whistles, and escaped down the Charlottenburger Chaussee. "That's how I plucked Pfiff," Kujath recalled, "out of the class war, model 'Red versus Red,' because I could see at a glance he was too small for it." He took him along to Brazil on his expedition into the heart of the Matto Grosso, where Pfiff earned his spurs as a tireless rider of the dwarfish *caboclo* horses. Now he led the way for me, striding bareheaded across the cobblestones in his white shirt, leather breeches, and knee boots. His figure suggested a wiry horseman (that's why he reminded me of Fitz). And in the context of the Pfauenhof a page.

As he led me past the two cars parked beneath the alcove, I queried, "More visitors besides the grandchildren?"

Pfiff switched on the flashlight and let the light play over the license plates, one of which bore a Geneva coat of arms. "Spanish exiles from Geneva. One of em's a big wheel. From d' Prado Museum. But tonight we're expectin' an even bigger wheel."

"Who?"

Pfiff switched off the flashlight. "Well, Trebla, I guess I c'n tell y-o-u-s . . . Valentin."

"Which Valentin?" I said, also whispering.

"D-e-e Valentin, man."

"What?!" I whispered electrified. "Valentin Tiefenbrucker?!"

"Dat's right. Four days ago he broke outa d' concentration camp at Dachau."

"My God," I whispered enthusiastically. "Great God."

"Aw get outa here wid yer great god, Mr. Austro-Marxist."

Pfiff peered up at the alcove window. So it seemed to me. Then I realized that he was actually checking the cirrostratus clouds that hung across the night sky like a titanic spider web. "South wind," he said. "No storm comin'. Tomorra morning at five he's flyin' out."

"Valentin—where to?"

"Not back to Dachau, dat's for sure, Comrade."

My upward glance remained fixed on the wooden shutters that flanked the bricked-up window. In the glow of the candelabras I noticed something that hadn't struck me during my earlier daytime visits.

Unlike the others, these shutters did not have the red and yellow pattern of wavy zebra stripes. I fitted my monocle into my weak eye, looked up at the alcove, and heard Pfiff's sudden laugh.

"Hehheh, d' Red Baron and his monocle."

"I keep telling you I don't wear it for any kind of snob appeal, but because my right eye—"

"Don't lemme kid ya, Tovarish. But what'r ya starin' up dere like dat for? Ya waiting for ol' Lukretia's ghost t' come spookin' out of dat bricked-up winda an onto d' balcony?"

"Whose ghost?"

"Lukretia, d'White Lady Lukretia Planta. Dat's our local ghost."

"Planta . . .? Ah . . . Your flashlight, Pfiff."

The thin bright beam of the flashlight moved slowly across the shutters. On both I discovered the same faded emblem. Yes, a peacock's tail. Where had I seen this before?

A few nights before. When in my concern over the silent de Colana house I had rushed into the backyard and up to the country lawyer's bedroom window. On the wall of the house above the window, barely visible in the stormy moonlight, the weathered sgraffito design. Not an hour after I had seen for the first time the Light in the Lake.

2   The Luzienburg's two towers were square and massive. Even the knight who built them must have planned to store grain in them. One of them at the end of the Pfauenhof had a few window slits, a longish gable roof and at ground level a romantically arched passageway leading to the adjoining courtyard, stairless despite the incline and high enough to allow a horse and rider to pass through. (Armored steeds had come and gone through here.) The little man let the light beam swing over the worn-down cobblestones and let me through the medieval passageway and across the narrow, unlighted adjoining courtyard; in front of me rose the steep and dark second tower, without a gable but with a broad balcony. Its massive Ghibelline battlement with swallow-tailed double merlons was chiseled into the subdued glow of the indirect light, and it too somewhat magnified in the reddish atmosphere of the south wind. Grandpa's cloud-cuckoo-land . . . Pfiff jingled a set of keys and pulled open a heavy iron door.

I stepped in behind him, across something like snow. Flour.

Wood and aluminum were predominant. A strange maze of spiraling ducts, rods, wheels, pulleys, flaps, hinges, which on workdays moved in esoteric rhythms in an interplay of mechanical jerking, rotating, sliding, ticking, rattling and humming—like the works of a gigantic watch whose every joint vibrated while a thin fog of flour dust blew through the mine-like shaft illuminated by caged-in lamps. Today the vertical labyrinth lay very still. Nothing vibrated, but the flour stayed on as an odorless, suffocating miasma in the sleeping mill, like snow on the floor of the dimly lit platform, across which we trudged noiselessly between full-packed, three-foot paper sacks. In the light they seemed to have the same reddish quality as the unfinished pinewood of the walls and beams and of Pfiff's straw blond hair. A brief memory of the Two Blonds flickered inside me. All that seemed to be far behind me. Yes, that's how it seemed in this moment as I was overcome by a strange euphoria.

Unlike the freight elevator, the Luzienburg's personal elevator was no more roomy than a medium-sized wardrobe. As it hummed slowly upward I became aware of the cause of my artificial euphoria—ephedrine. I was able to breathe freely in the cramped elevator, but the price was a confused feeling of not-quite-being-there. I felt wide awake in the midst of reality, but at the same time in something like an opium-high in which I was weightlessly gliding to some other destination. To think that this very elevator shaft led down to the loading ramp of the concrete colossus in the ravine Xana and I had passed by earlier. Kujath's architect had outfoxed the historical societies and proved himself a talent in camouflage by hiding the upper stories of the mill silo behind the unchanged façade of the castle's second tower.

"*Qué tal, qué tal,*" said Grandpa. "You speak Spanish, don't you?"

"Hardly."

"The last Homo-Hispano-Austriacus doesn't know Spanish?"

"I speak bad but rapid Italian."

"No Spaniard speaks Italian. Least of all a Basque. I'll talk French to them. They're leaving right away. *Je vous présente mon ami Trebla, anti-fasciste combattant!*"

Something struck me. For the first time since the beginning of our friendship, Kujath had neglected to embarrass me—by loudly introducing me to strangers as Giaxa's son-in-law.

At the same time I noticed Grandpa's pallor.

Swinging his large, overworked right hand, unmistakably the hand of someone who had done heavy work in his youth, he introduced me to Señor and Señora Ithurra y Azkue—whispering aside, he spelled out the double Basque name—and Señor Montez Rubio. The latter a slender man in his forties with an eagle's nose and small-clipped, graying moustache, the former two handsome young demigods in their early twenties, both dressed in discreet elegance, entirely in black. (Good; so my tuxedo wasn't obtrusive.) As I came in, it had seemed to me that the three had exchanged knowing nods.

They were drinking Fundadór from fat-bellied glasses and nibbling black olives. The tower studio, Kujath's cloud-cuckoo-land, an added story to the tower with a low ceiling and portholes in three walls like a captain's cabin and a French window in the fourth wall to the south, was free of flour dust and furnished in the exaggeratedly conservative style of a 1913 smoking parlor. Deep easy chairs of shiny dark leather around a smoking table with an inlaid amber tile illuminated from beneath. Next to it a set of French billiards with an oilcloth cover that gleamed in the light of a hanging lamp; the lamp's shade conspicuously fashioned out of the skins of coral snakes. On the walls a rack for cue sticks, bookcases, an open secretary overloaded with papers, a row of framed, yellowed photographs, mostly of the Amazon region, and a peculiar engraving. Grandpa, who spoke fluent Spanish and Portuguese, switched to perfect French, in which, however, his Berlin accent was more noticeable. The conversation centered on the loss of Castéllon, a town less than sixty miles north of the Republican capital of Valencia, on the fifteenth of June.

The young Ithurra, called Adan or Adanito by his wife, shaking his ebony-black curly hair in suppressed excitement—his nose small and finely shaped, his eyes a strange, greenish amber-brown (perhaps not unlike mine)—Adan, working himself into a fine fury, spoke about the Loyalists' defensive line (based on French defensive strategy) around Valencia.

"*Les fascistes*, even if they did reach the Mediterranean in April, Modesto will beat them back! Modesto, an extremely imaginative commander! Modesto, with his *Agrupacion Autonoma del Ebro*"—he swung his rather delicate fist while his very young wife looked at him full of tender sadness—"will hold the front against the murderous attacks by the Legion Condor of that morphine addict Goering. *No pasaran!*"

The three Spaniards rose gracefully from their deep easy chairs.

"Take a look at the older one," whispered Grandpa to me in German as he lifted the receiver of a telephone standing on the secretary. "He was the director of the Prado museum in Madrid; smuggled the whole Prado collection out of Spain at tremendous personal risk—to Geneva, imagine that . . . Hello, Pfiff? I'm bringing the Spaniards down now!—*Alors, mes amis*," he fell back into French, "I'll take you down in the elevator—no, I insist—but *comme vous savez* it carries only three people."

"I will wait," said the Prado savior politely.

The young Basque woman, who wore a golden miniature crucifix over her high-collared black gown, Señora Ithurra y Azkue, let an almost ecstatic glance play across my forehead. (I must have been mistaken.) Then she said with grave insistence, "*Vous descendez en avant, messieurs.* I will be the one who waits, *grand-pére* . . . so that I can take *un petit coup d'oeil*, another little glance at the valley from your *tour formidable.*" With that she flung a heavy lace shawl, apparently a genuine mantilla, around her shoulders and high-heeled her way out onto the balcony.

While Grandpa rummaged through the little drawers of the secretary looking for something, Montez Rubio shook my hand briefly with a polite, melancholy smile. *"Bonne chance, monsieur."*

I said, "Perhaps, *monsieur*, I will have the good fortune to visit you in Geneva and visit the Prado in exile."

The man from Madrid replied oddly: "I doubt that seriously. Even if you do come back alive, *monsieur*, which I sincerely hope, it remains quite uncertain how long I will have the pleasure of directing the collection. Farewell is all I can say, and thank you."

Grandpa had found what he was looking for, a small clip-on flashlight that he put on as he stepped out into the narrow entryway. Montez Rubio followed his host.

Even more odd were young Adan's words and gestures as he said good-bye to me. He shook my hand for a long time. In the light of the billiard lamp I discovered that his suit was of midnight blue gabardine and that a black mourning armband was barely visible on his right sleeve.

"Monsieur, it was an honor to meet you."

"Entirely my pleasure, *Monsieur*," I mumbled.

"I don't mean that just as a *façon de parler*. A great honor." (What could Grandpa have been telling them about me?) "I cannot explain to you now in passing why I myself cannot . . ." His amber eyes began to glint with dampness in something like angry sorrow or sorrowful anger. "I just want to tell you that Montez Rubio and I, a Basque Catholic, are Republicans with heart and soul and are convinced of our duty to join forces with the Communists against the mortal enemies of our young Republic. *Malgré certaines difficultés.*" (Does he take me for a CP big shot?) "I know little about you, but enough to make me admire your courage. Even if you are an atheist, *monsieur*, allow me to bid you farewell with the words God bless you! *No pasaran! Au revoir!*"

Quickly he turned away and I watched the two slight (compared to Grandpa) Spaniards follow their host into the narrow cubicle and heard the elevator hum down the silo. Then I heard something else. Soft footsteps—seemingly overhead.

I strolled out onto the balcony, to the tower's defensive platform ringed by a toothed battlement wall, and saw the young Mrs. Ithurra y Azkue standing with her back to me in one of the embrasures. Apparently she hadn't moved for several minutes.

Upon stepping out onto the balcony, you could see the jagged merlons with their swallow-tailed peaks, each looking like a squarish tower over twelve feet tall. Almost all were well preserved, but only traces remained of the defensive walkway that ran around behind the battlement wall at a height of about six feet. Since I had last visited the castle shortly after my escape from Vienna, Kujath had added another story to the tower studio—a pale brick structure no larger than a little garden house with a hatchlike door (closed at the moment and accessible only by means of a kind of vertical fire-escape ladder), and a slanting, studio-type skylight, from which a subdued greenish light shimmered out onto

177

the battlement. Now, now the light was fleetingly blocked by a human shadow, and I heard again the soft footsteps of the lonely pacer.

Was Kujath holding a prisoner in this airy "dungeon"? I imagined—especially under the influence of my ephedrine tablets—Grandpa to be capable of a great deal.

Now the south wind's night wore a touch of violet and the spider-web clouds were swept away; stars sparkled in strange magnification. The woman stood at one of the barred railings Kujath had built into the gaps of the battlement for the protection of his grandchildren. Her delicate but sharply cut pro-. file was engraved in the glow from the studio window. I leaned against the railing and nodded southward in the direction of a black violet peak that towered amazingly close at hand. "*Voila le Bévérin.*"

She made no move. Her voice was like Xana's but much rougher, yet still melodious—a very Iberian alto voice. "*Quand partez-vous en avion?*"

"Me? When do I take off?" (Holy Laudon, what could Grandpa have been telling his guests about me?) "I was—many years ago I was a pilot—in the war—"

"And now it is war again. And you will fly again. This time to Spain. To help our people."

(Holy Laudon, what *had* Grandpa . . .?) I chose my French words carefully. "*Madame—*"

"*Mademoiselle,*" she interrupted me, as unmoving as a tower lookout who has just spied the first enemy movements, "Adanito is my brother."

"Oh, forgive my mistake."

The shadow moved out of the skylight, then a brief hammering could be heard from that direction. The woman, this Miss Ithurra y Azkue, did not move a muscle. Only now did I realize how much she resembled the Basque demigod, except for her slightly longer, more pointed nose and her not curly, but smooth black hair cut short in an Eton crop. Trying to gloss over my mistake, I said—like someone talking about the distant past, "Once I took a trip with a lady and passed myself off as her half brother—to an Italian waitress. Even though I was by no means the lady's half brother."

"But?"

"But—her husband," I said somewhat hesitantly. "It was a long time ago," I lied. "Anyway the waitress thought we really were brother and sister. That's how easy it is to be deceived."

"Adan is my brother."

"Naturally, *Señorita. Naturellement.*"

"No! it's not natural any more."

"*Pardon?*"

She repeated in suppressed, rough-peaked cries: "Today—it's—not—natural—any—more—that—one—has—a—brother!"

I could hardly guess what she meant and didn't know what to reply. The eyes of Miss Ithurra y Azkue flashed with a peculiar brightness. In the diffuse light no longer blocked by the shadow of Grandpa's imprisoned Monte Cristo I could see that she had amber-colored eyes like Adan's. An odd color of iris—I'll be damned, it's mine! The sluggish vapor—that's it. Vapor of the south wind carried the sweet, animal-like smell of a blooming linden tree up to the parapet. Again the discreet hammering. The fabulous Miss Ithurra y Azkue, whose first name I didn't know, seemed not to hear it at all. Her elbows lifted toward me inside her mantilla. What was she doing? Unhooked the chain of her crucifix and after hesitating briefly, lowered it into my breast pocket. What was she saying there—without the least lowering of her rough melodious voice? "*En reconnaissance!* In gratitude! And give the Spanish soil my greeting."

At this moment neither question nor answer occurred to me. After a brief, this time almost desperate, hesitation, she pressed her strangely small, firm breasts against me and her turquoise earrings flickered like lightning bugs flying into my eyes and she kissed me with the sacred intensity of a mad woman, an intensity I found contagious. Not a question or answer occurred to me.

"*Notre terre brulée—et sanglante,*" the fabulous, though mad Miss Ithurra y Azkue gurgled into my mouth. "Our burned—bloody soil."

As the mill elevator began humming up the ninety feet from the ground floor to the top of the tower, in the light of the billiard lamp she repaired her bit of makeup in childish haste, whereby she did too much of a good thing. She didn't give me another look. Then Kujath stepped out of the small adjoining room, which contained, beside the elevator door, a small kitchenette. By the billiard table stood the little Spanish bourgeoise in black, her mantilla thrown over her Eton crop, her face an ocher-tinged mask, her mouth a red-bordered sgrafitto line. All reserve and silence, she nodded vaguely in my direction and high-heeled past the lord of the manor who as he departed recommended that I try a glass of Fundadór.

I crouched on the arm of an easy chair and sipped Spanish cognac and waited for Grandpa. Grandpa took his time. I got up and studied the yellowed photographs that hung on the walls: drilling towers in the wilds of Venezuela, rubber plantations on the Amazon, terraced jungles, peasants' huts on pilings in Belém de Pará, mausoleum-like houses in Manaus, snapshots in which a young robust Henrique Kujath could always be seen, riding on a small horse, paddling in a canoe on a wide, shoreless river or encircled by half-civilized river Indians. In some of them the Germano-Brazilian pioneer was so inconspicuous, despite his stature, so enmeshed in tropical growth that one had to search for him as in a hidden-picture puzzle.

Indeed, one curious engraving turned out to be a hidden picture—an oversized, pale-grinning skull. When you came within three feet of it the illusion ceased. Not a skull but seven naked, buxom ladies chained together in an antique prison—chained together, overlapping, intertwined—freshly raped Sabine women. (Not only her attacks of dizziness, but also the presence of this turn-of-the-century stag picture had caused Grandma to boycott the tower studio.)

I waited for Grandpa with my burning questions, but he took his time, and again there came the discreet hammering overhead and from deep in the distance a slamming car door.

All at once, above me, there was radio music. At first blaring, screeching, then purer, turned down to mezzoforte—the barcarole in Offenbach's *Tales of Hoffman.*

> "Beau-ti-ful, o night of love,
> O pa-ci-fy my long-ing."

sang a tenor. Grotesque, I thought. Fifteen minutes earlier this could have been background music for the shortest love scene I ever played—a scene torn from a drama unknown to me.

The gondolier's song broke off as suddenly as it had begun; then once again the gentle hammering. (Kujath's Count of Monte Cristo seemed to be an amateur radio builder.) Finally I heard the mill elevator humming up out of the depths, heard it and heard it, as if it was not coming from the ground floor of the tower but from the loading ramp of the concrete cellar built into the ravine 250 feet below me. I had time; I pulled out the necklace with the little gold crucifix. On the back of it was engraved:

M.I.y A.
S.Seb.1929

Apparently the girl M. Ithurra y Azkue from San Sebastian had received it for her First Communion and thus was not yet twenty today. Grandpa pushed his way out of the kitchenette, unclipped the flashlight from his raw-silk lounge jacket and with a disbelieving grin looked me over as I stood there wearing the monocle I had used to study the initials. He turned on the flashlight and shone it in my face. His dry guffaw sounded mildly reproachful.

"Oh man, Trebla-boy, you're a patented Casanova in your monocle and tuxedo!"

Mechanically I put away the cross and the monocle. "Seems to be a custom here at the Luzienburg."

"What is, you cunning Casanova?"

"To shine," I said casually, "a flashlight in my face and then make wisecracks about my monocle."

He clicked off the flashlight. "Who else did that to you? Pfiff? Who declared you an honorary member of the proletariat after February '34? *He* certainly didn't mean anything by it."

"I know. But you, Grandpa—I just have a feeling—*did* mean a little something by it."

"I'll tell you something . . . Brazil?" He plumped himself down in his favorite chair, pulled a black cigar box out of the hollow interior of his smoking table. "Holandeza by Dannemann? For cardiac cases."

"No thanks."

With a clipper dangling from his watch chain he cut off the end of the slim, dark blond cigar, sniffed it, twisted the mouthpiece between his lips before accepting the third match I held out for him. "I'll tell you something . . . I myself was never monogamous. My principle was to marry *once*. None of this American divorce idiocy. Instead a few little affairs on the side *à discrétion. À dis-cré-tion*. That means in such a way that it doesn't hurt mother. Not only that, but I was never a cradle robber. Kids under twenty are best left—"

"Excuse me a thousand times for interrupting you, Grandpa; but I wanted to ask you an important, a burning—"

"Just a moment, my son! The *caboclos* don't ride so fast." He puffed, put the burning cigar end beneath his duck's nose, sniffed the smoke like a tired epicurean, and knocked off the ash into an ashtray that was hinged to swing upward from the table's edge. "According to my EKG man in Chur I'm not even supposed to smoke cigars for heart cases. But 'what good is a dog's life?' What I wanted to say is, when you were wed to Miss *stud. phil.* Roxana Jacks-a the odds were ninety to ten for a marriage lasting no more than o-n-e year. Now your Xana has already gotten through eight years at the side of a very charming and equally crafty Casanova without the spectators in the third tier—and it's rude to look at a marriage any closer—being able to see any signs of discontent on her part. That, Trebla, seems to be a rather nice accomplishment of yours, and you know that not only my castellan, chauffeur, and secret messenger all in one—not only Pfiff holds you in high regard, me too . . ." Puffing. "Really. On the other hand the whole affair has a hitch . . ." Puffing. "You haven't got a child."

"All right. Now give me a cardiac cigar," I said nasally and in sudden irritation. With a not completely controlled movement I took one from the cubic box that Kujath held out to me. Something like puffing fury began to pump me up like a rubber hose that could burst. What right did anyone have to touch on this "topic," a topic even Xana and I avoided. I imitated the ritualistic motions Kujath had performed with his Holandeza. Then I said, full of embittered calm, "My friend and patron, you certainly didn't telegraph me down here from the Upper Engadine just because of this—hitch. Did you?"

"No."

3

Grandpa was by no means an aged fop, but he liked to call himself an "old romantic clotheshorse and tropical cavalier." His summer apparel consisted of a raw-silk suit with which he wore a stiff old-fashioned stand-up collar, a white ribbed necktie, and a vest of black piqué. He was no giant like Mavegn but still over six feet tall, broad shouldered and massive; across his Bacchus belly —he was no aristocratic tippler as de Colana had been but "a connoisseur of good Wuerzburg wine who savors one precious drop after the other"—hung a heavy watch chain, only silver, decorated like a veritable charm-bracelet. The tooth of an Onca tiger, a miniature hand carved from coral "not so much to ward off the Evil Eye as to remind me of the Brazilians and their marvelous superstitions" and two hazelnut-sized rubies "that I dug up myself in the Estado Minas Gerais; look how they sparkle, symbols of my political sympathies meant only for knowing eyes!" When I first saw him at my wedding in Vienna he was still wearing a turned-up moustache à la Kaiser Wilhelm; that's the "we've done it! model, even though Willy in Doorn has recently been wearing a pointy little beard of the model we've had it!" The moustache was his private joke "against my wife's nationalistic mishpachah; when I'm visiting in Potsdam I stand by the coatrack twisting my mustachios up to my eyeballs and then I hide my horny proletarian paws behind my back." In his sixties he wore his moustache longer and "droopier à la Masurian Paul who swallowed two squirrels." He never called Hindenburg anything but Masurian Paul and even though the last Reichsprasident of the First German Republic was an object of his salty scorn, Kujath's features betrayed a Wendish Alpine quality not unlike Hindenburg's. His large, round, seal-like head with its unprotruding, large-lobed ears was partly bald, partly *shaved* bald; one could imagine him as an illustration in a book about the Germanic tribes, as an Ancient Borussian with a pigtail resting on a bearskin swinging a hornful of mead, his chin dripping with the honey liquor. And yet for all his bullishness he was very well groomed and his years as a self-made man-of-the-world among Iberian and Amazonian peoples had given him a unique air of culture. Perhaps of ancient culture. Yes, perhaps this Heinrich Kujath, teamster's son from the Badstrasse in North Berlin had something of an Aztec chieftain about him.

"Now," he repeated. "At least it can't hurt you to take a look at yourself in the mirror—that one there in which my annihilated billiard partners only two years ago used to curse their own visages. Recently I haven't gotten so much fun out of billiards any more— and by billiards I don't just mean billiards."

182

Next to the cue rack hung the small Venetian mirror. I cast a glance into it and burst out in a quick, high (too high) laugh and began using one of the Kleenexes I'd bought with the ephedrine to wipe the lipstick off my mouth and chin.

"Not kissproof was it—the lipstick of that little Spanish charmer, who came flying slam-bam into your tuxedo-clad embrace," I heard Grandpa's blabbering (which he himself called "yacking"). "I'm awestruck; you seem to be a magician in that field. Considering that young Spanish girls are so damned unapproachable and particularly Maïtena who's from one of the most respected families in San Sebastian . . . inasmuch as . . . insofar as the word family still applies . . ."

"So her name is Maïtena."

"Don't even know the first names of the underage virgins you seduce, eh? Well, I must say."

I let myself sink down into a deep easy chair and picked up my Holandeza. "Listen, Grandpa. It's not *me* who's the magician. It's *you* who were able to conjure away the lady's unapproachability."

"M-e-e-e?"

"You. What kind of a flea did you put in those Spaniards' ears? Cross your heart, what did you tell them about me?"

"About you? Not a word. Cross my angina pectoris."

"You d-i-d-n't tell them that I'm a pilot on my way to Spain? That I'm a volunteer for the Loyalist air force or something?"

"I'm not completely looney, Trebla. I know full well that ever since you had that hole bored in your gourd you're no longer airworthy!"

"Bored in my gourd! Airworthy! Well said!" I smiled sincerely. I really fancied his Berlinese yacking. "Then how is it that this Señor Rubio, just like the brother of this Maïtena—hmm, at first I thought he was her husband—that both the Spaniards thanked me in more or less fervent terms."

"They thanked you? Am I hearing things?" Grandpa stopped puffing.

"And while you were taking the gentlemen down in your, pardon me, Lilliputian elevator, this fabulous Miss Maitena Ithurra y Azkue thanked me for my intended flight to Spain 'to help our people,' and before I could assure her that *grand-père* had been elaborating on reality in regard to my humble person she honored me with this red-brand of a farewell kiss that you yourself, *mon vieux*, wouldn't have been able to fend off with a saber at deep *quarte*—and with this little talisman she presented to an atheist."

"*Puxa!*"

Again I pulled out the featherlight necklace and let the gold cross dangle over the illuminated tabletop. "Or do you consider this the loot of an unscrupulous conjuring Casanova?"

"Poosha" was the Brazilian exclamation that Kujath uttered only in his rare moments of amazement. "Poosha!"

His worldly-wise, baggy elephant eyes stared wondering at the turning, glinting cross. All at once he leaned way back and laughed, at first more quietly than de Colana had ever laughed, really inaudibly, although the charms on his piqué vest danced. Suddenly his laugh became audible, swelled up to a roguish whinny and then broke off. He bent forward and pushed his cigar onto the ashtray: "Valentin broke out of Dachau last Wednesday. Imagine that. Out of Dachau. He's going to come by later this evening."

"I know. Pfiff let me in on the secret."

"That's fine. But let's keep it entre nous."

"Of course. Last Wednesday—that's tremendous. Really superb."

"Superb, no question about it," growled Kujath. The bit of color his youthful laugh had put into his cheeks now paled in a moment. The good tidings that a man had succeeded in outfoxing the machine-gun-bristling watchtowers and their black-clad, death's-head guards didn't really seem to fire his imagination. Pfiff had seemed to be depressed, not to mention the pallor and downtrodden manner of Señor Montez Rubio. Kujath, who had the tan complexion of light-skinned Europeans who had spent years in the tropics—Kujath's skin color tonight seemed to me as waxen as a church candle.

"Entre nous, ex-Reichstag-Delegate Valentin Tiefenbrucker entered Switzerland illegally across Lake Constance, and we're going to smuggle him out again tonight. Pfiff will drive him to a private airfield in the Jura where I've chartered a two-seat Fieseler-Storch and a French pilot. Everything strictly illegal," blabbered Grandpa. "If this gets out, the Swiss police will grab me quick as a wink for violating neutrality." The shadowy chieftain's-eye surveyed me almost tenderly. "But we two, *mon petit*, have already pulled off a thing or two."

"Valentin is flying to Spain?"

"On your honor, not a word. He's going to Army Group Modesto."

"I s-e-e-e. T-h-a-t's why. The fabulous Miss Maïtena misunderstood you, Grandpa. Inasmuch as she presumed Valentin was going into the Loyalist air force."

"Possibly."

"And then she mistook me for Valentin."

"That, Trebla, seems to be the joke. Which I didn't get at first. On the fringe of the Spanish tragedy a whimsical little comedy of errors." A cautious grin sprouted beneath his "squirrel tails." "C'est la guerre. War conjured you a kiss from the underage Spanish charmer."

"War conjures many kisses." I let the necklace clink onto the table top. "That belongs to Valentin. Please give it to him, will you?"

"Or better yet, you can give it to him yourself."

"Along with Maïtena's kiss? You can't ask that of me."

Grandpa's grin sagged.

"Aside from that I won't be able to wait for Valentin. Xana—"

His grin was wiped away. His large hands rose up pleadingly. His choppy

184

blabber: "You *must* wait for him!—I worked it out this way—I want you, eh, I beg you, in the interest of everyone, do me the favor!"

"I'd really like to, believe me. But Xana, you know, just got over a case of bronchitis. She's convalescing. And because we have to be back in the Engadine tonight—"

"Howso? Tomorrow our remodeled haunted house, I mean the Peacock Palace, will be all booked up, goddammit!" grumbled Grandpa. "But today we've still got five empty beds. Why, Trebla, why did you bring along Roxana? After I had telegraphed you explicitly to come solo."

"I . . . didn't want to leave her all alone up there. But most of all because I got *another* telegram; from Slovenia today just before leaving in our borrowed car to come see you. Signed by a friend of Giaxa's. What do you think of the text?—: 'Our dear old circus horse was requisitioned a week ago. Negotiating his release. Special delivery letter follows.' I assume this telegram has some connection with *yours*."

Grandpa sighed deeply. Two telegrams. The telegraph key in my forehead began pounding—this time, it seemed, almost audibly.

"Naturally, Grandpa, it could mean that they *really* requisitioned the old Lippizan, Giaxa Number Seven. But what could they do with an old horse like that in the Wehrmacht? It could mean *something else*."

Kujath's massive moustache tips seemed to vibrate. Then he spoke with the threatening expressionlessness of an Aztec mask.

"It *does* mean something else. They've requisitioned *both* of them, Jacksa *and* Jacksa. But please keep your head and be patient for just a little while longer." He popped open the face cover of his heavy pocket watch. "Not yet ten-thirty. Don't ask any questions now; spare me that for a few minutes, please. I've known it for days. Did you tell Xana anything about the Slovenian telegram?"

"Not a word. I tore it into a thousand pieces."

"Smart of you, Trebla. Not yet ten-thirty and Xana is asleep. *Die Burgfrau* let me know when I was saying good-bye to the Spaniards. Xana is on the divan in the Peacock Salon sleeping the sleep of innocents."

Did I want a bite to eat, he had asked me and I had replied that my hay-fever medicine had taken away all my hunger. With limp but not yet extinguished agility he had pulled a large napkin out of the hollow smoking table and spread it out on the illuminated surface and announced that some Malossol caviar (given for no particular reason by a Soviet delegate to the League of Nations), along with cold chicken, Milanese salami, and melon salad, couldn't hurt anyone. Everything to be found in the refrigerator next to the Lilliputian elevator (he said, quoting me). While I brought in the aforementioned items he arranged silverware, plates, and glasses.

"Fascist wine, you don't drink, right?"

"The stuff I took a while ago—"

"You mean your air pill. They prescribed me some air pills too, not agains hay fever but for cardiac asthma. Do yours work?"

"Definitely. But because they give me a rapid pulse I'd rather not have an wine."

"Have you got a rapid pulse, Trebla?"

I showed him my forehead. "Can't you see for yourself?"

"I'll tell you something. Because my oil pump doesn't work right my card ogrammarian in Chur told me I couldn't drink any more wine, but I can't just g back to the old days and start over—drinking one percent beer like Hitle mann—on the other hand, it's a hard job nowadays if you want to avoid fascis grape juice. German wines are all out; Chianti and Frascati are scratched. She ry is grown behind Franco's lines and you can write off Horthy's Hungaria vintage. All that's left is French wine, excepting of course some French spirit you can use for a rubdown. And how much longer can we enjoy antifascis French wine? Chablis, Champagne, Lorraine Vin Gris? My optimistic pre diction is two years. But it just occurred to me. I've got a bottle of 1929 Wuerz burger Schlangengrube left over from the days of the Weimar Republic. We ca risk that." Somewhat later: "Do you know Valentin personally?"

I said, "No, but early in '34 and last year we sent some messages back an forth. Not that it accomplished anything."

"An amazing guy, this Valentin, but no *homme à femme* like you. When look at you I realize why this Maïtena child *wanted* to take you for Tiefer brucker." Kujath sniffed the pulled cork, poured his glass an eighth ful dribbled some wine on his tongue, uttered a series of soft tongue-clicks lik those used to call an animal, then wiped his "squirrel-tails" with two pirouette of his right hand. "*Um bom vinho, amigo.* A noble fluid. Hope you're not ma at me for being mad at you just now."

"Not a bit."

"Just imagine I was elevatoring up and down and I elevatored back u right after I'd heard that Xana was sleeping in the Peacock Room and see you mouth all smeared with the lipstick of the Spanish charmer I'd introduced yo to not half an hour before—well. Everything's been straightened out—excep why you're wearing a tux. Are you staying at the Suvretta House up there o something?"

"No, with the postmistress of Pontresina in two furnished rooms. If w were going to have time, Xana wanted to do a little dancing in the Engadine o our way back."

Grandpa stopped in the midst of pouring, put down the bottle, and ben slowly forward. "D-d-dancing?" he whispered, he hissed, as if we were carryin on a secret conversation. "Roxana wanted to go dancing? So she really doesn' know anything about—?"

Mechanically I grabbed the bottle, poured it overful and emptied it withou

186

toasting my companion. "—about Giaxa's arrest. *Nothing*. I told you, I didn't show her that telegram from Yugoslavia. And since there is a strong chance, *must* be a strong chance of Papa-Rose being freed soon, isn't there? . . . *Isn't there*, Grandpa?!"

Kujath sank way back. Judging from the motions of his moustache, he was chewing something, even though he hadn't taken a bite. Then he asked with uncanny self-control, "Tell me, old boy, why do you say there *must* be such a chance?"

I had jumped to my feet. "Because those goons wouldn't dare take a man who—has made the whole world laugh—and put him—in prison—!"

The old tropical cavalier stretched out both his elephant-skinned hands. "Please now, Trebla, don't get so worked up about it; there's no point . . . sit down now. Have a little something to eat. It'll make you feel stronger. Then I'll tell you all I've learned about this awful affair in the last few days."

I exhaled: "That must be why you summoned me down here."

"What?"

"To tell me what you know."

"N-no, not just for that reason. We must wait for . . . wait and drink white wine. Now have a bite to eat." He poured himself a glass so clumsily that, with this one gesture, he reminded me for the first time of de Colana. In the second that I took the wine bottle from him the suppressed trembling of his hand passed to mine like an electric spark. (The cardiogrammarian in Chur must have known what he was doing when he prescribed abstinence for Grandpa.) I murmured, "Sorry that I just poured my glass full by myself and—"

"Cheers, Comrade-in-Arms! On to fikh-tory ag-henst za Frrenchies!" he interrupted me with an exaggerated rasping bark and a puppet-like forward snap of his heavy torso, something he must have scornfully borrowed from the patriotic relatives of the Kummersdorf girl. Again it rose up in me. In Memoriam Gaudenz de Colana—the roguish charm of his dueling fraternity manner. A brief noise overhead, which my host ignored. Then it came a second time, breaking out into a cacophony of screeches and roars that was turned down to the pleasant moderato Jacques Offenbach had intended: the barcarole from *Tales of Hoffman*.

"What's going on up there anyway?" I queried, pointing upward with my refilled glass.

"My Szabo is going on up there," Grandpa said gently.

"Who's Szabo?"

"A Hungarian Jew. A genius at building radios. He's set up a little experimental station above my cloud-cuckoo-land. At my expense. Also quite illegal. In an age of criminals we all have to get used to being gangsters, I guess." Sandor Szabo was developing an invention by means of which a secret mobile transmitter would be able to break into the broadcast speech orgies of Hitlermann. Not just with simple jamming. Unlike many inventors Szabo seemed to be no dreamer and had assured Grandpa that with his little "toy" he could interrupt transmitters as powerful as the Deutschlandsender with catcalls and music. "My Hungarian wants to be finished and ready to go by September for the Party Congress in Nuremberg. Just imagine, in the middle of all that ranting and raving we insert a little slogan of yours—a sharp little couplet—pointed and catchy—have you got anything like that on hand?"

"Sorry, my slogans are all at least as long as an *Iliad* Canto."

"It would have to be something like 'Whistle while you work/Hitler is a jerk!' Something like that. You can do *that*."

"I'm afraid not."

"Or we come bashing in with the beginning of Beethoven's Fifth. Tatata-tum!—Tatata-tum!" Grandpa sang sonorously. "Or in the midst of the vegetarian cannibal's hysterical shit-storm we broadcast Offenbach's heavenly barcarole."

"Your electronic genius has already tried it. Why the barcarole?"

"First, because it's my favorite aria and second, because," Grandpa winked in amusement, "it was composed by a non-Aryan."

"By the way that nice, sorrowful Mr. Montez-Rubio looks a lot like Jacques Offenbach."

"Really. He's from Granada. Tells me his ancestors were Marranos, also Moors. Did you know that in southern Spain the Jews and Arabs together built up a great culture and were the best of friends before the Sacred Inquisition got them into such a terrible scrape?"

"Yes."

"Today we're in the middle of a new inquisition. You *have* to be prepared, Trebla—because any day now *any* of us, great or small, rich or poor, hero or schlemiel, famous or nameless, could at any moment get into a terrible scrape. The most terrible, the last scrape. Are you ready for that?" he asked, bent forward, as if waiting to pounce. The amber glow muffled by the tablecloth threw shadows of his large moustache onto his face, and for a moment once again he reminded me of an Aztec mask, an ancient Mexican god concealing a dreadful secret. Before I could find a word of response he growled, leaning back, "Squeeze a little lemon on your caviar."

"What about those young Spaniards, Grandpa, the Ithurras."

"I imagine you're wondering why Adanito isn't serving with the Loyalists any more."

"No. I imagine that after the fascists took the Basque provinces last fall he set sail for France—"

"Right. But why didn't he set sail from there for Valencia to join his government as a leftist Catholic and strongly Republican Basque who served as a lieutenant under Nino Nanetti?"

"Nanetti-Nanetti," I murmured. "A young Italian? Commander of the

Garibaldi Brigade. Didn't he get killed in the Basque country?"

"Killed, right."

"Maybe Adanito had battle fatigue."

"No, señor."

"Or was wounded."

"No, señor."

"Then why is he sitting it out in Geneva?"

"Why Geneva?" came Kujath's mischievous echo. "Papa Ithurra, presently of Paris, was president of the Sociedad de los Estudios Vascos in San Sebastian. Was. Had a daughter, Maïtena, and four sons. Had. One, a famous pelota player, died in Asturia during the fascist offensive April of last year. Died. Two were snatched at 5:00 A.M. after the capture of San Sebastian and shot. By Falangists on the Monte Urgull at five in the morning. Shot. There remained to President Ithurra only daughter Maïtena and Adanito, the youngest. Whom he wanted to keep. Understandable for someone who's against bullfighting."

Maïtena: "Today it's not natural any more that one has a brother!"

The word "grotesque" hovered on my tongue, but I didn't say it. I put down my napkin, stood up and strode across the grass-green Mysore carpet—as if walking over short-cut grass—to the wall, where, flanked by two yellowed jungle photos, hung the sultry macaber engraving. The sardonically grinning skull. After I had approached to within five feet of it it turned into seven naked, half-frightened, half-sensuous women chained together—freshly kidnapped Sabine women. I turned about face and walked across the just mowed grass to the smoking table where Grandpa sat pagodalike. Turned around again. And again the death's head on the wall grinned at me. Again I strolled toward it. Again as I approached it changed into acrobatically intertwined, superimposed masses of generous, Rubens-like female flesh, a pyramid of succulent life. Then I went back to the smoking table and sat down without another look at the wall.

4 "Would you like a *cafezinho?* A mocha? On the Avenida Rio Branco in Rio we used to drink twelve, twelve *cafezinhos* in one afternoon—those were the days," blabbered Grandpa. "Today I can offer you only Kaffe Hag; that's coffee without any coffee in it, yet tastes like coffee. We live in the age of the illusion makers, that's the joke. And now tell me, my son, how *you* got into trouble with the Alien Cops."

"Beg your pardon, but didn't you want to tell me about the steps you took to get Giaxa—?"

"We've got time for that," Kujath cut off my question and again made the anachronistic gesture of pulling his big old silver watch out of his piqué vest and popping open the green-corroded cover. (No doubt it was a memento of his proletarian childhood, preserved with grim tenderness.) "Really, eh, we've, eh, still got time." From out of the smoking table he leisurely conjured up the pieces of a mocha service and a thermos bottle, from which he cautiously began pouring the steaming ersatz coffee. His large hand was trembling.

"I'm the waiter here," I said, tapping my tuxedo, and took the thermos bottle from him.

"How obliging of you, my dear Baron. How about another Holandeza?"

"Thanks, but tobacco doesn't help me much along with all this ephedrine. Nor does your Franconian wine. No doubt it's a fabulous year, but in my condition it seems more like a wine that doesn't have any wine in it, but that tastes like wine."

"Me it helps." It was true. Grandpa's eyes had taken on a bit of sparkle. Woefully his duckbill nose sniffed the cube-shaped cigar box. "And another Holandeza would help me too . . . but this old crock has heart troubles and will be seventy years old the day after tomorrow. Just let me get the hell out of the seventies! The death rate's too high . . ." Unexpectedly a bottle of Baselbieter Kirsch swung in his fist. "*Un café arrosé, monsieur? One* little drop won't hurt you."

I took the bottle out of his hand and "arrosed" the ersatz coffee by letting two drops fall into each cup.

"You seem to be a homeopath, my dear amigo. You could have allowed me a little bigger squirt." Grandpa emptied his demitasse in one gulp.

After I had given him a brief report on my correspondence with the Zurich Alien Police, my arrest that morning, the interrogation in Samedan, and my release thanks to the telephonic intervention of Miss Polari, Kujath declared: "That last bit of luck you owe to the fact that Mavegn was the go-between for the purchase of ten Breukaa's property. Even though the bullpens are closed today, I already know the story. You must have gotten that head bull really furious today, Trebla. They say he was on the point of sending you straight to the loony bin."

I squinted over at him. Was he staring at my forehead? I sensed a slight wave of gratitude when I saw him sniffing a Holandeza instead—almost platonically, as it were, without lighting it.

I acted a bit dreamy: "Maybe that would be just the thing for me right now. To put me in a loony bin, as you so lyrically call it, for a few weeks."

"How do you mean that?"

"But I can't leave Xana alone now."

"N-o-o-o! That you can't!" The shyness masked by Grandpa's tough exterior made a fleeting appearance. "Anyway it was the Zurich Alien Cops that sicked Samedan on you. Why did you have to pull their legs like that?"

"Maybe I was assuming they had a sense of humor."

"Zurich policemen have no sense of humor. Watch out. 'The granting of asylum is a unilateral act of goodwill on the part of the Swiss Federation.'"

"Hm."

"And I don't think they've got much goodwill left for you."

"Hm."

"If you'd been a good boy they'd have recognized you as a political refugee. But now, when Zurich *and* Samedan send their gripes about you to Bern?"

"Hm."

"What'll you do when your Austrian passport expires? The Republic of Austria no longer exists."

"*Austria erit in orbe ultima.*"

"Even in Rome the police don't understand Latin any more."

"A Reichs-pass was ready and waiting for me in the General Consulate of Greater Germany."

"For *you?* Of all things! What kind of a joke was that?"

I bent forward slightly. "A joke. My sentiments exactly."

"And what if they just drop you on the border—as a so-called foreigner without papers—drop you on the border like a lost umbrella?"

I used a stage whisper: "On *what* border?"

"Not the German or the Musso-Italian. There remains the French. Yeah. So long as I'm alive there's no cause to lose your hair about it. So long as the Miller of Luzienburg is secure in his watchtower he'll always be able to scrounge up a paper for you. As strange as it may sound, the fact is that wherever the world's on fire today it's not water that helps, but paper. And now ...," Kujath arose and began rustling about in the papers of his Biedermeier secretary, "... to the terrible and mysterious case of Constantine Jacksa." When he turned back in my direction he was wearing an enormous pair of horn-rimmed glasses that looked like something painted on his face. Placing an opened notebook upright on the amber tabletop, he began to blabber away without much concern for punctuating pauses.

"Friday immediately after news of Jacksa's arrest rushed to Bern with Pfiff; first stop Archie Crichton You-Ess trade attaché good friend requested strictest confidence since no German paper yet reported arrest of world-famous eccentric and premature announcement in foreign press could jeopardize release; using diplomatic channels Archie fired off letters to Charles Chaplin, Los Angeles; journalist Dorothy Thompson, Barnard, Vermont; Mr. Colingbee, General Manager, Barnum and Bailey Circus, New York City; author H. G. Wells, London; Rumiantsev alias Karandash National Circus, Moscow; de la Barre, President, International Performers Lodge, Paris; Colingbee to mobilize You-Ess Guild of Performing Artists; de la Barre to make contact with the German Performers Lodge—"

"Holy Laudon, you *were* active, Grandpa!"

"I also thought of Grock."

"Who played for Hitler . . .?"

"For that very reason, man! Thought of a coordinated protest as soon as the Nazios announced Jacksa's 'protective' arrest."

"You mean they took him into protective custody?"

"Investigation—arrest—police custody—confinement on suspicion—protective custody, it's all the same to them. I also thought of looking up the German ambassador in Bern. Koecher. I know him. Can you imagine what he told me under the table last March? Doctor Giuseppe Motta, Chief of the Political Department for X-years now, Swiss Foreign Minister, a pious Catholic from Ticino, five times president, last year too—anyway Motta asked Koecher to convey to the Fuehrer and Reichschancellor his personal admiration for the tactful way—tact-ful way in which the latter had annexed Austria. Stictly confidential disclosure of a strictly confidential disclosure. I see you're not very surprised . . . Koecher is from Baden, attended the Humanistic Prep School in Basel, speaks fluent Baseldytsch, which keeps him in good with the top Swiss authorities. I just met him recently on the Bellevue Terrace in Bern, greeted him with an outstretched arm, Heilitla! That seemed to embarrass him and he answered, 'Guete Tag, Herr Kujath, wia gooht's?' " Grandpa's bland chuckle. "But even if Koecher pretends to be a humanistic gentleman in the old Basel tradition, he can't do anything. The attachés around him are all fanatic party goons. Therefore I decided . . ." Now it was Grandpa who strode with silent, limp-elastic steps across the green Mysore carpet, back and forth between the smoking table and the puzzle picture which, depending on the distance, turned into grim reaper or female flesh. Unsure whether he was alluding to it: "You see, it's all a matter of distance. From my tower studio I can pull off a lot of tricks; but not everything. That's why . . . that's why I decided to make a personal visit to Prussia the day after my seventieth—to Berlin, home of my rusty cradle." Turned away from me, facing the puzzle engraving, Grandpa stood at attention and raised his right hand in the snappy casual Roman salute that Italy's *fascisti* had childishly (but at least with some historical basis) revived from the days of their former imperial grandeur—a salute that seemed awkward and provocative when imitated by their Neo-Germanic counterparts. The glow from the amber plate shone on the back of his seal-like head; only the tip of a bushy mustachio peeked out to one side and began to move as, without dropping his arm, he continued: "I'm not scared of dying. But you know what I am afraid of? Of being tor-tured-to-death. That scares me shitless, despite my seventy years. And they're watching me."

> "Beau-ti-ful, o night of love,
> O pa-ci-fy my long-ing.
> Swee-ter than the sun a-bove,
> O love-ly night of love."

192

Once again from out of Szabo's room the recording of an iridescent tenor voice that sang the beginning of the Barcarole and then stopped abruptly. Finally Kujath let his arm fall: "*Kammersaenger* Richard Tauber, five years ago the darling of Berlin. Had to go to London."

"W-h-o's watching you, Grandpa?"

"The Nazios." He collapsed into his easy chair. "Last summer I happen to look down from the tower here and see a lineman from the telephone company climbing in spikes up one of the poles along the wire that connects the Luzienburg to the post office in Tartar. Next afternoon I happen to see the same man stunting around on the same pole. Next day same thing. Because he's always working solo the whole thing doesn't seem quite kosher to me, and I take a look at him through my old telestereoscope—the same one I used to watch the Chavanté Indians, those harmless people-eaters along the upper Xingu. And what appears there in three-dimensional glory? Not a harmless people-eater, but a Nazio from Davos."

"You knew the man?"

"I'd spotted his mug a few weeks earlier. In the German Veterans Resort. At a Davos convention of the Volksbund of Overseas Germans, which I attended as a guest," he said, winking at me slyly. "Aha, fellow Teuton, so you're tapping my telephone, are you, I think to myself. I send Pfiff off to sneak down to Tartar and all of a sudden two gendarmes come zipping up here and arrest the pole-climbing impersonator." His dull chuckle. "Ever since that day I've had an atavistic aversion to afternoon phone calls . . . Still, I'd be willing to go to Berlin for Jacksa—where I have some acquaintances in the Bendlerstrasse. In the OKW, the Wehrmacht HQ up there, are two cousins of Miss Kummersdorf, that is one cousin and a nephew who belongs to the Reserve Army CHQ. And then I know a director in the Berlin Criminal Police Headquarters who helped me get Siegfried Heppenhein out of the concert camp at Oranienburg. Unfortunately I don't know anybody in Vienna . . . Do you know where the Hotel Metropol is located?"

"Beautifully situated on the Danube Canal as you come down the Rothenturmstrasse."

"Do you know who's taken up quarters there now? The Geheime Staatspolizei of Vienna. Stupidly enough I don't know a soul there."

"But I do."

"You?" drawled Grandpa.

"The lord of the manor is named Laimgruber."

"You mean *Leim*, like glue?"

"No; Laimgruber with A-I."

Grandpa maintained a stony listening pose as I related the contents of Stepanschitz's long letter and my concise reply. "Aha, aha. So that Reichs-Pass business was no joke. And this Laimgruber guy used what's-his-name Stefanschinsky to bring you home to the Reich and your only response to the offer was a request that he osculate your posterior."

"Yes."

"Well. Then. Then I suppose there is no point in trying to enlist the help of this Laimgruber fellow on Jacksa's behalf."

"No. But I've been asking myself—and now you—something else. Something else entirely." Stimulated by the long-lasting effects of the ephedrine and at the same time almost anesthetized, I felt it again for the first time: the gentle beating signal in my forehead. "Couldn't it be that Laimgruber has already done something on Giaxa's behalf?"

"How do you mean?"

"Couldn't it be that he, that he ordered Papa-Rose to be arrested *because* of my answer to Stepanschitz . . . ?"

Kujath bent slowly forward, so far forward that his face disappeared and the amber glow of the tabletop shone on his hairless round skull. I stared at his gleaming baldness. It seemed to me like the faceless visage of an oracle that had reached the ultimate expressionlessness before giving the answer I was waiting to hear. When he raised his head again I was shocked by the tired resignation in his shadow heavy eyes. No, he thought that was out of the question. In the Nazios' book there were already enough points against Giaxa. Had I forgotten his 1933 statement published in the non-German press where he refused to perform again in the Thousand Year Reich "even if it managed to last more than ten years?"

Grandpa lifted his huge hands, palms out. "And now, Trebla, you're eating your heart out, so it seems, trying to guess whether your carelessness might have been the cause of this horrible and mysterious affair. When years ago, even before the currency restrictions, I pleaded with your father-in-law to set up an emergency exit, to transfer his money to Switzerland in case one day it was all over with Austria—what did he do? Put all his circus-star earnings in Austrian banks. Despite the collapse of the Viennese loan agencies. Despite the Dollfuss-Schuschnigg farce. Everything. Except for a measly twenty thousand francs that he let me deposit here." He lowered his hands onto the amber plate, suddenly businesslike and obliging. "He gave Roxana joint access to the account, so any time you need something you can . . ."

I mumbled, "Thanks, not just yet," and continued haltingly. "Yes, he was—in one respect he was tremendously stubborn, Papa-Rose. You could—yes, you could almost say he had—an obsession."

"What was it?"

"Austria. Yes, or more exactly, Austria-Hungary, the Empire gone forever. Mmm, even though he'd made a living poking pantomimic fun at the old Imperial Army, he was still, still ruled by this obsession . . . *Austria erit in orbe ultima*—he had a sarcastic translation for that: Austria will be last. His obsession was to be *himself* the last—the last living piece of the old Austria—the last knight. Don Quixote was a clown on horseback too."

194

That's why he always was . . . set against leaving," Grandpa murmured.

"Yes, and that's why he was always—Holy-goddam-Laudon, why are we talking about him in the past tense?!"

Without answering he disappeared with his limp supple movements into the kitchenette and I heard a brief popping sound followed by his blabbering. "Shot like Robert Blum; they'd really like to shoot Leon Blum too; all Blums get shot like Robert Blum." He brought in a champagne bucket rattling with ice cubes and, before I could help him, set it down on the tabletop. "I dug up a bottle of Moët et Chandon I was hiding from myself—that's the kind of extremes they drive you into; we'll have to make do with white wine glasses; a little gulp of champagne is medicine for heart cases and also as sure an antidote to hay fever as pillow feathers. Did you ever try inhaling out of a slit-open pillow? Guaranteed to help. Tell me, this Laimgruber—"

"—has started something rolling. In my direction." I reported briefly the part of the interrogation where Mavegn had informed me of the recent request from the Vienna State's Attorney that I be extradited for trial as an embezzler of party funds and how I had recognized Laimgruber's flamboyant "L" on the documents in question.

Grandpa let out a kind of whispered whistle. "What sort of funds were they supposed to be?"

"Our party maintained a series of illegal regional offices after being outlawed by the Dolfuss gang. The office in District 1 was on the Blutgasse."

"Blood Street! *Nomen est omen.* And now they squeal to the Swiss police because you took off with the Blutgasse cash. Did you?"

"No."

"Would've been a good deed."

I said: "If I'd evacuated the money I would have deposited it with our exiled party headquarters in Brno."

"After deducting your expenses."

"After deducting my expenses. Stupidly enough, I didn't take along a single schilling."

"Obviously. Otherwise they would've tried to get you extradited back in March or April. They wouldn't have waited until June—until just after you passed the word to this captain that he could kiss your everlovin' ass."

"Right! Although I never said anything about 'ever-loving.' You ought to know your Goethe better than that, Grandpa. One week after I had sent off my answer . . ." I told him about the two blond "sportsmen" from Vienna who had turned up in the Morteratsch Hotel and of our encounters in the Roseg Valley and at the empty Chantarella station. Kujath had been turning the champagne bottle slowly in the ice bucket; now he lifted it out and, his hands shaking somewhat less, wrapped it carefully in a napkin.

"Ohboyohboy. Are you armed?"

"Walther pistol, caliber seven-point-six-five, loaded with three quarters of a pound of ammo, six shots in the magazine, one in the chamber, accurate up to twenty meters."

"Like shot from a gun, that answer," said Grandpa. I told him about my lonely target practice in the foggy woods below the Languard peaks and of the two human silhouettes that appeared and disappeared at the edge of the clearing.

"Boy-oh-boy, it looks like you're getting it from more than one direction. These two blonds that your Gestapo captain—what did you call him, 'Lord of the Manner'—Laimgruber sicked on you . . ."

"That's the big question. So you think he did?"

"Everything seems to point that way. That they're out to get you. One way or another. Out of sheer anger at your cheeky answer to their most generous offer. Out of pure, petty spite. First the bureaucratic gangsters try it with an extradition request on embezzlement charges—realizing that it's by no means a sure thing. Because nobody can be extradited without a decision of the Federal Court in Bern—expelled, yes, but not extradited. So they send out two freshly trained Viennese sportsmen to the place where your little greeting was postmarked. To Pontresina. Two charming blond man hunters with orders to trundle you down into the Lower Engadine under cover of darkness and from there to spirit you across the border by Martinsbruck. Remind you of the Jakob case? It's all been done before. And in case that doesn't work they've got instructions to rub you out. Whenever it's convenient. Assassination team with a time fuse. No need for Jewish hastiness. For hay-feverish resort patients, especially ones equipped with side arms, you can afford to take your time, let good old Viennese laziness take over and use the occasion for a little high-altitude vacation in the world-famous Alpine paradise. What's a week here or there, the German taxpayers are picking up the tab. Why're you smiling, Trebla?"

"'Cause I'm thinking: Who's the good man think he's telling all this to? But still—say, doesn't this whole thing sound like an adventure novel?"

"We're *living* an adventure novel, that's the joke. Too bad you provoked old Mavegn the way you did, otherwise you could get him to take a closer look at the facts, and so forth, on the would-be Messieurs Krainer and Mostny. Let the whole crew up there in on it: Criminal Commissioner, Alien Police, Court of Inquiry, *and* the Fedpo. Federal Police. But he'll never take a tip from *you.* Why don't you get out of Pontresina? Oh yeah, I forgot, your hay-asthma. Of course you'd be *safer* in Zurich, but . . . the Zurich Alien Cops are mad at you. Man, Trebla, it looks like you're really in a bind. So it looks. You know what? As soon as the idiot's ball for my seventieth is over I'll send Pfiff down to you for a few days. As a bodyguard. Meanwhile keep a sharp lookout; that shouldn't be much of a trick for an old Isonzo warrior like yourself."

"And you think they're only after me? Not Xana?"

Deliberately Kujath placed the napkin over the ice bucket. "O-only you. For the time being. Up to now they haven't been known to attack women in foreign countries. The time'll come. As soon as Hitlermann enters his total war into the business register of history." He pulled the napkin taut. "By the way I have another uninspiring piece of news for you. Giaxa's sister in Graz—your old Aunt Za—they grabbed her too."

The ephedrine kept on working. The conversation continued over Spanish cognac, Wuerzburg wine, Moet et Chandon—about the lost brothers of the young Basque girl and her mistaken goodby kiss, about the secret arrest of a famous equestrian eccentric, about the chances of being "accommodated" by an assassination team with a time fuse, about the official "nabbing" of an old aunt, and it all was enough to leave a man cold. Cold inasmuch as the drug killed the stimulus of the alcohol and left one feeling anesthetized, as if breathing under an ether mask (a sensation well known to someone having gone through repeated operations for a head wound). Ether too produced this temporary, numbing sensation of cold.

Only now did Grandpa come out with it. During his visit to Bern he had requested another friend, Mr. Miville, a respectable member of the Swiss Trade Commission in Yugoslavia, to interrupt his flight back to Belgrade at the Tezna airfield near Maribor and to drive across the nearby border to Radkersburg, i.e., into the Ostmark region of the brand-new Greater German Reich. Although he did not find Elsabé in the Giaxa home he did locate her at the country estate of Count Tességuier where she had sought refuge; she was all right.

"Aurel Tességuier! He's the one! Who sent me the telegram from Slovenia today. One of Elsabé's platonic admirers, a widower Papa-Rose used to play chess with. Used to."

"Anyway, your mom-in-law is well cared for at his place. Miville reported that, first, they actually did requisition Jacksa the Last, Papa-Rose's ancient Lippizan. Supposedly for the field artillery. As if the Wehrmacht really had any need for an old circus nag like that—what you said a while ago was absolutely right. Naturally this requisitioning could not be carried out without a loud protest from the owner in question. Next day they came again and took the owner into protective custody."

"Couldn't it be," my question burst out "—couldn't it be that they arrested him for that?"

"For that?"

"Yes, because he protested! Maybe he cussed them out *coram publico*. Papa-Rose hardly ever loses his temper, but when he does, the walls come tumbling down."

With a slight shrug of his shoulders Kujath left the question undecided. Mrs. Giaxa informed Mr. Miville that the authorities had taken her husband off to Graz, where, she learned the following day, her sister-in-law, Konstantin Giaxa's elder sister, the widowed Dr. Miliza Zborowska, had already been arrested.

"So they *are* out to get the family!"

"Don't get excited, Trebla."

"I never get excited. That's something I got over a long time ago."

"Ah-but-you-are-you-are, I've been watching the way you're starting to get all worked up about it. Now is not the time for that."

"And *when* is?"

Kujath let my question drift away as if I had meant it rhetorically. Then I followed up with "What *other* reason could there be for arresting Aunt Za?"—and he countered with—"After all she was well known as one of the first members of the Austrian Socialist Party."

"Yes," I added, "and every day she trips down the street to early mass with her fat little housekeeper Maltschi. And if you happen to see the old girl from a distance on her way down the Naglergasse in her wide-brimmed black hat, her long black coat, and her black doctor's bag you could mistake her for an under-sized country priest."

Well. Following up on Elsabé's report, Mr. Miville proved himself loyal to the assignment he (Kujath) had given him by renting a car and making a side trip to Graz where, not without courage and with the aid of a tip placed in the hand of a bartender in a tavern near the district courthouse, he had learned two things. Whereupon the trade commissioner went straight back across the border and informed Kujath by telephone the same night.

I said, "That must have been Popelka's Weinhaus."

"How do you know that?"

"Forgive me, but I too have had the honor of being locked up in the Graz courthouse. More than once. Popelka's place is frequented by all the guards from the courthouse jail."

Well, Mr. Miville had learned that the "little Frau Doktor Zborowska, who'd transferred thousands of the town's inhabitants from the womb into the light of day was, grotesquely enough, indeed a prisoner in the district court-house." About Giaxa's arrest the barkeep, an older man, at first claimed to know nothing. But finally he told the Swiss visitor behind his cupped hand that, believe it or not,"the greatest circus act in Austria-Hungary is under arrest. Horse and rider." Mr. Giaxa had been taken into custody at the end of the week but wasn't there any longer; he had quickly been transferred elsewhere; to Vienna, people say, to the Rossauer Kaserne.

5

"I've done time there too. Now don't get mad at me: but why have you waited 'til now to tell me all this?"

"Well I hinted that I thought he was in Vienna. Thought. That's why I asked if you knew anyone in the Hotel Metropol. Getting back to this Herr Laimgruber." Kujath pulled out his bulky watch again; it was clear he wanted to go no further with the Giaxa affair just now. "The two blonds he seems to have set on your heels—"

"Oh hell, in the long run all I have is a vague suspicion about those two." I recounted my walk to St. Moritz-Bad and how I had seen my supposed pursuers playing ping-pong with two young Orthodox Jews in caftans at the kosher-guest pension Villa Muongia.

"How 'bout that," said Grandpa. "What'll they think of next? You know, by the way, that blond Jews are not unknown . . . Were they staying there? Or had they just stopped by?"

"That I don't know."

"But it's important. In any case, if I were you I'd have asked the desk clerk or the bellhop a few discreet questions. Even if they were only there for a cup of coffee, a Jewish proprietor will always know which one of his guests is Jewish and which one a goy. The whole thing could be an absurd trick. 'Undercover SS men play with gentlemen in caftans to deceive Aryan victim.' Did I ever tell you about my Brazilian rendezvous with the blond snake?"

One Sunday afternoon the young German rubber planter Henrique Kujath, a recent arrival to the Amazon jungles, was stalking alone, armed only with a machete, along the banks of the dirty, mud-yellow river near his *fazenda*. Suddenly tired, he curled up for an afternoon nap on the riverbank. When he woke up he saw himself surrounded.

He had never seen a snake so huge before. It bore markings, but its basic shade was blond.

The blond snake had the diameter of a man's upper thigh and might have been seven yards long. He scarcely knew the species, but realized that snakes of this size were not poisonous. (A short time later, during a visit to Butantan, the world's largest snake collection in the city of São Paulo, he could verify that it was a giant boa constrictor, a variant of the anaconda.) At any rate he knew such monsters killed their prey by strangulation. And prey—if they felt threatened—included people too.

As the brand-new rubber planter raised his head from midday slumber his entire horizon was nothing but blond-gleaming, gently pulsing snake. The reptile's head, nearly as large as the young German's, only flatter, stood rearing back little more than a foot away from his face.

His first and last attempt to reach for his machete failed. The massive snake neck curled backward, ready to strike ahead and strangle.

Henrique did the thing that saved his life: he waited. He didn't move. Still half dazed with sleep, sitting halfway up, he waited, waited in an ever more intolerable struggle to remain motionless (a struggle even worse than his fear), waited, barely breathing, eye to eye with the blond-colored snake.

An endless period of time went by, a time that seemed to him like hours on end. He scarcely dared to take a breath, and feared he might be stifled by the sultry, tropic dankness of the afternoon.

At last the man succeeded in his rigid duel of delay.

With a monstrous, hesitant slithering, always stopping, flat head turning, ready to attack, the blond snake raised its siege. And slid away, now with surprising quickness, through the ferns and into the bamboo thicket along the river. As he gasped for air, the man was able to estimate the creature's length before it disappeared from view—around thirty feet.

The young *fazendiero* hurried back to his plantation. On arriving there he surprised himself by not reporting the nearly fatal incident to his Portuguese foreman or the Indios he employed. Instead he grabbed his English rifle and stalked back to the scene of the incident along the riverbank. And hunted about until he discovered the blond snake.

It was rolled up asleep on the swampy riverbank. Rolled up?

It slept coiled upward to a kind of pagoda, woven around and around into something resembling a laundry basket.

He killed it with twelve shots.

"Why," I inquired, "did you do that?"

"You mean, why did I run back there on my own with a gun?"

"To rid the area of the monster?"

"Ha! There was more than one anaconda along the river, and you couldn't have wiped them all out; anyway they hardly ever attacked people. There was a different reason why I kept the matter to myself and went back with a rifle. The whole thing was embarrassing to me. That was the joke—I was ashamed about having been afraid. That's right. 'Cause I'd been forced to sweat blood for hours on end by that beast—that's why. And that's the *only* reason why I had to shoot him."

"Beg your pardon, but I think that was a bit unfair."

"What?"

"Killing the thing while it was sleeping."

"Huh, what, unfair? Oi vay, my son. I see black for you in the jungle future we've got ahead of us. Black-black-black."

200

"Black-White-White-Black," I remarked.

"How's that?"

"A fleeting friend of mine used to say that."

"A fleeting friend? Is there such a thing?"

"There was. Last Wednesday he drove his rattletrap Fiat into Lake Campfèr."

"Gaudenz de Colana, Attorney at Law. I read it in the paper. Yeah, that good old dipsomaniac Avvocato Bow-Wow from Schoolhouse Square in St. Moritz."

"Did you know him, Grandpa?"

"For thirty years."

"At the risk of sounding sentimental, I think I was the last friend Dr. Bow-Wow had."

"Hm. After all, you were colleagues."

"In what sense?"

"Well, both of you were sort of, so to speak, has-been aristocrats, if you'll forgive my saying so. And what's more you are, if I'm not mistaken, *also a Doctor juris.* Why don't you use the title?"

"I don't like titles," I said. Then the telephone rang in the tower studio.

Kujath reacted with a jerk. Had he been startled? This time he struggled vainly to get up from his chair. The effort squeezed a muffled gasp out of him and I carefully grasped him under the armpits and lifted him, feeling his weight and his weakness, and he rumbled almost unwillingly, "It's all right, Comrade, thank-you-thank-you, I'll manage."

When he replaced the receiver his face was once again a wooden Aztec mask.

"Valentin," he said dully, "will be up here in a few minutes."

"I don't want to be in your way."

"You're not in the way. On the contrary."

"You mentioned a phone call I should wait for," I said, "perhaps with some news about Papa-Rose—"

"Please—just—wait—for—one—minute," spoke the Aztec mask. Then without warning the woodenness disappeared.

Out of the depths came a dull rumbling on wooden planks. "That's Pfiff going to pick up our late visitor from the post office in Tartar. Light up another Holandeza. I'll be right back up."

"Shouldn't I go down too and check on Xana?"

"Naw, just stay up here, my boy. Didn't I tell you, she's sleeping like a log."

6 While waiting alone again in the tower studio—not lighting a
Holandeza, but letting Maitena's crucifix dangle mechanically on its thin gold
chain in front of me—I recalled what I knew about Valentin; it wasn't much. He
was a few years older than I, a blacksmith's apprentice from Wasserburg on the
Inn, a Social Democrat; in 1916, as a private in one of the eight Royal Bavarian
Dragoon regiments, he was taken prisoner by the Czarist forces. Released at the
beginning of the October Revolution, he did not return to his homeland for years,
learned Russian, joined the Red Army in its successful campaign against the
White General Wrangel—but strange as it may seem, played no part in the installation of the Soviet Republic in Munich. (His legendary comment: "Nothing'll come o' that.") After polytechnic studies in Moscow he went back to the
mountains, but not the Bavarian Alps, to the Caucasian Soviet Republic of
Georgia (later renamed the Transcaucasian Soviet Republic) where, as a German engineer, he taught Georgian farmers how to go about repairing farm ma-
chinery. Rumor had it that his return home to Wasserburg about the time of
Hitler's Munich Putsch was for private reasons. His life's companion, a beautiful Georgian woman, had died in her prime. (Thereafter he remained a bach-
elor.) In 1925 Valentin Tiefenbrucker, also called Caucasian Val, became the
youngest delegate to the Bavarian State Legislature; two years later a delegate
to the Reichstag.

His typical Reichstag speech, with its brevity (he made sparing use of the
more hackneyed slogans of the class struggle) and its clever folksy dialectics (he
hadn't only learned Marxism, but had *become* learned *in* it as well), was a sharp
contrast to Hitler's hour-long black-magic carnival-hawker's spiel with its monstrous delusions of collective-Volks-grandeur interspersed with periodic attacks
of rabies—a contrast all the more bizarre in that both Valentin and Adolf had a
very similar dialect coloration to their speech. And as if wanting to ridicule the
Mass Hypnotizer of the Inn Valley even more, he adorned his upper lip with a
little black exclamation point of a moustache that looked like a conscious parody of the Fuehrer's "brush."

Shortly before the outbreak of our February defense corps revolt against
the Dollfuss regime the union leader Koloman Wallisch in Bruck and I in Graz
both received a secret message from Valentin (whom neither of us knew personally). "*Am presently staying incognito (as times demand) in Austria and am prepared to cooperate with you as an old billiards player with considerable experience at playing the red ball so that under favorable circumstances we might*

achieve a winning series of carom shots."

With the consent of Koloman Wallisch I passed on this offer to Major Alexander Eifler, Commandant of the Republican Defense Corps in Vienna. He turned it down. I had the dubious privilege of transmitting the refusal to Tiefenbrucker's cover address: NO BILLIARD PLAYERS NEEDED.

On my own I added: *Which Graz and Bruck regret.* The February battles with the Austrian Army, Police, and Gendarmerie, Heimwehr (the fellows with the rooster feathers) and the Austro-Nazi Storm Troopers (Tabernacle Bugs) were lost without Valentin.

Shortly thereafter we heard that he had returned to the Soviet Union, later that he had landed in a Siberian labor camp. Around this time a wave of purge trials against part of the Old Guard had begun to swell in the USSR. That these trials with their at times grotesque self-criticisms—incredible even to Sovietphiles—were a direct result of the installation and expansion of the Fascist regime in Germany was an obvious but seldom acknowledged fact. Valentin's name disappeared from the pages of the *Red Flag*. In February '37, when I was transferred from Vienna's Graues Haus to the internment camp at Woellersdorf, the *Pester Lloyd* (citing a "reliable source") announced Valentin Tiefenbrucker's execution. At the end of February '38 Valentin had breakfast at Smutny's Budweis-Beer-Restaurant near the Vienna State Opera and afterward played several rounds of billiards at Café Dobner on the Naschmarkt.

In those days Herr von Schussnigg had more important things to do than hunt Communists. And Valentin had not returned to Austria as a refugee, but rather as an agent of the Party. He maintained complete silence regarding his experiences in Russia. The coded messages, the secret chatter inside our ever more lackadaisical illegality reminded one of the drum signals of the very civilized Canadian Indians. Most of it was nothing more than gossip drummed through the forest. Thus I doubted the authenticity of a remark attributed to Valentin (which, though original, did not square with his well-known party discipline). "The trouble these days is that you never know for sure if you'll be gunned down by your friends or your enemies; but no doubt it's always been that way." Another one sounded more authentic. "I've come to Vienna to warn you. Inside of a month the Germans are going to march in here with trumpets and Gestapo."

This time it was I who tried to contact him. When I arrived at our secret HQ in Vienna/Brigittenau I learned that Valentin had made a side trip to the West Hungarian Komitat Sopron (in Oedenburg). Barely two weeks later the Wehrmacht rolled into Austria to oversee the "Birth of Greater Germany" amidst the frantic jubilation—we can allow ourselves the word—of a "considerable portion of the populace." The Gestapo didn't get Valentin until mid-April not far from Oedenburg; they got him for the first time while he was playing billiards in a Burgenland coffeehouse. After letting him sweat for three weeks in the Turkish Steam Bath at the Hotel Metropol they shunted him out of

Vienna by rail into his homeland. His homeland. Into the concentration camp at Dachau near Munich.

Now I would see him at last, in the Luzienburg. As I slip the necklace of Maïtena Ithurra y Azkue into my tuxedo pocket I hear the rising hum of the silo elevator.

"'Scuse me, Tiefenbrucker, if I go first," said Grandpa as he pushed his way out of the "Lilliputian elevator" ahead of his midnight guest.

During his ten-minute absence he had gone through a change. It was plain to see that he had literally gone through something. His facial color no longer yellowish but earthen gray. The squirrel tails of his long moustache sagged downward. Not only that, but the old man seemed slightly crippled. Yes, he seemed to be limping as he pushed between me and the billiard set on his way to the French window, as if he had nothing more urgent to do than go out on the balcony. In passing he hissed at me, "That's all!"

Then Valentin appeared out of the kitchenette. At first glance it wasn't clear to me why his emaciated but still stocky figure was surrounded by a radiant gleam from head to foot. Whatever it was he immediately reminded me of a portrait of a knight in armor. A certain portrait. Of a certain knight. Anything more particular than that eluded me at that moment.

He stepped up to me—amazing that his steps didn't clank! He took my hand and shook it powerfully—amazing that his arm didn't rattle!

He spoke with the slightly husky, warmly modulated, well-trained voice of a rural politician, in a polished South Bavarian accent. "Greetings, Trebla, greetings. At last! I'm really happy to meet you. Really. Or better yet, I *would* be really happy if this weren't such a stupid, godawful moment. The moment when we finally get to meet each other. There was a man who really made me laugh 'til I cried. The last time was, wait, yes, at the Circus Krone. And it wasn't a week ago that I cried *real* tears over this man, and it's a rare occasion when I cry. Trebla, my sincerest, my deepest, my goddam most heartfelt condolences: your famous father-in-law is no more."

7

Papa-Rose was dead.

Gul-Baba was dead.
Konstantin Giaxa was dead.
Giaxa & Giaxa was dead.

Obristi Obraski was dead.
Colonel Dubouboule and Colonel Mac Mac dead.
The Rákóczidetzky March was dead.

Beau-ti-ful, o night of love,
O pa-ci-fy my long-ing.
Swee-ter than the sun a-bove,
O love-ly night of love.
Times es-capes the pow-er of
My ten-der love's de-sir-ing.
Like a far de-par-ting dove
Time flees my ten-der love.

8

That had been my second hay-fever attack of the evening.

Still not recovered from his lameness, Grandpa had come reeling in from the balcony with a quivering hand stretched out toward the telephone. His muffled, snorting cry: Goddammit! He would tell that Hungarian to shut off his record-player racket this very minute. Shortly after Valentin's entrance the Barcarole, sung by Tauber, had come roaring down through the ceiling, turned up to a volume that transformed the gentle moderato into a distorted, crashing furioso for a few seconds. Then the radio amateur lowered the volume. My voice laboring under a new attack of breathlessness, I asked Grandpa to leave Szabo alone. The late guest, informed by his host in a few gasping sentences (as if he too were suffering from a hay-fever attack) about Szabo's experiments, agreed with me. Then Kujath collapsed into his leather chair while I washed down three more ephedrine tablets with the rest of my champagne and asked our guest what he would like to drink.

Valentin said, "I'd just like a beer."

In the refrigerator I found several bottles of real Pilsener and set one for him on the edge of the billiard table along with a glass. He put the bottle to his mouth like a construction worker and sucked the contents half empty. Then Kujath spoke. Haltingly he declared that this bad news was not merely a hard blow for all of us; a bolt from the blue; but for Europe and the whole world as well; for the world of laughter. A signal that the whole world would have nothing to laugh about for the next few years, no. Then he apologized: for not telling me the whole truth. "Naturally I suspected the worst. But I didn't know anything definite. And when Valentin, after arriving in Switzerland, called me from a telephone booth in Rorschach, I asked him. Because I knew that, after his own arrest, they'd taken him to Vienna first. I asked *you*, right, Tiefenbrucker?—if you happened—happened to know something definite about Jacksa. And you, you answered after a short pause that unfortunately you *did* know something definite. Right?"

The late guest, his whole figure a dull radiance, stood leaning on the billiard table and lowered his head.

Kujath: "I couldn't discuss the whole thing on the phone with Valentin. Too risky for him. And for me too. Not because of the Nazios from the German Veterans Resort in Davos who might have been tapping my line again. But because of the Federal Police, who've also been making their little spot-checks, lately in particular on Swiss 'paper' citizens of German origin. Despite the fact that I provide Swiss Counterintelligence with an occasional hot tip. That's secondary. Everything. Everything . . . secondary."

Grandpa fell silent like a big grayish yellow talking doll that had run down.

"I suspected the worst," he continued, now wound up again. "But human nature being what it is, you still hope. Until you get the bad news really slapped in your face. Also I wanted to keep you from running down to Xana and waking her up—just on the basis of my gloomy suspicions . . . Now you'll have to break it to her gently . . . gent-ly." Again the talking doll turned off.

"Yes." I heard the asthma voices crackle. They crackled in me, seeming to drown out my own voice. I looked at the late guest. "How did it happen?"

"Just a second, comrade. A quick question to my selfless benefactor. By when do I have to be out of here?"

Kujath: "By one. Pfiff has precise instructions. The private airfield where the pilot of this two-seat thingamajig—this Fieseler-Storch—is waiting for you—"

"The man's name is Liétard, if I understood right."

"Lietard. The private field is located in the Jura Mountains between Tramelan and Saignelégier, just a stone's throw from the French border. Twohundredseventy K-M from here. Pfiff can cover that distance with the Storch inside of four hours. Liétard wants to be airborne before six."

"In four hours I can get some halfway decent sleep. Then I'll catch a few more winks on the plane."

"If you can sleep in cars and airplanes."

"If need be I'll sleep under the gallows," said Valentin.

Sleep under the gallows, I thought. What a medieval way for a CP man to express himself. Slapping the oilcloth cover of the billiard table the late guest invited his host to a "little midnight joust." (That too a medieval phrase.) Kujath declined. In the last few days his hands had had quiveritis. Aha, said Valentin, did I want to play. A good round of billiards would calm the nerves—something all of us could use. I wasn't a billiards player, I protested. Aha, did we mind if he played a round of French billiards by himself, and Kujath said, Go on, go on; was he good at Russian billiards too, and Valentin replied that Russian billiards were uninteresting compared to French and as stupid as it might sound, ever since his arrest in Eisenstadt he had longed every day to sink a row of balls on a French billiard table . . . As diligent as a coffeehouse waiter expecting a tip, I rolled up the dark green oilcloth cover; the brighter green of the table surface now appeared; the late guest deposited the white balls, then the red one. Now, according to custom, he would remove his jacket. But no, he remained in full armor.

This impression of "armor" was created for the most part by his un-chic but obviously *sparkling*, brand-new suit of grayish black, metallic-gleaming fabric. He lifted a cue from the rack, and poked the air with it as if testing a sword. Rubbed the leather tip with blue chalk, caught my glance, and explained that he had bought the suit off the rack in Rorschach—first, because it was cheap, and second, because it was as inconspicuous as a black cat at midnight and third because it was very light and therefore just the thing for a transition to the hot June weather in Spain. Very light? With the heavy steps of a man in armor he paced back to the billiard table, bent forward onto his left arm and slid the cue between his knuckles. The unshaded light of the coral-snake lamp struck the brown violet pigment of his angular face. His nose seemed swollen; his constant sniffing was a clue that it was probably injured. But this very swelling of his nose made a certain resemblance to the Chancellor of Greater Germany more evident—especially if you imagined the forelock of a petty-bourgeois matinee idol in place of his stubbly shaven convict haircut. On the other hand, he was a much purer Dinaric type, completely without any tendency to strike jaunty poses. Suddenly without a trace of awkwardness he took his shot and stood instantly erect, surveying the green playing surface with keen eyes, and the double click of the red ball striking the two white ones could have been the subtle ticking of joints in a suit of armor. As he stood there, his cue lowered like a lance, he reminded me once again of a particular picture of a particular knight. Of a rustic South German knight—not one from the Thirty Years War, but an earlier one. Perhaps a warrior from those battles that provided Historical Materialism with one of its prime examples: the German Peasants' War.

Now despite the anguish of the moment I knew, I considered which portrait of a knight he reminded me of. A painting by Lovis Corinth. It depicted the actor Rudolf Rittner in the title role of Hauptmann's play *Florian Geyer.*

Last Tuesday Detention Camp Director SS-*Standartenfuehrer* Giselher Liebhenschl did us the honor of appearing in person at morning roll call. A real extra mean bullet-crapper he is. (Thus spoke the solo billiards player without raising his voice.) A worse tyrant than the Camp Commandant himself, who at the time was receiving instructions at headquarters on the Prinz-Albrecht-Strasse in Berlin. His deputy Liebhenschl is a dandy, a gentleman rider, a flower lover, and *bel esprit* who plays Chopin impromptus, quotes D'Annunzio, and prefers Helgoland lobster to roast pork and dumplings. In his own self-coined phrase, "a new-Germanic man dedicated to the timeless values of Western Culture, to the eternal idea of the Holy Roman Empire of the German Nation, a man, to his enemies relentless unto death."

I was already at the point of requesting Valentin to cut the details and get on with the story. Only his intense concentration on the billiard game held me back.

Standartenfuehrer Liebhenschl's exaggerated bellowing voice, a bombastic croaking, slices out over the three thousand shaven heads of the prisoners assembled at attention (the majority are away on "Special Details"). "Tomorrow morning on the Orient Express from Vienna a well-known personality will arrive to avail himself of our resort facilities! A personality who, in the prime of his career, commanded large sums of money for his appearances before the whole world—and who no doubt provided some of you gentlemen here with a few amusing memories!" It was one of Liebhenschl's humorous whims to address the prisoners sometimes as "gentlemen" and other times as "swine." "Greater Germany," echoes the falsetto growl of a whip-swinging Giselher Liebhenschl, "is no longer a circus ring for senile comedians who insist on undermining the martial will of the people! Interestingly enough we have a few other professional jokesters among us, albeit of somewhat smaller caliber! These will prepare a fitting welcome for our famous visitor!" The SS-*Scharfuehrer* Maerzhas reads off the names of five prisoners, all from Vienna, three of Judaic confession: the comedian and impersonator Neugroeschl from the Deutsches Volkstheater; the cabaret artist Gruenzweig from the Simpl; Paul Astor—actually Ashkenazy—who had made a name for himself during the twenties as a moderator in Berlin's Kabarett der Komiker. (Astor was employed in the camp as a pallbearer, remarked the billiard player between clicks.) The fourth, Leopold Habinger, stage manager for operettas at the Theater an der Wien, had the bad luck of being a Jehovah's Witness, and Jan Kejrschik, a circus hand of Czech descent, of being denounced as a Communist. "Just look at them!" croaks the Detention Camp Director. "Three Jewish swine, a Bolshevist swine, and a Jehovah's Witness swine! The reception committee for our honored guest! That will be a scene to remember!"

Toward evening the five of them are ordered into Liebhenschl's private quarters. Soon thereafter you can hear the sound of his Bechstein grand playing the famous cantata from the third act of Lortzing's *Zar und Zummermann.* Then a hesitant chorus joins in . . . That night, behind the backs of the guards, a restless whispering goes round the barracks from bed to bed: Who could this new man be who had earned such great sums for his appearances? No one takes the words "circus ring" literally. Most people guess it will be a film star. Four men are released to their bunks from the "opera rehearsal," the fifth, Neugroeschl, has not been so fortunate. The ex-comedian is a regular member of Detail 47-11. This group, named for the cologne, has the duty of transporting liquid manure from the sewage plant to the garden in used tin cans and old marmalade buckets. During the rehearsal Neugroeschl's "scent" arouses the displeasure of the camp director, who disciplines the prisoner with an overnight banishment to the bunker. In a depressed whisper the other four swear they still have no idea *whom* they are supposed to welcome with their acapella vocalizing.

For the next morning—that would be last Wednesday—most special details are cancelled. Everyone has to assemble for a special formation. After several days of bad weather . . .

I thought, bad weather in the Engadine, too, the beginning of last week . . . it gradually begins to clear. On Wednesday morning banks of fog—no longer cold—hang over the Dachau moors. The prisoners waiting in formation on the assembly field, thousands of gray-striped bodies, shaven heads—through the enclosing double barbed-wire fence charged with high voltage, they could see, for the first time in days, the Bullet-Crapper out for his morning ride. Stiffly clamped astride his dun-colored stallion Mjoellnir, the rider fades to a vague ghost of an image in the mist.

For two hours the men are kept waiting, and no one has the vaguest ghost of an idea who is coming to play the lead in this malicious scene to remember. The camp has two entrances; one behind the crematorium and the other, the main gate leading to the town, decorated with the slogan ARBEIT MACHT FREI, "Labor Liberates."

"Arbeit—macht—frei," the billiard player repeated, as if still more engrossed in his solo game. Click-click.

Finally the Detention Camp Director returns from his morning ride. He has his light pink, oak-leaf-trimmed dress uniform brought to him, obviously his costume for the impending scene, and positions himself as his own equestrian statue in the midst of the assembled prisoners as they stand in a U-shaped formation at the end of the long tree-lined entranceway to the camp.

Scharfuehrer Maerzhas, a towering galoot who is constantly teased by his superiors for his clumsiness and then takes it out on the prisoners, orders Gruenzweig, Astor, Kejrschik, and Neugroeschl (just released from the bunker) to form a rank to the front of the superb East Prussian stallion Mjoellnir. (Had he placed them *behind* the horse it would probably have cost them their lives.) The ex-stage manager Habinger has to stand at attention facing the four. Maerzhas presses a billy club into his hands.

We could hear Habinger asking: "Excuse me, with a club I'm supposed to—?" The answer, a boot kick in the shinbone.

There is the long row of barracks; the broad assembly field; the double row of lindens like the idyllic entrance to a rural estate (which, indeed, the camp at one time was). At the end of the entranceway the main gate fades into pale fog. Now it opens. First we notice shadowy figures: the guards by the gate, then five storm troopers, weapons slung over their shoulders, leading three civilians.

The eight come toward us down the road. Finally we can see. Two of the new men are handcuffed, the third is not.

(The rolling of the billiard balls. Click-click.)

The entranceway lined with tall linden trees is several hundred yards long. The storm troopers turn off with the handcuffed men and disappear behind a bunker. The unfettered man remains alone on the road. Then Death's-head *Standartenfuehrer* Liebhenschl's half-baked Lower Bavarian bread-face allows itself a grin. (The accent lay on *Lower*—here some of Valentin's Upper Bavarian pride came into play.) A grin that says flawless the way the whole scheme is running according to plan. His sweating dun-colored stallion glistens like gold in the rapidly warming sun now breaking through the fog banks; the horse chews foam that splatters onto the shoulder of the short "Jewish Detainee" Gruenzweig. But he doesn't dare move from the spot.

And the formation of beaten men, numbering in the thousands, along with its few hundred tormentors, and even the guards in the machine-gun towers—everyone stands staring at the one man. He promenades, yes promenades his way all alone down the tree-lined road. A finely built man—maybe he only looked that way because of the tall linden trees—not short, just medium height, slender, bareheaded, tieless, wearing a faded blue Styrian jacket, riding breeches, gray suede riding boots—

One thing I could not understand. Why did I avoid asking Valentin to make his story short and spare us the endless details? In that dreadful hour as I sat crouched on the arm of the easy chair facing the billiard table as if watching a small illuminated stage, never turning to look at Grandpa, who was not making a sound, my thoughts went something like this: Curious, how well this Communist billiards champion can tell a story—his descriptions so concrete, so exact, yet packed with so much restrained emotion—his attitude toward the place he just escaped from, the scene of so much suffering (including his own), so disciplined and objective, even at the very moment he is cursing it.

Was this the last of the Luzienburg's Midnight Tales?

I could not understand why I said: "Yes, in an outfit like that he rode out from the Murauhof every morning. They must have arrested him as he was on his way out to ride."

Kujath's voice behind me: "According to my informant they took away his Lippizan the day before. Did he have two horses?"

"No, but he used to exercise Tességuier's gelding."

Valentin rubbed chalk on the cue tip.

The new man has approached the reception committee to a distance of twenty paces, but still none of the prisoners has recognized him. He could be in his mid-fifties or mid-sixties with his youthful build and wrinkled face. Though smaller and wirier he reminds you of Bismarck with his rounded nose, his sharp eyes and bushy eyebrows. His face looks like tanned leather—

210

Instead of making a demand, "Please spare us Gul-Baba's portrait," I said, "From forty years of makeup."

"Aha, yes. The marked physiognomy of a—of a scientist."

"The circus *is* a science," I heard Kujath say.

"And still—which is remarkable considering how famous he is"— Valentin, half sitting on the table's edge, sets up the cue behind his back, ready to shoot—"not one of us recognized him."

"The audience," I lectured, "preserves the image of a clown's mask. His mask. Applied to Giaxa, the mask of Obristi Obraski."

"Godalmighty," murmured the Communist Reichstag Delegate, Ret., "Obristi Obraski . . ." He remained half sitting on the table's edge, his head turned, his cue at the ready. But he did not shoot.

"Without this mask," I continued as if we were engaged in a harmless chat, "he appeared only two or three times in the movies. The last time was in a Willy Forst film where he played a Major-General."

Now Valentin poked the cue forward behind his back. Click . . . "Wasn't your *father* a real Major-General?"

"He was," I said, "back in the days of the Empire."

"And your father-in-*law* did a satire on it. Interesting family."

"Onetime interesting family," I corrected him.

"Oi," said Valentin, turning to the blackboard and making some chalk marks. "I was standing right at the front so that I could see the Bullet-Crapper's face as he sat on Mjoellnir, and the faces of the reception committee. Strange that not even the actors recognized him at first glance, your father-in-law."

I had to get used to the idea that I would never be able to change the pace of his story, so I said: "He seldom had much to do with actors, with a few notable exceptions. But all the more with circus artists. He thought of himself completely as an artiste. Until 1933 he was president of the Deutsche Artistenloge."

"So that's why! It was the circus hand Kejrschik who recognizes him first. He can't control his amazement. In no time the name is out, even though *Scharfuehrer* Maerzhas gives poor Kejrschik a kick in the shins that almost knocks him over. The whispered name spreads like wildfire through our ranks, "*Who's* that? That can't be! Impossible! Giaxa in Dachau? Giaxa and Giaxa? Giaxa *without* Giaxa?*"

For the second time this evening the ephedrine did its job. My forehead registered a faster pulse. I could breathe easier and felt how once again the iciness began to surround me.

> *Praised be the day*
> *When you arrived among us*
> *Deedle-dum, deedle-dum, deedle-dum!*
> *To make us all so merry.*

So the five men of the reception committee begin to sing their meager chorus, the allegro vivace from Lortzing's *Zar und Zimmermann*. In place of a baton Leopold Habinger, who was formerly (that is, three months ago) the operetta stage manager at the Theater an der Wien, swings a rubber billy club. And Gruenzweig sings, spattered by the stallion's foam, and Neugroeschl, who was formerly (that is, three months ago) a popular comedian—ai, old Neugroeschl . . . one of the secrets of his comedy was the man's light-footed corpulence; now he looks like a half-empty sack. The night in the bunker did not agree with him. His spongy face shows bruises that look like spots of paint. One might have asked (but nobody asks—anyone who asks is punished), did he make his face up into a clown's mask, old Neugroeschl?

> *Deedle-dum, deedle-dum, deedle-dum!*
> *To make us all so merry.*

A steaming jet of water escapes the horse. Stationed on his flank, Paul Astor, once known as a charming and witty moderator, is soaked to the hips in horse urine (yet he doesn't move; anyone who moves is punished).

> *It was so long ago*
> *That none of us remembers*
> *Deedle-dum, deedle-dum, deedle-dum!*
> *That makes our hearts still gladder.*
> *Praised be the day*
> *When you arrived among us . . .*

And that is the scene to remember arranged by Detention Camp Director, SS-*Standartenfuehrer* Giselher Liebhenschl. The storm troopers giggle; and then from the ranks of the guards (composed primarily of greenies: habitual criminals) come a few trial sniggers. Liebhenschl, his own equestrian statue, looks around for the first time. The massed whispering ". . . axa . . . axa" dies on the tongues of the prisoners. Meanwhile not one of them smiles; not a peep nor a giggle, to say nothing of a laugh. Even though the guards with their unpunished trial-chuckles have proven that laughing is *not* forbidden in special cases. Liebhenschl's animated—no, animating—encouraging grin seems to say, For once every one of you is allowed to laugh, you swine, you public enemies! But instead a great silence hangs over the prisoners, and something sticks in the throat of even the Death's Head storm troopers: their own laugh. It is their duty to split their sides laughing at this special event arranged by the commander himself, but one aspect of the show doesn't go as planned. The bearing. The bearing of the still un-uniformed, un-numbered Prisoner X.

Of all those present Prisoner X fixes his gaze on the singer Neugroeschl who is standing there with his disfigured mouth like a badly made-up clown. Prisoner X, whom everybody knows and whom almost nobody recognizes. Prisoner X—with the deeply furrowed features of a tireless scientist and the clothing of a modest country gentleman—who himself looks nothing at all like a clown.

9

First a short hum of the silo elevator upward, then a long hum downward. Grandpa's funereal voice: "That's Szabo quitting for the day." The quiet rolling of the ivory balls; one click followed by nothing. Valentin left the snake-lamp's bright cone of light and stood in the coral glow of the shade, noting his score on the blackboard. He seemed to be playing a regular sixty-point game with himself. All at once I remembered another game of—Russian—billiards played on a smaller table by two friends of mine: the Two Blonds at Pizzagalli's Hotel. That belonged in another book.

"Valentin, did Papa-Rose—I mean my father-in-law," a strange word to me, "did he suffer long?"

Valentin, scribbling: "N-no."

Like a dutiful waiter anticipating an order I fetched another bottle of Pilsener from the kitchenette and Valentin took it. "Don't mind if I do." I sat back down on the armrest of the chair without looking at Kujath.

His Excellency the Bullet-Crapper intones from his highhorse with intentional loudness, "Well, Mr. Giaxa-and-Giaxa-and-Giaxa, how did you like the little musical reception your somewhat less world famous colleagues prepared for you? Nice, wasn't it?"

Prisoner X looks not at the rider, but at the horse. Like a deaf man talking to another deaf man he bellows out in Obristi Obraski's command voice, "That dun stallion will get a chill if he's not rubbed down right away!"

Scharfuehrer Maerzhas makes a face as if about to intervene, but Liebhenschl waves him off with his riding whip, dismounts, stamps jackbooted and stiff-legged (imitating his Fuehrer) up to Prisoner X and croaks, "How would it be if *you*—old horseman that you are—took care of that!"

"Why not!" bellows Prisoner X. "Here, Mr. Kejrschik, an old acquaintance of mine from the Circus Rebernigg, can give me a hand! *Servus*, Mr. Kejrschik!"

"Gree-eetings, Mr. Scha-sha-aksa," we hear Prisoner 4329 stammer. Once again Maerzhas, the gangling baboon, looks grim and ready to intervene. Once again Liebhenschl waves him casually back. "Fine. Why shouldn't number forty-three-twenty-nine help you? Give Mjoellnir a brushing!"

Prince Fugger in Augsburg had kept a part-Jewish riding master for his polo ponies who once made the mistake of coming to blows with a drunken "full Aryan" after the latter had called him a bastard. He now atones for that in Dachau. "Fugger's Bastard" (as he is called by the Storm Troopers) works as Liebhenschl's stable boy; quick as a wink he is on hand with the currying gear.

The eight-year-old dun stallion, a prizewinning steeplechaser, is a dangerously skittish horse. Except for the Bullet-Crapper and Fugger's Bastard, he allows no one to mount him. He doesn't bite, but bucks and kicks. Seen from behind, a truly savage beast: he lets fly the most brutal kicks when anyone comes near his hindquarters. On three different occasions unsuspecting new arrivals were murderously ordered to inspect Mjoellnir's hind hooves. Two clouts in the stomach, both lethal; the third victim is still lying in sick bay with an injured spine—

I heard Grandpa groan, heard his subdued bass voice: "'scuse me for interrupting, Tiefenbrucker, but I'm afraid I get the picture now. The way it happened. This whatsit-horse, Mule-near, or whatever his name is—"

"—caught Papa-Rose with a kick in the back," I heard myself say. "Right in his Achilles vertebrae. The grotesque part of it is—is that's exactly what he prophesied."

Kujath's voice behind me: "What's that—Achilles vertebrae?"

"In his army days, when he was serving at the Imperial Riding Instructors School in Hof Castle a remount gave him a vicious kick in the small of the back. After a few weeks he was back in the saddle again, but then he was transferred to the reserves, and even after many years his back would still hurt whenever he went on a long tour. Usually toward evening. Several times he had to cancel his entire act because of it. And once he said to me, 'Someday that back of mine is going to do me in,' and then explained dryly, 'Who knows, maybe someday I'll get cancer in that spot from all the years of irritation. In any case, while I'm working I always make damned sure I don't fall on my back. But if. If I ever got kicked in that spot again it would be something like . . . like you, Trebla, getting your second head wound."

Valentin chalked his cue tip with extra care. "Sorry, gentlemen. That's not how it was."

It was like this: Prisoners X and 4329 unsaddle Mjoellnir. Kejrschik *knows* the stallion's bad habits. You can see in his face, he wants to try to warn the new man. Before he can say a word *Scharfuehrer* Maerzhas roars at him. "Keep your mouth shut, I say!" Kejrschik blanches even more. Meanwhile Giaxa has brought the stallion's nervous weaving under control and raises his eyebrows suggestively. Kejrschik gets some of his color back.

Fugger's Bastard arrives with two pails of water. Giaxa holds the Prussian stallion on a short rein while Kejrschik pours water over its back. A trained

214

stable hand, Kejrschik pulls the curry comb onto his hand like a glove and curries the neck, the right flank, from the withers back to the croup, from the forearm down to the fetlock, and Mjoellnir, held fast by Giaxa, accepts it almost without moving a muscle.

And someone else lets something happen without moving a muscle: Maerzhas. Not applying the no-talking order to himself, Giaxa mutters incessantly to the dun stallion; now and then he gives a direction to the former circus hand. But Maerzhas doesn't make a move.

The uncouth *Scharfuehrer* is also—who would have guessed it!—only human. His friends and relatives (maybe even he himself as a boy) had marveled at the equestrian eccentric in Munich's Circus Krone, had laughed, clapped, and cheered—such things aren't so easily forgotten; he seems to feel this, for all his fanaticism, deep in his gangly bones. His questioning glance to the camp director remains unanswered. With the casual attentiveness of a degenerate Caesar Augustus watching gladiators battle to the death, Liebhenschl surveys the scene.

Just imagine how it looked (said Valentin, sinking another canon series): in gigantic formation the gray-clad army of prisoners, their ranks now rejoined on the double by Fugger's Bastard and by the reception committee except for Jan Kejrschik who, striped and shorn, continues to curry the dun-colored horse under Giaxa's supervision, like a harmless prison trusty allocated to a blue-jacketed country gentleman for morning jobs. As background scenery the tree-lined drive of an almost . . . almost idyllic country estate. Two figures clash with these homey surroundings: the Bullet-Crapper with his rose-colored uniform, his mirror-shiny riding boots splayed apart, the silver skull on his brownish black cap above his insipid face, his riding whip clamped beneath his arm, and lanky Maerzhas in his long, brownish black uniform . . . Some distance away a group of storm troopers; and manning machine guns in the wooden watchtowers even the guards stare expectantly—two of them through field glasses.

Up to the croup Mjoellnir allows himself to be curried by Prisoner 4329, then he begins to weave again. Prisoner X calls the other man over to him and shows him how tight to hold the reins. Throws a horse blanket over the stallion, slips the curry comb over his own hand, trudges along the horse's flank and begins (is there the hint of a smile in the deep creases of his face, or is it just an illusion?), begins to curry the hindquarters from tail to hock.

Twice Mjoellnir lashes out. But Kejrschik holds his muzzle in an iron grip, and the blows lack their usual murderous strength. Too, Giaxa evades the kicks with just the right moves—amazing for a man his age—and holds his ground like a bullfighter, close to the animal.

Then something unexpected happens. The spiteful hohoho of the storm troopers is nowhere to be heard. Instead, from the army of beaten men an involuntary, uncontrollable laughing flares up, born of a terrible, lonely second of joy.

(Valentin: "Awful. It sounded awful.")

"Silence!!" shrieks Liebhenschl, now turkey red, as the show begins proceeding contrary to plan. "Silence!!" roars Maerzhas's echo, which repeats itself in countless reverberations along the rows of barracks; "ilence-ilence-ilence!!" Echoing into the great stillness that follows the quickly stifled laughter. "Who was that laughing?!" shrieks the camp director. Utter quiet. Until Maerzhas reports. "The whole miserable lot of 'em, *mein Standartenfuehrer!*"

"*Ach so!*" shrieks the Bullet-Crapper. "The gentlemen think this is a circus, do they?!" Utter silence. Meanwhile Kejrschik has resaddled the stallion. "A cirus ..." repeats Liebhenschl, his tone now changed. "That was—that was your profession, wasn't it, Mr. Fratellini and Fratellini?" The obedient hohoho of the storm troopers—how dry and weak it sounds. The *Scharfuehrer* orders Prisoner 4329 to return to the ranks. Prisoner X stands alone next to the saddled East Prussian stallion.

"How would it be! If you gave us a little demonstration of your famous horsemanship?—even though a public enemy like you is hardly worthy of riding my splendid Mjoellnir—a personal present of the Reich's *Sportfuehrer* von Tschammer und Osten. You *deserter* from the year 1917! As you see, we are well informed! Or do you wish to deny the fact?! That you deserted the army in that year?!"

"I hope you're not implying," roared Giaxa in his Obristi-Obraski voice, "that I never faced enemy fire!"

Prisoner Valentin Tiefenbrucker, and no doubt many others, feels weak in the stomach. Only the Detention Camp Director seems pleased by this answer. He declaims, "After you had refused—something particularly shameful for a former active officer—to take up arms in defense of your fatherland you *did* spend some time at the front, though as a journalist for a Jewish Viennese newspaper. But after you had honed your pen into a dagger to stab the Central Powers in the back, and were punished once again by being transferred to a combat battalion, you deserted and escaped to Switzerland! We've made a detailed study of your memoirs! You joined the gang of international pacifists who came together there! In Zurich you even became acquainted with the deadliest enemy of Western Culture, with Le-nin!" ...

Grandpa's sepulchral voice: "That wasn't 1917 when Jacksa met Lenin in Zurich. But 1910, yes. Before Vladimir Ilyich went off to the Congress of the Second International in Copenhagen. Back in those days Lenin was still an unknown in the Big Circus while Giaxa was already a big name in the Little Circus."

The billiard balls rolled again.

Liebhenschl: "You will now entertain us with a little performance on horseback!"

"With pleasure."

"With pleasure?!"

"With pleasure."

216

"We are honored by your willingness, Mr. Rastelli and Rastelli!" Hollow guffaws from the storm troopers. "But watch out that my eight-year-old champion stallion, winner in a dozen jumps and steeplechase events—"

In this split second, Prisoner Tiefenbrucker thinks he detects something. Giaxa stiffens suddenly but unnoticeably.

"—that Mjoellnir doesn't cause you any difficulties! As a Dalmatian, or whatever Adriatic mish-mash you happen to be, you are no doubt unaware of the meaning of his name! Mjoellnir, that is the hammer of the Germanic god Thor! Thor's hammer! Mjoellnir means the All-Crusher! Understood?! Thor's hammer is not used to carrying retired circus riders! Understood?! All right! So watch out! It would be a shame if you broke your neck on your very first day with us!"

"O-oh, I break my neck only on very rare occasions," bellows Giaxa.

This time it is only a single man who bursts out laughing. Not a storm trooper, not a guard, but—as one can guess from the abrupt change in his spontaneous, uncontrollable laugh—a common prisoner in the rearmost rank. For as Prisoner X quickly hikes up the stirrups, the ecstatic laugh is transformed into an irregular scream of pain that moves slowly away. Apparently they are beating the man with rifle butts as they drag him off the assembly field.

The furrows in Giaxa's face are chiseled grooves in gray stone.

Then, as if by magic, he is in the saddle.

"The awe-inspiring image of an ancient—" Valentin searched for a word. I filled in: "—centaur."

"Right!"

Just for a moment the stallion rears and paws the air. Nothing but the brief prancing of an ancient centaur, at one with his four hooves. Now the mythical horseman paces ahead with measured steps. Prisoner Tiefenbrucker served in the World War as a Royal Bavarian Dragoon; he knows something about riding; Fugger's Bastard gapes wide-eyed with enthusiasm. The sneering masks of the storm troopers fall away, replaced by admiring stares. Only the Bullet-Crapper retains an expression of self-satisfied expectation that might be saying, Once Thor's hammer begins to swing, this centaur will have met his match.

In the open space before the assembled prisoners Giaxa improvises a riding ring. No great horsemanship here: walk, trot, gallop; traverse right, traverse left; figure eight, demi-volt, change of hand, full circle, halt, rest. Without warning, he rides out away from the formation at a restrained trot, down the tree-lined drive he had come up on foot only a short while before.

Scharfuehrer Maerzhas: "Where is he going?"

Forty-five minutes earlier another scene had taken place in the entrance drive. Two new arrivals were led away out of sight behind the bunker to the right of the drive. No one knew who they were, the poor devils (as Valentin put it), perhaps they had already been rubbed out. But the man who rides victoriously down the drive in the June sun—not to the bunker but to the out-

building on the left, where he turns and disappears behind it—*this* man everyone knows. It is a unique moment in the history of the Dachau Concentration
Camp: the man who rides down the entrance drive between the blossoming
linden trees, this centaur in a blue jacket, is the master of the estate *in persona*.
He is the Dachau of another time. Is Dachau the working estate-farm. Not
Dachau the state work farm. (Thus Valentin exhibited his brand of rural dialectics.)

Maerzhas: "Where's the bastard going?!"

Liebhenschl raises his eyes. The machine gunner on the watchtower nearest the front gate bends over his wooden railing and stares through his binoculars, keeping the rider in sight.

Then Giaxa reappears on the other side of a long storage shed, rides back at
a restrained trot through the acute angle formed by the loading platform and
the barbed-wire fence. Reins in the stallion and examines the long platform;
turns and rides back along the platform; reins in Mjoellnir again, stands up
briefly in the stirrups—an estate owner making sure everything is in order.

Now the Detention Camp Director snarls, "What's there to look at over
there?! Is *that* supposed to be great horsemanship?!"

Scharfuehrer Maerzhas blows his whistle, gives the tower guard an arm signal.

"Hey you!" roars the guard from his perch and waves vigorously at the rider to get moving. But the latter shows no sign of compliance, making instead a
close examination of a truck trailer parked against the end of the platform.

Valentin withdrew into the salmon-colored twilight of the transparent
snakeskin and pulled two more cue sticks out of the rack. Was he tired of his
solo play? Was he going to suggest another threesome? "Excuse me. But I'm
afraid I have to go into a bit more detail now."

"*More* detail?" groaned Grandpa behind me. "Is that *really* necessary,
Tiefenbrucker?"

"I think so. Otherwise I wouldn't bother you with it." Valentin laid two
cues side by side lengthwise on the playing surface. "Now watch this closely,
gents."

I heard Kujath sliding out of his chair. I catch his shadow out of the corner
of my eye. Now, like me, he is crouching on the arm of an easy chair.

"Keep your seat. I'm as farsighted as a turkey buzzard."

"Pretend that this is the double barbed-wire wall," said Valentin pointing
to the two parallel cues. Not a fence, but a real wall, a barbed-wire barrier
stretched between fifteen-foot concrete posts placed twenty feet apart. Atop
each post a metal bar slanting inward toward the residents of this monster cage,
with insulators on each bar to carry the strands of barbed-wire charged with
high-voltage current. In between, a twelve-foot-wide stretch of no man's land
and then a second cage of identical construction. Here (Valentin placed the
third cue slanting slightly away from the others, its tip touching the first cue,

and in the resulting small angle set two white billiard balls so that they touched the third cue as well as each other), here we have the long storage shed freshly filled with slabs of peat moss that the special details have cut out of the Dachau moors and placed in the shed to dry before final storage. Parked with its tail a few inches from the end of the fifty-yard-long loading platform, more or less as an extension to it—the truck trailer. Not like any of those parked down at the bottom of the silo here, but a longer one with four dual tires, its four sides lowered for unloading, its flatbed, like the platform, covered with bits of peat moss. Once again the rider trots back along the platform toward the assembled onlookers; again he reins in his horse to inspect the ramp end of the platform that points inward toward the camp. It slopes down to ground level as gently as a barn entrance, layered with dirt, covered with grass.

The tower guard places a megaphone to his mouth. "Get a move on, rider, hustle!" The rider takes no notice. "Hey you, clown!" the megaphone voice now roars with exaggerated distinctness. "*Clown!!* Get going!"

Lazily, at a beautiful, relaxed trot, Giaxa rides back. (Valentin rolled the red ball back along the slanting cue to the butt end.)

"Nice of you to have a look around our place, Mr. Hagenbeck and Hagenbeck," croaks the Detention Camp Director with a mildly reproachful glare at Giaxa. "Though I was a bit worried when you got so close to the wire! Which is charged with thirty thousand volts, in case you're interested!"

"Thanks!" bellows Giaxa.

"And now, where is the demonstration of great horsemanship you promised to present for our honored guests here?" Again the hollow guffaws of the storm troopers.

Then Giaxa forces the stallion up into a levade.

At first Mjoellnir rears wildly. Now it is the Bullet-Crapper's turn to react involuntarily, and he cringes back several steps. Maerzhas does the same. Whatever is good for the Deputy Camp Commander is good for the *Scharfuehrer*. Now the stallion bends back on its haunches, standing almost motionless on its hind legs, its forehoofs drawn in; the sun shines golden on its belly. Fused to its back, yet seeming to float in mid air, hangs the man in the blue jacket.

Liebhenschl: "Is that all?!"

Then Giaxa attempts a courbette.

"I'm sorry, but no untrained horse can do that," I heard myself say. "A proper courbette consists of six jumps that—"

"I know," Valentin interrupted me with calm certainty. "But he did manage three."

Three times Mjoellnir jumps forward in a levade—without going down on his front hoofs. Not at the *Scharfuehrer*, who, as if dreaming, reaches for his revolver, but at Liebhenschl. And everyone can see; now it is his turn to blanch as Thor's hammer swings toward him. A picture the army of prisoners will never forget: the terrified head-death's-headsman staggering backwards, holding the handle of his riding whip in front of his face for protection. ("A really stirring sight. I can tell you that.") Then Giaxa lets the stallion gently down onto its forehoofs.

"That's better!" shrieks the *Standartenfuehrer;* this specimen of the Master Race outshrieks his intolerable moment of fear. "That's better, Mr. Whatsyername and Whatsyername! But we want to see your real tour de force, your grand finale!"

"Grand finale? Ah, the grand *finale!*" bellows Giaxa's bassoon staccato. And repeats, this time to himself so that we can barely hear it: "The grand finale."

Slowly he unbuttons his jacket, reaches down with his right hand. Almost by itself the riding whip moves from Liebhenschl's still upraised hand into the hand of the rider. For a few endless seconds the old centaur looks down on the man in the rose-colored uniform. We who are standing in the front rank can only hold our breath. A strange, fierce resolve seems chiseled into the rune-marked stone of his face. Our stomachs grow weaker and our hearts pound. Is it possible? That the riding whip the Detention Camp Director has just handed to Prisoner X might slash down against his own half-baked, bready face—a boomerang? Then, without warning, the stone face of the horseman is brightened—by a melancholy smile? Yes. Yes: Giaxa squints merrily into the sun.

(Just then a line from another story ran through my head. A line from the little testament Gaudenz de Colana had left behind for me, scribbled on an outhouse wall in Sils Maria. *Abbé Galiani: Death is certain. So why should we not be merry?*)

What follows happens very fast, and is a complete surprise to everybody.

Giaxa rides out of the formation again. Not at a restrained trot, not to the entrance drive—he gallops headlong, straight as an arrow toward the storage shed he has just left. Twice he lets the riding whip crack down on Mjoellnir's flank. The horse reacts as if stung. *Ventre à terre,* in an outstretched gallop the dun stallion races toward the ramp to the loading platform, the rider lying flat along his neck like a jockey, the blue jacket fluttering from his back like a Bavarian cavalry standard.

Does the Bullet-Crapper *suspect* what Giaxa intends to do? "Shoot!" he shrieks. Still in a dream, the tall *Scharfuehrer* holds his hand on his holster.

"*Shoot!*"

As Maerzhas fumbles out his gun the rider gallops outside revolver range toward the ramp.

"S-h-o-o-o-ot!!" now roars the *Scharfuehrer,* whistles, signals in clumsy hysteria to the machine gunner nearest the storage shed. Quickly the guard depresses the gun in its mountings.

"*N-o-t* with the *machine gun!*" comes Liebhenschl's falsetto scream. "Watch out for Mjoellnir!! Carbines!!"

"Aim at the clown's back!! Watch out for the horse!!" roars Maerzhas. "Fire!"

The pack of storm troopers breaks up. Some rush ahead, stand, pull carbines off their shoulders and up to their cheeks. But not a shot is fired. Like brownish black tin soldiers, guns aimed, they stand as if thunderstruck.

The prizewinning steeplechaser has taken the grass-covered ramp without even slowing down. Now its flying hoofs drum down the long long loading platform beside the storage shed, *now Thor's hammer thunders.*

Even if it were possible in these flying, galloping, hollow-thundering seconds for a marksman to shoot the rider from his mount, the horse, without the guiding hand of its master, would certainly plunge from the platform and break its neck. The stallion's owner seems to realize this, and withdraws his order with a shrill cry. "Hold your fire!!"

But won't Mjoellnir lose his footing anyway? The fresh bits of peat moss covering the platform make the impossible possible, make the platform into an improvised racetrack. Thor's hammer thunders, up to the truck trailer parked like an extension to the platform, its sides lowered, its floor covered with scraps of peat moss. This trailer is like a springboard. Now Thor's hammer thunders a roll on a different drum. Yes, Mjoellnir dashes along the trailer bed, sparks flying amidst the spraying moss.

"That's insanity!" The half-choked howl of the Camp Director, "In-s-a-a-a-a-a--"

During the last phase of the story Valentin let the red ball skim along the top of the slanting cue, touched the two white ones with the red one, then flipped the red one out of his hand toward the two parallel cues and concluded:

All at once the giant formation of prisoners—three gray, living fortresses, hitherto motionless—begins to waver. A brief, inarticulate, mass cry from a thousand throats, and then the blue golden centaur *jumps*. A second mass cry, then a distant, horrible, squealing whinny that breaks off in half a second, and the centaur *hangs* high aloft in the electrified wire of the inner fence and begins to give off smoke. In the next second a third outcry that overwhelms the previous one; the centaur *bursts in two.* The blue-jacketed figure flies across the twelve-foot gap and is caught in the electric wires of the outer barrier, and he too begins to smoke a little in the glare of the June sun. Can a man be allowed to say such a thing? It looks, no, in the distance it looks no different than two facing spider webs, with two different species of insect hanging in them; on the inside a big yellow one, on the outside a much smaller blue one. Then the yellow one plummets lifelessly to the ground, taking the wire with it, surrounded by miniature bolts of lightning. The blue one remains hanging. Then comes the monstrously stupid, the godawful, terrible, nonsensical, completely and absolutely useless rat-tat-tat of the machine gun from the wooden watchtower.

10

To make us all so merry.
Deedle-dum, deedle-dum, deedle-dum.

For a dreadful period of time none of us said anything, and I thought I could hear them again, the "voices" of my asthma, until I discovered this time they weren't whispering in me. (The last dose of ephedrine was still working.) It was Valentin Tiefenbrucker's intensified snorting and sniffling, and behind me Grandpa's accelerated rattle. No one, so it seemed, would look at anyone else. Finally Valentin slipped off the spiral rings of nickel wire that had held up his shiny sleeves as he played, and commented, almost without a trace of Bavarian dialect but in a somewhat nasal tone (which, if you are not Viennese, means that you have a bad cold):

"If you've been through a world war, and a great revolution you've seen enough split-second tragedies. But a split-second tragedy like that—and a man—with a bearing like that—never. And even though it pains me deep down inside—today just as much as five days ago when I was forced to watch it—I couldn't help thinking then and I can't help thinking now. The whole scene had a kind of . . . classical grandeur."

"Strange, rkh, rkh, rkh," Kujath's constant rattle. "Strange that Trebla and I, that just before your arrival, Tiefenbrucker, we were talking about a, rkh-rkh, suicide epidemic . . . which seems to have broken out in the, rkh-rkh, Engadine. After your damned, really damned expressive description there can't be any doubt, rkh-rkh, that it wasn't an abortive escape attempt, but rather a rkh-rkh, spur-of-the-moment suicide, because that double hurdle—"

"Sorry," I broke in icily, still staring rigidly into space. "In my opinion it was a suc-cess-ful es-cape at-tempt."

"Oh man, Trebla, rkh-rkh, there you are sitting in front of me all dressed in black as if you've known all the time."

"All the time."

"If I—if I give you my condolences *this* time—there's not much point . . ."

"Not much point."

"M-a-n, you will have to," Grandpa's choking rattle behind me, "break it to Roxana as gently as possible."

"As gently as possible."

"With your natural tact."

"With my natural tact."

"And in the gentlest way possible, that's for certain."

"But *how* will you break it to her, that's the question."

"The question."

"Poor soul, I wouldn't want to be in your—rkh—shoes," he rattled, and I made a singsong echo, "I wouldn't want to be in my shoes."

Grandpa dragged himself past me. At last I looked at him again. With both his big hands he propped himself up on the flat edge of the billiard table. The bright cone of light revealed the discrepancy between his still-intact tropical cavalier's suit and his face, whose tint was now even more yellowish, whose eye sockets seemed even more violet, while his Hindenburg moustache had lost its shape. One tousled end hung almost straight down, which gave him a rather striking, almost Asiatic appearance. (From my World War and civil war experience I knew that it was possible for Germanic, Dinaric, and Romanic faces to take on an Asiatic appearance under severe stress.) It was no longer an Aztec mask; the outrage, the rebelliousness in this physiognomy reminded me of . . . the lead actor in the Russian film *Storm over Asia.* Kujath grabbed one of the two cues Valentin had used to represent the electric fence and bashed it down on the table's edge several times with all his remaining strength. "Tear up the wire, break-kh the wall, rkh-rkh," he rattled almost insanely in an outburst of senseless rage. To me it did not look senseless. His rattle became quicker, sharper as he thrust the cue into my hand. "Manoman, my biceps—rkh-rkh—haven't got any more oomph than a bathtub sponge; y-you b-bust this thing in two!"

"Ooi," said Valentin. "Too bad for the cue. Who's that going to help if you break it?"

"M-e, rkh. Go on, Trebla!"

I grabbed the billiard cue and banged it onto the table edge. It didn't break. I gripped it harder and thrashed it down onto the wooden edge. There was a bang not unlike a small caliber pistol as it cracked in two.

"Good!" At that moment Grandpa suffered the attack.

Valentin came round the billiard table with rustic haste: "Oh-oh, do you suffer from asthma *too*, Kujath?"

"Ha . . . hheart . . ."

The Miller of Luzienburg slumped into the arms of the escaped prisoner and I grabbed him around the knees in a corpsman's carry and we dragged the heavy man across the Mysore carpet (I could hear Valentin's own laboring wheeze) and bedded him down on the couch beneath the puzzle engraving, which I ignored. Valentin opened the collar of the seemingly unconscious man. Lacking cologne, I rubbed his temples with Fundadór, soaked my handkerchief with the Andalusian brandy, and held it under Grandpa's nose. He had stopped his rattling and breathed, almost hesitantly, almost reluctantly. His closed eyelids looked, in the dull amber glow cast by the indirect light from the smoking table, like two carved wooden balls. I began to have the sinking suspicion that he might just die here in a moment, here in his tower studio, without a struggle.

I was reaching for the telephone on the secretary to alarm Pfiff when I heard Kujath hiss. "Don't bother, Tre—" What followed was interpreted by Valentin, his ear bent close to the old man: The American pills in the drawer of the secretary, top left . . .

Barely half an hour later—it had already struck midnight from the church tower of Tartar—we were all leaning back in our easy chairs. The patient, after taking his heart medicine, had made an astonishingly quick recovery. The bringer-of-the-bad-news was telling us about his escape, which could never have been possible without the fracas caused by Giaxa's death ride. So that, I thought, is the last of the Luzienburg's midnight tales. Some ungraspable question I wanted to ask Valentin was shifting inside me, a question that swam around beneath the frozen surface of my consciousness and that I was unable to fish out of any hole in the ice.

All Wednesday morning long not a single note of Chopin echoes out of the Detention Camp Director's quarters. Instead, nothing but raging lectures. For a whole hour he harangues *Scharfuehrer* Maerzhas, who had stood there "like a lump of clay instead of blasting the crazy old Dalmation out of the saddle," dresses down the tower guard for wasting machine-gun ammunition on a dead man. The camp's walls have ears, the wooden barracks walls, the latrine walls, the sick-bay walls, the cement walls of the disciplinary bunker (spotted with brown stains that are not mold), the rocks in the gravel pit, even the man-sized, rusty shovels used to shove bodies into the crematorium ovens. On the barracks roads, the gravel pit, in the latrines, everywhere, The Incident and its consequences are whispered about by the prisoners and guards alike. Liebhenschl's lament for Mjoellnir, Thor's lightning bolt, done in by common electricity, the special gift of the Reich's *Sportfuehrer*, etc., along with caustic aspersions at "that traitor disguised as a circus act who passed sentence on himself"—none of this can divert attention from one fact: this masterpiece of the master race trembles to think what will happen when the camp commander returns on the weekend. Until then all leaves for the camp SS are canceled and they are ordered not to discuss the matter with anyone outside the camp, not even with the Political Division in Munich. "Get moving!" Now the slave-driver's bark seems to echo less loudly across the decks of the giant prison-galley Dachau. Early in the afternoon a special detail of nineteen prisoners and three guards drives out of the camp on a Moor Express. Not far from the north gate, near the so-called Game Preserve they have a breakdown. While repairs are being made, Valentin, without requesting permission, slips off into the forest to relieve himself. He hears the squad leader and the two storm troopers discussing The Incident in hushed, almost excited voices. One of them poses a question—(I too had a question to ask, but couldn't fish it out of the ice)—the same question that was whispered from barracks to barracks at noon. Why hadn't Giaxa, before his death ride—even the storm trooper uses the expression—given the *Standartenfuehrer* a good slap across the face with the riding whip? The squad leader cuts off the undisciplined questioner. If he'd done that, Maerzhas would have blown him out of the saddle with his revolver; it was only logical! They can't get over it, neither the old clown, nor his death ride, nor the logic of it all. Logical! Logical! echo the voices ever father behind the runaway as he creeps off into the buzzing June forest. Soon they will yell out his number, "report-report!" Carbines will be fired . . . To his complete amazement, however, he hears the Moor Express start up, hears its motor fade away in the distance.

From the underbrush by the forest's edge the runaway spies the swimmers. Now's the time to trust his luck. (A man has to have luck, even a man who believes in Historical Materialism!) Crawling back into the thicket, he undresses down to his undershorts—a makeshift pair of bathing trunks; buries his "zebra suit" and shoes; knots a handkerchief into an improvised bathing cap so that his shaved head doesn't give him away; clamps a long pine branch in his teeth to cover the tattooed number on his arm. Along the banks of the Amper by the Ampermocking bridge the water is filled with noisy swimmers. Scattered on the grass by the riverbank, the swimmers' clothes; leaning against trees at the forest's edge, numerous bicycles; Valentin is naked among the naked.

"Naked among the naked, I tell you, that's the best disguise."

Unnoticed by the bathing, sunning, playing throng, he selects his targets with lightning-swift decisiveness. The things he spirits off into the underbrush by the forest's edge combine to create an effect worthy of a clever billiards champion: a pair of sandals, the green shirt and cap of an *Arbeitsdienst* man, a Tyrolean hat, a rolled up pair of civilian trousers, a loden jacket. A ladies' bicycle disappears to complete the effect. A few minutes later a man in the cap and uniform of the *Arbeitsdienst* cycles over the Ampermocking bridge. On a bench in front of the Schusterhof sit two SS men, less absorbed in cleaning their rifles than in a lively argument: "This fellow, Shacksa . . ." That'll keep them occupied, thinks the bicyclist, but pretty soon they'll notice that I'm wearing a uniform shirt and civilian pants and riding a girl's bicycle. Soon I'll hear them yell "Halt!" behind me. But not a sound.

I, Trebla, could no longer follow Valentin at this midnight hour in the Luzienburg. Had the second dose of ephedrine numbed my consciousness? I tried racking my brain. There was still something I wanted to ask him in connection with this whole bloody business—what did, what did I want to ask him? *About this nightmare?* When I found him again he was rolling across the border of the Confederatio Helvetica near St. Margarethen, unbeknownst to German or Swiss customs, hidden in the brakeman's compartment of a freight car.

So that was it, I thought. The last midnight tale of the Luzienburg. Caucasian Val got up from his chair, and I sensed what he wanted and did the same, and he extended his hand and took mine, clasping it and shaking it vigorously, and I thought I could hear the gentle clanking of a suit of armor; I had to assume that he was saying good-bye now, and that I would never be able to deliver my question. But he said, a bit solemnly, sniffling a little more than usual,

"Without your papa-in-law's last ride I wouldn't be standing here now, god-dammit."

I didn't know what to say. I pulled out the golden crucifix Maïtena Ithurra y Azkue had given me and handed it to him, mumbling an explanation. He said: "I'm not much of a churchgoer, but in this case I'm honored." We heard Kujath clearing his throat and turned to him—was he starting his death rattle again?

The charms on the old tropical cavalier's watch chain rose and fell smoothly; he was breathing easily. But his expression, his stare, was peculiar. He stared over at the billiard table as if watching two champions he utterly despised as they played for the world championship. Not a rattle—this time it was more a singsong ritardando of indignation.

"N-n-no!—I—can't—stand—looking—at—it—any—more—Thththrow—it—ouuut!"

At first Valentin and I had to assume he meant (for some reason) the golden crucifix. But that wasn't it. *The concentration camp*, he insisted, had to be gotten out of his sight—and he meant immediately. He was referring to his own billiard table, on which Valentin had demonstrated The Incident. The cue stick he had used to represent the outer electric fence—on Grandpa's impetuous order I had been forced to smash in two. Now we had to get "the whole bloody-bullet-crapping-domain" out of his house. He gave no less exact orders on the way we were supposed to do that. The late guest switched on his parliamentary eloquence in an attempt to talk him out of this sheer nonsense. Kujath replied that, with all due respect to the USSR, this was not a collective farm; and I realized this was no senile whim or madness, nor a sudden drunkard's quirk à la de Colana, but something else entirely. Any back talk from us posed the danger of a relapse; there would be no way to avoid complying with Grandpa's categorical imperative. No sooner said than done.

"Okay now, boys. I won't be able to help you myself, now that my angina pectoris is acting up again. Pfiff will give you a hand."

With a shrug of his shoulders Valentin approached the billiard table. This time it must have been the resigned decision to do a little physical labor that brought back his dialect: "Watcha mean, Mista Koo-yat, wec'n doot w'thout Pfiff. A'mean, Trebla'n me, w're not s'flabby's y'think."

We took off our jackets (now I felt like a waiter straightening up the room after hours), and we lifted the table, one-two, whereby Valentin proved that his strength was undiminished, or perhaps even increased, by his ordeal in the prison camp. "Heave ho!"

"That camp has got to go," said Grandpa, enthroned pagoda-like in his chair, while out of the amber-colored gloom an image of death stared out above his shoulder: the puzzle engraving. (In this hour of bad tidings I asked myself the un-thought-out question: Isn't every death a kind of puzzle?) Carefully we turned the table upside down and the Bringer of Bad Tidings began unscrewing the four heavy table legs like a mechanic doing a routine job, while Grandpa announced without raising his voice, "This Dachau must go," and we lifted the heavy tabletop from the projecting edges on each end, and I was conscious how the second dose of ephedrine allowed me enough air to lug my end of the table out onto the balcony, and then two of the bulky legs. Scarcely had Valentin re-entered the tower studio when he put his steel gray jacket back on (like a knight, uncomfortable without his armor).

Kujath wasn't satisfied.

"As I explained to you gentlemen, this Dachau has *really* got to go; so over the side with it, and make it snappy! Let's clear this table clear out of here! *Tabula rasa!* Never mind the consequences—at worst the monster will crash down onto one of the little watchtowers, but they've withstood other bombardments in their day. So *tabula rasa*, chop chop."

As Valentin dutifully raised the first table leg over his head before heaving it through an opening in the Ghibelline battlement, struck by the feverish coppery gleam of the Domleschg moon that made his shiny suit (of armor) glisten, he was a Florian Geyer who put the one by Lovis Corinth to shame. Down below a thud, seemingly muffled by underbrush. While I was imitating him with the second leg I asked myself, What was it, what did I want to ask him?

The knight flung table leg number three down upon a silent enemy lurking below, and I tossed number four (more like a waiter getting rid of empty bottles).

From inside: "Go to it guys, tabula rasa! *Vamos, vamos!*

"He-e-ave. . .*ho!*" groaned Valentin.

The tabletop, this massive wardrobe, was hoisted onto the battlement. Then—far below, a crack like a short, flat detonation. Then the deep midnight stillness of the Hinterrhein Valley, a stillness deeper, it seemed to me, than a few moments before.

book four

Ghost
Train 2

1

At Grandpa's request I dug a map of Europe out of a drawer in the secretary, unfolded it, and spread it out over the smoking table, a map in the scale of 1:2,750,000 reinforced with linen so that the four corners stuck out stiffly from the table's edge. Large sections of Europe—Italy, Germany, Austria, Hungary, the major part of Spain—had been carefully painted over with a thin coating of black ink. Henrique Kujath, about to put on his horn-rimmed glasses, paused as the telephone rang. I handed him the receiver, "Hum?" he said. "Hum ... hum ... No cause for alarm. Just tell Heiner to crawl back in bed ... Yes ... That was *my* idea ... me, me myself, yeahyeah ... Hmm, it was all part of a wager ... Will do." Handing me the receiver: "That was Pfiff. I had to reassure everybody downstairs. The crash woke up my grandson No. two, Querfurt-Heiner, and he woke Pfiff. My ever-vigilant chauffeur-castellan thought it might have been a bomb planted by our Nazio friends from Davos, so I had to feed him that line about a wager. And Tiefenbrucker, I'm supposed to tell you you've got to get going via Freiberge in about twenty minutes."

"I'm ready," said Valentin.

"Let me have the telephone again, Trebla," said Grandpa. "Pfiff can connect me with Bern. With the night desk of the Swiss News Agency."

"May I ask for what purpose."

"Purpose? Man, I've got to pass it on!"

"What, may I ask?"

"What?! Well, hum, well, Jacksa's last ride. Make no mistake about it, the hoofbeats of that last gallop will echo around the world tomorrow."

Was the ice getting thinner? The old pounding in my forehead.

Valentin, almost without a trace of dialect: "I would wait a day or two with that. I want to be long gone before the news gets out. The agency will ask you where you learned the awful truth. And if you tell them you're smuggling the witness out of Switzerland so he can take up a job as a political commissar in Spain—"

"Rightrightright," rumbled Grandpa. "My IQ seems to have suffered under that last embrace from angina pectoris. But whatever happens w-e have to get the story out before the German midget, clubfoot-Goebbels. In such a 'special case' he'll *have* to make some kind of a statement. 'Short-term restraining seminar in concert camp; fatal accident on day of admission due to own negligence,' and *that*, of course, would not be 100 percent baloney. After all, it never hurts to grease a lie with a little squirt of the truth . . ."

"I told you about Liebhenschl's decision," said Valentin, "to keep the story under wraps until the camp commander's return from Berlin—which was set for Saturday."

"You mean he got the word out on Sunday?"

"I figure he'll do that sometime today, which is Monday."

"So today you think he'll get on the phone to the SS-Reich's Heini and the Reich's Propaganda Dwarf and try to make up a laundered version of the incident for Uncle Clubfoot's Story Hour?"

"That's what I think."

"So they probably won't come out with it before tomorrow, Tuesday."

"My guess," said Valentin.

"Of all days, it has to be on my seventieth; it never rains but it pours, r-kh . . ." (Was it only a deep sigh? or the first sign of another heart attack?) "So if I call the agency tonight, long after you've Fieseler-Storched your way out of here, I'll still beat the dwarf to the punch?"

"In all probability."

"And your escape, Tiefenbrucker? Don't you think they figure that *you* have already broadcast the news of Jacksa's last ride?"

"I doubt it. Look at it this way. The Bullet-Crapper would have liked to see his stallion give the famous newcomer a fatal kick in the head. That could indeed have been passed off as an accident—to quote you, Kujath—'due to his own negligence.' But by pulling off the incredible feat . . . against hopeless odds . . . of staying in *control* of the situation to the very end, Konstantin Giaxa screwed the Detention Camp Director in three ways. The last ride can't be doctored to look like an accident—he's lost his stallion, and me as well. On the other hand, they won't suspect I've managed to get across a heavily guarded border so fast. Instead they'll figure that as long as the Red bastard is still inside our Thousand Year Reich he won't dare broadcast anything. And it's true, I didn't whisper a word about The Incident, except to Wawrosch in Kempten, because he's from the circus. He'll keep quiet. Survival instinct."

"Then . . ." The Miller of Luzienburg surveyed me from the side. "Then you wouldn't mind if I informed the news agency tomorrow? Is that okay?"

"Fine with me." The throbbing in my forehead subsided; I couldn't tell them *how* fine it was with me. Now I would have some kind of leeway to "break it gently to Xana."

The departure hour (and if it passed without my being able to ask Valentin what I wanted to ask him? If only I knew! A question like the shadow of a great fish moving vaguely beneath a now thin layer of ice—I must, I must pull it out in time!). Neither of us returned to our chairs; as Kujath put on his glasses to point out the route of the Fieseler Storch across the bright, translucent surface of the map, Valentin bent forward beside him, fists on hips.

"Now look here, Tiefenbrucker. Your Pilot Liétard may fly into Toulon to refuel, or then again he may not—in any case, you won't get any trouble from the French. Then it's straight across the Mediterranean. He'll pass the Gulf of Lion on the right and avoid Barcelona as well, unless Hermann's Messerschmitts happen to take an interest in a harmless sport plane with French registration. He'll fly you straight to the mouth of the Ebro in the vicinity of—here—Cambrils. You should be with Modesto's Agrupación Autónomia del Ebro in time for lunch."

Adan Ithurra, the young Basque, I thought, had also mentioned Modesto's army group. Grandpa took off his glasses.

"Modesto, a brilliant commander, a man of fabulous morale, and to top it all off he's called 'the modest one'—under Modesto are two army corps, which include the Thirty-fifth Division under General Walters and the Forty-fifth under Lieutenant Colonel Hans, whose Eleventh International Brigade was attached to Walters's division."

"Hans Kahle," said Valentin. "An old friend of mine."

"If lady luck is with you—and even a historical materialist needs her, as you so aptly remarked—then you'll have *comida* with his staff. How's your Spanish?"

"*Salud, commandante.* I learned the bare essentials when I was in Russia."

"And the essentials of Russian you can learn in Spain from my friend Colonel Loti—but I guess as Caucasian Val you haven't much need of that. The commissar of the Forty-fifth, whom you're supposed to replace, is seriously ill. The man's name is Sevil."

For the first time since his attack a bit of a gleam, a bit of roguishness crept into the elephant eyes of the old tropical cavalier. His stand-up collar—we had opened it earlier—hung at the back of his neck, held only by the collar button; the ends stuck out horizontally above his shoulders. In the amber glow from the smoking table (still screened by the map of Europe) it looked like an ornament on some Asiatic idol. And as we stood there in his tower refuge, reacting to his farewell address, I couldn't help but fear this might be his swan song as well; in an ephedrine daze (or, more probably in shock) I couldn't follow much of it. Finally I said:

"You ought to go to bed, Grandpa."

"Naw, wait a minute up here in the ivory tower. I'm going to elevator down—go-on-go on, I'm back fit as a fiddle now—and tell the *Burgfrau* to wake Roxana." Suddenly he thrust his left hand down into empty space.

He buttoned up his collar, tied his ribbed tie, twirled his moustache à la Hindenburg. He had walked across the grass-green Mysore toward the anteroom, past the brightly lit vacuum where, at the stroke of midnight, the big French billiard table had stood. Obeying an old habit, he must have wanted to lean against it; now he grabbed for thin air, but caught himself before I could come to the rescue.

Waiting for the telephone to ring for the last time.

"Right!" Valentin added. "At Rail Inspector Punkosdy's place in Oedenburg, right, that's where I wanted to meet you. In Prague I told those pompous sourpusses in the Central Committee of the exiled Austrian C.P., I said now we mustn't lose any time getting in close touch with the Socialist revolutionaries there. But in Sopron-Oedenburg I get the word that Horthy's gumshoes are on my trail, so I have to lie low. But five weeks later they grab me anyway, in Eisenstadt. The gumshoes working for the brand-new State Secretary Herr Kaltenbrunner, head of Internal Security in Vienna."

"You know him?" I asked quickly.

"Old Bread-Brain!—he and I come from the same corner of the Inn Valley. Maybe that's why they did me the honor of showing me off to him in person, there at the HQ on the Morzinplatz."

All at once my ice-fishing rod jerked downward. "Morzinplatz, Metropol. Tell me, Valentin . . . did you happen to run into a Gestapo man named Laimgruber?"

"No. All I know is he was one of the SS-bigger shots there."

Was that the question that had been swimming beneath the ice? Had I hooked it?

On the spot where the French billiard table once stood we now stood and waited for the ring of the telephone. I never completed the thought: If Laimgruber had interrogated Valentin, then . . . And asked impetuously: "Were you tortured there?"

"Not me," said Valentin. In the furnace room of the Metropol they had only managed to knock his nose a little out of line—he sniffed demonstratively—but didn't break it. But by God, others hadn't been so lucky. The funny thing about it—apparently that blow on the nose had made him look even more like the Fuehrer than before, sad but true, but that may have been why he was never touched again. Neither in the Metropol nor in the Rossauer Barracks nor on the way to Dachau. "But what they did to the Jewish Reds on that last ride—God almighty!"

There, I had him!

The big, shadowy fish.

I, an inept angler, had yanked him out of the hole in the ice, and it was a deep-sea monster with a mouth like Moloch, and it flopped horribly and glistened in ghastly colors. Meanwhile I made conversation.

"I had a friend, a doctor who tended the poor in Graz. He was, as they say, 'only' half Jewish, but Red. —And dead. —He was bumped off on the way to Dachau or shortly thereafter. Probably in some unspectacular way. Did you ever cross paths with the poor guy, Valentin? The man was forty-one and had something of an El Greco figure about him and was named Maximilian Grabscheidt."

"*Max Grabscheidt?*" For the first time the rustic knightly face of the blacksmith's apprentice from Wasserburg blinked at me in shocked surprise—in an expression strangely similar to a little, half-stupid smile. "*Your* friend, Trebla?"

"As far as I know, my best."

Involuntarily he gave the hanging billiard lamp a little shove. The swinging cone of light struck my face several times—his—then mine—then his. No doubt about it, his horrified squint was directed, not at my eyes, but at my forehead.

For the last time on that south wind-heavy June night I stood outside by the tower's parapet and breathed the sweet, animal scent that welled up from the linden trees below, and beside me Valentin leaned his belly against the wall between the Ghibelline merlons, and I had taken one last ephedrine tablet to ward off the compact clouds of grass pollen that came sweeping in off the upland meadows with every gust of the south wind. (Perhaps also to ward off any ill effects of what awaited me: the last midnight tale of the Luzienburg.) Prepared for the studio phone to ring any minute, I stared almost unblinking across the straight course of the Hinterrhein to Riedberg castle, whose coppery dome seemed to have been blown closer by the wind; in the moonlight it flared like a weird fire in an old religious painting. My forehead (no longer of interest to my companion) registered a regular but very rapid pulse, which I diagnosed as one ephedrine tablet too many. Then my companion asked me something. Had I gotten the news of Grabscheidt's death from Kujath? My answer, negative. Not from Grandpa, who scarcely knew Maxim, but from St. Gall, the town that is, through the editor-in-chief of the *Ostschweizerische Arbeiterzeitung*, in which Dr. Grabscheidt had occasionally published medical articles. That was good. What was good? That Grandpa had gone down in the Lilliputian elevator; after the heart-attack episode he, Valentin, would not have risked telling the story in front of Grandpa ... I would understand. And as the dialect coloration of his speech abruptly increased (I began suspecting that his dialect was a defense mechanism to be used whenever he approached certain danger zones), he began telling it to me.

THE LAST MIDNIGHT TALE OF THE LUZIENBURG

Vienna, 20 May 1938, 0400 hours.

From out of the dark cells of the Hotel Metropol, out of the Rossauer Barracks, out of the Graues Haus, public enemies are being transported to the railroad station. Only a few of the prisoners suspect their destination. (For how many will there be a return ticket?) Out the small, barred window of the police van Valentin catches a glimpse of the lifeless Opernring in the morning gloom, trees with May-green leaves, Mariahilfer Strasse; so they're headed for the Westbahnhof. "Maytime in waltz-time/ Making two heartssublime"—Valentin can't get the poorly rhymed, schmaltzy waltz out of his mind.

At this hour there is only slight traffic passing by the Westbahnhof. A few market wagons that are detoured around the station. For a time the station square is sealed off so that the human freight can be transferred to the train without too much commotion. Transport of Jews and Communists to Dachau; the institution is inaugurated, without too much commotion. Which is not to say that an occasional gunshot is considered a disturbance of the peace. Circa 300 prisoners, 80 members of the death's-head-SS, 50 officers from the Vienna police force take part in the initial stages of this mobile massacre. The first casualties occur in front of the station. Two younger prisoners are shot in the back while allegedly trying to escape. "Maytime in waltz-time / Making two heartssublime." Valentin can't get the schmaltz-waltz out of his head.

The special train is made up of several tank cars filled with gasoline from Rumanian refineries, and four third-class coaches, their windows pasted over with black paper. On the platform there seem to be further escape attempts because more prisoners are shot in the back from short range. Within half an hour the transport has suffered eleven dead—even before it rolls out of the Westbahnhof. Meanwhile the station's first-aid service functions perfectly, without a trace of Viennese sluggishness. In his younger years Valentin saw many a man "die with his boots on," but today he experiences something completely new. He sees a Vienna policeman cry.

At the break of day the station lights are turned off, but nests of twilight still remain throughout the station hall. This is enough to give the scene a ghostly atmosphere—even to the eyes of an historical materialist. The policeman is no longer young. Instead of the traditional billed cap of the Viennese Police he wears a brand-new shako of the Prussian type that has just been introduced to the Ostmark. Valentin, as he is led handcuffed past the officer (who, though no longer young, is certainly no inspector), thinks he detects the man's discomfort with the chin strap of the new helmet: he tugs at it secretively. A freshly shot prisoner completely covered with a blanket is carried off the platform by the first-aid men—without a trace of Viennese sluggishness, amidst shouts of "make way," "please make way, gentlemen!" Thus they address the death's-heads men who carry on their business of producing more death's heads (which is what they are paid to do). And now the handcuffed Valentin discovers it, now, at this very second.

The no longer young Viennese policeman begins to cry.

To his horror the man only notices his so-called human weakness—this thoroughly unacceptable natural disaster in miniature that, at the very least, can cost him his position—notices it *after* it catches the eye of the man being led past him. His expression of momentary, compassionate distraction changes to momentary horror; his fingers move suddenly from the chin strap to his eyes, to the stubborn flow of hot wetness that is beginning to run down his cheeks. In the gray light of the station hall Valentin can see that suddenly and quite involuntarily the honest face of the policeman is virtually lacquered with tears. With two sharp, discreet jerks of his chin the man in the handcuffs gives the man in the helmet a command: About face! Forward, march!

The policeman turns and strides in a businesslike fashion across the track and onto an empty neighboring platform.

"If I ever get to Vienna again," interrupted the teller of the midnight tale, "and run across this policeman on the street, I'll be sure to buy him a beer."

"How was it with Maxim Grabscheidt, Valentin?"

"Didn't the phone ring?"

"Not yet."

The train, switched and left standing on sidings at every second village in the Vienna Woods, takes hours to cover the thirty-five miles to St. Poelten. But boredom does not become a problem. The death's-head detachment assigned to the part of the train loaded not with Rumanian gasoline but with warm blood, pulsing now in fewer than 300 human bodies penned up in 32 compartments—the escort of the *Kummerljudentransport (Kummerl = Communist)* —has its own way of passing the time. In each car several compartments are reserved for the SS, and in each compartment cases of beer and countless bottles of Slivovitz and Enzian are consumed by lamplight, since these compartments too have blacked-out windows. Occasionally the gentlemen, spurred on by their morning binge, make the rounds of the other compartments. In St. Poelten several cattle cars loaded with calves are coupled onto the train (the members of Transport 20 May can consider themselves lucky to be sitting on wooden benches; later "shipments" will be sent in sealed cattle cars). Also joining the train in St. Poelten: a Prussian *Hauptscharfuehrer*, a jolly fellow who evokes raucous laughter with the witty suggestion "Why don't we put a match to the tank cars and blow up the whole lousy lot of 'em? Of course it would be a sad waste of good gasoline."

The SS-detachment consists mostly of Austrians eager to prove their eagerness to the few others from the Old Reich. Broken down on a percentage basis the *Kummerljudentransport* consists of c. 15 percent Communists of Jewish descent, c. 15 percent Socialists of Jewish descent, c. 20 percent practicing

Jews from Vienna, c. 20 percent converts from Judaism to Catholicism who had been functionaries in Schuschnigg's and Starhemberg's National Front, c. 30 percent "Aryan" Communists and Socialists, among the latter V. Tiefenbrucker, the only Bavarian.

During halts in or near towns there are no beatings, and no shots are fired (there being no sense in frightening the brand-new citizens of the Reich with excessive screaming and gunfire). Only those inside the rolling prisons can hear the moaning of the wounded, the chuffing gasps of the locomotive, the plaintive mooing of the calves, and from the SS compartments, choruses of laughing drinkers, arguing cardplayers and raucous male singers (the song "Edelweiss" enjoying the greatest popularity). And when the train finally rattles on its way again, the rhythmic clacking of the rails (occasionally in waltz time) is broken by the sound of screams and gunfire, and the black guards come stomping, reeling in their jackboots down the corridor, down the electric-lighted passageway that looks something like a mineshaft—outside it is a bright May day. "Maytime is waltz-time / Making two hearts . . ."

One relatively modest prank of theirs: passing from compartment to compartment like conductors—punching noses instead of tickets, breaking one by one the noses of the shackled prisoners as they sit jammed together on their benches. Some of the "conductors" haul off with gigantic swings, other use housekeys or brass knuckles, other more sporting types have perfected the technique of smashing their victim's nose from above with a kind of reverse uppercut. The *Hauptscharfuehrer*, their comrade from the Old Reich, comes up with the idea of having the prisoners sing ("to raise their spirits") the song "I am a Prussian / Mark you my colors," whereby Prussian is replaced by Jew, colors by nose. In Amstetten some SS-men from Linz who have driven out to meet Transport 20 May join the death's-head crew. The closer the train gets to Linz, where the Fuehrer grew up, the more ruthless become the "countermeasures against reckless escape attempts." These "escape attempts" are made under various guises, for example when a prisoner asks to go to the toilet. "Number one or number two?" he is asked. If he answers "Number one," he is told "Go piss on yourself!" If he answers "Number two," he is told "Go shit in your pants!"

For most prisoners handcuffs have given way to foot shackles, one ankle being chained to a metal bar beneath the bench. Prisoner Tiefenbrucker, on the other hand, is allowed to stand in the corridor and use the toilet, for which purpose his handcuffs are removed. Is this embarrassing but welcome privilege a result of special instructions, his Aryan status, his somewhat legendary prominence, or his physical resemblance to Hitler? Are they already trying to make a guard out of him, a trusty? The *Hauptscharfuehrer* speaks to him in confidential tones—he is no "man of culture" like Camp Director Liebhenschl (whom he has yet to meet) but a stout, brutal but jovial Berliner.

"Ya don't have ta report ta me. Wanna cigarette?"

"I don't smoke."

"A beer, Tiefenbrucker? Whaddaya gawkin at me like that for? That's no joke, I'll treat ya to a beer."

"I don't drink beer."

"Now hang on there. Y-o-u, a guy from Munich, can't drink a beer?"

"I'm from Wasserburg."

"Y'know wat, Bolshevik Tiefenbrucker? I like ya, but don't tell'ny body. Lemme whisper in yer ear: my Viennese comrades here are a buncha bumblers if ya ask me. When ya come right down to it, these Austrians are all buncha soggy dishrags. All of a sudden they come on like a ton a meat, an can harly move, they're so muscle-bound."

(As a Reichstag delegate, Valentin had learned to imitate the Berlin dialect.)

All at once a prisoner in the same car makes his last mistake and loses, as we say, his head, raises a shrill voice in a cry for help. The cry is punctuated by a shot that seems insignificant amidst the rattling jolts of the train. The *Hauptscharfuehrer* shoves his way past the Linz SS-men blocking the corridor; now he is back at Valentin's side and growls. "A clear case—attempted mutiny. But t'start shooting at a range o' six feet . . . we Prussians 'r not t-h-a-t trigger-happy. Right through the heart."

After arriving in Linz, where the train is switched onto a siding in the main station for a two-hour wait, there is talk of a dozen men dead or dying. Here no station first-aid men rush to carry them away. Most of the Viennese SS have accepted the invitation of their Linz comrades to have an extended lunch in the station restaurant. The prisoners are virtually alone.

"Ham sandwiches! Hot wieners, Polish sausage! Beer! Coffee! Cigars, cigarettes! Newspapers, magazines! *Der Voelkische Beobachter, Das Interessante Blatt!*"

There they sit in their compartments with barred and blackened windows, penned up in their mobile mine-shaft underground: the still-living, the slightly or severely wounded, the half-dead and the dead. But from the station platform comes the hawking singsong of the peddlers. In one compartment a man groans from the aftereffects of a kick in the stomach, but in the next compartment the man with a bullet in his heart sits quite still, pitched forward, his ankle still chained to the bar. The man's name is Herzmannsky. It is rumored he is the former head of Children's Aid in Vienna II. (Of all things, Children's Aid, thinks Valentin.) Next to the dead man a living man, also pitched forward, who vomited from shock as the revolver bullet tore into Herzmannsky; on the opposite bench a man with his pants full; on the floor, pools of blood and urine; a compressed, fetid stench, barely breathable; the mooing of calves.

"Ham sandwiches! Wieners! Beer! Cigars, cigarettes!"

That is the worst thing of all, almost worse than the actual moments of torture and killing, the waiting in this combination death chamber and sewer lying motionless on a sidetrack of the central station in Linz, forced to wait and to listen to the familiar sounds of a Central European railroad station at noontime, to the sounds of life going on outside. A voice over the loudspeaker:

"*Achtung, Achtung,* the Orient Express, Paris, Strassburg-Munich-Vienna-Bucharest-Istanbul arriving shortly on track one—stand clear please! Express train to Bad Aussee now departing on track five; all aboard please, and have a pleasant trip!"

At the freight yard in Wels the cars loaded with calves are uncoupled and two new cattle cars are added. Contents: 80 prisoners from Graz, among them Maxim Grabscheidt, M.D.

Interrupting, I ask Valentin: "When did you see him?"

"See him? Not until later. During a stop in Traunstein. Not until hours later. It was already night, and after . . . it had already happened. But his voice, his voice I heard earlier, at the freight yard of Voecklabruck."

The Voecklabruck SS has driven out to meet the train at Wels and boards it to inspect the *Kummerljuden* on the way from Wels to Voecklabruck. At the Voecklabruck freight yard, mission accomplished, they hop off, plop-plop-plop and go off bellowing (the song "Edelweiss"). Now Valentin hears the *Hauptscharfuehrer's* Berlinese and the answer of a trainman in Upper Austrian dialect. They are discussing a bullet wound in the stomach.

"Thanks. So *that's* what it was. The Voecklabruck SS shot Maxim in the stomach and he suffered through the night—perhaps all the way to Traunstein—and arrived in Dachau a dead man. Thanks, Valentin, I'm not interested in any further details."

His sniffing this time is more like an irritated snorting.

"Wrong again, my friend. That's not the way it was. And the cursed details *must* interest you." It was no scene from an ancient myth like Giaxa's grand finale, but rather like something from a horror show in Montmartre, something from Grand Guignol. At any rate, when he arrived in Dachau, Dr. Grabscheidt was *alive* . . .

Isn't there a doctor among all these prisoners, Valentin hears the trainman ask. A small exchange develops between him and the *Hauptscharfuehrer*. The trainman is rather insistent that the man with the belly wound in the second cattle car be bandaged up, since it would "make a bad impression on our normal passengers to see blood dripping out of there."

Valentin hears the roll of a sliding door, and the voice of the *Hauptscharfuehrer*, "Are you a doctor?," and the answer of a sluggish, almost viscid male voice, "Until recently I was a doctor, yes" and the *Hauptscharfuehrer's* command, "Take off his handcuffs," and his jovial question, "What's yer name? Doctor Maximilian Grabshit? What. Oh I see, Grabscheidt. Well then, come on,

Maxie, let's go fix up a temporary bandage," and echoing steps.

Toward evening, during a stop at the freight yard in Salzburg, Valentin sees the *Hauptscharfuehrer* for the last time, as in a booze-drenched whisper the man confides, "Salzburg, Salzburg Festival, man I tell ya, I've had it upta here with the festival they've been putting on in this train. Sure you gotta knock the pris'ners inta line once inna while; sure you gotta crack down hard on escape attempts. But some'a my Ostmark pals here just don't seemta have all their marbles. The kinda festival they've been putting on here, man, I tell ya, it's enough to spoil yer appetite. I'm glad I'm getting outa this backwoods Alp-train. So long, Tiefenbrucker, yer basic'ly a true-blue German; have a good time in Dachau."

No SS men get on in Salzburg. This time, for a change, it's a troop of boys from the Hitler Youth who've driven from Traunstein to meet the train.

"It was a Hitler Youth brat who did it. A fellow Bavarian, a seventeen-year-old punk."

Valentin is not able to see how it happens. The "godawful details" are told him later by prisoner Julius Blum, former alderman from Brigittenau and longtime secretary of the Shop Assistants Union. Blum, who was arrested in Graz, shares the same cattle car with Grabscheidt; in the May twilight three HY boys inspect the doctor with a flashlight.

"Jeez, does it ever stink in here," says one of them.

"Why isn't he handcuffed?" boy number two asks an SS-man, who informs him, "He's been giving first aid."

The answer amuses the three uniformed boys.

"Are you a doctor?" boy number three asks prisoner Grabscheidt.

"I was 'til recently, yes."

"Report to me," says boy number one. Prisoner Grabscheidt gives no reply.

"He'll have to learn that," says boy number two and shines the light on the prisoner's face. "Not a Yid," he remarks knowingly.

"Are you a Jew?" boy number three asks prisoner Grabscheidt.

"I am a Jew."

Boy number two: "He doesn't look like one. Are you really a Jew?"

"I am a Jew" says prisoner Grabscheidt.

"Are you a Communist?" asks boy number one.

"I am a Communist," says prisoner Grabscheidt.

Boy number three orders him to sing the song "Edelweiss." The prisoner stares unblinking into the flashlight beam. Does he know that "Edelweiss" is the Fuehrer's favorite song, asks boy number two. Silence. Boy number three in a threatening tone: Does he know the song "Edelweiss" or doesn't he?

"I don't feel much like singing," says prisoner Grabscheidt.

Boy number three punches him in the face.

The man punches boy number three in the face.

"Listen, Trebla . . . he wasn't really in the Party was he?"

"No. And according to the Nuremberg laws he wasn't . . . even a Jew. What happened next?"

"Wait a minute. Then why did he say—"

"Maxim . . . Maxim was a man, if I may say so, with a tremendous supply of solidarity. I can't think of any other explanation. So what happened next?"

"Just a minute, I have to get this straight," said the Bringer-of-Bad-Tidings in a somewhat officious tone. "During my imprisonment there was any number of times I was tempted to do the same, but party discipline held me back from such pointless and suicidal one-man actions."

"That's your good fortune, Valentin. Maxim's mother, Kresenz, is a Styrian farmer's daughter; his father, Shoma, of Russian-Jewish origin, a dissident, also has a farmer's temperament; in his youth he worked as a field hand. Maxim looked like an El Greco saint, but there was also something of the farmer in him and maybe even something of a Cossack. He hit back when the HY kid hit him. What then?"

Then the telephone rang, yes, it rang. I didn't look at the Bringer-of-Bad-Tidings when he left the balcony to answer the phone in the studio; didn't look at him when he came back ("That was Kujath's driver, Pfiffke. We're supposed to be down there in five minutes"), didn't look at him as he finished the last Midnight Tale of the Luzienburg.

Boy number one, strongest by far of the three, an athlete, draws his ceremonial dagger and rams, while boy number two lights the spot, rams the blade into prisoner Grabscheidt's forehead.

Into his forehead.

The dagger—engraved with the words HONOR IS LOYALTY, this scalpel-sharp blade, plunged full force by the muscular arm of the boy athlete into Grabscheidt's head and throwing it back against the wooden wall—jabs through the skull above the nose bone and into the brain, and remains impaled an inch and a half deep.

"The exact same place, Trebla, where you've got that hole in your forehead. Christ! Now can you see why I was staring at you like that when you told me you were the man's friend? What a godawful coincidence."

"Godawful coincidence." (And that was our last dialogue in the castle tower.)

The most gruesome part of all this, the most phenomenal, horribly incredible thing: the victim does not collapse, he does not even lose consciousness. The uniformed youngsters hightail it without recovering their ceremonial dagger. Whose horn handle juts out of the victim's forehead like the single spike of a unicorn.

The former alderman and other inmates of the cattle car want to try removing the dagger, but the victim, as a doctor, refuses to allow it. If they did so, he predicts, obviously fully conscious, he would bleed to death in short order. The *Kummerljudentransport* rolls on toward Traunstein.

It was just after dawn on a May morning when the police van took me, ex-Reichstag delegate Tiefenbrucker, to the Westbahnhof in Vienna. It must be around midnight—we sit there without watches in our stinking mobile shaft, the living, the wounded, the half dead, the dead. The train halts again; it must be Traunstein; no hawkers' voices can be heard. From a church tower we hear it strike one, so it is the first hour of the morning, and under the famed cover of darkness come the stretcher-bearers, whispering like thieves, and take away the dead—but only these.

Outside a male voice. "Move him out of here!" Crunching steps across the gravel. Then two booted SS-men lift a man into our car.

Held beneath the armpits by one of the death's-head men he pushes his way through the corridor, unsteadily but under his own power. There is no such thing as a drunken prisoner. At first in the gray light of the corridor I fail to see what is wrong with him.

The booted men shove him into an empty compartment. One of them says to me, as if I were already selected as a trusty: "Keep an eye on him."

I feel weak. Not a bite to eat since early in the morning—how did the *Hauptscharfuehrer* from Berlin put it? It's enough to spoil your appetite. You can go without food for several days, as long as you get something to drink. But they never gave us so much as a drop of water.

When I sit down across from him in the compartment he says to me, "Don't be shocked."

Only then do I see what is wrong with him. The unicorn's horn sticking out of his forehead. Yes, as a Royal Bavarian Dragoon on the Eastern Front and later as a cavalryman in the Red Army under Semen Michaelovich Budienny when we were opposite Denikin and Wrangel, I saw of lot of unusual wounds. But never one like that. I feel weaker still.

I ask him if I can't help him; he says no, he's a doctor himself, from the Lastenstrasse in Graz, Styria; no thank you.

Even handcuffed I thought I could pull the awful thing out.

What then? Then he would most probably die following extrusion of cortical matter, he replied. It would be like upending a bottle and taking the cork out.

Maybe, I insist, I can get one of the guards to take off my handcuffs so that I can at least make up a bandage.

Really, thanks a lot, but as a doctor he was a specialist in bandaging. His own diagnosis: The knife could only be removed by surgical means—with another knife. By an expert doctor. Even then the chances were ten to one against his coming through.

We roll through the May night toward Munich and I can hardly believe it.

Hardly believe that he is sitting there on a wooden bench and talking to me. In a—perhaps even normally—sluggish voice that occasionally recedes in a kind of fade out.

No motor aphasia yet apparent, he diagnoses. What's that? Speech loss resulting from certain injuries to the lower frontal lobe. Naturally there was the acute danger of internal hemorrhage if one of the frontal arteries had been hit; and of course one of these could easily be grazed during extraction of the knife. It was a question of fractions of a millimeter.

His unusually large, dark eyes smolder in an ashen, corpselike face, a remarkably symmetrical face, yes, a face El Greco could have painted. Above his brow a barely visible thread of trickling blood, but out of his forehead grows the horn, and in the pale electric light its thin shadow cuts across the doctor's classical face like a threatening shadow of death.

Didn't he want to stretch out on the bench, I ask. No, he'd rather not. Reclining into the corner he sinks into sleep or unconsciousness. It must be somewhere past Rosenheim that a grimace of cramping pain comes over his face and his large dark eyes open. "I'm suffering from waves of severe headache," he tells me, and his voice never really returns from the fade-out. "Headache. But just let me be. You can't help me."

Testing, he moves his fingers, his arm, his torso, his leg, touches his face, sniffs. Olfactory nerve, he remarks sluggishly (but perhaps no more sluggishly than usual), motor control, auditory, kinesthetic, and vestibular senses, speech control, and trigeminal nerve—all still functioning, aha.

Yes, back there in Salzburg he had let his temper get away with him, yes. But he would not do our enemies the favor of leaving the scene without a fight. Although his chances for survival were slight, he wouldn't succumb for lack of will to live . . .

I ask him about his family. His parents had emigrated from Leoben to America at the beginning of the year, had gone to join his brother, a musician in Philadelphia; his wife had left him two weeks before the Anschluss and had sent their son Leo to Lower Austria, to a monastery school whose name she refused to reveal.

As we ride through Munich-Haar—it must have been Haar—he is still alive and fully conscious.

He is still alive, fully conscious, and more or less on his feet, on Saturday, May 21 at 11:05 A.M. Supported by Julius Blum and myself, he walks beneath the gigantic inscription *Arbeit Macht Frei* into the spanking clean Detention Camp Dachau (population 10,000 public enemies). Just back from his morning ride, *Standartenfuehrer* Liebhenschl greets us personally, clamped high aloft on his dun colored steed. No doubt he notices the dagger-pronged forehead amidst the wretched procession, but the pale eyes of the rider stare unblinking. It isn't worth a blink. As if an ox were being driven past him, an ox with a missing horn.

He is still alive, fully conscious, and more or less on his feet when, support-

244

ed by Blum and myself, he approaches the barracks to be greeted by a gigantic inscription on the roof:

THERE IS ONE ROAD TO FREEDOM
ITS MILESTONES
ARE
OBEDIENCE
ORDER
HONESTY
SOBRIETY
DILIGENCE
CLEANLINESS
TRUTHFULNESS
LOVE OF COUNTRY

The forty-one-year-old prisoner Maxim Grabscheidt, victim of an accident during transport, is brought to the sick bay. Surgery. Exit.

2

The Bringer-of-Bad-Tidings patted me gently on the back and I no longer heard the clank of armor.

Without another word he retired into the tower studio; soon I heard the upward humming of the silo elevator. I remained standing behind the Ghibelline battlement. (In a tuxedo, of all things.) So now I knew in what manner and by what means Papa-Rose and Maxim had met their ends—or rather first Maxim and then, not a month later, Papa-Rose. No ephedrine, no medicine in the world could help me now. For several moments I could not breathe. I could not bear knowledge. Because I was three thousand years too young. (In a tuxedo, of all things.) Because centuries ago European man had lost the ability of the *Iliad*'s warriors to mourn their slain companions with loud outcries of sorrow—the wild lamentations that let a man alleviate his grief. This elemental cry over land and sky and water had yielded to an introverted muttering of prayers. But what about those of us who have left praying behind us? I could neither wail, nor pray, nor weep. Perhaps it was more a kind of paralyzed fury than grief—this force that took away my breath and sight.

No doubt beyond the Rhine the dome of Riedberg castle still glowed beneath the south-wind moon, but I no longer saw it, I saw nothing more. One of my first reactions to being hit by that bullet fired from the cockpit of a Clerget-Camel fighter plane, a posttraumatic relapse that had recurred at ever-increasing intervals during the past twenty years, now appeared again. This "ocular nausea," the feeling that I was vomiting my eyes out of my head.

Down on the Pfauenhof, where only a few baroque candelabra were burning, we met Pfiff alone. Kujath's big black Horch limousine was now parked next to the well made famous by occasional waves of Lucretia Planta's ghostly hand. Beneath the walled-up alcove window stood ten Breukaa's Chrysler, now alone, but with the top up. His idea, remarked Pfiff, he'd also filled the American's tank. His breath smelled of coffee. The boss sent his best regards; he had fallen into bed exhausted; Mrs. Kujath had retired earlier. He wanted to know what we had thrown out of the tower studio and smashed during our stag-party; he thought he would wait until daylight to take a look at it, after his return from the Jura Mountains.

I left Pfiff unanswered because I saw someone huddled in the cabriolet, peered through the driver's window and discovered Xana in the front seat. She appeared to be sleeping.

Miss Slumber-Bunny, Lily-Arms, Elephantophile, Xana Coquelicot, Kuku-laps—with names like this I could never introduce my bad tidings. God-in-aw-ful-heaven. And in fact I did look up in that direction. Saw the roof silhouette of the Peacock Palace cutting through a segment of sky draped with an enormous veil of cirrostratus clouds; the moon, a diffuse wisp of gold. In his day Maxim had shown me many an X ray—for example, one of the tubercular torso of Franz Scherhack. Yes, this sky was like a gigantic, enlarged X ray of a human chest.

Xana's long, white-shimmering, bare arms were thrust into the rumpled crimson velvet jacket—something like a torero's cape (though she abhorred bullfighting)—on her lap. I couldn't see her face; in her typical pose of a shoul-der-kissing, female Narcissus it lay resting on her left shoulder, concealed by the iridescent, emerald green feathers on her gown straps, the feathers that reminded me of those on Bersaglieri helmets.

Under these circumstances it seemed wrong to wish the daughter of the great Giaxa a good-morning, Valentin had told me as we walked across the neighboring courtyard. We had shaken hands for a whole minute, during which time I had difficulty swallowing. After a few whispered words with Pfiff he ducked into the gleaming black Horch and waved at me—in memory of his days as a leader in the Berlin Red Front, and now perhaps somewhat ironically—with a raised fist, and I waved back in similar fashion. Pfiff strode once more across the cobblestones of the Pfauenhof like a jockey on foot; and again he reminded me of Fitz, the king's jockey stranded in St. Moritz. Would I please drive out first, he whispered, since he had to close the castle gate behind him. I could not give him a tip (as I could Bonjour), only my hand; then I slipped behind the wheel of the Chrysler and Pfiff closed the door with extra care so as not to wake Xana.

We left Tiefencastel and Tinizun behind us on the road to Julier Pass, and oncoming traffic was virtually nil. I brooded without letup about how, if Xana woke up, I would be able to tell her. Was she really sleeping? A night driver never takes his eyes off the road; and actually I didn't want to know whether she was really asleep or not asleep . . . After Tinizun, we had reached an altitude of approximately 4,000 feet—the oppressiveness of the south wind disappeared and it grew cool in the second hour of morning. My allergic vasomotor cramp began to subside naturally, and as the cabriolet passed a waterfall that plunged into the Julia River, the coolness of its roaring cut through the open window with such sudden freshness that I half leaned out, desperately sucking in deep breaths, guzzling the air and bathing my tortured bronchi in the chill freshness. Then she moved. Out of the corner of my eye I saw how, half asleep, she pulled the velvet jacket up around her shoulders before my right hand could assist her. Then she rested as before . . . Mulegns now behind us. Here in the Oberhalbstein the firmament no longer resembled a dreadful, oversized X ray, but was full of stars and banded with a sharply outlined Milky Way. The waning moon, too, this midnight riser on its creeping journey toward a daytime zenith, was no longer something bloated, no longer a bursting flame. Still shapeless, neither egg nor sickle, shining with a washed-out, sharply contoured whiteness, it peered down, it seemed, through the skylight window of a tunnel-like ravine.

Into which I drove. Then a roadside fence and a traffic signal (in daylight a construction site) narrowed the passage still more. At night the signal was set to a steady, yellow warning flash, and I stopped in front of it, flashing my lights at an oncoming driver, the first in many miles, allowing him to pass through first. He came dawdling along the fence, a little delivery truck in which the milk cans clattered audibly. A milk truck beneath the Milky Way. After he passed I heard him accelerate toward the valley and the clanging-together of the aluminum containers was transformed by the Doppler effect into the ever-dropping tones of receding bells. I engaged first gear and was about to release the clutch. But after one side-glance at the woman next to me my foot froze on the pedal.

During countless Giaxa performances and in the rehearsals for my own "Quo Vadis" premiere I had had occasion to study the weird effects of contrast lighting. But neither the staring of the bone-colored moon, nor the instrument lights of the Chrysler, nor the reflection of the headlights, nor the monotonous flashing-through-the-windshield of the warning light (yellow-on-off, yellow-on-off, yellow-on-off) could justify the chimera, the phantom vision, that now confronted me.

The crimson velvet jacket that had served her as a blanket was now fallen.

The Bersaglieri feathers on her left shoulder were broken, no longer fit to hide a sleeper's face.

It was a face that bore a dreadful, striking resemblance to her father's.

More dreadful than striking because it looked much, much older than his—much older than Konstantin Giaxa could ever become.

The face of an ancient, retired clown sitting by himself, rehearsing a grimace of pain.

A face weathered by thousands and thousands of makeup applications, a face scored with countless wrinkles graven in the clown's flesh by the Obristi-Obraski mask.

Hair, more ash gray than hazelnut blond, surrounded it like a matted fringe.

And the ancient clown face stared at me with half-open, hollow eyes, tearless, long-extinguished eyes like jelly—

Yellow-on-off, yellow-on-off, yellow-on-off.

For once a blundering chauffeur, I punched my right foot forcefully onto the gas pedal and roared carelessly past the construction site and out of the ravine, then without a look at my passenger and with a trembling right hand I switched on the car radio, twisting the knob until I found an all-night station where a thin, sometimes fading English voice with an Oxford accent extolled the virtues of the "Lambeth Walk," a dance of increasing popularity, ladies and gentlemen, inspired by the potters in the Lambeth section of London. Could sorrow destroy beauty so completely? *Did Xana know?*

He didn't want to be in my shoes, didn't know how to tell her of Giaxa's last ride—had Grandpa proved himself wrong and given vent to his blabbering impulse when he came upon her in the Peacock Palace? Not likely. Wouldn't Xana have reacted differently? Wouldn't she have wanted to cry on my shoulder? Wouldn't she have insisted on telegraphing Elsabé immediately from the Luzienburg? Torturing, silently gnawing questions, accompanied by the chirping of the all-night music: the Lambeth Walk, an English waltz, the *Schatzwalzer* by Johann Strauss . . . the Radetzky March.

The old, infamous Morse-code signal in my forehead. Giaxa & Giaxa's Rákóczidetzky March, Holy Laudon, must I be reminded of *that?* Not now. Again my right hand groped for the radio knob to turn it off, and was covered by another hand, a very light, very cold hand . . .

Past and above Bivio, up through the hairpin turns toward Julier Pass I raced with such verve that it seemed I wanted to match Kujath's No. 2, Dashing Detlev. I fixed my entire attention on driving, obsessed myself with it. My only interest was to distract myself by driving the four-wheeled, 200 hp torpedo, borrowed from the world's most boring Dutchman, to a height of 7,000 feet, to the height of the pass, to the top. Just don't look over at the passenger, I tell myself. The phantom face . . . Xana's and yet not Xana's, familiar and yet unrecognizable . . . was a chimera, a brief hallucination caused by the weakness of my right eye (a weakness most evident at close range), the diffuse lighting of the ravine, and not least by the overdose of ephedrine combined with the crazy assortment of drinks I'd consumed at the Luzienburg. Nevertheless I was wide awake, not tired; yes, my wakefulness grew and grew as the car gained altitude. The last dwarf pines on the roadside sank below, and now there was not a tree in sight—we had passed the tree line. Cold sliced through my open window, a veritable breath of ice. I rolled it up, leaving it open just a crack, switched off the radio, now chirping "God Save the King," and turned on the heat. Then my passenger began to move.

Over the discreet whine of second gear I could hear a lady's purse snap open. A Xana purse.

In nameless, stony solitude a shriveled, darkened house, the Hospice of La Veduta. Past La Veduta. Just before the top of the pass the big headlights caught three pillars posted unevenly alongside the road. I hadn't noticed them on the drive out, relics of baseless columns, untapered, Roman-Corinthian, with a functional, military simplicity: if I could trust Joop's lecturing, erected by the engineer cohorts of the Julian—Caesar Augustus. I stopped.

"Aviatishek." The woman's voice was bell-clear, not a bit hoarse from sleep. "It's all over with Bancroft's Feather-Elsie. My Bersaglieri plumes are shot. Both of them."

The clock on the instrument panel showed a few minutes past three. Over the ridge to the east, where the traveler crossing the pass would soon see the Upper Inn Valley, the Engadine open up before him, the stars were growing pale in an elephant-gray sky. No wispy clouds, no clouds of any kind: the very first sign of morning, the first hint of a sign. I switched off the headlights and panel lights so that my perceptions would not be influenced by lighting, turned off the motor so that no pianissimo rumbling could lull me, could distract me from my necessary observations. Not a sound of a motor far and wide. As if overcoming a stiff neck I turned my head, turned toward the passenger at my side.

In the circus-elephant gray, in the gray of the Alpine dawn, still ruled over by the gaunt half-moon, I observed that the woman had combed her hair, had powdered her nose a bit too white, but only this; had not yet put on her lipstick, had in the heated interior let her jacket fall completely from her shoulders. Many of the shoulder feathers were indeed broken. But that could do nothing to spoil the perfect harmony of the impression. The face of the woman, of the woman *not yet thirty*, was a bit vague in the ghostly elephant-gray, but was—strikingly beautiful. Had I been seized by madness down in the ravine by Mulegns—was I charmed by magic here? I could hardly trust my eyes. Pulled out my monocle and squeezed it in front of my weak eye.

Strikingly beautiful, if a bit vague in the grayness.

Hesitantly I reached out my hand and clasped her neck, which felt smooth and young. Her face rested soft in my hand as I felt my way up her cheek. Her eyes, if seen by a botanist, were tiny gentians opening in the early dawn. "You see," she said softly, referring to her damaged plumes, and I clicked "tsk-tsk."

Nothing more was said in that minute. The things I had encountered in the Luzienburg and near Mulegns—up here at seven thousand feet I pushed them out of my mind, down, down into my subconscious. And our fragments of dialogue could revolve around such trivia as "Even if the Palace Bar stays open 'til 4:00 A.M. after the ball, I can't go with these demolished feathers."

"Oh you poor thing; well then, let's just forget about it." After a while my hand gave her chin a reluctant caress to tell her that, like it or not, it had to move away. "I've got to check and see if Mr. Chrysler's 200 horsepower is boiling over or not," and she pulled back her chin and said, "Go take a look."

Outside it was windless and near freezing. I pulled up my tuxedo collar and pressed my lips tight, breathing the thin air through my nose. It was as if bull-like strength and a lion's courage were being pumped into me—a sudden feeling of vigor accompanied by a brief dizzy spell. Ye gods! Perhaps the sight of the three pillar stumps inspired this sort of vocative oath. Ye gods, what a titantic landscape. In contrast to Bernina Pass, this one did not have a really high-alpine character, especially not in this light. The rocks that formed the saddle had a kind of olive shimmer (perhaps moss) and were stacked up to form a pyramid only a hundred yards higher than the pass: the Piz Julier. Like the chott of the North African djebel, I thought. This could almost be the desert, and the peak could be a gigantic dune. I tapped the nose of the radiator grill. Barely lukewarm, okay.

Then I heard the first whistle.

Whistle.

Stood stock still, listened.

The whistle (I was fairly good at estimating the distance of sounds) originated on a boulder-strewn slope below the peak about thirty yards away. It sounded like the whistle of a patrol leader until recently asleep but now wide awake and eager to alert his men with the least possible noise. A lookout under cover behind a rock, for across the whole field of boulders there is no one to be seen in the elephant-gray dawn—a lookout under cover pipes out a thin but penetrating whistle into the prehistoric silence of the pass, where all one expects to hear is the winds of eternity (assuming you believe in it, that is). And look, look, no—listen, listen, across the highway, too late to be an echo, comes a restrained little whistle, a stealthy little answer to the first one. From the neighboring peak, called (I think) Polaschek.

This (I think) is *the* moment. The moment I may have feared yesterday, but am waiting for today.

A marvelous anger swelled up inside me, a beastly rage that could not impair my lucidity but would fight shoulder to shoulder with it—of that I was sure, as for the first time in hours I patted the narrow, bullet-packed leather strap that served as my rather unorthodox tuxedo belt. I was not alarmed; if anything in me was alarmed it was the chamber in my heart that held my concern for Xana. If only I hadn't dragged her along on my Via Mala, my evil way into the Domleschg! With a single leap I sprang to the open car door and ducked inside; switching off the parking lights I reached for the glove compartment and whispered, "Lie down, lie down flat on the seat quick, there's not a second to lose!"

Xana's trust in my instinct was complete—rock solid. My impulsive guess: perhaps she thinks I've seen—in the first light of the year's second longest day (tomorrow, the longest, is Grandpa's birthday)—thinks I've seen a rock that's *not* solid, a rock slide rushing straight down onto the parked car. In any case she drops obediently onto her side, bedding her torso on the driver's seat. (Another momentary reflection: torso, Italian, a stalk, a stem, how well the word fits her sinuous upper body—will it find enough room on the driver's seat?—this torso like a painting, not by an Impressionist but by Amedeo Modigliani.)

"What is it?" This first question of hers sounded not so much alarmed as politely interested. The Walther in the glove compartment—quickly but carefully I took it out, and as I did so, the pitch of Xana's questioning gradually rose to the level of insistence. "What *are* you doing? Why am I supposed to lie here? Is it a rockslide—? Listen, I don't want any rocks falling on my tummy now, not now—"

On her tummy? I thought in split-second bafflement, and whispered, as she raised herself halfway up, "Stay down!"

Quickly but carefully I shut the car door, and Xana, sitting halfway up, rolled down the window, one-two-three, and spoke in a lower tone again, calmly, politely: "Oh for heaven's sake, the slope isn't steep enough here for a rockslide." And I whispered, "They won't be shooting rocks at us, now quick, get down." And she asked: "What for? Why did you turn off the parking lights?" And I muttered, "Now it's *our* turn! Now we're going to get . . . our turn! But I'm going to spoil their fun—the blond bloodhounds—unless they've got tommy guns—in which case we've had it!"

There are precision jewelers who can build a three-master into a nutshell. If you want you can fit a great deal into a nutshell. And three minutes' time are like a nutshell in the fourth dimension with room for a great deal, for example a train of thought. As I sprinted the twelve yards to the nearest of the three column stumps the cold, thin air prickling my lungs like needle-thin icicles, the following thoughts flashed through my mind.

Xana is lying there in the car thinking over what I just whispered to her. That's the way she is. If I throw something at her she doesn't quite understand, she rarely throws the ball back to me in the form of a question. She ponders instead what did he mean? If Grandpa really did blurt it out, if Xana suspects or even knows something about her father's last ride, then she'll suspect or know what I meant by "our turn" . . . There won't be any Saurer truck in the game this time. For such things Men Clavadetscher obviously goes it alone. If the Innkeeper of Sils really did knock the Country Lawyer's Fiat into the lake with his Saurer he did it without accomplices. If he knows that I know he might be tempted to bump me off, as the saying goes, but he would do it alone. The quiet whistles from this side of Julier Pass and the quiet answer from the other side mean that at least *two* men are lying in ambush. Guess which two. And after listening to the Midnight Tales of the Luzienburg I can be dead certain about the mission those two are out to perform. Maybe after the first whistle I should have jumped behind the wheel and raced flat out toward the Engadine. But if they shot out a tire . . . Besides, after being forced to sit and listen to the last of these Midnight Tales and after being chased up every staircase, through every floor of Europe, up to here—to the roof of the world, you get the raging desire once and for all to *stand up and fight* . . . The cabriolet had originally been a four-seater; ten Breukaa had removed the back seat and installed a rack for paintings in its place. I could have taken cover next to Xana, but the field of fire from the car was poor, and my main concern was to divert the enemy's attention from Xana—to prevent the car from being fired upon.

Holding the Walther, safety off, in my right hand (as in a Hollywood B-picture or in wartime), I pulled my tuxedo jacket halfway off with my left, still sprinting, and let it hang from my right shoulder for several seconds. My feverish calculation: this old moon is still man enough to make my white shirt shine. The watchers ought to see it from their boulder hideouts and know that I'm moving away from the car.

Now dressed again in black, I reached the pillar stump.

The ancient stone of the column, which showed no evidence of fluting, was cold and rough to the touch—something like a toad. It was barely as tall as a man, untapered, and covered near the top with moss that felt like the cold, wet fur of a drowned dog. Although the pillar was no more than twenty inches in diameter it seemed to offer good protection. Wide awake instead of tired, I gasped the cold thin air after my twelve-yard dash in patent-leather shoes—air that smelled not of trees or mushrooms but of near-freezing dew and stone; I began to breathe easier, confident of my good morale, and I waited for the first shot or the next whistle.

And it came.

The next whistle.

And as I crouched down behind the column, my pistol at the ready, it hit me—the sudden realization that I had been completely duped, that I had fallen for a very effective illusion. Because this time the whistle was so near by that the whistler, had he been aiming a gun, would have had more than ample time to carry out his orders.

Laimgruber's orders.

"Albert . . . Al-bert!" her voice trembled from the abruptness of the cold that must have struck her as she emerged from the heated car. But despite its tremor, the voice had an undertone of severity. "What kind of party games are you playing anyway?!"

At first I could discern little more than her shadow backed by the dark silhouette of the Chrysler, a shadow with the faintest glimmer of cinnamon tint.

Then the soft clap-clap of her high heels approached across the asphalt highway and I saw her glowing dimly in the twilight like red phosphorus.

"Get back in the car!" I ordered. "I'm not sure yet—"

Ignoring my words she heel-clicked her way toward me and stopped only two paces away. "Oh yes you are," she said, less trembling but also less sternness in her voice, "you *are* sure. You were fooled by the woodchuck whistles. After we already know what they sound like—remember Roseg Valley?"

"That was in daylight. And why should woodchucks be whistling at three o'clock in the morning—instead of sleeping like the good groundhogs they are?"

" 'Cause you woke them up by stopping here. It's a chain reaction—can't you hear?"

Now from every corner of the boulder wasteland came the sharp, no longer camouflaged whistles, from pizzicato triplets to the drawn-out "wheee" of a boiling teapot. I crouched on one knee as if paralyzed.

"Come on. I'm cold. Why are you kneeling by that old Roman column, Trebla? Waiting for the Romans, hm? Are you one of Hannibal's old hangers-on waiting for them to come out of hiding?"

"You almost guessed it, my dear Elephantophile. I'm waiting for Hannibal's elephants to appear in this elephant-gray dawn. This time we're going to take Rome."

3

Next morning I decided to go on the offensive.

I must have slept no more than four hours; an overly bright mountain morning, a brilliant blue Monday peeked through the heart-shaped holes in the closed pine shutters, and Xana stood with her back to me, curved over the sink in her dressing gown and vomited with utmost discretion into the rushing water. Then the sound of the water ebbed away and I fell back asleep, and when I awoke again the bell of the local church was striking ten and Xana was asleep with her back to me, seemingly deep asleep in her pretty, sheer, dark red nightgown (which, in contrast to her new robe, was thoroughly attractive), and I asked myself if perhaps I hadn't dreamed the scene at the sink, and got softly out of bed, threw on my burnoose, took the Walther from the night stand, and crept over to my chamber. Sitting on a chair in the hall was a tray with breakfast intended for us, the coffeepot covered with the padded skirt of a rococo shepherdess: Madam Fausch's spectacular tea cozy. I didn't touch the breakfast, showered quickly, hurried back to my study, threw on a Pompeian-red flannel shirt and my Peyatchevich pants, yanked the cartridge belt out of my tuxedo trousers, slipped it on, shoved the Walther into the holster, shrugged on my corduroy jacket, buttoned the footstraps of my (then unfashionably narrow) Austro-Hungarian pants, one of twenty pairs Giaxa had given me as a wedding present, under the soles of my sturdy, reddish brown oxfords.

Ghost train Monday, 10:20 A.M.

"Pardon me, Madam Fausch, but could I trouble you with a special request?"

"What is it?"

"Could you do me a big favor . . . If any long distance calls come today—if *anyone* tries to reach me today, please do *not* call my wife to the phone. Tell the caller to try reaching me this afternoon . . . late this afternoon at the bar of Pizzagalli's Sporthotel in St. Moritz. Would you give that message to any potential callers?"

"Especially if they're female, eh?"

"Please, this is no joke. And if a special delivery letter or telegram comes for me, would you give it to me personally."

"Is Herr Baron expecting a *billet d'amour?*"

"Quite the contrary."

I hurried over to Confiserie Jann, ordered a cup of black coffee, inserted my reading monocle, and paged feverishly (as they say) through the Monday morning editions of several Swiss newspapers, braced to see the headline come leaping out at me: GIAXA DIES IN DACHAU. But nothing of the sort. MORE GERMAN TROOPS MASS ON CZECH BORDER! SUDETEN-GERMANS SAY: "THE DAY WILL COME!" What, according to Grandpa, had the Great Occultist told Quartermaster General Franz Halder as they rumbled along their way to Vienna on the Ides of March? "This won't make the Czechs very happy."

Ten Breukaa certainly had taken immediate measures to protect his Spahi from art-loving burglars. The wall that extended around Acla Silva from its vertical backdrop of pine-studded rock and enclosed the property like a stage set had been raised and topped with broken glass. The entranceway boasted a new barred gate, which, like the door to a bank vault, eschewed all ornament and was equipped with two special locks. An engraved brass plate warned visitors in four languages to beware of vicious dogs. I rang the bell and Bonjour, dressed in olive green breeches and a striped servant's vest, came trudging down the steps of the terraced garden, reining in two naked, humanly naked looking, gigantic Great Danes on a double red leash—one dog with deep black skin, the other spotted rose and gray. Behind this team, a lonely, waddling, silky-haired little black straggler—visibly intimidated by the intrusion of so much massive, canine nakedness: Sirio.

During lunch Joop had nothing to say about his recent Great Dane acquisitions, but could not resist informing me that if it hadn't been for Pola's telephoned intervention I would have ended up (as he put it) "in the asylum at Chur-Masans for a mental health checkup." I must have subjected Commissioner Mavegn, friend of Dr. Rothmund, the chief of the Swiss Alien Police, to a "highly undiplomatic provocation." To this I gave no answer, but eagerly accepted his invitation to an after-coffee round of chess. This ancient strategic game would pull me together. Would show me if I were fit to undertake my one-man strategy. If my intellectual reflexes were in order. If I was in form.

The women had decided to stay outside in the garden. For once the "lying Dutchman" had not assumed his place where, stretched out on his Récamier sofa, he could keep his eye on the portrait hanging over the English fireplace. Instead he sat in a Chippendale armchair with his back to the painting, while I took my place opposite him at an elegant little rococo chess table with inlaid Chinese motifs. The chessmen were Chippendale too, carved from mahogany in the English Far Eastern rococo style of the eighteenth century. Even though Joop still had a knight at the end of the first game and I was without a single officer, I had finished off his king (more like a potbellied warlord) with my superior force of pawns (more like giant coolies). Which seemed to annoy him.

"You and your mass attack of Chinese peasants—you were talking too much during the game," he admonished me gently, setting up his men for the next match; "that's distracting. Of course I've read about the Chinese communists and their long march. It was in the papers two or three years ago. Who was their leader—some peasant from Hunan—can't think of his name just now . . ."

"Mao Tse-tung."

"All right. He made a six-thousand-mile march with his people from Kiangsi to Yenan, *per pedes apostolorum.*"

"*Apostolorum?* That's not very appropriate."

"All right. Even if I weren't a convinced plutocrat hho-hho, I could share your, om, enthusiasm for this foot march only as an admirer of the Olympic Games."

I posted my victorious peasants for the second battle. "You said it, Joop. While all the admirers of the Olympic Games were reserving their hotel rooms in Hitler's Berlin—and helping make the swastika respectable—the peasant's son and ex-librarian Mao Tse-tung, along with P'eng Teh-huai, Lin Piao, Tso Chuan, Chen Keng and the nobleman Chou En-lai—"

"*Och zo,* a nobleman. More water on your mill."

"—were marching through the yellow dust into North Shensi to join the guerrilla units under Liu Chih-tan and Kao Kang."

"You are nicely informed," he said with weary irony. The second game began with a Spanish opening by me. Then, brooding over a perhaps decisive move—since my opponent, with his two rooks, was still quite strong—I looked up at the Spahi. Yes, now his eyes no longer appeared fearsome and disinterested, his eyes beneath their bushy single brow seemed to stare down at the chessboard with a touch of secret anticipation.

Then the moment of the daring thrust that would paralyze Joop's Chinese warlord in seven moves before he could bring his rooks into play.

After which I imagined seeing the minutest germ of a smile in the left corner of the Spahi's mouth.

But with certainty there appeared an ugly, angry smile on Joop's thin lips. The rosy polish of his bald forehead suddenly showed several white spots, and on his temples the chicklike fuzz he had toyed with during both games stood in ruffled disarray.

"*Barst!* You are nothink bot a dirty Commonist."

He loosed a tremolo of real vexation; even his excellent pronunciation, punctuated only by an occasional word of Dutch, began to suffer.

I took in his deprecations without batting an eyelash, whereupon he uttered a—still malicious—hho-hho-chuckle. Now I could hardly deny that I had worked together with the Communists, at least when I went underground after February '34. He too, I replied, Joop ten Breukaa of Amsterdam, would soon perhaps be forced to stoop so low as to work together with the Communists. "*Och zo?*" he said, and added a spiteful "*Geestig!*" Whatever kept me from joining the Party, anyway?

"Yes, well you see I feel our most important task is to bring three old Jewish giants under one hat."

His fallow eyes scrutinized me suspiciously. Did he think I was pulling his leg—about his father-in-law Isidor Popper who (ignored by Joop and last year deceased) had, together with his brothers Eugen and Sigi (all three of them tall men), managed a hat shop in Vienna's Taborstrasse . . .

"Marx, Freud, Einstein." I consoled him. Despite my insufficient knowledge I've attempted to follow these men who, as German-speaking Jews born in the last century, had remolded the face of this one. And all the Uncle Adolfs in the world couldn't change that. It was worth noting that all three of them had been forced to flee from German lands at one time or another. Each of them. Whether or not he was the old, sold-out, in-God's-own-image man, for whom "hell no longer offered consolation—"

"Trebla, om, you mean heaven."

"*Hell.*" For whom hell no longer offered consolation, because he'd already been through it at Verdun. Or whether he was the new socialist man who could no longer use his predecessor's out-mo-ded concepts of the absolute.

Now Joop's left nostril yawned . . . "*Och zo.* Trebla the pan-creationist, the preacher in the wilderness. As you see, I've read the preface to your poetry collection, Co-Co-Co——"

"*Cormorants of Lobau.*"

" —yes, I read it. An op-zord-ity." (Absurdity.) "A kind of eh-ehhh atheistic pantheism. *Geestig!* A home-brewed elixir from your own medicine cabinet, hho-hho. A Marxist-Freudian-Einsteinian-Pan-Creationist. Aren't you trying to be a few-too-many-things-at-once, Mr. Baron of the Barricades?''

As I set up my coolies for the third game, ten Breukaa arose with a fallow grin and stepped to the bookcase, then sat down again, flipping through the pages of a small, red, paperbound volume, all the time wearing on his face the expression of the master of a "hell that no longer offered consolation"—the look of a castrated Mephistopheles. "No doubt you know the *Communist Manifesto* in dozens of editions, Trebla.''

"Yes. I hope you're not going to rub my nose in Dunker's edition of nineteen hundred thirty-two ... with his epilogue about Germany being on the verge of a proletarian revolution ...''

"N-no, I just want to, om, establish *your* position, based on the *Communist Manifesto*, the way it seems to *me*. Listen to this, Roman numeral three, Arabic one, A. Omm, ommmm—'in order to arouse sympathy, the aristocracy had to appear to lose sight of its own interests and had to formulate its indictment against the bourgeoisie exclusively in the interest of the exploited working class. Thus it gained satisfaction from allowing itself to sing defamatory songs about its new master'—om, the bourgeoisie—'and to whisper more or less calamitous pro-phe-cies in his ear.' Hho-hho. 'In this way a feudalistic socialism was created, half lamentation, half lampoon, half echo of the past, half foreboding of the future, all the while striking the heart of the bourgeoisie with its bitter, cleverly devastating verdicts, always comical—*always comical*—in its to-tal in-a-bil-i-ty to comprehend the course of modern history.' Period. New paragraph. Hear, hear! ... 'In their hands they waved a flag of proletarian beggars' rags' hho-hho, certain aristocrats that is, quite nicely put, '... beggar's rags so as to rally the people behind them. But whenever they followed them, the people recognized ...' Hho-hho-hho-hho-o-o!'' Ten Breukaa erupted in a truly diabolical, eunuch's howl. '... recognized the old aristocratic coats of arms on their hindquarters and dispersed in loud and irreverent laughter.'''

I gave him a light, barely echoing slap. As I took an involuntary glance up at the Spahi, it seemed that I had looked a split second too late to catch sight of his broad grin.

Ten Breukaa had grown deathly pale. As a result, my handprint had stood out on his left cheek like a birthmark. We had both gotten up like actors in a slow-motion film sequence and stared at each other, and Joop was no longer an emasculated Mephisto. In his otherwise so tired eyes had lurked what American suspense and horror writers might call coldblooded murder. And the Spahi Farid Gaugamela had looked down on us with the same impenetrable aloofness he had preserved ever since that day in 1888 when he had posed for a certain Monsieur Gauguin.

Joop stared at me in an unchanged pallor with compressed lips until I asked him guilelessly what he intended to do—shoot me?

"*Och-man-loop-near-de-duivel!*" Now it came in furious bursts. "Do you think I don't have a gun in the house?!"

"Maybe you really would feel better, Joop, if you at least took a shot *at* me ... the way you did at that young sculptor-admirer of Pola's—what was his name? Haberzettl?—a few years ago in Vienna. You remember the story, don't you? The whole matter was forgotten by the police inspector. Or rather, the report landed in the wastebasket after you donated, if I'm not mistaken, three thousand schillings to the policemen's football club."

As suddenly as he had gone pale his color returned, overreturned. He grew lobster red.

"Of course I'm also prepared," I said, returning to the subject, "to give you your satisfaction according to the dusty rules of chivalrous honor. I mean a duel in Staz Forest. Pistols, heavy sabers, or Great Danes at twenty paces—I give you your choice."

Rapidly he regained his normal glossy coloration. "*Onmoglyk!*" he blurted at me, resting his elbows on the mantelpiece. "You are impossible! Get out of here!"

"I am impossible and will get out of here."

"I pity your wife."

I could not tell him how right he was, after the events recounted in the Luzienburg.

"When she was, om, ill, Pola sent our own doctor to see her. We were planning to take care of Dr. Tardueser's bill ourselves. That is now of course impossible. I will tell Pola you have decided to pay the bill out of your own pocket. Beyond that I believe we should keep this nasty incident to ourselves. Roxana is still welcome here." He used the mantelpiece as a support. "*You*, however, Trebla, I must request you not to show your face at Acla Silva in the near future."

"Yes-sir, aye-aye, sir," I said, standing at attention like a captain in the Fourteenth Dragoons taking an order from his division commander.

4

Ghost-train Monday, 2:40 P.M.

Without a word about the nasty incident, I left Xana in Pola's company. After a forced march of twenty minutes I reached St. Moritz-Bad.

"Listen, sir, what do *you* think about those bloody horsies?" Fitz asked me in his whining leprechaun's voice after tapping a salute on the long bill of his navy blue canvas cap. My patrol route led me past the Tattersall, as they called the riding stables here. I hadn't yet got a chance in daylight to inspect the building that had formed a shadowy backdrop to the solo-springboard act of that suicidal cycle-diver Zarli Zuan; with its onionlike dome and scaly wooden shingles, it resembled some church dedicated by Boris Godunov. The Royal Jockey, Ret., was wading around in the sand of the entrance. His dwarfishness was not of the chondrodystrophic type; his limbs were normally proportioned like those of the Lilliputian concertmaster Husseindinovich. A morose, fence-leaning onlooker, he glared into the riding school. In the center of the shadowy ring stood a riding instructor who, with casual but careful whipcracks, caused an iron gray horse to circle round him on a long rein, an iron gray that, in the half light, could not be distinguished from a Lippizan.

Behind him trotted two other horses bearing teen-age females in Texas cowgirl suits.

"D'you know, mister, what I would tell a chap who asks me to try out one of those bloody horsies?" Fitz continued, distorting his aged child's face, his almost Lilliputian visage, to a spiteful scowl. "I would tell him frankly, Fuck yourself, brother!" Fitz had hardly learned this mode of expression in Buckingham Palace or at Ascot Raceway. (Or, then again, perhaps he had!) "Once, long ago, I believed in horses as decent, powerful, intelligent human beings," the old "boy" grumbled on. "But I was terribly wrong. The whole bunch of them are stupid fucking bastards, even the thoroughbreds. Believe me, sir, I had to pay dearly for my error. Look," his little arm gestured lakeward, "at these fucking mountains they forced me to stare at ever since. Look at this fucking lake, this bloody fool Defila who'll never find the corpse of this poor bearded chap Zuan. But please, don't think all my swearing means that I'm a godless little old man. No sir. We, the Irish, are a goddamned fucking godfearing people. We had some trouble with the British, but, speaking for myself personally, I always respected the goddamned fucking law."

It became rather clear to me, a reluctant expert in post-traumatic disturbances, that Fitz had been suffering from just such an ailment ever since he gave up jockeying—a disturbance that manifested itself in his compulsive swearing.

"Yes, the fucking fish'll be sleeping in old Zuan's beard. These divers out there are bloody worthless arseholes and that bloody lake is goddamned deep." Yes, but in the winter it was all different. Then the lake could be just wonderful when it was covered with ice three feet thick, and there was skijoring on the ice in the bright February sun and the sleds and toboggans on the Cresta Run and the international skating aces on the rink at Kulm and the Curling Club—by the way his curling had been in top fucking form last winter—it was all just heavenly. Even the international horserace that took place on the lake every year looked heavenly. The steaming breath of the horses as they dashed along. It looked heavenly. But it wasn't. In reality it was hell. Yes sir. And the rich ladies and gents in the grandstands, if you looked closer—which a jockey rarely gets a chance to do—most of them turned out to be harlots and wolves, not worthy of kissing his royal Irish arse.

"I'm on Hurricane lying second. My Irish arse is riding higher than my head. I say to myself: 'Take it easy, my boy, don't get excited like a pregnant nun, Hurricane can do it. Now I'm lying a neck behind Exeter III and my mate Randy Tooley is riding like a fucking monkey on a tobacco tin. Heya, Hurricane, pass him, pass Exeter, you can do it! *Hurrican does it.* And then—"

The ex-jockey's croaking voice snapped off. Beneath the long-billed cap his pinched face, little more than a wrinkled apple, stared out at the chain of row-boats, outboard motorboats and two barges that formed a wide semicircle across the corner of the lake. On one of the barges a kind of crane was mounted. The purring of a compressor motor—no doubt supplying air to the divers—reached us across the water with exaggerated clarity. In the blinding afternoon glare the orange collar insignia on Defila's uniform flashed brightly. The dwarfish man seemed to stare out through the motionless chain of boats—much farther out into the lake to a point even with the distant shoreline rock where I had apprehended Xana on that May night . . . Had Hurricane plunged through the ice at that point? Had that been the end of Jockey Dylan Fitzallan's racing career?

He turned back toward the Russian church portal of the Tattersall, pulled out a short meerschaum pipe, began filling it, and made a last few sounds like the final cling-clang of a wound-down music box: "See you later."

"See you later," I replied with the same, pleasantly noncomittal English phrase.

Villa Muongia was situated on the lakeshore about a hundred yards beyond the Tattersall. On the left I passed by the long pier where, by the light of the waning moon, I had seen the rucksack-laden printer cycle his way to a watery grave. An ambulance from the district hospital in Samedan was parked near the landing. The crowd of onlookers had dispersed. The Sunday sensation was all over. I walked onto the little bridge leading to the Villa over the pool-like lagoon, then stopped halfway across. The lagoon, enclosed in black and grayish pebbles, seemed to breathe with the ever-so-gentle stirrings of the south wind. Dragonflies buzzed back and forth across it, almost invisible in the watery sheen. Now, as two days before, I bent down over the pine railing. From its gray black pebbled shore the underwater banks of the lagoon fell away steeply, almost vertically downward. The deep green to obsidian black surface of the lake, barely rippled by the mild Maloja wind, was as transparent as the glass of a wine bottle. The cold "breath" of the Alpine lake, where no one (except perhaps a Finn) could bathe, even in summer, rose up to meet me. Gazing down into the underwater abyss some seventy feet deep I thought I saw something directly below me.

A beard.

A black patriarch's beard like the one in the ad for hair grower.

I tore the sun-shade from my monocle. Could it be? Could it be that officer Defila was searching for Zuan's body out *there* and all the time *here* . . .? With a languid undulating motion the long straggly beard seemed to be nodding up at me. Was I getting seasick?

Casual whipcracks from the Tattersall.

"Mis-ter Fitz-al-lan!!"

The Royal Jockey, Ret., pipe clamped in his teeth, rambled around the domed Byzantine structure. "What's the matter?" I waved him toward me. He waded through the sand of the riding path; when he reached the shoreline promenade I recognized for the first time that his bowlegs caused him trouble in walking. Like a circus pony, I thought, with bent haunches trying, but not quite managing, to execute a piaffe.

"Have a look!" I pointed down over the railing into the bottle green abyss. Did he see it? Down there. *That.* That thing that looked like a long, black human beard.

"Let's see." He plucked the pipe out of his mouth, pushed himself up onto the railing as if it were an exercise bar and told me to hold on to him since he had no desire to take a bath, and I held him as one holds up a small child at the zoo so that he can see over the fence into a cage. (He must have weighed no more than ninety pounds.)

"No, it's not him," he remarked with dry decisiveness, sliding back down onto the bridge. "Certainly not this poor chap Charlie Zuan."

"But wait—don't you think it looks like a beard?"

"Fucking seaweeds, maybe."

Today the ping-pong table stood unoccupied in the less than modest (that is, neglected, but not totally degenerated) garden of the Villa Muongia. There on the shedlike entrance porch of the three-story chalet, the rust-covered enamel sign:

RIT. FAMILIENPENSION
MORDECHAI KATZBEIN-BRIALOSZYNSKI
PROP.
COFFEE, TEA, HOMEMADE PASTRIES, KOSHER CUISINE
SPECIALTY : GEFILLTE FISH

The shed's front door—a makeshift device to keep out winter cold, removable in summer (but not removed)—was yawning wide, as was the house door behind it; the small Maloja wind had them both squeaking in their hinges. From out of the stairwell came the high-pitched, peeping giggle of a young girl—a laugh so unremitting that it made one suspect the laughter was a female cretin. I stood and listened. About every thirty seconds an enormous thud could be heard, whereupon the ceaseless giggling broke into a falsetto squeal. I walked through the porch, parted a curtain that seemed to have been bought at the closeout sale of a coffin supply house, and found myself the unsuspecting witness to an idyllic scene whose actors might just have stepped from a Chagall painting.

The laughing girl made an impression by no means cretinous. She was a beautiful Jewish girl of the Oriental type, seventeen or eighteen years old, with veritable almond eyes, her bare arms a bit too slender, a pigeon-gray scarf tied beneath her chin. At first I couldn't locate the cause of her amusement. One question alone jolted through me: How can she? How, in the year 1938, can a Jewish girl so lose herself in carefree, jubilant laughter, laughter without a trace of hysteria; at the same time I was touched by her unsuspecting light-heartedness. In anticipation of renewed amusement her mouse-high peeping stuck in her throat, and she peered up the staircase. Which disappeared up into a stuffy darkness far removed from the bright daylight outside.

Suddenly, in a rush, something came sliding out of the darkness.

A young rabbi in a long caftan, with a black velour hat pulled down over his ears, locks at his temples flying, freckled face and curly sideburns. He must have practiced his stunt for some time because his form and balance were perfected to a T. In a flash he rushed sidesaddle down the polished banister, leaped off just before the newel-post, flew out across the floor and landed in a kind of crouch on the worn-out doormat by the entrance—just in front of my funeral curtain. I could have caught him.

The girl puffed and broke out in another fit of laughter.

"Pardon me," I said, stepping through the curtain. "Excuse the inter-ruption. Hello. Could I speak with Mr. Katzbein?"

Accustomed to the windblown squeaking of the front door, the girl was tak-en unawares, even shocked by my appearance. Now her laugh was stiffled to a hiccup, she raised one hand to her mouth and stood there, speechless and mo-tionless, as if doing a pantomime of the Habima play *The Old Marketplace*. The young rabbi, more than embarrassed, surveyed me from head to foot, whereby my monocle and the cut of my Peyatchevich pants seemed to attract the greatest interest. Then he hastily lifted his furry cap and with a graceful gesture pointed mutely at a button on the wall, above which the following hand-printed card-board sign was tacked:

FOR SERVICE
PING TWICE

Unsure whether the writer had written "P" instead of "R" out of ignorance or negligence, I pinged twice. The young rabbi escorted the young girl through the *pompes-funèbres* curtain and out of the house where she, I assumed, would start her giggling again; not a sound. The sight of my monocle—I put it away—and my scarred brow seemed to have touched her somehow. Then from the garden I heard the flat clicking sound of a ping-pong match.

Across from me a second funeral curtain was moved aside.

"Mr. Katzbein? My name is Colana," I said. "Excuse me. Could I ask you a few questions?"

"Come in—into the salon."

He wore a black silk yarmulke, a shiny gray jacket (that did not remind me of armor), and a nickel-plated pair of glasses shielding a gentle gaze full of both suspicion and kindness. The latter, at my mention of the name Colana seemed to gain the upper hand.

"Sit down, Mr. Colana."

"Oh thank you very much, it's not really necessary. I won't bother you for more than five minutes." From the window I had a view of the barren garden and the ping-pong table—the sight of the two players was anything but barren.

"You aren't bothering me. May I offer you a cup of coffee?"

"No thank you. Do you happen to remember a couple of blond fellows, mm in about their mid-twenties, who played ping-pong here about a week ago with two of your guests? Distinguishing marks, mmm—one of them had pimples, the other one didn't. Both of them were wearing knickers and pullovers, pullovers with a so-called Tutankhamon pattern."

"Tutankhamon . . . Tutankhamon . . ."

I turned away from the window, Mr. Katzbein took off his nickel-plated glasses, breathed on them, then put them back on, only to discover that he hadn't cleaned them yet, took them off again and cleaned them, muttering: "Blond fellows . . . one with pimples . . . one without . . . knickers . . . pullovers . . . Tutankhamon . . . Tutankhamon . . . Tutankhamon . . ." The name of the Pharaoh who ruled Egypt in the days when the children of Israel were being forcibly evacuated—the repetition of this name seemed to be causing a kind of auto-suggestion. All at once his unbespectacled eyes stared as emptily as those of a daydreamer. I said, "They call themselves Mostny and Krainer. And they're probably from Vienna." Mr. Katzbein woke up and put on his glasses. "Mostny? Krainer? I can guarantee you, they never stayed here."

"Then they just stopped by here. I happened to be walking by your place recently about teatime and observed this dubious duo at a game of ping-pong doubles. Their partners were the two young gentlemen in caftans."

"Caftans? Was one of them Candidate Zibebener out there?"

"Quite possibly."

"Then the other one must have been Candidate Schmuel Blitz who just sailed from Genoa. Mazel tov, aha, I've got it!" Mr. Katzbein gave his yarmulke a triumphant little pat. "Blond! Knickerbockers! Tutankhamon pullovers! Of course, Tutankha-a-amon!" His satisfaction over the perfect functioning of his memory expressed itself in a little singsong. "They ordered two cups of tea and were acting a little bit sneaky with each other."

"Sneaky?"

"Yeah, well—one of them—quite right—talked like he was from Vienna—"

"Not the other one?"

"The other one, the one with the pimple face, if I'm not mistaken, he didn't talk at all. I even remember what the other one called him. Schorsch."

"*That's* them."

"Well, this Schorsch fellow doesn't say a word. But his pal keeps on talking and talking at him, and all the time he keeps making these funny hand motions in the air."

"What's that?" I asked quickly. "Are you trying to say that he *habitually* moved his hands while talking?"

"You mean the way some Jews do? No, it was different. I kept asking myself, what kind of funny business are they up to? Like two plotters in Schiller's *Conspiracy of Fiesko in Genoa*."

"*Really?* That's what you thought?"

"Well, yes."

"And you didn't bother to think *why* these two came, of all places, to the Villa Muongia?"

"Why? Don't get me wrong, but I'd be a busy man if I had to ask myself 'why' every time a tourist from the spa comes in here for coffee or tea."

"Did you make any conversation with these two men?"

"Just the conversation you have when people order something. The one fellow says, 'Two cups of tea with lemon,' and I ask, 'How about a little pastry to go with it?' and he says, 'Just two cups of tea with lemon.' Otherwise we had nothing to say to each other. And during their game of ping-pong they called out the score, and at the end of the game the one fellow called out, "Thank you, gentlemen. Ping-pong-Heil!"

"What, ping-pong-Heil? Very interesting. In what sort of tone? Sarcastically or what?"

"No. Just the way you say: Ski-Heil. Then they paid the check and left, that's all."

"And they never came back again? . . . They didn't. And you don't happen to know where they're staying?"

"You'll laugh, but I think I do know. Right behind the Segantini Museum there are just a few houses on the road through the Suvretta Forest. It's a chalet, not a hotel or a pension, but there's a sign on it: ROOMS FOR RENT."

"One last question Mr. Katzbein. Could the two of them, in your opinion, be Jewish?"

The proprietor of Villa Muongia handled this question with a worldly nonchalance one could almost call blasé. "Jewish? You mean, because there is such a thing as a blond Jew? That there is; just look at young Zibebener. Or because Mostny and Krainer *could* be Jewish names. Waaall, they *could* be, *could*. But let me whisper something in your ear, Mr. Colana, a real Jew can tell Jews from goyim in his sleep. Even without kibitzing on the ping-pong game."

What followed seemed to me as condensed and abbreviated as a telegram, like a page from the war diary I kept on the Piave. (And never continued.)

No time to look at Segantini's paintings. House behind museum on road leading through Suvretta to Campfèr. Not chalet. Small garage, mechanic's workshop or something, living quarters attached. Sign by front door:

CHAMBRES SANS BAIN A LOUER ?/TOURISTENZIMMER ZU VERMIETEN. Door ajar. I ring. Knock. Nobody. Walk in. Call out, hello. Nobody. On left side of hallway small house altar with burning candle. I think first, Virgin Mary. Step closer. No, *Penitent Magdalena* by Reni, color print. Realize as I step closer, wrong— neither, nor. *Il Duce* Benito Mussolini on the balcony of the Palazzo Venetia. . . Colored poster illuminated by oil lamp. I think, Holy Laudon, if the Two Blonds have taken up quarters *here*, then Trebla's march route is right on target.

Reexamine my conclusion. Perhaps working on false premise. Until his betrayal of Austria, Mussolini was the patron saint of Starhemberg's Austrian *Heimwehr*. Garage owner perhaps *Heimwehr* contact man in Graubuenden. Something I'd already considered—perhaps the Two Blonds are Viennese "Rooster-Tails" (*Heimwehr* men) who've taken refuge in Switzerland from *Gauleiter* Globocnik's terror tactics. Even though I shot it out with the Rooster-Tails in '34 I'm not out to get them now.

Hammering from the workshop. Lead-glass window on the street side. No way to look in. Above the closed garage door a horseshoe and BICYCLES, MOTOR-CYCLES FOR RENT. REPAIRS. MOTORCYCLE RIDES & TRANSPORT. (The same in French, German, and Italian.) G. PARETTA-PICCOLI, PROP. Him! Paretta-Piccoli, "the Fascist," as he liked to call himself. Hammering stops. Roll-whack, up goes the garage door, out he comes in person. Smeared blue overalls, beret. (Grotesque! This is exactly the kind of makeshift uniform worn by the antifascist International Brigade in Spain before it was able to get old cast-off French, etc., army uniforms.) Fellow flaunts his hostility; not even a hello. I, also without greeting: Do Messrs. Krainer and Mostny live here? Shakes his head. I: You've driven them around in your side car more than once. He, pouting: Now that the season's started he's had plenty of passengers—taxi drivers don't know the names of their fares either. Basta. Off he goes through the garage door, roll-whack, down it comes. I'd like to knock again and ask him to lavish his affections on my posterior. Forget it, because Paretta has unconsciously told me where I can find the domicile of the Tutankhamon Twins.

Before he walked off he sent a rat-quick glance across the street to a house. Just up the road. A chalet, entirely of wood.

I give myself some time. Paretta shouldn't know that I know. Road traffic increasing. Stroll along the left side of the road a short way into the Suvretta Forest. (In countries where they keep right, always walk on the left, facing the oncoming traffic, which can be sidestepped if necessary with an occasional torerolike maneuver: nothing new for a professional leftist.) Turn about face, hurry back to the chalet. For once, the "rightists" behind me. THUSNELDA'S MOUNTAIN LODGE. ATTRACTIVE ROOMS FOR RENT. (The whole sign in German only.) BREAK-FAST & DINNER AVAILABLE. GERMAN & VIENNESE COOKING. THUSNELDA HUPPEN-KOTHEN, REG. SWISS MASSEUSE, PHYSICAL THERAPIST (FORMERLY GERMAN VETERANS RESORT, DAVOS). If a detective in a thriller, I'd let out a soft whistle, but since returning from Grandpa's I've lost the feeling of being in a detective story. This sanatorium, according to Grandpa's information: "The Nazi HQ for making Switzerland into one more province of the Reich." Now things are getting serious! I ring.

House girl with Swabian accent shows me into library. Goethe. Schiller. Klopstock, Moerike. As always cultural requisites in good German homes. No Heinrich Heine. Gustav Freytag, Felix Dahn. Warm, getting warmer. The master-race goon Houston Stewart Chamberlain: *Foundations of the Nineteenth Century*. Hot. Inconspicuous on the next shelf my fellow Austrian Kolbenheyer, Hans Grimm *Volk ohne Raum*. Hotter, hottest—Moeller von den Bruck, *The Third Reich*; Alfred Rosenberg, *Myth of the Twentieth Century*. (No *Mein Kampf*, probably on the night table.) On the music stand of a Bechstein grand a thick score of Wagner's *King* arranged for piano, open to the "Ride of the Valkyrie." No Fuehrer-portrait on the pine-paneled walls (after all she's a registered *Swiss* masseuse), instead *German People in the German Forest* by Max Zaeper, several Hanfstengl prints of Spitzweg paintings ("the Fuehrer's favorite painter") and, staring at each other from dead, plaster-cast eyes the death masks of Wagner and Nietzsche (who, it's well known, were friends at first, then later deadly enemies). The whole decor almost too perfect to be true.

The high point of it all, Thusnelda in person. An ankle-length gown of white linen embroidered with green and brown—early Germanic?—runes, a necklace of stamped bronze plates like the breast-shields worn by Amazons; sandals. Her head an ad for suntan oil: dark-tanned face gleaming as if shellacked, hair much darker than straw blond, braided above her ears in thick "snail" spirals, severely parted down the middle. Mid-thirties; type: Nordic-SS-child-bearer.

She: "Thussi Huppenkothen."

I: "Pleased to meet you. Adelhart von Stepanschitz."

"My pleasure as well. What can I do for you?" Seems to expect response. Do you massage men too? Surveys me: seems to react positively to my monocle with sun shield (which I had inserted again after leaving the Villa Muongia) and my manner.

"Pardon me—" I consider saying *Volksgenossin*, but say—"dear lady, might I speak with Mr. Krainer or Mr. Mostny?"

If she says certainly, one moment—what then? I can only beat a hasty retreat, since Thusnelda's Mountain Lodge is hardly a suitable battlefield.

"The gentlemen have gone out."

"Oh, that's unfortunate." So this is where they're staying! The state of things is becoming clear at last. The state of war. "You don't by any chance know where they went?"

"Are you a friend of theirs, Mr. von Stepan——?"

"-schitz. I've been sent here by a common friend of ours."

"Oh, I see. Yes, yesterday the gentlemen took a hike up to the glacier and so today they've decided to take it somewhat easier."

"Might I find them in Café Hanselmann?"

"Oh, definitely not. They went for a walk. Yes, now I remember ..."
"Thussi," previously of the German Veterans Resort, snaps two of her muscular
fingers. "Mr. Krainer spoke about wanting to go for a stroll by the lakeshore at
the foot of Piz Rosatsch—"

"Ah yes—in the Mauntschas."

"I assume that's what they call the area. Mr. Mostny went out ahead because Mr. Krainer had to wait for the long distance call he had placed earlier—"

A shot in the dark: "Vienna."

"Right. You *must* know the gentlemen."

"Casually." A second shot in the dark: "A call for Laimgruber?"

Thussi stares at me, the forget-me-not eyes bizarrely bright in her bronzed
face. The sight of my monocle again seems to have a positive effect on her.

"That I don't know. When Mr. Krainer was finished with his call I told him
his brother had already left and he got a little upset."

"His—brother?"

"Why yes? Didn't you know that Mr. Georg Mostny is Mr. Krainer's stepbrother?"

"Stepbrother, yes yes, of course."

"Well then. You also must know that Mr. Krainer doesn't like Mr. Mostny
to go out by himself."

I think something like, a two-man squad has to stick together until their
mission is accomplished, and mumble of course.

"So then. Mr. Krainer went off in a hurry to catch up with Mr. Mostny."

"Aha."

"Shall I give them a message?"

"Thank you very much, that won't be necessary. Perhaps I'll meet them
later at Hanselmann's after all. How long will they be here?"

"Until Wednesday, it seems."

"Day after tomorrow ... And then back to Vienna?"

This question goes too far. Frost on the forget-me-nots. "I'm afraid I can't
tell you that."

"All right. Do you message men too?"

Back down to the spa; double time; light, rhythmical slap of the Walther
against my hip. Fitz at his post between Tattersall and ominous pier. Have a
question on the tip of my tongue. Fitz doesn't let me open my mouth. Continues his grumbling. As if I hadn't even left him. No doubt Dr. de Colana had
been completely stinko, otherwise he wouldn't have driven into the Lake Campfèr. They found de Colana's body, but the corpse of this poor chap Zuan would
never be recovered. Zuan, too, had no doubt been stinko, otherwise he wouldn't
have pedaled his way into Lake Moritz. His (Fitz's) own grandfather had died
from drinking at the age of twelve; to be exact from drinking too much John

Jamieson, therefore he, the grandson, was always wary of alcohol. I, in a hurry: That's a good idea, Mr. Fitzallan, did two chaps just come by here, both blonds, probably in knickers and Tutankhamon sweaters? Fitz, stubborn at first: Were they stinko too? I, pressed but composed: definitely not stinko. He, Fitz, had seen them playing Russian billiards at Pizzagalli's the Saturday before last. Now Fitz remembers and makes the connection.

About half an hour before a blond fellow like that walked past the Tattersall toward Sur Punt. Aha, over to the Mauntschas? Yes sir. Alone? Yes sir; twenty minutes later the second one, also alone, walking much faster, almost running. Also toward the Mauntschas? Exactly. I: Before we had our chat? Fitz: Sure, sure, before that. And he supposed I doubted that his grandfather had drunk himself to death at the age of twelve. As quickly as possible I allayed his fears.

Ten minutes later I have the spa behind me, order my entire company—i.e., me solo—to fan out into the Mauntschas.

5

Ghost-train Monday, 4:05 P.M.

Corduroy jacket slung over my right shoulder, I climbed, following my nose like a hunting dog depending on his sense of smell. In that hour I placed a great, a terribly great trust in my nose. I was a hunting dog that had left the pack and gone over to the other side—to the hunted animals. And now in the name of all the hunted animals I was out to get the hunters. In that hour I placed a great, a terribly great trust in my Walther. I was the one-man-patrol Trebla on a penetration raid into no man's land.

The patrol turned off the path along the stream and ascended a trail paved with dead pine needles (no more larches) to the top of a foothill. Before sending my unit down into a densely wooded hollow, I took a look back and caught sight of St. Mo's lake at the end of a firelane, and all the way down the lane (the lakeshore remained invisible) not a person nor an animal nor a house—nor a boat on the visible section of the lake—could be seen. And the lake looked like a deep one—in accordance with the proverb about still waters being deep—and seemed to be covered with a kind of bottle-green opaque gooseflesh, as if it felt cold. A slice of thoroughly Nordic landscape—a fiord landscape. Up above through a narrow opening, a piece of the Piz Nair's barren crest and above it the exhaustingly cloudless fantastically cornflower-blue heaven of the south. Norway in Italy. But the Italian sky could not bring the fiord to smile.

Three enormous crows came sailing up the firelane, very slowly, soundlessly, barely moving their pitch-black wings. The three Norns? Mythological speculations had no place in a penetration raid.

One-man-patrol Trebla marched carefully into the hollow, the lake now out of sight, abandoned the abandoned path, moved at random into the trees of the wind-protected depression, trudging over moss-covered ground—only seldom did a branch crack underfoot. The pines grew relatively far apart and offered slight resistance to an off-trail advance—the only obstacles were rocks and boulders of various sizes. In times past they had cracked off of the Rosatsch Massif or had been loosened from the rubble of the slope and had flattened many a tree as they fell, but the wounds were long healed and the winds had covered the stones with humus, in which gnarled scrub-trees like dwarf pines and green elders had taken root, along with a few stunted stone pines. Of all these boulders the one that had fallen the farthest was the one Xana had crawled onto back on that frosty night in May after we received the news of Maxim Grabscheidt's sudden demise in Dachau . . . Not a very appropriate conversation topic for a unit on patrol. Or was it? After all, this story was a large part of the reason for this raid.

The larches, much taller than the stone pines, grew more and more prevalent, with their strange, spider-webbish, rather ghostlike green golden needles that simulated autumn. A distant, steady rushing sound, not wind blowing through the treetops, perhaps a waterfall on the Quellenberg. One-man patrol Trebla stalked around a long, scrub-covered chunk of cliff and suddenly found himself in a small clearing overgrown with stunted green alders. In the midst of it a lonely—grave?

JAN
1895 (Amsterdam)—1907

A squarish stone sunken in the forest moss, surrounded by a low, rust-eaten, wrought-iron fence, a black marble stone, too smooth for moss or lichens to get a foothold on it. No flowers on the grave, not even the withered remains, not even the ghost of a flower. Inscription in round Gothic letters whose gold leaf was still intact, though weathered to the point of complete dullness. The black marble gleamed timelessly.

JAN
1895 (Amsterdam)—1907

What might be interred here in this trackless wilderness? The bones of a twelve-year-old Dutch boy who died here thirty years ago? How? Was the poor child struck by a rock tumbling off the Rosatsch? The boulders had lain in this forest for hundreds of years. Or was he struck by lightning? More likely. Or did this Jan have an accident while sledding in the winter? No sled run here. And why no ornaments around the terse epitaph; no cross? Were the bereaved parents freethinkers? And was it allowed at all to bury an accident victim at the scene of his misfortune (especially in a country that made anything but sparing use of legal prohibitions)? Or was a dog buried here? Even more probable. A dog caught killing game by the forester and shot before his master, a tourist from Amsterdam, could intervene . . . I had to think of the stipulation in de Colana's will.

JAN
1895 (Amsterdam)—1907

I could have asked ten Breukaa if it hadn't been for our little spat; and if I weren't involved in a war right now. Joop, who lived not far from here, probably knew what Jan it was that rested here, child or dog . . . Suddenly one-man-patrol Trebla was seized by a feeling rather unbecoming to a military unit; a feeling of pity for the unknown victim lying underground.

Perhaps in peacetime this would have been the place to utter a small, pancreationist prayer.

Then the call echoed over from the slopes of the Quellenberg.

About a mile distant, it was inarticulate, but not a yodel. First a drawn-out "O-o-o. . .o-o-o!" Pause. "O-o-o-o. . .o-o-o!" Both times the final "o" dropped down a major third. Then a much shorter call, though far away, clearly insistent, even impatient, ". . . o!"

It could be the enemy. It could be Krainer looking for Mostny. One-man-patrol Trebla went into action. Rolled up the corduroy jacket and shoved it under a bushlike green elder, pulled the Walther out of its holster, extracted the magazine, checked for the six rounds plus one in the chamber, tugged the jersey down over the reholstered gun. Then the calling from the Quellenberg came again, now a bit closer it seemed; still impossible to tell if the "o-o" was really "Sho-orsh." Take cover immediately.

Not far from Jan's grave the massive piece of cliff once broken from the mountain's slope loomed long and nearly five yards high amidst the surrounding larches, cutting the clearing almost in half; it was flat on top and covered with dwarf-pines whose trunks bowed down across the rock, and on the sides was covered with clumps of moss that made it easy to climb: a kind of natural hunter's redoubt. Once on top the one-man patrol crept on all fours through the twisted branches, stretched out in the prone position, waited, felt well concealed. If the enemy passed by Jan's grave in search of his "missing unit"—even though the Peyatchevich pants were not exactly field gray, he would never see them. For a better view, crawl forward to the edge of the boulder's top, even at the risk of ruining the Peyatchevich pants. (They're not the only things at risk here. Besides, there's a reserve supply of eight pairs in Vienna I, Schoenlaterngasse—but then again, they must have been seized by Laimgruber long ago as "subversive material.") The flat roof the boulder measured about twenty-five yards in length. The one-man patrol had crawled his way nearly to the brink—

"O-o-o . . . o-o-o! (-o!) O . . . o! (O!)"

The caller in the forest. He had advanced audibly closer in the direction of Jan's grave, and his drawn-out call with its major third plus the following shout was now mimicked by a muffled echo. But as before he was marching too far out of range for me to hear an articulation like "Shorsh!" One-man-patrol Trebla, waiting at the outermost edge of the boulder's top, was about to utter the deceptive cry "Here!" so as to lure the caller into a trap—when he looked down . . . and froze.

Holy Laudon! Three or four paces from the foot of the rock lay the enemy. The enemy's "lost unit." Mostny lay, asleep, Silent Shorsh, his Tutankhamon sweater folded beneath his left cheek as a pillow, dressed in knickers and a flowered Salzburg shirt with rolled-up sleeves revealing a long, muscular right arm (the left arm pinned beneath his other side)—an arm reddened with a fresh sunburn, covered with blond hair. Yes, the pale-blond hair stood sharply out against the nearly lobster-colored, peeling skin. I was that close to him. So close that I could make out the flies walking through the forest of whitish blond arm hairs. Now the arm moved slightly in a sleeper's reflex to shake off the flies; now it lay motionless again, stretched out over the moss. His long, powerful hand, it too lobster red and covered with white blond hair, was open—as if the man were ready to reach for something in his sleep.

Two handspans away from the moss-clutching fingers lay a rifle. A relatively small, light weapon, obviously a Flobert carbine.

The fellow had taken off his shoes, so-called Tyrolean boots, and set them on the moss, heel by heel. A tall bastard, at least six feet six. And what long legs the guy has got, stockinged in patterned (not Tutankhamon) white woolen knee socks; what big feet—like a deformity. The sleeper's face is turned away, but not enough to conceal his relaxed, almost stupid expression. The acne on his face less obvious due to his sunburn. His shock of white blond hair, usually combed back, is mussed by sleep and hangs in shaggy fringes over his lobster-red nose, one long strand pushed out at regular intervals by the slow breathing of my sleeping enemy.

. . . Henrique Kujath hunted about until he discovered the blond snake. It was rolled up asleep on the swampy river bank . . .

He killed it with twelve shots.

"Why," I inquired, "did you do that?"

"Because I'd been forced to sweat blood for hours on end by that beast, that's why I had to shoot him."

"Beg your pardon," I said, "but I think that was a bit unfair."

"What?"

"Killing the thing while it was sleeping."

*"Unfair?! Oi vay, my son. I see black for you in the jungle future we've got
ahead of us. Black-black-black."*

I flicked off the tiny safety-catch on the Walther—the Walther whose iridescent mother-of-pearl grip gleamed in my half-open hand, two inches in front
of my eye. In a split second, as if I had never seen it before, I read over the
trademark stamped underneath the short barrel, CARL WALTHER WAFFENFABRIK
ZELLA-MEHLIS/TH. MOD. PPK KAL. 7.65 MM.

Grandpa Kujath was right: Unfair, huh, what?! I will shoot Mostny and the
shots will call Krainer to the scene, one-two-three, and then I'll shoot Krainer,
perhaps in front of Jan's grave, who knows, and it will be a routine operation (of
the kind *they* planned to carry out against *me*). One-man-patrol Trebla! Put
your finger on the trigger and think about a clown glued to the high voltage
wires in Dachau. And think of a poor man's doctor from Graz sitting in a cattle
car with a ceremonial dagger in his forehead. Think of an electrocuted clown.
Think of an electrocuted old clown and don't waste any more time.

The airplane came from Italy. It flew northward at considerable height,
an inconspicuous, pigeon-gray cross sailing out into the sea of air that was
framed within the motionless larch-tops of the clearing's edge, out into the path
of cornflower-blue sky that showed no sign it would ever redden into a summer
evening and finally turn pale. Although the plane's altimeter may have indicated 14,000 feet for its leap across the Alps, to me, lying on my stomach 7,000
feet below, its engine nose seemed shockingly close and, yes, threatening.

Glancing up briefly I got the feeling of wartime, the feeling of World War I
or II (the latter existing not only in Spain but even, it was clear, in the Mauntschas as well). The Royal Rumanian attack and reconnaissance planes I faced
while stationed at Brăila with the Thirty-sixth Recon. Co. were beneath criti-
cism; the Royal Italian fighters, on the other hand, which came flying singly
into the Brenta Valley and dove from considerable heights to attack Levico
(Eleventh Imperial Army) were often fantastically daring and deadly aerial acrobats—no less fearsome than the English flyers. Caught up in a sudden, involuntary reminiscence I thought, Tally-ho, there's another Italian acrobat sailing over the mountains; in a moment he'll dive . . . before our relatively slow
Brandenburgs can get airborne (without me; no longer fit to fly) . . . when I was
jerked back to reality by the surprisingly penetrating drone of the distant plane.
If the noise is enough to rouse the sleeping enemy . . . Now every second counts.

The noisy little cross sailed out of sight beyond the clearing's patch of sky.
But its droning ebbed away slowly. Dropping down, my gaze was caught by
some delicate, blood-red dots among the larch needles: female blossoms. The
moss next to Mostny's carbine was, I now noticed, spattered with four or five
such blood-red dots. Fallen larch blossoms, no doubt.

Blood-red blossoms, blood type B. The things that go through your head in decisive moments! Then suddenly it made sense to me. That could be tremendously important. What had just gone through my head. Every member of the SS has the symbol of his blood type branded under his left arm! I'd seen this once in Woellersdorf detention camp—on fellow internees, Austrian Nazis who had gone over to the Reich, to the *Austrian Legion* headquarters in Passau, and had been sent back as saboteurs and then captured. As was amply visible when they washed up in the morning, every one of them wore an A, a B, or an O branded inside and above his left bicep. The ones marked with a zero became special objects of ridicule for us, the interned members of the Republican Defense Corps.

I would give the tall fellow one last chance. Even if such generosity involved the risk that one-man-patrol Trebla might be wiped out. I would force him to show me his armpit. If an A, a B or an O turned up, then one-man-patrol Trebla would start shooting. Straight through the Peyatchevich pants would be the best way; yes, I meditated, my forehead still pounding, when I jumped down—not much over ten feet if I first let myself down on a tree branch—I'd best hold the Walther ready in my right pants pocket, otherwise it might fly out of my hand as I landed, and the snoozing galoot would wake with a start, grab his Flobert, amazed (for two seconds, no longer) that the prey he had pursued so long was so obligingly appeared for his own execution, and the abrupt end of this heroic story would be the no-man-patrol Trebla: Jan, 1895 (Amsterdam)—1907; Albert, 1899 (Olmuetz)—1938.

I clicked on the safety again and shoved my hand with the pistol deep into my pants pocket, grasped a sturdy pine branch with my left hand, let myself dangle from the overhanging limb, then dropped from the boulder and landed in a crouch on both feet, my left hand on the soft forest moss, not three paces from Mostny, grabbed his carbine and weighed it in my hand for a split second, in my left hand, while my right—thumb on the safety, finger on the trigger—clasped the Walther in my pocket, and a split second later I realized how strangely light the rifle was: this was no Flobert but an air rifle, the kind you give to a ten-year-old boy for target practice—and realized as well: the blood-red spots in the moss were not larch blossoms but little bolts fringed with red wool—toy bullets for a pneumatic rifle. But in the Mauntschas there were no woodchucks to fool, and nobody—no woodchuck and no straw-blond galoot was going to fool me this time, and I flung the air rifle in a high arc thirty yards across the clearing and saw the tall fellow, silent Shorsh, get slowly to his feet, an expression of sleepy stupidity, then boundless amazement on his long, lobster-red, spotted, peeling face, and bouncing back two or three steps I ordered him: "Take off your shirt! Hands up!" and heard the cry—not from the forest but from the tall fellow in front of me, a moderately loud cry, or better a helpless, shrill, gurgling attempt to stammer, a sound that struck the membrane of my head wound like a blow. For it was the throaty, inarticulate cry of a man who had no tongue.

6

Ghost-train Monday, 5:25 P.M.

I sat in Pizzagalli's bar on a long-legged stool over an espresso and three grappas (the latter taken in succession). Annette had informed me *un monsieur* had called at five o'clock and asked to speak with me. He had spoken German (not dialect), left no name, would try again within the next hour.

And so one tips a caffè espresso and nips three brandy chasers.

Hadn't I been *right* in assuming Laimgruber had set a two-man squad on my tail? My behavior that led them to suspect I was on the lookout. Then their strategic withdrawal to St. Moritz.

The night drive to the Domleschg. The midnight tales of the Luzienburg: Giaxa's last ride and Dr. Grabscheidt's last journey.

The false alarm I had given myself in the morning twilight on Julier Pass. My inability to tell Xana about Papa-Rose's end. Because of this my bad, miserably bad conscience, my sudden decision to go over from defense to offense, to avenge the sudden deaths of Giaxa and Maxim with the sudden deaths of two deadly enemies, and in this way, yes, to make up to my wife for not telling her.

My one-man-reconnaissance patrol to the Villa Muongia and from there to Thusnelda's Mountain Lodge. Where my last doubts were eliminated, where I became absolutely certain that I was hunting my own hunters.

And then: one-man-patrol Trebla moves out into the Mauntschas. Near Jan's grave, discovery of the Two Blonds—status as deadly enemy virtually dead certain.

And then, in the truest sense of the word, I fell upon the sleeping Shorsh.

And then?

The inarticulate, speechless cry of my victim.

The frantic, worried calling of the other man from the nearby woods: "Shorsh, where *are* you?!! What *is* it?!! *Wait,* I'm *coming!*"

My hasty retreat from the Mauntschas.

Conclusion: Laimgruber didn't do it. Everything is all right—that is, all wrong. He didn't send any killers to gun me down. Not yet anyway. Not these two blonds. Not them.

Last night in the tower studio of the Luzienburg, Valentin Tiefenbrucker's billiard-game report of Giaxa's last performance not only brought on Grandpa Kujath's heart attack but also a kind of temporary apathy in myself. So that after helping toss the billiard table overboard I was not all ears for certain parts of

Grandpa's blubbering "farewell address" (which seemed to help him recover from the attack), but only, you might say, half ears. ". . . measures to protect the genetic health of the German people and to prevent the transfer of hereditary disease; the extermination of 'unworthy' life, a special hobby of the Fuehrer's. As long as two years ago the Reich's chief medic, Dr. Wagner, said, 'To be ready for eventual war we must go forward with the program!' . . . Hitlermann is not about to let his private hobby out of his own hands. Planning and execution are transferred to the Fuehrer's own chancellery . . . Secret directive of *Reichsleiter* Philip Nebbish-noodle, or whatever his name is: *The blessing of euthanasia* may only be granted to those of German or racially related stock. May! By the way, Trebla," Grandpa blubbered out his cascade of horror, "did you know that they've already started performing these X-X's, I mean extermination experiments at the Waldesruh Sanatorium—in Purkersdorf I think—near Vienna?"

Uncle Adolf's X-X and Laimgruber's little black card file. I had been on the wrong track in my hunt for the hunters, as Albert Woodchuck-hunter-hunter in pursuit of the Two Blonds. I had overestimated Laimgruber's hostility, overestimated his zeal. The realization had struck me back there by Jan's grave at the moment I jumped down upon the sleeping Shorsh and heard his unarticulated cry of fear . . .

WE ARE NOT CREATED FOR THE TRUTH.
WHAT CONCERNS US IS OPTICAL ILLUSION.

ABBÉ GALIANI

This farewell message left for me by a dipsomaniac lawyer on the wall of an outhouse in Sils seemed to corroborate the evidence that, from the first moment I met the Two Blonds in Roseg Valley, I had been the victim of an optical illusion. Ever since June 2. For three weeks now. Even if I weren't created for it, the incident near Jan's grave should have left me in no doubt about the truth.

Why not assume that Shorsh really *is* named Mostny and the other man is Krainer, and that the latter really *is* his stepbrother, just as Physical Therapist Thusnelda told me. At the end of May the two stepbrothers arrive at the Hotel Morteratsch in Pontresina. Both Viennese, as revealed by their accents. *Their* accents? No, clearly not, just Krainer's, because no one ever heard Mostny utter a single word—just an occasional stupid laugh. (You don't need a tongue to laugh.) *A stupid laugh*, but *not a word*, neither on the veranda of the Morteratsch, nor during the first encounter in Roseg Valley, nor during the second encounter at the tramway station in Chantarella, nor during their billiard game here in Pizzagalli's bar (before de Colana drove me out to Sils). And today, Ghost-train Monday, Mr. Katzbein-Brialoszynski: "This Shorsh fellow doesn't say a word." And later on in the Mauntschas as I literally fell upon Mostny and he tried to call for help—tried and miserably failed—at that moment the scales fell from my eyes, as they say. Incredible I hadn't noticed it sooner; after all, I'd had a certain amount of experience with mutes. Not just from my acquaintance with a group of deaf-mutes in Graz who met every night in the trolley-stop shelter on the Jacominiplatz (many of them had done courier work for me in the years of party illegality). When I landed in the head wound department of Grosswardein Hospital I had shuddered to hear the animal-like, no—neither human nor animal-like utterances of men whose speech had been shot away. Then I had occasion to study the motor aphasia of brain-damaged fellow invalids, i.e., the most severe speech impediments, and to discuss causes and forms of muteness with Chief Medical Officer von Rohleder and later with Admiral's Staff Surgeon von Eiselberg (who performed my third operation in the Vienna General Hospital). Georg Mostny was no war casualty—too young. Nor was he a deaf-mute. I knew from my Jacominiplatz acquaintances that deaf-mutes could be very agile. Also Krainer had *spoken* to Mostny several times in my presence and the latter had understood—and even laughed in a way that sounded mean, almost vicious to me. If I had listened more closely I ought to have recognized: it was the laugh of a cretin.

Now that I had shaken off my optical illusion I was able to see.

Georg Mostny, Shorsh, is obviously a case of mutism. His constant silence, his doughy complexion, his belated case of teenage acne (rendered less conspicuous by his sunburn), how could I have overlooked these symptoms? Perhaps he had been an inmate of a Viennese sanatorium (it didn't have to be Waldesruh in Purkersdorf), when his relatives heard rumors about the Fuehrer's mercy-killing program. Then Mostny's frightened relatives send his stepbrother Krainer to get the patient out of the brand-new German Reich before this "beneficial" program can be initiated ... The conspiratorial sign-language Mr. Katzbein noticed them using—isn't that further proof?

If that were the truth: Krainer supplies himself with foreign currency and takes his retarded stepbrother to Switzerland. (Euthanasia refugees, the latest horror on the black-black market.) Perhaps the Engadine climate does Mostny good, or one of the two has hay fever. The Morteratsch in Pontresina is a reasonably priced hotel; but there across the street in the post office lives this guy with a pretty wife and an ugly scar on his forehead, and this guy begins to pester you for no known reason. Is it a Viennese Nazi on a hay-fever cure who could report your presence to Vienna? After asking himself this question Krainer moves with his protégé to St. Moritz.

Roses are red./ Violets are blue./ Who's the Nazi?/ *YOU!* A dreadful comedy of errors. That Krainer was playing ping-pong with his mute half-brother on the lawn of the Jewish pension. Playing. Isn't that considered therapy for this kind of malady? For Krainer it may just have been another guesthouse on the lake. Or did he, whose stepbrother was threatened by euthanasia, feel drawn to those facing a similar kind of persecution? And the fact that they were seen riding in a Mussolini-lover's side car? What should Krainer have to fear? Paretta-Piccoli has cheap transportation to offer, no more, no less. And the masseuse-landlady Thusnelda Huppenkothen, formerly of the German War Veterans Resort, Davos—a real textbook "*Nazesse*"? Now she appears as the last link in my false conclusion. An SS-assassination team sent by Laimgruber surely would never have decided to stay there—throwing caution and disguise to the winds. Perhaps Krainer was more interested in the landlady's main profession: physical therapy. Isn't such therapy recommended in cases of mutism? And when Shorsh, having escaped his protector's supervision, makes camp in the midst of the forest and I search him out the way Krainer calls out "Sho-orsh!" (one more proof that Mostny is *not* deaf); the way I jump down from the rock, grab the supposed carbine and, tossing it away, discover it is too light for a Flobert. A child's gun, a *toy* Krainer has given to Mostny—because play is part of the treatment for his condition . . . If that were the truth . . . And how could it be otherwise?

A confused prisoner in the hall of mirrors of a criminal age, I had mistaken a semi-cretinous fugitive from mercy killing for a specially trained commando agent of the master race. And I had come within a hairsbreadth of killing him. And the other one too. As the result—almost literally—of a Chaplinesque mistake.

At a nearby table Mavegn's bass voice echoed cavernously as if issuing from a glacial crevasse. "When I lead with clubs you don't play clubs, you play spades!" I heard his partner answer somewhat hesitantly that he didn't have a spade, then heard the police magnate growl, "He doesn't have a spade!" and his table-banging fist. "Dolt!"

The swinging doors to the bar stood open (hooked that way by Annette) and so I could see through to a section of the road leading up from St. Moritz-Bad. Beyond the embankment of the fork leading to Campfèr I saw the flashing black top of the Austro-Daimler limousine rising slowly. As slowly as if it were not being driven but being hoisted by an invisible crane. Behind the closed left-side window I recognized a bust portrait of Bonjour (profile) in his olive green livery, and in the back seat a figure, white on white . . . which my good eye was able to recognize—but not before two seconds had elapsed—as Xana . . . and during this space of time (there is space in even the smallest box) the driver and the passenger in their crane-hoisted snowmobile appeard to me like two dolls.

Vienna, Prater amusement park: A JOLLY VOYAGE TO AFRICA.

Sliding quickly off the barstool I asked Annette to come out and get me if the mysterious caller should ring again. Hurrying outside I shouted: "Bonjour!" an exclamation unlikely to draw much attention—just the cliché greeting of a loudmouth. Ten Breukaa's chauffeur switched on the left turn signal and steered over to stop in front of Pizzagalli's American Bar and gave me a mechanical nod through the glass (the right-side windows were closed too), like a man who felt out of place as a servant-chauffeur, a man unable to devote himself exclusively to his real profession of gardening. Maybe the Spahi Farid Gaugamela is not the only one who's out of place at Acla Silva . . . Only after I knocked on the right-rear window did the woman roll it down. Even though the glass separating driver and passenger was shut, she spoke rather softly.

"Bonjour—"

"*Bonjour, madame.*" God knows I had no desire to make bad jokes with her; I really thought she had greeted me this way.

"Bonjour just took ten Breukaa to the train station—"

"Joop traveling again? Out to get more Great Danes?"

"He got a long-distance call and then left immediately for Genoa. Without Pola."

"Why Genoa?"

"I think it's something about an old Dutch ocean liner the Italians want to buy."

This time I couldn't resist a bad joke. "Used ocean liner, like new, low mileage, for sale cheap."

What struck me was the pallor. The pallor of her small but *real* smile.

"Then Bonjour tanked up the car and now he's driving me home, and you're not supposed to come along," she said without reproach, merely confirming a fact.

She could know nothing of my recent military debacle, nothing about my waiting for a telephone call.

No foal's gaze this time. The young woman in white looked straight past me at a frog-green poster.

"I imagine you won't want to miss the festivities at the Innmuehle."

Holy Laudon, isn't it my duty now to *tell her everything?* Shouldn't I send Bonjour away and take Xana for a walk in the Suvretta Woods? (Pizzagalli's Bar was not the ideal place for revelations.) Give her Elsabé's long letter to read . . . or read it to her . . . and then, perhaps using Zuan's suicide as a starting point . . . tell her about Papa-Rose's proud demise . . . at first without going into the details? Without mentioning Giaxa's last ride on Giselher Liebhenschl's dun-colored stallion—

Dun-colored.

The dun-colored upholstery of the back seat over which hung the ends of a seven-foot-long white chiffon scarf I had never seen before. Xana had it pulled over her hair and tied beneath her chin.

"Where did you get the Isadora Duncan scarf?"

"Pola did me the honor. She's also got one for you that she's keeping a secret."

"Just as long?"

Her pale, almost white smile: "Shorter I think. In baby-blue."

"You've got to watch out for those long scarves when you're in a car. You know what happened to Isadora. This grotesque, long scarf trailed along outside a roadster and got wrapped around the rear axle and—"

"—strangled her, I know. But this car is no roadster." With that she cranked up the window and knocked on the glass partition. Rather awkwardly, Bonjour turned halfway around in his seat, and with her pale, white smile Xana gave him a graceful hand signal, and only now did I realize not just her nose, her whole face was powdered white, too white. The vermilion red was absent from her lips—had she, after taking an afternoon nap at Acla Silva, forgotten to put it on again and, instead of using lipstick, powdered her lips white? Yes, her lips seemed powdered too, and her powdered lips smiled at me from behind the window—which she suddenly rolled down again.

"*You* take care of yourself and don't let any woodchuck whistles get you going . . ." Something like an expression of deep thought crossed her face as if she wanted to add one last word (the name Trebla?) but had forgotten it. Then she looked straight up into my eyes, no, just a bit above them to my forehead and her blue irises stood out like spots of paint against the whiteness of her scarf and face:

"Your pulse is fast. I can see it. *Please* take care of yourself. I don't want . . ."

One of her famous pauses? But there followed nothing more. She cranked the window back up and Bonjour turned the car in front of the boccia lanes and drove off in the direction of the main road and Xana sat in the back seat, white on white on dun-colored upholstery, and said good-bye with a slight wave of her hand without turning around (she almost never looks back) and drove away surrounded by panes of glass, and I, with a bit of a lump in my throat, thought, Snow White.

"*Monsieur! On vous demande au téléphone.*"

I went back to the bar.

"*C'est lui,*" Annette said confidentially.

Ghost-train Monday, 5:55 P.M.

"I finally gotta holda ya, comrade." Pfiffke's voice, the voice of the Luzien-burg "castellan" and Kujath-driver, sounded muffled as if he were speaking through a wad of cotton or—hardly conceivable in the Swiss phone service—there was a fade out from a bad connection. "I'm callin' from down inna phone boot, 'cause I dit'n wanna use da phone up in da Burg. Ya neva know who could be plugged in dere list'nin, 'specially in de afternoon. I aweady tried ta get ya two times. Once at home and once at dis number dey gay-me dere. An I coult'n getcha anyplace. Not only dat but dey need me uppa-ta house so I coult'n juss waitaroun for ya da buzz me back."

"Hi, Pfiff. Do me a favor and go easy on the Berlin talk if you can. Otherwise I won't be able to follow you. Sure they need you up there today."

"Whadda ya mean, sure?" This sounded nearer, sharper.

"Well, on the night before Grandpa's seventieth I imagine you've got your hands full."

A fluctuation in the line, but no answer.

"Pfiff, you still there?"

"Yeah, I'm still dere." This sounded muffled again. "I wan-ned ta tell ya—we foun' it."

"What did you find?"

"Two-a da young guys from da mill an me. Da French bil-yerd. Da big bil-yerd table you tree gents trew outa da tower lass night. Not much lefta da big clunker; justa pile a sticks wid a green rag hangin' on it."

"You went all the way to a phone booth to tell me *that?*"

"Naw. Dat's not da reason."

"Well then, where's the fire?"

"Dere's . . . no fire any more."

"What's that? *Where* is there no fire any more?"

"It's burnt to a cinder."

"It? What's burned?"

"Well, hang on Trebla. Da Fieseler-Storch dat was takin' our friend ta Cata-lone-ya—"

"N-o!!"

"We got da news from Paris at eleven a-clock. It all happened b-'tween Tarragona and Cambrils, over a point o' land called Punta de Salou."

"Is Valentin dead?"

"Da Fascists got dere airbase on da B'learic Islens, you know dat. Well, da Heinies from da Condor Legion, our good ol' fellow Germans," Pfiff's voice seemed to gain strength from the increased speed of his blabbered imitation of Grandpa's speech, "always come roarin' over ta da main-land ta bomb Mod-esto's army—"

"I asked you if Valentin was dead!"

"Juss listen! Mon-sure Leotard, his pilot, comes puttin' across dis Punta de Salou, an somebody, some radio man, musta been asleep at da switch or a phone dit'n work or somethin', because da Republican anty-aircraft boys tink da liddl plane is a Condor-Heini tryin' ta sneak in, unnerstan? So dey shoot 'im down, an da pilot lans okay wid a parachute, but Tiefenbrucker's parachute gets hung up somewhere, an when da Modesto boys realize dey shot down da wrong plane an haul him outa da wreckitch he's still alive. Imagine dat, will ya, he was still alive, but not fa long."

I H...A...V...E H...E...A...R...D T...H...A...T A...L...L B...E...F...O...R...E says a Morse-like throbbing in my brow. "Holy Laudon! Holy-Holy-Goddam-Laudon! What did Grandpa say to that?"

"N-not much."

"What??"

"A little afta twelve . . ." Once again Pfiff's voice seemed to recede in a fade out. "We called 'is heart spesh'list in Chur—ya see—his heart, afta all dat excitement, de old cavalier's heart just gave out. A little afta twelve—"

"Your three minutes are up," an impersonal female voice broke in, "please deposit the amount indicated. *Les trois minutes sont écoullées, veuillez verser la taxe indiquée.*"

A click and the slight rushing noise was gone.

I waited in the booth for Pfiff to call again. After the bell remained silent for a while I lurched out of the red-upholstered interior and found the telephone book on a wall shelf, whipped out my reading monocle, and began flipping through the massive book in so-called feverish haste. Pfiff had said he was calling from down in a phone booth. I found TARTAR, which boasted scarcely more than a dozen numbers. One for the town registry office, the mayor, the schoolteacher (whose number bore the comment: *no messages taken*), a forester, a beekeeper, a road repairman, the Luzienburg Mill & Silo Inc., Kujath, Henrique, private . . . post office, public telephone . . . *that* number was worth a try. Then I heard the staccato ringing of the phone.

"For me, Annette!" I yelled and slammed the phone-booth door behind me. "Hello, Pfiff?"

"Sorry about dat, but in all da rush I fagot ta bring any change. Had ta go get some. Dat operator was right. His tree minutes. His tree minutes *was* up. Da boss died a little afta twelve. An of all days—da day before his birt-day."

"Jee-zus-god, that's awful."

"Awful? Naw it's all-*full*, all full o' *shit*, dat's what it is! It's one big, gigantic pile o' *shit!*" A snort. (Sniffing back mucus?) Pfiff's voice no longer sounded muffled, but now seemed swollen, almost to a grunt. 'Dey got our asses in a sling, Trebla, we've really *had* it! Dey're gonna flush us right down the sewer, dat's what dere gonna do! We might as well start diggin' our graves, I tell ya! Ya know, if I believed in God—I'd believe he was on da udder side."

"Take it easy, comrade," I said (making one of my rare uses of this form of address). "How is the Kummersdorf—er, Grandma taking it?"

"She's weepy, as usual: but at da moment she's not cryin'. At da moment she's bein' real strong about it all. 'We should've expected it all da time.' Dat kinda stuff." Another sniff.

"And Grandpa's daughter? Sedina?"

"Mizz Heppenheim. At first she had a tremendous bawlin' fit. But after half an hour she turns up in da Peacock Room wid a snazzy black mournin' dress. No kiddin'. She musta had it stored in mawt-balls juss for de occasion. Now she's passin' out champagne an caviar."

"Caviar?"

"Dat's what da boss ordered in case he died. 'Cause champagne would make da be-reaved reladives feel stronger. An because caviar is black."

"Hm. And his sons-in-law?"

"Da tree cripples, as da boss used to call 'em? Da disabled vet'ran, Querfurt, he's been takin' it real good. But de ex-race-driver von Preznicek and de exjudge Siegfried Heppenheim let everybody know dat as long as dere won't be any birtday party, d'least we could do ta celebrate is open up da boss's will. Da mayor and da town-registrar-guy got here almost as quick as da morticians, an at four a'clock da boss's notary an his lawyer came waltzin' in from Bern. An ta'morra already dey're s'posed ta read da will. Man, Red Baron, dere's gonna be some long faces aroun' here."

"How come?"

"Well, because of de-a-*mount*, dat's why. Juss between us, da boss used up one helluva lotta dough for all dem games he was playin'. *You* know what I'm talkin' about . . . Now comes da best part." The snort. "Da news of his dyin' musta spread like wile-fire in Bern, cause an hour ago da German am-bass-der Koecher called *pers*-nally ta tell Mizz Kujath how sorry he was." A crackling giggle, a crackling snort.

"Listen, Pfiff, of course I'd be glad to come to the funeral, but if Uncle Adolf's ambassador is one of the mourners—"

"Da boss is *not* gonna be buried."

"Cremated?"

"No. Da boss always said he dit'n wanna stay in Europe ta watch da radishes grow from da wrong side. Not in *dis* Europe. It's all spelt out inniz will. Dat dere's ta be no fune-ral. An his body's ta be shipped ta good ol' Brazil in a airtight coffin. An only one person is s'posed ta come along, dat bein' his trusty driver Pfiffke. An he's s'posed ta be laid ta rest in São João Batista cemetery in Rio. Right under da Corcovado; nifty neighborhood. He reserved hisself a place dere, even dough he's notta Cat-lick . . . wid-a little cash you c'n swing a deal like dat down in Brazil. Y'know dey don't bury people dere, dey walls 'em up. Cause o' da heat. Tree minutes 'r almost up; should I trow in anudder coin?"

"No, they need you up there. Just one more question. Grandpa wanted to get a message to the Swiss News Agency." (The one about Giaxa's last ride—which I left unmentioned.) "Do you know if . . .?"

"Right. This mornin' he tole me to connect 'im wid Mr. Saladin of da News Agency as soon as . . ."

"As soon as what?"

"As soon as we got da word dat Tiefenbrucker's plane h'd landed. Well it landed—

7

Ghost-train Monday, about 10:00 P.M.

"You're a bad apple," Miss Tummermut said as she made eyes at me. "A bad guy."

"He's not a bad guy, Verena," protested Lenz Zbraggen, the Handsome Soldier who now wore not a uniform but a phony elegant purple suit of the standard type, "Young Farmer at Church Social," topped off with a Turkish fez made of red crepe paper. "He's a nice guy, but he's a spy."

"Are you a spy?" Miss Tummermut gapes coyly with wide-open, piglet eyes.

"In this case I think it's more likely I'm a bad apple," I blab inanely.

"You're a nice guy, *but* you're a spy," insisted Lenz Zbraggen, hanging, like drunks often do, on a single subject or a single phrase. "Soldier Buddy is here to tell you. *I* am Soldier Buddy. *Soldier Buddy!*" Lenz roars it out suddenly amidst the *Laendler*-tooting, foot-shuffling, rude-shouting din of the dance hall in the Gasthaus Zur Innmuehle & Stadt Milano. Multiple cheers answer him from nearby tables. "You see that, spy? Everybody knows and loves Soldier Buddy. Only Captain Urs Xaver Dominik Vaterlaus doesn't love Soldier Buddy, and sends him off to be court-martialed."

"That's enough, Lenz!"

Balthasar Zbraggen's warning voice cuts through the noise. The younger brother stands up resolutely at the other end of the bottle-crowded table and brushes something hung from the coatrack behind him, causing it to swing: a carbine.

For the first time I notice the carbine hanging there and watch as Balz turns briefly to do something to it—apparently to check the safety. Attired like his brother in pseudo-chic civilian clothes and a party fez, he is smaller than Lenz and less broad shouldered, and his skull has nothing of Lenz's handsome Dinaric boldness, but the firm determination on his face belies the silliness of his headgear. He comes over and lectures Lenz for a few moments, but not in the local dialect. (Had Pola or the Tummermut girl told me that the Zbraggens came originally from Canton Uri?) At last Lenz replies, "Yes sir, Oh mighty Grand Mogul." The two fezzes move apart, and as Balz retires to the dance floor Lenz comments, "Guess who's the most gung-ho soldier in our whole battalion? Master Sergeant Balz Zbraggen." (He pronounces it like "Broca.") "He's always on the lookout. Keeps his eyes open. Watches out for everything. *Almost* everything. But even he couldn't prevent my accident the other day . . ."

"Oh, stop talking about that old accident of yours, honey," said the Tummermut girl. "Nothing really happened."

"No, but it almost did. It almost wiped out my company commander. And now Soldier Buddy has got to go to a court-martial."

"Don't think about it, honey. They're gonna let you live."

"Yeah . . .? You think so, Verena . . .?" In a strangely cautious tone, perhaps with an undertone of forlorn sarcasm Lenz speaks into the thick air ("you could cut it with a knife") of the dance hall. "Not a bad guy, that Balz Brocka, and very attached to me—"

"Even though *you're* your mother's favorite," said Tummermut.

"Whatever ... still, he's awfully attached to me, *but* he's a real watcher-outer. Spy, you've never seen a brother who watches out for his brother the way he does."

I think of the Two Blonds, of Krainer, who is his brother's keeper—a story that seems to be long behind me (as if it has ended long ago and not today, Ghost-train Monday), and I ask casually: "Lenz, do you know the story about the Clavadetscher brothers in Sils?"

"Sure. An old story. I was still in school then."

Miss Tummermut wants to know what kind of story it is, and Lenz, holding a half-full bottle of Malans, waves her off.

"An innkeeper in Sils Maria, Men Clavadetscher, went out on a wood-chuck hunt and shot his brother Toena, no ... Peidar, yeah, Peidar. A hunting accident that could happen on almost any fall day in these mountains. But if you happen to be on maneuvers and fire an MG bullet a couple of feet from the company commander's elbow, they take it for a mutiny or something."

"You're being silly, honey. Nobody ever said a word about mutiny."

"No, Verena?" asks Lens, again strangely vague.

"Did the examiner at the inquest say anything about mutiny?"

"No, but that *could* be the next step. If old Vaterlaus puts a flea—haha, if old Vaterflea puts a louse in his ear."

"Lenz, you're silly. And all this spy-business is crazy too. Alby here just happens to be a *Wunderfitz*."

"What am I, Verena?"

"A *Wunderfitz*, a guy who's always curious."

I: "That's true."

Lenz starts to pour me some Malans but I object. "Thanks, but I'll stick to Valtellina," and Lenz mumbles, "That stuff tastes too much like iron for me. I don't like the taste of iron." With that he bangs the bottle back on the table with such force that the glasses dance. "Goddammit, *I don't like the taste of iron!*" He stands up with a jerk, tugs his breast-pocket handkerchief into a rosette. Miss Tummermut presses a three-foot green teddy bear she won playing bingo—a dreadfully insipid thing—into my lap and then her imitation alligator purse, and smiles at me with her cute piglet eyes. Lenz says, "*Wunderfitz*, keep an eye on Balz's carbine."

The following seemed to happen in the same telegram-style I had used for my war diary. There are moments and situations whose rhythm is a prolonged staccato without rests or ritardandos; situations and moments that remind you of machinegun fire even though they occur only on maneuvers and not in real combat. And yet—even in the so-called traditional enclaves of peace—the entire situation and every moment of this year of our Greater-German-Lord-and-Fuehrer 1938 is latent war. In wartime, offense and defense are the order of the day, but there are idyllic interludes as well, contrasts to the great game of killing and being killed, idylls (some deserving sarcastic quotation marks) that range from great love affairs to the basest debauchery. When I was on the trail of my suspected pursuers—a trail revealed as false—from the kosher guesthouse Villa Muongia to the garage of motorcyclist Paretta-Piccoli and from there to the house of Thusnelda the physical therapist Huppenkothen—I had experienced everything in the shorthand style of my war diary. There is neither space nor time for conjunctions, nor even for many a verb. Verbs are action words, and what other actions had there been in the great Imperial War (where I received my schooling)? Just killing and being killed. Or expressed in more transcendental terms, killing yourself.

Monday, 10:45 P.M.

Starry night, fantastically clear, cool, frosty after the hot, stuffy air indoors, gentle night breeze off the lake, corduroy collar turned up. Where is Miss T. taking me, in this roundabout way to her apartment? Someone standing sentry-like by the railing of open air dance floor, drunk. Barfs over railing lined with colored light bulbs, between heaves atempts to yodel, curses in Romansh. Is T. heading for half-open wooden band shell? Too cold for dalliance there, and barfing sentry not exactly romantic. From the dance hall great popping of party-poppers. Upstairs, behind gable window, red light, notorious landmark, aha. *That* red light we saw night before last from Caduff-Bonnard's boathouse. She taking me there? T. answers: Not *her* room, she lives elsewhere, up there pharmacy student from Schwyz cramming for exams by "tango light" with record player. *Abbé Galiani: "What concerns us is optical illusion."* Maybe just small-town gossip about T., maybe she's no Zurich Whistle (whore), maybe just acts that way, really engaged to Lenz? We'll soon see. Ask her where's her room. Answers coyly: up by the Inn Falls, but we can't go there, too dangerous because of the owner (owner of Innmuehle Milano), incidentally, do I think she's part of Zurich life? Life? Night life, high life. Is there one? Sure, but she isn't part of it. If I want to risk a little episode with her, then not for money. I, somewhat stunned, baffled, charged up from the experience of so many deaths. In a word: horny. Toodle-oodle-doo farther away, waterfall closer.

A kind of mineral-spring bathhouse, bunkerlike, grass covered, windowless, iron door, T. has key, inside rather warm, T. digs little flashlight (Japanese) out of purse. A kind of junk room—old lawn chairs piled to stained cement ceiling, broken porch swing, long cushion on cement floor, dank stagnant air like indoor swimming pool. Subterranean rushing, T: "The Inn." I: "Hope there're no rats here." Green teddy, me, T. on cushion, she turns off flashlight, pitch dark.

Five-minute kiss, half my face wet from her warm saliva, my hand in the elastic cutout of her lamé dress. I'll be damned, no bra, so-called erect bosom (vulgar, super boobs), sweaty, warm from the dance hall. "Beautiful, oh night of love / Oh satisfy my longing." Memento of Offenbach's barcarole, blared out by engineer Szabo above Grandpa's tower studio. Away with mementos. I want to live, l, i, v, e, live it up, make a vice of necessity. Whispers drowned by the rushing water. I, louder: Let's get undressed. I can't *faire l'amour* with clothes on. She breathes hot in my mouth: All the way? Too risky. I: Can't we lock the door? She: Only from outside. Helps me slip off panties, refuses to remove garter belt, garters tight as bass fiddle strings, cut into her ample thighs. Unusually soft derriere, my hand seems to *feel* how rosy it is. "Come on, come on. We're like two greased pigs, huh? Come on, Albert, come on." Her damp little hand unbuckles my belt (without noticing the bullets in it), unbuttons, finds what she's looking for, but I'm too nervous, excited, overstimulated, and exhausted too. Mental and physical strain of last twenty-four hours. Super-boobs, super-woman, can't let her down now. She: "Come on, oh Albert, come on, come to me." Subterranean rushing, then T. squeaks as iron door flies open.

Classic case of being caught *flagrante delicto*. With my pants down. In the door frame, gently swaying male silhouette—drunkard? Lights cigarette lighter. Lenz Zbraggen with party fez! In left hand, cigarette lighter flickers in lake breeze; in right hand, carbine. From dance-hall party noises, toodle-doodle-doo of clarinetist. Firecrackers popping.

"Wellwell, this is where Soldier Buddy finds you. Wellwell." Five or six more "well wells". Switches, click, the carbines's safety off. (A familiar click.) Am afraid last hour has struck for T. and me. To be done in by Two Blonds or Men Clavadetscher, could have figured on that, but by Soldier Buddy? The (now suppressed) squeaking of Miss T.; holds green teddy in front of her as inadequate shield. Lenz's thick voice: "Wellwell, so it's you two. You double-dealing whore, Verena, you filthy whore." Strategically hopeless situation, but too awkward, unreal to paralyze me with fear of death.

You're at war. Last chance. (Used to last chances at war.) Feel for belt, Walther. Then iron door bangs shut, echoes through bathhouse like cannon shot. Once again pitch dark, now T. hugs my biceps, stammers short prayers unknown to any liturgy. Then second bang farther away. Not much different from firecrackers and party-poppers.

11:15 P.M.

Exit Soldier Buddy.

Shot himself in mouth with carbine. In just completed band shell. Ghostly footsteps trampling across hollow dance floor, people with party hats, draped with confetti, crowd around band shell with multicolored lanterns. Rumor spreads: Zbraggen's right foot bare, maybe pulled trigger with big toe. Ex-jockey Fitz lost in the crowd, Caduff-Bonnard waves to me like old friend. Here we are, the two of us, for another suicide. Sensational! Police Corporal Defila arrives first, shortly thereafter ambulance from cantonal hospital, Samedan, doctor in overcoat over white apron ("Nothing I can do here"), Commissioner Mavegn. Only witness to the suicide a drunk, a farmer from Madulain, barely coherent. No one seems to know Lenz went to the bathhouse. No one? If only she'd quit bawling so loud into her teddy bear! Balz Zbraggen out of crowd with quince-yellow lantern, quince-yellow face, party fez, confetti-strewn shoulders, to Verena. She leaves for home, sobbing, supported by *maître de plaisir* wearing earring.

Balz eye to eye with me, then to Mavegn.

Battlefield situation critical. Will Balz tell Commissioner about Lenz calling me a spy? Mavegn's patience might snap—after all I'm involved in another case of sudden death. (War is always a matter of sudden death.)

Mavegn first preoccupied with ordering removal of body. Owner of Innmuehle, fat German-Swiss named Koch, announces in four languages: Festival is ended due to tragic event. I look away as ambulance men stow stretcher. (Seen it too often.) Do I share blame for Soldier Buddy's death? Irrelevant question in wartime. Brother of fallen soldier (fallen soldier!) will prove that.

Seldom saw more peaceful corpse. Peaceful. Furious. Both at once. Verena and I have Lenz on our consciences. A slap in the face would suffice for Verena; not for me. He, Balz, could turn me in to the Fedpo (Federal Police) on suspicion of espionage. Considers not doing it because he wants me for himself. Would take suicide carbine and shoot *me*. I should count on it.

Enemies, professional killers, some disappear, others take their places— c'est la guerre.

On Ghost-train Monday, about 11:35 P.M. I stood near the eastern corner of Lake Moritz just beneath the dairy (darkened windows), the exact same place I had trotted past four weeks earlier in search of Xana.

The awful ballad of Lenz Zbraggen had ended on an unexpected chord. Brother Balz had turned once more to Commissioner Mavegn, whereupon the big man had approached me, followed at a safe distance by officer Defila. This time they'll have me remanded to Chur prison on suspicion of espionage, I had guessed, and under the suddenly different circumstances that might be the best thing for me. In the light of the multicolored bulbs Mavegn had, to my surprise, scowled and said, "Yaya, it had been a terrible loss for us."

And I had mumbled something like, "Terrible, such a handsome young man."

Ya-no, he hadn't meant him, Mavegn had replied; that had been a tragic act of fate. Now at least the fallible young machinegunner wouldn't face court-martial. (An Alpine glacier with feelings?) He had meant the owner of the Luzienburg in the Domleschg, Mr. Kujath, who was a friend of mine. No small loss to Graubuenden and to Switzerland. I remembered Grandpa's words. "Now and then we give Swiss Intelligence a tip," and apropos espionage it had occurred to me that perhaps Henrique Kujath was really one of the greatest behind-the-scenes operators of his time . . .

One thing was certain. Despite the fact that the Two Blonds had been revealed as harmless and that Men Clavadetscher (who did not even see fit to attend the Innmuehle festivities) had dropped out of sight, this time I had earned myself a *real* deadly enemy—Balz Zbraggen—who felt bound to take out something like blood revenge on me.

I had to get away. Right away. Away right away. Hay fever or no hay fever. It was unlikely that Zbraggen would pursue me into the flatlands. I had turned, not toward the station but toward the dairy, for the last train had already left and I hesitated to hire a taxi at the station. Stay out of St. Moritz tonight! I'd also made Joop my enemy (he was my class enemy to begin with, ha!), but I might run into his chauffeur in front of Acla Silva, and perhaps I could manage to charter Bonjour for a ride home.

Lenz starts to pour me some Malans, but I object. I'll stick to my Valtellina, and Lenz says, That stuff tastes too much like iron for me. Goddammit, I don't like the taste of iron! Suddenly it was clear to me. Even *before* the party, Soldier Buddy had toyed with the idea of shooting himself in the mouth . . . His brother would probably be involved with taking care of the sad formalities. And although I felt truly sorry for my new enemy (for I had learned from dreadful experience that it was senseless to pity the dead), I checked the Walther's magazine by the light of the Milky Way. What was a pistol against a carbine? That depended on the strategic situation, on the alertness of the opponents, and on luck.

Here, far from the phony lighting of the open-air dance floor, the Milky Way dripped with a magical brightness that glittered in the lake, from which the evening breeze no longer blew, and the lake, with Zuan's corpse anchored at its bottom, stretched out to such a flat, smooth mirror of the stars that it seemed a giant sheet of ice. I shivered. Yes, four weeks ago I had sprinted past this very spot; it had been colder then, dark and fog damp—not like now when the longest day of the year would soon begin. But I was cold today too. Four weeks ago the rock jutting out into the lake, the rock Xana had crawled onto, had been invisible, swallowed in fog. Today I saw it shimmering below me like a small iceberg and I felt chilled to the bone. Back then after reaching the rock virtually on instruments, I had quoted a line from a Punch and Judy show. Not the big one, the Grand Guignol, but the little one, Professor Salambutschi's Prater Punch and Judy show. "You see, madam, there is really no point in being sentimental." Back then, yes, right at that point I had begun my ride into the labyrinth.

And now the shivering gunslinger is riding out at the same place he rode in. You pay a five-figure sum for admission (it's inflation time), go through the labyrinth, then climb out and go away. Right away. But finding myself here at the very place I'd begun my ride, I sensed that it was not over yet. That I would have to climb aboard another car of the Ghost Train, (entrance not a hundred paces from the Prater Punch and Judy show): the NEW GHOST TRAIN AND HORROR LABYRINTH, entrance and exit side by side.

Laugh Laugh Laugh. Feigl's World Show. Madam Cumberland the Fortuneteller. Princess Hummingbird, World's Largest Lady. Laugh Laugh Laugh. Get Your Tickets Here. (Buy an Extra Ticket for the World's Largest Lady!)

Karl Homsa, four years my junior, best friend and first-class sculpture talent, son of a Czech bricklayer, stone-mason's apprentice and favorite student of Anton Hanak in the master class of the Vienna Art Academy, on a stroll through the Prater with me. Me, Albert who is studying law in Vienna—God knows why, if not merely to satisfy my father, Joseph Wenzel Ulrich Bogumil (the Austrian Republic had done away with noble titles), the retired general living in Graz. In the Eisvogel Café Karl charmed for us two good-looking country girls in thick peasant-skirts, children's nannies on a weekend outing. The Prater in a bizarrely impoverished postwar Vienna—an amusement park fascinatingly, not depressingly, degenerated, with a strange, colorful, shabby magic about it; rather phantomlike and queerly antiquated as well, weathered and tattered and yet at the same time painted and powdered, dolled up and jovial like an aging harlot; wonderland of flickering, spangled illusion, seemingly unchanged by a world war and the collapse of an empire, as if an ancient, paralytic hand were trying to write the year 1900. Karl and I, on our arms two Czech country maids with stiff-swinging skirts, stroll past the hippodrome, past the entranceway to the world-famous giant ferris wheel, the *Riesenrad*, waving and winking at Engineer Peizoeder, operator of its gigantic clockwork. If he shakes his massive, gray-derbied head, it means: Not today! If he stealthily holds up, say, nine fingers, it means: I can arrange it—come back at nine o'clock.

Meanwhile on this warm September afternoon we made do with a spin on the smaller, almost rococo-styled wheel, the GONDELRAD. CALAFATI, THE OLDEST MERRY-GO-ROUND IN EUROPE, over the entrance—like the god of a carnival temple, a colossal mandarin standing with a tremendous queue. "Oh yeah-ss, let's go over to Cally-Fatt, I even heard about him in Iglau!" FRANZ PUCHER'S OLD VIENNA GROTTO TRAIN. Johann Strauss Junior, a life-sized, lifelike doll, conducts the *Fruehlings-stimmen*-waltz. Karl's Iglau-girl: "Oh yeah-ss, let's go over'n see Strauss!"

Homsa: "Did you hear about him in Iglau, too?" WITCHES' SABBATH—CHILDREN BOARD AT THE REAR. The sudden changes in altitude on the roller coaster didn't do my forehead much good, and the rattle of the plunging cars reminded me of incoming mortar rounds, and I didn't want to remember things like that.

"Yeah-ss, let's ride the flying swing!"

Our flying, squealing country girls with their three to four petticoats were a sensation for the onlookers around the fence. In the neighboring seat, one man alone, somewhat older than myself, lean, pale face, hair combed back. I recognized him as an old comrade from the war, not only from the composed way he let himself be tossed about but from the polished wooden leg projecting from his windblown trousers. Every time around I thought, If that wooden leg flies off it will hit Johann Strauss right in the head . . .

My Iglau-girl: "Oh yeah-ss, let's ride the Ghost, ride the Ghost Train, Ferdy!"

"My name isn't Ferdy," I said.

"Then what is it?"

Homsa: "His name is Don Alfonso and he is the Spanish Crown Prince traveling incognito—a famous bleeder."

"You can tell that to your grandmother, Fritz."

"I'm not Fritz, I'm Karl," said Karl.

"And I'm not Don Alfonso, I'm Don Alberto," I said.

"Okay Bertie. Yeah-ss, let's ride the Ghost Train!"

"I've gone on enough Ghost trains," I said. A JOLLY VOYAGE TO AFRICA. NO GHOULS! NO CORPSES! NO GHOSTS!" Let's go to Africa first, that'll be good for a rest." In a four-seat coach disguised as a ship we rolled into a spacious viewing ground, and the trip to Africa was almost touchingly outdated. We found ourselves taken back to the days of Jules Verne. The leisurely rolling coach brought us to an automatic halt in front of illuminated show windows behind which life-sized puppets and replicas were slowly decaying: dolphins emerging from the Mediterranean; a dilapidated camel plus dusty Bedouins standing in front of the pyramids; half an elephant, its rear end cut off by the background bushes, and a weatherbeaten Fata Morgana; a flock of flamingos, a tiger that had seen better days; two lions that had been chasing the same painted antelopes for fifty years; an explorer in a checkered pith helmet being dragged by painted cannibals into a tublike soup kettle. (The scene still qualified as funny.) "Well, how did you like it, Mitzi?"

"Ludmilla's name is not Mitzi, it's Millie," said Karl's Iglau girl emphatically.

"Africa was a bore," said my baroque-hipped Millie. "Yeah-ss, now let's f-i-n-a-l-l-y go on the Ghost Train. I'm looking forward to the horror labyrinth so much!"

NEW GHOST TRAIN & HORROR LABYRINTH —over the entrance exit writhed a gigantic dragon of swamp green papier-mâché. ADMISSION 100,000 CROWNS. CHILDREN UNDER 16 NOT ADMITTED. NOT RECOMMENDED FOR PERSONS WITH WEAK NERVES OR HEART CONDITIONS. The establishment was built to look like a desert fort of the French Foreign Legion. Oversized skulls grinned from the loopholes. In contrast to Karl, who had been too young to qualify as "cannon fodder" for the Great War, I was not amused by the sight, but didn't let my feelings show. With my Iglau girl I got into a two-seated rail car secured with side chains; Karl and friend boarded the next one. Through an opening and closing double door we rattled into a dark space smelling of dust and glue, moved blindly up and down and around curves, and Millie, hugging me tight, was already screaming at the top of her lungs before the horror show began.

Sudden bursts of light like muzzle flashes in the dark, and a nine-foot-tall King Kong leaps down on us, his hairy arms outstretched, the car misses him by inches, as something like tracer ammunition explodes all around, and an escaped convict lunges toward us with a bloody knife. In contest with her friend behind us, Millie screams in blissful terror as if experiencing a glottal cramp. Now we run over an ancient beggar who shrieks hideously, and I hear Karl's youthful laugh behind me. Suddenly, like the cuckoo in a Black Forest clock, we rush out into Vienna's golden September afternoon and roll across an outer gallery of the desert fort and see above the Prater's roofs and tents the *Riesenrad* in its majestic turning, the *Riesenrad*, where afterwards with Mr. Peizoeder's help . . . And Millie says: "Yeah-ss, it's so exciting," and kisses me hastily on the ear, and, flap, we roll back through an opening-closing door into the dusty, gluey darkness. Now, it seems, the Ghost Train ghosts will get their turn: a white spook, combination Carmelite nun, maggot, and zeppelin soars down at us from the ceiling. Green-flashing light: a drowned man lifts his hands from a scummy pond. Red flashing light: a guillotine blade plummets onto a victim's neck. Yellow, flashing light: a life-sized robot in funeral attire slams a coffin lid on a white hand reaching out. Dying screams, bestial roars played on worn-out phonograph records. Darkness, in which something like hanging hair brushes cross your face—*truly* revolting. And suddenly someone in blue coveralls biting with true Viennese relish into a super-long hot dog—somehow the wrong door must have opened.

The toboggan tower, like the Cresta Run in St. Moritz, had its seasons and off-seasons. (At that time I wasn't yet familiar with the Engadine.) THE ARENA OF DEATH: Step right up ladies and gentlemen, the action never stops!! Even though Karl Homsa and I were short of funds we had managed to scrape together a couple million. In the Goesser Beer Restaurant Zum Walfisch we ordered *Salonbeuschel mit Serviettenknoedeln* (which sounds fancier than what it is: ground innards and dumplings); then the girls wanted to go to the theater Beim Leicht, the Prater cabaret where famous actors used to make guest appearances and where Pola Polari had made her debut as a chanteuse (before my time). But Karl steered the Iglau girls back to the giant ferris wheel and crossed engineer Peizoeder's palm with an even million. The latter took discreet measures to ensure that no one but Millie and I entered the eight-seat gondola, and that the next one was reserved for Homsa and friend. A clanging bell and the hoarse singsong of Peizoeder's announcer's voice. "En-*joy* your *ride, lay-deez* and *genn*-tlemen, and *do* not *lean out* of the *win*-dows, *please*," as my gondola reached the top of the giant wheel . . .

. . . as we peered down on the Praterstern—the statue of Admiral Tegethoff looking like some sort of knickknack—straight down into the illuminated spinning of the merry-go-rounds, the sparkling clangor of the orchestrions reaching us mezzopiano from below—down into the ravinelike, gas-lit streets of the imperial city, over there the chain of lights for the Nordbahnhof, over here the towering shadow of St. Stephen's Cathedral surrounded by vague reddish light . . . as we looked out on all this the *Riesenrad*, this wonder of the world (actually there were no more world wonders after the World War) *stopped*, thanks to a little obliging corruption on the part of the good Mr. Peizoeder.

Stood still. We hung in the sky above the carnival.

Now the watchword was *Hic Iglau, hic salta.*

I had told Millie I was from Moravia; a few Czech phrases made our bond still closer. The worn-out velvet bench of the cabin. In contrast to Karl I was not one for fast action. ("On the quick," Grandpa Kujath would have said, but I didn't know him yet.) Men who could do it, one-two-three on park benches or in stairwells, seemed somehow birdlike to me. On the other hand, because of my pulsing (at that time noticeably rosier) head scar, I felt I couldn't risk showing any signs of weakness. Up at this height I had to be at the height of my form as an unscrupulous open-air Casanova. How many petticoats were there in the Iglau peasant costume anyway? The girl insisted she didn't want a child and I assured her I would be careful, and she whispered, the whole thing was just crazy, but nice too; it was a little like being in heaven, yeah-ss, but for God's sake I should be careful, and I said, Don't worry, and she, Good grief, what if the thing starts moving down again, and I, Millie, I guarantee you, we'll be hanging up here over Vienna for at least eight more minutes, and she, oh Vienna, oh Alfonsichku, no, Albertichku, watch out, watch out, and down below the chaotic tooting of the orchestrions, the singing, laughing and whistling from the other stranded gondolas, and finally engineer Peizoeder's voice booming through a megaphone: "Lay-deez and gen-telmen, our minor tech-nical defect is now corrected, have a pleasant ride!"

The *Riesenrad* as fifteen-minute hotel.

But once . . . Karl Homsa had picked up two eighteen-year-old Croatian washmaids on the main avenue, and even though the story was that Croatian girls had too little of what our Czechoslovak nannies had too much of, namely underwear—that they wore nothing but their warm young skin beneath their skirts—despite all this I couldn't manage to work up the necessary lust. Perhaps my syphilis phobia (dating back to my days as a cadet) was coming out again, since Karl's latest acquisitions appeared far less trustworthy than the girls from Iglau. In any case I "left the Prater-profligate Homsa with his two Croatian strumpets in the lurch," as I put it (to Karl's amusement), when we met again later—he had taken a merry-go-round *à trois* complete with Peizoeder stop. I strolled out of the city of tents and stands, climbed onto an embankment that led past a kind of Prater city dump and out onto the summer green expanses of the Prater meadows; turning around I looked across the backs of the carnival booths and beyond them to the grayish violet tenement houses of the Praterstern, where above the roofs the western sky seemed to smolder with the dying heat of the sirocco day, an ominous glow like the reflection of gigantic fires burning over the horizon. The statue of Admiral Tegethoff, that symbol of former imperial splendor, looked from here like part of the amusement park, a Prater attraction like Calafati the World's Largest Lady. And just as motionless as the Prater's admiral stood the colossal wheel of the *Riesenrad.*

Not because Karl, with Peizoeder's help, was holding his Croatian orgy in the topmost cabin (it was too early for that), but because now, at the dinner hour, business at the Prater was slow. Only a few people moved among the booths, and the *Gondelrad,* the roller coaster, the merry-go-rounds all were standing still. The orchestrions, with their Strauss and Lanner waltzes, now were silent.

Only *one thing* continued in ceaseless motion.

On the flat roof of the desert fort alias Ghost Train—the stark back side of the building, not intended for the public eye, less carefully disguised—a sentry (on rails) trudged back and forth, back and forth. The life-sized soldier doll wore the tall blue cap of the French Foreign Legion and a burnoose like the one on Gauguin's Spahi Farid Gaugamela (I had not yet seen the original), but not in white, in crimson red. Had I approached the New Ghost Train from the Prater's main square I would never have noticed this sentry. Now I concentrated my good eye on the moment when the robot, having reached the end of his track, did an about face with a deceptively lifelike swing of his red cape . . . and with a strange sideward bend of his body, as if there were a worn spot in the mechanism, then jerked erect again and marched off across the roof in the direction of Admiral Tegethoff.

At the far end of the track the robot legionnaire again turned round with an elegant sweep of his burnoose . . . fell sideways . . . straightened up and marched jerkingly back in my direction. Only then did I notice it was the Grim Reaper.

DEATH AS A LEGIONNAIRE.

Perhaps a skeleton acquired from the dissecting room of Vienna General Hospital. Perhaps part of that army of wounded soldiers who died in World War I—only after it was over. Now a brightly uniformed desert sentinel, constructed of carefully cleaned bones, steel springs, ball bearings, electric wires, all in all a well-functioning machine.

And for minutes upon minutes I stared across at him in revolted fascination, watched him jerk back and forth in the fiery red twilight of a sirocco-day in early autumn, death on rails in the guise of a foreign legionnaire, moving back and forth, back and forth. And as I watched, it dawned on me that the war would go on, the war I had so recently left.

book five

The San Gian Road

1　　　　The three of them stood motionless on the steep driveway of Acla Silva, between the garage and the garden gate whose lamp no longer burned. So clean and bright was the Milky Way that the stocky man and the two gigantic dogs threw the ghost of a shadow onto the end of the road, a shadow that made all three appear inflated like balloons. Stepping closer I recognized Bonjour and, on a double leash, the two attack-trained Great Danes ten Breukaa had acquired to guard his Spahi, one spotted rose and gray, the other black and yellow. The astral illumination left them with color enough, and the same was true of the olive green livery worn by the domestic. (An appropriate term for Joop's gardener-servant-chauffeur.) I said, *"Bon soir, monsieur Bonjour."*

He cautiously returned my greeting, whereupon the rigid stance of both dogs relaxed a bit. To my question of why he hadn't taken part in the Innmuehle festivities, he replied in his Vaudois French, noticeably reticent, that *monsieur* was away on a trip and had ordered him to guard *madame* and the house. And above all the Spahi, I thought, then asked if he'd heard what happened in St. Moritz that night. His monosyllabic *"non,"* his patent lack of interest, confirmed my suspicion that Joop had incited him against me and probably had ordered him to keep me out of Acla Silva at all cost. So Bonjour would not be talked into driving me to Pontresina. In the distance a clock struck midnight. The pseudo-Scottish manor house was blacked out and so frosted by the sheen of the Milky Way that it looked deceptively Anglo-Saxon-Romanesque. The only light came from three windows in the second floor, glowing intimately through drawn, baby blue curtains.

"Po-la!"

The spotted Great Dane emitted something like a deep, interior rumbling.

I took two steps back: "Madam ten Breu-kaa! . . . Let me in just for ten minutes, please! . . . I've got some news for you!"

The first reaction from inside was from Sirio, a bright, childlike bark—sounding strangely comforting to me; then a baby blue curtain was pulled aside, the window opened and Pola's slender torso appeared. Is she wearing black? It flashed through me. Had the radio reported Giaxa's death on the late-night news? Wouldn't it be just like Pola to change immediately—

"Yes, Tre-bla! Good heavens, what are you doing here at midnight?"

"A thousand pardons, but something terrible has happened!"

Would she call down, "I know, I heard the awful news on the radio, Giaxa is dead in Dachau, horrible, what a dreadful horror," etc.? *And if Pola knew, then Xana knew . . .*

"*What* happened? When? Where?"

"Forty-five minutes ago at the Innmuehle Milano!"

"*Bonjour!*"

"*Oui, madame?!*"

"*Amenez monsieur au salon!*"

"*Parfaitement!*"

This "*parfaitement*" was contradicted by the face he made as he led me into the sitting room after unleashing the Great Danes into the terraced garden.

"*Bon soir, Monsieur Farid Gaugamela.*"

Bonjour went "*Hain?*"

"I was only wishing Monsieur Gauguin's Spahi a good evening."

His mien darkened visibly; obviously he thought I was pulling his leg. In the vestibule the house telephone rang and he trudged slowly out of the room, returned at his dragging, gardener's gait and spoke to me reproachfully, with such listless impudence that it seemed impossible he had ever talked so eagerly about the Monparnasse bordello Le Sphinx. "Madame has instructed me to make a fire in the fireplace and to serve you a whisky soda. *Avec de la glace?*"

"I'm an ice cube myself right now. I'd prefer a black coffee and an Armagnac."

"*Parfait,*" said Bonjour in a tone so flat I knew he considered my order anything but *parfait*. With visible reluctance he kneeled down in front of the English fireplace. And as he knelt there blowing the flames with the same gold-plated bellows used (according to Joop) three hundred years before in the cabin of Admiral Michiel Adrianszoon de Ruyter, he suddenly seemed to me like a priest performing his ritual before the altar of the god he served. And this god was the Spahi Farid Gaugamela who, thanks to the two attack-trained Great Danes, could once again assume his rightful place above the mantelpiece of the open fireplace. And as I had often observed with priests in service of their deities: the former had precious little to do with the latter. The priest took care of the ceremony, and the god stared out indifferently over his head.

From upstairs a chirping bark of jubilant excitement. The young cocker spaniel raced through the open double door into the sitting room with ears flying—he must have recognized my voice. Did one somersault on the Bukhara runner, another on the bedragoned carpet (Ming dynasty, sixteenth century, Joop had said), jumped up and up and up on me like a dark blue, silky-haired ball, stopping only for occasional attacks of joyful sneezing. Bonjour admonished him, but I declared that Sirio's playfulness didn't bother me at all, on the contrary, it helped me *dégeler*—thaw out. Exit Bonjour, peevish. Enter Pola.

Her entrance seemed noteworthy to me because of its total lack of showmanship, its complete untheatricalness. The lady of the house wore pajamas of dark purple, almost black terry cloth (or something similar), which, except for a brooch above her left breast, were as plain as a sweat suit. It made her look unusually pure and her puffed-up, slightly mussed, henna-red hair (intended to look uncombed?) made her appear even prettier than usual. Even her lack of makeup seemed spectacular. The exposed freckles around her small, pointed nose and the visible wrinkles around her caramel-pudding-tinted mouth led me to suspect she had spent fifteen minutes preparing herself to look like a country girl on her way to bed. Gold buskin sandals were the only luxury she allowed herself. A performance perfected to seem *not* a performance; Pola was acting so that she would look for once as though she were *not* acting. But perhaps I was being unfair, and she *really* wasn't acting.

Bonjour, now wearing white cotton gloves, pushed a small cart into the room: a small espresso percolator, demitasses, large-bowled cognac glasses, a three-and-a-half-liter bottle of Armagnac shaped like a tennis racket. "*Bonjour, le sucre,*" said Pola. His forgetting the sugar bowl did nothing to raise Bonjour's spirits. When he returned with it, Pola sent him off to bed before I could protest: after my clash with Joop the day before it would be pointless to try borrowing the Chrysler, but I had hoped Pola would encourage the servant-chauffeur to drive me home.

"What happened at the Innmuehle Milano, Treblatschi?"

"Mmmm . . . Your wood supplier, this fellow Lenz Zbraggen you sort of introduced me to at Pizzagalli's—"

"Soldier Buddy? The handsome one? My heartthrob."

"Your heartthrob . . ." Briefly I related the incident that had brought the Innmuehle festivities to a premature halt.

"That sounds like something he'd pull."

"Is that all you have to say about it?"

"What am I supposed to do, have a crying fit? If you've done as much theater in your life as I have, you reach a point then . . . where you just can't turn it on any more." She spoke without the exaggerated Viennese dialect she sometimes affected. "You just can't put on another scene. Even when you hear about a tragic thing like that. The people up here are just that way sometimes."

"What do you mean, 'that way'?"

"Just *that way*. Like they go off and shoot themselves at parties. Or they drive off into a lake—with a Fiat or a bicycle. After you've lived up here for months on end you get used to them pulling stunts like that."

"Stunts. That's a euphemistic way of putting it."

"It's the altitude, you know. The air. The thin air."

"I think someone else told me that not long ago."

"After a while it just pumps them full of . . . of some crazy force . . ."

"And I've heard *that* more than once since I've been up here."

"Not from me. At first, when you yelled from outside a little while ago that something had happened, I was really curious to know what it was. Or no. I just told myself. That I was curious. Actually it was just a pretext. For myself and because of Bonjour. A pretext for my wanting. For my wanting you to come in and talk for a while. And now? Now I don't want to hear anything more about that story."

"Thanks, Pola, thanks for being such a good old, mm—"

"A good old what?"

"A good old friend all these years."

"Don't thank your old Pola too much."

I sank into a Chippendale chair between the tea cart and the "East Asian rococo" chess table where Joop and I had had our falling out. Just for the sake of good manners, it seemed, Sirio had waddled over to Pola. She, after turning off the overhead light, had placed herself on the beautiful, asymmetrical Récamier sofa, hugging her knees as she nestled against the higher one of the two arms. In the glow of the indirect wall lighting (illuminating on the left a row of large Javanese marionettes in fantastic, disjointed poses, on the right a long glass case full of Etruscan urns and miniatures) Pola—tonight wearing no false eyelashes, but only a trace of lavender shadow around her definitely soulful Jewish eyes—began to cry a little. These were no stage tears. Her *bleu lavande* eye shadow dissolved and tinted her cheeks as it ran. Snapping out of her reverie, she pulled a platinum makeup case out of her pajama pocket and repaired her non-makeup with the help of a small batiste handkerchief, into which—as if for luck—she daintily spat. An atavistic gesture, so to speak, that harked back to her younger days as a small-time soubrette. Pola got up and turned off the section of wall-lighting behind the Etruscan showcase. "Too bright," she said with a voice grown somewhat thin. She began pacing back and forth in front of the Javanese puppets, somewhat wobbly on her thick-soled buskins, as if walking on stilts. (Without shoes like this, or high heels, she was actually small.) Now the young spaniel nosed against my leg. "Okay, come on." Though I said it softly he didn't have to be told twice, but sprang swiftly into my lap, climbed around on my upper thighs, on my Peyatchevich pants, turned around and around (the atavistic grass-flattening, bed-making gesture of all dogs) and finally curled up with a satisfied groan. I stroked his silky, young, shaggy coat from which sparks crackled, electrifying but calming as well.

"How do I get back to Pontresina tonight?"

"I'd tell you to go lie down in the guest room you had a few days ago. But today the situation is different." (You can say that again, I thought. Quite a few situations are different now compared with a few days ago.) "Xana and Joop aren't here. And if Joop found out from Bonjour . . ." She stilted past us to the sliding door, opened it, looked out into the vestibule, then closed it again.

". . . found out you spent the night here, he might shoot you." She said it in an indifferent, conversational tone. "You don't know how jealous he can be."

"So-o-o many people," I said, trying to appear blasé, "have tried to shoot me."

"When?"

"Well, during the war, for example."

"Sure," she said.

"Sure," I echoed.

"Sure, but recently?"

"Well, for example when I skied out of the Third Reich over the Silvretta."

"Sure, but not *very* recently—am I right?" she said with a hint of re-awakened interest.

I couldn't tell Pola about the stupid Tummermut episode or the threat of Balz Zbraggen's blood revenge.

"Stay for twenty more minutes then I'll call into town and get you a taxi. I know you're short of money. I'll contribute a little something. From my private piggy bank." Again she poured herself into the corner of the Récamier sofa (by Paul Labratut, Boulevard Saint-Germain).

I couldn't tell Pola that I had a well-founded, healthy fear of Balz Zbraggen. Or that I planned to leave the Engadine tomorrow. Tonight I had reason to fear Balz Zbraggen and St. Moritz, and everything connected with it—even a taxi stationed there—had to be off limits for me.

"I thought maybe you could get Bonjour to drive me to Pontresina."

"I already told Bonjour *bonne nuit.* He's already asleep—here in the house; Joop wants it that way while he's gone. Bonjour is sleeping next to Uorschletta." Her wistful laugh. "I mean in the *room* next to hers."

"Uh, to guard the Spahi better? Or your wifely virtue."

"Let's say, both."

"How about my sleeping in Bonjour's room over the garage?"

"Right now Mr. Haeberling is sleeping there. The man who brought Caesar and Brutus up here."

"Uh . . . wasn't that dangerous for Caesar?"

"Why dangerous for Caesar? They come from the same kennel."

"You mean from the same senate."

"What do you mean, senate? From the Uetliberg kennel where Joop bought them. And this man Haeberling from the Zurich Canine School is staying here a week to show Bonjour how to handle the giant beasts. By the way, this whole beastly business is your fault."

"Mine?"

"If you hadn't convinced Joop that *that* character over there—his Gauguin Spahi—might be stolen by art-loving burglars . . . You hear that?"

Outside a quiet tapping and clinking.

"On the other side of the house Brutus is prowling around on a half-mile-long chain, and on this side, Caesar. They don't bark very often, but that chain-clanking at night is enough to drive you batty."

"You can get used to almost anything, Pola. And one of these days Brutus will murder Caesar anyway."

"How did you get *that* idea?"

"You'll see." After a pause I said: "The Lying Dutchman has been traveling a lot lately. Where to this time?"

"To Genoa. To sell *Jan van Oldenbarnevelt.*"

"A painting?"

"No, not a painting."

"Or is he in the slave trade?"

"The questions you ask, Trebla. No, a steamer. A passenger liner that belongs to him and to the Nederlandsche Stroomvaart Matschappij. An old tub; I think they want to sell it to some Greek outfit. I *never* concern myself with his business deals, but I'm afraid not much will come of this one. Tell me, Trebla, were you two, ah . . . having differences?"

"Differences? There's always the difference between his income and mine . . ."

"Don't be so frivolous, especially on the night Lenz Zbraggen shot himself. You must have had an argument with Joop after lunch yesterday."

With our grudging gentleman's agreement still in mind I asked: "Did he say something about it?"

"No, but he must have been absolutely furious at you and must have bottled it all up inside himself. It's not like him; he's more the type for tremendous outbursts. You remember how he shot at young Haberzettl in front of our Cottage-Villa?"

"There we are back at the subject of shooting again. I wasn't there but Karl Homsa told me about it. And how the whole affair was squelched by Inspector Honsowitz."

"I don't know how you remember all those names."

"Remembering names is a specialty of mine."

"Orszczelski-Abendsperg died in '26 and two years later I married ten Breukaa and shortly after that Joop went on a business trip to Java where he'd spent part of his childhood, and because it was Fasching time in Vienna I threw a little house party in the town house we'd just moved into near Hohe Warte, an artist's ball with *real* artists, but also with aristos like Baroness Guepin. Joop telegraphed from Aden that he would be in Vienna in four or five days. How could I know he'd change his mind and take a plane from Cairo to Trieste."

"He really was a flying Dutchman."

"So we were living it up at the party until the wee hours of the morning—but it was no orgy—not in my house, I'm a respectable woman, you know."

"I know," I said without irony.

"If you're thinking of my merry widow days ... Well, those times were long past."

"So you were just a merry wife then?"

"Now come on, all I did was cuddle up to this fellow Haberzettl a little bit—really just a little; whatever you heard about it was probably blown all out of proportion ... and at eight o'clock in the morning as we're having our hangover breakfast Joop arrives via taxi from the Suedbahnhof after taking the night train from Trieste. He crosses the snow-covered yard and tries to open the front door—but it's chained from inside; the door opens only a crack. And then of all things Haberzettl happens to pass the door at that very moment—still good and drunk, carrying a dish of herring salad, and because he's never seen Joop before he says, 'Hey, what do you want here? You must have the wrong house. This is a private party.' And slams the door in Joop's face. Locks the poor man out of his own house."

"An awkward situation for the master of the house."

"What would you have done in his place?"

"I'd probably have broken in the nearest window."

"Joop is too reserved for that. Blasé or whatever you want to call it. At the same time he was fa-*na*-tically jealous of me and unfortunately he still is today. He goes with his suitcase to the garage where he keeps one of his guns. He got himself a gun license because the villa was fairly isolated. Here in the basement of Acla Silva he's also got a whole arsenal of the things."

"Yes, he hinted that to me."

"So he gets his revolver out of the garage and sits down under the arbor in the garden. Imagine that, in the February cold when he's just gotten back from the Red Sea. He waits-and-waits-and-waits. Slowly the guests begin to leave, but no one notices Joop. Last of all comes Haberzettl. Not that I had made the slightest concession to him—he was just a little party flirt, but not so easy to get rid of ... And when I finally get him outside ... the sun had been up for a while now ... my husband comes trudging through the snow with a gun in hand. First the young fellow thinks it's a Fasching joke, then he gets the scare of his life. Runs back to the house. Joop shouts *once*."

"And hits him."

"In the left cheek—of his behind."

"That detail I hadn't heard before."

"It was only a flesh wound, which I patched up right away—as you know, and who would know better, I was an army nurse who tended lots of wounded men. I had his pants rewoven. And Joop, now that his anger was spent—"

"Anger with a time fuse."

"—ordered a large sculpture from Haberzettl, and we agreed to whitewash the whole affair, but then one of our chambermaids went to the police anyway. Naturally I fired the girl, but as it turned out Haberzettl swore he'd attacked Joop and that Joop had acted in self defense, and this Inspector Hon-what's-his-name? Yes, Honsowitz, closed an eye to the whole affair after Joop said he was willing to contribute three thousand schillings to the Police Football Club. Why I'm telling you this shooting story after hearing about that awful Soldier Buddy incident, I don't know. I really don't want to hear one more thing about shooting."

"But Pola, I'm afraid we will."

Then she swayed over to me on her high buskins, bent over me, put her arms around my neck and kissed me in the middle of my forehead. My scar pulse felt the touch of her lips, which, for a few seconds, caused me a startling discomfort, as if someone were kissing my naked heart.

2

"At times I feel like a night-walker who believes in ghosts; every corner appears secret and terrifying."
F. M. Klinger

Was it the hallucination of a wrecked Austro-Marxist?

As I was leaving, Pola put a record on her phonograph, and "Wiener Blut" came waltzing out of the Chinese rococo cabinet. *Forte.* Her reasoning. It would hardly bother Uorschletta, who was hard of hearing anyway, but Bonjour *should* notice it. Even though it wasn't advisable to get Joop worked up (in view of our little feud) the servant-chauffeur should know that Madame and her late visitor had spent the whole time listening to records in the salon. By following the path through Staz Forest—I could hardly miss it on such a bright night—I would reach Pontresina on foot inside an hour; I just had to bear right past little Staz Lake, then I would reach the Plaun da Choma. And from there it wasn't far. Plaun da Choma? Where had I heard that name before? Oh yes. After my second encounter with the Two Blonds at Chantarella Station, I meet the country lawyer near his house on the schoolhouse square, and he—making a sober impression for once—gives me a ride in his Fiat to Pontresina, and when we've passed the Punt Muragl he points out across Flaz Brook Plaun da Choma ...

Pola had dug a blue woolen scarf out of her winter wardrobe and forced it on me along with a Japanese flashlight, slender as a fountain pen, and I hadn't been able to tell her I was planning to leave the Engadine that same day (Tuesday, June 21) to escape from a certain Mr. Balz Zbraggen. I had only mumbled something about not being sure when I could return the stuff. Don't worry, she'd said, the stuff was a good-bye present, and with that she had switched on the porch candelabra and the green-paned lantern on the garden gate and led me across the terraced garden, and from the left and right giant Great Danes had trotted up dragging giant chains. Sirio, obviously somewhat spooked by them, had walked beside me at a close heel. Pola, too seemed to place little trust in the Spahi's guardians; wrapped in a caracul baby-sheep jacket that reminded me of my old dragoon's uniform (Why must newborn baby lambs give up their lives to make such regalia? Though it hadn't concerned me as a boy-dragoon, I now felt an aversion to this senseless waste.), the lady of the house had hooked onto my arm and tottered on her buskins up to the little wooden bridge-cum-garden gate. Had unlocked the latter, given me a resigned kiss on the corner of my mouth and asked me to wait at the newly reinforced portal until she reentered the house. Sirio had given me two loving nudges with his cold-wet nose, reason enough for me to suspect he wouldn't have objected to coming along. I had waited until he and his mistress had disappeared into the house and the porch light and gate lantern were extinguished, then started out on my way, asking myself: Why in the world doesn't she go to bed? For once again I heard behind me the strains of Strauss's "Wiener Blut."

I didn't need the miniature flashlight. The brightness of the remarkably clear Milky Way seeped down into the pine forest and allowed me, as Pola had predicted, to find my way without difficulty. In this second hour of morning no one but me, the nightwalker, seemed to be abroad in Staz Forest—not a single pair of lovers, not one human soul. A distant sequence of short, ocarina-like hoots—were there screech owls up here?—just the proverbial thing to evoke eerie feelings. Yet curiously enough I didn't feel the least bit threatened . . . on the contrary, I felt rather cozy. The uncanny, the unfamiliar. Shielded from the night's chill by Pola's scarf I remembered that article of Freud's that appeared in *Imago* just after the war. Far from any human contact, my whereabouts unknown to anyone but Pola, I felt secure, unthreatened. Nevertheless, even before I sniffed the dull odor of planks from the bathhouse on Staz Lake I began to get the vague feeling I was being followed.

Hallucinations of a ruined Austro-Marxist?

Over Staz Lake—which appeared surprisingly small—the pine tops opened up to the sky, and I could make out the neat little old-fashioned bathhouse with its wooden cabins and diving board. Then I saw it again: the light in the lake. No. I really couldn't claim to have seen it again because Lake Campfèr, where I had seen *the* Light in the Lake, was so much larger than this mountain-forest pond, and this was no weird underwater illumination but merely the reflection of a waning moon that had risen just after midnight, a sickle appearing much leaner than the one I had watched yesterday from the tower of the Luzienburg. It had risen after my arrival at Acla Silva; and as I began my walk through the forest, it was hidden by the trees. Here and now it seemed like something a magician had conjured up, strange and yet familiar. Did it never cease to rise, this moon in June?

Professor Freud: It may be true that the strange, the unfamiliar is actually the familiar which has been suppressed so that the need for it is fulfilled by everything unfamiliar.

I listened and heard no more owl hoots, but something that *did* make me shiver a little.

"Wiener Blut."

Was it possible that Pola, instead of going to bed, was playing over and over again the same record she had put on when I departed, and that the sound of the Chinese rococo phonograph could carry through the forest across the distance I had covered in twenty minutes of walking? Was not something rotten in the state of Denmark? If there had been a single light showing in the lonely bathhouse I would have made the attempt to use the telephone and call Pola, "Hello there, say are you *really* playing 'Wiener Blut' over and over again or is that just another hallucination of a wrecked Austro-Marxist?"

PONTRESINA STATION/GARE/STAZIONE 3.9 km.
Plaun da Choma 0.8 km.

At the signpost I used Pola's flashlight for once, then left Staz Lake behind me.

Plaun da Choma.

Could that mean the lowlands of coma, the plains of coma, the last, unconscious struggle against death? Holy Laudon, how long might the country lawyer and his spaniels have struggled? Just as I asked myself this question I became aware that he was walking beside me. Yes, he and the patriarch Archie close by his heels were the first ones I "saw."

Professor Freud: We can no longer ignore the ground on which we tread. An analysis of cases of the supernatural has led us back to the old way of understanding the world called animism, a view characterized by the tendency to populate the world with manlike spirits and by man's narcissistic overestimation of his own psychological processes.

Plaun da Choma. The pine forest began to thin out and I got my first fleeting glimpse into the other valley, the sleeping valley in which Xana too was probably sleeping her strange deep sleep, and beyond and up to the few lights of the mountain station Muottas Muragl, lights that seemed part of the Milky Way, and some thirty paces to my left strolled *Doctor juris* Gaudenz de Colana, off the trail through stone-pines, larches and firs, paralleling my course, gait somewhat unsteady, closely followed by the old cocker spaniel Arcibaldo, and then I "saw" the other ones waddling along behind, Felice, Concetta, and all the rest of them. Disappearing behind trees, reappearing again. But all of them, man and dogs alike, had a kind of waterlogged, shapeless swollenness about them. All seemed drained of any color. All appeared pale and as white as grubs.

I stopped, touched in a familiar-unfamiliar way by this so-called apparition, having reverted to a state of "animism, man's narcissistic overestimation of his own psychological processes"—a reversion intensified by exhaustion, mitigated by overstimulation. For the same fraction of a second as I, the country lawyer and his cockers stood still, he resting on his grub white cane, his floppy white hat pushed up on his forehead, taking no more notice of me than his dogs did.

I listened behind me. No, Johann Strauss Jr.'s "Wiener Blut" followed me no longer.

As soon as I began to move, de Colana and his entourage did likewise. At the next turn in the trail I "discovered" a bicyclist on my right. He pumped the pedals with uncanny slowness, cycling at walking speed across the Plaun da Choma without track or trail, he too swollen, and grub white his clothes, his face, his patriarch's beard, his bicycle, his bulging rucksack. How long might the death struggle of the ill-fated printer Arli Zuan have lasted? About as long as that of his lawyer. Taking no notice of the latter or myself, he moved along—also in the same direction I was going, and I quickly grew accustomed to the fact of being accompanied but unnoticed.

Grandpa Kujath had not changed very much. He strode across the Plaun da Choma a short distance behind the last of the spaniels and next to another color-less figure. Judging from Pfiff's report, his coma had been a short one, and the grub white of his sea-lion head and his raw-silk suit was little different from the color, or colorlessness, he showed when facing me in the tower studio some twenty-eight hours earlier.

The other man was dressed in shimmering-pale rags. His white face seemed strangely erased, and yet I immediately recognized him as the ex-Reichstag delegate Valentin Tiefenbrucker. How had Pfiff said it on the telephone? "When the Modesto boys hauled him out of the burning Fieseler-Storch, he was still alive, but not for long." His black luster-fabric suit, burned, the white-shimmering rags, his singed, soot-smeared face, now as if flour had been thrown over it. Valentin.

He paced along next to Grandpa Kujath, and neither of them took any notice of the other.

My nightwalker's path began to run alongside a narrow, wedge-shaped grove of young trees, rows of saplings fenced in with shiny steel wire. There in front of me amidst the trees I "saw" the white rider on his white horse. He was riding at a walk, bareheaded, with the elastic firmness, that centaurian oneness with the horse that had characterized Giaxa to the end, and it, the horse, waded through the first risings of morning fog that wreathed the saplings, and even though it was Lippizan white, it was not—so I determined with my ex-dragoon's eye—any of the Giaxas IV to VII I knew.

Mjoellnir! It jolted through me—the East Prussian thoroughbred of Dachau's Detention Camp Director Giselher Liebhenschl—the dun stallion! All its golden color gone, depigmented like its rider and his clothing. What I now perceived, no, thought to perceive, no, perceived, caused me a real shudder. Close by the horse and rider pale fire licked back and forth . . . How long might their death struggle have lasted? Their electrocution?

This phenomenon, at least, offered an immediate plausible explanation: the steel wire bordering the young trees as it was struck by the beams of the moon . . .

All at once I saw his second horse.

This one *had* pigmentation, shimmering light brown, yes, a kind of dun color.

At the same time I became aware of the dull sound my own footsteps made on the "pavement," the countless generations of dead pine-needles underfoot. Giaxa's second horse heard it too. It alone heard it while the rest of the procession continued on at the same rate I was walking. It stopped and turned its head and stood in tense readiness, and I recognized plausible explanation number two, that it was a stag with very light coloration, a real one, an old stag (that much I knew as a passionate anti-hunter), a twelve-pointer.

Its branching antlers stood out as if engraved into the faint light above the young trees.

As I stepped toward it the stag jumped the enclosure—in an unbelievably elegant, youthful leap. A fading crackle of underbrush marked his escape route.

Paying no heed to this, Giaxa rode on. At a walk. At *my* walk. The sapling grove behind me. Behind us. Behind me. The thinned-out ranks of Plaun da Choma's pines; soon the trees would open up completely to reveal the sparse lights of Pontresina and perhaps the headlights of a long-distance truck (a truck, a Saurian, that was another chapter) on Route 29, the San Gian road, and the ghosts, according to ancient custom would vanish into thin air. But at the moment their numbers were increasing. Behind the bicyclist walked a man, larva white, swinging an equally white carbine—Soldier Buddy; his struggle could not have lasted more than a half second. But what about that of Dr. Maxim Grabscheidt, poor-man's medic from the Lastenstrasse in Graz?

At the wedgelike tip of the sapling grove he must have waited for me, and now he walked beside me, closer to me than all the others, yes silently upon the same gently falling forest trail whose skylight was the Milky Way, grub colored, with a shaven head (so they had even managed to drag the dying man to the camp barber!), dressed in baggy, gray-white-on-white striped prison uniform, his white lips touched with a strange-familiar-mysterious smile that might have said . . . *might* have said, Sorry, Trebla, that I can't notice you; I'm sleeping, sleepwalking, sleeping. But out of his forehead jutted the white horn-handle of a hunting knife.

How long might Maxim's agony have lasted, how many hours?

That was no longer secret and terrifying, that was unbearable; I didn't look at him again.

Hallucinations of a wrecked Austro-Marxist?

That night they escorted me home, the dead.

3

From Pola to Pina, who would have thought of that?

Puntraschigna. It occurs to the nightwalker: Romansh name for Pontresina, whose church bell now strikes two as he sneaks with silent soles up the post-office stairway. Quietly he opens the door of the tourist room that has been his chamber for four weeks now—and which he plans to move out of this very day. Against the wall, unlike before, a made-up bed. A slip of paper in the Remington: *Don't be mad because I moved your bed in here, but right now I need all the sleep I can get. In the event you ever do come home, sleep well, brother dear, you've earned it. X.* Ex period. Has she, who is so little concerned with getting wind of things, gotten wind of the fact (via village gossip? from the otherwise discreet Madam Fausch?) that he told waitress Pina, the melancholy Roman-looking maid from Valtellina, that he was on a hay-fever cure, not with his wife, but with his half sister? The connecting door locked from inside—rather odd of Xana, who so seldom locks her doors and suitcases. The nightwalker, too, needs his sleep after all the turmoil of Ghost-train Monday. He should simply shower quietly and accept the new sleeping arrangement. And indeed, he does take the shower. But in the third hour of Tuesday, yes, Tuesday the twenty-first of June, the first day of Greater Germany's first summer, this exile from the Reich is standing by the well in front of the Morteratsch Hotel, and it is still night, no cock has yet crowed, so that he might still be called a nightwalker. No cowbell clanging is heard either. Only the lonely watering trough splashes out its endless litany, sounding at this hour more lively than during the day, yet at the same time more tired. In this it bears a strong resemblance to the nightwalker himself. The careful footsteps of iron-cleated boots. Two heavily packed mountain guides, frequent visitors to the hotel's common room, trudge Berninawards, both smoking pipes, strolling at an easy pace. In the bright night they eye the man at the well with something like cautious mistrust. "*Salue.*"

"*Salue.*"

Their heavy boots toed slightly inward they trudge away, speaking Romansh in subdued tones. Talking perhaps about the shot that ended the life of that fellow Lenz Zbraggen from San Murezzan, horrible thing, that was, and "that character by the well was supposed to be involved" . . .? Improbable that these professional early-sleepers have heard about it already, but in any case the nightwalker is reminded of the argument he used to justify his current venture—that he had seen too many deaths, intensifying his lust. He knows where Pina lives. Should he attempt to make a window call? He gropes his way down the many steps running down the slope beside the hotel, and a late-hunting bat aims blind but dead-on at a fat moth fluttering madly around the single lamp above the stairs—snap, the bat darts off with his prey. The nightwalker cannot help comparing himself with this winged, late-night hunter. The last time he saw the country lawyer alive a bat was part of the scene, and when he unveiled Pina's marble white bosom behind Spaniola tower there was a whole swarm of them. *"Tanti pipistrelli!"* Didn't she tell him she lived alone in the first room at the foot of the outer stairs? Almost as swiftly as the bat he turns onto a concrete platform with empty clotheslines and a series of small wooden doors, each with a small rib-shuttered window (too small for window calls), the shutters of the first window halfway open. Out of the room's darkness the heavy ticking of a cheap alarm clock.

"Pina . . ."

Inside the small cry, the gasping whisper of someone roused from sleep: *"Chi va là?"*

"Il vecchio pipistrello."

The heavy ticktock of the alarm clock. Then: *"Chi? Che cosa?"*

The nightwalker collects his Italian. *"Il vecchio pipistrello aspetta fuòri alla porta."*

"C-o-m-e-e-e?" Inside, the whisper has changed to an indignant hiss. He repeats: The old bat is waiting outside the door. Now another sibilant sound: straw sandals sliding across the floor. Pina's marble pallor shines in the frame of the door-window. Face and nightgown seem made of the same material. The same thing true of her black hair, the heavy comb she runs through it and the "material" of her eyes, their stare by no means friendly. (Light enough to detect this.)

"Oh, Alberto." It sounded by no means friendly.

"La luna è oggi molto più magra, non è vero?" The nightwalker's attempt to embellish his window call with old bats and "meager" moons fails completely. She does not even deign to answer him in her own language.

"Go sleep, Alberto. I have-a get up inna two hour. I wanna sleep now."

"Is that all you've got to say to your old bat-man?"

"You go a-sleep." The ribbed shutter is pulled closed, lending a certain confessional atmosphere to the subsequent whispers.

"Non posso entrare?"

"No. You go home-a now, or you wake uppa da tree kitch-na girlss nexa door."

"The three kitchen girls will not wake up if you let me in. Inside I'll be as quiet as a little bat."

"You fly-a home now, *pipistrello*. Go back-a sleep wid your-a sister." The gruffness of her whispering!

"But I sleep solo."

"Sure-a, sure-a. You can go-da sleep-a wid your preddy sister. But maybe *il commissario* Mavegn don't-a like it."

"What do you mean?"

"Maybe dey take-a you to Samedan on-a Sunday 'cause-a you're *incestuoso*. 'Cause you did it wid your-a sister . . ."

"Me, an *incestuoso*? They've said a lot of things about me, but that tops everything. *Incestuoso* indeed!"

"You not laff-a so lout. You wake uppa da kitch-na girlss. *Va via*."

So that's what's itching her: Incest! The nightwalker whispers through the shutter's ribs: "I don't sleep in the same room with the Signora. Come over to the post office. See for yourself. *Dormo in una altra camera, capisce? La signora* is sleeping in her own room with the door locked. I couldn't get in there if I wanted to. I swear it's the truth."

Inside the ticktock of the alarm clock, then Pina's less harsh whisper. "You swear it's-a true, Alberto?"

"I swear."

Ah, this nightwalker, if only such deceitful honesty were his worst fault!

The quiet sliding of sandals moved away a short distance. Now I could hear an irregular splashing. What was Pina doing in there with the light off? Was she, now that she was awake anyway, washing some underwear she had forgotten, before going back to sleep? Hadn't she encouraged bat-man Trebla . . .

. . . I remembered the dream I'd had after my two-man drinking spree with de Colana: in it I had been a male animal, a little, soft, delicate, but very quick little animal . . .

Hadn't Pina encouraged me to think she'd let me in? I waited. And before he knew it the nightwalker was transformed into an early morning loiterer. While the valley remained submerged in night, its roof of stars had now grown somewhat paler and the mountains took on that first trace of steel gray blue I had observed from Julier Pass twenty-four hours earlier, just as I was about to be fooled by the first dawn whistles of the woodchucks . . . Then, only twenty-four hours ago, but what a distant, irretrievable "then," Grandpa Henrique Kujath, escaped prisoner Tiefenbrucker, and lumber dealer Lenz Zbraggen were all still alive. No, don't think about it now. What's there to do? Try hanging on the clothesline stretched out beside the row of doors? head downward like a bat? Or with my fingernails I could play a kind of arpeggio across the ribs of the wooden shutters, pianissimo, like a harpist. Inside Pina's splashing had stopped; the shuffling sandals came closer, then a gentle sliding back of the bolt. The door window opened inward. Bat-man Trebla whisked inside.

I shoved the bolt back in place, sniffing the rather pervasive scent of cheap lavender cologne and experiencing a great sensation offered me by the twilight of fading stars and first gray of morning that fell through the slats of the shutters. All things are relative. But at this moment it *was* a sensation for me. To discover that Pina had not been washing underwear but herself. That she was standing in front of me stark naked. Not absolutely stark naked; after all she was still wearing her straw sandals. She herself seemed unaware of her nudity until she noticed my surprise. Quickly she slipped on her long country-girl's nightgown. But it was too late. I was comparing her anatomy, and it was having an effect.

Was this Pina from Valtellina? Wasn't it really the young Basque maiden Maïtena Ithurra y Azkue, daughter of the director of the Sociedad de los Estudios Vascos in San Sebastian, Maïtena, whose eldest brother, a famed pelota player, was killed fighting for the Republic during Franco's Asturian offensive, Maïtena, who lost two more brothers—shot on Monte Urgull by the Falangists? No, don't think about it now. *Her* body could have shimmered like that if I had had her to myself at dawn in the tower studio. If the status she had mistakenly given me, the status of an escaped-Dachau-prisoner-volunteer for the all but lost cause of the first *Republica Espanola*, if my mistaken identity had suffered to overcome her resistance. *Her* body could have shimmered like this. The way Pina's had shimmered before she slipped the long nightgown over her head.

That was no Maïtena nightgown.

Pina bent down over the narrow bed to straighten it out. The early light that fell through the ribs of the shutters created a kind of magic unreality here, as if the bluish light of a quartz lamp were shining dimly in, or as if daylight were penetrating to the bottom of a glacial crevasse. As I got undressed, still feeling the aftereffects of the shower that had washed away the residues of Ghost-train Monday—a pleasant skin-prickling that kept me from feeling the chill of the room—I listened, slightly annoyed, to the heavy ticks of the big alarm clock as they echoed through the tiny chamber. Holy Laudon, how can Pina get any sleep with a racket like that going on.

By means of a simple trick, I managed to turn Pina back into Maïtena.

As she bent over the bed I pulled her rustic nightgown over her head, not forcibly, but with something like gentle suddenness. Pulled it up so that only her head and left arm and shoulder remained covered by it. Before she realized what was going on behind her back, she was at once disrobed and disguised.

The heavy ticking of the clock.

Now it was working again, the comparative anatomy. Bare shoulder, back, buttocks, thighs, all seemed as classically proportioned as if sculpted by Praxiteles in this bluish ice-grotto light that heightened and transformed the beautiful molding of her body. A body that could have been Maïtena's. With gentle suddenness I stretched my arms under hers and clasped—for the second time since a week ago (just *one* week?) by the tower on the Languard slope—her well-rounded, small, firm breasts. Was this Maïtena? And the heavy ticking of the clock.

Strange that she left it that way. That her right hand didn't simply free her head and left arm from the covering gown. Instead her right hand began another task. Slid past her hip and began, very cautiously, to touch my nakedness, so very cautiously that it might have been the touch of Maïtena's hand—in these times of war the deep-seated restraints of tradition were swept away. There, at last, after all the chaotic experiences of Ghost-train Monday, after all the unsatisfied lust of a man who has seen too many deaths, *it* began to awake. And as she touched, ever so cautiously, then felt, the experience drew from her an expression of combined dismay, respect, and delight in the rough-melodious timber of a young Latin woman's voice, in Romansh, Italian, or Spanish—*Yes, it could be Spanish!*—inarticulate beneath her long, draped "mask," a short sentence, half whisper, half shout.

And the heavy ticking of the clock.

—which sounded even louder. No, the kitchen maids in the next room would not be wakened by this stifled cry. With gentle suddenness I pushed her forward onto the edge of the bed and she kneeled down, thighs slightly spread, her sandals falling with dull flops (there was no rug, no bedside mat) onto the wooden floor.

Now give it to her from behind give it to her this young Basque charmer wants it in this position this situation you fell for her up there in the castle didn't you you old rascal can you believe a young Basque Catholic would let you in no questions asked between her Praxiteles-modeled thighs she lets you forward between thighs that must belong to no one but Pina this time not hot marble but hot *living flesh* pulsing to the rhythm of my well trained thrusting busily pushing back that must be Pina kneeling with her back to me willingly opening helping with her right hand bringing campanile in position that can't be the young Basque charmer how happy you'd have been last week to have only Pina now she stiffens of course she's had it already she stiffens and kneels there like an Egyptian animal statue no not a statue very living flesh on all fours living animal life and now pulls her covered head down harder her back sloping like a slide and now for her the second round begins while I what a self-controlled rascal am still fighting the first one and bent over on her rumpled gown and her free elbow she hasn't had time to free her head and left arm while she breathlessly gasps out again and again this incomprehensible sentence followed by the name Al-berto again and again: my name in Italian. *But also in Spanish.*

Was it Maïtena after all?

Suddenly, as if jabbed, I was sitting up in a strange bed; not Pina's but mine, though the surroundings were strange. My chamber, into which X. had banished me. (*In the event you ever do come home, sleep well, brother dear, you've earned it.* X. An oracle with an inborn gift for charming sarcasm?) The churchbell. Three strokes. Feels to me like 10:45. The excessive brightness of the forenoon shining through the shutters on the balcony door; *another* long, long, *over*bright day. Did it have to be that way? No . . . I would leave this place today or (at the latest) tomorrow morning! Just then I remembered the dream, the nightmare that had haunted me just before I woke.

Healthy is the man who dreams, nightmares or otherwise! Dreams are a vital regulative; nondreamers go insane. My first thought was, catch it, the *whole* dream, or it will escape, will be forever erased or remain a meaningless fragment in my memory. And it was such a typical dream . . . so typical of the situation I found myself—or was caught in.

I was standing on the little wooden bridge leading to the Villa Muongia, Mordechai Katzbein-Brialoszynski's kosher guesthouse, not far from the pier down which I had seen Zuan cycle to his watery death, and it was bright daylight and I was running away. Condemned for some reason, I had to get away from somewhere to escape a special kind of execution. Having arrived at my place of refuge, here and now, gazing down from the bridge into the deep, deep green water, I found myself in a familiar, yet changed, but nonetheless unlucky situation. One thing I knew: I had to get away, away even from here, in my pocket the dubious gift of an indefinite reprieve. (Exactly what kind of execution I faced and who was supposed to carry it out—these facts were as indefinite as the reprieve itself.) I had to get away, but where could I go—that was the question. Staring down into the deep green water (green from the mirrored pines?), I chanced to see the neckless lady.

The fish.

The lady.

The fish matron.

At first I took her for a female dolphin measuring seven feet or more. A stately female. As she swam up from the green opaqueness through the higher, iridescent levels almost to the surface, her sex never seemed in doubt, most of all because of her "attire." Dolphins are mammals like human beings. Because (according to family legend) a half-tame Adriatic dolphin had once watched over Xana like a kind of nursemaid, I was a dolphin lover. But dolphins, I reflected, staring over the bridge railing, lived in the sea and not in Alpine lakes. Thus it had to be a giant catfish, or more specifically, a female giant catfish. For I had no doubt about the sex of this underwater denizen. As I recalled my biology lessons in Olmuetz, it occurred to me that the catfish, though not a mammal, could move short distances overland—from one lake to another. Thus it was a kind of kissing cousin, so to speak. But dolphin lovers are not catfish lovers. I was not terribly attracted to this big-mouthed giantess who swam seemingly intentional pirouettes right under my nose, a completely neckless creature with a flat head and long black whiskers that snaked revoltingly as she turned. Fastened to her flat head (or growing out of it), a kind of silly, mundane Victorian bonnet with a

314

short veil like those worn by rich American widows at European resorts.

On her right front fin hung something like a handbag (or a mass of sea-weed?), which she kept swinging back and forth in a beckoning manner. She also moved her head to the side several times—again clearly beck-oning—causing her moustache to dance and (since she had no neck) half her body to move as well. And occasionally, with a kind of matronly flirtatiousness, she briefly let me see her massive, pale belly.

By means of this (most expressive) pantomime she was able to deliver the following message and invitation:

Come, dive into my realm!—but not to drown yourself like Zarli Zuan—and by the way I *know* where *he* is. You have nothing to fear, young man, either from the green water or my womanly charms—I'm really just being motherly; I'm much older, you know; you could be my son! Trust me, you won't drown!—you'll see how much easier you breathe down here than up above!—where you feel so confined and persecuted, don't you *Herr von*————? (She knew my name.) Come on now, jump right in, don't be afraid!

Quite literally, I fell for it. Took off my corduroy jacket and, still wearing my Peyatchevich pants, did a perfect headfirst dive into the deep green water. The slightest sensation of drowning would bring me straight back to the surface.

I didn't drown.

Thus a key point of the fish matron's pantomimic-telepathic message was borne out. My confidence rose as I sank, sank. Like a diver needing no diving lung, breathing normally as if I had gills—strangestrange, and yet, I reasoned, it had only been a few million years since my ancestors had been fitted with such equipment—and I swam heels over head some fifty yards into the depths until I reached bottom. Once there I saw no trace of the fish matron, nor indeed had I seen her on the way down. She had disappeared from the face of the earth (I mean the floor of the sea). Instead, in the refracted, dim emerald twilight of the deep I caught sight of the billowing black beard.

Yes, in the slight bottom-current it snaked up from a Something that re-sembled a human body tied on its back to the floor of the lake. Next to it the twisted wreck of the bicycle—Zuan's rucksack-weighted corpse!

Stepping closer (or gliding, since gravity was partly neutralized here) I real-ized my mistake. It was not a beard, but a bunch of water plants growing from an outcropping of rock. Nor could the bicycle be the one Zuan pedaled to his death. A bent and rusted velocipede from the early days of cycling, a "high wheeler" with its huge front wheel and tiny rear one, a cycle that might have fallen into the lake some fifty years before. Now I discovered that the lake bot-tom all around me was littered with household trash: broken bottles, rusty ket-tles with swarms of little silver fish swimming through the holes in their sides, a cracked bidet, half an iron bed intertwined with underwater vines, dented tins with still readable labels GUGGENHEIM'S MATZOS; some distance away a sunken fishing boat with the characteristic hoop frame for mounting a sun roof—the kind common on Upper Italian lakes and in Segantini's pointillistic paintings, rotted and black. On one of the hoops a shread of blackened canvas waved in the current like a black flag in gentle wind.

From that direction came the procession.

Half trudging, half sailing across the underwater trash-heap, and always heading in my direction as I stood by the "bearded" rock. In the lead something like a baldachin swayed and glided forward, and as it neared I recognized it as a once splendid, now sunken, moldering Engadine sleigh, seemingly modified to a kind of sedan chair supported by four bearers. In it sat the giant catfish matron. Down here her belly gleamed greenish pink like tourmaline. She didn't deign to look at me now, as if she had never swum her inviting, pantomimic pirouettes at the surface. Her monstrous mouth seemed painted with the latest lipstick from Elizabeth Arden. Her few long black whiskers waved and twined in spirals. Then the long train drifted past me, carried along in a gliding march tempo by the underwater current, sometimes borne up in small, swirling leaps like a slow motion ballet troupe. All men, of every age, bareheaded, emerald-green-on-green, but not corpses, not swollen, apparently not even drowned.

Except for the litter bearers all were shouldering chests that looked like children's coffins, clasping them with their right hands to keep them from drifting away. And from their mouths dangled small objects that, upon closer inspection, turned out to be miniature padlocks.

None of them spoke to me, but even if one had wanted to the tiny padlock on his lips would have made it impossible. But the occasional glances thrown my way expressed a dreadful resignation. Pain approaching madness. Or something resembling self-possessed horror.

And so the procession swayed, sailed, swirled, and sprang past me, obviously toward the center of the lake.

The feeling of blind trust I had felt suddenly changed to its exact opposite. I made a desperate attempt to push off from the lake bottom and swim back toward the bright day above me, the day whose refracted light seemed suddenly veiled in red. From some distant underwater bleeding?

But I had sunk too deep, too deep . . . the pressure of the water prevented the slightest upward motion. Then I caught sight of Zarli Zuan.

A straggler, yet unquestionably part of the procession, drawn by it, tied to it, not swollen (thus *not* drowned a few days before, not drowned!), free of his weighted rucksack, he pushed his bicycle along beside him. His miniature coffin on the luggage rack instead of on his shoulder.

Bringing up the rear, he could allow himself to pause beside one for a few seconds. And since the padlock on his lips (due to his patriarch's beard?) was rather loosely mounted, he was able to speak a few gurgling words that bubbled out of the right corner of his mouth:

"*Salue*, sir, so you're here too? *Excusez*, then *you* are also lost."

"Where," I also bubbled, "are you all marching to?"

"To our execution, monsieur."

"Execution?"

"Exactly. The giant beast—is going to eat us *all*."

"Beast? . . . The catfish lady?"

"Exactly, Hide and hair. The few bones left over go in the little coffin."

"You're carrying your own coffins to your execu——?"

"Exactly. *Your* turn will come in the next procession, *monsieur*. After *this* one is swallowed and, ah, digested by the greedy creature. By the way, her name is Dorothy."

"Dorothy?" I gurgled.

"Yes," gurgled Zuan. "Because she comes from the Dorotheum, the famous pawn shop in Vienna."

4
───

Pola came by with Bonjour and Sirio and abducted me to Alp Gruem. Return this evening. Don't wait for me but take good care of yourself. Χαῖρε. *Tender embrace.*

X.

The message, scrawled in pencil on the back of a laundry receipt, had been shoved under the connecting door; I scanned the text with my reading monocle. This legible, well-proportioned, simple handwriting seemed different than usual, slanted ever so slightly downward. Also several words seemed to lack the usual consistent-graceful balance, particularly the Greek *"chaire"* (something like *"ciao"* or *"so long"*). The door no longer locked. X's room—since yesterday hers alone—stood in complete disarray, a still life more grotesque than amusing and hardly attributable to a sudden departure for Alp Gruem. It looked almost as if burglars had ransacked the room. I washed, shaved, dressed and armed myself within seven minutes (but not carelessly) and hurried—ask Madam Fausch for the mail later!—over to Confiserie Jann. And began—even before the glass of black coffee stood steaming before me—to page through the Tuesday morning editions of the *Neue Zuercher Zeitung*, the Basel *National-Zeitung*, the *Tribune de Genève*—nothing, still nothing about Giaxa's end.

A slight sigh of relief.

Also nothing about the shooting down of a Fieseler-Storch and its passenger V. Tiefenbrucker, nothing, and nothing yet about Lenz Zbraggen's suicide.

LATE NEWS FROM THE NATIONAL-ZEITUNG:

Henrique Kujath-von Plessnow, the noted Graubuenden businessman, died yesterday at Luzienburg in the Domleschg, only hours before his seventieth birthday. Born in Berlin, Mr. Kujath, a true self-made man and pioneer, founded large rubber plantations in northern Brazil around the turn of the century, became a Swiss citizen in 1910 and shortly thereafter purchased the Luzienburg where he established a mill and silo. This operation involved a remarkable alteration of the castle—planned by Kujath himself and executed by a well-known architect from Chur—which was all the more notable for not being challenged by the Swiss Historical Society. (See tomorrow's edition for more on this many-sided personality.—The Editors.)

STOYADINOVICH MEETS COUNT CIANO IN VENICE. JAPANESE PLAN ATTACK ON HAIHAN. MASSACRE IN BAJADOZ. EXECUTIONS IN MALAGA. BURGOS JUNTA BECOMES NATIONAL GOVERNMENT. 70,000 IMPRISONED IN BASQUE COUNTRY, 20,000 EXECUTED. THE WEATHER IN EUROPE:

Yesterday's high decreasing, low centered over Gulf of Bothnia, falling barometer in the Faroe Islands, warmer, Tuesday night and Wednesday morning heavy thundershower activity in the southern Alps . . . So the long series of overbright days would come to an end. So what. I had to leave anyway. If Xana hadn't taken off for Alp Gruem our *départ* (as they say in this part of Helvetia) would have been today. *Départ*, départ. Check please.

MURSKA SOBOTA 20-6-38

ALBERT————POST PONTRESINA

ELSABES ADDRESS HOTEL ERDOEDY BAD VARAZDINSKE TOPLICE STOP AIRMAIL LETTER UNDERWAY TO YOU POSTE RESTANTE ST MORITZ

AUTES

First day of summer shortly before noon, the Pontresina post office more crowded than ever before in these four weeks, three windows in service instead of two, and Madam Fausch took me out of turn to hand me a telegram with the comment: now Pontresina had a real post office, not just a mailbox, and could I wait over there by the postal timetable, she had something to tell me. As I stepped back I noticed something in the expression of her mannish face that made me coin the dreadful compound: horror-hungry . . .

Fortune amidst misfortune—Elsabé is out of the Third Reich. Thanks to the initiative of Autes, Aurel Tességuier (there were doddering "aristos" and courageous ones, not to mention doddering, courageous ones), who had spirited her out of the country and telegraphed his success from the Slovenian border town of Murska Sobota. But what had inspired Autes to send his airmail letter, which, unlike his telegram, was to be picked up in St. Moritz? Most likely some news he wanted to keep from still-innocent Xana at any cost and therefore hoping to steer me away from her immediate vicinity. Did he know about Giaxa's last ride? Did he want me to absorb the impact of the death notice alone, so that I could get hold of myself and then break it gently to Xana sometime later?

This "break it to her gently"—an old song by now.

"D'you happen to know the widow Zbraggen who runs the big food store in Celerina?"

"No."

"Did you hear about the latest tragedy?"

"Hm?" (What and how much does Madam Fausch know about it?)

"That happened last night over at the Innmuehle Milano. Lenz Zbraggen, favorite son of the widow Zbraggen, shot himself with his carbine right in the middle of the dance floor."

"I heard about it," I said vaguely (instead of saying, I heard the shot).

"And what does Balz do, his brother and constant companion?" Her suppressed horror-hungry voice cracks like an adolescent's.

"Hm?"

"He goes straight to Celerina the same night so's to break it gently to his mother. And how does the widow Brocka take it all?" Pause for effect.

I waited.

"She wails and cries. 'Why'd he do that to me, my Lenz, my favorite son! If y-o-u had gone and shot yourself,' she says to Balz, 'by God I could've stood it better.' And what does Balz do then?"

My brow began to tick.

"Takes his dead brother's carbine into the bedroom. Fills the barrel up with water. Shoots himself in the mouth. Imagine that, the compression . . . His whole head exploded."

"Oh no, the Red Baron, it can't be true! 'Neighbor, your smelling salts!' What a small world! We meet again, here in this little mountain hut! And I thought Himmler had sent you to *Himmel* already!"

With these words she came slinking up to me in the navelike hall of the world-famous jet-set palace, Badrutt's Palace, dressed in a tiger-striped cocktail dress, high-heeling along with exaggerated, bumping swings of her hips—Black Charlotte. After describing for several minutes how she had escaped the "bad guys from the Morzinplatz" she suddenly winced. Pressed her silver-polished manicured claw in front of her cyclamen-red mouth. Spoke at a lower pitch, a toneless tenor. "Oh God, no, I've got to tell you how sorry I am, dear boy. In the name of all those thousands of people *he* made laugh I want to express my heartfelt condolences to you and your charming wife. How terribly, terribly aw-ful that *such* a famous artist had to go in *such* a ghastly way . . . Am I bawling? It may ruin my mascara, but I'm not ashamed to shed a tear at a time like this."

Karl-Otto Schwarzwild, alias Black Charlotte, was a transvestite from Berlin's famous homosexual nightclub the Eldorado, located on the Lutherstrasse near the Scala Variété, where Giaxa put in a guest appearance in 1931. One night following his performance Papa-Rose ended up in the Eldorado along with Elsabé, Xana, and myself. Blond Hansi, a gay fellow dressed as a buxom blond in a low-cut, white satin dress (and with such rosy smooth skin and such a cleverly mounted rubber bosom that no one outside the club would have taken "her" for a man), Blond Hansi greeted Giaxa from the stage of the pederasts' cabaret, and there arose a chorus of cheers from the audience. Later Black Charlotte sat down at our table, a slender creature with a bony chest exposure and a hook nose that seemed to bend down in front of her garish red mouth. In contrast to Blond Hansi she was uglier than sin. To the great Giaxa, Charlotte revealed her real-life identity: a young dress designer of Judaic faith. In the event of a Nazi takeover she planned to go to Vienna. A few years later I met Black Charlotte again on the Graben in Vienna. Dressed in an enormous Florentine hat she walked—high heeled, skinny legged—around the Plague Column looking for a pickup. Not that she made the slightest attempt to treat me as a prospective customer. She viewed Giaxa's writer son-in-law as a kind of colleague—to whom she revealed (a few minutes later in a prostitute's café near the Kohlmarkt) the nature of her present, almost bee-like busyness in Christian Corporate Vienna. Here, too, she worked days as a fashion creator. In addition she operated a salon where she introduced prostitutes to the dwindling supply of rich yokel-visitors from the Alpine provinces, convincing the latter that the girls were young countesses forced to sell their pristine bodies because of the impoverished condition of Austrian nobility. So that the provincial "guests" (mostly farmers who forked over copiously for the privilege of a gallant adventure with such titled young ladies) did not recognize the girls next day as they walked the Kaerntnerstrasse, the countesses all wore carnival masks. In the chic bars of *Grinzing* Charlotte used to latch onto normal cavaliers, passing herself off as a Paris cocotte on a visit to Vienna. And during the subsequent encounters in a one-hour hotel she was usually successful in concealing her sexual identity. Usually, but not always—though the normally drunken state of her suitors facilitated the swindle, she was occasionally exposed as a man and came away with a black eye. Several times, indeed, she was beaten so badly by a dissatisfied customer that she had to be taken by ambulance to General Hospital. But this put no damper on her bee-like activity.

That afternoon the sky had been covered with what looked like giant wads of cotton, and for the first time the famous Engadine air had grown somewhat compressed and sultry. Not only that but a slight burning in my eyes, the first warning of a hay-fever attack, had reminded me of Dr. Tardueser's prophecy. After about four weeks the grass will begin to pollinate up here. It had been necessary to pick up Tességuier's letter at the main post office, St. Moritz, to put on my flannel suit, to pocket my ephedrine, to put Pola's baby blue scarf over my arm, to cancel my accommodations with Madam Fausch (my burning eyes a good excuse) with the request that she tell my wife I went to the city to get an English antiallergy medicine not available here. Yes, for the last time I had boarded the spic-and-span little Bernina train to witness a spectacle that always rather awed me: a conductor of the Swiss National Railway in his immaculate midnight-blue uniform, his elegant shoulder bag of shiny red leather dangling on a long strap to his knees.

The last person I had expected to meet was Black Charlotte.

St. Moritz station, for the first time really bustling, hotel doormen looking like admirals in dress uniforms forming lanes along with servants wearing frog-green aprons. (What had become of the frog-green Miss Tummermut?) Increasing eye irritation; bought a cheap pair of sunglasses at a stand in the station. Toward the main post office, past the giant yellow box of the Grand Hotel; behind it that true *belle-laide*, an ugly-beautiful structure, *mixtum compositum* of Holy Grail castle, Tudor palace, and department store (perhaps an attractive sight when shrouded in the deep snow of an Engadine winter), where a taxi had just halted in front of its ostentatious main entrance. A female with short mink-dangles over a tiger dress. That black Florentine hat, that hip-jerking walk, those skinny legs on which she high-heeled through the revolving door with its attendant, a maroon-liveried bellhop. Off with the sunglasses: Holy Laudon, Black Charlotte?

At the cloakroom another maroon-liveried man had pantomimed accepting my scarf and beret. In the expansive Renaissance-furnished hotel lobby I'd found that my eyes had not deceived me; it was Black Charlotte in transvestite person, who sauntered over to me (just as she had in the Eldorado and later in the prostitutes' café on the Kohlmarkt) to give Giaxa's son-in-law her condolences.

So the news was out.

In the distance—the hall was so massive that the adjoining rooms seemed far away—an alto saxophone played "Night and Day," awakening some unhappy memories. The American hit had been imported at the very moment Uncle Adolf was coming to power. (Nevertheless, one of X's favorite songs.) The tears Black Charlotte was not ashamed to shed did indeed begin smearing the mascara on her left eye. Charlotte, washed by all the waters of the underworld, seemed to wince beneath my questioning gaze. Her lace-gloved left hand reached for her false bosom adorned with a (possibly real) diamond-studded clasp. Almost hesitantly her right hand pointed to the reading room.

Grotesque situation.

I thought as I bent over the table. Found myself with reading monocle at the ready in the company of a few newspaper readers at an enormously long library table that might have held the banquets of the Medici. All across it lay the gazettes of every imaginable country. I reached straight for the midday edition of the *Neue Zuercher Zeitung* (whose morning issue I'd scanned at Confiserie

Jann). The old "banker's aunt" as Kujath irreverently called it, though he praised its thorough news coverage.

CAMP ESCAPEE SHOT DOWN OVER REPUBLICAN TERRITORY

Telephone report from our correspondent in Valencia
(See our editorial on page 5.)

Moscow, June 21. AP/ag. *According to a report by the official Soviet news agency TASS, Tiefenbrucker's body will be transferred to the USSR to be interred in the Kremlin wall.*

About Giaxa's end—the events that had taken place in Dachau shortly before Valentin's breakout—nothing in the *NZZ*, nothing in the Paris *Figaro*, nothing in the London *Times*. Was it possible the transvestite had read it in a German paper . . .? I took down the *Frankfurter Zeitung* from its mount; on its front page, slightly restrained but no less revolting, the Fascist-German line; inside a cautious, perhaps ashamed, but more cosmopolitan tone. They did not support the *Voelkischer Beobachter* polemic against the Swiss border officials, but speculated that Tiefenbrucker's "alleged escape from protective custody in the Reich is questionable in the light of the undeniable fact that the Bavarian Communist died long ago in a Siberian labor camp." The Reich's Propaganda Ministry played its coordinated game with assigned roles, somewhat like the joke about a man involved in a civil suit who defends himself by claiming: "First of all you never gave me the bucket, second it had a hole in it and third I gave it back to you a long time ago."

Nothing about Giaxa's death ride.

On the edge of the table lay the Paris edition of the *New York Herald Tribune, European Edition, 51st Year in Europe.* My gaze stopped, riveted to the page: Giaxa, three times. The three snapshots showed him in 1926 during his American tour with Barnum & Bailey as honored guest at the Rodeo in Madison Square Garden, rising high in a levade, mounted on a fabulous white stallion, unquestionably Argon (Giaxa V), the horse I saw ten years later out to pasture on the little island near Hvar in the Adriatic. Rearing with beautiful ease, like a tree, his forehand raised high, Argon stood on bent haunches, his hocks actually seeming to flex, and behind the horse's head, espressing effortless confidence, the rider's face beneath a ten-gallon hat.

A bust portrait from the same series. The same huge-brimmed Texas hat. The likes of which I'd never seen him wear. His neckerchief hanging western style, he almost looked like a wise sheriff, but only almost: he was too much a son of the ancient Mediterranean to be really convincing in this new-world get-up.

322

The third press photo showed him as Colonel Dubouboule in the circus ring. The text filled more than a column beneath the large type of the headline:

KONSTANTIN GIAXA, 64, ECCENTRIC OF WORLD-WIDE
RECOGNITION, DEAD IN A GERMAN CONCENTRATION CAMP

*Nazi authorities declare: Accident while
horseback riding*

A laugh, a short, malicious snort through the nose. I couldn't hold it back. Those lie jugglers in Berlin! constantly throwing around a mixture of deception and half truths, and out of twelve bowling pins they toss in the air, one is the truth. The truth, in itself a lie. As if it were standard procedure for prisoners to go riding around in concentration camps like rich gentlemen cantering through the parks in Berlin.

So Kujath never had time to get the story to the Swiss News Agency, and the Americans had fished it out of another source. Or perhaps the Swiss *did* get it from Grandpa, but—not finding it opportune to be the first ones out with the story—passed it on to the *Herald Tribune*. I didn't need to read the long text.

Rushed into the central post office of the urban village. Much hustle and bustle in the main lobby. A long line stood in front of the window where letters were to be picked up. During all my days in mess halls, at latrines, in barracks and detention camps, at university offices, box offices and in the cells of bureaucracy I had been an enemy of waiting in line, and I had vowed to avoid these human snakes in war or peace. According to the timetable of the Bernina railroad, the next train to Pontresina, my train, leaves in half an hour. A row of phone booths reserved for overseas calls (all occupied) next to a few intended for local and inland calls. The booth had been pumped full of sickening cigarette smoke, so I left the door open a few inches, warned by the initial signs of my first Engadine hay-fever attack. My half-hour plan: call Acla Silva, get Tességuier's letter, depart. Ten horses would not keep me from setting off Xana-wards in thirty minutes. I knew ten Breukaa's number by heart. If he himself answers I'll ask him straightaway if he's heard about Giaxa's death. That subject would (at least temporarily) make him forget yesterday's little slap. I dropped ten rappen into the phone, dialed the number and waited, listening to the short ringing buzz as it repeated at regular intervals—when I was suddenly distracted by something else.

In the next booth someone was making a long-distance call.

The double wooden wall between us muffled the speaker's voice so that his rush of words dissolved. But the sound of the Viennese dialect was unmistakable.

The monotonous buzz in the receiver continued, and I hung up, pulled the clinking coin from the slot and inserted it again. Had I misdialed or would there be no answer, as before? Or should I let it ring longer until the near-deaf Uorschletta managed to reach the phone? My right ear heard the regular buzz while my left ear listened to the voice in the next booth. Then, quietly, I hung up again, completely lost in listening.

To a man's voice.

Not that it was a familiar voice. I was sure I had never heard it before. It was the tone and rhythm of the dialect alone: it rolled along, a kind of turbulent flood of words. As when someone who feels guilty tries to convince a superior, not with humility but with glib enthusiasm (behind which lurks the fear of punishment).

The flood stopped. Now the other party seemed to be doing the talking, and the man next to me supplied the answers. I became a listener at the wall. Yes, put my left ear right up to the wooden wall, and yes, now I could decipher individual words, spoken in a broad, popular Viennese dialect (a dialect, it occurred to me, so drawling and yet so terse that any phone-bugging agent of Swiss Intelligence, versed though he was in High German, French, English, Italian, and Russian, could hardly made sense of it).

"T'day—tawaylf—'marra—t'not—tawaylf—rawn tawaylf—'marraf shoa—shoa—d'red song-bee-itch—a gawna—rotted waylf—shoa—d'song-bee-itch—crawsta bree-itch—drav in—in da woo-uds—code fate—tagetha—blew-ud—d'song-bee-itch—sump spayshell—chest rot fer hay-im—rawn tawaylf—oh rot—oh rot—oh rot."

Translated: "Today—twelve—tomorrow—tonight—twelve—around twelve—tomorrow for sure—sure—the red sonofabitch—a goner—right at twelve—sure—the sonofabitch—across the bridge—drive in—in the woods—cold feet—together—blood—the sonofabitch—something special—just right for him—around twelve—all right—all right—all right."

The man stepped out of the booth without looking around, and peering through my partly opened door, I could see his back, his angular shoulders, and his knickers.

Could see.

The Tutankhamon pattern of his sweater, his straw blond hair.

The beret covered my identifying mark. I wore the sunglasses I had just bought (no monocle), and in a flash I pulled Pola's scarf out of my pocket and over my mouth as if suddenly suffering from a toothache.

Even if he turned around, even if the phone booth door didn't nearly cover me—he would never recognize me.

And he was not Krainer, not the speaker for the Two Blonds.

There was a kind of strange, intense probability about the situation, yet it was no longer grotesque.

A falsetto chirp cut through the confusion of voices in the post-office lobby: "Vienna, nine minutes," and the man shoved his way up to the window for long-distance calls and turned sideways as he bent down, and I saw his pimply profile.

Not Krainer, but Georg Mostny.

Shorsh, the mute.

The man who yesterday had uttered a totally inarticulate cry when I surprised him in the Mauntschas Forest. Mostny—whom I had taken to be a harmless, mute half-cretin threatened by euthanasia, whose family had sent him out of Greater Germany to save his life.

The mute.

5   Once again the following events, this time lasting for several hours, seemed at times to occur in a kind of telegram style, the style of my wartime diary.

Mostny left the window, Krainer nowhere in sight. Pick up Aurel Tességuier's airmail letter, postmarked Maribor, written in fountain pen, apparently in haste.

Complete text:

Maribor, 20 June
Dear Friend,

As I informed you by telegram I have taken Elsabé to Varasdin (Varăzdinske Toplice) where she is awaiting word from you at the Hotel Erdoedy. I presume she will fly to meet you in Switzerland within the next few days since she has obtained a Yugoslavian passport so that nothing should stand in the way of her leaving here. Her morale is not bad in view of the atrocious circumstances. She is composed, and perhaps even prepared to find out the worst. But as yet she is not aware that the worst has already happened a few days ago.

In Radkersburg and Graz (where meanwhile your lawyer has gotten cold feet) everyone professed to know nothing more about Giaxa's fate. Over the weekend the first rumors concerning his death began to circulate. To the disgrace of the Styrians it has to be said that most of these rumors were transmitted with a kind of malicious glee. That is how far the degradation of this misled people has progressed. It is all quite amazing when one considers that only a few months ago the same people were appointing him honorary mayor of Radkersburg, bowing and scraping, begging for autographs, etc.

So it was not a bolt from the blue, but one from clouded skies—nevertheless it struck me like real lightning when today I read the official letter sent to Elsabé: she had asked me to open her mail and if need be to report to her by phone from Murska Sobota (where my tree nursery is located). But I prefer to send this document neither to her nor to you.

The administration of Cc. Camp Dachau informs Mrs. E. Giaxa, née Countess von Hahnspor-Fermin—how precise they are!—via form letter of her husband's death on the day of his admission due to an accident for which he himself was to blame. Cremation already carried out; to meet resulting costs including shipment of urn to next of kin an advance payment of 392 reichsmarks and 75 pfennigs should be transferred to XYZ bank account in Munich.

During my fifty-three years I have seen many an official letter, but never the likes of this one. I must confess that while reading it I was forced to shudder. History, I need not tell you, is full of atrocities, e.g., during the persecution of the Huguenots there were more than enough. Nevertheless I simply cannot imagine that such things were ever committed so according to "plan X" and with such bureaucratic efficiency as here and now in this "New Reich."

What can I do, I who was honored to call myself the great Giaxa's neighbor, other than assure you of my deepest and most sincere sympathy—and even this may sound like an empty cliché under these dismal and disastrous circumstances. Write to me, Gospodin Autes, poste restante Murska Sobota, Slovenia, Yugoslavia. I refrained from sending this letter to your Pontresina address so as to preclude the possibility of it falling into the hands of your dear young wife. I am keeping the form letter; perhaps I will need it for an eventual payment of the bill. What should I do? Should I pay?

Yours, A. T.

So there still are some noblemen, in the literal sense. If Aurel Tességuier dried his ink on a blotter in the Maribor post office. If a Nazi informer got hold of it, he's a dead man. Listed in my notebook, telephone number of Vindobona Detective Agency, no private number for the private eye. Ex-private eye, meanwhile promoted to Gestapo big wig, no longer reachable under old office number, that's for dead sure. Woman at the window (not a character like Madam Fausch) hands me Vienna telephone book (still the old one), *Laimgruber, Heinzw., Hptm. i.R., W4, Porzellangasse 36*, tell her the number, wait. Porzellangasse ... wedge-shaped corner house, smoky restaurant, painted inn signboard with cracking darkened glaze: THE FLIGHT TO EGYPT. Donkey, baby Jesus, Joseph, Mary, rather in the primitive style of Henri Rousseau.

"Vienna, booth eight!"

Enter the phone booth Mostny just left. Close the door, pick up the receiver, wait. Out the little window catch sight of Paretta-Piccoli the Facist, pushing his way into the booth I was in minutes before. The tables turned, like in a cheap cops-and-robbers movie. "We are connecting you with Vienna, one moment please." Wait, switch the receiver to my left ear, listen to the next booth with my right. Paretta's words muffled by the walls but clear. Conversation in Graubuenden dialect with Jesumann's Garage in Martinsbruck. Jesumann, the garage owner? Martinsbruck the lowest town at the end of the Engadine, right on the Tyrolean, now German, border. If Jesumann finds a "sickle" with sidecar parked in front of the garage tomorrow morning could he take it inside for the night. Paretta-Piccoli will pick it up day after tomorrow. *Merci. Ciao.*

Paretta the Fascist leaves the booth and the post office without noticing the listener-at-the-wall.

Wait for my Vienna connection. (They're taking their sweet time.) Remember evening visit with private detective Laimgruber in office on Judenplatz. *"Trebla, you won't escape me! I'll get you yet! You'll be coming back to me, old comrade, alive or dead!"*

"We have the number in Vienna; go ahead please."

Telephone conversation uncut: "Hello there?"

"Heil Hitla, who is it you want?" a fat-whining woman's voice.

"Could I please speak with Herr Laimgruber?"

"Who izzit speakin'?"

"Prince Metternich."

"Prince Metternich?"

"Yes."

"Wal I'll be. Eh, this is the cook speakin'. Hanni."

"Tell me, Hanni, is Herr Laimgruber at home?"

"Fifteen minutes ago Herr Lieutenant Colonel drove out to dinna inniz Mercedes."

(Mercedes, Lieutenant Colonel. Quick promotion.) "To dinner, so early?"

"Yessah, he had an appointment in the Griechenbeisl."

"Ah . . . I'm a good friend of the Colonel's, and I've been trying to call him for some time now, but it was always busy. I presume because of the call from Switzerland we *both* were waiting for."

"I don't know nothin' about that. I just got home the moment Herr Lieutenant Colonel was gettin' inniz Mercedes."

"Thank you, Hanni. Good-bye then."

"Heil Hitla, your majesty."

Request the Vienna phone book again, find the Griechenbeisl restaurant on the Fleischmarkt, place another call.

"Your number in Vienna is busy; do you wish to wait?"

"I'll wait." Remember the Jacob kidnapping case. Berthold Jacob (family name Salomon dropped), Social Democrat, pacifist, living in exile in Strassburg, published a newsletter about German rearmament. Assigned to carry out the kidnapping: the turncoat Hans Kiepermann, until 1933 Geneva correspondent of the Social Democratic Party's official newspaper *Vorwaerts*. Kiepermann invited his former friend to Basel under the pretext of obtaining a passport for him. Late in the evening of March 11, rendezvous in a Basel tavern. Kiepermann had rented a Zurich taxi for twenty-four hours, put a German from Loerrach behind the wheel. The taxi with Kiepermann and Jacob raced past the Swiss border checkpoint at Kleinhueningen (the German tollgate, otherwise closed at night, was "accidentally" open) and into German territory. Trebla composed a ballad that was smuggled out of Waltendorf Detention Camp and published in Bruenn and St. Gall: "The Ballad of Poor Jacob and His Keeper-Mann."

"Vienna, booth eight please!"

"Restaurant Griechenbeisl, Heil Hitler, good evening," voice of a kindly, attentive Viennese waiter.

"Lieutenant Colonel Laimgruber, please."

"The Colonel is attending a meeting in the private dining room."

"Call him to the phone please."

"Whom shall I say it is, sir?"

"Prince Metternich."

"M-metternich? At your service, your grace. One moment please; it'll only be a moment, Your Highness."

Remember the entrance to the Griechenbeisl with a relief of a bagpipe player from the time of the Black Plague called *Lieber Augustin.*

"*Obersturmbahnfuehrer* Laimgruber, who's speaking, please?"

My suddenly ticking forehead. "The Red sonofabitch."

"*Who?* I was told, Prince—"

"Only a marquis. Perhaps from *Die Fledermaus.* A bat-man marquis."

"You seem to have the wrong connection, or are you some kind of nut?"

"No, I'm not a nut, see. Nor a not-see. You see?"

Suddenly his voice is knife sharp, close and clear, twice swelling up to a high-pitched shout: "You have the *gall* to joke with me, do you?! You're going to regret you did that! I'm having this call *traced!*"

"Let's cut out the games, Heinzwerner. Don't you recognize your old hole-in-the-head comrade?"

A gentle sniff through six hundred miles of telephone wire. Then Laimgruber's voice, vibrating with a kind of surprised cordiality: "*Trebla?*"

Beginning a restrained conversation is enormously hard. "By your leave, Herr Lieutenant Colonel, I mean *Obersturmbahnfuehrer*—what rank do you hold now, anyway?"

His answer, with its tone of sleepy amiability, sent shivers down my spine. "Come on now, old friend. *Obersturmbahnfuehrer* is the equivalent of Lieutenant Colonel in the police. Come on, come on, don't act so unfriendly. After all we're still old comrades-in-arms, despite everything that's happened since the war. Right? Isn't that right? Where are you now anyway?"

"Come now, old comrade, you know that better than I do."

"Pardon me. But how should I know that? We haven't seen or heard from each other, wait a minute, for a year and a half now."

"No? You mean you didn't get my, er, invitation that I sent you via Adelhart Stepanschitz?"

"Invitation? I don't have the slightest idea what you're talking about. Haven't seen Stepanschitz for weeks. I've been completely snowed under with work lately.

"I can imagine."

"I did hear some rumor about your being in Switzerland."

"What *other* rumors have you heard, old comrade? That the red sonof-abitch Trebla is curing his hay fever in the Engadine? By the way, I suspect this isn't the first call you've gotten from here today."

"What in hell is *that* supposed to mean?"

"Shortly before you left the Porzellangasse in your Mercedes you received a telephoned report from St. Moritz, right?"

A two-second pause; then with a click an impersonal, accent-free woman's voice cuts into the million-foot-long line. "Are you still speaking with Vienna?" and I say "Yes, I am," and then the click again, followed by Laimgruber's laugh.

"Hohohohoho, how did you know I'm in the Griechenbeisl and that I drive a Mercedes?"

"Maybe I took a few detective lessons at the Vindobona."

Through the long, long wire I sense his irritation. What is keeping him from hanging up on me? Instead, his deceptively jovial reply: "That's the old Trebla all right. Always joking."

"Yes, always joking. Let's assume that Stepanschitz *did* deliver my answer to your offer to take me back into the fold, back to the Reich. The answer I wrote, with a little help from Goethe, in my letter at the end of May. Where-upon you lost no time in sending two of your *thugs* after me into Switzerland. Those two nice boys Krainer and Mostny."

"Never heard the names."

"Those are their, mm, stage names you know."

"Stage? What?"

"The stage is the Engadine, the play a little liquidation drama."

"Liquidation—? What, according to your theory, is supposed to be liquida-ted? Some assets?"

"No, me."

"*You?* Treblahaha, you're really priceless."

"Really priceless. On the second of June the two wanted to carry out their mission, but they were foiled. Because I had my eyes open. Which they reported to you. Whereupon you ordered a sham withdrawal to the neighboring village."

"It all sounds like a little war between the tourists up there, hohoho. All that mountain air must be doing wonders for your poetic imagination. By the way, isn't this call getting a bit expensive for you?"

"It might be a lot more expensive for me *without* this call. Anyway, you send alias Krainer and Mostny from Pontresina to St. Moritz. The hay-fever cure takes one month. One month. So the two think to themselves: Honor is loyalty, well and good, but what's the *hurry* anyway? We'll never get another chance to spend a three-week expense-paid vacation in exclusive St. Moritz."

His gentle sniff somewhat longer. Through the million-foot wire a kind of noxious gas seems to creep out of the phone and into my nose.

Is it the stink of his annoyance transformed to the faintest decibels of sound? Was this my first direct hit? At the fast-rising death's-head man and police Lieutenant Colonel? (No doubt he's wearing civilian clothes to his dinner conference.)

I: "Hello," and his brief echo: "Hello."

Why doesn't he just hang up?!

"Apparently this Mostny-whoever-he-is was trained to play the part of a mute half-idiot. Yesterday I fell for the act. Otherwise *he* would no longer be with us today."

"I haven't the slightest idea what you're talking about, Trebla. *Who* would no longer be with us today?"

In the minimal interference on the line a slight sound-shift, as if we had passed through a short tunnel. (Probably the impersonal operator checking to see if I'm still on the line with Vienna.) "Do you remember Berthold Jacob?"

"Never met him," his voice almost shrill again (finally) with a touch of Adolfian hysteria.

"I'll introduce you. A Jew-boy, to quote you; a pacifist Jew-boy who was abducted into the Reich from Basel a little over three years ago. By a certain Mr. Kiepermann. Embarrassingly enough—for the Germans—the thing grew into an international incident. They had to give him back. The man they were so eager to have. Abductions via Swiss border *cities* turned out to be ineffective. Too many eyes. But out in the country—mountainous or otherwise—the chances for a smooth kidnapping appear a great deal better. Assuming that you were losing patience with your sluggish trigger-boys."

"To be honest." It *sounded* honest. "I have a good sense of humor. Particularly when it comes to old frontline comrades. But your tone, your tone is beginning to disappoint me."

A terrible laugh tickle in my throat. "Then, my easily wounded friend, let us call them your keeper-men, or better yet your little troupe of boy Schuhplattler dancers on a foreign tour."

His sniffing chuckle returns. "I can't get mad at you, Trebla, you're a real blast. You're Baron von Muenchhausen all over again. A real blast."

"—blast-blast, okay. But what if I'm not so easy to blast. What if I'm a woodchuck who doesn't *let* himself get blasted?"

"Now Muenchhausen has turned into a woodchuck."

"Remember our last fireside chat, old comrade? 'You won't escape me! You'll be coming back to me—alive or dead!'"

"Let me tell you something, Trebla. Some lost sheep aren't worth the shepherd's trouble to get back. Black sheep—or red ones."

"Red sons-of-bitches."

"You and your Red-sons-of-bitches. Haven't the slightest idea what you mean by that."

"Let's presuppose a coded telegram to your boy folk-dancers: Well how about some action, goddammit, after all these days of shooting nothing but your expense account. Bring'm back alive—back home to the Reich alive. Jacob was kidnapped from a Basel tavern. How about a rendezvous this time at St. Moritz leaning tower? About twelve o'clock at night. Rawn tawaylf . . . This time he'll be a goner, the Red sonofabitch. . . . a gawna . . . rotted waylf. There's room enough for two on a big motorcycle with sidecar"—I gush myself hoarse—"something special, just right for him, no, never, we haven't got cold feet, we'll get him together, tagetha, t'not, tonight, sure, chloroform him, for example, stuff him in the sidecar and roar out to Martinsbruck, if he moves we'll rap him one over his three-eyed skull, so that his blew-ud splatters, rot in da woo-uds, then crawsta breeitch, where the tollgate will accidentally be open, just as it was for Jacob, drav in, drive the Red sonofabitch right into the German Reich, Sieg Heil, and on the next morning an unmanned motorcycle with sidecar and Graubuenden plate is parked in front of a garage in the Lower Engadine . . ."

This time his silence costs me at least a franc. A silence that is no triumph for me. My sudden doubt: Hadn't I used far too little information to arrive at the *real* (or probable) plan of operation?

The impersonal female voice returns with a click: "Are you still speaking with Vienna?" and I: "Yes." Click; and now Laimgruber's voice, first muffled by a seeming fadeout, then clearer.

"Wait a minute, wait a minute, didn't I see your name just a few days ago in the *Reichsgesetzblatt?* If I'm not mistaken"—had his sleepy amiableness returned?—"you were not on the list of those deprived of German citizenship, no . . . Now I've got it! It was a call to active duty," his voice resounded in mild enthusiasm. "You were called upon to report for service in the Greater German Wehrmacht. Which would only be in keeping—haven't I told you that before?—with your family tradition. Now if *that* doesn't prove the fact that people over here are willing to let bygones be bygones." Mildly reproachful: "And you come to me with your fairy tales."

For a moment I felt short of breath, my eyes burned. "And *Giaxa?* Giaxa's—death—in—Dachau?—is—that—a—*fairy tale?*"

Now his voice will remove its mask; he will bellow through the million-foot line: "An old public enemy who got what he *deserved!*" And hang up.

Why doesn't he hang up?

Instead: "Right, no, that thing . . . I completely forgot about that . . . that you were related to him . . . Terrible story . . . I must confess I was stunned too when I heard about it. All you can say about something like that . . . a real case of bad luck."

I feel the sudden constriction of my bronchial tubes, the pounding in my head, the cold sweat beginning to cover my whole body, the receiver growing slippery in my hand: *"You* were *stunned! B-a-d l-u-c-k!"*

All sleepy amiability: "Look . . . look, my . . . look, I can tell you with a clear conscience that I knew nothing of the whole affair—"

"With a clear conscience."

"Yes, a clear conscience. The case didn't go through my department—"

"A clear conscience."

"Yes, sure . . . certainly, just look: I myself . . . I myself . . . when he was performing for Renz . . . it was a long time ago . . . I laughed 'til I cried tears."

"Tears."

"I would have contacted the Political Division over there in—"

"Tears."

6

Diagonally across from the main post office, on the terrace of the Stefanie. Wash down two and a half Merck's ephedrine tablets with a glass of Passugger mineral water. (The manufacturer of these bitter air-pills probably a descendant of Goethe's friend Johann Heinrich Merck.)

Ephedrine-in-Engadine works differently from ephedrine down in the Domleschg. I'm very much all there. Nothing blurs. Like looking through binoculars, you turn the focus until the image takes on super-sharp contours.

Breathing eased, eye irritation decreased. Reject idea of consulting Dr. Tardueser.

Two Blonds in the game again. In the endgame. Mostny *not* a mute, not sick. Fanatical, primitive (to judge from the talk I overheard), but not sick. On the longest day of the year, in the diffuse bright late-afternoon light on the Stefanie terrace, I learn how to breathe again and recall the phenomenon of the double shadow.

A lamp with two bulbs casts the double shadow of a wine bottle on the wall, one hard, one softer.

Krainer no keeper, perhaps not even Mostny's superior. Maybe *Mostny* is commander of the two-man team. Was informed of Balz Zbraggen's suicide—imitation of Lenz's death, the double shadow!—the ill-fated duplicity, the doubling of events—was on the verge of leaving my Walther in Pontresina. (Hadn't Maxim Grabscheidt's Dachau death found its double in Giaxa's death, de Colana's drowning in Zuan's, Tiefenbrucker's crash in Kujath's heart attack?)

A plus for the man sitting in Stefanie's wicker chair—gentle pressure of Walther (as so often recently) against right hip.

Everything relative. Quick shift in outlook. Things have changed in the

332

flash of an eye. Theater of war. Are there theaters of peace?

Yes?

Are there theaters of peace? (Rhetorical question.)

Theaters of war. Of them I knew several. The fortified triangle—the post-office, the Stefanie, and COOK'S TRAVEL OFFICE—the area that could be a theater of war. Despite the fact that Police Corporal Defila is directing traffic in it.

What if Mostny *did* notice his telephone-booth neighbor in the post office.

And told Paretta-Piccoli, alias the Fascist. Or is he proceeding unawares to rent the cycle for tonight?

Had Mostny sent Krainer out to find me?

My face half hidden behind a newspaper or Pola's baby blue scarf: a Sherlock Holmes caricature?

If Krainer really did pass by on his way from the nearby enemy headquarters at Thusnelda's house—came by in search of me . . . then this little theater of peace could become a theater of war—in the flash of an eye. Or a no man's land. Only for him—or for me. Everything relative. As before.

Pizzagalli Jr., Faustino, son of the Sporthotel proprietor, crosses the square. Taking his new pastel summer suit out for a walk—certainly the work of some noted Milanese tailor. Remove my sunglasses for a moment. As a monocle man, not much for glasses. Glasses-wearer Faustino gazes, no gasps over at me. Certainly he recognizes me. Turns away without greeting.

Snubs me, why? Because he's a sergeant in the same mountain regiment as the brothers Zbraggen . . .? Don't overinterpret people's behavior. Maybe just miffed to see a regular Pizzagalli customer sitting on the competition's terrace.

In front of the Cook Travel bureau Faustino runs into young man with unnaturally rosy face, surely under eighteen, suit definitely not tailored in Milan. Black. Farmer's Sunday best, but today's not Sunday. Mourning? Maybe son of Zarli Zuan?

I've seen enough boys with battle shock; this one shows same symptoms. Mixture of apathy and agitation on his face as he continues talking to Pizzagalli Jr. Put their heads together. Suddenly the boy looks my way. Face like a slab of bologna.

The concierge of the Stefanie lent me his train schedule. If the next Bernina train were on time, I could catch Xana before the Swiss evening papers hit the stands. If there was a Pontresina-Chur night train, Xana and I could pack our bags in a hurry and go.

Returning with the schedule to my round table at the terrace railing, found the next table occupied. Pizzagalli Jr.'s friend.

"You heard about vendetta?"

The moment he spoke to me in an awkward casual tone I was certain he had nothing to do with the Two Blonds, though the condition of his face reminded me of Mostny. (In your situation it's wrong to be certain of anything.)

The boy had placed several coins next to his Alpetta beer bottle. His face disfigured by a bad glacier burn. Georg Mostny, his skin had shone lobster red when I surprised him napping in the Mauntschas. But on closer inspection, the boy's narrow face seemed like a slab of bologna sausage, pieces of his skin peeled off and smeared over and over with something like bright yellow mustard.

Most heavily smeared with the burn salve, his lips. He seemed to move them as little as possible as he spoke. Had I heard about vendetta, he repeated, mumbling oddly, but with sharp consonants. "That's not just in Italy." His name was Andri Zbraggen. Brother of Lenz and Balz, the youngest and only remaining son of the widow Zbraggen-Tratschin in Celerina. He'd come off the mountain this morning where he had gotten this whore glacier burn and had heard what had happened in the whore Innmuehle Milano (he used "whore" as an adjective) and an hour later in his mother's bathroom. And he'd heard *enough*, I could be sure of that. Maybe they couldn't blame me directly for Balz's death. But if Lenz hadn't shot himself, then Balz wouldn't have blown his own head off. This godless whore bitch Verena Tummermut, Lenz shouldn't have had anything to do with her. But can you hold a female responsible? The real villain was me, that's why he would shoot me down.

Yes.

This very night.

His word of honor.

There'll be no escape for me, no.

Shoot me down with the same whore carbine that had sent his brothers to heaven. Then he (his father was from Uri, a Catholic) would go straight to the Celerina priest and confess his vendetta. To the same priest who refused to perform last rites for two brothers who died by their own hands.

A colossal bus from Birmingham stopped in front of Cook's; two dozen elderly English ladies disembarked from it, heads covered with overlong tulle-shawls à la Isadora Duncan. Andri disappeared behind the tulle procession. I rejected the idea of informing Commissioner Mavegn, with whom I'd just attained a *modus vivendi*. If I told the cantonal police what *modus moriendi* Andri had threatened me with, they would interrogate him. He would deny it.

Then came ten Breukaa, driving alone.

Up the street from the spa, in his open cabriolet, three golf bags jutting up from the passenger's seat.

(What a show-off!)

So Joop was back from Genoa, where he had unloaded a steamer, and since Pola had gone off with Bonjour in the Austro-Daimler he'd taken the cabriolet and played a few holes down at the spa. I jumped up and waved rather frantically at him from the terrace railing.

What I wanted to, had to ask him . . . Whether he had seen the Paris edition of the *Herald Tribune;* whether *it* was already common knowledge.

The gentleman driver noticed me. His greyhound face under the beige golf cap twisted into a grimace, yes, his long, pointed nose blanched suddenly. I was struck by a side-glance full of such completely unadulterated, concentrated hate that my waving arm froze in midair.

No, the lingering effects of the slap I'd given him yesterday could not explain the insane, angry stare he gave me as he rolled by.

A small rush hour between six and seven in the urban village. Ten Breukaa had signaled a right turn, obviously wanting to drive home via the station across the post office Bridge of Sighs. Just as obviously he changed his mind, signaled a left turn, broke out of the slowly rolling line of cars in the right lane—result: horn concert—and Joop rushed toward the intersection without regard for Corporal Defila's raised, white-gloved hand as it ordered him to stop. Defila's red cheeks stiffened into an officious glower and he brought his whistle to his lips.

A long whistle-chirp was about to fill the air.

Yet only a short chirp actually emerged. As if Defila had said to himself, the rich Dutchman from Acla Silva, a good friend of mighty Mavegn—let's close both eyes and let him get away with a little traffic violation.

Where was Joop getting away *to?*

It was almost out of the question that he wanted to play a second golf game at the other course near Kulm. Obviously the unexpected sight of *me* had caused him to change his itinerary. As if he had seen (as we used to say in our more Christian days) the devil. Trebla the devil.

The three golf bags next to him on the seat: clubs poked out of two of them; the third was standing on its head, bottom upward. Who would drive around with a golf bag set up like that—like a hat?

A short, snorting laugh rose from my ephedrine-cleared air passages. "Hee!"

Joop too?

Was ten Breukaa after me as well? Was he—wait a minute—the number four man to join the deadly feud? No doubt Andri Zbraggen's completely unexpected appearance would have shocked me, frightened me, without the sublimating help of Merck's ephedrine. Wasn't this becoming a kind of comedy of threats? And wasn't it almost perverse the way I began to be interested (or even entertained) by these manifold menaces. Which early bird would get the worm; which gentleman would pull the trigger first?

That I had sought admission to Acla Silva in the master's absence, that I had spent more than an hour with Madame in the salon, that phonograph music (first the "Merry Widow," then "Wiener Blut") had blared out into Staz Forest until 1:30 A.M., obviously an orgy for two. Bonjour could hardly have told all this to his master face to face. But if ten Breukaa had called from Italy early this morning (when late-retiring Pola was still asleep) Bonjour might easily have informed him of my extended midnight visit.

More than once Joop had sleepily boasted to me about his arsenal in the basement of Acla Silva, a Humbert, for example, and a Winchester Grand Speed. Considering the revolver shot he fired at the young sculptor Haberzettl after that party in the Vienna cottage-villa. Considering his pathological possessiveness and jealousy about the Spahi and Pola, one had to believe him thoroughly capable of another little armed assault. Of course it wouldn't do to stop right in front of the Stefanie, pull a rifle out of his upside-down golf bag and start banging away at me. Perhaps he planned, now that I had shown myself so unexpectedly, to ambush me on the way home. The notion of having an uneven duel with ten Breukaa—my little Walther against his double-barrel Humbert—caused me a second laugh snort. But the laugh died in my throat.

The Saurer truck, today covered with a massive arched tarpaulin, parked behind the Birmingham bus and Men Clavadetscher, owner of the Chesetta Grischuna in Sils, clambered out of the driver's cab. He was not here to read timetables.

Was it really only three days since the country lawyer had been laid to rest in Soglio along with his spaniel pack? Since I had driven to Sils alone and found that strange farewell greeting, the lines from Abbé Galiani, scrawled by a drunkard's hand onto the Chesetta's outhouse wall? Since I had watched the woodchuck-haired proprietor and been watched by him? Three days, for me three moons. The new sunglasses—to read the timetable, I had pushed them up on my forehead; now I pulled them quickly back over my eyes. But why? So that Men Clavadetscher wouldn't recognize me? Wouldn't it be more interesting to find out if he would snub me too?

Men recognized me despite the sunglasses. He didn't snub me.

Three baskets were hauled out of the rear flap of the tarpaulin cover, loaded onto a rack wagon and towed off by a hotel servant in a green apron. Then Mr. Clavadetscher came straight over to me. He wore a felt hat, mousegray windbreaker, knee-length black corduroy pants, high-laced boots. In this rather daring Alpine costume he looked like a mountain climber sliding across a glacier on a traverse wire stretched between his truck and my wicker chair—an imaginary wire—but the motorists approaching from both sides paused for a moment at the sight of this striking example of local color. The iris red of his albino eyes stabbed through my onyx-tinted sunglasses like sparkling rubies as he made the unconventional gesture of leaping up (with surprising agility) onto the terrace ledge and reaching out his hand across the railing.

"*Bum di, sen al vo que?*"

I could figure out the beginning with the help of a little Latin (*bonus dies*) as "good day"; the rest must have meant "how are you?," and taking a chance, I replied, "*Così-così. Come sta?*"

"*Così-così. Sta bene, Barone! Arriverderci. Au revoir, monsieur. Uf Wiedarluegga.*"

As he jumped down from the terrace—still holding my hand for a half second as if intending to pull me over the railing—he uttered a harsh, jovial laugh. About what?

Tôt ou tard
On bouffe bien
Chez Caduff-Bonnard

One of the numerous cardboard signs on the red-stained paneling of the tunnel-like Café d'Albana, signs on which Monsieur Caduff, *chef de cuisine*, acclaimed his Graubuenden and Franco-Swiss specialties. The tunnel's windows, hung with red and white checked material in imitation of a French bistro, faced, with one exception, the police station. (Not the worst thing to have next door in my situation.) At the only window looking out onto the schoolhouse square the Royal Jockey, Ret., sat across from me. Fitz sat there, his seat raised with the help of several magazines, a napkin tied (yes, knotted) around his neck, looking like a baby in a bib. He had removed his long-billed canvas cap, letting me see his completely bald head for the first time, and ordered *quenelles de brochet* plus a carafe of white Fendant from the waitress with the bad complexion. (Today she was less inclined to joke, appeared less a caricature of Xana.) I ordered the same, even though it would cause my ready cash to dwindle to a very few francs, and Fitz remarked dryly that that horrible twin suicide of those Zbraggen boys didn't surprise him one bit. Such things just seemed to happen up here. Did I remember the case of the famous Russian dancer Vaslav Nijinsky who—just after the war—went crazy during a gala performance in Badrutt's Palace? "Just imagine, in the middle of his famous dance number, I can't remember which, maybe that fucking 'dying swan' or something, he cracks up and has to be dragged off stage in a straitjacket—imagine, a dying swan in a straitjacket. Yes, the Zbraggen boys, Lenz and Balz, God Almighty, rest their souls. Mr. Caduff's pike dumplings aren't bad, are they?"

"No. By the way, I didn't know there was this third brother, Andri."

"Poor youngster." Fitz chewed. "I wouldn't be at all surprised if he takes the same gun tonight and blows his head off too." Chewing. "Or something else."

"What?"

"You see, the whole affair must have nearly driven him out of his head. Maybe he'll run amok and kill—if not himself, then somebody else."

"For example?"

"For example, his mother. Why are you smiling, mister?"

"Was I smiling?"

"Or maybe that piece o' dumplin' was too hot for you. Those fucking plate warmers. D'you think we had things like that when I was at Buckingham Palace? No sir." He poured a little Fendant into his delicate, tubelike glass.

"Yesyes, that terrible—crazy force."

"Where did you get that phrase?" I inquired.

"Where . . .? From the man who used to live over there. Il Avvocato Bow-Wow."

The de Colana house seemed unchanged with its closed shutters (even before his death the front shutters had always been closed) and in today's graying *heure bleue,* an *heure bleue grise,* blue gray hour, it looked like the prettiest Engadine house for miles around, especially since the urban village had hardly any of them to begin with. Just on the north side of the square was a similar, if much less imposing, structure (which I had overlooked until now) with a kind of barn door that looked rather primitive in these citified surroundings.

"Yesterday," Fitz continued, "I saw him again in the Innmuehle Milano."

"Who?"

"The young de Colana. I mean, just his *picture.* The painting on the wall by this Monsieur Paget. Showing young Gaudenz de Colana steering his 'Skeleton' into the Cresta Run curve in 1905."

"Oh really," I said.

"Yessir. The most treacherous curve on the whole icy course. A murderous fucking curve. But Gaudenzio took it with ease. He was a great tobogganer, yessir. And a quarter-century later—even after the old boy'd become a souse—he was a first-rate car driver. Tops. He could have started in the fucking Monaco Grand Prix. That's why it's so hard to understand"—Fitz shoved a little piece of dumpling into his little mouth—"how he could have driven his Fiat into the lake. If you ask *me*—"

"If I ask *you?*"

"—there was something fishy about the whole affair. Yessir."

He stated it, not in dreamy clairvoyance, but as a factual observation, and looked back at the Colana house—which appeared like a fairy-tale Engadine house in this longest "blue hour" of the year—then threw a random glance over to the distant corner of the square where the other, less impressive house and its primitive barn-door were located. This door was now open, releasing a warm glow of light, and before it stood a man in a stocking cap holding a lantern that cast a muted gleam scarcely different from the twilight. The man was peering down one of the little streets that ran into the other side of the square. Suddenly swinging his lantern he signaled in the direction of the street, all the while casting intermittent glances—toward Café d'Albana or the police station?

At a creeping tempo, lights out, the tarpaulin-covered truck growled out of the little street and then backed into the barn door. From his hat I recognized the driver powerfully turning the big steering wheel.

"Tell me, Mr. Fitzallan—do you know that man over there?"

Fitz switched off the table lamp in order to get a better look in the twilight; for a moment I thought he would climb onto the table, but he merely stretched out his neck, twisting it amazingly far to the side like a bird, to peer between the

338

curtains. ". . . the lorry driver? A certain Men Clavadetscher, tavern owner in Sils Maria."

Suddenly, in front of the barn door where the Saurer's radiator had just disappeared, something like a black swarm of oversized flies began to assemble. Ten men, some with black stocking caps, dressed in twilight gray and night black.

"I wouldn't want to have anything to do with *that* gang, nothing whatsoever," muttered the dwarf, switching on the light ostentatiously, sipping his glass of Fendant.

"Did you say a gang?"

"You can say that again. You, mister, were driven up here by fucking hay fever—please excuse my cursing, which I did *not* learn at the Court of St. James. But once your cure is over, I would get the hell out of here."

"I hope to do just that."

"You're an outsider here, even if you were briefly acquainted with Dr. Bow-Wow. Therefore I can tell you: All those men there are Men Clavadetscher's accomplices."

"Accomplices. So you consider Men criminal?"

"Men criminal," Fitz let out a small, dry giggle. "Maybe all men are criminal, if you let them be. Have you ever heard anything about organized smugglers and poachers?"

"You mean, Clavadetscher is the leader of an organized gang of smugglers and poachers?"

"In the last century his name was Gian Marchet Colani, Colan-i, King of Bernina. Today his successor is—if you ask me—Men Clava." He kept the "-detscher" to himself, peering at me suspiciously. "I just hope you're no more than a curious tourist."

"Nothing more."

"Not a reporter, newspaperman, travel author or anything dreadful like that?"

"God forbid."

"Righto, now listen here, Mr. Curiosity. Men and his gang will drive out of here, maybe in half an hour, maybe not 'til midnight. And as far as the illegal border crossing is concerned, there are several possibilities. They could drive out through Pontresina—"

"Through Pontresina?"

"Yes, and over the Bernina Pass."

"Know it."

"Righto, I'm sure you know your way around here, but you won't know the Val Fontana where the gang can cross the glacier at the border and clamber down the Valle Campo Moro to Chiesa on the Italian side. Anyway they hide the lorry in a barn or something, unload the contraband and get on their way. Or they drive out Maloja way and sneak through Val Muretto along the glacier across to Chiareggio. They can get to Chiesa that way too. It's all around the Monte Disgrazia you know."

"Bad Luck Mountain."

"You know it, I'm sure."

"Of course," I lied.

"Well. They have to reach Chiesa in any case, but the real unloading points are farther down in Bergamo, Berbenno, for example. There they spend the night and rest up from their ordeal and the next night they take off across the mountains again, and in the morning light they'll use the opportunity to combine business with business and go on a little poaching hunt—if they're not being tailed by the border patrol."

"Chamois hunting? Now, in the off-season?"

"No. Woodchucks. Munggs, as they call them here."

"Woodchucks? They've almost wiped them out here, even though they're inedible as far as I know and their fur is worthless. Why in hell should this gang bother to go and hunt woodchucks?"

"Don't get excited, mister." Fitz began working on a *meringue glacée* the size of his head. "Those fucking quacks in the canton of Appenzell."

"How's that?"

"These fucking quacks rub their patients down with woodchuck fat. Disgusting, isn't it?"

"Revolting. I'd never heard of that."

"I'm glad there's something you've never heard of." His dry, now cool, mocking but conciliatory giggle. Across the way the dark company had disappeared like a swarm of flies. As if sucked in by the mouth of the barn door that looked so false and out of place in its St. Moritz surroundings.

"Yes, this brother tragedy," I said, as if speaking to the "blue hour."

"I think we've sired that Zbraggen story enough." A drop of meringue jiggled on the tip of Fitz's nose.

"At the moment I don't mean t-h-o-s-e brothers. I was referring to a woodchuck hunt," I said into the gray blueness. "The woodchuck hunt that Mr. Caduff-Bonnard went on with Men Clava, as you call him, and his brother—what was his name?"

". . . Peidar. That's another story, an old story, one I'd rather not talk about. But where did *you* get wind of it? For a hay-fever patient you seem to know more damn inside stories."

"Doctor de Colana told me about it."

"Holy mackerel. Holy cow. Holy cherubim and seraphim," Fitz said stoically and daubed his nose with a napkin. "Doc Bow-Wow. He seems to come at you from all sides. As I always say, The dead never rest."

"Be that as it may, he told me this hunting story a few days *before* he died."

"I see."

"During a visit to the Chesetta Grischuna."

"I see. I hope the two of you weren't overheard by Men Clava."

Despite my ephedrine state, the inspiration came to me. "Smugglers aren't really criminals in my eyes."

"But woodchuck hunters you hate."

"Correct. I have one question, Mr. Fitzallen, mm. Do you really think this Men Clava—almost sounds like an American gangster name—capable of a ca-pi-tal crime?"

He poked at his iced meringue. "And I have one question, Mr. Curios-ity—why are you so interested in the local history here?"

"As a person who's studied law, I'm fascinated by criminal cases."

"Are you a lawyer?"

"No."

"Y'don't look like one, either. So just for fun you'd like to know my unim-portant opinion as to whether Men went out on that hunt to . . . bang-bang . . . his brother on purpose or not."

"I must confess to you that one reason I came to the Café d'Albana was to refresh Mr. Caduff's memory about the whole forgotten incident."

Fitz's squeaking French: "Tôt our tard/On bouffe bien/Chez Caduff-Bonnard . . . Chef Caduff is busy in the kitchen. But even if you come back some other time you won't find out anything from him. No, sir. He makes a point of not talking about this long forgotten affair."

"Why not."

"Maybe he's afraid."

"Of whom? Men Clava?"

"Maybe."

"But listen, Mr. Fitz! This is the most civilized country in Europe—"

"My good man, don't give me the same arguments as the bloody self-satis-fied Swiss. You don't really believe that frightful feeling of fucking fear doesn't exist here too—even if it *is* the most civilized country?" His features twisted into a grimace that made his face look like a shriveled apple, as if it were no stranger to him—this frightful feeling of fucking fear.

"What I can't figure out is—why should a gang of smugglers rendezvous right across from the police station?"

"You must never have read any detective stories or you'd know that was an old bandit's trick. You meet right under the eyes of the police who are busy looking for you everywhere else."

"And *what* do you suspect they're smuggling into Italy tonight?"

"Oh, let's say . . . fifty thousand Laurens cigarettes. Over hill and dale and glacier ice. Men Clava knows the secret ways across the glaciers. The smuggling season is short in the Alps. Winter and spring aren't any good because there's too much snow. Of course some try it on skis anyway. Now, at the end of June, just before new moon with a cloudy sky—just the way we'll have it tonight—that's just what the smugglers have been waiting for. When there's moonlight or clear starlight, the way it's been the past few days, it's not so good. The best time is the short and early autumn here in the Engadine. But in the fall there are too many licensed hunters in the mountains, even at night. Right now they've got their best chance."

"Are you tired of all my questions now?"

"Not at all . . . as long as they don't concern this old fucking story about Men and Peidar."

"Thanks. And what do you think they'll smuggle *back* from Italy tomorrow or the day after?"

"Oh, let's say . . . Etruscan vases and sculptures, stuff that's two or three thousand years old that the farmers in Tuscany dig out of their fields. It comes through Switzerland and is sent on—usually to those stinking rich American collectors."

"And how is this 'stuff' transported over the mountains?"

"You mean what kind of equipment do these fellows use—the ones you don't consider criminals? Beside the usual lanterns—which have to be real blackout lanterns—"

In my pocket, I thought, Pola's miniature flashlight.

"—there's *la gerla*. A cone-shaped basket. Or *la pricòlla,* a double sack that'll hold all sorts of things, tied over your chest and back. A kind of life jacket, you see. And we can't forget *le bedùlli*. All of this is Italian smuggler slang." The waitress with the pimply face clears the table; Fitz begins to stack beer coasters. "*Bedùlli,* felt soles, four or five layers thick, that the smugglers strap on their boots before they walk past houses in the middle of the night. Guaranteed not to make a sound. And finally *la càdola*."

"*Càdola*."

"A board on two poles to which several straps are fastened. You can strap it on so that the board sticks straight out from the carrier's back." He pulled out a gold mechanical pencil and began drawing on a beer coaster with his tanned, rein-gripping little hands. "On this you can tie up larger items."

"Tie up?"

"I mean tie on. On a *càdola* you could carry a grandfather clock over the mountains." He pushed the sketch my way.

"Looks just like a chair."

"Exactly. A legless chair, and you strap the back of it to *your* back."

"Could you, in your opinion, could you tie a person onto one of these *cà-dolas*?"

"If need be, of course. Somebody who's had an accident on the mountain or is suffering from frostbite . . ."

"No, I don't mean anyone like that. I mean someone who's by no means frozen—at least not yet—when they strap him to the chair. Not *yet*. Do you understand what I'm getting at?"

·

"No sir, sorry. I don't understand at all."

"Could you tie somebódy onto a *càdola* against his will and carry him a fairly long distance—"

"You mean *kidnapping*, American style?"

"I was thinking more of an adult victim."

"Oh. *Now* I know what you're getting at. The perfect murder!" Now a glass of coffee kirsch stood in front of him, and he gave out, as he breathed its stream, several chortles and giggles of delight. "Maybe you are a lawyer and you've never read a detective story, but maybe you'll just *write* one some day. It seems to me somebody once said . . . that you *were* a writer. The perfect murder. Now here I could give you a few tips. Even though I don't think much of scribblers. But maybe you're not a scribbler but a serious writer. Y'know, we Irish have always had a good supply of serious writers. Do you know James Joyce? I've never read him, but I'm told he's a bit indecent and confused. Are you indecent? I mean as a writer. Well, what business is that of mine? It could be 'The Perfect Murder of Bad Luck Mountain,' or 'Cassandra Peak,' if you prefer. The smuggler gang hauls its victim—a local or a tourist, what would you prefer? all right, let's say a tourist—into a covered lorry like that. To keep the man quiet they give him a well-aimed blow on the temple. Once, thirty years ago, I fell and hit my temple during a steeplechase in Auteuil; I was out for two solid hours . . . Scheherezade, favorite mare of His Majesty King Edward the Seventh, broke her foot in the fall and had to be put away. But then I have no intention of boring you with my fucking prewar calamities . . ."

Had this fall made Fitz so eccentric? Suddenly I became aware why I had such sympathy for the dwarf. For one thing he, like myself, had head trouble; for another, there was an aura about him of someone who had worked intensively with horses, those creatures (as Giaxa had explained to me on the little island off Hvar) that had served man for thousands of years, working and suffering for him, helping him shape his destiny and history, only to be threatened with extinction in the modern world.

He took a few birdlike sips. "Where did I leave off?"

"The tourist gets a knock on the head."

"Yes. Fine. Men Clava—the name will have to be changed, of course—drives his gang with their unconscious victim close up to the moraine of the Forno-Glacier, lying just across from Monte Disgrazia. It's a moonless, starless night in early summer and the gang—excuse me, all respectable citizens in your eyes—dismounts and marches off single file, perhaps wearing their *bedùlli*. The column of men with swinging lanterns . . . the rugged men, each trained to perfect physical shape, each carrying the *càdola* with the 'body' about three hundred yards, then the next man takes over the load . . . just imagine the picture. Good enough to paint. Or to write about; it deserves to be written down. So anyway, they come to the moraine. There they remove their *bedùlli* and rope themselves together. The column crosses the glacier, let's say in three groups of four men roped together, crosses the ice that Men Clava knows like the back of his hand. Until the gang comes to an appropriate crevasse, let's say eighty yards deep. And there they throw the victim in. Even if he survives the fall he'll be frozen in two hours while the gentlemen are on their way down to Bergamo with their cargo of cigarettes. You see the point? Who would ever be able to search every crack in the glacier? The perfect murder, you see. The missing man remains missing, literally vanishes from the face of the earth and will never be found again." Fitz's amused, chuckling cough. "Or will he?"

"What do you mean?"

"You know that glaciers *move*. In the middle of the twenty-first century our unlucky tourist turns up again at the Forno-Moraine. Reappears. Fantastically well preserved after spending one hundred and twenty years in the icebox, so to speak. Let's say he was wearing a gray flannel suit and a black shantung tie on the night of the murder—just like you—and there he is on display in this outfit, long after styles have changed, at the foot of the melting glacier. Why are you smiling? Come on, admit that you find it at least a little tiny bit chilling. Do me the favor."

7

Missed the last train to Pontresina. Still have 4 francs 20 in my pockets. Too little for a taxi. Tonight they won't guard my way home, the dead.

The leaning tower behind me and the Kulm Hotel and the Stadium of the 1936 Winter Olympics and the now-abandoned Curling and Toboggan clubs, and on the highway from St. Moritz to Celerina a gray guesthouse of who-knows-what category like a parody of the giant swank hotels in town, and now on the left the famous Cresta Run where de Colana once displayed his talents, and on the right the no less famous Bobsled Run, both abandoned, for it was summer. The beginning of summer. Thus there was still some traffic on the road that curved down in a gigantic loop between the two runs and on to Cresta and Celerina. Vehicles from every imaginable country. Therefore it was improbable that I would make contact with the enemy on this stretch of my night march.

With every step I came closer to Xana, or more precisely, I thought I came closer to Xana. X: one of the unknowns in my sinister little equation.

Wednesday, 22 June, 0005 hours. Car traffic on the highway has dwindled to nothing and Cresta-Celerina appears dead at this post-midnight hour. In contrast to the rather steep Via Maistra in St. Moritz the main street of this elongated twin village is quite level. Hardly anyone about on foot either, but numerous bats. Bats. I slip my Walther out of its holster and thrust my armed right hand into the pocket of my flannel suit jacket. Not that I had any intention of going bat-hunting. I have a certain weakness for these silent night-hunters, admire their ability to fly on instruments, feel no qualms as they loop down close to my beret. I decide not to pass through Celerina at a steady march. A cautious, promenade stroll is more advisable. Andri Zbraggen. Mountain ash in respectable, fenced front yards, a few handsome and seemingly authentic Engadine houses with wooden loggias. Shaded light from an occasional window. Streetlights with greater swarms of insects than on previous nights (tonight, relatively warm, moonless, starless)—thus the increase in bat busyness. Andri. The twitching of his burn-salve-smeared mouth was no good omen.

On the otherwise deserted street, pass two elderly gentlemen wearing berets. One of the men leaning lightly on a rubber-tipped cane. Frenchmen. As I pass them I hear this: "... *Mais il était formidable! Giaxa et Giaxa, tu n'as vu? Par exemple chez Bouglione? Colonel Dubouboule, ça alors! C'était unique, ça! Il m'a fait rigoler pendant quarante minutes, le vieux gars, et quelquefois j'ai eu le fou rire. Personne ne résistait à la magie de sa moustache rouge ...*"

"Sometimes I used to laugh myself silly over Giaxa; nobody could escape the magic of his red moustache"—on the main street in Celerina, of all places, I overhear something like that. How suggestive chance can be. Stay in the vicinity of the two Frenchmen, don't speak to them, let them stay on your heels, they give you rear cover. On the left, tennis courts, behind them the looming Cresta Palace, its rows of windows all extinguished but for two or three lights, and very muffled, perhaps trickling out of a basement bar, the sound of a piano, "Night and Day." One of X's favorites. Don't think of X, think of Andri, imagine him lunging out of the darkness at any moment, imagine him taking aim. Not that he would be likely to fire with the two Frenchmen behind you. But this rear guard won't be there for long. The fivefold tapping—two pairs of boots and a rubber cane tip—recedes in the distance, dies away. You are alone on the village street, alone with silent bats, seemingly alone.

But in reality?

On the left, the church, a towering shadow, then on the right, the house. The House. Probably because of a nonworking streetlight it is shrouded in darkness; not a glimmer from inside. Across the road a darkened filling station; four dull-shining gas pumps; every one good cover for a sharpshooter.

An Engadine house, elevated front door flanked by two staircases with wrought-iron railings. To the right and left the windows of the grocery store covered by roll-down shutters. Above them, legible in the distant light of the next bat-buzzing streetlight, the rustic flourishes of a sgraffito inscription, vva. R. ZBRAGGEN-TRATSCHIN—COLONIALS & DELICATEZZAS. Pasted onto one of the roll-down shutters a piece of paper edged in black. An obituary notice like those Catholics in rural areas sometimes hang out? In this cemetery lighting it's impossible to decipher the print—no, the handwriting. Perhaps it amounts to criminal negligence without having inspected the gas pumps across the street, but nevertheless I pull out Pola's Japanese flashlight and flick it on for a second. In steep, almost Gothic script.

Chiuso! Fermé! Voruebergehend geschlossen wegen Todesfaellen.
Temporarily closed due to death in family.

There it is again, another suggestive twist of chance. Or *is* it an accident? The faulty spelling makes it all but certain: an error in copying an unfamiliar text.

Nevertheless, the words "death due to family" grip me in a most suggestive way. Is this a trap? Mechanically flicking the safety off the Walther I whirl around and fix my gaze on the gas pumps . . . the four dull-shining gas pumps, looking a bit like a phalanx of knights . . . then with a few long strides I move off into the deeper darkness around the corner of the house.

I halt under what seem to be the arching shadows of giant, shuttered windows in a barn built onto the house. But it's not from there that I hear it; it's from the house. Out of the depths of the house, as if emerging from a deep cavern comes the camouflaged, muffled, dull yet hollow sound.

A horrid, never-ending utterance, one capable of chilling to the bone.

Swelling up and down. The yowling whine of an abandoned dog? Then it must be a *big* dog. Or . . . isn't that a *human* cry? Human crying? Praying, interrupted by something like the attempt to retch on an empty stomach, a gasping prayer in a language I don't understand . . . it could be Romantsch. Something repeated again and again—could it be *O Segner . . . il Segner.* (Oh Lord, The Lord.) Is there also the trace of a German accent? Dialect of Canton Uri? The most confusing thing—the swollen-bursting-breaking tone of the voice moves up and down over two octaves. Can't tell if it's a man or a woman. Straining to listen. Is it a prayer at all, doesn't it sound more like a litany—born of pain, helplessness, and yes, of rage—a litany of now whimpering, now yowling curses? (Against God?) A frightening question: Could they be laid out in this house, the corpses of Lenz and Balz, with their bullet-blasted heads (instead of in the basement of Samedan hospital, as was more likely)? Or are there—

—two voices? A woman's and a young man's? An argument during the deathwatch?

Straining to listen. No, just *one* voice. Perhaps a voice recently changed, perhaps Andri's voice . . . Is Andri at home?

From the direction of Samedan, crescendo, the clatter of hoofs on the village street, a lonely, primeval, outmoded clatter, doomed (according to Giaxa) to extinction in the forseeable future. A light carriage drawn by a black horse halts in front of the Zbraggen house. The horrid litany inside stops short. The coachman climbs sluggishly off of his seat and helps a woman dismount through the carriage door, a stately lady—as revealed by the intermittent, reddish glow of the side lantern—heavily veiled in black. Supported by his arm, she ascends the steps to the front door. No more than three words are spoken. I switch the Walther's safety back on and move off down the street. The carriage turns and passes by me at a trot, and the horse seems blacker than any I've ever seen, and only now the coachman notices me. For more than a moment he turns his face in my direction, pale and featureless, peering back at me over his shoulder, a little like a curious half-idiot—or does he take me for a potential customer?

Should I wave to him?

The coachman turns away and steers his rig toward the fork in the road, the one equipped with a large concave mirror where the roads branch off to Samedan (left) and Pontresina (right). Poking along under a bat-buzzing streetlight, the carriage seems somehow reminiscent of an old London cab, and the nearby steady splashing of a fountain reminds me that I myself must "make water" (as they used to say).

A few steps across the cobblestones and I am in a small, dimly lit square. The capacious watering trough, the old guard-stones, the authentic, perhaps whitewashed or rose-colored Engadine houses with their fortress windows and closed wooden shutters—all these things combine to create the timeless image of a Graubuenden village square. I toss three ephedrine tablets into my mouth—rather a big dose, but then, an ounce of prevention etcetera—and wash them down with water pouring ice cold from the fountain, then I imagine hearing something. The snoring of a sleeper? No, a regular, featherlight tapping seems to be moving about on the sleeping village square, audible through the sound of the splashing water, and I move away from the spigot to the other end of the trough, behind which I can take cover if need be, and diagnose the noise.

No louder than twenty decibels, aha, hoofbeats, perhaps a mile away already, diminuendo, aha, the carriage driving back to Samedan, aha, the black horse that delivered the Engadine's Niobe, Mrs. Zbraggen-Tratschin, to her door—the black horse is trotting homeward. Was she really the one who got out of the carriage? Was it she, the bereaved, grief-stricken, sorely tested woman? (What worn-out adjectives! and how much *more* worn out they would become in the next few years . . .) Or a relative? If it was the mother, then it was probably Andri who stayed home alone to cry (he's hardly more than a child after all), having realized the folly of his vendetta threat. But if it was the mother who sang that chilling litany . . . then Andri could be out on the prowl with his double-suicide carbine.

I could have asked the coachman *who it was* he drove here from Samedan. Too late. Three sluggish strokes from the nearby Celerina church tower. Quarter to one, and on the main street a short procession of cars moving toward St. Moritz with lowered headlight beams, and a big black tomcat who doesn't need to dim his headlights—for several seconds his eyes blaze malachite-green. Then the illuminated signposts, cases of opaque blue glass with transparent lettering: SAMEDAN (to the left), PONTRESINA (to the right). The fork in the road still inside the town, the almost N-shaped left turn (around an obstructing house) of the highway leading through Samedan to the Lower Engadine, and Trebla's road turning eastward, the San Gian road. In the V of the fork, the concave mirror designed to reveal the oncoming traffic to drivers approaching from south or north, the mirror, with its frame of red cat-eye reflectors, which I had passed by more than once in ten Breukaa's cabriolet. Walking on the empty right lane I head straight for the mirror like a slowly rolling vehicle and can see the distorted reflection of my head and shoulders, an image like those in the crazy mirrors of the Prater Fun House, an establishment not far from the Ghost Train. But that is behind me now. This night is not the ghost train of a ghost train, not a ghost train raised to the nth power, but raised to a chimera, an illusion of an illusion—for tonight *absolutely nothing has happened.* (The horrid, sobbing curses overheard at the Zbraggen house, and the carriage that stopped in front of it—those can hardly be called events.) On the other hand, there is something intensely real about the taste of the night with its unusual scent of sultry air. I pass closer to the mirror than necessary, and in the light of the signs I catch a glimpse of my face and a segment of empty road behind me. This half-pale, half-shadowy face appears not only warped by the fun-house mirror but strange and disturbing between the seldom worn beret and the borrowed blue scarf—like a painting by the great Norwegian expressionist Edvard Munch.

Celerina and the Inn bridge behind me. (Is the river at flood stage? Snow off the mountain peaks, melted under last week's cloudless skies.) A heavy cloud of young, blossoming grass blows at me off the Campagnatscha. But it can't get to me now. The ephedrine I took protects me and not just against pollen. I stick the Walther back in its holster. Now I am on the San Gian road.

8

"I eat nothing but stork meat."
Don't think about it.
About the World War.

> *Tôt ou tard*
> *On bouffe bien*
> *Chez Caduff-Bonnard*

Don't think about the Great War. The Great Old War. Better to think of the Peasants' War. The Four-Day Civil War. No, better not think about that either. Not about Franz Scherhack. But about the consequences. About the consequences of the Four-Day War for Albert Trebla—*that* you can think about. The long-term consequences . . . In ghost stories they always tell about a man walking cross-country on a dark night. Suddenly he senses (senses more than hears) that someone is following him.

The lonely night walker throws a panicky glance over his shoulder. His face distorted to an expression that might also have been borrowed from Edvard Munch.

The backward glance is no help to Edvard Munch's nightwalker. He discovers no trace, not the least trace of his pursuer's shadow. And then, after sensing the tapping footsteps behind him once again, he pulls himself together and halts. Turns around, in a fear-stricken, defensive pose.

But I felt absolutely nothing of the kind as I looked over my shoulder, stopped, turned about-face, and calmly scanned the six hundred yards I had traversed since crossing the Inn bridge. The few lights of Celerina looked far away, much farther away than they really were, as if we were separated by an utterly, utterly calm arm of the sea. For a second I mulled the spurious question of why no lighthouse stood there to give off its monotonous flashes of light.

Ha, we are in the mountains—those few lights and I.

But this silence. My overdose of ephedrine (that made breathing wonderfully easy) could not explain why, for a few seconds, I missed the gentle beating of the surf. Franz Grillparzer: *Waves of Love and of the Sea.* Here I was crossing the broad meadows of the level Campagnatscha, meadows where hundreds of cows had grazed until day before yesterday when they were driven up to their mountain pastures. It was the sleepy clanking of cowbells, near and far, that I missed.

Walking ahead you could hear the regular tap-tap-tap of *your own* leather soles on the pavement—which was freshly tarred in places. Now and then a little crunching sound of fine, tarred gravel when you walked over these places, a crunching sound combined with a strange feeling as if something were sucking onto the soles of your shoes, a kind of annoying, fleeting kiss you'd rather not receive. And you stopped for a moment once you had these miniature swamps behind you, and scraped the sticky tar and gravel off your shoes—like a restless stallion pawing the stable floor.

Rubber soles. Lonely nightwalkers with crepe soles and Edvard Munch fear on their faces, even those with rubber heels and leather soles, would be more likely to detect the tapping footsteps of their pursuer. Trebla wore neither crepe soles nor rubber heels. The regular tap tap of my footsteps on the San Gian road is very real and without the slightest echo. At my vigorous pace I seem to be almost flying along with—how curious!—a good, almost arrogant feeling of security. Even though I was resisting the thought of "I eat nothing but stork meat" and trying to suppress the memory of Brăila, 1916. But *this* little Brăila episode was not to be suppressed. Prisoners of war, young Rumanian gypsies, all illiterate, all unable (or unwilling) to tell the difference between left and right, are assigned to one of Mackensen's men, a Prussian sergeant. He drills them for all he's worth, but can't even keep the young individualists in step, whereupon this representative of Prussia's Glory hits upon an ingenious drilling technique. The sergeant, who must march his gypsy caravan down to the Danube every morning for duty (unloading ship cargoes), gives the order: every man must tie a handful of hay to his left shoe (the shoes themselves hardly better than hay), a bunch of straw to his right shoe. Left= hay. Right= straw. We the Southerners (Austrians) from the Thirty-sixth Reconnaissance Company (Weckendorfer is still alive, Laimgruber not yet our Captain) laugh ourselves half silly as the Mackensen sergeant marches by with his unit, bellowing out the march cadence in a cutting staccato:

> "Left!
> Left!
> Left! Right! Left!
> Hay!
> Hay!
> Hay! Straw! Hay!"

Haha.

> "Kiss my ass ya goddam wingflappers."

> "Hay!
> Hay!
> Hay! Straw! Hay!
> Hay!
> Hay!
> Hay! Straw! Hay!"

Nonexistent ladies and gentlemen! Despite the regrettable fact that we have no lights, cast your eyes upon the one, the only *(Princess Hummingbird, the World's Largest Lady* is nothing compared to him). *Trebla,* world's last living Social Democrat! See him marching down the road alone! . . . When it is all over with Hitlerism, Social Democracy as it was created and developed by its fathers, August Bebel and Wilhelm Liebknecht, will be no more. More or less purged (each according to national temperament) of the old, proud class loyalties, the new social democratic parties will become respectable and bourgeois, mm, hardly different from all the other late- or post-bourgeois parties around them, except perhaps for that honest respectability itself—a quality that will no doubt be distinctly lacking in the other parties. Nevertheless I hummed:

> "Avanti popolo / alla riscossa, / bandiera rossa / bandiera rossa. /
> Avanti popolo / alla riscossa, / bandiera rossa / trionfera—"

A curious spectacle. The son of an Imperial Austro-Hungarian Field Marshal marches down the San Gian road in the middle of the night humming the battle hymn of the Italian Reds. Perhaps Father Radetzky would turn over in his grave on Heroes' Mountain in Lower Austria. Or perhaps he wouldn't. Actually it's disgusting the way the living allude to such gyrations of the dead.

"Bandiera la trionferà / Evviva il socialismo e la libertà—"
The best, most rousing revolutionary song since the *Marseillaise.* Tap-tap-tap-tap-hay-straw-hay-straw.

Just to be decent let's try it in good Soci-German:

> *"Brueder, zur Sonne, zur Freiheit*
> *Brueder, zum Lichte empor—"*

(Jolly well meant but, sorry, I'm afraid it's just too sentimental to compare with *Bandiera rossa.* Or the *Internationale.*)

> *"A-v-a-n-t-i p-o-p-o-l-o / a-l-l-a r-i-s-c-o-s-s-a, /*
> *b-a-n-d-i-e-r-a-r-o-s-s-a / t-r-i-o-n-f-e-r-a."*

(Man, don't sing so loud.)

My greatest wish during the civil war was, as you might think, not to get my sights on Heimwehr commander Prince Ruediger Starhemberg. You might hate this good-looking playboy but you couldn't take him seriously. My most burning hatred I reserved for the Prussian Major Waldemar Pabst, who had come over to Austria from Weimar, Germany, and made a name for himself in those days—February '34—as Heimwehr chief of staff. (Supposedly he had a Nazi reason for not joining the Nazis—not racially pure.) If I had gotten him in my field of fire, this Waldemar, this double murderer who in 1919 was quartered along with the staff of the Guard Cavalry Rifles Division, in Berlin's fashionable Eden Hotel, and from there—perhaps over oysters and champagne—had ordered two people murdered: the half-Jewish Dr. Karl Liebknecht who as early as 1914 dared to vote against the war appropriations in the Reichstag. They pulled him into a car at night, let him get out in Berlin's snow-covered Tiergarten. "You're free to go, Herr Doktor"—*shoot him as he attempts to escape!* Well then, and what do we do about the little Luxemburg girl, Jewish Rosa? We'll show her what we think about *The Accumulation of Capital* (which she wrote); let's let that brutal little sailor boy Runge handle her. There is still no agreement among historians. Had Runge already shot her in the Eden Hotel (while Major Waldemar Pabst was popping champagne corks) and then dragged her body into the car (in which at least *one* navy officer was already sitting)? Or did Runge do her in in the car? In any case, a half hour later Rosa's body was floating in the ice-cold water of the Landwehr canal . . . Waldemar

Pabst, chief of staff of the Heimwehr, if only I could have seen the whites of his eyes. But during the four-day war I never get a glimpse of him. Instead I tie the wounded Franz Scherhack to my back and race over to Graz to the office of Dr. Maxim Grabscheidt. *Healed for the gallows!* And under martial law they execute Scherhack; Stanek, Secretary of the Styrian Metal Workers Union; Koloman Wallisch; Master Shoemaker Muenichreiter; Vienna Fire Department Captain, Engineer Weisl, inventor of the foam fire-extinguisher and the others. (But Albert, still young, aged 35, wounded veteran, son of a general—no, Old Austria was still too much a part of the Austro-Fascist regime for them to hang him.) Then the illegal SS-*Standarte* 89 kills Dollfuss in his office on the Ballhausplatz, and nobleman von Schuschnigg becomes Chancellor, and before he disbands the Heimwehr he politely suggests that the murderer of Liebknecht and Luxemburg kindly leave the country. Meanwhile Trebla becomes acquainted with two Graz prisons, four Vienna prisons, and a series of detention camps—1934, Messendorf near Graz; in late autumn one week free, then transferred by the police to the camp at Waltendorf. The latter is set up in a former school building. Police-cook Laibbrod, a female sympathizer who used to address me as "Mr. Comrade-Sir." There are Red and Brown prisoners in the camp, but to the Reds she deals out, whenever possible, a double ration of food. Also, two of the three guard shifts are inclined to be sympathetic. It's a merry scene when the visiting room is crowded. Whenever one of us gets the urge, whether with wife, life's companion, or lover, then a giant document cabinet in the camp office is cleared out—all but a layer of paperwork about mattress high. Shortly thereafter, while office work is suspended for half an hour, a more or less vigorous paper-shuffling can be heard.

"Mr. Comrade-Sir," whispers police-cook Laibbrod to me, "you're newly married, aren't you?"

"If you call four years newly married . . ."

"Anyway, you *look* newly married to me."

"Really?"

"Is it true your wife is Giaxa's daughter?"

"No, only his niece," I lied.

"Jack-sa!" Cook Laibbrod claps her pudgy hands together. "What I would give for an autograph from *him!*"

"Not so difficult to get."

"*Really?* Of course it wouldn't do to lock you and your lovely wife—I saw her in the visiting room—to lock you up in that dreadful cabinet."

"Of course, not to mention the fact that I'm allergic and would suffocate in that box within a few minutes."

"Mary and Joseph, Mr. Comrade-Sir! D'you know what I'm going to do? Strictly between us, but I'll fix up my room for you, put clean sheets on the bed—you just have to tell me *when* you and your wife want to take a—how do those Latins say?—a siesta."

352

Tap-tap-tap-tap. "Hay! Straw! Hay! Straw! Three cheers for the former Waltendorf police-cook Laibbrod!"

(Not so loud, Mr. Comrade-Sir.)

Apparently I was all alone on the San Gian road. Nothing and no one came toward me, not a car, nor a motorcycle, nor a bicycle, nor anyone on foot. This complete lack of traffic could have made me uneasy—instead I took it as something immutable. After midnight, truck traffic across the Bernina was extremely minimal. Trucks. Men Clavadetscher's truck. Where might that truckload of smugglers be sneaking about now? A man walking alone, now dependent on a single dot of light to get his bearings: the light of the Muottas Muragl aerial tramway. Such a calm, steady light; why not a blinking one? As an old wartime flyer I could imagine lighthouses on the mountains just like on the seashore. Where was my moon—this red specter of a waning June moon that had, literally, lighted my way home yesterday? Yesterday night, when they had escorted me home, the dead.

Tonight (whether because of ephedrine or not) I had no such escort.

I place my faith in nothing. Who said that, whose motto was it? The motto of the peasant knight Franz von Sickingen?—one of the very few historic figures who dared attempt a true German revolution.

I place my faith in nothing.

In very little.

And very much.

(Everything's relative.)

In myself.

No shrunken moon, not a single star, a sultry darkness never seen at these altitudes, better loosen your scarf. *End of the period of fine weather, thunderstorm activity in the southern Alps.* Not marching on rubber soles and despite my tap-tap-tap I now heard it. Heard it and saw it—the rumbling and flashing.

From a distance of more than ninety miles and from an altitude of more than five thousand feet below me the thunder grumbled out of the depths like a stifled growl from Hades, and the flashes were mere sheet lightning whose vague reflection haunted its way into the upland valleys. This display was on my right, while high above to the left shone the solitary star of the Muottas Muragl light, the only orientation point I could depend on, unless I wanted to use Pola's flashlight—which seemed neither necessary nor desirable.

Hay, straw, hay, straw, in July 1935, the Christian Corporate State lets me go free, for which I give them small reward. After two weeks that belong to Xana-me, I plunge myself into illegal work, become part of the political leadership of the Revolutionary Socialists in Styria. The ill-fated meeting in the quarry near Goesting. Two of my fellow conspirators are arrested. Later successful meetings in Preming's carton factory in Uebelbachgraben . . . At the beginning of 1936 I am part of the administration of the Autonomous Defense Corps in Vienna, acting as a contact man to the illegal unions. In Brigittenau, in the back room of a coffeehouse on the Danube Canal, the muffled call goes out for "*Kraxen*" (weapons). As an old journalist I establish three illegal plant newspapers. Though a hat-hater, I wear a marbled Tyrolean model to conceal my special identifying mark. Before the Christian State Police were able to confiscate my passport and doctoral diploma I'd had copies made (just in case) of both documents and had them officially notarized. Thus in June I am able to take the side trip to Hvar and meet the Giaxas. Shortly after my return to Vienna—Xana is still in Hvar and I'm spending the night (just in case) not at home but at a new hideout in a through house (house with several exits on the Graben—I get busted.

At 5:00 A.M. —it is already light out—two policemen haul me out of bed.

"What's your name?"

"Jonah."

"What's your *real* name, Herr Doktor Von———? Come along with us."

"If you have no objections I'd like to have breakfast first. Could I invite you gentlemen to join me? Coffee with cream, ham and eggs."

"Hem unt ekks, what's that?" asks one of them.

"English breakfast," informs the other one.

"Sounds all right."

And so I have breakfast with my arresting officers, whereupon they conduct me through the empty, sun-bright morning streets to the LISL, an extensive brick building, ERECTED MDCCCLIX, a somewhat macaber bombastic replica of the early Renaissance palazzo of the Dukes of Este in Ferrara. At 8:00 A.M., my first interrogation—by an experienced operator inclined to joke-telling.

"Well look at this, the infamous Trebla in the flesh. Do you know the joke about Count Bobby's Interrogation?"

"With whom do I have the pleasure . . .?"

"Police Superintendant Dr. Pfleger."

"Aha," I say.

"Where do you know me from?"

"We have friends in common and they've told me about you."

"Nice things?"

"Charming."

"All I can say is, remarkable. *You* are known well enough, it's sad to say, and I must report that I've heard very few charming things about your activities, *Herr Oberleutnant*—we always address war veterans with their proper rank here. When I look at you, a young man with an old, historic name." He leafed through a dossier. "Your father died at the end of 1929 . . . two days later your mother?"

"Flu epidemic."

"May I ask what party His Excellency, your father, voted for during the Republic?"

"You'll laugh, *Herr Doktor.* Social Democratic."

"You mean to say, Christian Democratic."

"No. Social."

"How could that be? It seems improbable that he would have been influenced by his son's opinions."

"Much simpler. Rent control."

"How's that?"

"He lost his quite modest fortune during the inflation. All he had left was the pension he was drawing in the pensioner's city of Graz. My parents couldn't be thrown out of their big house by the Paulus Gate where they lived on the ground floor. Nor could their rent be raised. Because of the rent control legislation passed by the Socials."

"It sounds almost plausible. Nevertheless, when you think, a retired Field Marshal of the Imperial Army—you can only say, remarkable. Had he no other family property? What about the family castle in southern Moravia? . . . Why are you grinning, Lieutenant?"

"Because the family castle was razed in the Thirty Years War."

"Aha. All I can say is, remarkable."

"Please feel free, Mr. Superintendent."

"What's that, please?—

"To say remarkable."

"You're a real case. Haven't you ever considered the fact that with your illegal machinations against the Corporate State you are playing into the hands of the Nazis? That you are helping to sell out Austria?"

"That's being worked out elsewhere."

"You mean in Berlin."

"Quite apart from that. In the foreign offices of Rome, Paris, and London."

My interrogator claps the dossier shut, then pats it with his hand.

"As a disabled veteran you will be granted certain privileges. Naturally it will be impossible to allow you to have another—what do you call yourselves—Revolutionary Socialist as a cellmate. That would only be encouraging subversive discussions. Nor will you get a Communist—he could pervert you even more."

"Eh-ooo don't be thilly!" I parody a homosexual.

"You should have been a clown like your—"

"Let's drop the subject," I cut him off.

"As you wish," says Police Superintendent Dr. Pfleger, almost affably.

My cellmate is a Nazi (SS-*Standarte* 89) and for weeks we do not speak a word to each other. Our only phonetic communication: occasionally we fart back and forth at each other, bunk to bunk. The summer is long and hot and one of my guards, Sedlatchek, pesters me because I undertake to wash my entire body (with soap): "Hey, Lieutenant, 'r you a whore?" Whereupon I submit the following written request to Major Kosian, the commandant at LISL:

TO: Commanding Officer, Police Penitentiary an der Rossauer Laende (Elisabethenpromenade)

SUBJECT: Cleanliness of exterior and interior portions of lower abdomen.

Since, following the excretion of fecal matter (commonly called shit) (i.e., after crapping) the posterior region (or asshole) cannot, even with the greatest diligence, be rendered entirely clean, the necessity arises to wash same with soap. For this reason I request to be allowed this privilege. At the same time I would like to point out that despite my interest in bodily hygiene I am not a whore, although Inspector Sedlatchek seems to consider me one.

Albert ———, 1LT., Prisoner No. 292

Two days later I get Major Kosian's dead serious reply: *Request denied.*

Suddenly an upward flash of sheet lightning, the reflection of an enormous lightning bolt. Perhaps down there in the Po Valley it had struck a night wanderer like myself. Or a poor animal. If only it had struck a Musso-Fascist. Curious. I don't even wish that a Musso-Fascist was struck by that giant bolt, unless he was not a poor animal, but a very big beast, and big Fascist beasts are unlikely to be out walking at this hour.

Without warning, illuminated by a quick series of distant lightning flashes from the Po Valley, the church shows itself to me.

Not the little church of San Gian, but a ghostly, gigantic church.

Abbé Galiani: What concerns us is optical illusion. De Colana's farewell.

For a few seconds the hill looked like a mountain, the high grass—its pollen powerless against my ephedrine—seemed as artificially green as a stage prop in an old Vienna theater. But the church made a different impression . . . seemed swollen, oversized, *real.*

The main tower with its pointed, long ago burned and never renovated roof, seemed as tall as the spire of Vienna's Minoritenkirche, while the modest little campanile behind it seemed nearly as high as the Heathen Towers of St. Stephen's in Vienna. A terrifying experience for me. If I had been sitting instead of walking I would have fallen off my chair. For the first time I was approached, no overcome, no overwhelmed, by a sensation of fear. Not a fear of someone who was pursuing me. Or might be. Or could be. A fear of my own capacity to exacerbate my own fantastic visions.

One more, perhaps the last, great upward thrust of the sheet lightning . . . distant warfare is also sheet lightning, and close combat is thunder and deadly, crashing bolts . . . but it is always light. Don't think about it; don't think about the Old Great War—

And it stood there on my left as I marched past, *the gigantic church of San Gian—*

A feverish thought. Could it be that the same Merck's ephedrine . . . Goethe's friend Merck . . . that had made me feel strangely absent after listening to the next to last Midnight Tale of the Luzienburg, that at this altitude a sizable dose of this drug had a different effect on me, an effect not unlike opium? That was my only fear at this moment—the fear of losing control over my own senses, fear of a possible drug-induced loss of reality—something I could under no circumstances afford on this night.

Not this night, this night that followed the first day of summer, 1938.

Perhaps humming would help.

"*Avanti popolo / alla riscossa / bandiera rossa / bandiera rossa—*"

The sheet lightning was dying away along with the distant growl of thunder, reduced now to the last weak snarl of a watchdog that had barked itself hoarse at a lonely stranger passing its farm in the dead of night. High up to the left the unchallenged, invulnerable light from Muottas Muragl. "*Avanti popolo / alla riscossa, / bandiera rossa / trionferà.*" I seemed to have the whole San Gian road to myself, and I marched ahead, and the thunder from the Po Valley growled more and more softly, a watchdog that had returned to its doghouse for good, and then there was only the quiet echo of my footsteps, and as I looked back over my left shoulder (unlike Xana I was not superstitious about looking back)—in the last sulfurous upflaring of sheet lightning, without the slightest background noise—I recognized the very humble, tiny little church: San Gian.

Walking along, letting imagination take over, you're writing about the past four weeks . . . with flashbacks into the past forty years, sorry, you're only thirty-nine, anyway no longer young, you write a novel in the first person, and if fate overtakes you on the San Gian road, then the work will remain a fragment. Regardless of length. No extermination.

Sorry, a Freudian slip in my monologue. Naturally I meant no termination.

Ephedrine, Merck, Darmstadt. Johann Heinrich Merck, Darmstadt, Goethe's friend. *The Sorrows of Young Werther.* You can. This short novel. That started a suicide epidemic in its day. Proves the point: You *can* write a novel in the first person, with the last few sentences, after the unnatural death of the narrator, in the third person . . . *No clergyman went with him.*

Those were the days. (De Colana was a special case.)

When a man who died an unnatural death, for example a death at his own hands, brought on by a psychological dilemma, when such a man (or body) was not accompanied by a clergyman.

Those *will be* the days, *these* already *are* the days when there is no question of a clergyman accompanying the bodies who become bodies because they refuse to place their bodies at the disposal of the disposers to be disposed of—not to mention all the other violent deaths.

A sudden hollow reverbation of my marching steps, then a rushing sound not far below. That had to be the bridge over Flaz Brook, the stream now near flood stage, flowing down toward the young Inn. Out of the darkness below a few drops of spray flew up to touch my right cheek like fleeting, friendly cold kisses.

To check my turn into the Samedan-Pontresina road (nearly a right angle) I used Pola's flashlight twice, each time for barely a second. And remembering the little dwarf church I had just left behind in San Gian, a church blown up to enormous proportions by a flare from the depths, I was gripped by the memory of another looming shadow. A Christmas Eve shadow. One of the largest churches in Europe—even without the help of optical illusion: St. Stephen's Cathedral, Christmas 1937—until further notice the last Austrian Christmas.

The LISL, the Police Penitentiary an der Rossauer Laende with its eight towers adorned with imitation Ghibelline battlements, despite Major Kosian's abrupt refusal of my special hygienic request—the LISL a sanatorium compared to Vienna's Landesgericht I, called Graues Haus, whose doors were, unbeknownst to me, yawning to await my entry. First, they generously let me loose on probation—after all I'd only been sent up for four months' police custody. The good side of this coin: I run no risk, after six years of matrimony, of becoming a marital cripple. Xana keeps picking me up at the prison gates for a new honeymoon (so to speak) each time I am released. Whenever the agents of the Christian Corporate State show up to arrest me again, she automatically withdraws to her parents' home in Radkersburg, where she maintains a kind of love affair with her mother. (At least I keep telling myself that my only rival is Elsabé, since Elsabé seems terribly jealous of me and Xana—all of which is bearable under the heading Strange Family.) The mild November evening when in the men's room of a wine restaurant in Vienna Nussdorf I meet my former captain and commanding officer of the Thirty-sixth Aerial Reconnaissance Company, Heinzwerner Laimgruber. That evening in January when I visit him in the Vindobona Detective Agency on the Judenplatz. A few days later I'm arrested again, sent to the Gray House, "On the special instructions of Edmund Glaise von Horstenau, Minister of Justice." I reject the idea that Laimgruber could have been behind it all.

"Hay! Straw! Hay! Straw! Hay! Straw! Hay!"

One-month's detention in Vienna's Landesgericht I, the Gray House. Compared to LISL, not only gray but gruesome. No more special privileges for disabled veterans. Receipt of packages with books or food prohibited. Rations horrible. Bugs. The ancient faded nineteenth-century carpet patterned all over with roses (of all things, roses!)—

"Come with me to Varăzdin / While the roses are still in bloom—"

—and covered with stepped-on bugs. The oldest, palest specks perhaps original nineteenth-century bugs. Far more lively, the bugs of the Christian Corporate State—

"Come with me to Graues Haus / While the insects still crawl the floor—"

Most of my fellow inmates try to keep themselves clean. But only Lysol will help against bugs, and so I organize a chant. "Lysol! Lysol!" And after one of the guards, à la Sedlatchek, has stared a hole in my head (as if to convince himself that I already had one), we get our Lysol. Exit bugs. A mean little trick concocted by Minister of Justice Edmund Glaise von Horstenau deprives me of the chance to enjoy the Schuschnigg government's new amnesty. The latter applies to all Red and Brown delinquents who acted with idealistic motives. (Bombers excepted. And such cowardly brazen tricks as bomb-planting we left to the Adolf supporters anyway: How can you tell *whom* you are blowing up?) They have discovered that I entered and departed the country on a falsified passport . . . to visit Giaxa on the island of Hvar . . . and that is, according to the State's Attorney . . . "fraud. The accused, whose passport was officially confiscated, went off on his merry way to Yugoslavia using a notorized duplicate—charges, by the way, have already been filed against the notary in question. Thus the accused has defrauded the state of its custodial authority."

My merry way! Despite the earnest situation I feel a laugh tickle in my throat. The State's Attorney is already using (as a kind of last rehearsal, so to speak) perfect Nazi jargon. My imprudent activities were all the more reprehensible since my ancestral name had gone down in the history of the Holy Roman Empire of the German Nation. He never mentions the word "Hapsburg," but declares instead that the treasonous ideology with which I had aligned myself was responsible for the Spanish Civil War. But the revered General Franco, thanks in large measure to the energetic support of two great statesmen determined to safeguard Western Culture (discreetly, he avoids mentioning their names), will put an end to the threat posed to Europe by men like me. And as the State's Attorney declares that I have placed myself in league with Red-Spanish nun-rapists, I give out with a whooping laugh that earns me a rebuff from the presiding judge.

The sentence: four months' confinement not including time spent in detention. The gallery of rogues I am assigned to is comparable to the *Strafuni* detail (soldier convicts) I commanded as a seventeen-year-old cadet on the Piave—two pickpockets, two professional shoplifters, three suitcase thieves, thirteen common burglars, and the burglar king Pepi.

Pepi has a face like something out of a Daumier album. "Docter," he addresses me with a confidential wink that says, the two of us are the only real "bosses" here. "Docter, I—"

"Forget the titles, Pepi. When I was sentenced to jail I lost my doctorate. Automatically."

"Makes no dif'rence a me. Fer me you's a docter, and a docter stays a docter. An' becuz you'n me's gonna be ouda here 'fore long—I been in her a long time ya know—I wanna make ya an inter-esting propy-sition. You gets aroun' a lot, I know, wid rich people an poor people. I 'magine you knows rich people in town dat you likes. Doze ones don' int-rest us. But den dere might be some rich people dat you don't care 'bout so much. Doze ones we oughta talk about."

"How do you mean that, Pepi?"

"Waitaminute, docter. And den dere muss be *some* rich people you juss can't *stand*. Doze are da ones we's after. Now wid dis lass cata-gory of rich guy you draws me a plan of his house, where da safe is, an' everyting. Where dey keeps deir jools n'da like. An' den you asks dem casual-like when dey plan ta go on vay-cation. An' den you calls me up from da telephone boot—I'll give ya my secret number. An' if da job goes good you gets a turd of da loot."

"You know what, Pepi—"

"Na, come offit, Docter. If ya don't needit for yerself—den yer party dat's been outlawed an's gonna stay dat way—dey always c'n use da cash."

After spending every night for *four* months with *four* people in a cell designed for one man, I am released not into the real world but—after spending a single day with Xana—into the detention camp at Woellersdorf near Wiener Neustadt. The camp is set up at the former Mandl munitions factory, and there we are treated (relatively speaking) very well. Aside from being voted into the illegal camp executive committee on the second day after arrival, I was also appointed barracks leader by the camp commandant, First Lieutenant of the Gendarmerie and physician, Dr. Anton Hruby. He is concerned with the well-being of his prisoners. To diminish their sexual frustrations, he orders them to play hard daily rounds of volleyball (the illegal executive committee does not join in; they have more important things to do) and has saltpeter mixed with their food. To negotiate improvements for his patients he makes personal calls at the Federal Chancellor's Office to see Schuschnigg (but not Glaise Horstenau, whom he discreetly abhors). This good man Toni Hruby accepts the fact (and, it seems, willingly) that the prisoners deceive him. For example, our old trick of smuggling in illegal newspapers as material for guitar builders. When during a sultry summer hot spell I suffer from one of my post-traumatic headaches, he orders me to spend the morning in bed; my breakfast is served to me there, and strangely enough I find on the tray copies of illegal papers published in Czechoslovakia, the *Arbeiter-Zeitung* from Brno, the *Red Flag* from Prague.

"*Herr Lieutenant*, what would you like for lunch today?" asks the camp cook, a fellow Social detainee from Crete, a furniture-mover's neighborhood in Vienna's tenth district. "Liver dumpling soup, pot roast, pudding?"

Before long there are two First Lieutenants in Woellersdorf: 1st Lt. Toni (official commandant) and 1st Lt. Trebla (unofficial commandant). "If old Glaise knew about this!"

Lone walker on the midnight road past San Gian, you will . . . must . . . had better reach Punt Muragl soon. Valley station of the aerial tramway.

The better my relations with the camp commander become, the worse they are with a certain (very certain) group of fellow internees, Social big shots who accuse me of collaborating with the blackshirts (Hruby) as well as with the blood Reds (Communists) of Woellersdorf. Holy Laudon, when I think of these pale pink fatheads . . . the way they sabotaged my (almost proto-communist, ultra-egalitarian) distribution of food packages . . . and to think that these very bossocrats ... *after* the Adolf era ... could ever come to power again in Austria ... One September day Dr. Hruby takes my arm and, almost delightedly, shows me a copy of *Le Populaire*. "Read what they wrote about you in Paris—by the way, I'll see to it that you get out of here in October."

> *Albert* ——*, ex-aviateur, ex-aristocrat et*
> *socialiste révolutionaire autrichien*

At the end of October 1937 I am released.

But First Lieutenant of the Gendarmerie Dr. Anton Hruby is dead. They got him too. He was not unreligious, definitely a conscientious Christian who would have been embarrassed to call himself a liberal Catholic. Very shortly after the birth of the Greater German Reich he is said to have offered armed resistance to those attempting to arrest him.

> *Tôt ou tard*
> *On bouffe bien chez*
> *Caduff-Bonnard*
>
> Early, late, from near or far,
> You eat so well
> At C.-Bonnard

A small disappointment awaited me at Punt Muragl. Naturally the Muottas Muragl funicular railway, just reopened, was not operating at night. Nevertheless I had hoped to find the valley station lit with at least a single lamp. Riding past (but never up from) this little mountain station, I found it just slightly reminiscent of a small Buddhist temple. Now the place was pitch dark and emitted only a barely audible humming sound. A transformer turned almost all the way down? Whatever it was, the tone, unlike the rushing of Flaz Brook, buzzed at me in an unfriendly way, like a wasp flying around my left ear.

Aha, and even the light from the mountain station Muottas Muragl was no longer a consolation. What did that mean, no consolation?

It meant that it shone no longer. From here, Punt Muragl, it was no longer visible because the mountain was slightly hunchbacked. The little temple. Wouldn't it make an excellent ambush point? Therefore I'd best make tracks without attempting to put some light on the subject with Pola's flashlight.

Now it was indeed like walking through a tunnel, although the analogy was not quite perfect. A man walking through a tunnel could hear the rattling approach of a train in time to press himself against the cold wall and save himself. Here on the road beyond San Gian with lightless Punt Muragl at my back there was no cold wall to take refuge against. As strange as it may sound, I wasn't really *concerned* about taking refuge. But rather about testing. A series of hypotheses. A series that, as such, might be imaginary. Yet one element or another in this series might be real, might have consequences. An incredibly bizarre, no burlesque, idea—that perhaps the only *correct* name in my complicated crossword puzzle might be . . . Joop ten Breukaa. March tempo undiminished I groped my way along through nothingness—nothingness without light, without heat, without cold. Man's will is his heaven (old proverb). Or his hell. Drag your Hades just another half a mile and then—if you are lucky, and despite all the bad and worse that have happened around you and have left their mark on you, you do seem rather favored by the gods—you will see the scattered few lights of Puntraschigna alias Pontresina. Oh, you and your old hypertrophic reporter's curiosity and your old revolutionary spirit, both of which were often enough at odds with your survival instinct. Isn't that pathological? Am I sick? An obsessed, sick man? Oh go on! (I *am* going on!) Well anyway, all great heroes have a small hole in the roof. And with at least one hero this is literally, i.e., physiologically true. One thing I hadn't done, I hadn't *bragged* to anyone that I would undertake this solo march on the San Gian road . . . no, I had not bragged anywhere to anyone about it, and therefore, while striding through the remaining stretch of Egyptian darkness, I could rightfully declaim, *How glad I am that no one knows / My name is Rumpelstiltskin* or *You will never guess who I am, I am Josef, your Emperor.*

On the right, rather close at hand, the lively rushing of Flaz Brook again. Why was it called that? Senseless question. Why shouldn't it be called Flaz Brook? The names of European rivers and streams: Inn, Reuss, Rhône, Marne, Maas, Main, Mur, Drava, Po, Don—Europe's flowing waters did not have names like Mississippi. Also following me now, a humming sound, different from the mechanical wasp-buzz that had greeted me at Punt Muragl. A diffuse sound, seeming to come neither from the right nor the left, diminishing in a kind of fadeout and then returning, and even when *there,* so soft as to seem intended for the phenomenal ears of bats alone (those blind night flyers) . . . Perhaps the vibrations of telephone wires strung between poles I could not see. Not a single tone but a polyphonic texture of sound covering several octaves. It sounded like music.

. . . Mozart?

In mid-October 1937 I'm a free man again and am living with Xana in our attic apartment on Vienna's Schoenlaterngasse next to the Basilisk Inn—almost as if nothing had happened or would happen—and am obsessively typing out the first act of *Love and Love* on my old Remington. Type it out right away, right away—like Hemingway's, my dialogues come rattling straight out of the typewriter (strange that he never wrote any plays). The time, 1937, place, Vienna. The plot—a revolutionary Socialist becomes—out of love for his party—a burglar of rich men's homes. He meets an unusually pretty working-class girl whose father was killed in the February battles, whereupon she became a fallen woman walking the avenues around the Prater. Now the man's love for his party comes into conflict with his love for the girl. I envision a play about a grotesque idealized underworld with mildly surrealistic local color and contemporary relevance. In mid-December Giaxa had sent me a terribly nice handwritten note inviting me down to Radkersburg for Christmas. But almost three writing years lost in arrests, jails, and detention camps weigh heavily on my soul, and though my heart is heavy too, I decide to let Xana go to Radkersburg alone while I spend the Christmas holidays at the typewriter. Not excluding Christmas Eve. But as the Pummerin, St. Stephen's giant bell, calls and calls for Midnight Mass across the city's snow-padded roofs in its deep-deep-dark, more ghostly than comforting, strange, sublime-sounding voice, the play *Love and Love* grinds to a halt. Soon I am pushing my way along with a maelstrom of coat-muffled churchgoers through the main portal of the cathedral.

Of all Gothic cathedral interiors (Chartres excepted), St. Stephen's is just about my favorite. But on the cold Christmas Eve of 1937 the enormous cavern, its floor crowded with thousands of wool- and fur-packed creatures, is filled with a foul miasma that makes me mildly nauseated—as if the grayish mass had suffered some kind of collective flatulence and relieved itself with a thousand-fold fart that hung in the nave, slightly perfumed with incense, like a cold, gigantic cloud.

How long can I stand to breathe in this miasma? On the other hand I am gripped by the premonition that this is the last time I will be in St. Stephen's. The last time. And so I let the splendor of the distant, tinkling-mumbling ceremony wash over me from afar across the thousand candles of the great midnight cathedral, letting myself slowly drift with the undersurface current of the crowd like a swimmer floating in the paralyzing mire of a mud bath.

"*Kyrie eleison . . .*"

Strains of homophonic music pouring down from vaulted heights—not music by the cantor of St. Thomas in Leipzig, the Lutheran German Johann Sebastian Bach (who was usually performed on this holy night in St. Stephen's). The few oboes and horns, the cautiously employed drums and trumpets (they would be less cautiously employed for Uncle Adolf's grand entrance), the discreet use of the giant organ, the strings without the bumblebee-hum of violas, the choir with only four parts, proclaiming its own personality with a strongly accentuated Kyrie eleison—now it begins, young Mozart's C-major Mass, the *Coronation Mass.*

Mozart pitted against Bach on a kind of fatherland front, isn't it ridiculous? Isn't Uncle Adolf, the man they are standing up to with this musical gesture—isn't he a latter-day compatriot of Mozart's? (To think that the same piece of land could bring forth *him* as well as *him!*) And wouldn't Mozart have done better to accept the Prussian king's offer of a well-paid position as court composer—instead of continuing to work on a small salary for the emperor in Vienna—only to have his still young body thrown—one snowy December day barely

150 years ago—into the *allgemeine Grube,* a poor-man's mass grave, never to be found again?

"*Gloria . . .*"

O ye gods, no, O God, what simple, sincere, almost naïve solemnity lives in this Gloria with its broad, concluding Amen . . . Amen . . . Amen. As far as I am concerned, a man fighting with a mild case of nausea. My deep, my great love goes out to this man buried in his frozen mass grave. His thousand-faceted song moves my heart more strongly than Bach's cooler universality, his nondualistic, well-tempered, mathematical music that soars above human passions. And as the Credo begins and as its center movement, where the singing of the modest choir weaves strangely, tenderly, sweetly, mysteriously through the figurations of the strings, glides down upon me from above, I stand there, the ex-Christian, deeply stirred, and smell the rank odor no longer. I grew up as a Catholic; now I feel myself at home in church for one last time.

"*Et incarnatus est . . .*"

An inexplicable hope wells up, seeming to pass by my deep, empirically rooted pessimism, a *wonder*-ful, senseless hope. It continues through the majestic Sanctus, the charming Benedictus, up to the joyful Hosanna. Then it is disturbed.

Theodor Innitzer, seemingly miles away, posted at the high altar with his back to the congregation, looking with his vestments and pointed miter like a giant turtle standing on its hind legs, its long pointed head stretched out of its shell. His Eminence Cardinal Innitzer, Archbishop of Vienna, would offer no resistance to the newest form of hosanna, the shout *Sieg-Heil.* No impassioned Nazi like Suffragan Bishop Hudal, he *was* a Sudeten German. Perhaps one could make a more favorable prediction if he had come from some other part of the Danube Empire—not from its German-speaking Sudetenland fringe. The Sudeten Germans seem enchanted by Adolf's new Reich—even to the ranks of our Czech sister party.

"*Hosanna! . . .*"

And who in this crowd surrounding me would offer any resistance to the Hitler hosanna as it rolled across the border? *Who?* Wouldn't half of them, far more than half of them, be ready overnight to implant the four-times-broken-cross beside the Cross of Christ while chanting the new hosanna with a thousand voices?

"*Hosanna! . . .*"

Once again the army of damp-coated worshippers begins to irritate my nose and once again I am immunized against the miasma by my distant, immortal friend Wolfgang Amadeus. At the same time I recall how I had enraged my catechism teacher in Olmuetz, when as a nine-year-old I had asked why God had chosen a lamb instead of a lion (Father Patchafirek: "To fulfill the prophecy, you dunderhead!"), yet I allow myself to be spun inside the beautiful, earthy sadness of the Agnus Dei as it filters down, sung by a lonely, sweet soprano that

I immediately fall in love with. Is that church music? Isn't it rather the countess in the opera buffa *La nozze di Figaro*? with her sweet resignation: "*Dove sono i bei momenti*"—"Only too quickly you have departed" . . . (How true.) "Farewell, farewell" . . .

"*Dona nobis pacem! . . .*"

They are always begging for it. For peace. At the same time they are destroying it, the schizophrenic beggars—begging in their hearts (less than in their heads)—give us war!

Don't think about it. Not now. Let yourself be moved for just a minute more. Only too quickly it will have departed.

"*Dona nobis pacem! . . .*" The giant organ's crescendo, in its gleaming, truly gleaming tones, swells within me. Peace? Are we not *the last*? Not just Giaxa (& Giaxa VII)—all of us here in the midnight cathedral or outside in the Christian Western world, in the hypocrisy of this fraudulent Holy Night—would not all of us, major, minor, or anti-Fascists—assuming we saved our skins—be the last representatives of a rather extraordinary, circa 300-year-old age that began with Galileo . . . and would now, within a few years or decades . . . come to an end? Or are we the forerunners of *the first*? That is the hope within hopelessness.

The organ of St. Stephen's resounds alone in an adeptly improvised Mozartean final cadence, but in its resonance—the memory within memory—

I see the night motorcycle ride from Bruck to Graz in those February days of martial law. Tied to my back with a clothesline, Franz Scherhack, whom Maxim Grabscheidt had just cured (TB), now with a bullet through the lung; he coughs up blood onto my neck as we roar by the rolling mill. Then they come and take Franz away . . . who could have tipped off the police? . . . out of the doctor's basement hideaway on the Lastenstrasse and drive him to the gallows. *Healed for the gallows!* Then it offends my nose for the last time, the stench. The stirred feelings of an ex-Christian are smothered and die. He cannot stand another minute in the cathedral (only too quickly have you departed), a thousand pardons, dear Mozart . . . The thin shower of snow has stopped; it is a cold night, fifteen degrees. Everything closed along the Graben. Deep in the Naglergasse a lamp glowing glowworm green. Is there a bar open down there? There is. And in that place I will be offered a double Christmas present of a kind seldom received by anyone. But no matter; I will turn it down.

Had the telephone poles moved away from the road leading out of San Gian? The soft humming of what must have been telephone wires—this polyphonic humming had turned into Mozart. Now it was gone.

Sheet lightning. Reflection of a thunderstorm so distant that its rumble, its doghouse growl was no longer audible. Yet there is also such a thing as post-sheet-lightning, the last, silent signals of a far-off storm. In the light of one of these I discovered the Plaun da Choma on my right.

The Coma Plains. Plains of agony.

Whose agony? Agony? To translate the Romansch "Plaun" with "plains" was probably correct; but to interpret "Choma" as "coma" most likely went too far. And yet this mistranslation had taken root in me some time earlier, more than two weeks before when Gaudenz de Colana had given me a ride in his rattletrap Fiat following my abortive trip to Corviglia and had introduced the place *en passant* with his hoarse voice, "*Plaun da Choma, my dear Black-White-White-Black. Plaun da Choma.*"

De Colana; the natural association: Sils, Chesetta Grischuna—Men Clavadetscher. And as I thought of him, yes in the same second I heard something. . . Flaz Brook was farther away now . . . something at least two miles away; coming up from in front of me and to the right, perhaps in Roseg Valley . . . I stopped.

"Wwwummmrrr." Silence. "Wwwummmrrrrrr."

A car engine that didn't want to start? Hardly. More likely a truck trying to remain undetected . . . driving a short stretch, stopping; driving on, stopping.

Could it be . . .

What the Royal Jockey, Ret., told me in the Café d'Albana . . .

Could it be that smuggler-poacher Clavadetscher . . . in the Roseg Valley, where I had seen the first woodchucks on June 2 . . . that the poachers . . . so as not to draw attention to themselves with gunfire by day . . . were setting woodchuck traps by night?

"Come with me to Varăzdin / While the roses are still in bloom—"

Papa-Rose's widow Elsabé. Elsabé as a widow, inconceivable. Yet Elsabé was in Varăzdin, in the Yugoslavian resort of Varăzdin; a ray of hope, if one could speak about rays of anything in such a darkness . . . this meant literally not symbolically the darkness of this road, the kind of night this was. Unlike last night one did not enjoy the luxury of being escorted home by the dead.

The recently dead.

Over there to the right they had accompanied me through Staz Forest up to the clearing—Plaun da Choma.

Valentin Tiefenbrucker. If perhaps his end had come in a completely different way than was assumed. If the Republican flak battery on Punta Salou had *not* brought down the Fieseler-Storch by mistake. Isn't it absurd to think that in broad daylight anyone could *mistake* a Fieseler sports plane for a recon machine of the Legion Kondor? If information had reached the Trotskyite POUM (Partido Obrero de la Unificacion Marxista) with its HQ in Barcelona's Hotel Falcon, or if information had reached the POUM militiamen at the Punta Salou flak battery that party-liner Tiefenbrucker, who had survived the great purges in Stalin's Russia (Grandpa Kujath: a result of the persecution complexes of our times—complexes, alas, often justified) without a scratch, is flying to Modesto. If in the course of this civil war, which would soon come to an end because Spanish democracy had been betrayed and sold out (for free) by the great democracies—in the final phase of the war—animosity was sure to increase almost organically, as it were. What if Valentin were not the victim of an accident but had been shot out of the sky and burned in the course of a family quarrel between Republicans—after having escaped from Dachau and from the Detention Camp Commander Giselher Liebhenschl—

Once again my blind advance came to a halt.

The purring sound of the truck—coming closer—the same truck I thought I'd gotten a fix on a few minutes earlier—right twenty degrees, southwest, range two miles, in Roseg Valley? Now it seemed to be coming straight out of the south, driving steadily—from Bernina Pass? A lonely, steady rumble coming out of the valley, ever closer. For three or four minutes the sound dropped an octave lower (slowing down?). Was the truck being driven through Pontresina? Now the big, glaring headlights came into view, obviously approaching faster than the top speed of any Saurer truck. That could *not* be Men Clavadetscher's smuggler bus! Suddenly the whole highway was transformed to a double track of blinding-white, block-long rods of light, no, the Saurian, the Saurer from Sils could never drive at such a tempo. Perhaps this border country was crawling with smugglers on this first night of summer. Perhaps Men had switched vehicles.

By the roadside on my left two pines on the lower fringe of the wooden Schafberg slope. Involuntarily, yes, unintentionally I leaped across the roadside ditch between the trees and saw something I had never seen before: a speeding vehicle with antlers.

A steel blue gray metal beast, the front of its cab mounting sixteen-point antlers, hurtling by me at over 65 mph, letting me feel the gust of its wake as it passed. Pickup truck. Geneva plates. Sign on door just visible in headlight reflection: INSTITUT ZOOLOGIQUE DE CAROUGE.

And then the old darkness.

This time I used Pola's little flashlight again to get back onto the road. Get back on the road. Get going home now, home that's not home. You and your blind march, and your damn desire to *put more light on the subject,* to provoke provocations, to hunt hunters.

What if you came home without anything happening to you on this road. What would you look like then? In that case, in that non-case your status could be listed under a heading no one has ever used for you, neither friend nor foe—Grade-A Number One Asshole.

Because Xana *must* have heard or read about it by now; certainly she *knows* about Giaxa's last performance.

Thus it may justifiably be maintained that it would be highly disconcerting if nothing highly disconcerting happened to you on the San Gian road. And that means within the next fifteen minutes, for in that span of time the first small lights would begin to show behind the massive body of darkness on the left—Munt da la Bês-cha, the Schafberg. I gave the Walther a gentle pat in its holster, as if calming a nervous horse.

Small lights—small light, after Midnight Mass, walking across Vienna's deserted Graben, past the monument that has stood there swelling with baroque pride for over 250 years, as if the plague had been some kind of festival. From the plague-festival pillar a view down the narrow tunnel of the Naglergasse; deep inside, the small green light—perhaps there you can get something to warm you up. So you let yourself drift down the tunnel street you've seldom entered; along its length runs a bent wrought-iron railing. To what effect one hardly comprehends—the abyss guarded by the railing is exactly three feet deep. OSIRIS-BAR. The sign outside an illuminated (and somewhat dilapidated) green sun. The two—obviously inseparable—whores are named Vilma and Ehrentraut, and this, their place of business, is actually closed, and actually I've walked in on a private party celebrating Christmas around a fir tree crowned with an illuminated crescent moon of Isis. Everyone is slightly tipsy, and the sparse-haired barkeeper confides in me that he's had seven Cointreaus against doctor's orders—he's a diabetic. "D'ya know what—in the springtime I got bees buzzing around my barn door." The two clearly inseparable whores are without male companions. Their motto is obvious at a glance: We don't need husbands; we don't need pimps. We watch out for each other (without being lesbians). They look as alike as twins, both about five foot six, both corn blond, more than buxom, definitely qualifying as fat but at the same time strangely well proportioned. I'm not a type who arouses sympathy and (as far as I can judge) have never—even in my worst moments—been considered pitiful. But Vilma and Ehrentraut (nickname, Traudl), the more they pour real Polish Kontushkovska into their relatively enormous bodies, the more unprofessional ("We don't work Christmas Eve") pity they lavish upon me. First because, of all times, he's got to spend Christmas Eve without his family, and second because he's really a good-looking guy and third because he has such a *darling* scar on his forehead.

"Did ya just get that in Spain?" Vilma wants to know.

"Oh gwan," her colleague corrects her, "can't ya see? The scar is *much* older than that. Maybe he got it in the World War."

Vilma: "He looks too young for that."

"Maybe he went to war when he was just a kid." With that, fat Ehrentraut smacks a big fat kiss onto my forehead and, because her lipstick isn't kissproof, draws a big laugh from the Osiris clientele. Various mirrors on the wall show me in this greenish gleamy glimmer the kiss-print looks like a "bullet hole" worn by an actor in a horror play. Blood makeup. Théâtre Grand Guignol, Montmartre.

From high out of the southeast . . . even a blind man could make out the direction once he knew the course of the San Gian road . . . from the direction of Bernina Pass the exact same thin humming sound, then a thicker, buzzing, slowing down, then (getting closer) accelerating . . . not a truck. A pickup. Holy Laudon, *not that*. It rushed toward me, acoustically not unlike an artillery shell, rrroommm-wheee, the great headlights projecting two immense, long poles of light. This time I sprang to the right, behind a guard stone. The pickup truck, enamel blue—above the cab stretches a broad, branching pair of giant antlers—sixteen pointers. The driver seemed to notice my existence for he braked slightly, then floored the throttle again. The grayish blue beast with antlers rushed past me, and in the glow of the headlights I could decipher INSTITUT ZOOLOGIQUE DE CA——, and then the tail-lit Geneva license plate.

Involuntarily remembering Grandpa Kujath's jargon—it was a real slap in the phiz. (If things kept going like this, if *I* kept going like this for all un-eternity . . . since according to Professor Einstein eternity is a lot of rubbish . . . and every so often, forever and ever, a bluish pickup truck called INSTITUT ZOOLOGIQUE DE CAROUGE passed by me fitted with a giant pair of stag antlers, *that* would be a new variation on Dante's *Inferno*.)

The last Christmas of the First Austrian Republic—or the Feast of the Egyptian sun god Osiris, or the Feast of the Persian sun god Mithras or the old Germanic Yule Feast of Winter Solstice: Vilma and Ehrentraut hold a short, whispered discussion, then give me a discreet signal with a double nod of their heads. And so I follow the two tubbies out into a small courtyard—covered by a skylight but frosty enough. To say nothing of the garbage cans.

And then they lift, slide, flip up their long knit skirts together, side by side, in double, synchronized motion. Through the dusty art nouveau rosettes of the bar's back window shines the green Isis moon or Mithras or Osiris sun, and by this light I watch as two double pairs, yes two *double* pairs of woolen panties slip downward in a twin, concerted, pantomimic motion so perfect as to seem almost rehearsed. Hocus-pocus, halleluja, keep your hands to yourself. Two circa-thirty-year-old female posteriors that would have inspired P. P. Rubens blazon forth before my very eyes—cheek beside cheek, a voluptuous two-part, no four-part masterpiece, you might say. Now both of them bend forward, legs spread wide (reminiscent, in a way, of women's gymnastics), as they rest their torsos on the (apparently) just emptied trash cans.

"You can go ahead and bang us," speaks Vilma's profile.

"Both of us. From behind," Ehrentraut's profile.

"It won't cost you a cent," Vilma's profile.

"Because it's," Ehrentraut's profile, "a Christmas present. Ya understand? Now come on. You bang me first, then Vilma."

"Well! . . ." Vilma's profile, "How long do we have to stand here with our asses in the air?"

"Or are you afraid we've got the clap?"

"Don't you know we get regular checkups?"

"You think we'd risk landing," Ehrentraut's profile, "in the city hospital?"

"Ah, but ladies, my dear ladies . . ." I move my hands like a kettledrum player rolling a pianissimo across his double instrument.

The voice of the diabetic barkeep from inside: "Vilmaaa! Telepho-one!"

In a moment Vilma is dressed again and struts out of the dim courtyard without a word. Ehrentraut waits a few moments longer before saying, almost gruffly, "Y'know, I don't like people that don't accept presents. But, poor baby, maybe you weren't just shot in the head, maybe they got you somewhere else too—"

Haha there I heard it, heard it before, no doubt about it, from the direction of Bernina Pass—Morteratsch, the third approaching purr of an engine, slowing, accelerating, now humming up an octave higher . . . not a car, not a truck, but something in between. A pickup. Woe is me. Woe is me if it has sixteen-point antlers on the roof. Even if two little chamois-horns should poke up from the cab it would be disastrous for my mental health.

The pickup truck (or whatever it would be) purred closer and for a moment its big headlights made a raised platform of blinding light on the San Gian road. Unlike its two predecessors this one dimmed its lights and reduced its (circa) 65 mph tempo, obviously in deference to me, the lonely roadwalker. Despite his lowered lights I could make out INSTITUT ZOOLOGIQUE DE CAROUGE. But most important, *no* antlers projected above the cab.

Also for the first time I got a glimpse of a shadowy driver-profile with a hand raised from the wheel in a brief wave (which I returned). Look at that; on the San Gian road, a human shadow waved to you.

Now I was no longer walking blind. The first lights of my destination began to blink. Which aroused unexpectedly mixed feelings: hope and misgiving. In the almost complete darkness, sense impressions limited to the contact of the soles of my shoes with the road, I had felt safer.

Though I knew I would soon reach the fork in the road leading down to the station, I misjudged it by at least 100 yards. Not only that but the still accelerating Carouge Zoological Institute on its way to San Gian and the rushing sound of Flaz Brook (now nearer once again) drowned out the motor noise that approached the station road. All at once a single headlight came into view as if bursting, as if flashing out of a cave a few yards in front of me. *One light* that could only be a motorcycle. A light not dimmed but brightened. A terrible, round sun shot toward me.

I was terrified.

So there they come! On Paretta-Piccoli's Zuendapp with its sidecar and 20-plus horsepower! The two Keeper-men (Jacob case), the Two Blonds, *both* of whom can speak!

I had my Walther out, at the ready, safety off and roared into the rising yowl of the motorcycle:

"Come on, you keepers! Come on, *you keepers!*"

A high-pitched horn; a motorcycle sans sidecar whose driver had turned on his bright light only after seeing a nightmare: me.

A curse in Romansh was all that remained as he buzzed off in the direction of San Gian, yet his "sun" had lit the way into the Great War.

To a memory: the way this war had begun for me. I secured the Walther but left it swinging in my right hand like the handle of a walking stick.

And now that you see the Light in the Darkness, the first lights of Puntraschigna (real Romansh name for the place—Pontresina just a modish Italian figure of speech, like San Murezzan was with its modish Germanic St. Moritz—yes, as you near the end of this road you should come as close as possible to the truth, yes, that you should), now that you have the fork in the road behind you and the second of terror behind you; now that the few lights of the town's north end, the lights of Larèt shine like faintly pulsing signals, constantly dimming slightly, then brightening. Not hard to diagnose the cause even a quarter-mile away—Pina's *pipistrelli, molti pipistrelli,* the swarms of bats, which were unusually busy on this rare, starless, sultry night. Even at the foot of the valley where lights marked out the small station square I could see with my good eye the subtle but obsessive, ceaseless fluttering of the bats. Bats were also part of the scene on summer nights in the imperial capital.

"At all cost avoid thinking about the war." This rule no longer held sway. Fall 1913, I am a student at the Olmuetz prep school. My father takes me with him to the hunting lodge of the pretender Franz Ferdinand, archduke of Austria-Este. It is the hunting season, but this is not the reason for the—very brief—Sunday visit. Obviously papa has something very pressing to discuss with the heir apparent and Franz Conrad von Hoetzendorf, chief of the Austro-Hungarian General Staff. Both Franzes have brush haircuts (resembling, in hindsight, that of Hindenburg, at that time still a nonentity). By comparison my father's haircut seems almost Biedermeier, à la Johann Strauss Jr. One didn't have to be a fourteen-year-old secret agent to overhear the subject of their conversation: the Magyars. The Hungarians-Hungarians-Hungarians pours out of the Hunters' Hall like a litany, interspersed with Tisza-Tisza-Tisza (the Hungarian prime minister). Outside on the Danube Meadows—meadows that in reality are mottled green-yellow-red-leaved forests—a *battue,* a hunt with beaters, is taking place for stag, deer, wild boar. I know how to ride. The nasal, nonchalant suggestion of *His Royal Highness the Inspector General of the Entire Armed Forces:* that I should join the hunt. Casually suggested, half through the nose, in passing. A bit of blond turned-up moustache (not as jagged as that of Wilhelm II, who at that time is anything *but* a nonentity) pokes out from his long cheek. My answer to this totally disinterested piece of advice: a kind of Chinese mumble in which the words "your Royal Highness" sound more like "Yu Roi Hai."

Of course I leave unmentioned the fact that I would rather go sit on the toilet than chase wild pigs. (My earliest poems were composed in such leisurely isolation.)

I stroll through the antler-spiked hallways of the palatial lodge, urged on by the desire to locate a toilet without asking a servant. And thus I find myself in the Pretendorial, Grand-Ducal, Franz-Ferdinandian bathroom. I stand before the bidet of the Heir Apparent's Lady, née Countess Chotek, "morganatic Sophie," like a scientist before an unexpected discovery. The bidet rimmed with a strip of copper bearing an engraved wild-boar hunt—less baroque than realistic.

In the distance the ti-ta-ta-ta of hunting horns. Barking. Gunshots.

Not ten months later the heir to the throne Franz Ferdinand and his wife will be bagged (as they say) in Sarajevo, and the Great War will begin. To be more precise, a welcome excuse will be provided to begin it.

Also somewhat later, not three years thereafter, at the sight of all the corpses, all the violent deaths I see during the war, it will come back to me like an obsession—the memory of the boar hunt on that bidet and the distant horns.

A few months after the visit to Franz Ferdinand's hunting lodge my father falls from his horse as it slips on ice. Fractures thigh; is retired with the rank of Brigadier Lieutenant Field Marshal; when the war begins, has himself reactivated as an instructor, takes command of the garrison at Josephstadt. A provincial nest on a Bohemian plateau north of Koeniggraetz (Hrade Králové)—three-fourths of the population military, one-fourth whores, innkeepers, and store owners. In the war the secondary HQ of a howitzer regiment whose fledglings blast away in training until the walls shake. A troop of the Fourteenth Cavalry also receives training here before being transferred to the Southern Front as divisional cavalry. I am a volunteer dragoon cadet.

The woman.

A woman with an orange fur piece and a light flowing evening gown had come on stage—hardly 200 yards away. Her face would not yet be recognizable even if I used my long-range monocle—but there was no time for that anyway. Judging from hair color—the standing figure had now grown larger as I approached—it *could* be Xana. The pose could be hers too. Could. Two things spoke against it: first of all, she had no such ball gown, and second, she was afraid, unlike . . .unlike Pina, she was afraid of bats—had an almost atavistic aversion to their constantly swirling, dead-sure, eyeless flight, an aversion no amount of reason could overcome. Thus it was improbable that she would be standing, waiting to meet me under the hanging lamp of the last house in Larèt, lower Pontresina.

From my point of view, the *first* house. I remembered. The house belonged to a dentist from Basel who practiced up here. The lantern was suspended in the claws of a feathered, green-corroded dragon claw—talon of a basilisk, the mascot of Basel. On Vienna's Schoenlaterngasse we had lived next door to the Basilisk. The stage, otherwise empty. It had to be a woman who had been stood up for a late-night rendezvous.

And then the trenches began to appear, row after row along the roadway, these nearly man-high banks of peat moss or fertilizer or whatever it was, visible in the bat-flickering lights from the station below and the street ahead. The long earthworks I had noticed when de Colana had driven me home following my unsuccessful Corviglia trip—driven me home without spaniel cortege and unusually sober in his rattletrap Fiat.

"*O sole mio . . .*"

"I eat nothing but stork meat."

After his troop of divisional cavalry has been decimated, Albert————, alias Trebla, has "the silver" (i.e., the Silver Cross) pinned on his blue gray chest by the Commanding Officer of the Fifth Army—a rare spectacle in view of the rather modest nature of the award. No doubt Field Marshal Svetozar Boroëvíc von Bonja does it as a favor for T.'s papa, a fellow FM. Then with the rank of Cadet Acting Officer T. makes a three-week guest appearance with Schoen-burg-Hartenstein's Sixth Division of the Third (nicknamed The Iron) Corps. Little by little the Corps is transferred down from Galicia until in November 1915 it is positioned along the Isonzo front. It has succeeded in helping hold the cornerstone of the Doberdo positions—Monte San Michele. *The iron wall of the Iron Corps proves once again immovable*, etc., as the war correspondents would say. (K. Giaxa did not take part in this campaign.) Later they would report: *But at the end of February 1916 the main body of the Iron Corps is collected to help form two assault armies for the great spring offensive to be launched from South Tyrol. These preparations proceed unhindered despite enemy attempts to disturb them with a diversionary attack in mid-March 1916.* (Or something similar.) That is the fifth battle of the Isonzo, and into the very midst of it (the area around Monte San Michele, San Gabriele, Monte Cosich) T. is placed—no, inserted—into an enormous honeycomb, 250 feet long, 50 feet wide, 16 feet high. T. is able to spend a relatively calm first week as an orderly on the staff of the Corps Artillery dug in at the rear of the Doberdo positions in a spacious underground bunker built by General Janecka, a heated, electrically lighted place where officers lounge and sip coffee as if they were in the Imperial Café on Vienna's Opernring. Aside from the jolts of Janecka's mortars firing overhead, the only disturbing noise is the constant tick-tick-tick of a rather worn-out telegraph, for the incessant noise of the battle—in the end there will have been five or ten or a hundred Isonzo battles—sounds in this café no louder than the buzz of a neighboring beehive. But then T. receives orders to join the Counter-Sapping Operations on San Michele, i.e., to combat the Italian efforts to undermine Austrian positions; also to ensure that the repeatedly blasted telephone line from San Michele to the Imperial Café is repaired as quickly as possible. As a schoolboy, T. enjoyed the challenge of climbing the back face of the Ortler. Mountainclimb he can. But he has never been trained as a sapper or a telephone lineman, and so he climbs into the natural cave (enlarged by blasting) whose inhabitants are typical of the motley assortment of men thrown together to form the rear guard of the Iron Corps. Commanded by a first Lieutenant from the Twenty-fourth Rifle Battalion are remnants of the oldest infantry regiment in the Imperial Army (the Eleventh), of the Ninety-sixth Croatian Infantry and the South Dalmatian Militia. Thus T. enters trench warfare along the Piave. Those were the days! The *honeycomb* war.

   The Honeycomb War.
   Was there ever a beehive—and San Michele is nothing but a giant enlargement of one—whose buzzing inhabitants were at war with each other, honeycomb against honeycomb? Well, pleasant or not, the drones are killed off here, but are we the drones? Aren't we in reality de-masculated by war? And

some are *literally* emasculated when they (following a childhood instinct not to fill their pants, and trying not to foul their cavern) hang their buttocks out the side tunnel to relieve themselves. Shot in the groin. T.'s predecessor as Counter-Sapper fell victim, not to a sapper's charge but to pneumonia. (They took him to the rear on a mule. Maybe he's still alive.) Unfavorable weather for war, this end of March. Not unfavorable enough. Up in the mountains, on the chalk cliffs of Tyrol and Friuli, it is snowing. Bad weather conditions, but the worst thing, it occurs to T., is how brave *we* all are. And by "we" he means neither one of the opposing forces, *but all of us* in the Doberdo positions. General Luigi Conte Cadorna's Alpini and Bersaglieri are brave and Lieutenant Colonel Stephan Duic's Bosnians are brave, and the Hungarians, Lombards, Slovaks, Sicilians, Carinthians, Tuscans, Croatians, Piedmontese, Dalmatians, Venetians, and Viennese, all these races and peoples in all the honeycombs of this dreadful beehive called Monte San Michele, Monte San Gabriele, Monte Cosich—*all* are brave. Outside the hole of our honeycomb (close as it is to the Adriatic) it is raining. And the rain makes the pools of man blood and mule blood that have collected on the rocky trails and on the once pine-covered (now barbed-wire-covered) plateaus, makes the pools overflow, and sometimes the honeycomb's inhabitants can see a running curtain of reddish water in front of their window.

Strangely enough the honeycomb war tends to subside during long periods of rain. Sunshine, snow (Russian winters excepted), even fog, are better conditions for war than steady rain. Is it the old, legendary fear of the flood that brings about this hesitation or is it the ancient slogan Keep Your Powder Dry—the artillery barrages usually let up during such lengthy downpours, and T. is playing chess (holding strictly to the rule: a piece touched is a piece captured) on an ammo crate with a cadet from the South Hungarian Thirty-fourth Division. The cadet, whom T. is supposed to help reorganize cable repair operations, has already lost eight men in this endeavor. Three dead, five shipped out wounded. The South Hungarian maintains artillery fire that is comparable to cuckoo calls in springtime. When one sequence has ended, it's not hard to estimate when the next will begin. T. refuses to have birdcalls be even *mentioned* in such a context, for now it is early April and the rain outside the cavern is getting warmer and there is a touch of spring in the air, and the rain will stop and the honeycomb war again will gain the upper hand—the upper hand raised to throw a grenade. The Alpini will come down from upstairs and will be repulsed—onethousand-twothousand-threethoursand-throw!—with hand grenades. But more often with machine guns, which now have gotten their last oiling (anointment? literally, extreme unction). Whose barrels jut out of the caverns and, oiled for the last time, are blasted to pieces by a 48mm mortar shell from Janecka's positions—more or less from the Imperial Café. Yes, to repulse an Alpini attack from upstairs an Austrian shell blows away Austrian machine guns. And the quiet corpses (of Catholics who receive no last anointment), and the wounded that scream, cry, and pray, and the dying who lie there beside men who have returned to their card games, lie there until, once dead, they are

374

heaved out of the honeycomb to be splattered onto the rocks, man and mule, by shellfire—like paper dolls or squashed flies. In the midst of this T. plays chess with the young Hungarian from the Thirty-fourth who can't get the cuckoo's call out of his head—the cuckoo's call of artillery. And there is something Easter-like in the air of this honecomb-destroying April. And the rain stops entirely. And the night battles begin, and from the direction of the Adriatic the monstrous, colored incandescence rises once again—rockets, blue, red and green, like a fireworks display in the Prater.

And a morning. A splendid April Sunday morning after a night of attacks from honeycomb to honeycomb with fire support from howitzers and mortars. And a tenor as beautiful, as fantastically beautiful as the tenor of a young Caruso (one of the Dalmatian militiamen informs me *iurnata* is a Neapolitan word), a solitary, young, magnificent voice sings into a pause in battle so perfect it seems prearranged.

"*Che bella cosa 'na iurnata a' sole / Un' aria serena / Dopo la tempesta / Un altro sole / Piu bell' oine / O sole mio / Sta in front a te ...*"

Through the peephole in the side tunnel, T. sees five storks moving northward and thinks, What devil-of-all-storks has possessed them to want to nest in *this* Europe? Where are they flying? To the little old mill by the brook? God, they'll be blasted to hamburger there. T.'s immediate reaction to "O sole mio!" and the migrating storks: He stands at attention before the honeycomb's commander, the Carinthian First Lieutenant named Kotz.

"Sir, request permission to be served a plate of *spaghetti alla Napoletana* with stork meat! How's that? You don't have that here? In that case, sir, I'm afraid Cadet Acting Officer———must leave this position. So long, Lieutenant Kotz!"

For the second time the woman stepped out of the stage-set house with the basilisk lantern at the north end of Pontresina, and with my good eye at a range of one hundred yards I recognized Xana.

What I had taken for a fur stole was her camel's hair coat. Xana had no eagle eye. The road stretched out so darkly in front of her that she had certainly not yet seen the shadow marching toward her. Also, standing under a lamp, it is difficult to see into the dark.

I could have pumped my lungs full of air and shouted out to her at the top of my voice ... the way I had yelled up to the Italians after leaving the San Michele honeycomb. That risk I had taken; this one I refused to take. Especially now when I was almost out of the tunnel—almost,̦ but not yet. And Xana would doubtless recognize my voice and run toward me—*into* my tunnel, the San Gian road. And if the action started then?

Behind the long, well-stacked layers of peat (or whatever), behind these almost man-high ramparts, a sharpshooter could be lying in wait. Just one? And what if in his eagerness to get his man he fires, not just at me? What if Xana becomes an opportunist's target? DANGER!! UNAUTHORIZED PERSONS PROHIBITED IN TUNNEL.

Or should I risk a hundred-yard dash to Xana? The street rose slightly toward the entrance to the village. Such a sprint might turn out to be the greatest stupidity, no the worst denial of instinct in my entire life. Thus quiet, quiet up the hill without the hay-straw cadence.

And here San Gian and San Michele become really, no sur-really one. *One.* Steeply down hill. T. ignores a shrill command, takes off.

Climbing down from Michele he sees no archangel Michael flying overhead, not an archangel Gabriel soaring above the neighboring mountain—even though the latter was the angel of death in the Apocalypse—and there was no point in trying to find an angel over Monte Cosich. "*Amici,*" he yells at the top of his voice up to the honeycombs on the top floors, "*mongio solamente carne di cigogna con spaghetti alla Napoletana!* Stork meat with spaghetti! I eat nothing else! Understand, *amici?*" Alpini faces under helmets stare out of the upstairs windows and T. thinks, they'll be too surprised to shoot this obviously cracked-up kid, and they *are* too surprised. He hears men laughing up above—Italian laughter has a timber all its own. The escapade can't be classified as a classical desertion because he reports back as an orderly to his staff officer (Imperial Café): "Yes sir, there is no archangel Cosich and I eat nothing but stork meat." In close confinement near Klagenfurt: "I eat nothing but stork meat." The order directing him to be transferred immediately to the Klosterka in Tyrnau (oldest military asylum in the Empire) is cancelled after father's intevention, and T. is sent to Professor Wagner von Jauregg in Vienna. Brief résumé of the diagnosis (the patient himself is not informed): typical case of battle shock. (The English enemy's term most accurate here.) Not suited to trench warfare. No signs of dementia praecox, no history of childhood disturbance, schizophrenia or paranoia. Allergic (hay-fever). Hypersensitive, inclined to rebellion against existing conditions. Recommendation: reassignment to front line in non-close-combat role with opportunity for free development of personality, e.g, aerial reconnaissance. So Trebla goes, not to the Klosterka in Tyrnau but to an accelerated flight-training course in Wiener Neustadt. There he spends most of his free time in a concert café on the Boehnergasse with a gilt-lettered sign in its window:

AFTERNOONS CLASSICAL

EVENINGS CLASSY MUSIC

Then Brăila, December 4, 1916, the day I'd tried to forget, to suppress for over two decades now. Trebla, now part of the Thirty-sixth Reconnaissance Company, promoted to lieutenant under the chief pilot, Captain Weckendorfer (Weckendorfer crashed, Laimgruber his successor), pilots his Brandenburg reconnaissance biplane along the Black Sea coast between Constanta and Varna and has left the peninsula of Cavarna below and behind, and the thick blanket of stratocumulus clouds over which he flies is like a giant snowy desert warmed by the winter sun, and because he is flying almost straight south by the compass *the other plane comes straight out of the sun,* at first a flashing point, rapidly growing, yes, on this endless field of white, like a fairy-tale sleigh.

There is no intercom. T. thinks, could that be a British fighter penetrating alone this far out from his base in Saloniki? The smallest risk would be to dive straight down, at least as straight down as a Brandenburg *can*, down through the cloud cover. Then observer Corporal Humonda shouts from the rear seat—he must have made careful use of his telescope—he screams against the whistling wind with a piercing falsetto voice and Czech accent: "Loo-ten-ahhnt saaah!—Th-a-a-t's *not* a Fokker!—N-o-t a *Cher*-man!—*Not* a *frent*-ly p-l-a-a-ane!—Et's an *Ink*-lish-man!—A Clare-zhay *Ca*-mel!—Let's go d-o-w-n! Rah-t a-w-a-y! A C-a-m-e-l!"

Soon enough T. can verify with the naked eye—although a first-rate pair of German Goerz field glasses dangles from his neck—it *is* a Clerget-Camel fighter.

Humonda's falsetto scream (he seems to have bent closer between the whistling guy wires): "Loo-tenant sah!! A Ca-mel—with checka-board pat-tahn—I already got a picsha of it—what's the use—if we don't go *down?!*" Observer Corporal Humonda is right. If this Camel, this single-seat RAF fighter, climbs to 15,000 feet with the intent of getting on our tail, we are dead ducks. The best thing to do: dive straight down through the clouds. Down there the coastal batteries of the Bulgarian-Austro-German antiaircraft would offer protection from such a pursuer.

The real-unreal-surreal moments of one's life.

Across the endless blanket of stratocumulus cloud, an endless, sunlit steppe of snow, the Clerget-Camel approaches like a sleigh. Climbs 1,500 feet higher, a sleigh sailing over the snowdrifts. Pulling the stick back against his chest, T. climbs to the same altitude. Were the other plane to climb up into the sun now, there would be nothing to do but follow Humonda's pleading advice, push the stick forward and descend to safety in a kind of downward glide, the only dive T.'s crate is capable of. But there is something like magnetism at work now. T. is not flying a crate, but is guiding a sleigh of his own. And the two sleighs maintain their collision course as if drawn together by mutual gravitation. At the same altitude. T.'s left hand swings his Goerz glasses in front of his eyes, and he sees a face above a yellow scarf.

If this were not wartime we could drive past one another like two sleighs or two cabs on London's Piccadilly Circus or two fiacres on Vienna's Praterallee. But we will *not* drive past each other because this is war.

War.

And what counts in war is *getting the other man*.

In completely unstealthy fashion, as if according to the hallowed rules of a knightly joust, he attacks me *front on*, and I get—get a burst of machine-gun fire peppered over at me and something strikes the middle of my brow. No pain. Just a dull bump; then the numb feeling of local anesthetic over the root of my nose. I *must* shoot back. The Brandenburg reconnaissance biplane is fitted with a single machine gun, not a flexible one but one mounted to fire through the propeller hub. The cursed Brandenburg can only aim and *hit* if its whole body is aimed in the right direction. A flying rifle whose only secret is that its body must be held as steadily as an aiming rifleman's in order to shoot, to shoot back, to hit the target. Oh you poor reconnaissance bastard!

You poor reconnaissance bastard!

I threw myself down on (and behind) one of the last ramparts at the end of the San Gian road and aimed my Walther flash-quick at the shadow of a small haystack where someone had fired on me, and in the same split second I fired back, aiming with my whole body, and the shot whipped through the night, and from nearby came the sudden barking of a wakened dog; then two or three others joined him. For a short time. Then silence, the great silence of the mountain valley. Crouching low I ran along the last heap of peat moss (or whatever) and thought, a numb feeling of impact growing in the middle of my brow, I thought, *right in the same spot, my "old wound" where they got me before,* but why, why is there no curtain of blood falling across my eyes?

"Did you see that—did you hear it?!" I gasp. "They were shooting at me; let's get out of here!—get away from this light!"

"Nobody shot at you. Anyway not just now."

I had grasped Xana's shoulder through her camel's hair coat. (Camel, the Camel—hadn't it wobbled strangely in the air after the exchange of fire? Perhaps I had *really* shot through its rudder controls before I sank unconscious into Humonda's arms.) Holding Xana, I tried to pull her out of the bat-flickering light of the basilisk lantern.

With a gentle twist of her shoulder she shook me off.

"*You* were the *only* one who fired. I saw you and heard you and saw you. The way you threw yourself down on this manure pile or whatever it was. Threw yourself down and fired. Why were you shooting at a haystack, Trebla?"

Yes, she must have gotten up around 1:00 A.M., put on her devotional dressing gown, thrown her coat over it, without getting the least bit ready. Her face was covered with face cream. Under the basilisk lamp—the fluttering bats seemed not to worry her any more—her features shone like silver.

"'You see, madam, there is really no point in being sentimental.' Do you remember, Trebla? You told me that. A month ago. When I ran away from Acla Silva that night. Because they killed Maxim Grabscheidt ... When I ... when you found me on that rock by the water. That's when you said it. A line from the Punch and Judy show of Professor Sa——"

Hot from running, I pulled Pola's baby blue scarf halfway off my neck: "Salambutschi."

"My father is dead." (She didn't say Papa-Rose.) "But I'm not going to poison myself. Not going to poison myself in despair. I'm in my third month, a mother-to-be. It must have happened just after you came over the Silvretta. And then, up here—we've hardly spoken to each other for four weeks. Hardly at all, right?"